Starling

Southern Watch, Book 6

Robert J. Crane

Starling
Southern Watch, Book 6
Robert J. Crane
Copyright © 2017 Ostiagard Press
All Rights Reserved.

1st Edition

This book is a work of fiction. Names, characters, places and incidents are products of the author's imagination or are used fictitiously. Any resemblance to actual events or locales or persons, living or dead, is entirely coincidental.

The scanning, uploading and distribution of this book via the internet or any other means without the permission of the publisher is illegal and punishable by law. Please purchase only authorized electronic editions, and do not participate in or encourage electronic piracy of copyrighted materials. Your support of the author's rights is appreciated.

No part of this publication may be reproduced in whole or in part without the written permission of the publisher. For information regarding permission, please email cyrusdavidon@gmail.com.

Prologue

Before

Lucia Fiore was used to taking a punch.

She knew the taste of blood in her mouth, knew that hard sting of shame mingled with the fear of what was going to come next. Knew the pain that radiated out from her eye when she got hit, the sting that had left scars in her red eyebrows.

"You needed to straighten up," her father, Jim, would say afterward. "You needed some discipline, put you back on the straight and narrow. You deserved it. Right?"

"Yes," she would always say, cradling the spot where he'd hit her, trying to protect herself. Every time.

*

The 2003 Ford Explorer rattled as it left the dirt road south of Fort Oglethorpe, Georgia. Lucia's father was in the driver's seat, head down, neck straining as he craned it to look down the road. He was squinting too, forgot his sunglasses again. He did that about half the time, and always griped about it.

"We could go back and get 'em," Lucia's mother said in that quiet, plaintive way she had. She didn't speak up often. Like Lucia, she'd been conditioned to stay quiet.

"I ain't wanting to do that," her father said, continuing his squint. "It's forty minutes to Chattanooga, and I just want to get this over with."

Everyone settled into silence. It was the safest course, Lucia knew.

The sun was shining outside, bright and cheerful. Lucia could almost imagine birds singing in the trees as they passed, heading toward Battlefield Parkway. The rear shocks on the Explorer had gone to shit a while ago, so Lucia rattled in the back seat, feeling like a pebble in a coffee can that someone was shaking hard.

That was okay though. She'd been shook a lot worse.

"Goddamned sun is killing me," her dad said, fiddling with the sun visor. It wasn't having any effect, because the sun was too low in the sky and the visor couldn't cover it. They were still heading east, yet to make the turn north, and her dad looked like he was flinching.

"You want me to try mine?" Lucia's mother asked, already hopping to reach for her visor.

"What's the fucking point of that?" Her dad gestured. "The sun's straight ahead on my side. What fucking good is it gonna do for you to dick around with your visor? You fucking stupid?"

Her mother seemed to recede, as though trying to melt into the window and door on her side, subtly inch away from Lucia's father. Lucia watched from the back seat, taking it all in but trying not to be too obvious about it. It wasn't like her dad would turn on the radio or give her anything else to entertain herself—like a cell phone. Her friends all had them.

"Fucking stupid all around me," her dad muttered, and blinked away from the sun in his eyes, casting a glance back at her. "And you. Did you go out last night?"

Lucia felt like she'd been tagged in the middle of the forehead by a rogue softball. Not too hard, but enough to stun her and make her stammer when she answered. "J-just for a little while."

Her father gave her a hard look before turning his attention back to the road. "I suppose you went out with that goddamned devil worshipper, Lara, again?"

Her mother turned around and sent her a scalding look. Lucia felt it burn, set fire to her cheeks. "She's—not a devil worshipper."

"So you were out with her last night?" Her mother adopted a tone of stern disapproval, jarred out of her torpor by something to pick at. Lucia knew that feeling, the relief that came when the crosshairs shifted off of her.

"I was back before ten," Lucia said, almost begging. It was a plea, in her mind, one for them to leave her the fuck alone, or better still, give their blessing for her to get out of the house and draw a free breath every now and again, one not supervised and under their roof.

"Sixteen years old and you're hanging out with a devil worshipper all the time." Her dad just shook his head. Even petrified, waiting for the inevitable assault, verbal or otherwise, a thought crossed Lucia's mind that she wouldn't have shared even if he'd threatened to bust her in the jaw: *We don't even go to church.*

"Ain't right," her mother said, shaking her head. "That girl's momma—Brenda Black—I knew her when we was coming up together. She wasn't right as a girl, and she ain't right as a woman, and it's rubbed off on her daughter, sure as hell. Apple didn't fall far from that tree." Her mother sat up straight now, no need to seek shelter from the door or window next to her now that her father was nodding along.

"I thought I told you to stay away from that girl and her fucked-up family," her dad said. He didn't deign to look back at her until after he got no reply the first time. His eyes were flaring, and not just from the bright sun. "You hear me?"

"Yeah," Lucia said softly.

"But you went out with her last night anyway?"

"We just went and saw a movie," Lucia said.

"What movie?" her mother asked.

"*It Follows,*" Lucia said.

"What?"

"It's … it's a horror movie."

"You're polluting your mind with that stupid shit," her father said, pushing down the dashboard cigarette lighter until it clicked. "Fucking monsters and shit. Ain't real. What a waste of time."

"Well, I don't have anything else to do," Lucia said, lowering her face to stare at the aged upholstery.

"Oh, I'll give you more to do," her mother said. "There's always more laundry could be folded. Vacuuming."

"I already do all that," Lucia said, and instantly wished she could reach out, seize the words from the air and shove them back down her throat, even if they choked her.

"Did you just sass your mother?" her father asked, head whipping around in a frenzy. He beat her—but sass? No, that was not okay, Lucia thought, keeping her eyes on her ragged shoes. "After everything we do for you? I work my fingers to the fucking bone putting food on the table, putting clothes on your back—hey, you look at me when I'm fucking talking to y—"

She looked up just in time to see the flash. She thought maybe it was the glint of his wristwatch as he moved to smack her, but she didn't get a chance to tell for sure because the world rocked around Lucia, everything spun, and suddenly she was upside down. She'd been knocked around by punches before, but this wasn't like that.

First she thought maybe she was dead, then for one heart-stopping moment she realized, *This isn't death …*

This is ...
It's ...

A big semi trailer smacked into her side window and sent shattered glass raining into Lucia's hair. It had already run over the front of the car, grinding it beneath massive wheels, her parents disappearing beneath those enormous, relentless tires as she watched it happen in less than a second. One moment her father had been there, yelling, escalating, finger pointed, about to smack her—

The next, he was just gone, the body of a tractor trailer and its running board sitting where her parents had been a moment earlier.

Lucia just sat there, blinking. The roof had been sheared open, silence flooding in from outside of the vehicle, a ticka-ticka-ticka mechanical noise repeating in the ears deafened by Armageddon a moment earlier. It was as though the big semi had just decided to park itself in the front seat of their vehicle, miraculously appeared right there, after only a second of wrenching and tearing and squealing of metal, replacing her parents with this new, superior, mechanical god for her to pay her homage to—and fear.

She took a breath, then another, and somewhere outside the car, now open to the sunny day, she heard someone scream, "Jesus!" She didn't see Jesus though; all she saw were her knees, a little bloody, her shoes, still scuffed and dirty, and a missing front half of the old Ford Explorer.

Lucia extended a hand experimentally, feeling for the door. Her palm landed on the plastic surface, and she brushed off the broken, pebbled glass and then went for the handle. She tried it, and it squeaked but failed to open. She pushed, and it yielded, making a rough grinding sound, metal against metal. It squealed and then fell with a clatter, the hinges missing.

She tried to shove across the seat and get out, but something resisted. It was the seatbelt, clutching tight against her neck like a noose. Lucia blinked, reached down, and hit the button. It snapped free easily, zipping back to the seat and hanging there. She shoved along and out of the car, legs failing to hold her. She hit the ground and a sharp pain came from her knee; a little cry of, "Ouch!" escaped her lips.

It was a little like when she'd hit the floor after a punch from her dad, but nowhere near as bad.

"Holy living fuck," a guy said, waddling up to her. His pants were held on by a belt around his waist that sat just above a wide, exercise-ball-sized storage area of a gut. "Are you okay?"

Lucia stared at him for a second as she wobbled to her feet. She stared at her canvas shoes. "Yeah," she said. The world sounded muffled, still, around her. She looked up and blinked at the big man. "I think so."

"Jesus," he said, and looked past her.

Lucia looked with him, knowing what she'd see but also knowing that it'd be so much worse for seeing the whole picture.

The Ford Explorer looked like it had been cut in half, but it really hadn't. The tractor trailer had just run over the front, mashing it down to a foot or so of height, somehow shearing it and crushing in the roof just in front of where she was sitting so that it had broken cleanly and simply hung there, like an awning, instead of mashing her to paste when it crushed the car.

"I swear God must be looking out for you." The big man touched her, put a hand on her shoulder, and she could feel the sweat on his palm as he brushed down her arm, like he was trying to convince himself she was really there. "I wouldn't have believed anyone could survive that."

Lucia just stared at the wreck, strangely numb. Her parents ... they had to be dead—there was no way a human being could fit into the inches of space that were left under the big tractor trailer's treads. Little drips of blood or oil, dark liquid ran out of the metal beneath the truck, and she dimly knew that it was probably what remained of her only family.

"Yeah," she muttered, staring at the dark liquid as it dribbled out like blood across her chin after she'd taken a punch. "I guess so." Already she could hear the sirens in the distance, like church bells, ringing out as they approached. "Maybe He is."

Day One

"… see, when you use the Prep Scrub, then the Pre-Shave Oil, then put on the Shave Butter, and use an Executive razor—that's the $9 option—"

"I thought these razors were a dollar? Wasn't that supposed to be the whole point of this club?" Keith Drumlin said, letting the hose he was using to wash off the pavement hang limply as he focused on what Nate McMinn was saying. This was how it went with Nate and his talking, which slowed down Keith's progress by a good half or so. He wanted to be mad, but he did enjoy a good chat with Nate. It kept his mind off … other things.

"Well, the cheapest option is a dollar a month," Nate said, doing his own part to scrub some of the gore off the street of Midian's town square. The whole place smelled like blood and turds, vomit and God only knew what else. "But the really good one—I mean, really good—is like $9, but trust me, you want it. You use the Scrub, the Oil, the Shave Butter, and then the Executive Razor, and I'm telling you …" Nate made a sweet sighing sound that was at odds with the fact that he was wearing a jumpsuit coated with human excretions all down the knees and legs. "It's like the finger of Jesus rubbing across your face. It's so smooth, so sweet. It's like not even shaving at all. Smoother than a Vince Gill ballad."

"Shit, that is *smooth*," Keith said, trying to wash a pile of—what the fuck was that, anyway?—down the nearby drain. There was a lot of stuff in the square that needed to be washed down the drain. The streets still ran with blood all around the perimeter, and the grass had an unhealthy crimson tinge to it, made it look funny in the early morning light.

"They got a lot of other stuff too," Nate said. "Expanded products lines and the like. Shampoos and soaps without sulfates."

Keith stared into space. That was a new one for him. He almost didn't ask, for fear of sounding ignorant, but curiosity overcame embarrassment. "What the hell is a sulfate?"

"Probably some shit they only care about in Cali-forn-i-a," Nate said. "Anyway, it's awesome. You should join the club."

"Huh," Keith said, directing the hose toward a spot of bile and trying to wash it down the nearest storm drain. It was stubborn, refusing to bow to his sprayer's water pressure, steadily applied to it. "Reckon that's a lot better than what my daddy taught me to do to save money on razors."

"What's that?" Nate asked, looking up. The bristles of the scrub brush in his hand were red. They hadn't started that way. They'd been white as a wedding dress when the two of them began their labors this morning.

"Well," Keith said, "my daddy ... he heard on Clark Howard that your razors last longer if you towel 'em off after you shave. Keeps 'em from rusting. He could use one blade for six months, because he would take his hair dryer and dry it after every time."

"Wow," Nate said. "That seems extreme."

"You ain't kidding," Keith said, sniffing. Man, it just stunk around here. Lots of little pieces of people were spread all over the place, parts the demons had cut off or ripped off, parts that couldn't be identified. There just wasn't time enough to deal with all this. The funeral homes in Calhoun County were already filled to capacity. Keith had gotten notice of at least fifty he needed to go to himself ... including his dad's.

Including ...

This was why he was here now, washing off the square. Talking about razors and close shaves was a hell of a lot better than sitting around his mother's dark house, eating casserole and fried chicken and talking in quiet voices to friends and relations and well-meaning folks who wanted to tell him how sorry they were. Any distraction at all was better than sifting the ashes of whatever feelings were tickling him inside, in those idle moments when he had a chance to think about it all.

He wondered how many people had even stopped by. There were an awful lot of dead people in Calhoun County right now, and specifically in Midian. The folks around here had a support system. Whenever someone died, folks stopped by with food—casseroles, store-bought meat and cheese trays, cakes and pies. When you lost someone, you ought not to have to worry about cooking. Keith remembered going to a hundred houses where folks would just stop in, all day after someone died in the family. They had tables full of food. That was the Midian way, the Southern way. "We take care of our neighbors," Keith muttered under his breath, "and ourselves."

He hadn't seen a full table yet in his momma's house. It wasn't just this one incident, where a Halloween event on the square had gone hellishly wrong, some sort of crazy demons busting out and taking over people. He'd heard the tally on how many people had died, but it kept going up as they identified the pieces of folks.

And there were a whole hell of a lot to identify.

"Jesus," Nate said, holding up a severed finger. "Should I even save this?"

"I expected more," Keith said, shaking his head.

Nate frowned at him, then the finger. "More what? More knuckles? Cuz this one got severed right at the—"

"Naw, not that ... more of everything," Keith said, shaking his head. "I expected more people to care how many of us got killed. I mean ... kids and women and old folks ... we lost a *lot* of people at Halloween. You watch the news, right?"

Nate looked gobsmacked. "Uh ... not really."

"Well, you know that things happen out there in the world, right?"

"Well, yeah," Nate said, looking quite abashed. A bird chirped from a tree in the middle of the square. That was surprising, Keith figured; unless it was a carrion bird, in which case, boy, had he picked the right place.

"Lots of bad stuff happens, right?" Keith asked. "And the news shows up and they report on it, all, 'You wouldn't believe the shit that happened today in' ... I don't know ... 'Dubuque, Iowa. There are twelve people dead after a bronco escaped from the rodeo and gored a bunch of people standing in line for a Porta-Potty.' You know, they thrive on shit like that. News of the weird."

"Okay, yeah." Nate nodded along. "Yeah, I heard about that." He guffawed, low. "How much would it suck to get gored while you're standing in line for the shitter?"

"It'd suck. A lot. But my point is, crazy shit happens everywhere. And it gets on the news." Keith extended a hand to sweep it over the whole square. "How many people d'you reckon died here now? A couple hundred? And have you seen one news truck?"

"Hell, I heard the sheriff couldn't even get the Tennessee State Patrol or TBI to show up," Nate said, now sounding sullen.

"That's my point," Keith said. "We have all these people die, and no one from the news or the state or the federal government shows up?" He waited, trying to make his point by silence. "Ain't that a little weird?"

"Well, it was a *demon* attack," Nate said. "Not exactly the sort of thing the news would tend to want to talk about."

"And that's another thing," Keith said. "I saw with my own eyes what happened here … and I still don't fully know what I saw. People going crazy and tearing into each other and shit?"

"Man, if that ain't the work of the devil, I don't know what is," Nate said.

"See, I seen shit like that before on TV," Keith said. "Or in the movies … there was one called *Kingsman*—"

"That movie was *awesome*," Nate gushed. "That limey motherfucker could really kick some ass."

"But you know what I mean, right? Where they had that weapon that turned everyone on each other?"

"Yeah," Nate snickered, "in the Westboro Baptist Church. He killed every motherfucker in that place, like a boss."

"I think they called it something else in the movie," Keith said. "Probably didn't want to get sued."

"We all knew what they were talking about though," Nate said with a low chuckle. "For all our differences, I gotta say—is there anyone that don't hate them?"

"I don't hate anybody," Keith said. "I just don't like everybody. But my point is … this shit here was right out of a Hollywood movie, you know? Neighbor turning on neighbor, wife turning on husband. Divide and conquer."

"Well, shit, we got conquered all right," Nate said uneasily, looking around. He lifted up his scrub brush, red liquid running from it in a long drizzle. "We flat out got our asses kicked, man. If we were a turtle, we'd be on our backs right now, shell down, belly up, and asses vulnerable to whatever coyote wants to come along and take a bite."

"Yeah," Keith said, the hose dripping on a patch of sidewalk that wouldn't come clean, no matter how much he sprayed it. The blood had soaked in good. He hadn't seen his daddy on the square. He wondered where he'd fallen, if it had been here? Over there, maybe? Keith shook it off, and focused on the conversation. "It wasn't on the TV."

"Nope," Nate said.

"Tennessee Highway Patrol didn't show up. TBI didn't show up. FBI didn't. News didn't."

"Nope."

"I always felt like there's a lot out there I didn't know," Keith said, putting a thumb over the end of the hose to try and focus the spray.

It squirted out around his thumb in a sprinkler pattern, but the red on the sidewalk failed to diminish. It was ingrained in the concrete, and no matter how much he washed, it did not fade. "Like maybe people out there—out past the boundaries of Calhoun County—people in Nashville, people in Washington, people in New York and L.A. ... I felt like they knew things I didn't know."

"Well, yeah, Keith; they got college degrees for that—"

"Not what I meant, jackass," Keith snapped, the hose still going to little effect. "I mean, I felt like ... they knew things about how the world worked, the government worked, the press worked ... things they didn't tell me, tell you, tell us. Like they were in it all together, and in their little coastal enclaves—"

"Fancy word."

"—like it was a big club, and we weren't invited," Keith said. "We weren't good enough." He looked at the blood spot. "We didn't belong. Now I'm seeing this shit—this ... I don't even know what ... spilling out all over the place in the streets of my own town, and ... I'm wondering ..." He looked east, settling his gaze toward the sheriff's station that was out on Old Jackson Highway. "I'm wondering if there isn't an elite in our town that knows more than they're telling us. That's keeping us in the dark because we're ... not good enough." Keith's hand shook, but he couldn't tell if it was fear or rage that moved it to do so.

Nate was quiet for a moment. "Well, I mean ... they told us it was demons that did this. Demons that possessed people—"

"Maybe it was," Keith said softly, the spattering sound of the hose splashing against the concrete a steady rhythm. "Maybe they're right. Maybe they're telling the whole truth. It's like I been locked out of the club so long I don't know how to trust someone when they finally claim they're inviting me in, you know?"

"I think I know," Nate said quietly, the splash of the water running out of the hose the only sound in the early morning square. "I felt that same thing before too. Like there's a club and you'll never be part of it. The cool kids." He put the scrub brush down. "But I do gotta ask you ..." He looked up at Keith with earnest eyes. "Do you really think it's all true? That demons ... really do exist and they're in Midian right now, raising all manner of hell?"

"I think so," Keith answered honestly. "Would Sheriff Reeve lie to us? He's one of us, after all, not from somewhere else ... though who knows what that means anymore, cuz that cowboy ain't from around here, and they seem to be listening to him. Awww, hell," Keith said, finally turning the hose to somewhere else, somewhere that it would be put to better effect. Little chunks of flesh washed into the grass, the smell of rot rising as the morning air became warmer. "I been wrong before though."

They kept working in the silence, both of them still pondering that last statement, as they tried their hardest to clean up the mess of their town square.

*

Mack Wellstone was practically shaking. He was in the woods with his dad, on the first day of gun season for deer, something he'd been looking forward to since he was a little boy and first understood that his dad left to do something mysterious and fascinating every November. He'd pack the car and vanish from their family home in Knoxville for a weekend or longer, coming back grizzled, his usually smooth-shaven cheeks replete with a few days of beard growth, a wide smile for his son and wife when he got back, a sort of placid calm fallen over him that was different from when he spent a week away traveling for work.

Mack Wellstone had been looking forward to this day for almost his whole life. He'd been in the woods before with his dad, been out stalking deer in this very place—not too far from a cabin outside Midian, Tennessee—but always in the off season, maybe the summer, when it was hot and the sun was cooking them from overhead. Not like this, all bundled up against the cold, heavy camo jacket and a blaze orange vest over it. He felt like a traffic cone in the middle of the autumn woods, but his dad had assured him that deer couldn't see blaze orange, and his dad knew everything, didn't he? Mack was still young enough to believe that in his gut, even if intellectually he knew otherwise.

"Shhhh," his daddy said, nodding once to his foot. Mack had accidentally crunched a leaf as he'd stepped. It hadn't rained here in a while, apparently, and there wasn't a lot of dew on the ground. His dad had warned him about that, said if they were going to stalk prey they needed to be quiet, because a deer could hear you coming from a long ways off.

Mack trod more carefully with his next step, though he still crackled a leaf underfoot. He grimaced, but when his father looked back, he was grinning. Whew, he wasn't mad at all. That was a relief.

His dad beckoned him forward, and they headed for a nearby tree. His dad was all done up in camo as well, his own blaze orange vest and his head capped with an orange toboggan hat. He sat down against the bark of a large tree, and Mack followed his lead, taking the rifle off his shoulder, checking to make sure the safety was still on, and then leaned it up against the trunk before sitting down next to his father, nervous tension making him want to get up and run a lap around the clearing in front of them. That'd spook the deer for sure though.

"When are we going to see one?" Mack leaned in and asked his father, whispering nice and low.

"We might not," his dad said, "at all."

Mack shifted restlessly, crunching another leaf. "Oh," he said, trying to bury the disappointment. But that was hardly definitive, was it? It meant they *could* still see one, after all. Could see a whole bunch of them, maybe.

"Listen, son," his dad said, leaning in and putting a big hand on his shoulder, giving him a firm and reassuring squeeze. "It's not all about seeing a deer or even killing a deer—I know you want to, and I understand, because I was like you once—it's about getting out here in the woods and being part of nature. It's about seeing the sun come up, hearing the woods coming alive, smelling that fresh air." Smiling, his dad drew a deep breath to illustrate what he was saying, then froze, making a face. "Ugh."

"What?" Mack took a sniff of his own and almost gagged. What was that? It was sharp, and stank like eggs left out in the sun all summer.

"Sulfur," his dad said, coughing lightly. "Yuck." He swiped a water bottle out of his pack and took a drink. "I know there's an old paper mill in Midian, but ugh, that is rank. I don't think I've ever smelled anything quite that rancid out here before."

Mack agreed. "It smells like somebody didn't cover up their latrine when they were done." He'd read all about digging latrines in an old Boy Scout handbook his dad had given him.

Mack's dad laughed. "Yeah, it does smell a little like th—" His dad froze, listening. Mack imagined he looked a little like a deer who'd caught wind of something, and wondered why he'd thought such a strange thing.

Then Mack heard it as well. A leaf crunching behind them.

His dad held a finger to his lips in warning. Then he slowly started to turn, trying to look around the tree they were leaned against …

Mack tried to stay quiet too. It wasn't easy; there was a bed of dry leaves all around them. He watched the placement of his hand as he leaned his weight, trying to keep his old boots from crunching dried leaves as he got to one knee. Mack picked up his gun.

He leaned around the trunk of the tree, watching his dad do the same on the other side. The sun was up, but the canopy of the woods intercepted most of its rays. There was another crackle of leaf, loud as a shot in the clear, quiet morning air.

Mack leaned out, slowly. He wanted to see what was coming. Could be a raccoon. A squirrel, maybe. Or ...

It could be a deer. A big, twelve-point buck. His dad had promised to let him take the first shot.

Mack looked out beyond the tree, keeping his head closer to the ground. He knew that a silhouette could betray his position to his prey easier than almost anything. He kept his movement slow, and knew his dad was doing the same on the other side of the tree. Mack leaned, his abdomen unhappy with the way it was twisted. He didn't care. He needed a look.

The rifle in his left hand, weight leaning on the right, Mack tilted his head around the tree trunk.

And saw ...

What the hell was that?

It walked on four legs. It was the size of a dog, maybe a Labrador. Its coat was shining, shimmering black though, and darkness seemed to melt off of it like smoke off dry ice.

Mack peered at it, not sure if he was seeing what he thought he was seeing. That sure as hell wasn't a buck. Or a doe. Or even a fawn.

"The hell ...?" his dad whispered. He wouldn't have spoken if it had been a deer, Mack didn't think.

The black thing—whatever it was—lifted its head. Its eyes glowed a ruby scarlet, that strange shadowy-melt drifting off it. It cocked its angular head toward his father, and made a noise.

It was like a hissing bird call, high and low at the same time. It followed it up with clicking noises.

Mack just stared. He'd never seen anything like this, not even on TV.

Another sound mirrored the creature's call, and then another, off in the distance. There was a rustle in the leaves nearby, and Mack turned his head slowly.

It had been loud.

And close.

One of the black, shadowy things was coming out of the woods behind them.

"Dad," Mack whispered, and the thing looked right at him.

"Shit," his dad said, holding steady and still. "Mack, don't move."

The one that had emerged from the woods behind them stared at them with those ruby eyes. There was no trace of a mouth on its pure-black head. A long, thin tail waved behind it, like it was balancing the creature.

Leaves crackled. Another one came into view to his dad's side.

An aura of menace floated in the air. Mack could see his father's tension in the way he held his gun, the intensity with which he watched the creatures. A worried rumble crackled through Mack's belly.

"When I tell you to," Mack's dad said in an even voice, "you shoot the one coming out behind us here. I'll get the one to my right. Then we'll both turn and get the last one, if it ain't scared off by then."

"Okay." Mack clicked the safety off. He'd been ready to shoot something this morning, but he wasn't expecting it to be these ... things. "Dad ..." He hesitated, and his dad looked at him. "You think these are in season?"

His dad sat there uneasily, hand gripped around his rifle. He stared at the one that was looking right at them, tail cocked and ready to spring. "I get a bad feeling about the way these things look. I'll take a poaching ticket if it comes to it."

Mack readied the rifle. He drew a bead on the one in front of them, its shoulders down, butt up in the air like it was going to spring. The rifle was a .243, one his dad had borrowed from his uncle. Mack looked through the scope, trying to breathe like he'd learned. He exhaled, one finger just barely on the trigger once the reticle was settled on the creature's shoulder. *Just like a deer,* Mack thought.

"Shoot," his dad said. "I'll go as soon as you do."

Mack stroked the trigger softly and felt the gun bellow in the morning air. The rifle shot was a deafening crack in the still woods, barrel leaping up as the muzzle flashed.

The black creature took a stumbling step back from the hit. Mack figured he'd got it in the shoulder. He waited, watching, as it curled in on itself.

"Aieee!" His dad's scream tore Mack's attention away from the creature he'd shot. His whipped his head around, looking to see—

One of the creatures had his dad against the tree. Its jaw was open, a shadowy line broken by Mack's father's face buried in sharp, shadowed teeth. Blood was dripping down, and another scream tore the morning. Mack's dad's rifle was just out of reach, his struggling fingers trying for it and failing. The creature had him, pinned him, a cracking sound emerging between his father's screams.

Mack raised his gun on instinct and fired. The flash blinded him for a second as the barrel rose. The black thing snapped back like he'd kicked it good. It let loose a whimper that sounded like a car with the muffler fallen off.

    Mack just stared. His dad was bleeding, one hand shaking as he tried to staunch the flow, the other still reaching for his rifle. It was a few inches from his fingertips. Mack watched as he labored for it, almost had it—

    A hard blow knocked his father sideways as something struck. It was the first creature, then one that had been around the tree. Mack was supposed to shoot it, but he'd gotten distracted.

    He couldn't shoot it now though. It was half-hidden behind the tree, and the part that was visible had his dad in its jaws.

    "Dad!" Mack shouted as the thing ripped into his dad's leg. A warm geyser of red steamed as it splashed onto the orange and brown leaves, wetting them where before they'd been dry.

    "Oh, God!" his father yelled as Mack tried to bring his rifle to bear. It was so close, but the shot was tough. It was twisting, shaking his father like he weighed next to nothing. Mack could barely see the thing in the scope. His mind was running away with him. He was reacting fast, crazy. He'd just shot two times at two different animals.

    They'd been attacked by animals. In the woods. In Tennessee.

    What the hell were these things?

    "Mack, look out!" His dad's dull, pain-tinged warning tipped Mack off just in time. The first beast he'd shot was coming up now. It staggered a step as it leapt at him. Mack didn't have time to fire.

    He dodged.

    He rolled as he fell back. It was all instinct, just trying to get out of the way of the train bearing down on him. The thing was big, bigger than any dog he'd seen.

    It breathed on him as it passed over. Its breath smelt of that same stinking scent—sulfur, his dad had called it? Like rotten eggs.

    Mack brought the gun up and fired without even looking through the scope. It roared, the stock slamming him in the upper arm. He hadn't had much of a grip on it when he'd shot. He'd eyeballed the thing, and it hit right in the thing's hindquarters. Ass shot, Mack thought. Normally he would have laughed at that.

    There wasn't much to laugh about now.

    His dad was still screaming. That other thing had him and was pulling him, yanking him behind the tree, the rifle lying lonely and forgotten across the dry leaves.

    Mack fired again at the shadowy creature he'd just shot. Another hit, both to the critter and to his upper arm. That'd be a bruise later, he reckoned by the dull ache in his bicep. Not that it mattered.

    The shadow creature had ears like a cat, pointed at the tips. He could see it now that it was closer. Its skin looked like nothing he'd ever seen—like a black cloud, fuzzy and indistinct. It snapped its head around at him, red eyes on his.

Mack gulped. The thing was mad.

"Oh, Godddddd!" his dad yelled as the thing tore him loose from the tree. He disappeared behind the trunk. There was a tearing sound, sick and wet. The screams intensified, even as they became more choked and guttural.

Mack stared into the red eyes of the thing stalking him and fired his gun again. It flinched, staggering as it hit the tree.

But the red eyes never left him.

Mack's ears were ringing. His dad's screams had been muffled by the percussive rifle shots that had deafened him. The black creature opened its mouth at him, just a few feet. It was snarling, but he couldn't hear it.

He tried to shoot again. Nothing happened.

Empty.

Mack pulled the trigger again, fruitlessly. Again. He couldn't even hear the click.

The shadow cat rose up on its haunches. It could smell blood—his blood. Mack remembered the hunting knife at his belt and pawed for it. It was buttoned into the sheath, and he couldn't work the button—

The cat leapt. Damn, it moved fast too.

He wanted to close his eyes. Knew he should. He couldn't hear his dad anymore.

Mack couldn't stop looking though, his eyes fixed, wide, on the thing. That thing was death, he realized with a sick pit in his stomach.

Death was coming.

And there was nothing he could do to stop it.

*

Lafayette Jackson Hendricks had dealt with all kinds of shit in his time. Twenty-five years old, he'd spent time in Iraq during some of the high points of the war, had a night in New Orleans that had somehow ended up an even more memorable hell than his time in Iraq, and since then ...

Well, since then he'd bummed around the world fighting demons.

It wasn't an easy gig, especially given some of the shit he'd seen lately. Some of the things he'd run across in Midian, Tennessee had turned his stomach in ways that it hadn't been turned in the sandbox.

In Iraq, though, he'd faced flesh-and-blood men. Men who bled.

Men who died. He'd looked down the sights of an M-16 at them, pulled the trigger, and watched them dissolve into blood, bone, tissue and brains.

Now he faced an enemy that didn't dissolve at all when he pulled the trigger.

Hendricks had an AR-15, the civilian model of the weapon he'd carried over there, slung across his chest. It was a new addition to his gear. He'd used one a few months back, one that was property of the sheriff's department, but this one was new, only fifty rounds put through its recently-virgin barrel. He'd been the one to break her in, to get the sights the way he wanted them.

Now he peered down the red-dot sight at what was up ahead, and let loose.

It took multiple trigger pulls to crack out multiple shots. That might have made him sigh at any other time; the three-shot burst setting on an M-16 was handy when you were trying to fill the air with a high volume of bullets. Not as good as an M249 SAW for it, but the M-16 did a decent job of fire suppression.

He wasn't taking any fire here though.

Hendricks peered through the sights as he ran, minding his footing, firing and moving. His red dot was settled on a black target, some demon slung low to the ground like a fucking jungle cat.

He pulled the trigger again as he hurried forward, loosing another three shots. He had a thirty-round mag, and he figured he could close the distance before the hellcat—that was what it was, after all—managed to shrug off the effects of the rifle shots.

"COWBOY is moving in," Hendricks said over the open channel as he advanced, trying to put the damned thing down. It had been about to sink its demon teeth into a fucking kid dressed in camo and blaze orange.

"Understood," came the voice over the other end of the radio connection. This rig wasn't too different from what he'd used in the Marines.

Hendricks peppered the beast again, really let it have it. He knew the demon wasn't going to die from what he was doing, but it surely didn't feel too good inside the thing's shell, either. He was plenty happy to put a hurting on it. He was only about twenty feet away now, and the kid that had been about to be the cat's lunch was looking pretty grateful, now prone. He was on his belly, staring up at Hendricks like God Himself was advancing on the kid's position.

"Keep your head down!" Hendricks yelled. The kid ducked and covered like a good PFC when a drill sergeant shouted at him. The

AR-15 rattled out another bellowing chorus and came up dry. He'd already gone through thirty rounds? Shit.

It was time to get up close and personal anyway.

Hendricks let the rifle fall back gently, making sure no part of it swung to cock him in the nuts. Nothing could ruin a man's day like a mag to the boys. While he brought the AR back with one hand, he drew his sword with the other, bringing it out so that the black hellcat could see what was coming for him. Its red eyes locked on the holy blade, some primitive intelligence evident in the creature's hissing reaction.

"That's right, motherfucker," Hendricks said. "Your essence is about to taste air."

The hellcat didn't like that. It hissed in that otherworldly screech, like a whisper combined with a shriek, and it must have decided it didn't want to die backed up against a tree because it came out swinging at him.

That suited Hendricks just fine.

He swung the sword as the cat came at him, paw extended, shadowy claws visible like glowing black teeth. It was swiping for him, desperate. Not desperate enough to retreat, but crazy enough to come at him even though he had the reach on the sucker.

The blade caught it mid-paw as it tried to swipe the weapon down. Maybe it was gambling that he was just some dumbass out for a walk with a regular sword on his belt. Bad gamble, Hendricks figured, but who knew how smart the hellcat was?

The thing screeched as the holy implement made contact with the demonic skin. It had seemed to be almost smoking black, its skin alive, undulating like a cloud from a smokestack.

The skin stopped moving the moment the sword found home. It blanched, switching from black to a pale blue, then almost white as it evaporated. The essence in the core of the demon made a shrieking sound as it left this plane of existence behind. Nothing but a puff of white smoke heralded its passing.

Well, that and a hellacious burst of brimstone even worse than the stink the damned thing dragged around normally.

Hendricks watched the thing pass with a jaded eye. He'd snuffed his share of demons—his and a hundred other peoples' share, because very few people on Earth hunted demons. "Stay down, kid!" he shouted, giving the boy who still had his head down little in the way of attention as he galloped past. There were more hellcats, Hendricks was sure, and close by, because he could see the blood trail—

Hendricks stopped short as he came around the tree. It wasn't a pretty sight, what he saw. "Fuck," he whispered, his sword still dangling from his hand.

*

Lauren Ella Darlington was sitting at the breakfast table in a whorehouse, her daughter beside her, French toast sizzling on the nearby cook top. She was eating it too, and it was delicious, the flavors of cinnamon and maple syrup sweet on her tongue. She'd half expected it to be tasteless or unappetizing, but no.
This was the best French toast she'd maybe ever had in her life.
Here in this whorehouse.
Sitting next to her daughter.
While the madam cooked for them.
And one of the johns sat across the table.
Hell if these weren't the craziest days Lauren had ever lived through.
"Would you like some more, dear?" Melina Cherry asked Molly, Lauren's daughter. Her voice was a low purr of the sort that was not at all out of place given the madam's profession. Her beautiful, slightly lined olive skin was exposed down to the cleavage by her nightdress as she leaned over to slide another slice of the French toast onto Molly's plate after receiving a nod in reply to her question. The madam switched her attention to the only man at the table, and Lauren looked at him reluctantly. She'd been trying to avoid eye contact with him throughout the entire meal.
Unfortunately, Casey Meacham hadn't shared her reticence to talk given the fucking awkward circumstances. "I think it's gonna be a fine day," he said as Melina Cherry slid two more slices of the French toast onto his plate. Casey had already devoured at least two—maybe more; Lauren hadn't been watching closely—and set to work cutting these up, his knife clinking against Ms. Cherry's beautiful china.
It wasn't that Casey ate like a pig, Lauren told herself. It wasn't that he stuffed dead animals for a living either, though the smell of the taxidermy chemicals was pretty strong on him even now, in spite of the smell of night sweat and sex that she hoped—really, really hoped—Molly couldn't place. It was a nauseating combination that threatened to make Lauren chuck her good—no, amazing—French toast all over the red and white checkered tablecloth.
No, it wasn't any of those things that made her feel like a virgin whore in a room full of horny johns, a metaphor that felt awkwardly appropriate for where she was at in her life at the moment.

It was the fact that they were all sitting there around Ms. Cherry's table, Casey in nothing more than his boxers and a white, stained, wife-beater t-shirt, every single one of them knowing he'd paid Ms. Cherry for sex the night before and probably—okay, definitely, because the walls weren't thick enough to keep back the sound—fucked her for literally hours while Lauren and Molly tried to sleep. Tried, and failed, because ...

Well, because they were spending their time trying not to imagine Casey fucking Ms. Cherry.

Five times.

"Yeah," Molly said softly to Casey's proclamation. "Probably not gonna be a fine day for some of us."

Lauren cringed. Maybe the fact that it was today had a little something to do with their inability to sleep. Though the loud sex hadn't helped matters.

It was a shame too, because with the exception of Casey's visit last night, the whorehouse had turned out to be a surprisingly nice place for Lauren and Molly to hang their hats. It had started to feel ... not like home, but like a refuge from all that was going on out in Midian.

And then this fucking guy showed up.

"Oh, yeah, sorry," Casey said, cramming a bite of French toast into his gaping piehole. "Foh-god ab—"

"Casey, darling," Ms. Cherry said sweetly, "please. No talking with your mouth full."

"Thass whut I sed tu yu lass night!" He guffawed as he finished swallowing some of his mammoth bite. His amusement faded. "Anyway, yeah ... forgot about the funerals today, sorry."

His words were like a tiny stiletto knife, pricking Lauren in the heart.

Today was the day.

Today was the day they were going to bury her mom.

"How many funerals are there today?" Ms. Cherry asked. "I know Sheriff Reeve's wife is at noon, and your mother's—" she met Lauren's gaze with true regret "—is at two."

"Alison Stan's is at four," Lauren said, a little numbly. She hadn't had much time to grieve on that one. Not that she knew Alison Stan terribly well, but she'd been part of the watch they'd formed in Midian to fight back, and it had stung all the same. "Some others too ... so many I can't remember." She put a hand over her eyes for a second and laughed mirthlessly. "It's a bad sign when you have scheduling conflicts because you've got so many damned funerals."

"It is a bad sign," Casey agreed, cutting up his French toast, eyes on the plate. "Like seeing one that says, 'Toilet Out of Order' after you've just dropped a massive deuce."

Molly cringed visibly and pushed her plate away. "Ya know … I'm not hungry."

Casey stared at her. "You're a teenager, right? How old are you again?"

Lauren stiffened. This was prime Casey, inquiring about the age of her daughter. She could see this one coming and started to try and head it off, but too late—

"Umm … sixteen …" Molly said, regarding him carefully.

"Hm," Casey said. "You should say 'literally' more often, shouldn't you? Isn't that hallmark of your age group?"

Lauren just stared at him, and a slight flush of relief reached her cheeks. "That … was way less bad than I thought it was going to be."

"Anyhoo," Casey said, turning his attention back to his French toast, "you're turning into a right pretty little thing. When you hit eighteen, you let me know and we'll celebrate." He looked up, mouth full again, eyes twinkling. "Cuz you'll be legal," he managed to get out around a mashed piece of crust.

"And there it is," Lauren said.

"Casey," Ms. Cherry scolded, shuffling around as she turned off the cook top. She gave an apologetic look to Lauren. "You have to forgive him. He's a very sexual being."

"Yeah," Molly said under her breath, "we kinda heard that last night."

Casey looked at her expectantly. "And?"

She blinked a couple of times. "We … 'literally' … just heard that last night?" She tried it out experimentally.

"That's how you do it." Casey nodded, and turned back to his food.

Ms. Cherry looked like she wanted to weigh in on this, but she paused, one arm draped around Casey, looking past them all to the open door. Lauren turned her head and saw, with a lot of surprise, the fourth occupant of the whorehouse, standing in the doorway, her hair in a tight ponytail, pale skin free of makeup. She was a pretty thing, as Casey might have said—oh, God, Lauren wondered, wishing she hadn't—had Casey had her, too? Probably, she had to concede, shivering in revulsion.

"Lucia," Ms. Cherry said, smiling warmly at the girl standing in the doorway, "why don't you come in and have something to eat, darling?"

"Not very hungry," Lucia said quietly, but she edged in anyway, mouse-quiet. She had the shifty gaze that Lauren associated with abuse victims, that worried look that was always seeking out the direction of the next attack. She lingered at the edges of a room, of any conversation. Today was no exception; she made her way toward the fridge and opened it, but didn't turn her back to any of them for more than a second or so, as though she thought they might fall on her in a rage. She emerged with a can of Coke and opened it with a long, chipped pink fingernail. She seemed to freeze as she regarded the damage, then took a long, shuddering pull of the drink, watching Casey the whole time.

"I made French toast," Ms. Cherry said lightly, plainly trying to entice the girl.

"It's very good," Molly said in the way she had when she was trying to draw in a stray cat to pet or feed. She took a bite, apparently to illustrate it, even though she'd previously shoved her plate away.

Lucia regarded her and Lauren in turn, her expression inscrutable. In that way, she wasn't totally dissimilar to Starling, the entity that apparently claimed use of her body at times. Lauren might not have believed that if she hadn't had conversations with Starling, who was quiet but not shy, and Lucia, who was quiet and shy. The eyes were the real difference. Lucia's were always darting around, and Starling's ...

Well, Lauren couldn't even remember exactly what Starling's looked like.

"You should have a bite or two," Ms. Cherry said, sounding like a mother hen. She'd been that way to Lauren and Molly too, always gently coaxing rather than applying death-grip pressure, the way Lauren's mother would have.

Oof. Just thinking about her mother caused Lauren a pang of pain, of regret. She couldn't believe it was today.

"Okay," Lucia conceded. She moved the chair back just a hair, barely enough that a piece of paper could slide in between it and the table, but she damned sure fit her skinny self in there when she sat down. She put the Coke down in front of her, eyes flitting over to Casey. "Hi," she said, without any of the normal nervousness that Lauren associated with her. She sounded pretty okay with him, which Lauren—who did not find Casey anywhere in the same neighborhood, or even continent, as okay—found surprising.

"Hey, Lucia," Casey said with a mouth full. "How you doing?"

"Good," Lucia whispered. She smiled faintly. "Heard you had fun last night."

"Always do," Casey said brightly, lifting another full fork. "Did you have a quiet evening?"

"Things have been very quiet of late," Ms. Cherry said with a frown, still hovering behind Casey. "Which is surprising."

"A lot of people just died," Molly said, looking somewhere between shocked and mortified. "I'd think that would ... uhh ... depress business ... for you?"

Ms. Cherry shook her head. "People deal with their grief in different ways."

"It's true," Casey said, nodding sagely. "Last time I went to a funeral, I got laid afterward. Girl I went with pulled the truck over and fucked me right there at the entrance to the graveyard. Went right at it like she was going to tear my clothes off." He shook his head, and did a full body shiver of delight. "I think when there's death all around you, it's a natural instinct to do something so life-affirming—"

"Please cover your ears, Molly," Lauren said, feeling the desire to collapse on the table. She'd never considered herself any kind of prude—it wasn't like she got pregnant at sixteen through immaculate conception, after all. It was the messy kind of conception, and surprisingly fun considering how many of her friends had been fooling around at the same time and had nothing but half-hearted shrugs to express themselves over it. Or horror stories. There were a few of those.

"Well, maybe he's right," Molly said uncomfortably—but still too comfortably for Lauren's taste. *You're sixteen, for chrissakes* ... "Maybe when people see that much death around, they just sort of ... look for things to ... cheer them up." She shrugged at her mother, way, way less creeped out than Lauren would have hoped.

"Is there a physiological component to it, y'reckon, doctor?" Casey looked right at her. "I mean, men get boners regardless, you know? The desire don't go away unless you take the one-eyed snake by the neck and just wrestle it right out of 'em—" He illustrated the point with a hand gesture. A horrifying, horrifying hand gesture. She barely restrained herself from covering Molly's eyes.

"Jesus," Lauren said. She glanced at Lucia, who was daintily picking at her French toast. "Do you have anything to say?"

Lucia stopped, fork halfway to her mouth. "I've ... never had funeral sex. Or wanted to." She looked around the table like she'd gotten caught having funeral sex, then eased back in her chair and slowly pushed the fork to her lips. The bite was minuscule, maybe the size of the first knuckle of Lauren's pinky, and she chewed it slowly.

"Humans are funny creatures," Ms. Cherry said sympathetically to Lauren. "We don't all react in the same way to tragedy, to grief. We don't all carry around the same ... mores, I think you call them? We think differently, we are different, we react differently, yes? Some turn from pain, some ..." She looked at Casey, slightly pointedly, and he blushed. "Some embrace it. In any case ... you have grief, my dears." She looked at Molly and brushed a hand down her hair. "Hopefully today will help you deal with it ... at least a little." She smiled sympathetically and drew her silken, somewhat see-through robe together before she swept out of the room, looking as elegant as if she'd been at a ball.

Casey watched her go. "Got-damn!" He tossed his napkin down in the plate and stood, causing Lauren to jerk her head away rather than look at what was protruding from the flap of his boxers. "I got to go get me some of that fine lady." And he swept out of the room in a hurry, feet tapping their way up the stairs after Ms. Cherry's more relaxed, quiet pace. Lauren heard a giggle halfway up the stairs and a whisper, and then the pace increased for both sets of footsteps until a door slammed.

"Ohmigod," Molly said, her eyes wide. "Did you see—"

"It's like the sun during an eclipse—tell me you did not look directly at it," Lauren said, horrified.

"It was like Medusa," Molly said, her eyes narrowing and her tongue protruding in disgust. "I couldn't look away! It was like a snake rising out of one of those wicker baskets when the charmers play their song! But—I mean—it was HUGE! I don't even want to think about one of those going in—"

Lauren almost threw up the French toast right there. "Stop. Just ... stop. Don't think about it."

"How am I NOT supposed to think about it?" Molly asked, her eyes tightly squinted shut. "Oh, God, I thought about it again!" She shuddered, full body, her legs crossed tightly together. "AHH! Again!"

"Yeah, Casey's not a small guy," Lucia said quietly. "You'd think ... maybe he talks big because he isn't, but ... no." She shook her head, the red ponytail snaking down her neck, brushing against her shoulders. "It's all right though." She looked right at Molly. "Most guys aren't ... I mean, he's *unusually* large—"

"I don't think that helps!" Lauren said.

"Oh, whew, I think ..." Molly said. "I mean ... porn stars, I can kinda get, maybe through practice and building up the, um, stretching, but ... Jesus. That thing! It looked like a bodybuilder's arm holding a cantaloupe in his hand—"

"Please stop talking about it," Lauren hissed. "Just ... stop."

"It gets easier with time," Lucia said softly. "And, yeah, practice, I guess." She pushed her French toast away from her, too, and picked up the Coke, drinking a long pull from it. Her lips were cracked and dry, almost bloody. "Not that you need to worry about it anytime soon." She stood up and paused, glancing at Molly almost sadly. "I hope."

"Uh ... thanks?" Molly asked, looking up at Lucia with her eyes narrowed suspiciously. "Why would I need to wor—"

"You don't," Lucia said, shaking her head, breaking off eye contact and heading for the door. She disappeared behind it as quietly as she'd come in.

Molly stared after her. "Uh, Mom?"

Lauren was wary, expecting where this was going. "Yeah?"

"Do you think she's kind of been slapped around or someth—"

"Yeah." Lauren didn't mince the words. After a breakfast conversation that had covered funeral sex and ended in a massive erection, what was the point of denying that Lucia had almost certainly been abused at home—wherever that was for her?

*

Archibald "Arch" Stan swept his sword through the neck of the black-shadowed cat demon. He was already sweating from having dispatched a couple of the things. These were a little new to him. He'd dealt with fire dogs once before, but shadow cats? Well, it was all variations on a theme, he supposed, as he cut the head clean off the accursed demon.

He'd been late to this party, that much was obvious by the state of the woods around him. There was a whole lot of blood in the midst of all these downed leaves, autumn in full, blazing glory out here in the woods. He recognized the smell of an intestinal tract torn open, and he tried to breathe through his mouth. He didn't have any desire to add his lunch to the ground with all that blood and guts already spilled.

The hellcat screamed one final time as he caught it in the neck. The scream cut off partway through as the holy blade sliced down and hit the earth, severing a leaf or two in the bargain. The cat shrieked and hissed, but it wasn't the mouth making the noise. It was the essence of the thing, exposed to air now that he'd broken up the shell that contained it here on Earth. It let loose a stink of brimstone and sucked up into itself like a balloon that popped and shrank into nothing.

Arch would have made that same movement—sword through a demon neck—a thousand times this morning if he'd had enough obliging targets. They didn't seem to want to oblige though, there being only two of them when he'd showed up. The man they'd been picking at when he'd come out of the woods was plainly dead, his heart's blood run out through his open neck a few minutes past. One of them had locked a jaw on him and ripped it hard while the other had done the same to the man's guts. It didn't paint a pretty picture, but it had certainly painted a picture—one that was heavy on the red.

"Fuck," Lafayette Hendricks said as the cowboy stepped out from behind a tree, his boots crackling on the dry, fallen leaves as a gust of blustery wind blew through, stirring Arch's jacket and causing the cowboy's knee-length black drover coat to whip at the tail.

"That's all you ever say," Arch observed, probably a bit more irritably than he might have under normal circumstances.

"Sorry," Hendricks said, sounding genuinely contrite for his profanity.

That didn't make Arch any happier. He gave the cowboy a raised eyebrow and a flat look that held in his anger. "Don't do me any favors, okay?"

"Sorry," Hendricks said again. "We, uh … we got a kid over here."

Arch just stared at him. "Say what?"

"There's a …" Hendricks jerked his head toward the tree so hard that he had to catch his cowboy hat before it came falling off. "This guy had a kid with him."

That caused Arch's belly to bubble. He caught himself before he said something that might have been offensive, though no doubt the cowboy would have been amused. "Son of a gun," he said instead.

"Son of him, more like," Hendricks said grimly, and stepped back around the tree.

"Call it in," Arch said, coming up after the cowboy, hot. "I'll talk to—" He rounded the tree and found the boy, all decked out in camo and blaze orange, his face white as a bleached sheet. "—him."

"Which him?" Hendricks asked sourly. "The boy? Or your God, who I guess was totally cool with this happening?" Hendricks froze, teeth gritted together and mouth open in a grimace, eyes tightly shut. "Sorry. I'm sorry. That slipped out." He opened his eyes again, gauging Arch for reaction.

Arch didn't react, just stared at him coldly. "You gonna call it in or not?"

"Yeah," Hendricks said, stepping back, coat swaying as he moved. "Yeah, I'll call it in. You … do whatever you need to do." And he stepped away, putting a finger up to his ear and touching the thumbswitch. "Home base, this is Cowboy. Responding to the … to the screaming and gunfire we heard up in the woods … we have a male subject … down …" He kept from saying "deceased," Arch noticed, though based on his furtive looks at the boy, Arch wasn't sure it would have broken through just now. "And we have a young boy … teenager, I think … we'll be heading down in a few minutes."

"Roger that, Cowboy," Brian Longholt's voice crackled through Arch's earpiece. He could see by Hendricks's reaction that it had come through loud and clear for him as well. "What do you want to do about the … 'down' guy?" Brian was a smart guy; he'd plainly gotten the inference. "Ambulance or morgue wagon?"

"The latter," Hendricks said quietly. "You got a GPS position on us?"

"Roger that," Brian said. "I'll get … Yuval Simon heading your way. Looks like he's up in the rotation." It was sad that they even had a rotation of mortuary operators that they were having to call lately. Arch grimaced, a temporary respite from the look of fury that he was pretty sure he was wearing all the time of late.

"Ten-four. Cowboy out." Hendricks stepped back over and nodded at the boy who was quivering against the tree. "I thought you were gonna give aid and comfort while I called it in?"

Arch just glared at him, then let his furious look dissolve as he knelt next to the boy. "Can you hear me, son?" He waved a hand in front of the boy's eyes.

The boy's gaze snapped to him, and he spoke loudly, as though his ears were ringing from rifle shots. "Yes."

"My name's Arch Stan." Arch pulled back his coat's lapel to reveal his badge pinned on his uniform. "I'm with the Calhoun County Sheriff's office. What's your name?"

"Mack," the boy said, still loud. "Mack Wellstone."

"Okay, Mack," Arch said, speaking a little louder, to match the boy's speech, "we need to get you out of here. Can you walk?" He'd looked the boy over for injuries, but none were apparent, no hints of dark liquid against the camo pants or top, or the blaze orange vest.

"I think so," Mack said, looking past Arch to Hendricks. Mack frowned, but if he had a comment about the man dressed like a ranch hand who was lingering in the clearing, he didn't give voice to it.

"Come on then," Arch said, offering a hand. Mack took it, and Arch helped him to his feet. The boy wobbled a bit, but he stayed standing. He really wasn't a boy, Arch reflected. Probably only a decade or so younger than Arch himself, but Arch had experience that the boy—it was how he thought of him—hadn't had until today.

And Arch had it by the ton, now.

"We were supposed to go hunting," Mack said, staring off into the distance. This time he spoke pensively, in a normal tone of voice. Arch figured maybe he thought he was whispering, because he didn't look like he wanted a reply. He glanced at the tree. "My dad ... is he ...?" He looked at Arch, searching for a reply.

Arch knew Mack was fully aware of what had happened, so he just shook his head. "I'm sorry."

Mack took it like a champ. No, he wasn't a boy anymore. Arch wondered how much of the disemboweling he'd seen. Hopefully not much. Arch's words were apparently enough to convince Mack that his father was dead; there was no need to show him and remove any doubt that might have persisted.

Doubt was a fine thing. Arch would have a killed a thousand demons for a whisker of doubt for himself this morning.

"Come on," Arch said, putting an arm around Mack's shoulders to steer him out of the clearing the long way. They might have to walk an extra half-mile or so, but it'd be worth it not to show that boy his father's body.

*

Hendricks trailed behind Arch and the boy a few yards, keeping his eyes skinned for trouble. It tended to find them whether they wanted it to or not, especially lately, but he'd had enough of trouble sneaking up on them long ago. He had their six, he figured, watching their backs while he and Arch escorted the boy out, taking a meandering route out of the clearing on their way back to the police Explorer.

"It's gonna be okay," Arch said, causing Hendricks to roll his eyes when he was sure that neither Arch nor the boy was looking at him. How the fuck exactly was it going to be okay? Hendricks wondered. He'd lost a father too, and he didn't remember feeling it was okay, and damned sure not five minutes after his dad had died.

"Okay," the boy said wearily, just walking along, guided by Arch's hand on his shoulders. "What ... what were those things?"

"Wild dogs," Hendricks said loudly. He and Arch had been half a mile away, checking out an old cabin that was boarded up after getting a tip that it was a possible demon's nest. They'd heard gunfire, and enough rounds in a row to be convinced it wasn't just some good ol' boy with a loose trigger finger trying to put down a buck. No, it had sounded more like a day in Fallujah to Hendricks, so they'd come a-runnin', arriving a few minutes too late to save the day. The boy looked back at him quizzically. "Rabid," he added, layering on the bullshit because he knew Arch wouldn't lie.

"Was it really dogs?" The boy turned his head to look at Arch. Arch's sour-ass expression flickered as he gave Hendricks another nasty look. He was full of those lately. Of course, he had all the reason in the world to be in a foul mood. Losing a beloved wife tended to do that to a body, Hendricks knew through hard experience. "Looked more like demon cats to me," Arch said tightly.

That apparently mollified the lad, because he didn't ask again, just put his head down and kept walking. He hadn't even brought his rifle or pack with him out of the woods; apparently he thought Hendricks and Arch were badass enough to keep trouble at bay.

Or, more likely, he was back to the default mode of civilized humanity, assuming there was no trouble immediately at hand. Dumb thinking, Hendricks thought. There was always trouble about, even in those so-called civilized bastions of America.

"What'd you have to do that for?" Arch asked, whispering it low to Hendricks, turning around enough to give him a drink of the fury waiting behind the big man's eyes.

"Most people don't want to hear that their daddy got—" He caught an especially scathing look, and backed off from saying it flat out. "Well, they don't want to hear the truth of how what went wrong back there ... went wrong." That was about as much as he could talk around the subject at hand, Hendricks figured, and it damned near made him dizzy trying to do it.

Arch gave him what might have been a grudging look, but the steel in his voice hinted he wasn't backing down an inch. "White lies are still lies, you know."

"Maybe we should discuss this later," Hendricks said, glancing behind them again. The woods were quiet now. He hadn't seen hellcats before, but he'd read about them. They didn't tend to travel alone, which suggested to him that there might be more somewhere else in these woods. That'd turn hunting season right on its fucking head, wouldn't it? "You know, instead of finishing that other conversation we weren't having."

Arch frowned at him. "We weren't having a conversation before."

"Exactly," Hendricks said. The big man was usually brighter than this. Hendricks had figured Arch would have taken a drink or something after losing Alison, but no—the bastard was back on patrol, throwing himself into it. *That was how I handled it too,* he thought. Embrace the world of demon hunting or face the fact you lost what was most important to you in this world?

Easy choice.

"You make no kind of sense." Arch shook his head, brushing off Hendricks. The Explorer was visible ahead at the edge of the woods. So was that looming, boarded-up cabin. Arch's attention focused on it for a moment, and Hendricks could read the hunger in his eyes. He wanted to go crashing in, do what they'd come here to do, maybe poke holes in a few demons.

"We've got to get the boy back to HQ," Hendricks said, trying to defuse that bomb before it went off. All they needed was to save this kid from one patch of trouble only to go stumbling into another.

Arch stared at the old cabin for just a few seconds too long. "All right," he said, like he was struggling to convince himself. That was worrying, at least to someone like Hendricks who had seen this particular road up close and personal and knew where it led. "All right," Arch said again, resigned this time. He broke eye contact with the old cabin and turned his body toward the Explorer. "But ..."

"We'll come back, yeah," Hendricks said. Well, fighting demons was at least a productive way of handling grief, wasn't it? A hell of a lot better than balling up in a little ball and crying, that was for damned sure. It'd all come out sooner or later anyway. Arch could bury his feelings for now—like his wife—but unlike Alison, hopefully they wouldn't stay down there forever, moldering in some cold and worm-laden grave.

*

"They're bringing in the survivor," Brian Longholt said, fidgeting with the radio headset he was wearing. It caught his hair a little and pulled, the only thing he really disliked about this new rig. It had shown up wrapped in a big blue ribbon that advertised Amazon's Echo just a few days after—

Well ... a few days after.

"Glad to hear we had a survivor," Sheriff Nicholas Reeve said. He didn't put much feeling into it, but then, Brian understood that—sort of. Reeve was like a man carved out of stone, especially lately. His voice had been alive before, but now it was like a harsh whisper, which Brian considered a natural side effect of having demons possess your wife and kill her, then turn loose on your town in a goddamned frenzy of violence right out of the French Revolution, or the Bolshevik Revolution ... some kind of fucking revolution. There had damned sure been enough blood in the streets.

"Not too many of those these days," Brian said, adjusting the headset again. Two more pulled hairs. Ow.

"Seems to me we had plenty of them in the square a few days ago," Reeve said. He just sounded dead, like all his wisecracking good humor had left him. He was still here, still doing the job, but if there'd been light in the man's eyes, someone had doused it with a fucking fireman's hose, just pissed all over it until the candle was out.

Brian got that too. He was feeling more than a little of it himself, and he hadn't even been hit as hard as Reeve.

"Do you know if Dr. Darlington is stopping by?" Reeve asked, rubbing at his freshly-shaven cheeks. Brian eyed them; there was a nick or two on the older man's face, probably the product of shaving with a shaky hand, and for the first time in days. He had to look good for the funeral, Brian supposed.

"Before, uh … the service, yeah," Brian said, tap-dancing around that one. He feared to say it for some reason. *Before her mother's funeral. Before your wife's funeral. Before …*

Before Alison's funeral.

There were damned sure more funerals than that. Brian's fifth-grade teacher, Mrs. Waldman, had died in the square. His pal Jacob Reading's mother had died too, along with a dozen other people tangentially involved in his life. Midian had been kicked squarely in the balls, and they all felt it.

But the three that he was feeling most acutely were Vera Darlington … Donna Reeve …

And his sister.

"Good," Reeve said, causing Brian to jolt in shock until he realized that Reeve was talking about Dr. Darlington stopping in, not the deaths of the people they cared about. "I don't need to be worrying about this … shit—" he waved his hand vaguely in the direction of the detention cells "—with everything else going on."

Brian glanced in the direction he'd waved his hand. He knew full well what the sheriff was talking about, of course. It was another little detail that he didn't want to consider at present, that man sitting in the cell block in a catatonic state. If it had been up to Brian, going with his gut, he would have left the man in there and never spoken about him again. He wouldn't have been able to avoid thinking about him—the bastard—but he was pretty sure he would have been content to let him rot away there, out of sight, out of mind.

And the bastard was pretty damned surely out of his mind.

Or, rather, a hell of a lot of minds were out of him.

They didn't even know his name. He was just a guy, medium height, medium build, vacant expression. Just a guy without fingerprints on record, without a mind of his own, who was sitting in a cell as he had been for the last several days, slowly starving to death with no desire to eat the food they put in front of him or drink the water they'd left for him.

He just sat and stared, all day and all night, no difference in how he was when he was awake from how he was when he slept—if he slept.

And although a tiny shred of guilt wiggled in his psyche ... Brian was mostly okay with the fucker wasting away like that.

Because he had, after a fashion, killed Vera Darlington. Killed Donna Reeve.

Killed Alison.

He'd done more than that, of course. Brian knew through hard experience, though he was fighting it on every level, that whatever was in that cell wasn't the thing that had killed those people. He knew because a piece of what that man in the cell had carried had wormed its way into Brian's brain, had taken over his body the way it had presumably once taken over the nameless man in the cell. It had walked him around like a man, made him talk like a man ...

But that thing was not a man, and what it had used him for ...

"Jesus," Brian whispered.

"It hits sometimes out of the blue, doesn't it?" Reeve asked warily. He had charcoal-dark circles under his eyes, well earned, Brian suspected, if the sheriff's sleep experience was anything like his own of late. "You'll be thinking about anything but ... and then it just comes down and cold-cocks the fuck out of you from nowhere."

"Yeah," Brian whispered. There was a lump in his throat the size of Cleveland. Ohio, not Tennessee.

"Anyway," Reeve said, looking away, "glad Dr. Darlington's coming in to deal with Johnny Doe so I don't have to."

"She's going to ... uh ... put in a feeding tube, I think," Brian said, wiping his eyes with the back of his hand. A couple tears leaked out unintentionally. He didn't fucking care if Reeve saw. "And an IV, again."

"Great," Reeve said, though he didn't sound like the sentiment was anywhere in the neighborhood of great. Pretty fucking far from it, actually. "Let me know when she gets here. Or when Arch and Hendricks come dragging in with their survivor. Reckon I'll have to call the kid's parents—or parent, maybe?" He shook his head. "Whatever's left, I suppose."

"Will do," Brian said, still brushing at the back of his eyes. They wouldn't stop now. They never did, whenever he thought of what those demons had done to him ...

What they had made him do.

"I'll be in my office," Reeve said, not looking back at him. Maybe he didn't want to see a putatively grown man cry in front of him. Maybe, like Brian, he was feeling it enough that watching would have set him off. The sheriff wasn't the sort of man who evinced grief in the sight of others, near as Brian could tell. Brian didn't care anymore. What they'd done …

"I've got to go to the hospital later," Brian called after him. "Before the …"

Reeve didn't look back, just waved a hand like he got it. He probably got it. They all got it, after all. Grief. Hell. Demons. They were all in the thick of this together, after all. He shut his office door and left Brian sitting there, manning the radio. Calls would come in. They always did. Brian would be ready, would do his shift until it came time to leave for the hospital.

"Fuck," he whispered and mopped at his eyes.

"And kid," Reeve said, opening his door. "Way to be in here … you know, given what's going on … what's gone on … with your sister … with your dad in the hospital and whatnot …"

Brian looked up at him, the world blurry through the veil of tears. "Well," he said, "you're here even though your wife died and you're facing a recall vote next week."

Reeve just stared at him, stock still. "Someone's gotta do this job."

"Yeah," Brian agreed. Reeve just nodded and shut the door, disappearing behind the glass that said SHERIFF on it in big golden-shaded letters. "And I guess we're the only ones who will."

*

"I'll be back in a few minutes," Lauren said as she walked out the door of the house. The *whore*house, she corrected, the thought of its purpose especially clear in her mind after listening to Casey doing … whatever … with Ms. Cherry. No, not *whatever*, Lauren told herself. She knew damned well what he was doing. Everyone in the house did, because they were not quiet, and even Molly wasn't innocent enough to ignore the paroxysms of pleasure being shouted through the thin walls.

"Umm, I'm coming with you," Molly said, attaching herself to Lauren's arm. Lauren didn't wonder at her clinginess; they'd lost her grandmother and been rendered essentially homeless in one stroke.

"Don't get me wrong, I'm happy to have your company," Lauren said as they navigated around the big back bumper of Casey's truck, "but—"

"OH GOD!" Molly burst out, eyes squinted shut and her tongue out like she was about to heave. "OH GOD, OH GOD!"

"Like I didn't hear enough of that being screamed before we walked out the door," Lauren said.

"Look!" Molly threw out a finger at the back of Casey's truck, and Lauren's eyes followed the natural line to a bumper sticker written in flat red: *Unless you're trying to form a human centipede, get off my ass!*

"Gross," Lauren pronounced. She was pretty sure it was in last place for nastiness this morning though.

"'Gross' is an understatement on the level of saying that Othello was kind of set up, *The Vampire Diaries* was kind of dramatic, and *Batman Vs. Superman* kind of sucked."

"Fair point." Lauren shook her head. "You know, living in this whorehouse actually wasn't bad until Casey showed up."

"I know, right?" Molly shuddered. "He literally …" She froze, then blinked. "Oh, God. He's got me saying 'literally' now, Mom. He's literally got me saying literally."

"There, there," Lauren said, opening up the car door. She almost said, "At least it can't get any worse," but stopped herself just in time.

*

Erin Harris kept her silence in the nave of St. Brigid's, looking sidelong at the door with her hand at her side, fingering the grip of her Glock 19. It was probably weird to be holding onto the grip of a pistol in the entry to a church, but she didn't care. These were weird times, and they called for crazy measures like making sure you had a hand on your gun in church.

She thought she heard something outside, a squeal of car tires. Probably just her imagination. She thought she'd been hearing the squeal of car tires for months, after all.

Father Nguyen was doing his thing, right in the middle of the altar. If the crosses had been upside down, Erin might have thought it was some sort of satanic ritual, something she would have been more enthused about attending than a mass before this whole hell crisis had come roaring into Midian, Tennessee. It would have sounded fun, flippant, outrageous and rebellious to her youthful, inexperienced ears.

Of course, that was before she saw demons murder people, before she'd been possessed by one and committed atrocities while under its control. Before she'd come back to herself on the town square, doused in blood like it was a baptism for that rebellious occult ritual.

Now ... she had about as much interest in that as she did in sitting on a cold steel fence post without her pants on. Which was to say none. At all.

This ritual she was watching now though ... it had been dimly interesting a few hours ago, when it had started. But she'd long since lost her enthusiasm for it, and was ready for it to just be done. It felt like she was standing in the world's longest line, and her patience was out, she was tired, she was about to have to go to a heap of funerals that she had no interest in attending ...

Father Nguyen got to his feet at the altar, and Erin blinked. Maybe he was done? Hell, that would be nice. She'd been here all damned night watching his back just in case a demon somehow made it past the tuned-up security that the Father had put in place around St. Brigid's. Erin didn't know how likely that was, but it wasn't deemed worth chancing.

"Your holy instrument, my lady," Father Nguyen said, picking up the item from the altar. He spoke fairly quietly most of the time, but now he was loud enough that she both heard and understood him from all the way back where she was standing. St. Brigid's was not a small country church by any means. He started down the aisle toward her through the sea of pews.

A chill wind whipped at the garbage bags taped up over some broken stained-glass windows on one side of the church. Erin glanced at them from where she leaned in the doorway. She'd been told that she herself had done that, leaping through them to escape while possessed. She vaguely recalled it, but it had been during the period of time when she'd been so damned worn out from mentally fighting the multiple souls that had jumped into her head and sat on her will that she'd zoned out while they possessed her.

Other times she remembered clear as a blue-sky day.

They were uniformly the times when the demons had used her body to do terrible, terrible things to the townspeople of Midian.

"I've been seeing lots of unique choices," Father Nguyen said as he advanced toward her with the weapon in his grasp. "Casey Meacham had me consecrate a tomahawk, but this ..." He shook his head. "This is unique." He extended his hands, cradling the weapon carefully.

"You've never seen a baseball bat with nails driven through it before?" She took it from him and slung it over her shoulder, taking care to avoid the tetanus shot that would be required if she accidentally poked herself with one of the jutting nails. There were about twenty of them driven through various parts of the bat, giving her a lot of room to swing the thing around and put some holes in demons.

"Not as a blessed holy instrument, no," Nguyen said. "I'm fairly certain they're mostly used for doing work that is not God's."

"So are most weapons, I'd imagine," Erin said, looking at the Louisville Slugger emblem that was marred by a nail poking through. It had been her brother's bat, but he didn't need it anymore since he was off in the Army.

"Indeed," Father Nguyen said. "Now, if you'll excuse me ..." His shoulders slumped slightly. "I need to prepare for a funeral mass, and ... just possibly ... sleep for a few minutes beforehand."

"Go with God," Erin said with a fair amount of sarcasm. Nguyen either missed it or chose to ignore the insult. Erin didn't care either way. She hadn't ever really been much of a faithful person, and having a demon in her head had done surprisingly little to turn things around. Shouldn't she have been alive with the spirit or something?

She didn't feel alive with anything except deep cynicism and a vaguely nauseous sense that she'd been used and abused to do some shit right out of a horror movie to people she cared about. About half the survivors of the square were probably feeling about the same now, she reckoned, but she didn't care about them either. It was every woman for herself as far as she was concerned, and the dark hole she'd felt growing within over the last few months at this crisis had only gotten deeper and darker in the last week. Sometimes she woke up in the middle of the night and felt like she was drowning in an ocean of darkness and couldn't get to dry land no matter how she struggled.

She wanted to blame it all on Lafayette Hendricks, and really, part of her thought it'd be simpler if she could. But that part warred with the reality, which was that her hometown had been doomed to a showdown with the forces of fucking evil before the cowboy had even showed his perfectly sculpted abs around these parts, and they'd probably have been a hell of a lot worse off at this point if he hadn't come.

That burned. A lot.

She'd had fun with him. He was a pretty good lay once they'd gotten past that first time. She could tell he was a little rusty—well, she'd suspected, anyway, later verified by his own confession: Hendricks hadn't fucked anyone but her in years. She couldn't say the same, not that it had seemed to matter to him at the time.

But now he had gone his own way, she was heading hers, and she couldn't help but feel this miserable sense of anger and rejection.

They'd left her behind after all, when he and Alison and Duncan had blown town, hid out in the country in a house with no plumbing or air conditioning or anything else. While she was sitting in a hospital recovering from a car crash that should have killed her, the four of them had gone off and had a grand adventure. Resentfully, she knew that wasn't the case, but it was still like a thorn in her heart she couldn't extract, the feeling that Hendricks had left her behind.

Not that she'd thought they'd get married or anything. God, she wasn't that over the moon for him. He was sullen, moody, a pain in the ass, and that fucking bag of his smelled like toxic waste from all his dirty laundry.

No, she hadn't thought they'd get married. But she didn't think they would flame out over her saving his life and damned near losing her own in the process. She didn't figure she would have been so goddamned angry over something she understood—that he had to leave town when he did, and that he couldn't have come for her—but she was. She was so fucking furious, and had been for as long as they'd been working together again. The anger she'd felt toward him was almost as heavy as the fury those fucking irate demons had felt toward the townsfolk of Midian when they'd taken over her body. They'd used that too, her anger, and she'd felt a righteous fury when they'd done those horrible things with her hands. Totally misplaced righteous fury, but it had been there nonetheless.

Shit.

She slung the baseball bat off her shoulder, careful not to nick herself in the face as she did. Yeah, she wanted to throw some hurt with this thing, pop a few demon motherfuckers. She probably wouldn't even be thinking about Lafayette Hendricks's face when she was nailing—haha, she thought, that was kinda funny—those demon cockwaffles ...

Probably.

*

Jason Pike had been the County Administrator for Calhoun County for a few years, and he couldn't imagine a more satisfying job, or more thrilling place to be right now. After all, this was the opening act of some pretty grand shit right here; they'd had a complete and total catastrophe in the square in Midian just last week—something he'd orchestrated himself—and now who knew what they were heading for next?

Oh, sure, it wasn't all sunshine and daisies—or maybe entrails and blood sacrifices. The square event was supposed to be like a ringing of the dinner bell for all the demons in the area. Pike had planned it to be a slaughter, but it was supposed to be more of a demon buffet rather than a chance for some ages-old legion of demons to air whatever grievances they had with local law enforcement.

Pike shook his head. He was sitting in his office, in Culver, about forty minutes from Midian, looking out the window on the woods out back. The County Administrator's office was on the second story, and as far as views went, he had the best in the county. He'd seen to that. A man at the top ought to have a few perks, after all, oughtn't he?

And Jason Pike was at the top of this county, that much was sure.

He had a pretty comfortable chair too. The last county administrator had skimped in that department, bought some ragged old thing that would have been okay for a meeting room in the council hall, but wasn't fucking fit for a County Administrator to rest his ass on all the live-long day while he was working to solve problems. Well, solve some and create others. He'd fixed that shit right off, bought a several-hundred-dollar seat, overstuffed and padded, that did the trick nicely. He spun in it now, leaned back, thought about putting his feet up.

In his most private, unguarded moments—and this was definitely one, with his heavy wooden door tightly shut—he pondered the opportunities laid out before him. It was a narrow road he walked, trying to slice off one piece of the county at a time, making sure his duly dull constituents didn't get wise to his act. He had a plan, and it wasn't to get run out of town on a rail before the fun really began.

There were certainly opportunities. There were nglashii harbored in a nest out near the National Forest, according to Pike's sources. Nglashii were two-legged, three-headed chaos-thrivers. They didn't tend to show up to a hotspot party until it was time for the big show to begin. As much as he regretted his little sacrifice going awry in the square, it hadn't been all in vain. The demons here might not have been able to participate thanks to that damned possessed bastard stealing the thunder, but it had raised a few eyebrows in the underworld, and sent a bunch of demons stampeding this way. The other hotspots were slowly dying out now, and this place was starting to look more and more appealing to the crowd he was looking to attract.

"County Administrator," Jenny beeped in on his phone.

"Yes?" Pike asked, putting those weighty thoughts on hold.

"Your wife is on line two."

"Thank you, Jenny," Pike said, leaning forward to pick up the phone. "Hello, Darling Darla." He'd had that special name for her for years.

"Jackass," she scoffed, but he knew she was smiling. "Are you sitting behind your desk, contemplating masturbation?"

"I was actually considering my evil plan," Pike said with a little amusement. His wife had a filthy mouth when she wanted to. Not when the kids were around, though.

"Well, that's a form of onanism. Intellectual, but still."

"It does feel good when I do it." He chuckled. "Are you checking in on me for any specific reason?"

"I wanted to let you know," she said, getting to it, "I'm not in the mood tonight, so make sure you fuck Jenny before you come home. Or if you're in a hurry, have her suck your cock." There was that dirty mouth. She sounded almost entertained by this suggestion. Well, she had been entertained by it before, when she'd watched while touching herself.

"Because you're closed for business, got it," Pike said. She was awfully damned considerate to give him a warning. It was more than most wives gave their philandering husbands, after all—willing consent for him to despoil whoever he could sink his dick into, and happy in the knowledge that he was doing it. Sure, it came with a price—her doing a little despoiling of her own—but he didn't really mind.

He knew at the end of the day, she'd always come home to him and he'd always come home to her. They had a tie that united them that went far beyond the physical, even though they still fucked like rabbits.

That tie was power. They both craved it like he craved a lick of her nipple right now.

"Have you called Sheriff Reeve yet?" Darla asked, dry amusement in her voice crackling like fall leaves.

"Every day," Pike said. "He doesn't answer or call back for some reason."

"Maybe it's because you set up the event that resulted in the death of a shit-ton of people in his tribe and never showed up for it. Made you look a little guilty."

"Well, hell, I am guilty," Pike said with a smirk. "But how would he know that for sure?"

"Reeve never struck me as a man who was overly concerned with proof."

"He is a bit lacking in the refinement that might have come from a higher education," Pike said. "I wonder sometimes if he's even heard of Miranda Rights."

"Who is this Miranda?" Darla asked. The woman was damned funny when she aimed to be, and she usually did. "Does she have a tight ass?"

"Not as tight as yours, Darling Darla."

"You have a silver tongue. Watch where you put it."

"So ... not up this Miranda's ass, then?"

"Mmmm." Darla let out a long sigh. "Maybe I am in the mood after all."

"That was a quick turnaround. You want me to hold off on dumping my load in Jenny?"

"Nah," Darla said. "Go ahead. It'll be a fun challenge getting you interested again. But make sure you call Reeve. It's very important you hedge—"

"I know," Pike said, nodding along. "I need to appease the man ahead of the recall—in case he wins."

"He and that little Boy Scout Troop he's formed are a real threat to what we're doing here," Darla said. She sounded hot. And menacing. Menacingly hot, like she'd shoot Nick Reeve right in the head if he was in front of her. "You need to make peace, to throw them off the scent until you can deal with him."

"Well, gosh, Darling Darla," Pike said, "I'd sure like to, but short of walking up and capping the bastard or waiting for the recall to drag his ass out of his chair, I'm not sure how to approach that particular problem."

Darla paused, clearly giving it some thought. He could almost imagine her blond hair tossed back over her shoulder, pale blue eyes darting around in thought. She had just a slight bit of fat built up around her body from child birth, and it didn't do anything for Pike. He didn't dare say a word about it; the old saying about a woman with extra pounds living longer than the man who mentioned it was probably true, especially in the case of his Darla. "No, I suppose it'd be too much to shoot him in the head, even for this county right now. Which is why you need to make peace with the man. Keep in mind that as far as he knows, you're not involved in demon goings-on. One of them stabbed you with a holy blade, didn't they?"

Pike held up his hand, looking at the bandage where Alison Stan— that cunt, devils take her fucking soul—had jabbed him with a knife. "Indeed they did."

"So they probably just think you're an asshole politician. Take advantage of that. They're probably decent people." She snorted a little. "Get in their blind spot. They're worried about demons right now, not people."

"Reeve's been in law enforcement an awfully long time," Pike said, looking at the closed door to his office. "He might see a little farther than the rest of his merry band."

"It doesn't matter," Darla said. "Snow him for a few days, and maybe the recall will take care of it."

"I don't think even a recall is going to pull this man out of the fight," Pike said. "I don't think the fucker is just going to pull up stakes and leave Calhoun County."

"Maybe not," she said, "but it'll diminish his base of support, and events are likely to take care of him given enough time. No man can fight a demon army forever."

That was true, wasn't it? "As always, my lovely, you have wisdom."

"I've got more than that," Darla said. "Call Reeve. Make your peace. Swallow your ego and, later, maybe I'll swallow your cock if it goes well."

"Mmmhmmm," Pike said, staring at the door. "I'll get right on it. If he'll take my call."

"Maybe you should dial 911."

"Ooh, that's clever, my dear."

"I'm a clever girl. And Jason?" she asked sweetly.

"Yes, my darling?"

"I want to taste Jenny on you when you get home, you hear me? Give it to her good." And she hung up.

Pike nodded, replacing the phone in the handset. How could he argue with his wife over something like that? He stared at the phone for a minute and tried to decide which to do first, fuck Jenny or call that bastard Reeve. He decided on the former, imagining Jenny bent over his desk, the thought of her ass smashing against his pubic bone giving him an immediate chubby. He flicked the intercom switch with a smile on his face. "Jenny, would you mind coming in here for a minute? We need to go over the schedule for next week's events."

She'd know what that meant.

*

Brian stared at the teenage boy as Hendricks and Arch brought him in. He had a sick look on his face, as one might when they'd seen a parent murdered in front of them. It wasn't too hard for Brian to imagine what that felt like, since he'd recently damned near seen his father murdered in front of him, and by his own hand, no less. At least the boy wouldn't have to deal with that guilt, though he'd probably be working through some of his very own.

"Gentlemen," Sheriff Reeve said somewhat formally, coming out of his office to greet them. Brian cast him a long look. They hadn't spoken for the last half hour or so, however long it had taken Hendricks and Arch to make their way back to the sheriff's station. It had been a good silence, the kind Brian used for processing through the steady river of horrendous emotion that seemed to pulse through his veins with regularity of late. Reeve bent over to look the young man in the eye. "What's your name, son?"

"Mack Wellstone, sir." Damn if he didn't have manners, under those skinny shoulders. He was wearing a blaze orange vest of a kind that Brian associated with trips where his dad had wanted him to hunt and he hadn't wanted to.

Brian felt a hard pang in his heart at the memory. He sure as hell wished he'd done more hunting now; he might have been better prepared to be out there with a gun and a sword instead of sitting in the sheriff's station with a wicked limp, playing Felicity Smoak to the cowboy's Oliver Queen—but without the played-out sexual tension.

"I'm sorry about your father, Mack," Reeve said, and Brian could tell the man felt it, more emotion bleeding out in his voice right now than Brian had heard from him over the last week. "Where are you from?"

"Knoxville, sir." His voice was flat.

"Do you live with your momma and your daddy?"

"Yessir." It was painful to listen to the conversation; the boy was shut down, responding only when spoken to, like he'd been rendered insensate by watching his daddy die. How much had he seen, Brian wondered? Not that he needed to see it to be scarred by it.

"Could you write down your momma's phone number for me?" Reeve picked up a pen and pad from the desk next to him and handed it to the boy. Mack Wellstone didn't hesitate; he wrote down a number immediately and handed pen and pad right back to Reeve, his expression still unchanged.

"I'll go give her a ring," Reeve said, retreating slowly. "These fellas will keep you company until I get back, all right?"

Brian glanced at Hendricks and Arch, both of whom were pretty damned quiet. Hendricks had his hat down, trying to hide his sullen expression. Brian couldn't quite figure that one out; the cowboy had less cause than the rest of them to be upset. He wasn't from here, wasn't watching his own hometown go straight to hell in a handcart. Even Arch didn't look quite that grim, and Lord knew he had more reason to.

"Hey," Brian said to the boy, whose gaze slid over to him easily. "I'm Brian."
"Hi," Mack intoned. The kid really wasn't feeling much, was he?
"You hungry?" Brian asked.
"No."
"Want something to drink? A Coke or something? RC Cola? Moon pie?"
"No." The kid didn't register emotion at all. That was probably for the best.
"Okay. Let me know if you change your mind." Brian paused for a second. "You want—"
"For chrissakes," Hendricks said, rolling his eyes back hard, "leave him be. Jesus, people."
Arch shot Hendricks a look that would have burned through a lead-lined shield. "Would you kindly stop—"
"Yeah, yeah," Hendricks said. "I took the Lord's name in vain, I know."
They fell into a dreadful silence. There was a clear tension between the two of them, and they'd been thick as thieves only a week ago. That was the effect of losing Alison, Brian figured, feeling another sharp stab to the heart. At least Arch hadn't completely come apart on them. That would have been extra shit on top of a crap sandwich, given what was going on. He was soldiering through though, wasn't he? Brian snuck a look at him, but Arch just looked neutral. He clearly wasn't shut down, but that was down to his faith, wasn't it?

He was probably praying his way through or something. Brian didn't have the luxury of believing to carry him through this shitshow.

Reeve came out the office door again a few minutes later, opening it quietly. "I talked to your momma," he said, making his way over to Mack again. "She's on her way up from Knoxville." He tried to meet the boy's gaze, but Mack was fixated on the gun rack on the far side of the room. "Shouldn't be too long."

"I shot that dog," Mack Wellstone said, looking at the guns. "Shot him a few times." He sounded curious, trying to explain something he couldn't quite work through. "He didn't die though."

"Probably just missed," Hendricks said quickly.

"I didn't miss," Mack said with the first stirring of emotion he'd exhibited since walking in the door. The denial was hot, the boy's eyes narrow enough that Brian would have labored to squeeze a dime through the slits that remained. "I hit 'em, but they didn't die." He looked over at Hendricks. "And when he shot one, it hissed like a balloon with the air coming out."

That prompted another uncomfortable silence. "I'm sure it was just—" Reeve started.

Brian coughed loudly, to cut him off. "Don't gaslight the kid," he said under his breath. Everyone heard him.

Reeve just stared at him. "Gas-what?"

"Gaslight," Brian said, but no one knew what the fuck he was talking about, plainly, so he lowered his voice and tried to explain. It didn't matter, of course, because Mack Wellstone could hear every word he was saying. "Gaslighting means trying to explain away something to make someone think they're crazy when they're not."

Reeve shot him a look of—not even daggers, more like swords. "I am not—" He stopped mid-sentence, giving Brian a *you idiot* look. "Son," Reeve said, turning back to Mack, "I'm sorry about your father."

"What happened to him?" Mack asked, a little less dully now. His brain was re-engaging, the primal response that had resulted in him freezing finally letting loose.

"Nothing good," Hendricks answered under his breath, the most honest goddamned thing any of them had said to the boy so far.

"I'm not sure," Reeve said, and though that was probably literally honest in that he and Brian hadn't gotten the exact details, they were sure as shit clear on the general cause.

"That thing wasn't a dog," Mack said.

"We don't know exactly what it was," Reeve said.

"Huh." Mack settled back on his heels, still staring at the gun rack in the corner.

"Your momma's gonna be here in an hour or so," Reeve said, clearly trying to walk him back from these precipitous questions. "Why don't you grab a chair and sit for a bit? We can get you something if you want—"

"Not hungry."

"You want a Co—"

"Not thirsty," the boy said, but he did wander over to the nearest chair and plopped himself down, still staring at the gun rack in the corner of Reeve's office. It had glass covering it so that someone couldn't just walk up and grab a weapon. Brian was wishing it was lined with steel right now.

Reeve followed the boy's gaze, finally, and seemed to make the connection. "Uh huh," he said. He didn't do anything obvious, but Brian figured it would be on his list to shut the door to his office given how hard the kid was staring at his guns. "Well. We'll just wait for your momma to get here then," he said uncomfortably.

The emergency line rang, something that was a pretty regular occurrence, and Brian flipped the switch to route it to his headset. "911, what's your emergency?" he asked.

"Hello," said a playful voice, one that raised his own eyebrows, "this is County Administrator Pike, and I need to talk to Sheriff Reeve."

Brian frowned. "I'm sorry, this is an emergency line—"

"It's an emergency," Pike said coolly.

"What is your emergency, sir?" Brian asked, doubting that whatever Pike was playing at—probably trying to break through and talk to the sheriff, who had made it clear he had no desire to talk to this bastard—rose to the level of actual emergency.

"I got a serious problem over here," Pike said, still cool as a freezer. "Let me talk to Reeve."

Brian froze, trying to decide what to do. "Listen, Administrator Pike, this is an emergency line—" He caught Reeve tossing his head back in despair.

"And this is an emergency, I told you."

"Just put him through to my office," Reeve said, gesturing at the door. He was going to have to close it anyway, wasn't he? Brian figured the despair had finally gotten through to the man.

"Hold for a minute," Brian said, clicking the button to shut Pike off. The line blinked bright red. "You sure? I can 'accidentally' disconnect him."

"No," Reeve said, shadowed in profile in his doorway as he stood there, looking back at Brian out of the corner of his eye. "I suppose I've avoided this long enough." He shut that door behind him, and a moment later the red phone line stopped blinking furiously.

*

His name was Aaron Drake, as far as anyone in this world knew. It wasn't his real name, of course, but demon names weren't often exchanged because of the power they held, so he went by Aaron Drake, which was a fine enough appellation. It had a sort of old-world prestige to it, reflecting well on Aaron Drake's standing in society.

Ah, society. It was the true measure of human sophistication that they didn't just scrabble in the mud with their fingers anymore, or chase animals and carelessly roast them around the fire. He recalled well the days of primitive man, when fire was their greatest accomplishment. At the time, cooking meat had been the new thing. Then someone had discovered salt and spices, and things had taken another step. At some point—Aaron Drake could scarcely remember that far back, though he had been there for it—crops had come into play, along with sowing and reaping, and the culinary arts had taken another leap forward.

Drake had been there through it all, watching every change made by these humans with approval. His own people certainly hadn't made any great strides in making food better or more impressive. They all varied in what they ate, after all. Some enjoyed the same foods as humans, some liked to eat humans themselves, others dwelled in the sewers and enjoyed excrement—mostly that of humans. Drake didn't understand those creatures any better than a human understood a dung beetle—it made sense that someone would fulfill that function, but it made his shell crawl to contemplate being one of them.

This last twenty years or so, though, with the rise of American cuisine to new heights ... these had been heady times for Aaron Drake. Suddenly, a home-cooked meal at a ma and pop diner wasn't necessarily cause for despair. Now they were places where chefs took pride in their efforts and often tried to elevate them beyond simple greasy spoon offerings. Previously, America's primary alimentary virtue had been the sheer volume of food available; now it had somehow become a place where food was plentiful *and* exceptional. Spices, preparations, recipes—what had once been simplistic was now revolutionary, the citizenry seemingly obsessed with the culinary arts, attempting creations in the privacy of their own homes that might once have been the exclusive domain of the executive chef of a restaurant in one of the major metropolises.

Now, cuisine was everywhere.

And Aaron Drake couldn't have been happier, though he did feel his options here in Midian, Tennessee were limited. Leave it to the hotspot to open in a place where there wasn't a single Michelin star to be found. The diner on the square had plainly been left behind in the food revolution that had spread across America, and there wasn't a Trader Joe's or Whole Foods to be found within an hour's drive.

Drake sighed, a sad, throaty sound. He hadn't had a good meal in Midian since Duchess Kitty had left town so abruptly. Her party had been exquisite, a perfect breath of New York cuisine brought to town for one brief, blessed moment. It was a curse that she'd fled so quickly, without hosting another gathering, but that was to be expected. The quality of the local parties had gone precipitously downhill since then as well.

And oh, how the hunger had risen within him since then. Why, it felt like he was practically starving.

The key to the entire food revolution had hinged on two concepts, Drake knew—one, the ingredients available to amateur chefs were now infinitely better than they had been before. Now a normal person could get veal or duck breast or at least USDA Choice beef or goose liver pate in the proper store. Along with that came other possibilities, such as fresh thyme, ginger, things that in the fifties might have been taken for being exotic diseases rather than what they were—sophisticated flavor-improving opportunities. Second, and perhaps more importantly, techniques were being disseminated over the internet to people who would never have had access to them before. Suddenly, a housewife in Toledo, Ohio could get the same basic culinary training that was once reserved for a master chef in Paris. Of course, the master chefs of Paris were busy pioneering new techniques that would make their way to housewives in Toledo in five years, but the principle still allowed for a rapid diffusion of knowledge, and now any diner owner could add in a touch of sophistication that would have been impossible only a few decades earlier.

It was a wondrous time to be alive, especially for a gourmand like Aaron Drake.

Of course, the ingredients available in Midian weren't quite top shelf. That lack of access to a Whole Foods down on the corner made it less desirable of a location than New York or Los Angeles. But there were ways around that, weren't there? Some of the spices he could get on an extended trip, and vegetables could keep for a few days.

It was the meats that lost their flavor first. Farm-to-table was becoming such an important part of the chain of knowledge, and while there were farms around here ... Drake had a taste for something else—something slightly more controversial, something not available at Trader Joe's or Whole Foods.

There was a shop in town—every town, sort of—that could deliver what he wanted. At a price, of course. Drake contemplated paying the asking price for the meat he was looking for, but he wasn't an exceedingly wealthy demon. He had funds, of course, as one should after living for as long as he had, but they weren't of a sum that he could afford to never work again. A service that delivered fresh meat of the type he wanted, the sort provided by Spellman to various locales and hotspots, wasn't cheap. Not at all.

No, his was a problem of supply. He had the demand, but he didn't want to pay the asking price for that meat, which shouldn't have been rare or lacking in supply—there were seven billion of them, damn it!—yet it was. This was why he came to hotspots, because oftentimes there was a sudden excess of supply, bodies lying about, going to waste.

He'd thought that after the incident on the square, he might have been able to sneak in and pick up a few fresh pieces, a few little things to soothe the hunger of an aching belly tired of pork and beef and chicken ... but no. No, they'd closed that place up tightly, leaving Aaron Drake to skulk meekly around the edges of the police barricades, seeing no way in to collect a liver here and there, maybe a severed leg for a sumptuous roast. There was human veal too, but that was right out, a terrible disappointment to see it go to waste.

Drake was the sort who didn't want to get his hands dirty. He didn't mind involving himself in the preparation, or even occasionally the butchery, but he didn't want to trouble himself with the law, which could make his life disproportionately difficult. He didn't like physical confrontation, especially in a town with demon hunters in it. Threat to his life was a frightening prospect, not something he cared for at all, no.

Yet the hunger was there, and needed to be sated. His desire for a filling meal, something other than chicken-fried chicken—ugh—was rising. He only needed one, at least for now, something well raised, with a little marbling, something simple that he could slaughter and savor, going through unique preparations in order to scratch that itch he felt after a long time in the food desert that was Midian, Tennessee. Meat he could season, something he could prepare and then sink his teeth into, moist and delicious ...

Yes, that moment was coming. And soon. His hunger could not be contained any longer.

He needed to eat.

*

Sheriff Reeve stared at the blinking light only a second before facing his fear and picking up the handset, hitting the hold button as he did so. "This is Sheriff Reeve. What can I do for you, County Administrator Pike?" He put a cool emphasis on the man's title, figuring he'd at least start off polite.

"I was calling to apologize to you personally," Pike said, unctuous as ever. He was an ingratiating fuck, either looking for the right thing to say or, once you'd gotten on his bad side, the thing that would most piss you off. "Obviously, things have changed after what happened at Halloween."

"Have they?" Reeve asked, cooler still.

"I bear a considerable part of the blame for holding that event," Pike said. "I know that. And even more for denying that there was something going on in this town, even though you were telling me that things were ... unbelievable."

"I was telling you that demons were attacking us," Reeve said. "You ready to believe that now?"

"Well, I'm closer to ready," Pike said, and Reeve could sense some discomfort. "I didn't see it with my own eyes, obviously—"

"Obviously." *Because if you had, your own eyes would probably have been ripped out and splattered across the square with half the crowd you brought there, you dumb fuck.*

"Look," Pike said with an aura of patience, "we're in a shitstorm, no denying it. I'm calling you up, hat in hand, asking, 'What can I do for you?'"

"Other than knock this stupid recall business off?" Reeve asked with a sour taste in his mouth.

"If I could do that, I would in a heartbeat," Pike said, smoothly, maybe even sincerely. Reeve couldn't tell, not with this one. "But that's out of my hands; it's mandated by the signatures I collected. Talk to any lawyer; they'll tell you. I, uh ... well, I set the wheels in motion, and even an injunction couldn't stop it now."

"Well, then I reckon there ain't much—"

"Hold it," Pike said. "Listen ... there's other stuff I can do for you. I know we've been arguing about budget—"

"Since day one."

"And it's not like I can just pull money out of my ass, but ... this is an emergency. It doesn't hurt us if we overspend a little in the process of trying to save this county from ... well, from whatever—"

"Demons." Christ, was this guy serious? Hundreds of people dead over the last few months and he was still talking like it was business as usual, budgets and spreadsheets. Maybe he was sincere, but talking about helping with the fucking budget? It was probably a mark of how ingrained in the bastard's personality penny-pinching was that this was the approach he took in trying to get Reeve's attention.

"Yeah, demons," Pike said, sounding pretty uneasy about it. Well, it was an uneasy sort of subject. "My point is ... I want to help. Is there anything I can do?"

Well, he certainly sounded sincere, Reeve had to concede. Entrenched in being a bureaucratic prick, but maybe sincere in his desire to help. Brian had shown Reeve that everybody might be able to help, at least in their own way. It might not be standing out on the line, swinging a sword like the cowboy, but someone had to man the radio, someone had to keep the lights on, didn't they? "I appreciate the offer," Reeve said, somewhat grudgingly. "Lord knows we could use some help. I expect there's more you could do if you were of a mind to."

"Well, I'd love to be of help," Pike said. "All I'm looking for is a chance to be of assistance." Reeve could almost see the bastard smiling in his office, and something about it made him uneasy.

"Great, well … start with that budget," Reeve said, wondering what Pike's idea of unlocking funds would look like. He suspected it would be pretty minimal compared to what Reeve actually needed. "Then … we can talk again after." The nice thing about it would be that maybe Pike would get off his back for a while.

"Next time, we should meet face to face," Pike said.

"We'll figure something out," Reeve said, fully intending to blow him off. He didn't want to see Pike, not ever if he could avoid it, no matter what part the man had to play. The son of a bitch had still arrogantly scheduled Halloween, against all logic and advice, and hadn't even shown up to see the slaughter. He might not have been a demon, or controlled by a demon, but he was damned sure lacking in judgment. Reeve hung up, figuring that was as good a capstone to their conversation as any. That nagging question about where Pike had been could wait, at least a little longer.

He stared at the phone for a minute after he hung it up, wondering how much time he'd have to recover from this conversation with Pike before he'd have to try and navigate another. The County Administrator was a persistent son of a bitch, so probably not long. It'd probably be at least a couple days, though, before the bureaucrat got his purse strings untied and started doling out money. The watch could use a paycheck or two in their capacity as informal deputies, some meals and stuff. Brian Longholt had been paying for a lot of that on ol' Bill's credit card, but Reeve didn't feel too sanguine about that lasting, given Bill's vegetative state.

It took Reeve a minute to realize that there were raised voices coming from out in the bullpen, and he slumped against the headrest on his chair. Did this shit never end?

*

"Lying to the kid doesn't do him any favors," Arch said hotly, digging in, feeling like he was arguing with a stone wall. Hendricks's face suggested he was pretty much a stone wall, less emotion than Arch at this moment, and for a lot less reason than Arch had. For some reason, that got under Arch's skin.

"Telling him the unvarnished truth doesn't do us any favors," Hendricks said. "Do you want him to explain to his mom why you're laying out what happened to his dad?"

"Jesus, Hendricks," Brian said, looking pretty damned uncomfortable. The kid was watching them all from the waiting area, listening to them talk about him without saying a word. "Gaslighting him seems kinda shitty—"

"Stop talking in fucking hipster dipshit code," Hendricks said.

Brian blinked at the cowboy. "Fine. Trying to convince him he didn't see what he saw after he already lost his dad? Dick move. It's not even a flaccid, half-measure dick move, it's a full-on, mighty erection straight into the unlubed orifice move—"

"That's enough," Arch said, blanching at the graphic nature of his brother-in-law's—well, former brother-in-law, now—description of events. "We don't need that kind of talk in addition to all that's going on—"

Brian must have bit his tongue, because he made a face but kept his peace. "All I'm saying," he finally allowed, "is that Arch is right, and lying is a shitty thing to do, especially under these circumstances."

"Why don't you shove it up your fucking pussy-ass hole?" Hendricks asked, favoring Brian with a look of utter contempt. "This isn't tiddlywinks, you little bitch, this is a war with otherworldly forces, and in case you missed last week's episode—we're fucking losing."

"I didn't miss it," Arch shot back. "I noticed, trust me."

Hendricks adopted a slightly chastened look. "I—I'm sure you did."

"It didn't escape past me, either," Brian said. "And you probably shouldn't be teaching this kid new words after—" He glanced at the kid, still watching them all. "After what happened."

"He's probably heard the words 'pussy,' 'ass,' 'bitch,' and 'fucking' before," Hendricks said. "You pussy-ass fucking bitch."

"Hendricks!" Arch said, furious now.

"Jesus," Brian breathed. "You don't ever let up, do you?"

"What in the blue hell is going on out here?" Reeve asked, opening his door in a rush of furious air. He wore a look like a storm cloud. Arch felt the look on Reeve's face was probably mirrored in his own—weary, personal grief looking for an outlet.

"Vocabulary lessons for the pussies," Hendricks said, causing Reeve's eyes to burn a little brighter.

There was a squeak as the entry door opened in the lobby area and

Lauren Darlington stepped in with her daughter. Both of them were dark-haired and leaden-eyed. Arch had known them before all this, and they'd been lighter then. Well, Lauren had always been irritable with him, but when he'd watched her unobserved, she'd been a pretty happy person overall, especially when with her daughter.

There was none of that now; both of them looked bleary, the weight of grief clear upon them. Molly looked a bit worse for the wear, but then, the girl had suffered through some rough times even before she'd killed her grandmother while possessed, hadn't she?

"Why are you all shouting about vaginas in here?" Lauren asked, looking irritated. She shot a look back at her daughter, who closed her eyes and giggled slightly, giving her an impish look that broke through the weary sadness for an all-too-brief moment.

"Uh, maybe they were talking about cats," Molly said, eyeing Mack Wellstone, who was glancing at her and Lauren with vague interest.

"No, it was definitely about vaginas. I like to shout the virtue of vaginas everywhere I go," Hendricks said, causing Arch to close his eyes and shake his head. There was no changing the cowboy. "I'm a big fan of them, you see."

"An admirer from a distance, I'm sure," Lauren said coolly, delivering enough reproach that the cowboy couldn't miss it.

"Who's the new kid?" Molly asked, probably to defuse the rapidly increasing tension.

"I'm no doctor of gynecology, like maybe you are," Hendricks said, not letting the moment escape him, wide grin plastered on his face, "but I've examined my fair share up close." Arch was pretty sure that Hendricks knew that wasn't Lauren's specialty, but since when had the cowboy ever let facts hold him back? "Call it a hobby of mine."

"Yeah, I doubt you lack the ability to go pro," Lauren sniped back. She wasn't one to back down from a snark-fight, Arch knew by experience.

"Seriously," Molly said, "are you two going to just pee all over each other in an attempt to mark your territory for most sarcastic? Because I'm the teenager here and I will batter you both to hell with my natural ability if you keep giving me reason." She jerked a head toward Mack Wellstone. "I ask again, imploring you both to remember you're putatively adults before I'm forced to pull out the nuclear snark on your amateurish, aging asses: Who's the new guy?"

Lauren and Hendricks exchanged a sullen look. There was no particular antipathy between them that Arch knew about, but they were both strong personalities and tensions were running high all around. He decided to insert himself into the peacemaking process:

"We picked him up in the woods this morning. His name's Mack. He, uh ... lost his dad."

That caused both Lauren and Molly's faces to fall. The Darlington ladies didn't lack for empathy. "I'm so sorry, Mack," Lauren said, looking at Mack sincerely.

"Yeah," Molly chimed in, nodding at him. "I lost my grandmother last week, so I, uh ... kinda know how you feel."

Mack Wellstone seemed to take it all in like a sponge taking in water, but without any visible swelling effect. "Thanks," he said after a few seconds. He kept his eyes on Molly though.

"I'm gonna head out for a bit," Hendricks said, even as he headed for the door. "If you need me, call me." He slowed a little as he approached the door; Molly and Lauren were still standing just slightly in the way. Molly launched herself aside with all the urgency she might have put into dodging a gunshot. Lauren moved a little slower, met eyes with the cowboy, challenging him before she moved just a few inches aside and put out her arm toward the door, as if proffering a formal invitation for him to walk through it. Her eyes were alive with the sarcasm she wasn't giving voice to, as though daring him to be a smartass about it.

Arch cringed, but Hendricks just smiled and detoured around, tipping his hat excessively as he went. Thankfully, he was apparently confident enough in his manhood not to start World War III over her goad. Arch let out a sigh of relief. It was just as well; he'd had about enough fighting for the morning—at least of the variety that didn't involve stabbing holy objects into demons anyway.

*

Lauren didn't have a lot of patience for the Marine-turned-demon hunter. He probably wasn't a bad guy under normal circumstances, but her appetite for testosterone-laden bullshit had run out around the time her mother had died, and Hendricks managed to annoy her on a near-constant basis now. Especially lately, he seemed to have evolved from being a slight pain in the ass to being an absolutely huge one. Maybe it had something to do with being raped by that demon Duchess, but that would have to be someone else's cleanup. Lauren had enough to deal with.

"Doctor," Sheriff Reeve said, gracious as ever, "thanks for coming." Whatever his failings, Reeve, at least, had manners.

"No problem." Lauren had a bag over her shoulder with the stuff she needed. Well, some of it anyway. Once she got the feeding tube in, she'd leave it to other people to figure out what to pour in, but she had a protein shake for the poor, mute bastard to start out with, since he wasn't eating and she could only do so much with an IV. "I'll get to work if you—" she looked at Molly "—want to hang out here for a few minutes?"

"Sure," Molly said, sounding pretty indifferent. A lot of the spark had gone out of her daughter. It was disquieting, but it couldn't be helped at the moment, and anyway, it was a funeral day—how much spark should she have expected today? "Have fun."

Lauren frowned, clutching her medical bag against her side. Putting a feeding tube into an insensate patient wasn't something she would have considered fun, unless it was the demon who had killed her mother, and she was inserting it rectally, perhaps with mildly acidic lubricant. Even that probably wouldn't be fun, though it might at least be at little satisfying.

"You know where you're going, right?" Reeve asked.

Of course she fucking knew. She just gave him a look that stated the obvious. "I think I can find my way," she said coolly. He didn't mean anything by it, but she'd been here a few times before, after all, to care for this particular patient.

Lauren made her way down the hall, leaving behind the stilted conversation in the bullpen. "So … Mack …" Molly was saying. She dodged into the holding cells and shut the door behind her before she could hear where the conversation was going. Probably nowhere good, because Molly was not among the world's great small-talkers.

The sheriff's station only had a few holding cells, and Lauren pressed the button to let herself into the area, prompting a buzz from a nearby speaker. Someone was sitting inside, staring up at the ceiling, and Lauren nodded as she came inside. "Hey, Sam."

Sam Allen was a local tow truck driver, and pretty well looked the part, save for he wasn't wearing his jumpsuit today. He looked pretty bored just sitting here, staring up at the ceiling. He glanced at her without a lot of interest. "Hey, Lauren. Here to feed him?"

"Yeah," Lauren said. "I'm here for his health, not mine."

Sam chuckled. It wasn't that funny, but he looked like he'd been here for a while, and he didn't even have a smart phone to entertain him, apparently. "I'll let you in. Gotta lock the door behind you though."

"I know the routine."

"Can't chance this bastard getting out," Sam said.

"Why?" Lauren asked. "He's demon-free."

Sam's face darkened. "He killed a lot of people, Lauren. A whole lot of people."

She turned so Sam couldn't see her roll her eyes. The man in the cell hadn't killed anyone, as far as she knew. He had carried a demon the way a person might carry a virus, and that demon had killed a lot of people. She didn't expect Sam to understand that though. Hell, she might have understood it on an intellectual level, but she still had trouble coming to grips with it on an emotional one.

The man in the cell didn't make it any easier on her either. Sam unlocked the door to let her in and she found him there, sitting on the cot, staring through her. She probably should have pitied him, should have viewed him as a poor unfortunate, but she couldn't, not entirely. She could mouth all the excuses to Sam about how he was no guiltier than any sick patient with an infectious disease, but the truth was …

Lauren hated the man in the cell. And she didn't even know his name.

"Hello," she said, trying to stay professional. He wouldn't answer, and that was just as well, because the thought of carrying on a conversation with the man who'd brought the demon to town that had possessed her daughter, had killed her mother, had ruined her home …

Well, it was a lot to stomach.

"Can you hear me, sir?" She asked mostly as a formality. He didn't give any sign that he'd heard her, and he hadn't since he'd been here. He just stared straight ahead, didn't really respond to stimuli like light or pain. Pinching him, even hard, had no effect. She'd stuck him a few times with IV fluids, and she hadn't been particularly gentle on any of the sticks, but he hadn't reacted. The man was in a catatonic state for all intents and purposes.

"Of course you can't," she muttered under her breath. Why would he start talking now, after all? He had remained silent as a damned stone for the last few days, there was no reason for him to begin gabbing now. The man didn't even twitch, or scratch himself. When he urinated—which he did rarely—he just pissed his pants. Lauren didn't love the smell, though it was mostly the scent of sterile agent lingering in the air now. Someone must have cleaned him up, otherwise the place would have just stunk of urine.

"Anything to declare?" she asked, her gloves snapping as she put them on. She needed to take a few stats—blood pressure, heart rate and all that—before she could just cram a feeding tube in. "If you have anything pressing to add to the conversation, now's the time." She went about her work, not expecting a response and not getting one. She read out his blood pressure and heart rate as she took them, then pulled the pulse oximeter off his immobile finger.

"I don't blame you for not talking," she said matter-of-factly as she ran her hands over his neck, feeling his glands; demon possession might cause cancer, and she'd be the first to document it. It wasn't like she could publish the data anywhere, but nonetheless, she felt she should have it. "I expect some of the guys who have come in here to watch over you have probably said some shitty things." She glanced unconsciously over her shoulder at Sam, who was behind the glass, staring at them distantly. He couldn't hear them, as far as she knew.

The man in the cell said nothing, did nothing—just stared straight ahead.

"I'd be ashamed if I was responsible for the death of a mess of people. I mean, who wouldn't?" She was being conversational, though she wasn't sure why she was doing it here, now, with this man. "Especially if you didn't really do anything to deserve it. I mean, we don't even know how you came in contact with the demon—demons, I guess, since there were a fuck-lot of them in you." She sighed. "I wonder how many there were. Hundreds? Thousands? A million?"

She turned, and thought she heard something, a whisper so low it might have been the squeak of her shoe. She spun back to find the patient—

Sitting still, staring ahead, not a sign of movement on or around his body.

Lauren stared at him for a moment, trying to decide—had he actually talked? Probably not, right? That must have been her shoe or something else, because this—this motherfucker—he hadn't opened his mouth, surely. He was still silent, not a hint of sound passing between his lips.

She shook it off. "Whatever," she said, dismissing it as a thought, as anything but a word from the man before her. "I'm almost done anyway, but if you've got anything to say, you'd better say it now, because pretty soon there's going to be a feeding tube down your throat, so conversation? Yeah, it'll be a problem."

She stared at his blank eyes. Inserting this feeding tube was an exercise in pointlessness. Why preserve the body for a mind already gone?

"Any last words?" Lauren asked, getting the tube ready. It was an NG tube at least, rather than one she'd have to stick down his craw. It still wouldn't be much fun to insert, like trying to snake a garden hose down a bumpy crevasse. "You sure?" she asked the impassive mien as though he'd responded.

He didn't say a word.

"Okay then," she said and propped his head back. He offered no resistance, another sign that he was brain dead. She readied the hose—

She thought she caught a hint of movement in the eye, which had thus far failed to so much as follow her anywhere around the room. She looked right at his pupil, but it stayed fixed now, looking up at the ceiling. She'd imagined it, right? This guy was a vegetable, as much of one as Bill Longholt at this point—more of one, actually, because Longholt was supposedly at least moving and groaning—and even moving his eyes seemed out of this guy's reach.

"I'm just losing my goddamned mind, that's all," Lauren said to herself, and started the slow work of inserting the feeding tube. At least he didn't resist, though part of her—a very small part—sort of wished he would, just so she could reassure herself that she was not losing her fucking mind and that he had, in fact, moved.

*

"Arch," Barney Jones greeted as Arch came in the door of the Jones family home, a rambler out on the edge of Midian. Something was cooking on the stove, as it usually was no matter what time of day he dragged himself in. Barney was seated at the table just inside the entry door under the carport, along with Braeden Tarley. Tarley was a young, bearded, swarthy white man; Jones was old and black, dressed in clothes that marked him as a reverend—Arch's preacher, no less. Jones and Tarley looked like they'd been talking before Arch had come in, and he could feel the uncomfortable remnants of an interrupted conversation heavy in the air as he stood there.

"Olivia working on something in the kitchen?" Arch asked. Tarley had taken a hit the same night Arch had, losing his little girl to those demons on the square. Now he had demons of his own, in his head. That was the reason Tarley was staying here, and the reason Jones had offered Arch a spare bedroom as well. Arch had taken him up on the offer at the time mostly because the shock of the situation had taken over and he'd been unable to make a decision for himself, but now that he was on his feet again, he was about ready to move on out.

"She is," Jones said with a friendly smile. "She might need a hand." Arch took the hint and walked on through to the kitchen via a swinging door, feeding the illusion that he didn't know he was being asked to leave without being really asked.

"Good to see you, Arch," Olivia Jones said, stirring something on the stove. Arch took a deep sniff and caught a batch of gravy going, light brown and bubbling with flakes of pepper visible in its surface. Biscuits were baking in the oven, and Olivia was tending a pot of green beans with a wooden spoon in her other hand, alternating between the two pots. There was already an abandoned skillet sitting in the sink, handle jutting over to the other side like a telephone pole sticking out of the earth after a serious storm. Fried pork tenderloin was laid out on a paper-towel-lined serving dish on the counter, smelling like a little slice of heaven.

Arch loved the smell of down-home cooking. His mother-in-law had done this well too, and Alison had been on her way to being able to craft a meal worthy of his raising. Arch felt a little hit inside, right around the heart, when he thought of his wife. He didn't reckon that'd go away anytime soon, but as much as it troubled him—and it did; he woke in the night breathing heavy and crying—his grief was mitigated in the light of day.

He had faith Alison was in a better place now, that he'd see her again once the veil had lifted. He missed her terribly, like a great, empty, gaping gash had been carved out of him. The Book said they became one flesh, and they danged sure had. He sometimes found himself starting to say something to her and then remembering—she wasn't here anymore.

"Give me a hand stirring here while I get the biscuits out?" Olivia asked, keeping focused on her work.

"Yes, ma'am," Arch said, taking a deep, hard breath. It wasn't easy to draw that breath, to focus on food. He suspected Olivia didn't even really need his help, like the gravy couldn't stand a minute without stirring. The funeral was coming in just a couple hours, though he'd been trying to ignore it all day. All week, really. He'd been successful largely because his mother-in-law had been busy caring for Bill, and Brian had been distracting himself with work at the sheriff's station as well, but it was getting harder now.

Of course, there'd been no shortage of demons to distract either. Not in Midian. Not right now.

Arch worked on the gravy; it was good and thick, not runny like Alison's had been. She lost patience with it, didn't give it time to reduce the way she should. He mentally slapped himself for thinking like that. Who cared that she didn't make the gravy the way he'd had it when he was growing up?

Why did that matter now?

Arch swallowed his thoughts along with his grief, and brought up the spoon. He caught a little gravy on the side of his hand, and it brought her to mind again. It didn't take much to stir thoughts of her. This time it was seeing that little pale blob on his dark skin, reminding him of how it looked when he held her hand, their fingers intertwined.

He hurriedly pressed the finger to his mouth, tasted the salty, peppery goodness of the gravy. He went back to stirring, listening idly to Olivia humming as she pulled the biscuits out of the small countertop oven behind him. Arch drew a ragged breath, trying not to think about it anymore as he gave the green beans a stir.

"Make sure it doesn't burn, Arch," Olivia said.

"Yes, ma'am," he said, not really listening to her.

His mind was elsewhere, remembering a day in the park, before this had all happened …

"Do you ever think about leaving Midian?" Alison asked, breeze stirring her fair hair over her shoulder, little strands of yellow whipping like they were playing in the wind.

He'd stared at her, at the single freckle standing out on her nose. It hadn't been there at the beginning of summer, but it was there now, a little kiss from the sun. "No," he said, shaking his head.

"We coulda stayed in Knoxville." She wasn't wearing her sunglasses, and when the sun came out from behind the clouds, she squinted, looking at him narrowed-eyed—but not in an angry way; like she was trying to pick him out in the brightness of the day, the sun causing the green hills around them to almost glow.

"After college? I s'pose," Arch said. "I never wanted to work for a city department though. And your folks are here."

"I know." She seemed a little restless under her skin, like she wanted to get up and move but forced herself to stay seated. "Midian's home, but …" She stared off into the distance, out of the sun, so the lines around her eyes relaxed somewhat.

"But what?" He'd never had much ambition to leave, but she'd been the one that most wanted to stay when he'd mentioned other possibilities—Knoxville, Atlanta, Charlotte, Raleigh, Charleston … he'd never fought hard for any of them because of her.

"Town's not what it used to be," she said, shaking it off like a bad dream she was waking from. "Not a lot of jobs moving to Midian. If the paper mill goes …"

"They been talking about the town going under if the paper mill leaves since we were in elementary school. Ain't happened yet."

"Yet." Her fair hair and occasionally blank look seemed to give people who didn't know her the impression that Alison was some dumb airhead. She wasn't, not even close. "Daddy says it'll happen eventually. Paper's less of a need, and they've been bleeding jobs for years, not hiring new workers to place the retirees." She glanced at him. "It'll happen."

"Well, we'll deal with it when it does," he said. "But for now … you got a job at your daddy's store, and I'm deputy, so …" He smiled. "What's there to worry about?" He looked into that pretty face, and suddenly it was jarring, and he was back in Barney and Olivia Jones's kitchen, and he realized he'd never … never really see her again …

"Arch," Olivia said with an excess of patience, "didn't I ask you not to let the gravy burn?" She was standing at his side, looking past him. The gravy wasn't just browned, it was blackened, stuck in great chunks to the bottom of the pan.

"I'm sorry, ma'am," Arch said, a lump in his throat like he'd swallowed an apple whole. He handed her the spoon and retreated, disappearing up the stairs into the darkness of pulled curtains, ignoring the smell of burned food, hurrying into his room so he could close his door and weep in privacy for everything that he'd lost.

And he'd lost danged near everything.

*

"What can you say about a woman like Vera Darlington?" Pastor Richards's question echoed through Lauren's head, through the church, which was empty except for a scattered handful of mourners.

It wasn't supposed to be like this. The candles were burning on the altar, and the cross was hanging, empty, above it.

And the pews behind where Lauren and Molly sat in the front row were damned near as empty as the cross.

How had this happened? Lauren wondered. Her mother had lived in Midian her whole life. She had friends, she had acquaintances. This church should have been bursting at the seams. Did people not know when the service was? Surely not.

No, it had to be something else. Her most loyal friends were here. But a lot of her most loyal friends …

Well, they had grandkids and kids, and those folks … they'd been disproportionately represented on the square at Halloween.

They'd lost their kids and grandkids in some cases, had watched other people dear to them die. Midian of late was a buffet of grief, a gluttonous all-you-could-eat-until-your-belly-exploded sort of affair.

How many funerals had been held in the last week?

Too many to count.

How many people had lost someone? More than one someone? A friend, a spouse, a close family member? Almost everyone.

Who wanted to go to a steady number of funerals? Who wanted to spend every day like that?

Apparently not the people of Midian. It wasn't as though she didn't understand; Lauren hadn't been to any other funerals either. But looking around the few remaining pews, she counted eleven people. Less than a dozen.

This church should have been full! They should have been celebrating her mother's life in force, with stories and testimonials about the effect of Vera Darlington's life on those around her.

Instead they sat in a mostly empty church, Lauren weeping delicately into a tissue as she puzzled her way through the mystery of the poor attendance.

"… I think Vera would have been glad to see the faces gathered here today," Pastor Richards said, and Lauren cringed. That was a line he used at every funeral, and it irked her that he'd trotted it out given the shitty attendance. Richards didn't take any notice of her cringing though, just looked down on her and smiled. "Lauren, why don't you come up and say a few words?"

Lauren blinked. She'd met with Richards a few days ago and he'd mentioned something about having her say something, hadn't he? Fuck. She hadn't thought about it since. Living in the whorehouse, trying to fight with the watch, she had enough to keep up with. The only thing she hadn't had to deal with was work, but that was because she'd let them know her mother died.

Robot-like, Lauren made her way up to the pulpit, wondering what the hell she was doing. What the fuck was she even going to say? She put her hands on the sides of the pulpit unsteadily, gripping the white-painted wood surface, and stared out at the small assemblage. She knew all of them, every single one—

Except for one guy, dressed in a black suit and tie with a white shirt for contrast, who was sitting at the end of the second row on her left. He had jet black hair, was probably somewhere in his thirties, and watched her attentively, giving her an encouraging smile when she took notice of him. He straightened in his seat in the pew, his long face immediately going back to the typical look of a mourner, with eyes downcast.

"I knew my mother … all my life," Lauren finished lamely. Constructing a sentence at this point was like shitting a brick, with all the strain that would entail. "She was … a good woman. She taught me ... lots of things." *But not how to avoid being a moron when speaking in public, apparently,* Lauren almost said, feeling a couple beads of sweat breaking out on her forehead just above her hairline.

"I ... I don't know what to do anymore," she said honestly. She picked a spot on the side of the white-painted church wall and just stared at it. It was easier than looking down at the audience. Miss Cherry was in the second row behind where she and Molly were sitting. "I guess I'm kind of like a millennial, because I never left home. After I had a kid, I needed all the help I could get, and Mom ... she was always there for me." Lauren looked at Molly, but only for a second. If they locked eyes now, she'd become a weeping mess, Molly would become a weeping mess, and Lauren just needed to get through this. "She raised my daughter so I could become a doctor." That hurt to say out loud because she couldn't remember if she'd ever made that confession to her mother. Lauren blinked, a profound realization dawning on her. "I wouldn't be where I am today if my mother hadn't been there. I'd be ... I don't even know. Working at the paper mill, maybe, which would have sucked because yellow hard hats are terrible with my complexion. Not in my color wheel at all." She stopped. What the hell had she just said?

Molly was looking up at her, shaking her head. No, that didn't make sense. What were you supposed to say at a funeral? You were supposed to give comfort or something, right?

"Uhm, well," Lauren said, stumbling to get back on track, searching for her next thought. They were in a church; maybe some scripture from her youth would make some sense right now. "As Jesus said," she began, "uh ..." Nothing came to mind. Mental constipation again? Dammit. Something sprang up and she just said it: "'The night is dark and full of terrors.'"

Lauren froze, catching the puzzled looks from her audience. Molly had her head down again, just shaking it, somewhere between disappointment and laughter. "That, uh ... might not have been an original Jesus quote," Lauren had to admit.

"Pretty sure that's from *Game of Thrones*," Pastor Richards chimed in from where he sat behind the pulpit. "The Red Woman says it."

"Christ, Reverend," Lauren said, looking back at him, "is that really appropriate for a man of God?"

Richards shrugged. "You have to relate to your flock, Lauren."

Lauren turned back to the small crowd in the pews. "Uhmm ... I really suck at this. No lie. You all can tell. I don't do a lot of public speaking. I haven't exactly committed my life to Jesus either, at least not since I got re-baptized when I was twelve. I've spent years learning how to treat broken legs and diagnose a sinus infection. I ... I don't think I've believed in God since I was a teenager. I got pregnant doing something that's—I dunno, I hear it's a sin, but it's fun, more fun than going to church, so I keep doing it—and so we parted ways, and I haven't looked back, and, for all I know, God's not sorry to see me go either." She stared down at the red carpeting that adorned the floors. "My mom still went to church though. Almost every week. She was faithful. Probably prayed for my soul, even though I didn't care to hear about it. I'm sure she did, now that I think about it. I'd catch her praying sometimes—not like she hid it, but she'd do it mostly at night, before bed. She gave up on saying grace around our house a long time ago." Lauren blinked, just staring blankly at the floor. "I wasn't nice about her belief. I made fun of her for believing in some man in the sky that told us what to do. I thought it was stupid, and I had to make her feel stupid too. Had to let her know how smart I was, how I was in on the scam and she wasn't ..." She blinked. "I don't ... I don't mean to insult anyone here, because ... well, I was just ... I was a bad daughter. I was an asshole. My mom gave and gave to me, raised my daughter, and I ... God, I was an ungrateful shit." Lauren's eyes watered. "I wish I could tell her ... that I'm sorry. I still ... probably ... don't believe like she believed ... but I hope for her sake ... she was right."

Lauren sniffled and walked away from the pulpit. There was scattered applause, light as the audience, the strongest clapping coming from that man in the second row at the end with the long face. He only met her eyes for a second; then she had to look away, because her tears were blurring everything, and she just needed to get back to her seat so she could weep without worrying she was going to fall on her damned, ungrateful face.

*

Hendricks found his way back to the hotel, driving a purloined SUV. He was doing a lot of that, lately, taking cars that didn't belong to him. It didn't really matter, because the one he had taken belonged to people slaughtered in the fucking Charlie Foxtrot on the square on Halloween. But it felt sort of blasphemous, even to him, a decided unbeliever, to fuck with these peoples' car by removing the child safety seats in the back.

Yeah, he left that shit alone, adjusting himself so that his sword's scabbard ran conveniently out of the way. It twisted at his belt, bending it at an unnatural angle and making him glad it was a short ride from the sheriff's station to the Sinbad motel where he was staying.

"This whole town is a shitshow," Hendricks proclaimed to the empty car, catching sight of one of the child seats in the back of the SUV as he looked in the distorted, child-watching addition to the rearview while making the turn into the motel parking lot. What had happened in Midian had been a sick, fucked-up experience from start to finish, one that had gotten under his skin in a way that no previous adventure in demon hunting had. He'd seen some fucked-up things since picking up this job, but now he was past cow demons, past demons that burned hookers with their flaming, acidic jizz, they'd galloped past the demon that knocked up every woman in a small town with his super sexual demon powers, met a real royal of demon blood who'd … well, she'd fucked his shit up bad, he knew, and had suffered through an attack by a collective of demons that possessed human bodies in an effort to massacre the whole town. That was to say nothing of the other minor shit they'd dealt with, like the stupid goddamned bicycling demons. Those pissant fuckers; he wished he could shoot down their flock with an M-16 again, the stupid cheesedick fucking flock of wannabe birds.

Hendricks left the keys in the ignition as he turned off the SUV. He didn't care if anyone stole the already-stolen car, frankly, but he doubted anyone would. Part of him hoped for it just so he could stop looking at the car seats in the back every time he glanced in the rearview, because the guilt that sprang on him every goddamned time was almost like acidic demon jizz, eating him alive.

He unlocked the door to the motel room and stepped into the shrouded darkness. It was grey and overcast outside, and the Sinbad had blackout curtains. They looked like they had been manufactured in the seventies, but they still worked, although they stank of years of smoke and industrial-grade cleaning products. They kept the light out good though, and Hendricks stood there in the darkness, waiting for a sound.

"You here?" he asked, calling out to the darkness. He hoped she was; he had a yearning for her.

"I am here," Starling said, already in the bed. She stirred, slipping out from between the sheets, another shadow in a room full of them. He could see the slight red glow to her hair, the dusky shadow of her eyes as she caught a line of light that escaped the gap between the curtains. Her breasts were illuminated for a second as the light slid across her chest, and he caught a hint of her totally shaved pubis as she stepped through the beam slowly, lingering probably to rev him up. She did seem to like revving him up.

"Good." Hendricks shed his coat, tossing it aside, then set his hat on the dresser. That left him with a t-shirt and jeans, once he'd kicked off his boots. They had a little dirt on them from hoofing it through the woods this morning, but he didn't care. Housekeeping did a shit job in this place, but a little dirt and sand hadn't bothered him since he'd done that tour in the sandbox.

"Why is that good?" Starling asked, hesitating just out of his reach.

"Because I want to bend you over and fuck the shit out of you, that's why."

She stripped off his t-shirt for him, unbuckling his jeans, her lips on his. They were soft, not something he would have anticipated when they'd first met. She caught his earlobe in her mouth and it drove him wild as he worked his way down her neck. He had been semi-hard before he'd even walked in the door, anticipating this. She greeted him like this as he came in over half the time lately, about as much as his poor, worn-out ass could handle.

She didn't make much noise, barely a breath taken, and when she did, it was almost like she was doing it as a cue for him. She didn't really require much warm-up either, almost always slippery as a lubed-up rubber whenever he put a finger in her to check. She smelled different than the other girls he'd been with too, had a musk about her that was a couple degrees off. Not that every woman smelled alike or anything, but the way Starling smelled ...

Well, it was good enough, not off-putting at all. She could have smelled like a rotten carcass when he'd first started fucking her and it probably wouldn't have put him off until he'd gotten his fill of getting laid with her.

So far, that wasn't even close to true. He still loved her pussy.

He bent her over the bed, already out of his jeans, and entered her. She made a little noise that approximated satisfaction—he supposed; it was hard to tell. She was a perfect fit for him as his cock slid into her. There was a slight height mismatch, but Hendricks just bent at the knees so it worked. He could have had her get on the bed, but he wanted to stand, wanted to put his hands on her, wanted to pull her to him, ram his rod home over and over again.

He did too, giving it to her. She was mostly silent, her breath a little less steady than usual, punctuating her apparent enjoyment with the occasional noise to mark her arousal. Hendricks had a hard time getting a full read on this lady, but if she was acting, it didn't bother him too much; she at least *seemed* like she was enjoying herself.

Hendricks was damned close, pushing those last few long, sweet strokes until he clutched tight to her hips and held himself inside, that biological reaction along his dick compelling him to finish ejaculating here, deep inside her, where it felt the best and where it would be most likely to produce a baby, presumably. He'd wondered about that, whether he was imagining it when he felt that momentary urge to pull out and ignored it in favor of the pleasure his member sought. He'd perhaps enjoyed the thought of what that biological reaction might result in a hell of a lot more when it had come with his wife. He'd tried to ignore it when he was fucking Erin, but now …

Now, with Starling … he just didn't give a damn anymore. He answered the call of his cock and blew his load in her every chance he got. Why did it even matter at this point, after all? The town was all gone to hell, he was halfway gone to fucking hell himself …

What did it matter anymore?

"Goddamn," Hendricks whispered, his breaths coming as hard and fast as his thrusts had been a moment earlier. He'd gotten some cardio done here. He and Starling had done more exhausting workouts, ones where they'd started on their feet and ended up against the wall with her on his cock, holding her up as he slid in and out of her, or ones where they'd moved all over the bed, taking turns riding each other. She did pretty damned well on top compared to other women he'd known, but she didn't seem to have much trouble switching it up either.

"Why?" Starling asked, and it took Hendricks a moment to decode her reaction.

"Just a saying," Hendricks said, his dick still in her, though it was losing its fullness now. He could feel his penis retreating, its work done, load expelled. He exited, cringing as he did so, the edges of the head sensitive to the bare friction, though Starling was still fully wet. Some days he could get recharged for another go, some days he couldn't. Getting old, he thought as he finished pulling out of her, tapping the head of his penis on her ass as he straightened his knees, which ached from being bent uncomfortably during their fuck.

He could see the glistening drip of cum he'd left on her ass, catching the light and sparkling slightly. It was small, just a few little dots left behind, the majority sitting inside her. He collapsed past her onto the bed, body protesting as he ground his dick into the sheets. He didn't care about that either; it annoyed him to pick the flakes out of his body hair later, but that was a problem for another time, inconsequential next to the sudden desire to sleep that had been dumped on him by the hormonal release that had swept down after climax.

He waited to see if Starling would say something else. She usually didn't. There wasn't much need for words between them, though Hendricks was starting to feel the desire to talk to her, just because he could sense her in the darkness, standing there, watching over him. She did that, and it felt good, helped him sleep sometimes when he imagined other shadows in the night, things lurking in the inky darkness.

He drew a long breath, sinking into the cheap, thin mattress, looking at the shadow of her lingering above him. "You can lay down with me, you know. It's not like we didn't just do the most intimate damned thing we possibly could."

She cocked her head at him in the way that she did. Studying him, maybe. "Do you feel intimate with me?"

"I …" Hendricks didn't know quite how to answer that, so he fell back on being crass. "Well, I did just stick my dick in you and blast off a few good squirts of baby juice, so, yeah, I'd say we've been pretty intimate. You've had my cock in your mouth, in your ass, and I've been fingers deep in your snatch." He had done that, but had stopped short of using his mouth at any point with her. Not for that. "Not sure how much closer we could get, physically."

"Is physical intimacy the only kind you know?" Her voice was as toneless as ever, but Hendricks froze in bed as he was about to adjust himself.

"It's … I mean …" He felt himself grow a little flustered. He'd blown a wad in her; what more was there? Long walks on the beach, reading poetry to each other, waking up on Sunday morning and eating brunch after a leisurely fucking romp in the sheets? "It is what it is," he mumbled.

He'd had those other things with another woman, after all. The thought of revisiting them now, those feelings, those emotions … here? In the middle of Midian, and the storm of hell blowing through? It wouldn't be too long before the only leisurely brunch would be demons snacking on the few fucking survivors, if things kept going the way they were.

"What is 'it'?" Starling asked. Damn, she had that way about her. Naive or something.

"I mean we are what we are," Hendricks said.

"And what are we?"

"Lovers, I guess, is the polite term," he said, getting more exasperated by the second. Why did she have to define this? Erin had gotten the same way after a while, but at least he'd wanted something then. Now …

The specter of Kitty Elizabeth—that goddamned cunt—was like a shadow behind him, and Hendricks turned his head, just to make sure she wasn't there, that she hadn't somehow come back to Midian just to lurk over him in the darkness, stick a hand on his face, push him against the bed and—

Hendricks thought he smelled sulfur, nearly threw up in his mouth at the memory, and shivered in the cool motel air. His dick was limp now, and it would have been just as limp if he'd remembered Kitty Elizabeth in the middle of fucking Starling. It had happened before, and when it did, he'd fake getting there before he lost it completely, thrusting a few more times as he mimed the noises he made when climaxing just so he could get out of her, get away, get into the shower and wash himself clean as he could get, down to the red and rubbed-raw skin.

Starling didn't smell like a normal woman, but at least she didn't smell like that.

"You remember her," Starling said.

Hendricks froze for a second. "Which her? Erin?" He doubted she meant Erin. Doubted she meant Renee either, but … why the fuck would he talk about this with Starling, of all people?

"The Duchess." Starling stood there like a black hole in the middle of the room. "She hurt you."

Fucking understatement, Hendricks thought. "She carved out a little damage, yeah." He shrugged. "I've been through worse." But that was probably a lie, because he wasn't sure he had. He damned sure couldn't remember having nightmares like this, even after Renee, even after his tour in Ramadi.

Hell, even dying hadn't done a number on him like this.

"Have you?"

Another shrug. "I've been through a lot," Hendricks said.

Starling kept her silence for a few minutes. Hendricks tried to close his eyes, tried to get to sleep, but it felt futile. "Christ," he muttered. It was the middle of the day, after all, and the tranquilizing effect of the orgasm had apparently already evaporated. Shit.

"Would you like me to open the curtains?" Starling asked. Her eyes glimmered in the dark.

Hendricks stared at the ceiling, at the line of light that made its way in a long diagonal across the white popcorn coating. "Why? Are you leaving?"

"Soon."

This didn't bother him too terribly much. He wasn't going to be able to find his way back to hard, not this afternoon. Maybe this evening, but not now, not after goddamned Kitty Elizabeth had just invaded his mind again. He nearly retched once more at the memory of her, of what she'd done to him. It was fading; that was the only good news. A week earlier and he would have found himself on all fours over the toilet, heaving up his fucking guts at the thought of her, of her touch, her knife, her ... her fucking cockroach of a clitoris rammed into his mouth, writhing against his tongue as she ground her pelvis into his face.

He kept his eyes open, trying not to picture those eyes, the purple veins sticking out of her legs and face as she'd crushed him into the ground in that fucking pull shed of hell. He felt a phantom ache in his toes where they'd regrown after she'd done what she'd done. "Yeah," Hendricks said, remembering that Starling had asked him a question. "Open the curtains." *Don't leave me in the dark*, he didn't say, as she shuffled over and they screeched open, Starling hiding her naked body in the shadows still cast by them, her pale skin and tight body suddenly visible for an instant, her red hair hanging over her shoulders. He could see the little dab of cum he'd left on her ass, just to the right of the crack, glinting slightly as she turned.

She stood there for a moment, naked, breasts visible and on display, her legs slightly spread so that he could see the perfect slit that worked its way from her pubic mound down. He focused on it, staring. He seldom examined her in the light, but he did now, staring at her crotch, bare and hairless, staring at it until—

She was gone a second later, the curtains just there where she'd been standing a moment earlier, bare, swinging slightly from where she'd moved them at his request. Hendricks lay naked on the bed, alone, looking out at the grey day, on the empty parking lot of the Sinbad motel, feeling small, miniature, now that his silent sentinel was gone.

"Don't leave me in the dark," he murmured, almost like a prayer. *Don't leave me in the dark*, he said once more, this time in his mind.

Don't leave me in the dark ... with her.

*

Reeve didn't really want to go to the funeral, didn't want to acknowledge what it meant any more than he wanted to have another damned conversation with Pike. But he was bound to both, it seemed, bound to a duty he didn't particularly care for. Sometimes a job was like that; sometimes life was like that, he reflected.

And sometimes ... well, for fuck's sake, you just had to eat your way through a shit sandwich when you were in the middle of it because there was just no other way out.

This felt like one of those times, he thought, sitting in the front pew of Barney Jones's church. He could have picked any church in town to go to, because really, he and Donna hadn't had close ties to a church in years. They'd gone to the Methodist church across town, one that was predominantly white, when the kids were young, but that was probably five or six pastors ago. They'd gone weekly back then, but somehow the fire had gone out of Reeve's spiritual life when the kids were teenagers. Once they were out of the house and a new, less motivating pastor came, a lot of his motivation to drag himself out of the house on the Sunday mornings when he wasn't working vanished.

So here he was, having the funeral for his dearly departed wife in Barney Jones's church because ... well, why not?

"Are your children coming, Nick?" Barney asked him. The man's eyes were compassionate, and he had a hand on Reeve's shoulder as he looked him in the eyes. They were in the small office off the main sanctuary, a dark room with a few sets of the pastor's robes hung on the wall next to a speaker that emitted a slow, dirge-like song. Reeve suspected that was the church sound system, playing whatever was going on out there, giving the preacher a cue for when he was expected to take the stage, as it were.

"Hell, no," Reeve said, then remembered who he was speaking to. "I mean ... no. I haven't told 'em yet."

Jones's eyes went wide, then he nodded, once, as he got it. "You don't want them to come back to Midian."

"Not now," Reeve said, shaking his head. "They got out, you know?" They'd gone on to build lives elsewhere, away from here. This wasn't their hometown anymore, by choice and for good reason. "No reason to drag them back now."

"When are you going to tell them?" Barney asked. Probably a reasonable request.

Reeve rubbed a hand over his bald head, feeling the slick, oily skin. He hadn't showered in a couple days. He was living in the sheriff's station, after all. "When we've driven the damned demons out of town. When they call and ask. I don't know."

Jones nodded. "I got to warn you ... funerals right now ... they're not as well attended as ones you might have gone to in the past."

Reeve stared past Barney's shoulder. "What are you talking about?"

"There's liable not going to be a whole lot of people here."

Reeve frowned, then got it. "Too many funerals lately."

"We have suffered a fair few," Jones said. He was parceling out his thoughts carefully, feeding out his warning to Reeve. "I think folks are a little worn down, like a boxer going into the late rounds."

Reeve raised an eyebrow at that. "Can't blame 'em. We are staggering, after all." He drew a breath. The little waiting room they were in was dark. On a table nearby lay a metal tray for carrying communion grape juice in the tiny shot glasses, as Reeve thought of them, and a covered dish for the pieces of bread. Reeve stared at it. Midian had sacrificed enough flesh and blood to fill a thousand of the damned things. *We've been having a communion of fucking crows,* he thought dimly, *pecking at what's left of us.*

"You should go on out," Barney said, ushering him toward the door behind him. Reeve didn't argue, just walked out the door, which shut behind him automatically, and paused for a second as he looked out over the near-empty church. Jones had been right; there was only a scattering of people.

Well, that was all right, wasn't it? He'd gotten the town to agree to fight together against the demons, after all, but outside of a fight, the idea of sitting through who knew how many funerals? Shit, that was a special sort of torture, wasn't it?

At least it wasn't a funeral mass, Reeve reflected as he took his seat. Arch was sitting there in the second row, and so was Braeden Tarley. Reeve wasn't entirely sure why Tarley was there, especially since they'd had words when they'd spoken last. Erin Harris was there too, a few rows back, in her deputy's uniform, looking somber. She had a baseball bat with nails driven through it leaned against the pew next to her. He might have commented on it, but hell, he knew why it was there, so he just let it pass. He had his holy dagger on his belt too, and suspected Arch had a sword on his, though he couldn't see it.

The world sure had changed.

Reeve cast one last look behind him and saw a familiar face in the fourth row. He stared a second too long, and the subject of his attention caught his gaze and blushed, looking away.

She was as smartly dressed as ever, her suit darker than usual. He eyed Lex Deivrel and wondered what she was doing here. She'd been of some help recently, which was an unusual turn in an antagonistic relationship that stretched back years. He caught her eye again, and this time she looked back evenly at him.

Reeve turned back to the front just as Barney Jones came out. He walked quietly in front of the pulpit, and Reeve caught motion out of the corner of his eye. He glanced over and saw a guy sitting there in the front row, all the way down at the end. Tall, lanky, raven-haired, dressed in a black suit and tie, with a white shirt and a long face, he met Reeve's eye for a moment without guilt or guile, and then nodded once, expressing his condolences with a look.

Who the hell was that? Reeve barely had time to wonder before Barney Jones started up, and he listened to the man extol his wife's virtues with one ear while his cop's brain tried to work out who the unknown man in the front row was. It didn't take long before emotion forced him to put the thought on the back burner and devote himself, entirely, to keeping himself from breaking down in public.

*

Erin Harris didn't know quite how to take the fucking disgraceful showing at Donna Reeve's funeral. She'd known the woman forever, as had a great many people in town, and the fact that there were maybe fifteen people in attendance was like a personal insult. She'd talked to Arch and Braeden Tarley beforehand—Arch looked pretty okay, surprisingly, but Tarley was a fucking disaster, barely able to string a sentence together without lapsing into a blank look followed by a deep swallow and haunted shaking—and had heard what Barney Jones had been telling people, about how Midian was trauma'd out or whatever.

Yeah, that was bullshit.

Sure, she hadn't gone to many funerals herself, but dammit, didn't people see? Reeve had hosted that meeting to pull the town together after the Halloween slaughter to try and—well, to *unite* the fucking town. The fact that they weren't here for this funeral, that they weren't showing up like they usually did, weren't filling peoples' houses with fried chicken and sandwich platters and potato salad—dammit, it was a shitty omen for a town that needed to pull together. Yeah, maybe they were mounting some effective patrols and shit now, sending people out to fight, but the fact that they weren't backing each other up in the moments like these …

Well, hell. It was a bad day for Southern hospitality, that's what it was. If her mom hadn't left town a couple years earlier, she would have been ashamed to see it come to this.

"We all knew Donna," Pastor Jones said, his powerful voice not needing a microphone to resonate to the highest corners of the wood beams in the ceiling. "We knew she was a good woman, a good servant of the Lord."

Erin might have found herself cynically raising an eyebrow at that if

Donna had still been alive and someone said that about her. Not that Donna Reeve was a bad woman. Hell, she wasn't; she was a damned good one, one of the best. But had she and the sheriff even gone to church these last few years? Erin had never heard them say a peep about it.

That was the problem with someone dying. They always had to paper over the bad spots in someone's past in order to make them sound good. Erin had understood that once, but that had been before a flock of demons had come to roost in her head and made her kill her fellow fucking townsfolk in the process. She remembered how long she'd had to work to scrub the blood off her hands after Halloween.

She'd imagined her own funeral a few times since Halloween, had pictured herself eating her Glock. The only reason she hadn't was because she couldn't seem to muster up enough care one way or the other to pull the trigger. So she'd sat there one night, teeth clenched just behind the metal sight, taste of grimy, dirty gun oil permeating into the back of her throat, urging herself in a calm and reasoned voice to just do it, put a bullet out the back of her skull, make sure and hit the base of the spine so it would well and truly be over and the blood she squirted out the back of her head would be the last she'd shed.

God—if that bastard existed—knew she'd certainly spilled enough of other people's.

She took a breath and could almost smell that gun oil still, almost taste it on her tongue, bitter and greasy. It was like a mark on her, like the bloodstains she couldn't see anymore, branding her. She wondered dimly if it would follow her all her days, and how long those days might last. She'd once imagined guilt to be a crushing weight, but it wasn't really like that. It was more like one of those damned little dogs, constantly biting at her ankles while she tried to walk.

It just kept taking little bites out of her flesh, a little bite here at the ankle, the next at the toe. She was bleeding as she walked, trailing it behind her, draining slowly, leaving a clear path of red for someone to follow her.

No one was going to follow her though. They were all too busy fighting demons and trying to keep themselves together. That was why they weren't here, weren't supporting each other by going to the funerals. Everyone had reached their limit, everyone had given what they could give. They were all taxed out. Shut down.

That, Erin understood. It came over her slowly, and she looked away, down the row toward the stranger in the black suit and tie, very plainly dressed, tall with a long face. She didn't know him, and she didn't care to know him either. He wasn't particularly handsome, nor was he very young, and while she certainly wouldn't have said no to some comfort right now—and had some ideas already churning in her head about where she might find some after this goddamned funeral was over—he wasn't her type at all. Not that that always mattered, but she wasn't drunk enough to make an exception in his case. Not at her boss's wife's funeral. Not today. Not even if he had the biggest cock in the room, a tongue that could reach his eyebrows and a willingness to use both without regard for any orgasmic interest of his own for the next six hours.

*

Nora Wellstone was probably in shock, she thought, hands clutching tightly to the wheel of her car. She hadn't started the day expecting anything big—her son, Mack, and husband, John, were down in Calhoun County, Tennessee, going hunting together for the first time. It was a rite of passage in her husband's family, one that Nora found as mysterious as the fetishistic girlie magazines that John kept in the bottom of his underwear drawer. But Nora didn't try to understand hunting any more than she tried to understand her husband's fantasies about Asian women. She just left them all alone and went about her business.

Up until this year, Mack—the light of her life and the main reason she and John were still married—had stayed home with her when her husband went to the woods in the first weekend in November. She'd enjoyed her time with Mack. He'd grown up so fast, and those weekends were a nice way to reconnect, to eat TV dinners and forgo cooking and cleaning and all the other crap she hated but did for the good of the family. It was her weekend to relax, to enjoy Mack, and let him break from routine.

She hadn't been happy when John had pronounced this as the weekend Mack would make his entry into manhood. There was a small trace of regret that her baby boy was going to be going with his father rather than staying with her for the weekend to keep her company, but that was balanced out by the fact that she could go see the new Sandra Bullock romcom and meet her friends for drinks at Cheddar's without worrying about what Mack might get up to without her for the evening. She could get tanked on margaritas, reconnect with her girlfriends about everything from jobs and work to men and sex (she was barely having any, like most of them), Uber home, and sleep in the next morning.

She'd been out for a nice lunch at Chipotle when she'd gotten the call from the unknown number. She'd taken it because that small mother's instinct had cried out at her that it might, just might, be an emergency involving John and Mack, though she didn't really believe it—

Until she'd heard the cool words of the man on the other end of the line, telling her that John was dead and Mack was sitting in the Calhoun County Sheriff's office, waiting for her to come pick him up.

She hadn't cried, surprisingly. Maybe it was because she and John had been mostly staying together for Mack. Maybe it was because they hadn't had sex in almost a year, and when they had, it had been mechanical, over quickly, and left her wondering afterward if he'd been picturing an Asian woman when he closed his eyes for most of it.

Maybe the tears would come later. After all, they'd been married for almost twenty years. That didn't just pass without some emotion, did it?

Nora clutched the wheel tightly as she drove down the interstate, the grey sky hanging over them like a ceiling on the world and Mack sitting next to her like a black hole of silence, sucking in every word she said without radiating any out in return.

"Mack?" she offered again, trying to get something, anything out of him. He glanced at her, attentive enough to watch her, waiting for her to say something more than his name. "Are you …?" She didn't bother to finish.

Why should she? He'd watched his father die this morning. How could he be okay?

Nora tried to figure out what to say next. She hadn't gotten much in the way of information about how John had actually died, and Mack wasn't talking. The sheriff had promised the body, had given her the number for a funeral home, but she was unwilling to deal with it today. He'd been polite enough to ask if there was anyone else he could call for her, had told her that no, she didn't need to identify the body if she didn't want to. She didn't want to, was too stunned to press any further. She'd just collected Mack and gotten out of there, wanting to get home where she could process this—this unexpected event, this emotion that was cracking its way through her walls.

"Do you want to talk about it?" Nora asked lamely. She almost cursed herself for it as soon as she said it, bumping down a side road. She didn't know Calhoun County like John had. He had been born and raised here; it was why he came back here to hunt on a spread his parents had. It was the only contact he had with them, she thought ruefully, seeing them once a year for a few minutes as he went up into the hills above their house. She hadn't even thought to call her in-laws, she realized dimly. Well, that was all right. They all hated each other anyway, so fuck them, they could wait.

Mack didn't reply. She steered the car around a gentle bend, keeping it right at the 45-mile-per-hour speed limit. She didn't even see the small, black obstacle on the back road until her tire hit it and burst, sending the car into a sudden, unexpected lurch to the left.

*

Aaron Drake frowned, almost guiltily, at the trap he'd set on the country road. They were deep in the woods, here in the back country of Calhoun County, a little ways out from the town of Midian, where Drake had rented his temporary home. He'd constructed a plan, considering carefully exactly what he wanted to accomplish, and how best to achieve those ends.

In pursuit of those ends, he'd sought out a blind corner, a sharp S-turn that would come up swiftly, and then placed a piece of plywood two feet by two feet filled with heavy roofing nails onto the road and covered it up as best he could with fallen leaves.

It had taken some time to construct his little trap, it was true. He'd acquired the needed items when he'd made a trip into Athens Chattanooga to visit Home Depot as well as Whole Foods. A little sweat—not that he sweated through his shell—and a little ingenuity, and soon he had a device able to stop a car.

Drake had planned this well, putting his own vehicle one turn ahead on the road, leaving the emergency blinkers flashing as though he, too, had hit the same obstacle. He merely sat there and waited after that, listening to the wind whistle through the woods around him for almost a half hour before the first sound of a car's engine made its way over the hill to him like sweet music. Then came the sweeter sound of a tire popping. He waited patiently until he saw the car crest the hill, still slaloming as the driver tried to regain control.

*

"Shit, shit, shit!" Nora said as she guided the car toward the shoulder, pressing slowly on the brake now that she'd gotten control of the wheel once more. This was not her day, was it? Next to her, Mack was white as a glass of milk, having now experienced his second big shock of the day. As a rule, she tried not to swear in front of him, but she was obviously failing.

Well, hell. She'd lost her husband and her tire today. And if Mack hadn't heard the word "shit" before, she'd eat her own tampon.

"You all right?" she asked Mack as she got the car back under control and limped it to the shoulder.

"Yeah," Mack said, shuddering a little. The tire going hadn't been too loud, but the rim hitting the road hadn't been quiet.

"Let me pull over and call a tow truck," Nora said, steering the car gently to the side. She frowned; there was a car ahead with the emergency flashers on as well. That made sense, because whatever was in the road was pretty big, and if it had flattened her tire, it made sense it would flatten another, right?

"You think that guy popped a tire too?" Nora asked, mostly to herself, figuring Mack probably wouldn't answer.

"How do you know it's a guy?" Mack asked, and Nora pointed.

They guy in question walked along the shoulder, looking desperately out of place in the woods. He was wearing wingtip shoes, a sky-blue dress shirt, and an expensive coat that ran all the way to his ankles. He had a bulge at his midsection and was balding, hair combed over. He seemed soft to her, or as John would have said—before he died— he looked like a pussy. John always was a pig.

The man made his way alongside their car and gestured for Nora to roll the window down, which she did, unthinking. He was so effete, he didn't look like he'd be any kind of a threat at all. "Hi, did you hit the thing in the road?" she asked.

"Yes," he said, his voice high, "isn't it just dismal?" He gave a little shudder. "The quality of the roads around here is really cause for concern." He leaned over, and smiled, immaculate teeth looking like they'd been bleached regularly. "Is everyone all right here?" He smiled across her at Mack.

"We're fine," Nora said, looking down. Where had she put her cell phone? "Have you called a tow truck yet?"

"Mmm, no," he said, and when she looked up in surprise, he said simply, "No signal."

Nora felt her stomach drop. Oh, God. There were enough hills in Calhoun County that she knew there were places where cell service was impossible to get. It'd be just their luck to have blown a tire in one of those spots. "Who's your provider?" she asked, looking down again to rummage through her coat pocket for it.

"It doesn't really matter," he said pleasantly, and something about that caused her to hesitate as she fumbled through her right and left pockets simultaneously, both hands tied up in the action.

"Why doesn't it m—" She didn't even get all the words out before he hit her in the back of the head and rammed her face into the steering wheel with such force that the airbag exploded. Nora, already reduced to painful semiconsciousness by his attack, was whipped back into her seat, knocked cleanly out by the force of the blow and the airbag. The last thing she thought before she went out was—*God, he's strong for a little pussy.* She didn't even have time to curse herself for thinking like John would have.

*

This plan had worked perfectly, Drake thought as he rammed the woman's head into the steering wheel, accidentally deploying the airbag. Her eyes fluttered as she went out, but she was most definitely out, a trickle of blood running down her forehead. He ran a finger across the wound and took a lick.

Mmm. Savory.

"Well, all right," Drake said, reaching for the door handle. This was a job well done, and—

A squeak caused him to freeze. What was—

Footsteps pattered across the pavement behind the car, and Drake listened.

The kid!

Leaves crunched as the boy—it was a boy, wasn't it? He hadn't really noticed—ran into the woods. Drake peered after him, the cloudy afternoon reducing the woods to darkness and shadows. The boy hit the tree line and kept running, disappearing into the boughs.

Drake sighed. He hated to exert himself. Checking the woman again to make sure she was unconscious and would be for a while, he made his way to the shoulder of the road and stepped off the pavement.

Leaves crunched under his impeccably tailored shoes, the sound like some bastard chewing with his mouth open. It was a disquieting sensation, the idea that things here had once been living and now, through a natural cycle, died. He knew that his prey were on just such a cycle, but he preferred to focus on the slaughter that he inflicted. The natural part, caused by the gradual expiry of their lives …

Well, ugh. That was unpleasant. Like old, tough meat.

Drake worked his way down the short embankment to the slight ditch below. The woods lurked in front of him, the sound of the youth's crunching footsteps going somewhere within. How far away was he now? It didn't sound too far. Drake could run, try and catch him. It wouldn't be too hard …

He peered into the woods. It was so dark. There were so many leaves. Worms, working on dead things. Naturally expired things. Composting.

Drake plunged forward, crossing through the tree line as though passing some invisible barrier. His shell felt as though it were crawling, as though bugs were landing on him with wild abandon, buzzing around his head, caterpillars and worms crawling up his body.

He took a halting step forward, listening. The footsteps had faded; he couldn't hear them any longer.

Drake stood there, listening, watching for movement. The boy had to be here. He had to be. How could he escape?

"I needed this," Drake murmured. He had recipes, plans. Ideas to sate the hunger, the low growl in his essence. Sure, the woman would suffice for now, but he didn't want to have to do this again tomorrow. He wanted time. Time to experiment with his kitchen, such as it was. It was something he was looking forward to, to achieve some culinary mastery.

He sniffed, trying to catch the scent. His nose was not a nose, per se, but it was good enough at catching scents. Better than a human one, in any case.

Drake wrinkled his nose at the smell. Death. Rotting leaves, some sort of animal dung; all of these flooded his senses. The cool, autumn air pricked at his shell, and the sound of wind running past him was almost overwhelming.

The boy was out there somewhere. He was young, lacking some of the marbling to be found in an older human, but not as rangy as the truly old ones, the ones approaching natural death. He could smell the boy in the distance, somewhere, dirty, sweaty, that earthy aroma of fear permeating him. Drake liked the fear, the adrenaline flavor. It gave humans a more … succulent taste. Well, there was really room for either—he could go for a human that had been run relentlessly, adrenaline changing the taste as it seeped into their meat just before death. But he'd also like ones that had died soundlessly, without time to panic or react, like the woman in the car. He wanted to try both, do a little … taste test.

But the smell of death ahead of him was daunting. Nature, in all its horror—that was not for Drake. He took a step back toward the car. Sure, a taste test would be nice, but really, was it necessary? Now? He didn't want to have to run, to chase the boy through the woods. That would be … undignified, wouldn't it?

Drake shivered, the cool air running over the surface of his shell in a gust. No, it was time to be thankful. Best to quit while ahead. He shrugged at the thought of chasing the boy through the woods and contented himself by removing the woman from the car, carrying her prostrate body over his shoulder and tossing her into the trunk. She'd suffice for now.

*

Arch had lingered after Donna Reeve's funeral because his wife's was next. He'd parked himself in the front pew and stayed there, thoughts coming slow and steady, prayers right behind them, trying as best he could to work through the moment with the Lord at his side. He dug his fingers into the velvety cushioning, feeling the smooth cloth against his hands as he spoke to God in his head.

Barney was out there somewhere, probably in his office or the little room off to the side of the pulpit, thinking things through. The man was delivering a lot of eulogies lately. Every clergyman in town was. Arch wondered how much thought they were putting into each eulogy. Some, like Barney, actually knew well the subjects of the funerals. Others ... maybe they didn't. Though Barney hadn't known Donna Reeve well, probably, just in passing.

A click of the door at the back of the sanctuary caused Arch to turn, breathing a quick, "Amen," to wrap up his current chain of prayer. A stubby, suited figure was making his way slowly up the aisle. He stopped next to Arch, hands thrust deep in his pocket.

"Duncan," Arch said, looking at the man who was not a man at all. "You're in a church."

"Don't think it doesn't pain me to be here," Duncan said, looking like pins and needles might be prickling at his shell. "Not as bad as St. Brigid's now that Father Nguyen has turned up the holy juice, but ..." He looked around and evinced distaste at the empty cross hanging at the front of the room. "The symbology alone causes some ... discomfort."

"Reckon it'd be tough for an unbeliever of your sort," Arch said, simply and without ire.

"I'm not an unbeliever," Duncan said. "I'm a knower, see? I know if what you believe is true, I don't need the faith you have."

Arch just nodded at that, turning his attention back to the cross at the front of the church.

"You know how many so-called believers over the years have asked me whether there is a God after I told them what I just told you?"

Duncan asked. He looked at the cross, blanching faintly, as though it had a klieg light shining down into his eyes.

"Quite a few, I'd imagine," Arch said. "Which is why you referred to them as 'so-called believers.'"

"Yep." Duncan was quiet for a moment. "But you're not so-called. You're a true blue."

"I try," Arch whispered, feeling wrung out.

"You succeed," Duncan said, tearing his gaze away from the cross. "She believed too, you kn—"

"I know."

"Not quite like you did," Duncan said, "but her faith was strong."

"I know."

Duncan hesitated. "You think you're going to see her again in the … next life?"

Arch blinked, then turned his attention to the demon. "I know I will."

"Good," Duncan said, nodding with obvious discomfort, taking a step back from the cross. "I'm sorry, I can't stay. This is just …" He waved a hand at the cross. "It's too much."

"Thank you," Arch said, looking back at him. "For not testing my faith at this hour. For not … rubbing it in, as others might." He meant Duncan's partner, Amanda Guthrie—though he still thought of her as Lerner.

"I may be a demon," Duncan said, "but I'm not much of a devil." And with a last nod he turned and made his way out of the church, relaxing visibly the moment he passed through the doors and into the autumn afternoon outside.

*

Brian had carpooled to the funeral with his mother, who had torn herself away from his dad at Red Cedar down in Chattanooga to come. It was another difficult choice in a life full of them lately, Brian supposed. Stay with the partially brain-damaged husband or bury your daughter? Gosh, what a decision.

It didn't help that the church was so damned empty. Brian hadn't been to many of the funerals, but Alison's, thus far, was probably the poorest attended he'd been to. The first two rows were mostly filled, and after that there was only a scattering of people throughout the rest of the church.

He leaned back against the wooden, felt-lined back of the pew and remembered a thousand uncomfortable church sermons spent in pews just like this, listening to sermons and mentally poking logic holes in the arguments. Some pastors couldn't construct a theological argument to save their souls (*hahahaha*, Brian thought, *so true*) but others ...

Well, he'd been to Barney Jones's church a couple times with his parents after they'd switched once Arch had come into the family, and Jones ... he was not one that could easily be argued down. The man came up with arguments like an addict came up with excuses.

"Brothers and sisters," Jones said, sweeping out of a door to the left of the pulpit and taking his place, his robes black and his vestments white. He clutched the pulpit, leaned down, and looked right out at the congregation, not even going from notes. "We are here to celebrate the life of a beloved sister in Christ, Alison Longholt Stan."

Brian cringed a little. He looked around, tuning out Jones during the next part. Sheriff Reeve was a couple rows back, his bald head bowed and shining. He'd already had his wife's funeral today. Erin Harris was sitting not far from him, looking more serious than he'd ever seen her, a baseball bat handle resting next to the pew against her. It took Brian a minute to realize that she'd probably had it consecrated, that she wasn't off to a softball game or something after this.

Hendricks was much farther back, his hat off his head for once, staring straight ahead at the preacher. He looked pretty blank-eyed, like he wasn't paying too much attention to what Barney Jones was saying.

"'... blessed are the meek, for they shall inherit the earth.' But I think we all know Alison wasn't meek. Quiet until you got to know her, yes. She was reserved, but her spirit was a beautiful thing, full of life and energy. She was a vivacious young lady who loved her family, who embraced her duty to protect her town with a steadfastness that does glory to Him ..."

Brian kept looking around, trying to avoid coming up with mental arguments for Barney Jones. It was his sister's funeral; he didn't need to pick any intellectual fights at the moment, and he was trying to avoid those these days in any case. Too much fighting of the regular variety to do.

His eyes settled on a man sitting a few rows back. He had black hair and a black suit with white shirt beneath it, set off by a black tie; he looked like a villain from a black-and-white movie. But then, the villains had all been pretty one-dimensional back then, hadn't they? And ugly, that was a hallmark of that era—villains were physically unpleasant as well as cacklingly evil.

This guy wasn't hideous; just thin with a terribly narrow face. He looked a little swoop-necked, like a bird or something. He wasn't familiar at all, and Brian didn't spend any more time trying to place him. He just listened to Barney Jones as the preacher drew the eulogy closer and closer, made it more and more about Alison, and he tried to hold in the feelings rising within.

*

Erin was consciously trying to avoid looking at Hendricks in the manner of a woman who had just broken up with a guy and was trying to reassure herself she would be fine without him. Sure, they hadn't been together for a few weeks now, but still, there was a lingering, nagging question in her mind as to whether they might get back together, whether there might be some kind of hope for them in the future.

Maybe?

He didn't seem to be looking at her either, which was fine with her. He was looking straight ahead, paying attention to what Barney Jones was saying, which surprised her, because she knew that while she might have been agnostic, he was pretty firm in his total non-belief.

But here he was in the church, listening politely, head down slightly, eyes up and forward. She kept stealing glances at him out of the corner of her eye, occasionally reaching out to touch the baseball bat, reassure herself it was there in case shit went down. Was it likely to happen during a funeral? Well, hopefully not, but it was tough to tell in Midian these days.

She looked to the side, and there was that guy again, the skinny one in his suit with the long face, the one that had been at Donna Reeve's funeral. She'd never seen him before today, had she?

The thin man looked sideways at her and smiled, as if sensing her attention toward him. She didn't return the smile; she was in uniform and felt plenty all right glowering suspiciously in his direction. He didn't react, just kept smiling and went back to paying attention to the preacher.

"... and pray the way You have taught us to pray, oh Lord ... Our Father, who art in heaven ..."

Shit. She hadn't even noticed Jones had started a prayer. She hurriedly bowed her head and started murmuring along.

*

Lauren strolled in through the front door of the whorehouse, Molly trailing behind her. "My feet hurt," Lauren complained, kicking off her heels and sighing in relief. The shoes that Ms. Cherry had lent her, literal hooker heels, pinched like hell.

"You look about two sizes too big for Ms. Cherry's shoes, that's why," Molly said, taking off her sneakers. It was all she had because neither of them had gone back to their house since ... well, since.

"Hey, if you think we should have hit up our own wardrobes, you should have said so," Lauren retorted.

"No thanks," Molly said, paling slightly. Lauren knew she remembered what happened, but she didn't want to press. It wasn't as though Molly had wanted to slit her grandmother's throat, after all. It was those goddamned demons that had done it. "Though we are going to have to get some clothes soon. We can't just keep raiding Ms. Cherry's closet forever."

"Have you seen her closet? We *can* live out of it forever. We *should*," Lauren said. The woman had style, taste, and a lot of extra clothes in various sizes for reasons that Lauren didn't want to delve too deeply into.

"I'm amazed how much she has that fits me," Molly agreed. "Though most of it is a little lower cut than I prefer ..."

"Oh, it's you." Lucia spoke from just behind the curtain to the living room. She was barely visible, scarcely more than an eye and her legs in view behind the parted cloth. She was standing in shadow, which was something Lauren had noticed that she and Ms. Cherry did quite often before greeting a "guest."

"Yeah, just us," Molly said. "Did you do anything, uh ... fun ... while we were gone?" She blushed as soon as the words were out of her mouth.

If Lucia caught her discomfort, she didn't let on, answering with a shrug of her thin shoulders. "Mostly just sat around and watched TV. Only one customer, and he didn't stay long."

Lauren waited a second, two, then three. "That's nic—" she started.

"Why didn't he stay long?" Molly asked.

Lauren blanched. Here was another problem with living in a whorehouse: her inquisitive sixteen-year-old daughter was now asking questions about the business.

"He just wanted a blowjob," Lucia said with another shrug of the shoulders. "In and out in less than ten minutes."

Molly's face was a study in cascade reaction. "Wait, so he just wanted you to—"

"That's about enough," Lauren said.

Molly was making a face. "But ... I mean ... he just wanted that, not—"

"Please stop asking questions."

"But I want to know why—I mean, why a guy would only want that when he could have so much—so much more." Molly waved a hand to indicate Lucia's crotch. "You know?"

Lauren frowned, putting her hand over her eyes. "I—this is ... it's so wrong ..."

"You want to know why he just wanted a blowjob?" Lucia asked, regarding Molly with a sort of world-weary amusement.

"Well, yeah," Molly said, flushing. "I mean ... I thought guys wanted to get laid, you know?"

Lauren thought about thrusting her fingers in her ears and humming really loud until the conversation was over. It wouldn't help. She'd imagine it, and that might be worse than what was playing out in front of her.

"Sweetheart," Lucia said, unflinching, "men just want to get off. Some men want to get off by getting laid, yeah. Some would prefer to see a woman on her knees in front of them, working them between her lips until—well, until they get there."

"You said it so politely too," Lauren muttered.

"But I thought oral was just a warm-up!" Molly said. "You mean ... they actually ..." She lowered her voice to a whisper. "... get there ... like *get there* ... in your mouth?"

"Yes." Lucia maintained that dry amusement.

"Really ...?"

"Okay, please stop," Lauren said, closing her eyes. There was no way to imagine this worse.

"Wait. Mom, have you ever—"

"I'm not answering that," Lauren snapped.

"Oh, God, you have," Molly said, mouth falling open. "You totally have. How often—"

"NOT ANSWERING!"

"Do a lot of guys like that?" Molly asked. "To skip, you know, straight-up sex and go for—"

"Enough!" Lauren seized Molly by the upper arm and started to drag her away. "Lucia ... seriously," she shot back, "kindly—not—with my teenage daughter!"

"That's a pretty basic thing to learn," Lucia said quietly, "what guys like." She eyed the two of them. "I'm guessing you knew at her age."

"I also knew what it was like to be pregnant at her age," Lauren snapped, trying to pull Molly away, away from this conversation. "I'm trying to keep her from learning how that feels too."

"Blowjobs don't cause pregnant," Lucia said with a barely contained smirk.

"I don't want to get pregnant," Molly said, mostly going along with Lauren but still looking back at Lucia, "but, I mean … Lucia and Ms. Cherry are, like, sex experts, and it's stupid for me not to take advantage of their knowledge while I'm here—"

"NO," Lauren said again, practically dragging her upstairs, toward their room.

"But this is really interesting!" Molly said, turning to her with a slight pout. "Why can't you and I have conversations about sex like that? You know—honest, engaging, fact-based—"

Lauren felt her blood run cold. "Because if your grandmother wasn't already dead, hearing you and I talk about oral sex would have pretty much killed her." She caught the blush from Molly, the hot shame at the invocation of her grandmother's name, on this day of all days, and the slight resistance she'd been putting up faded instantly, allowing Lauren to drag her back to their room and shut the door, both to the whorehouse and the conversation that her daughter had been wanting to have.

*

"No one among us is irredeemable," Barney Jones said, his words a little like nails screeching on a chalkboard to Hendricks. Hendricks hadn't spent a lot of time talking to the preacher since he'd joined the watch. The pastor was a little evangelical for his taste; not too over the top, but a few degrees too warm with the spirit for him to want to spend much time with the man. "The apostle Paul was originally known as Saul, a persecutor of Christians so virulent that he was among the chief of them to hunt down believers."

Hendricks kept from rolling his eyes, but only just.

"One day," Jones said, raising his hands up above the pulpit theatrically, "Saul was walking down the road to Damascus. Here he was, the fiercest enemy of the Christians. He walked along, and was struck blind by the Lord—"

"If only your Lord would strike me deaf right now," muttered Hendricks, rolling his eyes and getting a nasty look from an older black lady a row ahead of him. He shrugged in mild penitence, then let his gaze drift around the church.

He didn't know any of these people who weren't with the watch. He'd been in town for a while now, but he hadn't done much socializing. He'd run across a few people in the course of fighting demons, but really, his wasn't the most social of occupations. He'd talked more with people here in Midian than he had on any other job, but that wasn't saying much.

   He caught Erin looking at him again. God, that was annoying. She was playing a fucking teenage game with him, he could feel it. For his part, Hendricks considered them done. He was getting his pussy elsewhere at this point anyway.

   He blanched inwardly at the slight swell of guilt that presented itself after that thought. Sure, maybe he'd felt something more for her at some point, but that was damned long gone now, wasn't it? Fucking a crazy redhead without complication was way better, wasn't it?

   Sure it was, he told himself, but his guts churned, telling him something slightly different.

   "… and through this man, Saul, God gave us this lesson—that no one is irredeemable. That every man has his part to play, his choice to make. That among the flock are welcomed even those who once hunted the flock. Saul became the Apostle Paul. He went from dogged hunter of Christians to a leader of the church in its incipient form." Barney Jones looked around. "I see dark days. I see people willing to fight. Alison Stan was one of them. I knew that girl since she was a little thing, long, long before she stepped foot in my church with Arch, who would become her husband. Alison and I had a few conversations about her faith." Jones smiled. "It was strong. Alison believed. John 3:16 says that, 'Whosoever believes in me shall not die, but shall live forever.'" He looked over the parishioners. "Alison believed …"

   Hendricks barely suppressed the eye-roll. Maybe she had believed, but he didn't. He believed in a whole lot of nothing after death. That the brain died, the body died, and the consciousness was just gone. Black, empty nothingness. Hell, he'd wished for it when Kitty Elizabeth had gotten hold of him. Wished for an end to it, for his lights to get switched out, for his struggles to be done. Another life after this? Shit, this one was more than enough. Sure, they said eternal peace or bliss or whatever, but really, that didn't sound any more believable than anything else they professed.

   "… and the thought of redemption for some us seems like a … like a distant sort of idea." Jones was smiling again, down at the flock, and it made Hendricks queasy. "We go about our daily lives, and maybe the Lord isn't much with us, isn't much in our thoughts. We can make our way without him, after all. We can do what we gotta do, get through the day." Jones raised a clenched fist. "Get caught up in the concerns of man. Live our shallow lives, looking for the things that'll keep us busy, keep us … entertained. There are things aplenty to preoccupy a man in this world."

Hendricks listed a few of the more fun ones off in his head: *pussy, beer, whiskey, pot.*

Jones went on: "It is easy to walk through the world preoccupied by those concerns, by the pleasures of the flesh. They offer a respite from the pains of the day, from the pains of being human." Jones gave a knowing smile. "We've all had bad days. We're looking at a lot of 'em in both directions right now, forward and backward. It'd be easier for a body to lose hope. To think, 'Heck, why bother? There's fun to be had, and what's the point of fighting on? Of … believing?'"

Not a terrible point, Hendricks thought. Other than sheer orneriness, maybe a desire to cram a sword into the face of every single demon he could. Those were reasons, weren't they? They'd carried him along this far.

"Man can act for himself, selfishly. That's one way to live life." Jones slumped dramatically. "It's a terrible way to live your life though, driven by crass desire, moving from one pleasure to the next, these shallow compulsions the only thing that gets you out of bed in the morning. I knew a man in my youth who struggled with drink. His eyes were bloodshot, his nose a red bubble on his face." Jones mimed a bulbous attachment. "I came around an alleyway corner one morning and found him there, drinking deep from a bottle of rotgut. He was retching, gagging up and spitting, the smell of sick just terrible in the air. I watched him wrestle with the nausea, the desire to heave up his guts. Just when he got hold of himself, with a little drip of spittle still making its way down his chin—he took another drink. 'What are you doing?' I asked him. And he looked up at me, not even noticing I was there before, and he said, 'If I can get past the gagging on the first bottle, the rest of the day goes just fine.'" Jones shook his head. "Friends … we need not go through our days gagging our way, dragging our way, through to the next pleasure. That man in that alley … he was focused on his pleasure, not realizing he'd lost himself long ago. If all you do is chase your satisfaction, you'll find yourself strangely unsatisfied. There are other people in this world, people who could use your help. Even the worst of us have our moment on the Damascus road where we can keep going—pursuing power, pursuing lust, pursuing our … our own selfish desires …" Jones turned solemn. "Or we can seek redemption. Become better. Be washed in the blood of the One who forgives us when we do our wrongs. We all do wrong. No man is perfect. We all fail. We are all by turns terrible, and that's all right—not that we do terrible things, but that we can be forgiven for them …"

"Oh, for fuck's sake," Hendricks said under his breath, drawing another nasty look from the lady in front of him. She reminded him a little of his former mother-in-law. He didn't say what he was thinking, probably because she did look like Renee's mom: *I didn't realize I was coming here for a fucking sermon.*

*

Nora Wellstone woke up in darkness, stone blocks surrounding her on all sides. Chains bound her to a table. She tried to move, but the table squeaked beneath her, the legs slightly uneven. The chains rattled in the darkness, the sound unsettling her further.

Her head felt foggy, like she was still coming out of a deep sleep. She had a little double vision going too, the lone bulb hanging overhead resolving slowly into one filament, then diverging again into two. "H … hello …?" she asked the darkness, rocking experimentally once more.

What had happened? She'd been in the car with Mack … they'd blown the tire … she'd pulled over …

What had happened next? It was vague, a blur, and she recalled … wasn't there a man there? Yes, a man who'd … he'd been pulled over too, hadn't he?

"Oh, you're awake." A squeak behind her, just out of her field of vision, which ensured she couldn't turn her head to look far enough to see him. His footsteps suggested he was on a set of stairs, descending slowly toward her. "Good." He sounded pleased about this.

"Wh … where am I?" she asked, catching sight of him finally. Her vision was blurry around the edges, and the grey concrete block that made up the room wasn't very clear, wasn't easy to see. "Where is … where's Mack?"

"I take that to mean the boy that was in the car with you," the man said, coming around into her field of view. He was carrying a … a …

Oh, God.

"I don't know where he went," the man said, lips pursed together. He didn't look terribly pleased, nor terribly upset one way or another. He looked vaguely troubled, as though thinking carefully about something. "I wish I did."

"What are … what are you going to do with me?" Nora asked, her thoughts slow, like a drip from a coffee pot about to run out of water.

"Nothing you're going to enjoy," the man said emotionlessly. He was eyeing her, the hacksaw in his hand, and he brought it down slowly, where she could see it, until it rested on her throat. Ignoring the pleas, then the screams, he started to saw, teeth biting into her flesh as the warm blood began to run.

*

"The service was nice," Reeve said, lingering near Arch, who was taking condolences with his head held high. Well, what else could he do? He was a man, and the point of this was to give folks a chance to grieve Alison's death. Arch was grieving in his own way, in his own time, and danged sure in his own place. He needed to be strong for others right now.

"Thank you," Arch said, as gracefully as he could. It was kind of Reeve to say, especially given how poorly attended things had been. Arch didn't really know how to explain that, other than by the attrition of folks worn out by grim events. He'd be pretty happy never to contemplate another funeral, but the only sure way out of that was to get to his own, and quickly.

"I like the flowers," Erin said, sidling up to join their conversation. She'd been watching at a distance for a little bit, easing into their small conversational circle just like she might have at work.

Arch glanced at the flowers. The arrangements were spread out all over the church, and he realized dimly that they were the same ones that had been here for Donna Reeve's funeral. "They're nice," he said simply, not interested in commenting further. Why bother? There were a lot of funerals, and if no one was getting the attention they deserved, at least they all had flowers.

"Arch," Erin said, leaning in toward him and putting a gentle hand on his arm, "you gonna be all right?"

Arch nodded slowly. "I'm not entirely all right now … but I will be." He kept his voice strong. It was surprisingly difficult, even though he thought he maybe had a handle on himself now. Well, the mind was a powerfully self-deceptive thing. "He'll see me through."

It would have been impossible not to notice the slight tightening of Erin's face at his comment, but she didn't say anything. He suspected he knew what she was thinking though, and that was fine. He felt a little bad for her; he didn't imagine what he was going through would even be possible without help from above. He reckoned he'd be reduced to nothing, a shattered pile, like glass you could sweep away with a broom, had he not been able to pray his way through. What was he supposed to do if he didn't have that? Try and muscle through the grief alone, with a shattered will and the feeling he'd been carved in half?

"Well, good," Erin finally said, but her tone suggested otherwise. It was her somewhat condescending way of saying, "I don't understand what you've just told me, but I'll smile and nod politely like I do." Arch was used to that by now, but at least Reeve had the grace to keep his own feelings about the matter hidden. He was probably feeling about like Arch was, but the question Arch had was … how was he muscling through?

Or was he at all?

*

The woman had taken a while to die. Aaron Drake had stood over her all the while, after opening her neck a little more gradually than if he'd meant to kill her with maximum expediency. It had been calculated on his part because he'd wanted to sample the meat tinged with the soaked-in adrenaline, and the way he'd chosen to access this particular steeping method was by letting her bleed to death very slowly.

So he'd sawed her neck open, teeth of the blade biting into pale skin, red welling up within. He'd cut all the way to her throat because he didn't want to hear the screams. Instead, she'd made guttural, hoarse noises as she'd bled to death, a little bit at a time, over ten minutes or so before she lost consciousness.

It hadn't thrilled Drake to watch, but he'd watched it nonetheless. The gasping, slurping sound she made while trying to scream might have been disquieting had he viewed her as something other than a piece of raw food that was not yet ready to eat yet. As it was, he merely found it distasteful, but listened to her last attempts at words as her carotid artery and jugular vein pumped out over the course of several long minutes, sluicing thick, red, dark liquid down their respective sides.

When she lost consciousness, he ended it quickly, raking the saw back and forth with all his strength until she was very definitely dead, her head nearly severed. Her eyes were slightly open, a little glassy, and Drake sighed, a little ripple rolling through his essence. He'd worn an apron, fortunately, for this was a very messy endeavor.

He set to work immediately, using a knife he'd purchased specifically for the purpose. He'd let her keep her clothes on for her death, figuring that stripping her of her dignity wouldn't contribute enough to the fear to make it worth the corresponding increase in flavor. Once he'd removed the chains, he shredded the clothes off methodically, the way a nurse might in an emergency room.

Once the carcass was naked, he set to gutting it. He didn't have any use for the stomach or intestines, so they all came out after he made the cut, carefully pulling back the skin of the belly and then slicing into the abdominal muscles, careful to avoid poking into the intestines. The stench was already powerful, but a simple error here would make it infinitely worse. He was gloved now, and cut the stomach out first. He pulled it, all the way down to the intestines, all out in one stringy mass. It was a modest challenge, slopping the organs into a wash pail at his feet, until finally he reached the colon at the end of the long string. He used a zip tie to bind it shut tightly, then severed it from the external exit at the anus, letting the last of the digestive tract slop uselessly into the wash tub.

Next he removed the lungs, which really hollowed out the chest cavity. There were, perhaps, some things he could do with a lung, recipe-wise, but they seemed a pointless exercise in keeping the waste to a minimum. He didn't feel the need to do that; he wanted the choicest cuts of meat, and when he was done with this one, now that he'd seen how easily it could be done, he'd simply find another prey and start again. No point in eating lungs or trying to make a human version of haggis when there were so many fish in the sea around Midian, as it were.

Next, he began the process of skinning. It took longer than he would have thought. He removed the head entirely, not bothering to skin it. He dumped it in the tub with the other discarded parts, the glassy eyes staring up at him, barely open. He looked back at them in amusement, then draped the flesh he'd removed from the chest over them, to stop their staring. It was slightly unnerving, having your dinner look back at you.

It took a long while to remove all the flesh from the body, but he was a surprisingly deft hand at it. He didn't get it all in one long strip, but he did eventually get it all, leaving a mass of muscle and bone. He severed the feet and hands at the joints and tossed them in as well; too difficult to make much of anything with those. They stood in the pail at awkward angles.

Then, he removed the reproductive organs. He couldn't imagine a use for them, nor for the spleen, not any he'd care for, anyway. It took time and patience, but he carved them out. His fingers ached from the precision work, but it would be worth it.

Next, he started to carve into the cuts of meat. He wrapped the liver carefully, then the heart. They had some real weight to them, as Drake held them in his hands, marveling at their freshness. These were things he could cook with—that he could make magic with.

He flipped the carcass over, splotching blood onto the table. It was a messy business, butchery, but these were the sacrifices one made for truly high-quality meat. The smell was a little rank, a pungent aroma of irony meat that seeped into his nose. He ignored it and began to trim the backstraps, the tenderloin. These were the best cuts, and he took his time, was delicate with them.

He was careful with the meat of the legs too. He severed the legs one by one, then divided each into upper and lower, placing heavy pressure on a larger knife to break through at the knees. He made sure to leave the bones in; they'd really add flavor when he cooked them. He wrapped one carefully in thick butcher's paper and left the other bare. He had plans for this particular cut tonight. The one he wrapped in paper, he scrawled an "F" for "fearful" (not "female") so that he would know when the time came for a taste test.

It was methodical work, dressing and preparing the animal. The pieces he couldn't quite remove whole were cut into meat for a stew. He broke apart the ribs, removing the spine as best he could and dropping the bone joints into the bucket. He knew, more or less, which pieces were the most flavorful, but this was a chance to refine his flavors, find the best uses for each in a way he hadn't experimented before. He took the cuts he'd wrapped and put them into the quietly humming freezer across the basement room.

Drake surveyed what remained. The pelvis, the arms. He cut off the buttocks—the flanks, rather—and tossed the bones. He cut the arms as he had the legs, wrapping them and putting both into the freezer and shutting the lid once more. Barbecued human wings, he thought with amusement. An interesting recipe to try.

He scooped the rest of the waste into the wash basin and pondered it for a moment. If he'd been desperate, perhaps he might have come up with another use for these excess parts, a stew or something. Well, not the digestive tract, but perhaps the rest. As it was, he had no desire to eat any of it. It was all substandard, and he intended to dispose of it at his earliest convenience. He had a few ideas for that.

He whistled as he attached a hose to the laundry sink in the corner of the basement, and then washed the blood down the drain. He didn't care if a CSI lab found traces of blood in the future; human law enforcement troubled him less than demon law enforcement did. In a town this hot, surely the OOCs would have better things to do than worry about one demon killing a human or two at a time? He'd be safe unless he was caught with the pieces, probably, and he didn't intend to be caught with either the remains of a human or a live one. Part of the key to that was appearing normal, not giving them reason to come look for you.

The crimson-tinged water ran red across the concrete floor, illuminated by the single bulb. It trickled into the drainage grate quietly, burbling as it washed away the traces of what Drake had done. He felt untroubled by the act; excited, actually. Not from the deed itself but from the anticipation of what was to come.

When he finished, he shut off the water and placed the end of the hose in the sink to keep it from dripping everywhere. Once done, he grabbed the leg and a rack of ribs, and carried them upstairs atop the wash basin of disposable parts. It was heavy, but he didn't want to have to make more than one trip.

Once upstairs, he took care not to drip on the wood floors. It wouldn't do to leave a mess up here. He carried the wash tub outside to the far end of the yard. He'd rented this house when he came to town, a little three-bedroom on the edge of a wooded area. He didn't spend much time out here, preferring the great indoors to the great outdoors, but he'd looked around enough to know that beyond the high, wooden privacy fence behind the house was a tract of woods that didn't get much traffic.

Drake took the cuts he intended to use that evening and slapped them onto the table next to the preheated Kamado grill, its rippled surface shining in the back porch light. That done, he carried the tub to the far end of the yard and hefted it up, dumping the remainder over the fence. He had little fear it would be discovered, and suspected that by morning most of what he'd just disposed of would be gone, picked over by every manner of creature, from raccoons to vultures to worms. Possibly even some irribasha, slithering, wormlike demons that were drawn to the smell of blood and fear and sometimes even excrement. Other demon carrion eaters were likely around too, and if he was lucky, they'd take care of his disposal problem for him.

He carried the tub back to the rear of the house and set it down with a clatter on the weather-stained concrete patio. The rack of ribs waited next to the grill, and he quickly added a spiced rub that he'd prepared before he'd gone hunting for the meat, putting a thick layer on it.

The Kamado was puffing clear blue smoke out its top, that faint hint of charcoal. He wasn't sure if he should use apple wood chips or mesquite—maybe hickory?—to give this particular meat a little extra flavor. He'd try each of them in turn, though not today. Today he'd try apple wood; he filled a large plastic cup with water and tossed a couple handfuls of wood chips into it to soak. He loved adding the wood chips; they popped and fizzled in the charcoal bed, filling the air with a heavy wood smoke for a few minutes as the moisture burned off, white mist piping into the air. Drake sighed in anticipation.

He'd be cooking the ribs using the 3-2-1 method. The ribs, by themselves, with indirect heat for three hours at about 250 degrees. Then he'd take them out, smell their rich flavor, and wrap them in foil, giving them a little bath of apple cider. Two more hours on the grill then, and remove them from the foil. He'd need to sauce them up, top and bottom, and put them back in for an hour, opening the grill after a half hour and slathering them with his favorite sauce again to glaze. Three hours, then two hours, then one hour, and the ribs would come out delicious, juicy, and flavorful.

His mouth was already watering.

This was how they cooked it down here, wasn't it? Barbecued everything. He would give this a try, experiment a little, see how he liked it. After all, what was the point if he couldn't attempt something new and different? Tomorrow, he meant to try a more traditional preparation, a steak-like cooking of the flank and tenderloin, but for now, he'd embrace the local flavor.

Drake stared down at the earthly remains of Nora Wellstone—he'd gotten the name from her driver's license, dimly interested—and smiled. Yes, he'd embrace the local flavor—in more ways than one.

*

Erin's hands shook slightly on the wheel as she drove home from Alison's funeral, her pulse hammering, as it always seemed to these days when she drove. It had been bad since the crash, but ever since that demon had jumped into her mind ...

Well, that didn't bear thinking about. She just kept her foot on the accelerator, maintaining even pressure and keeping control of the wheel. She was just driving.

No big deal.

She'd taken the long way home from Alison's funeral, wanting to be alone with her thoughts for a spell, because she damned sure had more of them than she cared to carry with her, especially since it was nearing closer to bedtime and the last thing she needed was another sleepless night. She had just turned a sharp corner when she saw the car pulled over on the opposite side of the road, abandoned.

She was in the police Explorer and steered it off to the side of the winding road, picking up the mic and cueing it. "This is Harris, over." She figured she'd go through the watch channels rather than the more formal—and likely unmanned—sheriff's office.

"Harris, this is HQ, over." That sounded a little like Casey Meacham to her, probably doing his shift as radio operator for them. "Go ahead, Erin." At least he sounded somewhat professional.

"I have an abandoned car on Faulkner Road," Erin said, "about a mile past Derry's farm. Need you to run a plate for me." She gave him the license plate number, then waited.

"Roger that," Casey said, concentrating. "Ms. Cherry's running it through the computer right now; it'll be just a minute." He paused, and his voice got a little lower. "How were the funerals, Erin?"

Erin felt her cheeks burn a little at that, opening her door as she grabbed the big, heavy Maglite and clicked it on. It wasn't all night yet, but dusk and the tall trees that lined Faulkner Road made it dark. "Hardly anyone there for either Donna or Alison's. It was a real fucking disgrace if you ask me."

"Shit," Casey replied. "I wanted to be there, but I drew this shift, you know? Guess people are getting tired of funerals, huh?"

Erin bit back her first, angry reply. "Well, unless we get our shit together, they're not gonna stop anytime soon." She took slow paces up to the car's window, shining the light in and keeping an ear out for any noise other than the whistling wind making its way through the trees.

She stopped, staring into the car. The airbag had been deployed, the loose, white bag drooping down, deflated, looking a little like a used condom. She peered in, staring at the surface.

There was blood on it.

"Shit," Erin said, keying the mic on her collar again. "HQ, we've got blood at the scene in this abandoned car. Whistle me up some backup, will you?"

"On it," Casey said tersely, the wash of static hitting her ear as he let loose of the transmit button.

Erin hesitated, looking around furtively. Had she heard a rustle in the underbrush, or was that just the wind? She shone the light around, trying to catch sight of anything moving.

Leaves danced as she brought it around, casting long shadows behind the trees at the edge of the road. The beam of light spilled ahead of her, giving Erin something else to focus on as she nervously dropped a hand to her pistol and drew it to low rest. Getting out of the car without the baseball bat had been stupid, reflective of her police training, not the current realities.

She pointed the Glock down, finger running along the rectangular slide's smooth surface, and brought the flashlight arm beneath the one holding the gun, wrists crossing together, sleeves brushing against each other. She kept the flashlight and gun pointed in the same direction at all times and swept around, making sure the path between her and her car was clear.

It was. A few leaves scraped the shoulder of the road as they blew past, and she hesitated only a moment before taking action.

She broke into a furious run, covering the distance between her and the car in seconds.

When she reached the door, Erin swung the flashlight and gun around again. She threw the door open quickly, swinging the flashlight and gun around again to check her six.

Nothing.

She felt exposed, like eyes were on her. The thin edge of panic was wedging itself into her mind. It reminded her of when she'd been in Rafton Park, and those demon bikers had rolled through right in front of her, following the trail along the Caledonia River. They had been a black swarm, ominous and loud, breaking the quiet with the mechanical whirring of their bikes.

Here, nature was the only sound. She didn't trust that though. She jumped into the driver's seat and clicked off the flashlight without thinking, tossing it into the passenger seat. It clunked in the floorboard and she flipped the car lights on, slamming her own door shut behind her. It echoed in her empty cruiser, and she wheeled to make sure nothing had snuck into the back seat while she'd been out, ready to tear into her like something from a horror movie.

Whew. It was empty, the caged rear compartment silent, light casting ominous net-like shadows on the seat.

Something moved ahead, a shadow slipping behind the stopped car. It was there for only a second, disappearing before she could be sure it wasn't her imagination.

"Fuck," Erin swore, snatching up the baseball bat so quickly that one of the nails snagged on the seat. A ripping noise filled the car interior, and she swore again. "Goddammit."

Now she wished for a knife, something small, compact. She fumbled for keys and started the car, not wanting to be caught out here without an easy escape in case whatever was out there really was more than her imagination.

She should check it out, with the baseball bat, shouldn't she?

Someone was going to have to, sooner or later.

Fuck that. That was dumb. What if it was a demon? The baseball bat was for a melee, but if she got jumped here, it wouldn't necessarily be a melee. Demons were stronger than people, after all. The damned thing might end up taking away her bat and ripping her to pieces with it. Or its own claws, if it had them.

"Let's not do that," she murmured. Backup would be coming, probably soon. If she needed to check things out, why not be smart about it?

Erin put the car in drive and wheeled it around hard, stomping on the accelerator. It surged forward, headlights illuminating Faulkner Road's leaf-covered pavement as the high beams spread out from the front of her vehicle.

Nothing but the leaves moved, that and the rustling boughs overhead. She turned the wheel and brought the car around hard in front of the abandoned vehicle, blocking the road but casting the lights over the ground in front of the other car.

Did something move again? Or was that just shadows slinking away from the high beams?

"Dammit," Erin breathed. Once again she wasn't sure what she'd seen. Could it just be a trick of the lights?

Or was something moving around the car?

The quiet but ever-present muffled engine noise kept her from being able to hear footsteps, or breathing other than her own that might have been taking place outside the vehicle. She couldn't smell sulfur, but the air conditioner was on recirculate, and the heater's smell was the only thing she could detect, that warm, blowing air carrying the heavy tinge of pine from the air freshener hanging from the rearview mirror.

"Sonofabitch," Erin muttered, peering out the windshield. What the hell was she supposed to do now?

*

Brian's phone buzzed, and he checked it as he walked into Red Cedar hospital. It was a simple text message of the sort he got frequently nowadays, a group text that went out anytime one of the watch reported danger.

ABANDONED CAR ON FAULKNER ROAD, BLOOD IN VEHICLE. OFFICER ON SCENE, REQUESTING BACKUP. ANYONE NEARBY?

Brian furrowed his brow. This one was coming from the dedicated cell phone they left in the sheriff's station, always plugged in so that they could dispatch help at all times. It was getting toward late in the evening, and people would be winding down. They had a dedicated night shift now, and if they felt they needed more help, they could always start ringing people up, but …

This didn't sound too serious, and Brian wasn't exactly combat ready, even without his limp. He put his phone on Do Not Disturb mode and pocketed it, noting that a couple text messages had already joined the stream, announcing imminent backup for Erin. That was good. Even if they weren't attending all the funerals, the town had pulled together in this regard. He slipped the phone into his pocket and wandered over to the elevator, catching it just as it was about to slide closed.

He slipped inside, eyeing an orderly dressed in blue scrubs. He didn't give her a lot of notice, save for catching the yellowed fingers on the right hand. Smoker, then. He almost opened his mouth to say something to her about bumming one, but the truth was, he didn't really like to smoke cigarettes. Weed was his vice, or it had been before all this demon mess had happened. He'd given it up when he'd joined the watch, figuring it was more important to have a clear head going into possible danger.

"Fuck," Brian muttered, drawing a curious look from the orderly. She blinked at him, and he said, "Sorry. I was just … thinking about getting high."

She raised both eyebrows at him and smiled like he was crazy. "That's nice," she said with a heavy amount of sarcasm. Yeah, he probably would have reacted the same way if a stranger in an elevator had said something weird like that to him.

The elevator door dinged and she walked out, giving him a last look over her shoulder as though he might stalk her out. He rolled his eyes. If he'd said, "I was just thinking about getting drunk," would she have evinced the same reaction? Probably not, but alcohol was legal in Tennessee.

He got out at his floor and wandered down the hall, still thinking about how nice it would be to get baked right now. Not enough to make him paranoid, just something to take the edge off. It had been a few weeks since he'd last smoked out, and they hadn't been easy ones.

Brian paused outside his father's room, putting a hand against the wall, mentally steeling himself against what he'd find inside. His dad had been alone for a few hours now, since his mother had gone to the funeral and headed home afterward. He'd offered to relieve her here, the better to … well, to get the hell out of town.

He couldn't get away from his thoughts though.

"Hey, Dad," he said as he came into the quiet room. The heartbeat monitor still beeped quietly, but his father was moving a little, head bobbing up and down. He couldn't quite fix on Brian. Instead his eyes drifted around, meeting his gaze only occasionally, as though he couldn't control his muscles enough to keep them steady.

Brian was getting used to that. His father had suffered a traumatic brain injury, after all, a bullet gouging its way up from below his jaw, tunneling through the bone at the top of his mouth before entering his brain and then exiting at the top of the skull.

It was a miracle he'd survived, really.

Brian didn't believe in miracles though. And even if he had, he damned sure wouldn't have called the state his father was reduced to any kind of blessing.

"Had dinner yet?" Brian asked, not expecting a coherent reply. He didn't get one. Bill Longholt moaned, moving his head up and down on a slight diagonal, the only manner of reply he could make these days.

"Yeah," Brian said, nodding for no reason. His dad might have been making sense to himself, but Brian doubted it.

This was a fucking shame, Brian reflected. He and his dad had had their fair share of arguments, of fights, of disagreements, especially since he'd come back from Brown. "I wanted to spread my wings," Brian mumbled, ignoring the grunting noise his father made. "Guess I picked a bad time."

He hadn't done much wing-spreading though. No job, no girlfriend. His life had squarely landed in the shitter since he'd come back to Midian. Hell, he hadn't wanted to come back anyway, but it wasn't like his dad was going to keep paying for him to live elsewhere in the country, forking over cash for an apartment when Brian didn't want to get a job and bash his head against the wall doing stupid, meaningless shit work. He'd wanted to do something intelligent and meaningful, and failing that ...

Well, failing that, he just wanted to get high, watch TV, and contemplate finding something that would matter. Something that would stir his passion.

Fighting demons had felt like the ticket, oddly enough. It had been the thing that had gotten him out of bed long before noon lately, which ... hell, even classes hadn't gotten him out of bed before noon. Now he was fighting the good fight for Midian, a town he hadn't wanted to come back to, but ...

Jesus, what a fucking series of hits they'd taken. He'd figured out where the last one was coming, but not nearly in time to stop it. He considered himself lucky, after a fashion, that he hadn't seen the slaughter on the square. He'd had a couple nightmares about it nonetheless, because maybe imagination was as bad or worse than seeing what had happened. He didn't, couldn't, know for sure, but he'd woken up sweating and screaming a couple times in the basement, clutching a pillow and his holy dagger, scared shitless that demons were coming in through the windows to get him.

"It's bad, Dad," Brian said, loud enough his father could hear him. If he was listening. The grunting and head-bobbing continued unabated, and Brian closed his eyes. "The town is ... fucked. So many people have died the last few weeks." Brian rubbed his eyes. "Reeve says it would have been worse if I hadn't figured Halloween out, but ... I don't know. It's such a goddamned disaster that it's hard for me to feel like I did any good. And the number keeps ticking up. Hundreds dead ... how do you call that a win? Alison dead?" He choked back that heavy lump in his throat. "In what mirror universe does that sound like victory ...?"

His father's grunts grew in pitch, and his head rocked harder back and forth.

Brian stared at his dad. "You understand about Alison, don't you?" There was no change in his father's manner. "Maybe? You know?" He watched for a sign, any, but there was no change. His dad started to settle a little, eyes still drifting wildly. His eyes were glistening though ...

Brian got out of the chair and drifted over to his father. He tried to look into his eyes. There was still a blood-tinged bandage under his jaw and at the top of his head. The dressings were being changed daily, but what good was that going to do? Stave off infection, maybe. But to what end? So his father could live this life—a fucking vegetable's life, grunting from now until his end?

"Alison's dead, Dad," Brian said, catching him carefully on each cheek and holding his head in place. His father's eyes darted still, unsteady. Brian tried to bring himself around, tried to match their twirl, but he couldn't. They moved too much, wouldn't hold still. "She's dead."

A mild grunt answered him, and Bill Longholt's eyes rolled up as he tried to pull against Brian's hands. Brian let him go, let him pull away. He saw the source of the glistening now, the very small tears at the corners of his father's eyes. He teared up a lot though ... for all Brian knew, his dad had no memory of who Alison was, let alone had any reason to be sad about her death.

"Welcome to hell," Brian muttered to himself, turning his back on his father for a few minutes to close his eyes, let his own tears flow unimpeded and unwatched. His father might be permanently handicapped, but Brian still couldn't bring himself to show weakness in front of the man. It just felt ... unseemly for some reason.

*

Reeve came over the last hill as his high beams illuminated the police Explorer stretched across both lanes of Faulkner Road like a barricade set up at a right angle with the abandoned car on the side of the road. He saw the flat tire on the abandoned car, the front left wheel sunk all the way down to the rim. Erin was in her the Explorer and he caught a perfect picture of her, baseball bat leaning across the top of her steering wheel.

He couldn't blame her for waiting in the car, and she was peering at him where a minute before she'd been looking out the front window at ... something. He wouldn't have been able to see it, hidden as it was by the car, except—

Reeve applied the brakes; he could have sworn he'd seen something in the shadows along the far side of the abandoned car as he pulled in behind it, figuring he'd cover the back and right side of it. Erin had the front pretty well lit up with her own headlights, but ...

Was there something lurking in the shadows along the side farthest from the road?

Erin's voice crackled in his ear, his radio flaring to life. "I swear to God there's something moving around here." He could see her looking at him from within her vehicle, though now the abandoned car was positioned between them.

"I thought I saw movement a minute ago too," Reeve answered back. "On the far side over here, maybe moving toward the woods. Get a look at anything?"

"No," Erin said.

"We got a few more of the watch inbound on y'all," Casey said, breaking in. "PRIEST is on the way; so is WRECKER." That was Sam Allen's codename. "Oh, and DRUMLINE, but he's probably ten minutes out." That'd be Keith Drumlin.

"What do you think?" Erin asked. She was staring out at him through the car, partially bisected by one of the dark metal strips between the windows. "Wait for backup?"

"I like numbers on our side in a case like this," Reeve said. "But ..."

"I don't like 'buts.'"

"I like butts," Casey said. "I'm an ass man."

"Jesus, Casey," Erin muttered over the open channel.

"The driver of the car might be out here somewhere, hurt—if that blood on the steering wheel don't mean they're dead," Reeve went on. "I hate to leave someone like that, not knowing what's happened to them."

"Shit," Erin said. "That's a damned good point."

"Casey," Reeve said, "did y'all—"

"I got a match back on that license plate—well, HARLOT did," Casey said. Reeve twitched a little bit. HARLOT had been Melina Cherry's choice of a code name. The fact that one of his biggest supporters in this endeavor was the town madam … well, it didn't quite sit right with him, but what could you do? "Registered to a John and Nora Wellstone of Knoxville."

Reeve blinked. "Goddammit."

"What?" Erin asked.

"That's the mom of the kid that Hendricks and Arch brought in this morning." Reeve felt almost physically pained. "She drove in to pick him up and must have tried to get back to the interstate this way." He opened his door and killed the ignition, decision made. "I'm getting out to take a look."

"Knew you'd say that," Erin said, and he saw her open her door as well, the sound of her engine idling greeting Reeve as he stepped out into the brisk evening air. She didn't key the mic for the next thing she said. "What do you want to do?"

"Keep your voice down, for one," Reeve said, keying his own and speaking quietly into it. He slid his sword out, gripping it tightly. "We don't know if there's someone watching us, or if it's some*thing*."

"Aye aye," she said with a fair amount of sarcasm, hefting the bat, "though I'm pretty sure given we've lit the scene up like a fucking night game, it probably knows we're here."

Reeve didn't care to argue that point, because it was a damned fair one. "How far out are PRIEST and WRECKER, HQ?"

"Uhmmmmm," Casey said. "I guess they're not online with comms yet, huh? I could text 'em, but …"

"Never mind," Reeve said. A thought occurred, and he swore, loudly, and not into the mic.

"What?" Erin asked, dispensing with her own.

Reeve drew a sharp breath. "If the mom was driving …" He took a few steps to come alongside the abandoned car. Sure as shit, there was the deployed airbag, and there was the blood, like someone had taken a blow to the head. Those bled like crazy, even when they weren't too serious, all the capillaries in the skull.

"Yeah?" Erin asked. There was a rustling of leaves, and they both jerked. Erin shone a light, keeping the unwieldy baseball bat clutched in her other hand, looking more tentative now that they'd heard something.

Reeve tried to search out the source of the noise, peering along the beam of Erin's flashlight. Nothing was there, was it? She swept the ground toward the woods slowly, and that rustling sound came again. "I'm wondering …" he said, trying to see into the dark. Even with two sets of headlights and her big flashlight, it wasn't an easy task. Night was falling.

"Yeah?" she asked, barely breathing.

Reeve just stared, still trying to see something, anything, really, out there. "Where's the kid?"

*

Hendricks stretched, the long, lazy stretch of a man who'd just gotten his rocks off good. Starling was a hell of a lay, giving head like a champ in order to get him hard like a rock, then she let him piston his way in and out of her for almost a half hour before he finally came, dropping a load inside her without so much as a word of protest that he was firing live ammo. Starling was wearing a hooker's body, but Hendricks didn't worry too much about pregnancy or STDs in this case. Why would he? The kind of STDs he was most apt to catch could be wiped out by antibiotics, and he doubted a practiced hooker got into bed in the mornings without taking the pill.

It wasn't the attitude he'd had when he'd had things to live for, but … what the hell did it matter now anyway? It was a measure of how few fucks he gave, psychologically, that the ones he gave literally didn't trouble him, consequence-wise. So he blasted Starling full of his semen without giving it hardly any thought, just an idle musing now and then in the shower as he washed the strange smell of her sex off his cock.

"Was that good?" she asked. She didn't sound insecure about it, or as if she truly cared. It was a question as disinterested as any other she asked, devoid of the sort of emotion he might have gotten from Erin under the same circumstances. She didn't want to cuddle afterward either, and that suited him just fine.

"Worked for me," Hendricks said. It had been pretty good, yeah. He hadn't had much urge built up, but she'd damned sure gotten him hard in a hurry. "You?"

"Yes," she said simply. He couldn't tell if she meant it, and wasn't sure he cared. It was pretty hard to get a read on Starling, to know what she was thinking, why she was doing anything.

"Good," he said, probably meaning it. He hadn't asked her why she'd suddenly started sleeping with him. Now that he thought about it though ... "Hey—"

He turned to find her already gone, just vanished, as though she hadn't been lying next to him a moment earlier, breasts and body exposed, totally unlike those chicks on TV post-coitus. The lower temps in the motel room didn't seem to bother her, though her nipples were pretty decently erect most of the time.

Well ... now they were just gone, but still.

"Figures," he muttered. He doubted he could have gotten it up for another round anyway, but it was kinda nice to have her around, have her watching over him. He wondered idly what she was up to now. Probably back to being Lucia.

That thought prickled at him a little bit. First she'd showed up to warn him cryptically about stuff. Then she'd started saving his life. Now she'd taken to sucking and fucking him.

What was next? A marriage proposal?

Hendricks guffawed lightly at that thought, then slipped out of bed. He was headed to the shower when he saw his phone's screen light up. He'd put it in Do Not Disturb mode when he'd come in and found Starling waiting for him, barely getting that done and casting it aside before she'd dropped in front of him and taken his zipper down, pants to the floor, deep-throating him before he'd had a chance to get more than half hard.

He snatched up the phone and woke it up, taking a look at all he'd missed. Thoughts of a shower flew right out the fucking window, and two minutes later he was dressed and in the car, putting the purloined SUV in drive as he floored it out of the Sinbad's parking lot toward Faulkner Road.

*

Lauren had stepped out of the parlor to return a call, getting hold of Ms. Cherry for a basic breakdown of what was going on out on Faulkner Road. She'd missed the text message string while she'd been in the bathroom, crying a little. Shit, she had kept it all in during the funeral, but this was her mom, for fuck's sake.

She'd come out to find Molly missing. Well, not missing, she realized as she stepped up to the door. The sound of the television going in the parlor was a strong indicator that Molly had just decided to do something other than read or be alone with her thoughts in the room they were sharing.

Lauren understood that. She didn't much care for the idea of being alone with her thoughts right now either.

She had made it to just outside the parlor archway when she heard the faint snatches of conversation under the TV's raised volume, almost as though someone had turned it up to cover a whispered conversation.

"So … if a guy … does that … in your mouth … what does it taste like?" Molly's voice was curious and maybe a little disgusted.

"It's called cumming." Lucia's tone was even, almost amused. "And it's not a good taste. You want to move his tip to the back of your mouth when he's about to cum, because otherwise you—I mean, your taste buds are on your tongue, right? So if you move it to the back of your mouth, when it comes squirting out, you don't really taste it as much and you can just swallow it right down—"

"Ewwwwww!"

"—without, you know, getting sick," Lucia finished. "Guys don't really like it when you start gagging. It's a turnoff."

"Gagging?" Molly asked, somewhere between revulsion and awe. Lauren was feeling sick too, but for a different reason. "You really get sick? From what, the taste?"

"Unless your guy has been drinking a lot of pineapple juice, yeah," Lucia said. "It's a pretty distinct flavor, pretty nasty."

"Wait … pineapple juice? What?"

Lauren closed her eyes and shook her head.

"It changes the taste so it's not so bad. Asparagus does the opposite."

"So … I mean, I've heard the old … I don't know, sayings about 'spitting or swallowing' …"

"Don't spit."

Molly's voice broke in after a short pause for reflection. "But if it's nasty, why would I want to—"

"Look, it's all about what you're trying to do," Lucia said. Lauren barely contained her nausea. "If you're actually trying to give the guy a good time, pulling it out of your mouth or stopping before he's done? It kills it. I can't do that in my job. I have to keep going until he's done and practically begs me to stop. If you're trying to please the guy, don't quit until he's done, don't spit, because that's—I dunno, guys get offended or something. Definitely don't gag."

"But it sounds so fucking gross!"

"It is," Lucia said, "but ... I dunno, you get used to it. Just do what I told you to do, and you won't taste it so much. Finish it until he tells you to stop. Swallow if you can, because the taste doesn't go away if you spit, and he'll be all glowing and flattered if you do. Unless you hate him, in which case ... why are you blowing him in the first place, unless it's for money?"

Lauren's eyes almost burst out of her head. "Oh, God," she whispered. Now her daughter was getting career advice from a prostitute.

"Is there some guy you have in mind for this?" Lucia asked, sounding like she was sort of dimly enjoying herself. This was older sister advice, except from a goddamned hooker.

"No," Molly said, and she sounded serious. "It's all theoretical, I guess. I'm just curious."

Lauren took a halting breath, and the nausea subsided a level or two. It was still there though, kind of a twisting feeling in her stomach at hearing her daughter ask a pro on how to give blowjobs and pleasure a man with her fucking mouth. Or by fucking her mouth. A new swell of sickness hit Lauren's belly, settling in her guts.

"It's not a bad way to start with a guy," Lucia said matter-of-factly. "Instead of losing your ... you're still a virgin?" She sounded pretty definite, like it wasn't really a question.

"Yeah," Molly said with obvious discomfort. Lauren felt that gut-twist again; Molly had nearly lost it to a demon only a couple months back, against her will, and though she was coping well, it was still a sore point, Lauren knew. Trauma didn't fade like bruises. It stayed long past any physical signs.

"Oral is a good way to start," Lucia said, sounding like her voice was drifting off, dreamy. "Guys like it. Well, most guys do. It's quick and easy, less messy than, you know, fucking. You can do it in a car without contorting your entire body against the wheel, and it feels good for him."

"Uh huh." Molly sounded a little far away too. "So ... if it's so good ... why don't guys just go for it ... you know, all the time?" She was speaking in a hushed whisper once more, probably hoping they wouldn't be overheard. Either that, or she was ashamed to be asking.

"Variety," Lucia said. "I think? I don't know. Different guys like different things. I have customers that are in the mood for oral one time and anal the next. Then maybe they want straight sex the next time. One guy just likes feet, another likes me to use my hands and then let him spray all over my belly. I don't know how guys think, I just know how to do what they want."

"Huh." Molly sounded like she was processing it all. "But what about—"

Lauren leaned against the wall a little too hard, and her back made a thump. She froze, and the conversation came to a halt. Shit, she thought, and knew she'd been heard. No point hiding it now.

She came around the corner, looking right at Molly. Why shouldn't she? Lauren was in charge of her, in charge of protecting her, and this—this—abominable conversation? No part of it sounded good to Lauren. None of it. "We have to go," she said hoarsely.

Molly frowned at her. "Go? Go where? It's—"

"The watch is—there's a car on Faulkner Road that—" Lauren was so flustered she couldn't finish a sentence. "Come with me," she finally said, exasperated and wanting to make it an order rather than a question or request.

"You want me to come with you on a call?" Molly leapt to her feet. She didn't even cast a look back at Lucia, instead bursting into a goofy, geeky, uncoordinated run. Well, there was a reason that Molly wasn't an athlete. She dodged past Lauren in a second, bare feet thudding along the floor as she hurried to put on shoes.

"Wow," Lucia said mildly, her green eyes registering very little surprise. "I thought you were trying to keep her out of harm's way." It came out not as any kind of indictment on Lauren's parenting, more like a gentle—even amused—commentary from a detached outsider who didn't care what happened one way or another.

Lauren didn't know what to say to that, so she didn't say anything at all. Instead she whirled, ready to go gather up her weapons and try to corral her daughter away—far away—from this goddamned hooker who was not just educating her about the facts of life, but about the finer points of giving blowjobs for fun and profit.

*

"So we're looking for a kid?" Erin asked, quivering clear down to her legs. It was just getting darker and darker, the clouds above covering the skies. It was pretty damned unsettling, especially since she and Reeve had both been seeing things out here. Really fucking unsettling.

"We're looking for a kid, at least," Reeve said, holding his sword, tip pointing up, her high beams glinting off it. "Mack Wellstone. His mother's name was—is—Nora. His dad died this morning out in the woods."

"From what?" Erin asked, trying to keep her voice steel-chord taut to keep the worry from bleeding out. She was no chickenshit, but this was not exactly a calming stroll in the woods. It was a tense watch, waiting for backup to show so they could start sweeping for a kid and facing ... well, hell, God only knew. Demons, probably.

"Hendricks and Arch dealt with it, I don't know," Reeve said, his gaze still sweeping around their lighted perimeter. "They didn't say in front of the kid, and I didn't have a chance to talk with them about it afterward."

"Goddamned Hendricks," Erin said under her breath. She meant it. The cowboy was supposed to be a demon expert, but he was about as useful as two left shoes when you were in a hurry to get out the door. "They didn't even give you a hint?"

"They might have had some other things on their minds," Reeve said, keeping his sword pointed toward the woods. "I might have too." His voice was low and rough, and veering toward choked.

That was probably the closest the man had gotten to acknowledging he'd gone to his own wife's funeral today, Erin realized. God knew he hadn't shown a sign of it elsewhere.

"Just keep our perimeter tight for now," Reeve said, just as leaves crunched out in the woods.

Erin spun, her Glock held tight, and her desire to put her finger on the trigger held at bay by years of her daddy teaching her not to put it there until she was ready to shoot. Her stomach warbled, rumbled, a queasy hint of worry like a chaser fighting with the shot of fear she'd just taken against her will. The bat was hanging from her other hand, heavy as shit and threatening to drag down her aim.

"Shit," Erin said, tracing a path over the lit parts of the road, the headlights giving her a little to see by. "This is all we need, a goddamned search for a wayward kid when we're in the middle of demon-infested woods."

"Hard to say if demons are infesting the woods," Reeve said.

"Well, they're in the town," Erin shot back, slowly spinning to cover one hundred and eighty degrees extending behind her car but careful not to point her weapon close at Reeve. "It's not exactly a stretch to imagine them out here, is it? Especially since this kid was already attacked in the woods by something this morning."

Reeve blinked a little at that. "Shit. Yeah. You're right. Guess I just don't want to think of—fuck."

"What?" she asked, frowning at him as she tossed a look over her shoulder.

"The woods were always my sanctuary this time of year," Reeve said tautly, his own gun clutched in his hand. "Any normal year ... I would have been out this morning for opener. But instead, we get this. Maybe I was just hoping, giving all the hell we've seen in town ... it'd steer clear of my damned woods."

Erin chuckled against her will. "You were hoping we were up against a bunch of goddamn city-slicker demons?"

Reeve hesitated, then laughed. "Yeah. Like they'd draw a border at the edge of the woods and be afraid to cross it. 'There's no Chardonnay or goose liver or shit in there!'" He laughed again, then stopped. "Goddamn." He looked right at her, and there was an empty look in his eyes. "They're gonna take everything they can from us, aren't they? Every last goddamned thing, right down to our lives."

"Looking that way," Erin said soberly. She couldn't really see his face fall, but she knew the words had hit him nonetheless, and felt required to say something more. "But we're not gonna goddamn let them, remember? Not without a hell of a fight."

"Right," Reeve said, and returned to scanning the dark woods, eyes alert for movement, the two of them listening for any unusual noises. But he didn't sound convinced.

*

"Honey, I'm home," Pike said as he came in the door of his ranch-style brick house. It was after seven, which was when he usually came in, past the time when the kids—they were five and two—were in bed. He preferred early bedtimes for his kids, mostly so he didn't have to put up with too much of their horseshit in the evenings. He put in some time with them in the mornings and on weekends, but he didn't have much interest in them at this age. The five-year-old, he conceded, was starting to get interesting, but the two-year-old ... eh. Wiping asses and talking baby talk bored Pike, and the sooner they got through that into the point where they could hold decent conversation about something that wasn't related to toys or kids' games, the better.

Darla agreed, he knew. They'd weighed the pros and cons, and decided in favor of having kids, but Pike was most definitely finished at two. He doubted he had the patience for any more because he barely had the patience for the two he had. The kids went to bed early by mutual accord; Darla didn't have much patience for the bullshit parts of parenting either.

"How'd the peace talks go?" Darla asked, swinging her pretty blond head around the corner. She'd had some nice curves even before they'd had kids, and those were more accentuated now. Her breasts were quite a bit bigger too, though Pike was ambivalent about the belly fat she'd picked up. There was a time when she'd had abs, a tight little stomach that made him pull out and blow his wad on her, white splattering on her pearly skin. The sight was hot enough that even after he was done he immediately wanted to fuck again, in spite of the pain it caused his prick to try and force himself to go on once he'd blown his load.

That was what Darla was good for. She was from Illinois, originally, hearty Midwesterner stock, but without any of the puritanical bullshit that Midwesterners sometimes picked up. She loved cock, loved to fuck, loved to go all night and push him past his limits. She was as libertine as they got, in touch with her feminist side, in touch with her sexuality, and ready to cuss like a fucking sailor at the drop of a hat. She sucked cock like a champ too, had given him head on their first date because she'd been on the rag at the time. He'd watched her face as she'd teased him, savoring his roller-coaster of emotion and arousal until he'd exploded in orgasmic relief after forty-five minutes of insane, teasing buildup.

He'd known right then that this woman was the one for him. The fact that they'd had their first three-way a week later at her suggestion had cemented the decision.

He thought about how much he'd gotten laid before Darla had come along, and it couldn't hold a candle to how much he'd gotten laid since. She had zero possessiveness about him, practically handing him the keys to the chastity belts of women he couldn't have hoped to fuck before he'd met her. She could whisper a word to him, some little secret, some angle he could take after talking to a woman for five minutes, and ten minutes later the woman's dress would be in a pile on the floor and he'd be balls deep, thrusting into her until he reached that sweet climax. All because Darla would show him the way.

Goddamn, did he love that woman.

"Went well," Pike said. "I gotta throw Reeve a budget bone in order to make good, but that ought to be no big deal."

Her eyes flickered as she nodded. "Small price to pay. You probably won't even have to live up to it over a whole fiscal year, and anyway, who cares? It's not your money."

"Exactly." Pike smiled.

She returned the smile, an element of lasciviousness in it now. "Did you fuck Jenny?"

"Six ways to Sunday," Pike said.

"Good." She sauntered over to him and kissed him, unbuckling his belt. She broke off and let his trousers drop to the ground.

She chased his cock around in her mouth for only about ten

minutes before he moaned and squirted in the back of her throat. She took it all down, smiling mischievously around his piece, holding it in there afterward, rolling her tongue in a way that caused him discomfort now that he'd gotten off. He grunted, but she kept her lips firmly anchored on his dick. She did this sometimes, smiling as she slipped it out and gave him a lick up to the sensitive head. "I like the taste of her. Her and you, together."

"Jesus," Pike said, sweating. Was it hot in here?

"I'm thinking about going on," she said, and deep-throated him again. Pike grunted; the prospect was pleasant and yet unpleasant. He had that painful, after-orgasm sensitivity from head to the bottom of his shaft, and Darla damned well knew it. But he knew better than to say anything, because she didn't mind doing unpleasant or even painful things to him, and this was the least of them that she might try if she were in a playful—or hateful—mood. She slipped her lips up and down him again, tickling the back of her throat with the head of his penis.

Pike gasped again.

She pulled it out, gripping it firmly and giving it a squeeze. A little dot of semen dangled at the tip, hanging like it might drip. She looked at it, then at him, and he felt like he was being watched by a shark. She took him into her mouth up to the tip and gave him a hard suck. He tried not to moan again but did, and she smelled his weakness, squeezing the base of his shaft and running her lips tightly up and down him again, wringing amusement out of him at his expense.

Goddamn, did he love this woman.

"Admit it," she said, pausing and taking his dick out of her mouth, dragging it across her cheek, where it left a trail of saliva and a thin thread of clear ejaculate, "you wish I'd swallowed the cumshots that made our babies too, don't you?" She looked up at him with devilish amusement.

"It gets easier every year," he gasped, avoiding the answer while trying to get control of his breathing. She was being really rough with his shaft, like she was trying to suffocate it, but Darla had always been rough—in blowjobs, in sex. He mostly didn't mind, though he had drawn a line that he knew she exceeded with other partners. "As they grow up, I mean. They're not quite the needy little bitches they were when they started out."

"You're such a selfish prick," she said, squeezing his dick mercilessly hard again. She rubbed the head on her chin, leaving another droplet there and grinning at him. "Stop being selfish, prick, and give me another squirt."

Pike groaned. He still wasn't through the refractory period where his dick would be recharged for another round, but she was pushing through that painful interregnum with everything she had. "You know, I do have my limits."

That was the wrong thing to say. Her eyes lit up, and she looked up at him without raising her head. A hand that had been cupping his balls a moment earlier snaked through his legs and up before he could protest.

He grunted, but squeezing did nothing to prevent it; she sunk a finger up his ass before he could pucker shut, and then she squeezed his dick so hard he thought she'd break it off. "I'll tell you what your goddamned limits are," she said, burying her finger up to the knuckle in his ass as she captured the head of his penis in her mouth again and then deep-throated him.

It went on like that for a few more minutes as the pain in his cock subsided the longer she went, turning back around to pleasure again. She didn't go easy on him in the other end though, putting a second finger up there, then a third, loosening him up as she went, drawing him into her with one hand and pushing into him with the other. She avoided the delicate spot of his prostate, knowing he wouldn't hold on after that. She liked to make him suffer, after all, and she'd prolong it as long as she could.

No, she took him in and out of her mouth agonizingly slowly, smiling when she pulled him out, torturously blowing him while working her way up to squeezing her fist into his ass. She worked the fingers in and out of his anus until she managed it. It was hardly the first time, but she could have—and had—gone much rougher rather than allowing time to work up to the whole hand.

At least she didn't have big hands, Pike reflected as she buried herself up to the wrist like a puppet master. She moved it, brushing his prostate, and he clenched.

Now he was caught between pleasure and pain again, some perverse combination of the two. She was doing just enough service to him in the blowjob to keep him hanging on, watching him for signs of weakness while also keeping an eye on him to make sure he wasn't having an entirely awful time. When she'd first started to push his boundaries in this way, he had relented mostly because she'd done so many things for him, had opened up new vistas of sexual pleasure he couldn't have dreamed of with other partners.

She'd also only started with one finger, and a small one at that. None of this whole-hand shit.

But he took the good with the bad; took the endless, delicious, explosively wonderful blowjobs with the unlubed fistings, took the hours of fucking with the occasional golden shower she required of him, took the anal with ...

Well, with anal. With her strap-on. It wasn't as bad as the fisting, at least.

She finally let him cum, and he let loose, painfully this time. It squirted in her mouth and she devoured it as his legs wobbled beneath him. He'd been standing for so long, and she'd done a number on him all the way around. He telegraphed his collapse and she grinned, removing her hand with a little more gusto than she needed to. Pike dropped to his knees on the wood floor carefully, trying not to injure himself. He could tell by the look in her eyes that he was going to need to be gentle to himself, because she had no intention of being so, at least not tonight. She was like that sometimes.

She unbuttoned his shirt and cast it off, kissing him. "You know what I want, don't you?"

He nodded, somewhat resignedly. "Yeah."

She snuck around behind him, clearly awakened now. "You're not going to tell me you're too tired, are you?" She nibbled his ear, whispering in it as she did.

"No," he said—but he was tired. Damned tired. He could have gone to bed right then, the sleep hormones flowing through his bloodstream, leaving him exhausted.

"Good." She whispered in his ear, "Let's go to the bedroom." And she slapped him on the ass with the hand she'd just had up it, and walked off with a stride that suggested she had plans for him—for that ass of his.

It'd be the strap-on tonight then.

Jason Pike sighed and picked himself up off the floor. He slid off his shoes and left his pants puddled right where they were. There was no point fighting it, even though he was tired. She was going to tax his ass tonight, in spite of her saying she hadn't been in the mood. Well, she was damned sure in the mood now, a very specific sort of mood, one that happened at least once or twice a week, one he had long since grown accustomed to—and even perhaps, very slightly, to enjoy.

It was the cost of his marriage.

"Get your sweet ass in here," Darla called, and he could hear her moving about in their bedroom, putting it on, clearly ready for him.

"Goddamn, do I love that woman," he said, caught somewhere between ecstasy and fear. Odds were good he'd be feeling a lot of both of those emotions until the evening was over, and he shuffled toward the bedroom in order to get it over as quickly as possible.

*

"Hope things ain't got too crazy down there yet," Barney Jones said as they whipped around a corner hard. Arch held on, the *oh snot!* bar tightly held in his grip. Whose bright idea had it been to let Braeden Tarley drive? The man still looked half-traumatized, and definitely favored one arm—the one that hadn't been dislocated on Halloween. But the other half of him was made of fierce determination, his focus tight on the road ahead.

"Why, you want to be there for it when all Hades breaks loose?" Arch asked as Tarley about flipped the truck over taking the next turn at ninety. He hadn't involved himself in the watch yet, probably because Barney had been keeping him out of it. Arch considered that wise, but when they'd run out the door tonight after getting the text blast, neither of them had had the heart—or the time—to tell Tarley to get back in the house.

"I feel uniquely qualified to deal with hell," Barney said with a slight smile that Arch saw when Tarley brought them out of the turn so hard that Arch was whipped around enough to get a glimpse of Barney in the back seat of the pickup, bracing himself. "In a way maybe the rest of y'all ain't."

"I'm gonna give it," Tarley said, the knuckles of his ruddy, calloused hands white on the wheel. Between them on the seat lay a big old wrench, which glinted in the glare of a streetlight as they turned down Faulkner Road. Tarley caught Arch looking at it and they both stared at each other blankly for a moment.

"You know that won't kill 'em, right?" Arch asked. Tarley hadn't done this before; he probably didn't know what demon fighting entailed.

"Good," Tarley said, slaloming the pickup around another curve. "Because I just want to hurt 'em. Over and over. I'll leave putting them out of their misery to y'all."

Arch traded a look with Barney as they went hard into the next turn, Tarley treating the truck like this was NASCAR. Pastor Jones just shrugged, and Arch wondered again just how wise bringing a man as scarred as Braeden Tarley into a battle like this was.

Tarley slammed on the brakes and brought the truck to a squealing, skidding halt. Arch felt himself surge forward, that moment of weightlessness before the seatbelt jerked against his chest making him fear he was on his way through the windshield. "What are you doing?" he almost shouted.

Tarley was unfazed. "The hell is that?" He pointed through the windshield.

"Well, I'll be," Barney Jones said. Ahead, just around the next bend, red and blue lights were flashing, but here—here there were only the truck's headlights, low-slung floodlamps casting additional illumination along the hard-bitten surface of Faulkner Road. And right there, just in front of them, was a patch of leaves that had been partially swept away to reveal...

"Is that a bed of nails?" Arch asked.

"In plywood, I think," Barney said. "Should we get out?"

"We need to clear the road," Tarley said. He grabbed his wrench and was out of the car before Arch could finish telling him that this was a bad idea.

"There could be demons out here!" Arch said, opening his own door and jumping down over the truck's running board, hitting the hard pavement below with a thud.

"Good," Tarley said, striding toward the trap in the road. He reached it and stopped, giving it a shove with his foot. It made a scratching noise against the pavement, like sandpaper on a rough surface. He gave it another shove and it moved a foot or so, then another, as he pushed it toward the underbrush carefully, probably trying to avoid needing a tetanus shot.

Arch scrambled around the side and gave him a hand—well, a foot. Together they shuffled it off the shoulder and it toppled into the ditch at the side of the road. When it landed, Arch squatted over it, keeping an ear out for trouble, though he couldn't hear much over the low rumble of the idling engine.

There had to be a hundred nails driven into that plywood. It was like a makeshift spike strip of the kind cops deployed when they wanted to stop a fleeing suspect in a car chase. He hadn't seen one since the academy, but there were a couple back at the station for use in case of emergency.

"What do you reckon this was for?" Barney Jones asked. He'd reached Arch just as Tarley had turned around, heading back to the truck with a purpose. Arch watched the mechanic go and realized they needed to follow, and quickly, because patience didn't seem to be something Tarley had much of right now.

"I don't exactly know," Arch said, though he had a few dark suspicions about it. "Come on. We need to get to the others." And he hurried to follow Tarley. Reeve and Erin were waiting just around the bend, after all, and they wouldn't have called if they hadn't thought help was necessary.

*

Hendricks brought the SUV to a squealing halt after another ugly curve, his headlights catching the two police cruisers and the wrecker laid out in the middle of the road. There was another vehicle pulled off to the shoulder, dimly lit under the flashing glare of red and blue. It was a civilian car, not one of the watch's.

He hopped out of the purloined SUV as Erin turned to look at him. Her face evinced relief for about a half second, then got hard again. "Didn't know you were coming," she said, sounding about as pleased to see him as if he were a demon.

"You call, I come," he said, then regretted his choice of words immediately as soon as they were out. Her eyes narrowed as if wondering if the double entendre was deliberate. He changed the subject. "What's the situation?"

"The Situation is a guy from Jersey," said Sam Allen, a tow truck driver carrying a tire iron that Hendricks hoped had been consecrated. It was getting damned hard to tell what was consecrated nowadays, with the watch resorting to all sorts of weird-ass weapons. Erin had a bat with nails driven through it over her shoulder, like she thought she was on *The Walking Dead*, or maybe just trying out for a fucked-up softball team.

"Abandoned car," Reeve said, "blood on the inside. Belongs to the mother of the kid you rescued from the woods earlier. Don't mean to seem squeamish, but we've seen motion in the woods."

Hendricks stared at Erin, who was still giving him that look like he'd stuck his hard-on up her ass without warning. She seemed to be daring him to say something ugly in response to that, but he wasn't going to give her the satisfaction. "Reasonable precaution," he said, taking care to strip any sarcasm out of his reply. "Any sign of the kid or his mom?"

"No—" Erin started to answer, the thinnest hint of relief showing through on her face before squealing tires sounded around the curve ahead and a pickup truck came rocketing to a stop, missing Erin's squad Explorer—Arch's car, usually, but they were sharing it now—by about half an inch.

"Found a trap in the road back there a hundred yards or so," Arch said, jumping out of the passenger side. He seemed mostly business, but also maybe a little relieved for some reason as his feet hit terra firma. The big bastard even stepped down from the truck without needing the running board, something Hendricks decided he wouldn't care to try if he was riding in that sucker. "Bunch of nails driven through plywood."

"Explains the pancake nature of these tires," Sam Allen said, motioning toward the abandoned car. "Four flats at once? That ain't usual."

"I seen that happen to your momma's car before, Sam," the driver of the pickup said as he came hopping down. Hendricks didn't know the man well, but he knew his name was Braeden Tarley. He'd caught the sad-ass story after the square, about how the man had lost his daughter to the demons. "Hard to say what caused it, but it happened as she was pulling out of KFC. Couldn't understand her when she tried to explain, because she had a dozen biscuits crammed in her mouth. Frame was bent like a damned U too."

"Dick," Sam Allen said with a good-natured smile. There was an aura of relief about the tow truck driver, like he was glad to hear his friend make even as obvious a joke as a "yo mama so fat..."

"I know you like the dick, Sam, but I ain't in the mood," Tarley said, sweeping on past the tow truck driver with a slap to his shoulder. Sam Allen just grunted his amusement. "Where the demons at?"

"Ain't seen any quite yet," Reeve said, easing in. They were forming a small perimeter now, using the vehicles as cover, like circled wagons. Hendricks didn't love that idea, because demons didn't really use ranged attacks or guns, so cover was more or less useless. The vehicles were just an obstruction to seeing anything coming. He was about to say so when Reeve shouted, "Mack!"

A rustle in the underbrush up the slope from the road caused Hendricks to whirl. He had his sword out already and noted the other members of the watch had their weapons in hand too. Good instinct. His eyes played over the tree line until they were drawn to motion, a small figure springing free from a bush and warring with gravity as he came down the slope, fighting not to go tumbling.

Yeah, that was Mack, all right, and he was hauling ass.

"What is it, kid?" Hendricks asked, already advancing on him. Erin was moving too, and so were Reeve and Arch, hurrying forward around the abandoned car to try and meet the boy as he came skittering down the slope, arms pinwheeling, reminding Hendricks of a time he'd chased a couple demons down a hill, probably not too far from here.

"Something's out there!" Mack shouted, gasping as he ran down the hill.

STARLING

"Lotta things out there, probably," Hendricks said, hustling to be first as Mack hit flatter ground and surged past him, not slowing as he made a beeline for Reeve. Hendricks raised an eyebrow as the kid hid behind the sheriff like the bald man was his mother's skirts or something. He stopped short of grabbing Reeve around the waist, at least. Not that Hendricks would have blamed him. Losing your dad would be bad enough, but the fact this kid's mom was missing now too, and nothing but a bloody steering wheel to show for it? Beyond shit luck. Midian luck, as Hendricks was starting to think of it.

"What happened to your mom?" Arch asked, stopping between Hendricks at the start of the embankment up to the tree line and Reeve, who was still hanging not far from the ditch off the shoulder of the road. The sheriff was standing still now, focusing all his attention on Mack, putting a gentle hand on his arm, trying to calm the kid down. At least Arch wasn't yelling at him.

"It was some chubby guy," Mack said, surprisingly coherent. He wasn't screaming, wasn't crying, wasn't doing anything besides hiding behind Reeve and breathing hard from his run. "We pulled over after the flats, and there was this other guy parked. He smashed my mom's face into the steering wheel. I ran." He seemed pretty even about it, all things considered. Not everyone could witness their mom getting assaulted and avoid going to pieces.

Reeve spoke slowly. "Mack ... did you see what happened next?"

Mack shook his head. "He chased me into the woods. I hid in a log until—until I heard those things coming—"

"What things?" Erin eased up next to Reeve, muscling in on his territory.

Mack pointed right at Hendricks, then Arch. "The ones from this morning." He took a breathless gasp. "The ones that got my dad. I can hear them out there." His voice dropped low, and now he pointed back up the embankment toward the woods. "They're coming."

*

Lauren came rolling up on the scene just as Reeve was manhandling that kid from earlier up out of the ditch next to the shoulder of Faulkner Road. She peered, bringing the car to a stop as Reeve carefully opened the door to his squad car and pushed the kid inside, saying something she couldn't hear before he shut the door. He'd been wearing a mask of gentle reassurance, but it vanished the second his back turned on the car, and Lauren got out just in time to hear him start barking.

"How many of those things do you s'pose there are out there?" This was directed at Hendricks, who was definitely lacking his usual cockety-cocksureness, coming back onto the road with his sword drawn and a wary look cast all around, but especially at the shadowed tree line overlooking the road from up a nice slope.

"We got three of 'em this morning," Arch answered for the cowboy. Tense, tight, pissed off. Lauren was feeling a little softer toward the big man since Alison had died, though she was far from his biggest fan.

"Three of what?" Molly chirped, already out of the car. Lauren blinked at her; something had changed in her calculation since showing up here. Something about the sheriff's bearing was all wrong. Too tight, too tense, especially given how many of them were here.

Sheriff Reeve did a double-take at the sight of Molly, but to his credit, he answered. "Demon cat-things that Arch and Hendricks faced off against this morning." He cast a molten-lead look at Lauren. "Is this bring-your-daughter-to-work day? Because you might have picked a bad one."

"I was starting to get that feeling," Lauren said, her stomach clamping up again. God, it was like someone had wrapped a rod around her upper intestines and was rolling it hard, trying to squeeze the juice out of both ends. "How bad are we looking at?"

"Uh ... real bad," Erin Harris said, and everyone looked at her, which was a mistake, because she was pointing up at the tree line. The second of delay as everyone processed her motion, then followed her pointing finger up to the tree line, where there was nothing but shadow—

No, wait. *Shadows.*

Hundreds of them.

"Fucking shit," Hendricks said, brandishing his sword.

"Funky butt loving," Arch said, and everyone stopped, breaking their gazes from the shadowy demons to look at him.

"I'm gonna go with the cowboy on this one," Lauren whispered, staring up at the hundreds—thousands?—of demons staring down at them. With a shaking hand, she drew her squirt gun filled with holy water and pointed it. Right now she was wishing she'd brought the heavier version, with the dual water tanks to strap to her back.

A growling echoed over them, like the sound of metal scraping concrete, a bizarre howl from bizarre creatures, and then, almost as one, they poured down the slope, like shadows slipping out of the trees.

*

"I do love a good night of fucking," Darla said, stretching across the bed and flopping her wrist across Pike's face. He was tender, real tender, all around his anus, but if he gave even a hint of weakness, she'd bend him over and given him another half hour of hell, until she'd rubbed her own clit raw against the other end of her toy, so he just clamped his mouth shut. "You fuck Jenny, I fuck your ass with hand and toy … I love it all. I just love fucking."

"Oh yeah?" Pike pushed her hand away carefully; it wasn't the one she'd recently had buried up to the wrist in his sphincter, fortunately.

"Yeah," Darla said, almost glowing as she stretched. After she'd finished with what she wanted to do to him, he'd had to get it back up and get her done, and that hadn't been comfortable either, but he'd done it. Gingerly.

Pike smiled thinly. It was all he could manage with the throbbing feeling in his ass.

She flopped that hand on his bare chest again. "Seriously. There's nothing like it after a hard day of parenting and talking baby talk and shit."

Pike wrung out a raw chuckle from his exhausted frame. "I thought you liked parenting."

"I like the thought that someday our kids are going to grow into interesting people," Darla said. "But right now? They're fucking boring as hell. The only good thing about them is going to the park and admiring the asses of these moms in their tight yoga pants. And every once in a while you get a hot dad in between all these skinny-jeans-wearing metrosexuals that probably had to find a sperm donor to knock up their wives." She laughed viciously at her observation. "Or maybe they like to watch a real man give it to her, like you do."

Pike bristled a little; being cuckolded was her fantasy, not his, but he went along with it when she wanted him to. "Did you like the taste of Jenny tonight?" he asked pointedly.

"I did." She stretched again in satisfaction. "Honest to God, I don't know where you found a hot little piece of ass like her in the backwoods of this hellhole county. The only thing that could make her any better is if she was wearing my naked thighs as her earmuffs." Darla laughed again. "But I think we both know she doesn't go that way, which is a damned shame." She ran her hand—still the clean one, thankfully—over the thin layer of chest hair he sported. "Guess I'll just have to keep getting some secondhand snatch."

"I asked her once if she'd join us," Pike said, adjusting himself in the smooth, cool, silky satin sheets.

"What'd she say?" Darla asked, now still.

"I don't think she took me seriously," Pike said. "And I don't think she swings that way. Shame, I know, because I'd love to give it to her from behind while she is burying her face in you. It's what I was thinking about while I was fucking her over my desk today, actually."

"You dirty bird," Darla said with mock accusation. "Keep talking like that, sailor, and I'm bound to get randy again. Might have to take it out on you."

"You might have to take it out on a dildo, I think you mean," Pike said, "because I expect I'm about done for the night. I'm not as young as I used to be."

She snuggled in tighter to him, pressing her sagging breasts against his arm and his chest. "I know. I'm not either. This gravity shit ... I hear it only gets worse from here." She ground her right breast against his ribs, then stopped, suddenly serious. "But Jason ... if we can pull this off ..."

"I know," he said quickly, nodding up and down on the pillow. "Getting old's not going to be a worry if we thread our way through this particular needle."

"I want my body back," Darla said, rubbing against him again. "I want your body back. Your dad bod's okay, but I liked it better before, back when we could fuck all night and you'd still be hard again in the morning without me having to throw a finger up there to get you going."

Pike shuddered involuntarily. "Yeah. I miss those days too." *But maybe for different reasons.*

"You gonna make your peace with Reeve?" Darla asked, propping up on an elbow to survey him better. "You gonna keep kissing his ass to get his little brigade of holy terrors out of the way? Just for a little bit, you know."

"Oh, I know," Pike said. "And yeah, I'm kissing his ass. As best I can, anyway. He's suspicious, of course—"

"Of course he is," Darla said, leaning up, letting her tits hang right in his face. They'd been a lot smaller, more pert, before she'd had the kids. Now they dangled a little, reminded him of cones that pointed down at a forty-five-degree angle. Her nipples had stuck straight out before. "You dicked him over hard and set up a massacre on Halloween. He'd have to be a grade-A fucking moron to ignore all that when you say a couple of sweet things to him about—what, the budget?" she scoffed. "I mean, he's probably dumb, but I doubt he's *that* dumb. And as long as he's been in law enforcement, I doubt he's gullible. Met a few too many liars to survive and thrive, even in Midian, without figuring out how to smoke them out."

"Yeah, he's no fool," Pike said. "But I think he wants a little diplomacy. Maybe he wants to believe the best of people. And I can work with that—at least for a little while. All it'll cost me is a little pride."

"What's pride?" Darla said, slapping him in the chest with the hand she'd just stuck up his rectum. She laughed, her face going blood red from chin to hairline, leaving pale, white traces where her hair met her scalp. She cackled loudly, that funny sound she made when she got real tickled.

Pike took his eyes off her long enough to stare down at his bare chest where she'd slapped that dirty, ass-smelling hand. She just kept laughing, and he was damned near ready to throw up. Gross.

*

"Well, here we go," Hendricks said as the shadowed beasts came rolling down the hill like an evening thunderstorm. They sounded like danger, that clang of a thousand hissing voices distorted by demon voice boxes making a high-pitched cry that caused even his spine to shudder. Yeah, Hendricks, veteran of Ramadi, kicker down of doors, the man who died in New Orleans at the hands of a couple punk demons—even he got the chills listening to the sound of these demon cats ululate, like hell's own army of jihadis rolling down at him on four legs.

They bounded with a fluid grace, these cats, which was a creepy thing to watch. He'd seen animals in zoos, had a couple cats that hung around his house when he was a kid catching mice and birds. They moved fluidly too, but not like these things. There was definitely something otherworldly about the way they bounded, almost too smooth for the human eye to follow.

"You guys maybe should have mentioned in your text that everything was going to shit out here!" Lauren Darlington screamed behind him. Hendricks heard the faint sound of feet pattering against the asphalt; he presumed the doctor was rushing to evac her daughter. It was never smart bringing civvies into a war zone, which was one of the reasons he'd worked alone.

The smell of sulfur was rank, sweeping down with the cats like a foul wind off the embankment, like ten thousand corpses had rotted in the woods with old eggs bundled up in their carcasses for extra flavor. Unbidden memories rose in Hendricks's mind of running his tongue over dead flesh, over a clit that was rubbery and stiff, unnatural—

He shuddered again, gagged right there, and steadied himself.

"You gonna be all right?" Arch asked from next to him.

"Hold tight in formation!" Hendricks said, trying to get back to a level place. He was a loner, not a leader, but spitting that shit out helped him stop thinking about the stupid shit he shouldn't be thinking about with death charging in at them. That was the shit that got people killed, head up their own asses, thinking about a Jody back home when they should have been focused on kicking down a door and clearing corners.

"What formation?" Braeden Tarley shouted. The man was brandishing a wrench, face all twisted and pissed off. Hendricks had seen that look before too. Hell, he recognized it from his own face after he started demon hunting.

"Hang together," Reeve said, taking over for Hendricks before he could spit out some clarification for the dumbass. "Watch each others' backs—"

The sheriff didn't even get a chance to finish that happy thought, comrades in arms looking after each other and all that happy shit, because there came the shadowcats, teeth and claws glinting in the day's last light, and that shadowy essence rolling like a black cloud beneath their skin.

*

Arch could see the threat coming, plain as day, but somehow he didn't care all that much. If he lived, he lived, and he'd go on fighting. If he died, well, he died, and he'd go down fighting. The tickle of the cool dusk air across his skin didn't bring any fear with it; if anything, he was anticipating the coming battle. His sword was clutched hard in hand, knuckles wrapped around it tight, raised and ready to start the fight proper.

He had it in mind to stab rather than whack, figured the way they were coming at him, he'd get more mileage if he thrust rather than swinging it down like he had to behead these foul things. He didn't; he just needed to let a little air out of their balloons, and they were charging in plenty fast to impale themselves on his weapon without him having to do much about it.

The first came leaping at him and Arch went low. They moved fast, faster than him, but once they were in the air, they were committed, and he swung his sword's tip around to greet the shadowcat.

It got a look on its face like it was intelligent enough to know what was coming. It barely touched the tip when it screeched like metal on metal, then evaporated in a cloud of smoke. Arch tweaked the tip subtly to the right and greeted another one of these cursed things. Three leapt at him as the sulfur cleared from the first one, and this time he swung the sword.

The blade caught one in the belly and vaporized it, another in the ribs and it went to smoke; the last he hit with the edge and it curled into black puffs of rank sulfur just in front of his face. He inhaled it and coughed, eyes burning from the stink but unable to spare the time and attention it might take to really focus on expelling it from his body.

There was no time for that. Two more came at him, and Arch eyed them through the tears that were welling up from the smell. He'd never had a demon blow up quite that close to his face before, or if it had, he'd never had it smell like that. They stank, but these demon cats were somehow worse. "What have you been eating?" he asked as he spun to deal with another one coming at him from a forty-five-degree angle, heading for his ribs. He caught it in the face with the tip of his sword just in time.

As many of them as there were, as immediate as the threat was, somehow Arch's head was a turn back, at that device they'd discovered in the road. Who would have planted such a thing? To what purpose?

And what did it have to do with all these demon cats?

*

Erin was swinging for the fences. It was a little like playing a game of kickball with four thousand yipping dogs. They were everywhere, absolutely fucking everywhere, leaping and biting and trying to rip her to pieces. She'd lost a little skin on her elbow, the road rash sensation burning like crazy. One of them had missed her face by the width of a kitten hair, flying by as she ducked. That sucker had slammed into the side of Sam Allen's wrecker and left an indentation the size of an exercise ball.

"Motherfuckers!" Erin swung the bat, not putting a whole lot of backswing in it because she didn't have a ton of space to swing this time. Lauren Darlington and her daughter were just behind her, the girl doing a hell of a lot less screaming than the mom.

"I should have left you with the hookers to learn about BJs and rusty trombones and God knows whatever else!" Dr. Darlington screamed as they went past behind her, fleeing for a vehicle. Erin didn't have the conscious thought to tell them that this was a stupid idea, because if one of these things could put a dent in Sam Allen's door the size of a jumbo deluxe manhole cover, they weren't going to have any issue blasting through a car window.

"What's a rusty trombone?" Molly Darlington asked as a light splatter of water hit across the back of Erin's neck, cool and refreshing. Something screeched like a speaker on overload at a goddamned rock and roll concert, and Erin turned her head in time to see a hellcat bursting into flames with a squeal like it had just had its balls dipped in acid. "Never mind! Learning about putting penises in your mouth would be a lot less dangerous than this!"

"What the fuck is wrong with this town?" Erin muttered, burying nails in the side of a cat then reversing her swing and clubbing the shit out of another shadowcat as she brought it back over her shoulder. Even a privileged little prissy cunt like Molly Darlington was learning some fucked-up lessons about life now.

*

"God, let it only be one penis in your mouth!" Lauren shouted to—well, probably to everyone because she was having a hard time keeping her calm.

"At a time?" Molly fired back. They were scrambling toward the police cruiser, toward the illusory safety it provided. Mack Wellstone's face peeked out of the back, eyes wide as he took in the shitshow going on around them.

"EVER!" Lauren shouted, encouraging Molly along with a hand on the small of her back, the other pointing the squirt gun loaded with holy water at anything that came close. She squirted a hellcat surging at Sheriff Reeve while his back was turned, and she caught it flush, a blast to the face that caused it to burst into flames and then evaporate into darkness. "I hope you find one guy that you really love, and that when you put his dick in your mouth, it's the first and only dick you ever put there or anywhere else on your body! Including in your hand! And you can wait until a reasonable age, like maybe or fifty or seventy—it's the new thirty—until you lose your virginity."

"When did you go Puritan on me, Mom?" Molly shouted, hunching her shoulders as she ran, like that would protect her, keeping her head down. "You were always the one that made fun of those other moms, the ones who practically bought their daughters chastity belts and locked them in high towers and never let them hear the word 'vagina' while you were dropping it in casual conversation and talking about what an innovation the pill was to modern life—"

"Jesus," Sam Allen said, turning his head to look right at Lauren. "That's a mighty fucked-up upbringing—"

A hellcat shredded Sam across the back, screeching as it hit him, claws flashing in the scattered headlights reflecting off the road. Sam Allen's upper torso went rolling off and his lower body fell a second later under the furious onslaught of two hellcats. Blood sprayed at Molly and Lauren, spattering them like they'd walked into a PETA demonstration wearing full mink.

Molly screamed as Lauren turned her squirt gun on the hellcats that had shredded Sam. A little piece of his entrails was thrown into the air as the hellcats screeched and burned, bucking wildly. It landed in Molly's hair, and to her credit, she didn't scream, though Lauren wondered if she even felt the wet, slick piece of intestine tangled in her hair to the right of her face.

"I'm not winning any mother of the year awards today," Lauren said, yanking Molly back a step as a hellcat sailed in front of them, clearly anticipating them running. Lauren smacked it as it went by, causing it to twist and spasm in fury, a lot like a regular cat that went nuts for no apparent reason.

"Seriously," Molly said, looking right at her. "You're fucking losing it, Mom. Why does it matter what hookers teach me about sex right now, with all this shit going on?"

"Because it fucking does!" Lauren screamed and pushed her again toward the police cruiser, Mack Wellstone waiting just inside. Lauren's heart was beating at a million miles an hour, and she snapped off another shot, laying down a line of holy water fire at a trio of hellcats trying to run over Sam's corpse. They screamed and burned, and in Lauren's head it felt like she was doing the same, the same words repeating themselves in her mind over and over again: *Just let me get her out of here and safe. Just let me get her out of here and safe ...*

*

"WRECKER is down!" Reeve shouted when he saw Sam Allen get ripped in half by those motherfucking demons. He would have hoped he'd be detached about it, but he wasn't detached at all. The blood was ripping through his veins so hard his temple was throbbing, the sound like a drumbeat in his head. The Darlington girls were heading for the cruiser where he'd shoved Mack Wellstone, which didn't seem like such a hot idea to him, but he didn't have a lot of time or mental space to think why it wasn't.

The goddamned hellcats kept coming too, another wave of them rushing down the hill. He imagined them lined up from here to the county line, and it made him shiver as one of them just about took his legs from beneath him. He nicked it just in time, and it vaporized with a hiss and screech, reminding him of back when he and Donna had cats and he'd stepped on one in the middle of the night. He'd never liked those damned things, always been more of a dog person, and this was cementing it for him.

"They're trying to flank us!" Hendricks shouted. Reeve spared a glance out of the corner of his eye and saw the cowboy was right. They didn't have a very wide line, after all, just the few of them, and Sam had already fallen. Funny how he'd walked into this thinking they were making a show of force.

Now Reeve figured they were making a last damned stand. That was how fast this thing had turned on them.

"Out of the frying pan and sucked into the damned mouth of hell," Reeve said, swinging his sword, clearing out two of those shadowcats as he did so. This holding action was just about to fall apart, he realized, seeing a few of the hellbeasts circling wide around, trying to sneak in behind Arch. If they made it in ... the whole damned line was going to fall down one by one, like Germans to Alvin York.

*

Hendricks knew what was coming from the side, just past Arch, but there wasn't a lot he could do about it with a shit ton of hellcats coming from his front. They were still rampaging their way down the slope in hella numbers, storming out like they were in infinite supply. He was falling back slowly with the others, trying to figure out if there was any kind of safe ground.

Nope. He didn't even need to look around. There was damned sure no safe ground here. These things could jump like they had a spring in their ass that was wound tighter than mouse's cunt, and the likelihood they were just gonna back off and let the survivors of this clusterfuck alone was about as likely as him getting a blowjob from Erin.

Goddamn, did he want another piece of Starling. What was it about scratching that itch with her that only made him want more of it and more frequently?

A hellcat came screaming at him from just to the side of Arch, crossing right in front of the big man at a moment of ultimate distraction. Arch was already slashing up two of the fuckers and moving to try and save that damned Braeden Tarley, who was hammering one with a wrench that was doing both jack and shit to his foe. Definitely not consecrated, because the mechanic was giving the hellcat some hell of his own and it was squealing but resolutely refusing to burst into a cloud.

The charging cat shot right past Arch and collided with Hendricks, sending a shooting pain up his leg. Thankfully it had gone kinda sideways to try and escape Arch's attention, and even though it was squirming, it didn't have a claw handy to tear into his ass with. Instead it just hit like a fucking Mack truck built for a toddler, and his knee gave out and his ass went down.

"Fucking cheesedick motherfucker!" Hendricks shouted, half hoping someone would hear him and half just to shout because of how much it hurt when the damned thing rammed him. His knee had buckled and was screaming at him like he'd done a week's worth of hopping on it and then given it a rest by ramming his sword between the joint. His ass joined the angry fray a moment later as it kissed asphalt, sending a numb sensation up his spine, compressing all the way up to the back of his neck and giving him a feeling like someone had just turned down the volume on the whole world. Or was that just a sudden ringing in his ear?

He didn't have a lot of time to figure it out, because a shadowcat came at him from the left, claws bared, and his sword was on his right side, angled way wrong. He ripped his 1911 out of its holster and fired from the hip, something he never cared to do because it tended to be hideously inaccurate. This wasn't high noon at the OK Corral though, guns drawn at fifty paces; this was a fucking fiend from hell heading right into his face to snack on his nose, eyes, and probably his goddamned tongue too, and he was attached to all those parts. He thumbed the safety without a thought, the hammer already back, and just let loose, running through the entire mag in about five seconds.

The hellcat took the rounds to the face like a dog that's just been kicked in the gut. It made a noise that Hendricks couldn't hear, ears ringing and his brain already numbed from the landing, its jaws wide, blackness looking therein in such a way that it made the damned thing's shadowy coat seem blacker by comparison. The hellcat didn't stop for long, shaking off the attack, but it gave Hendricks enough time to shift off his aching right side ...

He brought the sword around and jacked that motherfucker in the face with a good stab. There was a real satisfaction to ramming a pointy object into a demon and watching it go poof, but he didn't have a lot of time to enjoy it right now. He ignored the stink as best he could, holding his breath even as the stench threatened to crawl up into his sinus cavity and settle there like it was the Willamette Valley for shitty smells, a promised land in which they could stink forever.

"You enjoy that, fuckstick," Hendricks said, and then he caught motion out of the corner of his eye. A hellcat was coming at him low, just out of his blind spot, and he wasn't real likely to get that sword back around in time to deal with it.

*

Arch felt like splitting his time between saving Braeden Tarley's backside and trying to keep the shadowcats from sneaking around his own rear end was a losing endeavor, somewhere on the order of trying to run down the clock from the opening whistle of the fourth quarter when you were up big rather than keep playing and winning the way you had all along. It was defense, and he didn't care for that at all.

"These damned things won't die!" Tarley howled, beating the living snot out of one of the shadowy creatures with his wrench. It was making a mewling noise, one of the most horrible sounds Arch had ever heard, and trying to rise as Tarley was hammering it over and over again where the spine would have been on a normal cat.

Rather than reiterate the point he'd tried to make before about them needing a holy sword to fall easily, he instead said, "I've killed them without a consecrated weapon before. They're just real tough to do that way." It was true; he'd killed a demon in his own bathroom by breaking its shell. It hadn't been easy though. Not at all.

"Hey, Arch, behind you." Barney Jones didn't even shout it, just said it, loud enough to be heard—and Arch heard it, and spun right away. He slashed one in half as it evaporated, smell once again threatening to choke him. Jones was hanging out a little behind him; Arch hadn't heard the pastor approach, but there he was, doing a little creeping behind the lines of his own, coming over to block these things from getting around behind them. He was doing a pretty fine job of it too, vaporizing two of them while Arch was looking.

A flurry of gunshots went off to his right, and Arch flinched at the sound. Hendricks was ripping off a few rounds again, it seemed, but Arch didn't have time to worry about that. He had three coming right at him, splitting their attention, and another going for Tarley. This was getting wild, but strangely, that fear that should have consumed him in this sort of fight, that feeling of real peril, of being overwhelmed, of having everything going wrong all around ... it just wasn't there.

Not when they started trying to slip around the side.

Not when he heard Hendricks resorting to the desperate use of his pistol.

And not now, when three of them were coming at him from three different angles, trying to get him to commit and split, keep him from landing the kill on all three of them.

The exhilaration of knowing he was fighting a holy war, of knowing that the cause was just ... that was still there, though not as strong as it once was. But that healthy fear, the one that had told him that this was real, that the danger was ever present ... it was gone.

Arch realized, as the hellcats sailed toward him, gracefully slipping through the air like black holes in motion, trying to split his focus so they could split him into pieces ... that maybe he just didn't care if he lived anymore.

And that it might just be easier if he didn't.

*

Lauren was operating on autopilot, the objective fixed in her mind and all her thought driving her toward it—get to the damned car and get Molly locked away. It was the lizard part of her brain that was moving her ahead at this point, nothing else. There was no calm analysis or assessment; no time for that shit. She had to move, and move now.

"How can there be this many demons in the woods?" Molly screamed. "Where did they come from?"

"Hell," Barney Jones said from somewhere behind her. "Right from the depths of—"

"I've already had one sermon today!" Lauren shouted. "I don't need another!"

"I think you do, if you're mistaking the word of God for *Game of Thrones*." Jones shot her a knowing look. "I'm not saying that show is evil or anything, but it ain't exactly holy."

"Jesus!" Lauren shouted as two hellcats went scooting past, inches from her, on their way to wipe out Arch. "I fucking hate small town gossip!" How had Jones already heard about her stupid fucking eulogy slip?

"That's taking the Lord's name in vain, Lauren!" Jones called over his shoulder as he put the end to another cat. "One of the ten commandments, right up there with, 'A Lannister always pays his debts.'" Jones sent her another look, twinkle in his eye.

"Asshole," Lauren said under her breath as another hellcat went screeching by, howling at the top of its lungs. It seemed not to notice them, because it was bounding past without a glance their way. They were only a dozen feet from the car now, and Lauren didn't even bother squirting the hellcat because she was low on ammo, the squirt gun getting perilously lighter with every squeeze of the trigger.

That was some bad news, given what they were up against here.

"We're almost there!" Lauren ducked even though there was no reason, running low toward the door of the police cruiser. She spun as shots were fired, long, loud ones, and turned immediately in the direction of the sound, squirt gun raised. It was the cowboy, fending off one of the hellcats, but he had it under control, more or less. She turned back to her mission. It was right there …

She yanked the handle and started to deposit Molly in the back seat of the car when a hellcat shot out of her peripheral vision on the right and smashed into the front windshield, obliterating it completely with its landing. It screamed inside the car, the confined space and open door acting like a funnel for the screech, causing Lauren to shut her eyes tightly against the blast of sound as though it were an actual attack. It was worse than any concert she'd ever been to, a hell noise that called to mind the image of a bridge collapsing around her as she fell into a canyon below.

"I don't think the car is safe!" Molly made herself heard over the cataclysmic noise.

Mack Wellstone scooted out of the backseat and hit Lauren right in the gut with a shoulder as he did so, the kid plainly becoming accustomed to watching out for himself. The smell of sulfur hit her hard in the face, almost as hard as the sound of the demon screeching.

"No shit," Lauren said after taking a moment to recover. Mack was already hightailing it away from this mess, off the other side of the road and away from where these things were flooding out of the wood. The hellcat was thrashing in the front seat, pieces of stuffing raining in the car's confines like it was snowing. Spiderweb cracks were already present in the Plexiglas divider between the driver's compartment and the back seat, and the hellcat had only been rustling around in there for a couple seconds. Lauren's face hardened. "Let's get the fuck out of here!"

Molly just stared at her in disbelief. "How?" She yanked Lauren's arm. "That thing just tore into the car to get to Mack. We get in our own and one of those comes in like that …"

She didn't really have to finish the thought, because it was obvious as slash marks started to appear in the back of the seats as the hellcat tunneled through, apparently panicked by the tight confines of the vehicle. If they got in a car and one of those made its way in, they'd be better off throwing themselves into a giant blender. And marginally less likely to die.

*

Erin was tearing her way through this horde of demonic kittycats, but she wasn't having much fun doing so. She had a nasty feeling that death could swipe a shadowy paw out for her at any second, striking her from the rolls of the living. These things were starting to break through their line, and the damnation of it was, she didn't even know if they were really all that serious about the sheer killing, or if they were just having some fun and accidentally killing as they did so. Like a bunch of kittens on catnip, and the watch were their balls of yarn.

But the strength of these things was such that being their ball of yarn meant your ass got unspooled pretty quick. And God help you if they decided to rake you with their claws for shits and giggles, because then you'd end up like Sam Allen.

"We're breaking!" Reeve shouted as the line started to fold. Kitties were coming in on the side now. Not Arch's side, because Barney Jones had moved himself over to deal with that and was doing so admirably, but the other side, the one where Sam Allen had been stationed before he'd been ripped up. Now Reeve was trying to keep them out himself but was falling back on all fronts. Erin wasn't going to hang out up front while everyone else was moving back, nossir. She was having a hell of a time fighting these things anyway, and getting the fuck out of there before she was left exposed was right up there on her priority list with not taking one to the cornhole—at least, not on the first date. Or second. Or ever again, if she could avoid it (goddamn sweet-talking Clayton Mackey and his promises that it wouldn't hurt).

This, though—this would hurt a hell of a lot worse if she got it wrong. It'd be a lot worse than not being able to sit right for a few days. Sam Allen was a great illustration, his guts all strung out where the hellcats had torn him apart. It reeked of shit and sulfur now, at least on this end of the line, and Erin didn't want to add her own to the pile.

"What a fuckup," she said, swinging the baseball bat low and then up to catch a hellcat when it came at her in mid-air. It dissolved into that shadowy blackness shit that they became when they'd gotten the air let out of them, and she whipped the bat back around and caught another, creating a whirlpool of ebony that popped and left her with a sulfur stink that covered up the shitty evisceration smell of Sam Allen's corpse.

"Holy Christ, fall back!" Reeve said, and he bumped into her, giving her a rough shove that he probably didn't mean anything by, but which damned near got him a bat to the side of the fucking head. Erin's brain was processing everyone as a threat right now, and it took a hard pull on the mental reins to keep from attacking him.

Reeve shoved past her as he slashed his way through two more of those hellcats. A swarm of them were after him though, at least a dozen. Erin started to go after him, not for revenge this time but to help, but something swiped low across her shin and she screamed, because *holy fucking shit!* the pain was suddenly worse than anything that lying Clayton Mackey had done to her ass.

It was a small gash, the tear across the front of her pants leg, but it was already running dark crimson in the twilight, and she staggered back, trying to keep from keeling over there and grabbing at it like a kid with a skinned knee. This was a fuck-lot worse than a skinned knee though, a gashed-up shin. The hellcat that had done it had already moved on, joining the scrum that was forming in front of Reeve. They smelled blood with him, apparently, the weakest link, because he was swinging hard, clearing out the space in front of him, falling back to the police cruiser and slamming his back against it in retreat, exhaustion obvious as the sweat poured down his face, and the strain showed when he took his aim at another of those fucking things and gave it hell with a hard swing.

He was failing though, and he knew it. He was panicked too, giving it everything he had in order to kill the hellcats stacking up in front of him to leap. They were coming low and high, and fast as fuck too, the slippery little shits. He was barely staving them off, and Erin was about to hobble toward him to help when she caught motion out of the corner of her eye streaking toward her—

It wasn't a hellcat, thank God.

It was a fucking car—a pristine white Land Rover, the squeal of its tires on pavement only a few feet away as it streaked past, aimed right for the pack of hellcats in front of Reeve. She caught a glimpse in the window as it shot past, and it looked a hell of a lot like Ms. Cherry was waving at her from the passenger seat and Casey Meacham was in the driver's seat.

Which would explain why she thought she heard someone shout,

"DIE, MOTHERFUCKERS!" as it went past, slamming into the pack of hellcats in front of Reeve and sending them flying through the air like a kicker sends a football on a good punt.

Reeve just sat there against the cruiser, chest heaving, Casey drawn to a stop in front of him. The window rolled down and Ms. Cherry popped her head out. "How are you doing, Sheriff?" she asked.

"A little better now that you're here," Reeve said, and then a hellcat claw ripped out of the cruiser beside him, nearly cutting his ass in two. Reeve scrambled away, fumbling for his weapon and thrusting his back against Ms. Cherry's Rover, jabbing at the hellcat in the police cruiser and catching it on the paw. It screeched and dissolved, and the police cruiser's door fell off where it had ripped it off the hinges. "Never mind that bit about being better," Reeve said. "I think I might still be kinda fucked up."

*

Lauren was about ready to hyperventilate, panic, freak out and maybe die of an overactive heart when Casey and Ms. Cherry came screaming up and smashed into a pile of hellcats, sending them flying through the air like confetti. One of them hit a tree squarely and dissolved, shell broken, a demonic piñata spilling darkness for half a second before it was gone.

"Fuck yeah!" Molly shouted, pumping a fist as the hellcat trapped in the police cruiser ripped its way out the other side and was promptly killed by Sheriff Reeve, who thumped against Ms. Cherry's car. Molly had her head down and so did Lauren, like they could duck and cover on this side of the car and somehow it'd be all right, like these fucking things weren't scrabbling all around them.

Oh, here came one now.

"Watch your mouth!" Lauren shouted, dousing the incoming hellcat as she yanked Molly up.

"Oh, for fucking real?" Molly asked as Lauren steered her around the trunk of the car. "Sam Allen is torn in half over there, and you're still worried about me saying the F-word and talking about blowjobs?"

"I'm trying to protect you!" Lauren squirted at a demon that slithered past, like it was trying to keep its head low. It screamed at the contact of the holy water and flopped down on its belly, burning up and smoking off a second later. "From everything!"

"Good fucking luck! The town is in the middle of a demon invasion and we live with hookers! Also, I've known the word 'fuck' since I heard you say it when I was four!"

"Well, fuck it all!" Lauren screamed, stopping just past the trunk of the cruiser. The back of Ms. Cherry's car was just sitting there, and so was Reeve, huffing against the side of the vehicle, winded like he'd worked hard, which she supposed he had. "I have had about enough of these demons, this bullshit, your language, and—"

Something moved out of the corner of her eye, and she caught sight of it as it was slithering toward Hendricks, who was down, on his side, quartered away from the hellcat that was coming at him. He could see it, she knew, but there wasn't a damned thing he could do to stop it from taking his head right off.

Something flashed between the demon and the cowboy, and suddenly there was a person there where nothing had been before. Red hair shining, eyes hard and furious, dark as the dusk itself, Lucia—no, *Starling*—lashed out, and the hellcat shattered as it flew backward from the blow, the woman's fist breaking it into pieces with a single blow.

"—and her," Lauren finished, heat boiling off her statement. She stared at the hooker-turned-savior, and felt only loathing for the woman, in spite of how little she knew about her.

"Wow, Lucia just saved Hendricks's day!" Molly said, gushing like a groupie.

"That's not Lucia," Lauren said tightly, "and she's not a fucking hero, okay?"

Another squeal of tires greeted them, and a car surged around the last curve and blasted another herd of hellcats like tenpins, scattering them. The OOCs came flying out before the thing was practically even in park, throwing themselves into a fight with those truncheons, the weapons rising and falling and drawing a great many hellcat screams.

Other cars were pulling up now too—Father Nguyen, Chauncey Watson—the rest of the watch were arriving, and the hellcats were on the run.

"Holy shit, Sam," Braeden Tarley said, staring at the ruin of Sam Allen's body. Lauren watched him sag like his wrench weighed a ton, blank eyes on the corpse, nose twitching at the scent of death and shit and piss.

Lauren's eyes settled on Starling again, as she lashed out almost absentmindedly and killed another hellcat, sending it back to—well, to where it came from, Lauren supposed. Starling offered a hand and Hendricks took it, and she pulled him to his feet as Lauren watched. The shadow kitties were gone, retreating back into the woods from whence they came, the trees rustling madly up the slope.

"The fuck that's not Lucia," Molly said, wrenching her arm free of her mother's grasp and hurrying away toward Starling and Hendricks. Lauren just stood there, frozen in time like she'd been the one to get slashed in the back by one of those things, not Sam Allen. She wanted to throw her mouth open, put her head back, and howl at the sky like a werewolf, just vent all that fury and sadness and all the other shit emotions right out.

But nothing came out except a choked noise, and instead she just kept standing there, watching her daughter as Molly threaded her way over to Hendricks—and that goddamned hooker.

Or whatever she was now.

*

"Holy fuck, Lucia, that was badass on a stick!"

Hendricks turned his head to see Dr. Darlington's too-cute-for-her-boots underaged spawn walking up to Starling with a fucking glow on her face. It was probably only a notch or two off what Hendricks himself had been wearing only a few hours earlier, but maybe a degree or twelve lower on the lasciviousness scale. This was pure admiration, not the unbridled lust he tended to display when he jammed his face into Starling's collarbone after the act, wet hair against her skin and neck as he lay, spent.

Starling cocked her head, as she tended to do, and Hendricks wondered how she'd take the compliment and the wrong name. She seemed to need a second to process, which was funny to him given how fast she moved and thought during a fight. "Thank you," she finally seemed to decide, which was weird too, because since when did Starling give a fuck about manners?

"How did you do that?" Molly asked. Hendricks just stared at her; she was acting like he wasn't even there, like they hadn't been in the middle of a conversation when she came rolling up. "I mean, you busted that thing up with one hit!"

Hendricks kept his mouth glued shut like a good grunt, waiting for the answer. He doubted it'd be satisfying, and it sure enough wasn't: "I just did," Starling said, sounding a little uncertain, which was also curious. Then she turned back to him, as though that would just close up the conversation with Miss Underage-and-Inquisitive.

"You are so amazing," Molly gushed, and Hendricks couldn't help but grin a little. This was funny to watch, the honor student gushing over the hooker-angel or whatever.

"Yeah, I bet you want to be just like her when you grow up,"

Hendricks cracked, and then saw Dr. Darlington stalking over, a boiling-oil look on her face. He kind of internally shrugged; if the goddamned Al Qaeda insurgents hadn't killed his ass, what did he have to fear from some bleeding heart, feminazi, mamabear country doctor? Even if she did have an ass that raised her overall fuckability rating up to a hard 8 out of 10.

"Why would she want to be like me?" Starling asked, head cocked like she was genuinely curious. Another weird one from Starling. Not that she never asked questions, but that was a weirdass question for her to ask.

"Because you're a stone badass," Molly said. "And because you know stuff."

"Like the optimal number of times and the angle for ramming a dick in your mouth before it spurts," Lauren Darlington spat out. "Or the position guys like best during sex. It's doggy style for most." She shot her daughter a nasty look. "See, sweetie? I know those answers too, but I'm a little too refined to share them all with you."

"Yeah, you're a real lady in the parlor there, Doc," Hendricks cracked.

"Nobody fucking asked you, asshole," Darlington shot back.

"Hey, I was just sitting here minding my own beeswax when your daughter came up gushing over Starling," Hendricks said. "You can go ahead and take your little family squabble on down the road and it won't pain me a bit."

"I can't believe you won't let me fucking breathe for five seconds," Molly Darlington stepped in, "when we just survived that—that—that—"

"Shitshow," Hendricks supplied.

"That fucking shitshow, thank you, yes," Molly said, pointing at Sam Allen's corpse, "which you led us into because you were too damned up your own ass trying to keep me from finding out about dicks."

"Jesus," Hendricks said, fighting the urge to take a step back. He'd known a sixteen-year-old girl or two with the mouth of a trucker—hell, he used to have crushes on them—but this was kinda disconcerting now that he was older and a little more world-weary.

"I think you know about dicks," Lauren said. "I'm trying to keep you from thinking that sucking one or fucking one for money is a good career path, that doesn't involve—oh, I don't know—drug addiction, sexually transmitted diseases, violence—"

"Yeah, way to go on steering me out of violence," Molly said, chucking her head toward the corpse again. "Really dodged that one.

Now I'll never see a person dismembered with my own eyes. Or—and I'm just spitballing here—" the sarcasm was flowing now "—watch my own hands slit a dear family member's throat."

"Fucking shit," Hendricks said, taking a step back for real this time. This was getting goddamned dark, fast.

Lauren visibly paled, like she'd had milk poured all over her face, or been filming a bukkake. Then she got mad, also like she'd filmed a bukkake, but unknowingly. "This place … it's going to kill us. Destroy us."

"You're just now realizing this?" Hendricks asked. "Fuck, did you graduate last in your class or what? For chrissakes. And I let you treat me as a patient? Fuck."

She ignored him. "Get in the car, Molly."

"You sure?" Molly's voice still dripped with sarcasm. "Because last time you tried, that worked out real well, since we ended up here—"

Lauren reached out and grabbed her daughter by the upper arm, latching on and digging in like her fingers were claws. Molly grunted, but Lauren started pulling her away.

"See you later, Lucia," Molly said, going along with her mom pretty submissively, though the look on her face said defiance was in the cards. Probably, also, a cold spell once they were in the vehicle, if Hendricks had to guess. "You can tell me more about sucking cock back at the house." She mimed the dick sucking motion, popping her tongue into her cheek while holding up her hand with thumb touching her forefingers like it was wrapped around a big shaft. It gave Hendricks an instant boner kill, because it looked gross and goofy when the schoolgirl did it. "And maybe I'll see you later too, Marine." And she made the motion another couple of times before Hendricks jerked his head away, wincing at the image.

"Are they going to fight now?" Starling asked as she watched them walk away in silence. "Should we stand back and let them?"

"I don't think they're going to fight the way you're thinking," Hendricks said, "but yeah—I ain't getting involved in that. No way." And he shuddered again. That teenager was fucked in the head—and hopefully nowhere else, for her sake, her mom's sake, and hell, everyone's sake. "Grow the fuck up," he muttered, and meant it.

*

"Man, I did a number on my back, crashing like that," Casey Meacham's voice echoed down over the road and the ditch, "and not a good number, like 69."

"Oh, you poor thing," Melina Cherry breathed softly, causing Arch's ears to ring a little and his nose to curl like he'd smelled something terrible. Which he had, because Sam Allen had been ripped open, bowels exposed to the air, but that wasn't what he was reacting to when his nose curled.

"You weren't even fucking joking about those things," Braeden Tarley said breathlessly. The mechanic's shoulders were heaving with his recent exertions, traces of blood drizzling down the side of his face. What had happened there? Arch wondered and then discarded the question, realizing he didn't much care. The man seemed all right, and that was good enough.

"No, Arch was dead serious," Pastor Jones said, offering Braeden a hand. The mechanic took it, and Arch realized he was limping slightly, putting some weight on Jones.

"Let me help you there," Arch said, hustling over to relieve the pastor. He took up some of Tarley's weight as Tarley threaded an arm around his shoulder. There was a wide gash up the mechanic's thigh, and Arch wondered how that had gotten there. He hadn't seen anything take a slice out of him, but then, there had been a lot going on.

Jones eyed Arch, a little mischief mixed in with his smile. Arch had an idea there was a message Jones wanted him to get, but Arch ignored it and turned away. He flicked his gaze over to where Duncan and Guthrie were chasing off the last of the hellcats, truncheons held high like cowboys—or a cowgirl, in Guthrie's case—running off a pack of wolves.

"Those guys are demons, right?" Tarley asked him.

"Yessir," Arch said.

"But they're helping us?"

"Demon law enforcement," Arch said. He still wasn't entirely sure that he understood the idea behind the Office of Occultic Concordance, but he couldn't deny that Duncan had made some use of himself in this fight. He was a little less sanguine about Lerner—now Guthrie—but she'd done some good once upon a time as well. "Reckon this sort of thing we just saw violates some demon law about keeping trouble on the down-low."

"How'd that shit on the square fit into demon law?" Tarley asked, storm clouds and resentment brewing not far beneath his surface.

"Probably blasted it all to heck and gone," Arch said.

"Hmph," Tarley said, and that told Arch all he needed to know about Tarley's feelings on demons and their law.

"They're helping, Braeden," Jones said diplomatically.

"They're demons," Tarley said. "Thought you'd be against that sort of thing on general principle, Reverend."

"You might think I'm supposed to be against hookers, and murderers, and idolators and adulterers as well," Jones said, "and I am against all of those things. I hate the sin, hate it with the fire of conviction." He jerked a head toward Ms. Cherry. "But I love the sinner, because He loved the sinners. There's an act, and there's a person, and I can see the difference between the two because I have eyes and a mind of my own that reasons and thinks and learns. Yes, perhaps our friends over there are demons. Perhaps they're even evil, I don't know. But they do acts of good right now, and when I see them commit an act of evil, well, I'll call them out on it, just the same as I might call out you for getting a little too wrathful and a little hastily unwise just now." He gave Tarley an arched eyebrow. "Next time, perhaps we should get you an instrument of God if you want to fight the devil?"

Tarley just nodded, and Arch started to help him shuffle back to the truck. "Reckon we should have the doc take a look at this," Arch said, peering down at Tarley's calf, where the gash was dripping on the pavement.

"That might be a problem," Jones said, staring straight ahead.

Arch looked up to see where he was looking. Sure enough, there was Dr. Darlington behind the wheel of her car, her daughter visible through the passenger window, fury on her face as the vehicle peeled out, heading back down the road toward town.

Arch did a frown of his own. "Hope she don't run into that trap we found."

"She'll be fine so long as she doesn't cross the lane and run into the ditch," Tarley said, grunting from his wound as he fussed with his pants leg, "and, really, she'd have bigger problems than her tires if she did all that."

"I suppose," Arch said, brow still furrowed in thought. He'd mostly forgotten that nasty little trap while they'd been in the fight. Now that they were out of it, though, he found his mind heading back to it, and wondering …

What happened to the woman from that car?

He looked around. Come to think of it … what had happened to Mack Wellstone?

*

"How's he doing?" Addison Rutherford Longholt asked as she walked into the hospital room. She asked that every time she came in, and Brian dutifully answered it every time, always the same way.

"About like always," Brian said, not looking up from the magazine in his hands. "Sleeping, for now." He still had a dull ache in his leg, probably from sitting too long, but standing up and exercising it now would just make the problem worse. They were up on the fourth floor, and he could see the quiet Chattanooga streets outside the curtains, the street lamps snapping on.

"Did you hear the ruckus on your phone a little bit ago?" his mother asked. "Thought mine was about to explode like one of those James Bond devices while I was driving."

"You're getting the watch's text message alerts?" Brian raised an eyebrow at that. His mom was not much of a fighter, at least not with weapons.

"Seems wise to pay attention to what's going on around you, doesn't it?" Addie wore a thin smile that vanished when her eyes played across the room and settled on her husband's sleeping form. The whole place had that antiseptic hospital smell to it, and Brian was sick of it. He felt like he could almost taste it, and it disgusted him all the way down to the base of his stomach.

"Better than walking into an open manhole, I guess." Brian let his eyes dance over the *Entertainment Weekly* lying across his lap without absorbing a single word from the page. He'd been trying to read it for a half hour now, but he kept having to reread the same paragraph over and over. He still didn't even know what it was about. He looked at the picture. Oh, right. Another gushing profile of Kate McKinnon. Well, she was funny, he supposed, though he hadn't seen her in much.

"How long are you staying?" Addie asked, causing Brian to forget what he was reading again. "Not the whole night, surely?"

"I dunno," Brian said, taking a breath and triggering an inadvertent yawn. "The nurse says Dad doesn't do so well when he wakes up and no one's here."

Addie absorbed that, unmoving. "I suppose that makes sense."

Brian leaned his head back against the vinyl headrest on the visitor chair. "Really? Because it doesn't make much sense to me. He's a fucking vegetable."

His mother's face went stiff as a death mask. "You take that back."

"Why?" Brian asked, exhaustion seeping out. How long had it been since he'd slept a full night? Hell, even a half night? "His brain ended up on the ceiling, Mom, or at least a lot of it did. I should know; I saw it happen. Now it's just a question of which kind of vegetable he is. I'm leaning toward maybe a stewed cabbage or something, myself. Soft and mushy—"

"What a disgusting thing to say about your father," Addie snapped, making her way over to the window and drawing the curtains violently, the rings clicking against the rod. "And he is still your father, in spite of whatever you might th—"

"No, he's not," Brian said, putting the web of skin between his thumb and forefinger squarely against the bridge of his nose and leaving it there, massaging his temples as he did so. "My father was a man with thoughts of his own. Lots of them. Opinions. Insights. Persuasive arguments, even. This?" He pulled the hand off his face to sweep it toward the sleeping figure on the bed. "This guy ... this vegetable ... he doesn't have opinions. Persuasion? Insights? Pffft. He can't even feed himself."

"You don't know what's going on in that head of his."

"Very little. I know very little is going on in there." Brian laughed mirthlessly.

His mother stood there, looking at him, her expression impossible to read. He'd known her his whole damned life, imagined he knew her well, but this ... he had no idea what she was thinking now. How could he? She'd never lost her daughter before. Never had her husband reduced to this. Brian had seen her go through a lot—the loss of her own parents being the biggest thing he could think of, but ... this?

This was so much worse. By leaps and bounds. No contest.

"You don't have any hope," Addie said, sounding mildly surprised.

Brian made a snort of derision from deep in his throat. "Well, no shit. My dad's lost all higher brain function and—well, you know the rest that's going on. Hope's a pipe dream right now, Mom." He snorted again. "Actually, a pipe dream right now would be a full pipe of green that I could smoke."

"As satisfying as I'm sure that would be," she said, a ragged edge of anger in her voice, "it doesn't solve the problem."

"A fucking team of top-class neurosurgeons can't solve this problem, Mom. Remember? We talked to—"

"Hope doesn't just come from doctors, son," Addie said. "And if you wait for your circumstances to improve before having hope, your life is going to be a terrible waste." She turned away from him, fiddling with the curtains she'd just closed, parting them slightly to look out on the Chattanooga streets. "Hope doesn't come from the events. There's always something going wrong in the world. You don't have to do anything other than flip on the news or pick up a paper to know that."

"I get my news from Twitter, thanks."

"Then you're just as ill-informed as anyone else, I reckon," Addie said with a shrug. "But you're missing my point. Your father and I went round and round about this when you first came home. 'He needs a job, Addie,' he'd say, like that'd make a grown-up, responsible man out of you."

Brian's lips puckered in irritation. "Gee, thanks. I thought I was grown-up."

"If you've got to run to marijuana or beer or drugs anytime things go hard for you, son," Addie said, looking over her shoulder at him, "you've got a problem that just getting a job isn't going to fix."

"Nope, the reefer madness doesn't solve any problems," he said dryly. "Unless there's a Cheetos invasion, or we're drowning in Visine. Then it's a perfect cure for what ails us."

"You had no hope," she went on, ignoring him. "You didn't know your place in the world, what you were here for. Coasting along like you had no engine—"

"Well, I'm a human, so technically I don't have an engine."

"—no reason to move," she said. "No hope for finding the thing you were meant to do in this world, in this place. And I think you're still there, struggling with your role in this watch."

"Well, right now I'm mourning a dead sister and brain-dead father, but ... sure. Let's talk about my lack of direction."

"It's not about a career," Addie said, sighing. "And that's what you never got."

"I suppose I need to find my passion, huh? Like the career counselor said?"

"You need to find something that gets you moving in the morning," she said, "something that gives you a little fire in the belly. But I don't think it's just an issue of motivation. You've got no h—"

"Hope. Yeah. Heard that." He put the *Entertainment Weekly* down as he stood, the sound of pages whiffling in the chair as they slid back toward the seam. "So, why don't you tell me ... what gives you hope at a moment like this? When everything's—I'm sorry, but ... fucked. Everything's fucked!" He said it with such violence it surprised him. "Irredeemably, irretrievably *fucked*." He paused. "Do you know the difference between optimism and insanity?"

His mother stared at him warily. "No. What's the difference between optimism and insanity?"

"I'm sincerely asking," Brian said. "That's not a line from a joke.

I'm trying to figure it out right now, because it seems to me this hope, this optimism, whatever you're trying to suggest—it's a complete denial of reality. Like you expect Dad to just spontaneously heal, hop out of bed tomorrow and be fine and dandy, shake our hands, go back to ... puttering around in his study or handling guns or something. And that's not going to happen. Not that. Not the other thing—"

"What other thing?"

"Alison," he said tautly. "She's not coming b—"

"I damned well know my daughter's dead, son!" Addie said, losing her patience at last in a bout of breathless anger. "And I'm not blind or ignorant of the prognosis your father has received. But what you're missing is that optimism isn't denying reality, or failing to understand that bad things will happen, or preparing for one in case it does. Optimism is trying to find the bright spot in the darkness, trying to see how things might get better, having a belief that they will get better—"

"Demons have invaded our town, Mom," Brian said with bleak amusement. "Literal demons. They killed Alison. They did this to Dad. He's not going to get out of that bed ever again. He'll be lucky if he can string together two words. You think things are going to get better?" He let out another bark of terrible laughter. "How?"

Addison Longholt drew herself up to her full height, which was not considerable, even compared to Brian, who was on the short side. "I don't know yet. That's sort of the point of life. You don't get to see what's around every corner."

"I hate to say it, Mom, but—spoilers! It's only going to get worse from here."

"You don't know that."

He sank back into the chair, picking up the *Entertainment Weekly*. "Yeah. I kinda do." And he went back to trying to read, but he had no more luck than he'd had before.

*

"Mack!" Reeve called out, shining his light into the woods. He was being real careful, had more than a few of the others backing him up—Hendricks, Starling, the OOCs, the Guthrie half of whom was eyeing Starling with something just this side of lust, it looked like. It would have been vaguely interesting to watch her continue to size the redhead up, maybe, if this had been a dirty movie.

But for now, his focus was on Mack Wellstone and his whereabouts.

"I dunno," Hendricks said, sword glinting in the light of a dozen flashlights scanning the woods, exposing thin pines, twisted and dead-looking in the artificial white light of the headlamps. "If I was that kid ... dad dying like that, mom apparently getting ... well, whatever happened to her ... and then this shit? Pffft. I don't think my feet would touch the ground between here and the next county."

"He's just running scared," Guthrie said, still looking at Starling appraisingly. "Any one of you meat suits would be after what he's seen today."

"'Meat suit'? You're calling us 'meat suits'?" Keith Drumlin was giving a wary eye of his own to Guthrie. "So ... does that make you a something else?"

"On a form, I'd have to check a box that said, 'Something Other Than Human,' yeah," Guthrie said. "That is, if you meat suits weren't busy being blind, ignorant, and discriminatory against your non-kind and steadfastly refusing to notice us."

Drumlin edged a step away. "So ... you're a demon, then."

Guthrie seemed to find amusement in this line of inquiry. "Yeah ... and if you get too close, I'm gonna eat your eyeballs too."

"Because ... you're a demon, and that's what demons do?"

"No, idiot," Guthrie said, "because I'm a black lady, and that's what black ladies do."

Drumlin let out a small snort of amusement. "Hmph. I've known black ladies, intimately in one case. Ain't never seen one of them eat an eyeball. So I think that's the demon in you talking."

Guthrie rolled her eyes. "Ain't nothing in here but demon, idiot."

"How long are we going to blunder around looking for this kid?" This one came from Hendricks.

"You scared, cowboy?" Erin stepped into the conversation.

Hendricks just smiled, hat down and shadowing his eyes. "A little, yeah. Not that I don't enjoy your company in the dark woods, Erin, but I get the feeling if we went for a moonlit stroll right now, we wouldn't be alone for long, if you know what I mean." Her face tightened up, but she didn't interrupt him. "There are an awful lot of these things out here, lurking in the dark. Now I know everyone's instinct here is to go charging in after this kid, and hey, I get that. First into danger, been there, done that. But given what this kid has run into ... if we go out there and try to execute a normal search pattern, it means we've got to split up, or at least form a line with a gap of twenty to fifty feet between us, right? Then march in?"

Reeve chewed the skin inside his cheek. "That's usually how it's done."

"Well, let me tell you a little something you already know about that sort of formation, in these woods, tonight—it's a real good way to get a whole lot of us dead." Hendricks's voice was low, and dead earnest at last.

"That cowboy's not wrong," Casey Meacham said.

"Kind of a chickenshit," Erin said tightly, "but ... no. Probably not wrong."

"Hey, if you guys want to go marching in, I am right there with you," Hendricks said, chucking a thumb over his shoulder. "I will be like—maybe five steps behind Erin, because like two guys and the bear, I only really need to outrun her, not those things, but—still, I'm with you."

"You cock face," Erin said.

"Sheriff?" Nate McMinn asked, stepping up next to him. "What should we do?"

Reeve let out a low sigh. Hell if he hadn't seen more of his damned constituents wiped out in the last couple weeks than any time in all his years in law enforcement—combined. But this kid ... this Mack Wellstone ...

"First we lost his daddy," Reeve said, "then, somehow, we lost his mom ... and now ..." He put a hand on his forehead and wiped at the thin sheen of sweat there. "Hell, I think these things done wiped out the whole family in one day."

"Not the first time that's happened in this town lately," Hendricks said, and he sounded a little huskier than usual.

"Won't be the last either," Guthrie said, almost cheerfully.

"Now *you're* being a cock face," Duncan said.

"Unlike the cowboy, I haven't had any cock in this face," Guthrie said. "Trust me, I'd remember."

"We could rectify that real quick, if'n you got an interest," Casey Meacham said, sidling up.

Guthrie gave him a sour look. "You should stick to hookers, guy."

How had it come to this? Reeve wondered. Now he wasn't just dealing with losing people here and there, piecemeal. That shit on the square had kicked off a whole new level of wrong in Midian.

The apocalypse seemed to be getting closer all the time, but now it was taking more than baby steps forward.

"Should we try again tomorrow?" Keith Drumlin asked. "Maybe in the daylight—"

Reeve just shook his head. "I'm gonna issue an advisory: everyone needs to stay out of the woods until such time as we can clean these things out." He started to bury his face in his hand again, then stopped when he realized showing despair wasn't a real smart way to lead. "And we do need to sort them out, quick."

"Yeah, it's hunting season, and my business is at stake," Casey said. "If I don't stuff some deer, I ain't gonna be able to stuff Ms. Cherry, if you know what I mean."

"What a terrible tragedy," Guthrie said with mock sympathy.

"Hey, man, I don't think you know how much money that injects into the local economy," Casey said.

"Please don't tell us about your stimulus package," Duncan said.

"Heh," Hendricks said, "he 'injects' it with his 'package.'"

"Yeah, that's the joke, cowboy," Duncan said. "Way to ruin it by shaking all the subtle out of it."

"Oh, I get it," Drumlin said. "Yeah, that's pretty funny."

"Let's get out of here," Reeve said quietly. Somehow, everyone heard him, and they started to turn back toward the edge of the woods. Reeve stayed, staring into the darkness between the trees, listening for a hint of something—some sign that Mack Wellstone was still alive out there, hiding, maybe. "Mack!" he called one last time, and listened to the sound echo through the woods. But the only response he got was the sound of his compatriots shuffling through the dead leaves, and after a minute he turned and followed along behind them, feeling like he'd left a lot more than just that boy in the woods tonight.

*

Arch was looking over the abandoned car real carefully, wondering if a clue was sitting in plain sight, something he wasn't noticing with just his usual police observation skills. He knew a few things, after all—that a man tugging at his pocket or his pants meant they could be holding a weapon in there, that if someone's eyes were darting around furtively, they could well be lying. There were always little tells, things about human behavior that gave you away.

But what could you deduce from a car sitting on the side of the road, airbags deployed and popped, and a little spot of blood on the steering wheel?

Heck if he knew.

"They hit the trap back there," Arch said, trying to work it out in his head. Why was this so important to him? This particular thing, this part of the incident? They'd just been attacked by a solid several hundred cats from Hades. A kid was missing.

Why was he fixating on this abandoned car?

He looked around; even Barney and Tarley were off in the middle of the road, manning the defense, waiting to hear if someone shouted from the search party that was up in the woods. It had seemed too foolish to send everyone in, given what they knew was lurking out there.

Why was he focusing on this?

Because he was the only one who was paying attention to it. It was calling out to him, and him alone.

"You say something, Arch?" Nate McMinn wandered over, hands on his hips, looking at the woods past him like they were going to burst open and deliver another herd of psychotic shadowcats any second. And in fairness, they just might do that very thing.

"Working through something out loud," Arch said, putting his head in through the car window. "She hit the trap back there—"

"Wait, there's a trap back there?" Nate asked.

"Piece of plywood filled with roofing nails," Arch said. "Can you think of any reason it'd be sitting in the middle of Faulkner Road?"

"Piece of roof blew off a truck, maybe?"

"Maybe," Arch said. "You see much construction going on around here?"

"Well, they're building that new subdivision out on the south end of town," Nate said. "But ... I don't reckon they'd be anywhere near here. Someone could be doing a new roof, hauling the junk to the dump ... but that's in the other direction ... unless it's one of the folks lives down here ..."

"Seems unlikely, doesn't it?" Arch asked.

"There's some ... improbabilities, I guess," Nate said.

"A trap makes more sense," Arch said, "but let's assume you're right for a second. One of the people down this road lost a piece of roof with a mess of nails in it. Either way, Ms. Wellstone and her boy hit it, right over there." He gestured around the curve behind them. "They slide around the corner, come to a stop here." He stood back up, careful not to bump his head on the car as he extricated himself. "Something happens. The son says she was attacked. Ms. Wellstone's head got rammed into the wheel."

"You're thinking demon," Nate said. "A demon did it."

"Could be a human, I guess, but it hardly seems likely a human's going to start stalking and killing people when we're in the middle of a demon invasion," Arch said. "Yeah, I'm thinking demon. And then they carted Ms. Wellstone away while her boy ran off in fright."

"Well, hopefully they find him—" Nate started to say, then turned his head to where the would-be rescuers were coming back out of the woods. "Oh. Well, that don't look good." He raised his voice. "Hey, Keith! What are y'all doing?"

Keith Drumlin shook his head at McMinn. "We're not going after him tonight. Too many of those things in the woods, we'd have to string out and make ourselves tempting snacks for those hellcats."

"Well, damn," Nate said. "That's a shame. You reckon that boy will make it through the night out there?"

Arch took a hard breath. Mack Wellstone had run right into those woods in the midst of that fight, and there were hundreds of those shadowcats out there, maybe thousands. They ran faster than a human, way, way faster, and Mack Wellstone probably wasn't taking time to be quiet. It was an ugly conclusion, and it turned Arch's stomach to come to it, but he reckoned that one was going to turn out to be a "like father, like son" sort of ending. "I don't expect he's still drawing breath even now, but if he is ... he won't be for long if he stays in those woods."

"Shit," McMinn said. "Man, I knew things were bad after what happened on the square, but I didn't see this demon cat thing coming. I mean, people we know being possessed and tearing shit up is crazy, right? But this is like a whole different level, you know? You can kinda ... imagine something bad happening with people. People do terrible shit all the time, all over the world. But these things ...? They defy explanation. Like every stray cat in the county got dipped in darkness and got big, and started killing shit." McMinn shook his head. "A plague of them damned things just descended on us."

"Yeah," Arch said idly, looking back down at the steering wheel with the spot of blood. How was it that McMinn was laying out a terrible scenario, a herd of those things, rampaging through the woods ... and here he was, the only one wondering about this other mystery? A disappearing woman—why was that the thing that sparked his interest in all this?

Well ... he had just had a woman of his own vanish from his life ...

Arch shook that thought off. "It's a terrible thing," he said to McMinn, putting a hand on the car door. Everyone else was going to be focused on this other threat, these cats, and he'd be involved in the solution on that, whenever it came up. But this ... he looked down at the blood spot again ... Ms. Wellstone's disappearance was all set to be one of the things that slipped through the cracks of Midian County's justice system right now, and something about that he just couldn't abide. *I'm going to find who did this to you,* he said to himself, not wanting to say it out loud and have McMinn question him about it. It was a faint thought so far, a little flicker of a flame, this desire to see justice done—on this, at least.

But it was his, dadgummit ... this one little task was his, and he'd see it completed if it was the last thing he did.

Because it just might be.

*

When the car bumped onto the onramp for the interstate, Molly finally shed her silence. "Where are we going?" Her brows were arched, staring intently at the road.

"Chattanooga," Lauren said. She was white-knuckling the wheel, shoulders hunched.

"For the night?" Molly asked.

"No," Lauren said, steering the car to merge with the light traffic heading south on I-75. "For good."

"What?" The anger was back now, Molly's face catching a passing headlight from oncoming traffic and her mouth going wide in an outraged O.

"We're out of here," Lauren said, trying to sound casual even though her heart was hammering in her chest. "This is crazy. We're crazy if we stay. So ... we're out. No more living in a whorehouse, no more attending funerals like this is a film festival and we want to catch as many as we can. We're out. Done. Gone. Not going back."

"But Midian is *home*." Molly's whispered voice was choked with outrage. When Lauren didn't immediately reply, Molly started to build some steam. "Grandpa died here. Grandma—this is home. This is where our home is—"

"But we don't live there anymore," Lauren said, changing lanes to slide between two monstrous semi-trucks rolling their way down the road. "Do we? I don't want to go back to our house; do you?"

Molly flinched as though she'd been slapped. "No, but that doesn't mean—"

"Kid, the town is crawling with demons. They're literally swarming out of the woods now." She gripped tight the wheel as she drove. "There's nothing we can do about that, so ... why stay?"

"The watch is doing something about it," Molly said, sitting up straighter in her seat. "That's the point of us being there. To fight back with the others."

"They can fight back just as well without us." *Without you,* she didn't say. Whether they'd be all right without a doctor ... well ... The important thing was getting Molly clear of this mess.

"But Grandma and Grandpa died there—"

"And you think they'd want us to too?" Lauren asked. "Like ... right now? Because we've had some near misses, and I don't love the idea of continuing to push our luck." She lowered her voice. "I know you remember the Summer Lights Festi—"

"That's low," Molly said. "Of course I remember."

"I almost lost you, kid," Lauren said, steering the car back into the right lane and slowing it down so she could focus on what she had to say. "That demon—do you know what he did to his victims? Impregnated them. I heard all about it from Hendricks a little while back. He hit a small town in Alabama and knocked up this girl with demon puppies. When they came out, they'd burned everything, killed everyone. Hendricks and Alison saw it with their own damned eyes—nothing left in the town but burnt-out buildings and a crazy girl with her dog babies."

"Sick," Molly said, evincing distaste and pushing it aside quickly. "But that doesn't mean we should—"

"That was almost you," Lauren said. "You almost ended up—God, how could I have been so stupid to let this go for so long?"

"Just because you think I was about to become a one-woman demonic puppy mill—"

"I don't 'think' it, okay? I know it. That guy—Mick or Mike or whatever his fake human name was—he was going to rape you, seed you with those things, and let the town just burn. Like he'd probably done a thousand times before."

"I kinda doubt a thousand towns have dropped off the map in America," Molly said sullenly, looking away.

"I don't," Lauren said. "The point is ... I thought I was going to—I was so scared for you that night. And when you came out of it safe and sound, I guess—I don't know, I was so stuck on the idea of demons that I got ... obsessed. Medically interested. But I screwed up because instead of following my curiosity I should have been looking out for you. And this town, Midian ... it's not a safe place for kids."

"I'm fine, okay—"

"Yeah, but I don't think Mack Wellstone is," Lauren said. "Abilene Tarley sure as hell isn't. Dozens of others—I mean, Jesus, you were on the fucking square, you saw what happened—kids died just like anybody else in that hell—"

"Stop, just stop! You're—you're so scared all of a sudden—"

"I'm reacting reasonably to a dangerous situation, okay?"

"You're—you're acting like a chickenshit. And I don't need—"

"You need to be safe. Secure. Not have demons coming after you to rape you and rip your flesh off and turn you into a weapon to destroy your own damned family—"

"Well, I don't know how much good I'd be of a weapon after they ripped my flesh off—"

"I'm fucking terrified for you, kid, don't you get it?" Lauren's restraint burst, and it all came flooding out at once—the fear, the anger, the tears she'd held back while they were being chased around by those hellcats. "Every damned day. And yeah, I know, I know—learning about blowjobs and fucking and—hell, even meeting a human boy and having underaged sex with him every night at this point isn't exactly a grave threat—"

"Ew, Mom!"

"—but don't you get it? I'm freaking out over the little stuff because the big stuff—goddamn, it's fucking daunting. Every day in Midian right now brings some fresh, sulfur-stinking hell of the sort that Dorothy Parker couldn't even have imagined ringing her doorbell. It's non-stop, and it's not going to get better. Every day I have to be afraid. So forgive me for freaking out about boys and hookers talking to you about the beautiful and natural process of deep-throating a dick until it spurts in your mouth—"

Molly made a gagging noise. "Seriously, you can stop anytime."

"—all salty and warm and sticky. You know what it tastes like? It tastes like—"

"Ohgodohgodohgodmakeitstoppleeeeeeeease—"

"—like liverwurst and ass all ground up together with a jerk of flavor like what I imagine rat piss tastes like—"

"Jesus save me."

"These are the things you don't ask," Lauren said. "And it doesn't really matter. At this point, I should be ecstatic if you live long enough to suck a dick or two. Hell, twelve, though preferably not all at once."

"This is so fucked up. Why is this so fucked up? Why are you being so fucked up?"

"Because if you make it that long," Lauren said, breath coming out raggedly, along with her words, "to deep-throat a few cocks—"

"Please stop saying that!"

"—or to have real, honest-to-God, terrible first-time sex, to feel that hurt—you know, down there—"

"Fucking shit, Mom. This is so—this is just fucked."

"—and then, you know, you work your way through that shit phase until it starts to get decent, then good, and, God willing, really, really, mind-blowingly good, because you know what you like, and what works for you—"

"I want to not be listening to this, but it's like a car wreck on the side of the road as you pass. It's an auditory car wreck. I can't stop listening. There are even screams in my head."

"—because sex can be so, so good. So good. And even better if it's with someone you really like or love—and I want that for you. More than anything, because if you get to it—it means you made it, kid." Lauren felt the tension start to bleed out of her. "And after these last few days, weeks … shit … that's all I want for you at this point. For you to make it so that you can feel that knee-quivering sensation of having the lights go out for you when you hit a big, big O with the right guy while riding his—"

Molly buried her face in her hands. "Of all my childhood traumas, this may be the one that scars me longest."

"—huge dick," Lauren said. "Because of course it should be huge in this imaginary dream of hope I have for you. I've only ever wanted the best for you, and this—I mean, a huge dick would be best. Not the first time, but you know, work your way up to it. Because it would mean *you survived*." She laughed and cried a little at the same time. "And honestly … that just doesn't seem likely to happen in Midian. Not this week. Not this month. Not this year. I don't think anyone who stays is going to make it out of there alive, and kid—I want more for you than for you to die at the teeth of some goddamned demon hell army. I want you to be able to lose your virginity. To have a happy wedding day at some point—"

"After I've taken like fifty or a hundred huge dicks in all my orifices, probably, at the rate your standards are presently decaying."

"—and maybe, someday, ruin sex for your kids the way I'm doing for you, right now." Lauren sighed. "But that's not happening if we stay in Midian. It just won't."

"You don't know that," Molly said, but she was desperately pale again, and her reply was weaker.

"If you take fifty to a hundred huge dicks in Midian, I mean just by virtue of the population skew, you're going to be scraping the bottom of the barrel to make that happen. I mean, we're talking dregs here—"

"Fuck off about the dicks, okay?" Molly said. "I'm a virgin and I intend to stay that way for the foreseeable future, all right? Enough of the dick talk!" She deflated. "Real talk now, please?"

"Dick talk isn't real talk?"

"I'm serious."

"Dicks feel pretty real. Huge ones, especially. So real when they're—"

"Fuck! Stop acting like a child, Mom!" Molly stared out the window.

"I don't want to die, but ... Jesus. Leaving home? I mean, seriously?"

"You saw what happened back there," Lauren said. "Those things ... how many there were?"

"Yeah, but ... that's not ... insurmountable," Molly said. "Is it?"

"I wouldn't want to ... surmount it," Lauren said lamely. "Like a—"

"If you make a huge dick mounting joke I will open this car door and bail out on the interstate, and when the State Patrol finds me, I'm going to say I was kidnapped by a crazy lady who wanted me to fuck a hundred huge dicks."

"We were staying in a whorehouse," Lauren said quietly. "I feel like this might not be stretching the truth too far if we'd stayed there longer, if only by neglect."

"Ugh," Molly said. "Prostitution is not like an STD; I wasn't catching it, okay? At no point did I say, 'Hey, you know, Lucia seems like a totally well-adjusted and put together person; why not take career advice from her?' I was just ... curious about things. Mysterious things." She made a sour face. "Things which you have taken any mystery and allure out of, completely. Grossly, even."

"Seriously, the taste would gag you. Liverwurst and ass and yuck."

"I didn't want to be like Lucia, all right?" Molly hunched lower in her seat. "I just wanted to know things. Maybe I felt the bite of mortality, of the town sliding ... and I was curious."

"Mortality's bite doesn't have much to do with a teen being curious about sex, kid. It's kinda written into your hormones."

"Whatever," Molly said. "So ..." She seemed defeated, which was maybe a worse look on her than her curiosity, her trauma—any of the other things she'd seen on her daughter's face these last few weeks, or before that, going back to when she was a child and fell off her bike and started to cry from the wrist sprain. "What now?"

"I have a friend in Chattanooga," Lauren said. "From work. Elise. She's in private practice, so she's loaded. We can stay with her."

"And then?" Molly asked. "Then what?"

"I should probably go back to work," Lauren said, "before I get fired. And then ..." She stared straight ahead, into the dark, unknowable night. The road curved ahead, around a big hill. Trees waved on either side, and there were only a sparse few lights in this section of the freeway. "... and then ..."

"Then what?" Molly asked.

Lauren opened her mouth to answer but found she didn't have one. "I don't know," she finally said. "Whatever comes next."

*

It felt like defeat, that walk back from the edge of the woods, like taking the kick in the teeth and running away, which rankled Erin. There was a ripple of anger running hot under her skin that had been there since even before those fucking assholes had co-opted her body to do murder. But that hadn't made it better, had it?

Nope.

No, it had only made it worse. It was a raw sort of itch, and she wondered if fighting alone would scratch it. Before the demons had hit town she'd gotten that kind of restless desire every now and again, and she'd drowned it with alcohol and fucking, which seemed like a sensible plan in a small town. Beat getting married.

"Such a shame," Duncan said, jarring Erin out of her reverie. When she looked at him blankly, Duncan elaborated. "The kid, I mean. He ran from one kind of trouble that he might have survived—" he made a hand motion to envelope the perimeter of cars that was set up like circled wagons on Faulkner Road "—into another kind he couldn't hope to."

"You don't know it for sure," Erin said. She wouldn't have laid any money on the boy making it through though. She didn't have much to begin with, and certainly not enough to waste it on sucker bets.

"Oh, we know it for sure, sweet cheeks," Guthrie chimed in. Getting used to Lerner as a black lady was tough, but whenever she piped up like this, it got easier to accept. "A tween versus hundreds of snarling v'k'thw'sh? Even your ex—" Guthrie jerked her head to indicate Hendricks, who was walking along with Starling at his side, engaged in some kind of deep conversation "—could figure out who wins in that scenario."

"We've just been calling them hellcats," Erin said. "Or I have."

Duncan kind of blinked at her. "Hellcats works."

"Rolls off you peoples' tongues easier," Guthrie said.

"Why are they here now?" Erin asked, and then chastised herself as she caught the pitying look from Guthrie. "Just the hotspot?"

"'Just the hotspot,'" Guthrie said mockingly. "Sweet knees, the hotspot is not 'just' anything; for demons it's everything. It's the sweet call of momma singing you home on a Sunday afternoon."

Erin gave him a little sneer. "I kinda doubt you've got a momma that sang you home on Sunday or any other day."

"Just trying to talk to you on your level, kiddo," Guthrie said with a savage smile. "A hotspot's a big draw, especially for these barely sentient types like your so-called hellcats. They can feel the thrum of that shit on the other side of the planet. Hell, these probably swam the Atlantic to get here, because they're normally indigenous to Africa and I doubt anyone would be dumb enough to try and round them up for importation."

"What is it about a hotspot that calls you demons?" Erin asked.

Duncan, less of an asshat, took it on himself to answer. "It's just something hard-wired into who we are. Like a dog whistle, we can hear it—or feel it, more accurately. It's a pulse in the soul, or essence, or whatever you want to call it. It's instinctive."

"So you feel it too?" Erin asked.

"A little," Duncan admitted. "Not like these things though. Like I said, it's an instinctive thing, and for those of us a little more evolved than animals—"

"Which doesn't include your species, obviously," Guthrie said matter-of-factly.

"—it's less of a main event and more of a sideshow we can choose to ignore," Duncan said, giving Guthrie a reproachful look.

"Like the sex drive of men, it's constant," Guthrie said with a smirk. "Women? Not so much, maybe, but just like guys are always thinking about the same thing, low-functioning demon intelligences are always looking for hotspots. They're the equivalent of getting laid."

"It's always an illuminating conversation with you, Lerner, or Guthrie, whatever you're calling yourself between vapes," Erin said.

Guthrie just grinned. "Nice pushback, kid. You're learning. I could almost get to like you, even after that time you got me thrown back to hell."

"Really?" Erin shrugged. "I guess, like a woman's sex drive, I'm just not feeling it." She gave Guthrie a nasty grin which was met by a guffaw that sounded otherworldly. "So, these things ... how do we get rid of them?"

"Same as any other demon," Duncan said. "There's just ... you know, more of them."

"You're not kidding," Erin said. "What else are these things going do? I mean, with that many of them running through the countryside?"

Duncan looked more than a little uncomfortable at that question. "Well ... they usually aren't together in such high numbers. These ... hellcats ... they're pack hunters, but packs are like—"

"Five," Guthrie said. "Usually no more than five. It's a small, social unit. I've often pondered—"

"Shut up," Duncan said. "No one cares about your ponderings. The point is—this is unusual, to say the least. In a group of five, hellcats can raise some pretty big havoc. Attack farms, wreck cars ..." He nodded to the police cruiser that looked like it had been shredded from the inside out, pieces of metal and glass strewn across the asphalt. "A few hundred though …"

"Shit," Erin said, shaking her head. Of course they had another cataclysm ramping up. Why would they get a break for a day or two during a demon invasion, after all?"

"I think she's starting to get it," Guthrie said. "But don't worry, kiddo—now that you've all seen the problem, I'm sure you'll—I dunno, assemble the army, saddle up the cavalry—whatever it is you loons do."

"We're with you, by the way," Duncan said. "Because Guthrie won't say it. We are."

"Hell no, I wouldn't say it." Guthrie looked mildly affronted. "Why would I voice support for riding into a battle with hundreds of these things with meat suits as our backup? We'd be better off with a glarhnsanng at our backs."

Duncan didn't blink. "These things … they're the clearest, most present danger, and to have them all together like this? A formula for speeding up the entropy around here. If you mean to take them out … we'll help, because this is right, square in the middle of our mission."

"Shit," Guthrie said mildly. "Committing us to action again. You twat. Or rather, lack of twat."

"Great," Erin said, looking for Reeve in the middle of all this. He needed to know about this, and fast. Not like he didn't already see the way things were going, probably, having witnessed the shitstorm that just blew through with those hellcats, but still. If the OOCs were onboard, this thing was plainly the big crisis of the moment—if they could even narrow it down to just one in Midian right now.

*

"You know what the sad fucking thing is?" Hendricks asked Starling as he meandered away from his awkward as hell discussion with the doctor and her soon-to-be terminally fucked daughter. "I think that girl used to be normal. This is what happens when you stay in a shitbox town that's going straight to hell."

Starling just did that thing where she cocked her head at him, like she didn't understand his use of the word 'shitbox.'

"I have a hard time understanding exactly what you understand," Hendricks said, shaking his head. "Honestly, before we started screwing, I would have wondered if you even knew what fucking was." She stared at him. "I mean, your other persona clearly does, but—"

"What she knows, I know," Starling said.

"Well then, Lucia must be real dumb not to understand some of the basic things people have said to you over the last few weeks."

Starling stirred, looking at the ground. "What she knows, I know ... but I don't understand everything she knows."

"Well, now we're making some progress," Hendricks said. "So, you take a body for a drive, but you don't quite ... get everything? The comprehension part of it? Is it a little like you're overlaying your personality on top of hers?" He felt a mild discomfort. "Does she even know you're doing anything with her? Because she didn't seem to know your name the time I asked her—"

"She knows who I am," Starling said simply.

"Then why didn't she—" He stopped himself. "Yeah. Why would she say anything? 'Yeah, Mister, I've got a random angel being stuck in my body.' Like there ain't enough crazy shit already going on around here."

Starling just stared at him.

"Well, I suppose it's about time to call it a night," Hendricks said. The search was off, which was probably disappointing to a few people, but he found it kinda hard to get exercised about it. Yeah, it sucked that Mack kid was out there, alone, probably dead or dying, but—

"He is an innocent, isn't he?" Starling asked.

Hendricks chewed on that one for a second, even though he knew who she was talking about right away. "Mack? Yeah. I'd say so."

"Why did you leave the child to roam the woods?" Starling asked.

"You know why," Hendricks said, feeling a little stung by that question.

"Prudence," Starling said.

"How about 'not getting everyone killed to chase a kid halfway to hell and gone through the woods'?" He scuffed a boot against the pavement and it scraped loudly. "You saw what's out there."

"Slightly less than a thousand of the creatures you call hellcats ... and a scared child," she said tonelessly.

"Fuck," Hendricks said, squeezing his right hand tight. "Is he going to make it through to the morning?"

She didn't even blink. "No."

"How far away is he?" Now Hendricks's interest was raised. Starling had always shown a talent for appearing and disappearing close to his sorry ass, but the idea that she could track others? Never occurred to him.

"Far," she said.

"Like ... minutes away? Or farther?"

"Out of your reach," Starling said.

"That mean he's treed? Like a fox?"

She didn't reply to that.

"Fuck," Hendricks said again. Now he was questioning this decision. "I gotta—"

"There is nothing you can do," she said and seized him by the shoulder. It wasn't rough—not any rougher than she'd been in the bedroom, at least—but there was a commanding amount of force applied to his shoulder. He didn't quite know how to take it; if it had been a dude doing it, he would have decked the motherfucker.

With Starling, though ...

"There is nothing you can do," she said again.

"Then why'd you ask why I did it?"

"Because I am curious about you," she said, and strangely, that admission prompted a stirring below his belt. It didn't take much thinking to figure out why—it had been a while since a woman had shown a real interest in him.

"I could say the same about you," Hendricks said.

Her hand was still planted on his pec, like she was afraid he'd charge past and go after little Mack. "It is curious to me ... how easily you fit into the role of hero."

He narrowed his eyes. "Every time I think you might be wending toward a compliment, you take a left turn into something that feels like a passive-aggressive insult."

She cocked her at that too. "You are a hero."

There was a sinking feeling in his stomach. "I'm not feeling too much like one right this second, given I might have just condemned that boy to die."

She processed that for a moment more and said, "But if you had all gone, you would have all died."

She sounded so certain that it eased his mind, just a little. "You sure about that?"

The answer came back unreserved. "Yes."

His stomach still churned with unease. "Well, all right then." He turned and stared back into the woods nonetheless. This was the shit side of regret, always wondering whether you're making the right call in tough situations. But this quasi-divine—not that Hendricks believed much in the divine, but still—this being that seemed to know shit that he didn't know about—she said he was in the right on this one, no matter how shitty it felt to walk away from a person in need. How much shittier would it have been to walk most of the watch into an ambush?

It was probably the right call. He could imagine them working their way through the woods, twigs and leaves crackling beneath their feet as they shone their lights the next twenty, the next thirty feet ahead. They'd be calling, "Maaaaack!" in loud, echoing voices over the hills and hollows in these woods, stringing themselves out in long lines to cover the most ground. Hell, they probably wouldn't even hear the approach of those things until it was too late.

Hendricks's stomach twisted like a hellcat had run one of those shadowy claws over it, and he shuddered, imagining his intestines spilling out into his hands, trying to push them back in, slimy and slick, the stink of rotten food and shit roaring up his nostrils unstoppably while he fell to his knees.

Yeah, staying out of those woods was wise, at least for now. He'd settled it in his head, and started to turn to Starling to say so, but ... hell if she wasn't gone, leaving him standing in the same spot without a damned thing to do.

"What's the matter?" Erin Harris called out at him from behind her car. She was watching with a smirk. "Your imaginary girlfriend disappear again?"

"Guess so," Hendricks said, her comment causing his cheeks to burn a little now that he'd left most of the warring emotions over calling off the search behind. "It's all right though. I *imagine* she'll appear again later tonight, on my dick. Better than a booty call." He smiled, guessing this was going to go over like a lead balloon.

Erin froze for just a second, and he watched his smartass bomb strike home. She probably was being an asshole, making that comment when she didn't even know the two of them were knocking boots. Erin was good for one of those every now and again. She turned away, either because she was trying to be the bigger person or because she didn't have anything smart to say. Hendricks didn't give a fuck about trying to figure out which. He just headed for his purloined SUV to get back to the Sinbad motel.

Because Starling probably would show up later for some dick, and he wanted to be ready.

Interlude

Two Years Earlier

Raymond Creasy had that look about him that screamed bad boy. Twenty-two, denim shirt over his tanned muscles—she'd seen him with it off, and those tattoos, purrrrrrr—and how he wore those jeans. Mmm. It was enough to give Lucia a yearning to get closer, and get closer she did.

He was the best thing about her new digs. New mom, new dad—not even close to same as the old—new neighborhood, new school, new friends. She'd been fostered because no one in her family wanted to take her in. Her grandma was too old, and her aunt was busy raising eight kids of her own as a single mother.

So here she was in her own little new world, mom and dad dead and her staying with Michael and Karen. But two doors down was Ray Creasy, and he liked to drink beer and work on cars with his shirt off. He had his own house that he was renting, he drove a badass Chevelle from the seventies—she didn't know much about cars, but it was hot, like him—and here she was on a Saturday night without permission, sitting in the Chevelle on an old dirt road, sipping beer with Ray in the back seat and listening to the crickets outside.

"You sure this is okay?" she asked. "Don't cops get mad when you got an open beer in the car?" She sipped again. It was tangy, Michelob Golden. She suppressed the desire to spit it out the window. She'd been working on it slowly for a while and it was starting to get better.

"You're from the Georgia side of Chattanooga, aren't you?" Ray asked. He looked pretty damned amused about it, like he knew something she didn't. He lifted the beer and guzzled it, draining the rest of it in one. He damned sure liked those things; every time she saw him he had one. Amazing he managed to keep a six-pack of abs given how much he drank. Her dad had taken down a six-pack a night and was working on storing his own keg on his belly before he'd died.

"Yeah." A flash of insecurity made the car heat up for Lucia. He could tell that? She felt out of place again, like he knew she was Georgian and was judging her for it, but also like he could smell her virginity in the small space between them, another thing for him to not like about her.

Fuck, what *was* there to like about her? She looked away. She was stupid, ugly, her mouth was too big—

"There's no open container law in Tennessee." He touched her chin, turning her face back to him. "They call it the 'Hold my beer' law. You just hand your beer over to the person in the passenger seat and boom—no problem here, officer."

"Yeah, but I ain't legal to drink," Lucia said.

"So you'd get an underage ticket—who gives a shit?" Ray laughed. "I'd pay it for you."

That sounded pretty fair to her. She took another sip of the beer, but ended up letting about half of it wash out of her mouth and back into the can. Her tongue rubbed against the sharp edge of the can's mouth; felt like she was going to cut herself.

She lowered the can and found Ray right there, tight against her. His shoulder was pressed to her left arm, his hand on her bare knee. Lucia was wearing short shorts, and his fingers rubbed against her smooth skin where she'd shaved her legs for this date. Her foster parents didn't know where she was; she hadn't taken her cell phone along because she didn't want to hear the steady buzz of it going off, and it was easier to say, "Oh, I just forgot," than to try and explain why their worried calls went to voicemail for the next two or three hours.

He was warm against her, and he pushed his lips against hers before she almost had a chance to swallow that foul-tasting beer. He shoved his tongue in her mouth quickly, parting her lips just as she got the last of it down. She kept from choking on it and looking like the stupid idiot she was, accepting his tongue as gratefully as she could given the surprise of it showing up and probing all the way back to her tonsils. She forced her eyes shut until he finished, leaving her with the taste of beer and a little excess slobber dripping down her chin.

"Ahhh," Ray said as she opened her eyes, and she heard something rattling. She looked down and saw him fumbling with his belt, unfastening it with one hand, beer still clutched in the other. He went to the button of his pants next, then the zipper of his jeans made its way down with a staticky noise to reveal his yellow-striped boxer shorts beneath.

Lucia got this sick sense of dread, like she'd known this was coming but she wasn't really ready anyway. She put on the brave face, though, because she didn't want to disappoint him. Ray reached into the slitted gap of his boxers and from it he pulled out his dick.

Lucia had seen a dick or two on TV. They'd never really elicited any response but, "Oh, gross," from her before, the thought of that mushroom-headed noodle getting anywhere near her a slightly repellent one.

But now she kept her face as straight as possible. Ray had his fleshy instrument out, and it didn't look too big, maybe a little wider than a couple of her fingers put together. He presented it to her, hand wrapped around its base, like it was some kind of gift. He was grinning widely, and wagged it at her. "Come on then," he said, like she was supposed to know what he meant.

She did know what he meant though, or at least she thought she did. A blowjob, right? She froze in place for just a second, a little loop going through her head:

I don't want to put that thing in my mouth.
But—
I want him to like me.
But—
I really don't want to put that thing in my mouth.
But—
I really, really want him to like me. Really, really—

She went for it. It felt halting, awkward, filled with the lingering worry that he was going to *know*, somehow, how nervous and sick she felt at the sight of his penis. She touched it first, and it felt sticky, sweaty, the hot Tennessee night making Ray sweat even before they'd gotten in the back seat. The Chevelle's air conditioning didn't work all that well, after all.

She paused as she got close, getting a full whiff of the dick now. It smelled funny, like an armpit but a little worse. It wasn't like she smelled good down there, either, all the time, but this was different, it was—

Now the regret was settling in, now that she had a hand on his dick and it was poised about two inches from her lips. Did she really have to do this?

I really, really, really want him to like me.

She opened up her mouth and shoved it in, trying to remember what she'd heard Virginia Jenkins say to that group of girls in seventh grade about giving head. It was a long time ago, but it was all she had in terms of firsthand experience, and it basically boiled down to—

form your lips into an O over the surface of his dick and move your head up and down fast.

Lucia did just that, trying to ignore the taste, which was sweaty, like an old gym sock right under her nose as she breathed through it, and ran her mouth over his shaft, burying her nose briefly in his slightly damp pubic hair with each lift. It was like sucking on a lollipop that had been dipped in dirty underwear, and then it started to ooze from the tip, this salty, nasty—

She came up for air and felt like she was going to gag, holding it back with everything she had in her. She hadn't been able to look up at Ray's face during, because he was seated and she'd been thrusting her mouth right into his lap, but she looked up at him now with watery eyes. His dick had tickled the back of her throat, damned near getting the gag reflex.

He was leaned back, smile wide on his face. "Mmm," he said, like he was stirring awake, his eyes coming open, "that was a good start."

Oh God, she thought, how could she do any more?

As if he could see her frozen, deer-in-the-cock-headlights look, Ray opened his eyes again and leaned forward, planting his lips on her neck. That actually felt kind of good, tickling a little. He worked up to her ear, put his tongue in it. That didn't feel so good. He landed a pawing hand on her breast, grabbing at her small tit through the bra.

"Mmmmhmmm," Ray said, tugging at the bottom of her tank top. She let him lift it up over her head, moving her arms to allow it. It was better than the thought of going back down on that cock of his.

Once her shirt was off, he threw it in the front seat and ran his hands up her sides, rough palms and fingers running over her ribs and back to her bra hook. He fumbled for a couple minutes, cursing under his breath in her ear, the smell of Michelob Golden almost enough to start her retching after all.

Her bra popped loose with a surprising amount of force, especially considering there wasn't much beneath it. Ray pulled the bra off and Lucia tried to cover herself, blocking one nipple with a hand and the other with an elbow, breathing in sharply as she did so, instinctively.

She caught herself in the moment, his tongue still working its way through her mouth. She didn't want him to know she was a virgin. She just needed to be cool, to let him see her tits as they were, no big deal. It wasn't like she could augment them here and now, anyway.

Lucia pulled her hands from her chest and opened her eyes; his were still closed, but a second later his roaming hand found her right nipple and pinched it, drawing a sharp prick of pain and discomfort. She stifled the urge to take so much as a sharp breath to indicate the pain, even as he twisted slightly on the nipple.

I want him to like me.

His hands didn't press and twist for long; they moved south, to the button of her jean shorts. Lucia's breaths were coming in short gasps now, a panicked feeling running the length of her like she was going to burst into flames at any second, like hell was going to reach out and get her for this. This was wrong, wasn't it? Letting him feel her titties, putting his dick in her mouth, and—and whatever happened next—

But I want him to like me.

He opened her fly button and cranked down the zipper of her shorts with surprising violence; the teeth let out a squeal. Ray was breathing heavily now, his face moving to her neck, kissing her, leaning into her. He struggled with her shorts, trying to rip them down while she was still sitting on them.

Lucia lowered herself back, thumping her head lightly on the door of the Chevelle. It hurt, but she didn't let it distract her. Ray's weight was on her, then subsided as he pulled at her shorts. She lifted her hips and they slid off, leaving the soft, cotton panties a half inch below their usual spot, her crotch feeling curiously bare even though it was still covered from sight by the underwear.

Ray snatched that a moment later, dragging it off with the shorts. Both ended up in a pile in the floorboard, and Lucia glanced at them forlornly. "Looks like the curtains match the carpet," Ray said with a grin, like that made any kind of sense.

I really, really, really want him to like me …

"You ready?" Ray asked, and before he'd even finished asking, he was on top of her, poking at her crotch with his dick. It felt like someone was stabbing her with a pen, but a little softer. He missed and hit the bottom of her right butt cheek, then fumbled around, adjusting, grabbing at himself—

Then he hit the right spot and Lucia tensed, because it fucking hurt.

She wasn't hardly wet at all, but he shoved it in. He had his head back again, his abs rock-hard but not looking nearly so hot now that he was this close and right above her. He pushed in and she winced, tensing from the top of her head all the way down to every toe, the muscles reflexively tightening.

"Oh, yeah," Ray said, and shoved in deeper. It felt like he was covered in sandpaper. Lucia opened her mouth in anguish but choked back the cry of pain that threatened to come tumbling out. Ray opened an eye, saw her, and grinned. "Feels good, huh?"

No, it feels fucking horrible, like you're ripping my vag in two, Lucia thought, but she kept from saying it.

It only got worse. He leaned in, pulling out and pushing it back in. He started slow, experimentally at first, and she got a little wetter, but the pain—*fuck, shit, the pain!*—it didn't get any better. He was sweating, droplets coming off his chin and dripping right onto her face, her belly, and all points between. He bent over her, going for the neck again, as he thrust in, pulled out. Each time felt like he was using a hot poker to push into her. Was this supposed to be natural? Were people supposed to do this all the time?

WHY?

Lucia bit her lip and held back the tears as she lay there. He was going faster, faster, and it was like someone had taken a dry jackhammer and applied it to her pussy. Ray was letting her have it, and it was hard to believe that this little stump of a thing that had fit so easily in her mouth was causing all this pain. He sped up and it got worse, and Lucia wondered for a moment if she was actually going to die from it. Could you die from sex? It felt like it.

The raw, tearing sensation, like she was being split in half, only seemed to get worse the longer it went on. She was breathing tightly, afraid to let it out or take it in, like that, too, would cause her pain. A tear rolling down her cheek; it was all she could do not to scream. Ray was on top of her, his flat abs pressed against her, and she tried to restrain herself. She wanted to shove him off with both hands, get out of the car, find a cold spring and just sit in it. He increased the tempo, like a drummer going into a long, painful solo, the music turned up so loud she couldn't stand it anymore.

Lucia was sure her vagina was going to split open, that she was going to scream any second, was going to die screaming because this was just so—so—so horrible. It had been impossible to imagine a baby coming out of that hole before, and maybe even more impossible now. His dick was so small compared to a baby, how would that even work …?

She let out a little cry, a whimper, and Ray went faster still, his ass pistoning up and down as he thrust into her. How long would this last, this fucking hell of fucking? Forever, she thought miserably, her legs bowed and getting stiff from having his body between them at this angle, her back feeling the milder pain of a seatbelt buckle pinned against her ribs just above her kidney.

Ray's weight was crushing, the pain was agonizing. Was this what torture felt like? Maybe she deserved it. She didn't say anything, didn't dare to. She tried to arch her back, to at least get the seatbelt buckle from biting into her, from getting worse as he leaned more and more heavily on her.

"Unnnnnh!" Ray bucked, thrusting himself deep inside her and holding there for a second, then pulling it just slightly in and out, over and over. It felt like variations of torment, like he'd wedged a jagged rock up in her pussy and was poking it around. Then he collapsed, his weight dropping upon her and his head coming down on her collarbone. That sent a shooting pain up her neck and down her arm, but it was minor compared to the agony of the hot poker he'd shoved up her pussy.

"Ohmigod," Ray said, just lying there still, finally. He was still in her, it still hurt, but at least he wasn't actively ripping her in half anymore.

Lucia waited, that sensation like the inside of her pussy was being pinched by a thousand angry vises not fading like she might have hoped. "What?" The word was tense and tight, like she was feeling.

"Sorry I didn't last longer," Ray said apologetically. "I guess you got me all excited with that warmup."

Longer? she thought. *Thank Christ you didn't!*

He pulled out, and it hurt, but fuck, it felt so much better a second after he had. It was like she'd birthed that jagged rock, and while the wounds remained, at least the goddamned rock was gone. She sat up and winced as Ray pulled back, his little dick already sagging, shiny and wet with blood. She stared at it for a second, and her stomach sank.

I'm not a virgin anymore.

Then, with a breath of relief, the first she'd felt in a long time—*I'm not a virgin anymore.*

"Next time I'll last longer, I think," Ray said. "You could just come over to the house, you know. Next time. It'd be easier." He looked kind of thin and emaciated now that she looked at him in the faint light of the instrument display and a street lamp past a couple of dogwood trees.

Next time? she thought. *You think I'd willingly rip my pussy in half again?* But she said, "Yeah. That's a good idea. Making it easier next time."

I want him to like me.

"You did pretty good on that blowjob," Ray said, fishing for his own underpants in the floorboard. "But I could teach you a few things to make it even better."

"Okay," she said. He handed her her panties.

"Can you put those on?" He pushed the panties into her hand and looked down. "I just don't want you bleeding on the seat. I didn't know it was your time of the month."

"It's n—" She caught herself just in time. "Sorry."

"Oh, it's fine; it was good," Ray said, breezing on like it was no big deal, watching her as she slid the panties on. She felt the ooze of blood and something else—warm, sticky, drying like concrete along her pussy lips and in the cotton crotch of the panties as she dripped into them—his cum, she realized with a start; he'd just cum in her. Like he could sense her thoughts, he said, "It's so much better without a condom, ain't it? God, like a whole different thing."

"Oh," she said. She hadn't really thought about it. It wasn't likely she'd get pregnant after all, was it? Not this once.

He was struggling back into his pants. "Yeah, ain't nothing like this." Fastening his jeans, pulling his belt snug over those abs. They didn't look so impressive now, and it wasn't just the light. Something about the way they'd looked when he was looming over her, pushing into her like he was stabbing her in the pussy …

They'd lost some of their appeal, and she looked away as she picked up her bra and put it back on nervously.

His eyes roamed over her, like he was trying to drink her up, and she paused as she picked up her shorts and tank top from the floor. She watched him watch her and asked, "What?"

He kind of shrugged. "Nothing much. I was just thinking … maybe you want to go back to my place? Have a couple beers. We could maybe do this again a little later, when the mood strikes …"

Lucia did everything she could to reel in her immediate reaction.

I want him to like me.

But I really, really, really don't want him to put that fucking dick knife in me ever, ever again.

"I gotta get home," she said, the soft fabric of her tank top rubbing between her thumb and forefinger as she rustled it nervously. It was right there, in her hand; if she could just get it on, it'd protect her. It'd be like it was before; she'd be a little sore—okay, a lot fucking sore—but he wouldn't have that—that thing—where it could get into her again, stabbing its way inside her sex over and over again. "My foster parents are already gonna freak."

"Yeah, I get that," he said sheepishly. "Mike's a little … he's wound tight. And I wouldn't want to put up with the shit he has to put up with from your foster mom." He shook his head like the mere thought revolted him. "Karen's a real cunt. Heh. Karen the cunt. I don't know how you deal with her, either."

Lucia just shrugged. "Where else could I go?"

Ray said it faster than she could sense the trap she'd walked into. "You could stay with me for a while."

She just froze. About five minutes—and a fucking lifetime of pain ago—she would have wanted that. In a heartbeat. Now, though ...

Shit, he'd want to fuck again at some point. Hell, he already suggested he'd want to go again *tonight*.

Lucia barely held back a hard shudder as her brain turned the gears quickly. "I'm still underage," she said, and watched him freeze. "I wouldn't want to get you in trouble." He relaxed a little at that. "And you know my foster parents would—"

"Yeah." Ray nodded along. "Mike wouldn't let that stand. I bet he's a scary-ass motherfucker in court." Mike was a lawyer, and Lucia figured Ray had it pretty right.

"I should get home," Lucia said, shuddering a little at last.

"I'll drive you," Ray said, and he smirked again. "Wouldn't be fair to make you walk after that, I guess." He barked a rough laugh, and Lucia tried to smile. She wondered if she actually could walk, with this throbbing pain between her legs, and the aftereffect of feeling like someone had spread hair gel into her pubes and let it dry in there. Her stomach quivered as she started to get out of the car to move to the front seat with Ray as he eased in and started the engine. She blanched as she sat down wrong on the seat; how long was this going to hurt?

And how the hell could she possibly be expected to do it again?

*

Lucia slipped into the house through the front door like a trespasser. It felt unnatural, this place, the finely upholstered sofas, the chairs that were so stiff and uncomfortable to sit in, the curtains that hung regally from the rods to make the image of the house from the outside appear a flawless, antebellum paradise.

But inside ... fuck, this place crawled, for Lucia.

"I hear you," a scratchy female voice sounded from the kitchen. A light clicked on ahead of her, and there she was—Karen, the queen bitch of this place. Skinny, ragged, a cigarette flaring from between wrinkled lips. That was a bad sign. Mike didn't usually let her smoke in the house. Special circumstances, Lucia guessed. "And now I see you, dragging in at midnight like a goddamned whore." Her thin lips parted as she transferred the cigarette to her leathery hands, which bore the signs of long sun exposure and age.

Lucia didn't lip off; instead she just dragged herself in, kept her head down. Her vagina was still pulsing with pain, and she avoided taking any long steps because she knew she was faintly limping. She just stood, steady and still; thank God the pain was already starting to fade, something she had thought impossible. She damned sure wasn't ready to contemplate a "next time," but knowing that at least it didn't fucking scream forever gave her hope that someday she'd be able to sit normally.

"Ain't got nothing to say for yourself?" Everything about Karen screamed "white trash" except the house. Her straw-like hair hung limp over her long face, uneven strands half covering her lined forehead. "Whore."

"I'm not a whore," Lucia mumbled.

"What's that, whore?" Karen made a show of leaning forward, putting a hand up to her ear, brushing back the aged straw to expose a dotted ear that probably had skin cancer growing on it. Lucia didn't know much about skin cancer, but that growth on Karen's ear just didn't look right. She didn't say anything about it, though, because honestly, she was kind of wishing Karen did have skin cancer. Nothing fatal, of course; she didn't wish death on the woman. Just something debilitating that would get her the fuck out of the house for a little while, maybe put her in a bed for a while after that. "Does your dick-sucking mouth have anything stupid to say?"

Lucia flushed hard red.

Karen noticed and seized on it. "I knew it! I knew the moment I saw you, I said to myself, 'This girl's been off whoring. She's been sucking dick.' And now I know I's right." She advanced on Lucia, taking a drag on the cigarette, the tip flaring orange as she puffed on it. "Did you use a condom? I bet not. If you end up getting calved, heifer, I ain't paying for it. The government don't pay me near enough to deal with you squirting a little white trash baby out of that pussy of yours—"

"What's all this?" Mike's quiet voice sounded from up the stairs. A light came on up there, and Lucia's breath caught in her throat.

Thank God. Mike was always the more even of the two of them, though it wasn't like they were talking every day and eating ice cream like besties. He always seemed to put the damper on Karen's white trash crazy tendencies, and Lucia let out a little sigh of relief as she saw his skinny, hairy legs come into view down the steps. He was wearing a pair of gym shorts that looked hastily thrown on; his white t-shirt was tucked inside the waistband in the back but not the front. His hair was short, usually slicked up and combed back, though his hairline was full and thick, no hint of loss. He was a good-looking guy—for an old guy.

There was a flicker of disappointment in Karen's eyes that matched the waning burn of her cigarette as she withdrew it from her mouth. "I caught this little whore dragging in just now."

Mike paused at the base of the stairs. "Come on, Karen. She was probably just out a little late. It's only—" he checked his watch "—hell, it's not even eleven yet."

Karen took a long, judicious puff of cigarette, running her eyes up and down Lucia in disgust as she did so. "Just look at her. You can tell she's been out fucking someone. Who was it? Was it that man from down the block? I seen you looking at his ass like you wanted to crawl up in his crack and wear it like a mask."

Lucia blanched, involuntarily, in disgust. She'd tasted the front of Ray's crotch now; no way did she want to go to the backside. "Ewww."

"Don't you say 'eww' to me, girl, like I can't see right through your whoring ass—"

"Karen," Mike said with the air of a man who had been woken out of a sound sleep. He blotted at his eyes and yawned as he worked his way over to them, bare feet tapping against the tile floor. "Come on. Be reasonable."

"Do you want to get stuck paying for her fucking?" Karen's voice was like a screech.

"She's sixteen. She's been here for a couple weeks; I doubt she's been fucking already," Mike said with some amusement. He looked right at Lucia. "You haven't been fucking already, have you?" He smirked, like using Karen's own words against her was the funniest thing in the world.

For some reason … Lucia couldn't get the word, "No," out just then. A part of her brain dimly thought she should just say the easy lie; and it should have been easy. She didn't know these people. Karen, in particular, hadn't been very kind to her. But Mike …

Well, he kinda had.

The lie halted at her lips, froze there, died there. She wanted to say it, to give birth to it, but she just … couldn't. Instead she just froze for a second, then hung her head and didn't look at Mike.

"Hmph," Karen said, ringing out her little snort of triumph.

"Wait a minute." Mike drew a little closer. "Did you—have you—you actually were sleeping with someone tonight?"

Lucia stirred, taking her gaze back up again; she'd stared at the floor for a few seconds. "I was—I don't—I mean, I …" There was a crushing feeling inside her, like she was back in that car, steel bending all around her from impact.

"She did it!" Karen crowed. "She did it—probably with that

dumbass mechanic that's always outside with his shirt off to show everybody how much he works out. What's his name—Roy?"

"Ray," Lucia said.

Mike just stared at her, his face a cipher, partially shadowed in the night.

"It was just this one—" Lucia started to say, but was stopped when a thundering blow clipped her right in the jaw.

It felt like she was in the car accident again, except this time without the protection of her own vehicle, like the semi had slammed right in her jaw. Her legs went weak and wobbly, and she staggered and hit her knees. Pain surged through her kneecaps and blood welled up in her mouth. It drowned her tastebuds in that coppery flavor, dripping thickly out between her lips.

Lucia's head ached like someone had sledgehammered her just below the jawline. She opened her mouth to speak but blood and drool came dribbling out on the floor next to her and across her hand, which was planted palm down on the white tile. She felt like she'd given a blowjob again: she was dripping and gagging. Dark liquid dripped across the tile and onto the dark grout that crisscrossed it. Agony surged through her jawbone as she moved it and she tensed her neck, which ached all up and down it.

Dazed, it took her brain a moment to realize what had happened.

Mike had punched her.

"Ohhhhhh!" Karen shouted in exultation. "How'd that feel on your whore mouth? Bet you won't be sucking dick again anytime soon!" Her feet danced into Lucia's vision for a moment, then a sharp pain screamed in Lucia's side like she'd been shot in the ribs.

Karen had kicked her. That was what had happened.

Lucia tipped over, cradling her side, trying to protect it under her elbow like a bird shielding itself with a wing, and held loosely to her jaw with the other. She thumped a hip to the ground, lying stretched across her side and curling up rapidly, instinctively, against the next attack. A hot rush of emotions ran through her—fear, like a crashing wave of hot water. Shame, that she had brought this on herself. And then that nagging worry that she deserved this, all those little stomach-deep feelings dug in like a trench line around her belly, setting up for the long haul. Like she hadn't already had enough to think about.

"I'm so disappointed right now." Mike's face appeared above her, fuzzy through her nearly-closed eyelids. "I thought you were better than this."

"She was a whore through and through," Karen said. The cigarette was still dangling from her fingertips, and she flicked the ash down at Lucia, who covered her face as it landed on her hand. It burned, stinging for a few seconds, but nothing like the pain in her jaw. "I told you that." Karen snorted. "You're just pissed you weren't the one who got her virginity."

"Shut the fuck up, Karen," Mike said, "or you'll be on the floor with her."

"Oh, don't play that game with me, Michael," Karen said. "You know you're going to need me to lie about how she got this way."

"We found her on the lawn," Mike said. "That's the story, got it?"

"Yeah, I got it. You want to hit her again while she's down?"

Mike didn't answer, but Lucia felt it a moment later, a hard, cratering blow that felt like someone had taken a steam shovel and just ripped a stretch out of her back just above her left buttock. She tried to scream, but it came out a muffled shriek instead, through her shattered jaw. Then she heard a series of soft, urgent cries, and realized they were coming from her own throat.

"You should hit her in that pretty face," Karen said. "Take out some of those teeth. That way, she comes back, she won't be able to bite you when she's sucking your dick."

"I'm starting to think you might be a little jealous of her, Karen."

"She's just a whore cunt," Karen spat on her, literally. Lucia could feel it on her hip, exposed where her tank top had risen during the assault.

Lucia curled up in a ball, trying to keep everything tight, keep them from having any other places to hit. She was whimpering, she dimly realized, a low, continuous whine. Karen kicked her in the leg, but lightly compared to what Mike had just done.

She deserved this, Lucia realized dimly. This was her punishment for everything. For getting her parents killed. For sucking Ray's dick, for letting him fuck her like that. This was the penance. This was the price.

She'd earned this.

"I don't want to hear a goddamned squeak out of you," Mike growled somewhere above her; she could hear him even though she'd buried her face in her hands, trying to compact herself as tightly as she could. "Not one."

She said nothing. Why would she? This was hers, her pain. Her punishment.

Mike's fingers sunk into her hair, and she drew a deep breath as he forced her to her feet, yanking her along, back toward the door. "You're going to lie outside for a while. I better not hear you. Then we're going to come find you, and when we do, we'll call you an ambulance." He stopped, yanked her around and ripped her hands from her face. "Look at me." She tried to guard her face again, but a strong grip clamped onto her wrist and pulled her hand away. "Open your eyes. Look at me."

Lucia strained against eyes that didn't want to open. She managed to get them thinly slitted, enough to see Mike staring down at her. She could smell his breath, the faint aroma of toothpaste still on it from his pre-bedtime ritual.

"I'm a lawyer," Mike said, staring down at her with deep pools of black in his eyes. "Remember that. I've got lots of clients that owe me favors. If you tell the police I had anything to do with this, I will have your whore ass shanked in jail. Got it?" He stared down at her out of the shadows that shrouded his face. "Nod your head if you understand."

Lucia nodded, once.

"This girl knows when she's beat," Karen cackled. "Not too dumb. You know, for a dumb whore."

"You just keep your mouth shut and everything will be fine," Mike said, his face in the shadows. "We'll get you taken care of. Just don't. Cross me." He shook her once, for emphasis, then grabbed her by the hair again and dragged her out.

Karen's feet tiptoed over to the door, and she opened it quietly, as though she were afraid any sound would alert the police. Lucia took that all in as Mike dragged her over the metal threshold and it hit her shoulder, bumping it like a punch someone had aimed to deaden it.

The pain was spreading from her jaw, all up into her head.

"Just wait right here a few minutes," Mike whispered as she felt the cool touch of the stone front step against her cheek and he finally relinquished his death grip on her hair. "I'll be back for you, and we'll make it all right." Now his voice was soft and soothing.

He shut the door behind her, leaving Lucia alone on the front steps, bleeding quietly onto the concrete. "Clean this shit up," Mike's voice echoed through the door, "while I shower off."

"Shit," Karen said, "why would I want to go do that? Get whore blood on me?"

"Because if you don't, you'll be lying out there next to her, Karen, and you fucking know that. Maybe it's been too long since I reminded you of your place in this house."

There was only a faint squeak in the house, a foot scuffing against the tile. "I'll—I'll get it cleaned up." Now she sounded appropriately cowed, Lucia realized dimly.

She touched her lip and brought her fingers away. Blood drenched her fingertips. She reached out and pressed them against the concrete, not making a sound. It left a dark impression, a black-looking fingerprint on the concrete.

I deserve this, Lucia thought as she lay there on the concrete porch. There was no light overhead, only the street lamps to give her illumination. Her neck ached. Her jaw throbbed where Mike had hit her. Her vagina no longer screamed, the lost virginity now the least of her pains. Funny how it had felt like it would be the very death of her only half an hour earlier.

She lay there for an hour, two—she could hardly tell—thinking about everything she'd done in her life to get to this point, to deserve this pain—and it passed like an eternity of torment in the dark.

Day Two

"... and it turns out that this Night's King? Well, he's been made by ..." Nate McMinn's voice droned in the early morning still.

The sun rising over Midian cast a flat glare on the wet pavement of the town square, the splash of the hose going, Keith Drumlin doing his level best to wash off the stains. It had been two weeks since Halloween now, two weeks since the damned world had come to an end. A week since he'd seen that crazy shit go down in the woods with those hellcats, seen a goddamned demon rip Sam Allen in half like something out of a fucking horror film.

The body count kept ticking up and up—an attack on a hiker last week that came wandering in off Mount Horeb with his skull open, half his brain eaten out. A body they found in the south end of town with the pieces scattered all over the road like he'd been pulled apart for sport. Shit, Keith had seen crazy crap before he'd joined the watch, but since ...

He'd hit his quotient for fucking lunacy. And that was absent the nightmares, which came with alarming frequency. He found himself thinking about one now, hands shaking on the hose, water squirting everywhere. "Shit," Keith muttered under his breath, getting it back under control.

"So, they're all charging after 'em, and we finally find out where Hodor got his name—" Nate stopped, lifting the flat push broom he had in hand, the end speckled with dried and crusted blood. "Keith? You listening? Did I lose you?"

"Sorry, Nate," Keith said, adjusting the hose to close it, only a drizzle making its way out now. "I wasn't paying attention, no. Got lost in my own thoughts."

"That's a shame, man. I was just bringing you up to speed so you can pick up the next season."

"I don't care about that right now," Keith said with a shake of the head.

Nate stared at him dumbly. "Well, you should. The sixth season of *Game of Thrones* was the best damned season of scripted television I've seen in a long fucking time. That sumbitch moved in a way the last five seasons just didn't—"

"That's because they took it out of the books and started making shit up as they went," Keith said, waving him off. "Without some author slowing you down, your television writers can write fast and make a lot of crazy shit happen." He shook his head again. "I don't care about that though."

"But you watched it religiously up until this last year! We used to talk about it all the time!"

"Yeah, but we got other shit going on now," Keith said, mouth feeling dry as a West Texas gulch in August. "And I used to catch up on it once summer was over." He waved a hand around to indicate the square. The blood was long dried, the remaining pieces of corpses putrefied. They both had a special solution rubbed on their upper lips to defray some of the stink as they cleaned. "Summer's over, and now this is the shit that we get, right? Can't even enjoy deer hunting season for fear I'll get ripped into pieces like that dad last week." He frowned. "They ever find that kid?"

"No," Nate said. "Don't reckon they ever will, either. Those damned critters were fucking vicious. You see what they did to Sam?"

"I ain't seen anything but that when I close my eyes this last week." Keith shuddered in the morning chill. "Sam didn't deserve to go that way."

"Hell, that kid didn't deserve to go that way! He was just hunting with his daddy, and boom! Then he got hunted, *with* his daddy. Then attacked with his momma, and soon enough ..." Nate shivered. "Shit, Keith. Is this what it's going to be like from now on?"

"I don't know, man," Keith said. "Maybe. Hard to say. I ain't never been part of an anti-demon militia before. Guess I don't know what to expect other than what I've seen so far."

"I reckon that is what we are," Nate said, straightening his posture, like he'd just woken up to the fact that he was part of something cool. "An anti-demon militia. That's badass."

Keith gave him a jaded look. "Until you get cut in half like Sam, sure."

"You got a real good point there," Nate said, and put the broom back down, scrubbing at the concrete. The problem was that everything had dried and crusted, and it didn't want to come off so easily. And there was a lot to be scrubbed—piss and shit, blood by the gallons.

"This is depressing as fuck," Keith said, and this time, Nate took notice of his murmurings.

"I been saying that a lot lately," Nate said knowingly, getting back to sweeping. "That, and 'I just don't know.'"

Keith tried it out—"'I just don't know,'"—experimentally, like. "Yep, it fits," he decided. "For pretty much everything."

Nate paused, looking up at the sun layering streaks across the horizon. "Yep. That's why I just keep saying it." He surveyed the mess around them uneasily. "Reckon we oughta get back to work."

Keith stared at the detritus around the square. Two weeks, and it was still in a fearful state. "You know, Nate ... I'm starting to believe this might be a lost cause."

Nate didn't stop scrubbing. "You talking about this little project of ours? Or the whole town?"

The sun was coming up, bright orange. Keith swallowed heavily. He would have spent his nights here too, if he could, just to get away from the quiet, empty house. But then he'd be out on the quiet, empty square, so he bore the nights in anticipation of getting out in the mornings, of doing this. Feeling the whisper of fall air on his skin as he sprayed the rivulets of gore off the town square, once the proud centerpiece of Midian, Tennessee, and now ...

Well, now it was the site of their saddest hour.

"I might just mean both," Keith said, his mouth a little dry, hands feeling a little weak. But he went back to work anyway, alongside Nate, opening up the hose valve and trying his best to clean up the mess around them.

*

Reeve woke to the radio playing the Dean Martin standard, "Ain't Love a Kick in the Head," and he had to agree with at least part of that sentiment. He definitely felt like he'd been kicked in the head, and as slow recall came rolling over him with the return of consciousness, he started to wonder if he'd be feeling kicked in other places, too, as the day went on.

Because it was election day. Time to see whether or not County Administrator Pike's little effort at ripping him out by the roots was going to bear any fruit. Wouldn't that just be a bitch, trying to fight this war without the office, without the cars, without the funding that Pike had just pushed through for him to put some of the members of the watch on staff.

At least Pike had come through like he'd promised during their conversation last week. He might have kept those purse strings tighter than a nervous virgin's thighs up until recently, but he'd loosened them up a little in the last few days. Not enough to get at the honey pot, but then Pike wasn't totally in charge of that.

Reeve rubbed his bald head and turned over on the cot where he was sleeping in the back of the station house. A dim light seeped in under the door and informed him that it was well past daybreak.

He swept his legs over the side of the cot, ignored the cracking of his back and knees as he realigned things, adjusted himself so as to stand. He was still in his clothes, because he'd be damned if he'd be awakened in the middle of the night to deal with a crisis in bunny slippers.

Soft voices made their way through the thick door of the supply closet. He concentrated, trying to hear what they were saying. He could hear Arch out there, and maybe Brian Longholt too, though it was tough to tell from here. Reeve stood, caught his balance by shoving off from the cinder block wall, and toddled his ass on over to the door to open it up.

"I'm sure he wouldn't mind seeing you," Brian said as Reeve opened the door and damned near fell over from the brightness shining in through the windows. Shit, they were blasting him like someone had set up klieg lights outside. It was just the sun though, nature's version of the same.

"I don't reckon I'd want to see me if I were him," Arch said, arms crossed over his chest. The big man was wearing his uniform, standing like a pillar in the middle of the bullpen area. "I don't expect I'd aid his recovery. More like remind him of his daughter being gone." His tone suggested that there was no emotion below the surface, none at all, which was a feat even for the stoic Arch Stan.

"I doubt he's operating on a high enough level to work through all that," Brian said, turning back to the dispatch radio. "You'd have to see him to understand. It's … not pretty." Brian glanced up at Reeve. "Morning, Sheriff," he said, all business again.

"Any calls in the night?" Reeve asked, trying to compose himself as he shut the door to his bedroom/supply closet behind him.

"Minor stuff," Arch said, a statue barely coming to life to answer. "More sightings of those shadowcats—"

"Hellcats," Brian said with a wide grin. "Hell. Say it, Arch."

Arch just gave his brother-in-law—former brother-in-law, now?—an icy gaze. "More of 'em," he said. "Out near Rucker's place.

Probably a couple packs. Gone by the time we got out there."

Reeve grunted. "Why didn't you wake me?"

"Figured you needed your rest for today," Arch said. "And besides, we ain't had a clash with them since last week out on Faulkner Road."

"Could come at any time," Reeve said, working his way over to the coffee pot. He could smell the brew. Smelled old and stale, and he gave no fucks as he poured a big old cup and watched it sit there, not a hint of steam.

"Sorry I missed that little throwdown," Brian said. "All I've heard the last few days is you guys talking about it. Sounds like an epic showdown between good and evil."

"Really?" Reeve did the slow turnaround. "Because to me it seemed a lot like us almost getting wiped the fuck out and then having to basically surrender our decency in order to leave a twelve-year-old to die in the woods alone." That still stuck in his fucking craw, that they'd left Mack Wellstone out there to get ripped apart by those goddamned hellbeasts. And he must have gotten ripped up good, too, because no one had seen hide nor hair of the boy since that night. Over a week in the woods with those things prowling around and not a sign?

Shit, Mack Wellstone was deader than the U.S.S. *Maine*.

"Better than taking an entire crew into infested woods and pitting them against those hellcats on their own territory," Brian said. The fact that the lily-livered Ivy League pussy was on his side wasn't much of a balm to Reeve's butthurt over his own choices. Logic didn't sell half as hard to him when it carried a whiff of cowardice, and this thing stunk of chickenshittery. "Unless your goal was to get our town's only line of defense good and dead."

"No, that's not my stated fucking objective," Reeve said, sipping the cold coffee. It was shit, but he didn't care because he wasn't drinking it for the flavor. He was drinking it to stave off the five-alarm headache he'd be experiencing in the next hour if he didn't quaff it down. "But my oath was to protect people, and leaving one to twist in the cold woods? Not my finest hour."

"But getting ripped into pieces in the woods by devil dogs would be?" Brian asked. "Doesn't sound that fine to me."

"Devil cats," Arch said, and when Brian shot him a look of mild amusement, he said, "Hendricks, Alison, and your dad faced devil dogs before. Just being clear about it."

"I've faced a couple devil dogs in my time," Brian said seriously. "I imagine as a long-standing officer of the law, you probably have too; am I right, Sheriff?"

Reeve didn't want to find that amusing—didn't want to find anything Brian said amusing—but this stupid joke did actually draw a smile. "I have. But I prefer Little Debbies. Those oatmeal crème pies just kill me."

"One artery at a time, yes they do," Brian said, arching his eyebrows, pleased as punch that someone had gotten his joke. Arch was just shaking his head. "Ready for the election?"

"Ready as I'm gonna get," Reeve said, feeling across his bare head again. That headache was starting, even though he had a cup of coffee in his hand. He took another long pull, figuring he'd better hurry up and get it down before that throb started feeling like a bullet in the skull; otherwise, even without the election, this was going to be a bitch of a day.

The jangling bell over the door caused all three of them to turn to see who was coming in, a silhouetted shadow highlighted by the sun behind them, showing a thin figure with a box in hand that started to clear as he stepped inside and was lit by the overhead lights.

Reeve stifled a sigh. Of all days ...

"Gentlemen," County Administrator Pike said, brandishing the box in his hand, "I hope you're hungry, because I brought donuts, on this most auspicious of days. Peace offering." He gestured toward Reeve with it.

Yep. Reeve rubbed his forehead. It was definitely going to be a bitch of a day.

*

Hendricks awoke in the cold light of day, abs feeling the strain from—well, from the fucking he'd been doing lately. It had taken a little while for him to get sore, but yesterday he and Starling had gone for two rounds, the second one lasting well over an hour and progressing into something approaching a workout. By the time he'd finished, he was exhausted, spent, and pretty sure he was shooting blanks from the days of increased sexual operating tempo.

He looked down, and noticed he wasn't even approaching hard. No morning wood here, probably because he'd drained the damned thing of all its sap with the help of that fiery redhead.

Hendricks scratched his crotch, feeling the sticky reminder that he'd been balls deep in Starling last night all matted around his pubes. He was a little surprised it hadn't rubbed off on the sheet, but then maybe he'd slept on his back the whole night. Kinda unusual, but—

Hey, was that a weight on his shoulder? He looked down in surprise to find Starling's hair glinting in the darkness, catching a little light from the gaps in the curtains. That was a little weird. She stirred and looked up at him, eyes fully open, like she hadn't slept a wink all night.

"You're still here," he said as she sat up in bed, her small breasts hanging pertly right in front of him.

"I was not required elsewhere," Starling said. He was getting used to her lack of emotion, though it had taken awhile, especially during sex. She made some noises, but they were nothing like the more human partners he'd had over his lifetime.

Still, her pussy was sweet silk, and he didn't mind the quiet in exchange for her active nature. She didn't just lie there and take it; she made it a mission to wring some joy out of his ass in the process. He couldn't be sure, but he thought she was getting there, too. At least it seemed like it, in her limited emotion sort of way. She did roll her eyes and shit, and make a weird noise deep in her throat when she got what he expected was close. Not that that was a sign of any sort he could hang his hat on.

"So that's what it takes to get you to spend the night?" He ran a hand through his tangled hair, thought about touching hers, but somehow that felt ... weird. Indecent, overly familiar ... something. He would have laughed at the fact that he'd fuck Starling nine ways to Sunday but feel strange about making an intimate gesture toward her like that, but he didn't want to do so in her face, and it wasn't that funny anyway.

She didn't react to his question. "When I am required elsewhere, I must go."

"I s'pose," he said, rolling out of bed and heading for the bathroom. "Good thing for me your other half doesn't have a busy schedule today."

"Why?" She appeared behind him in the bathroom door. "Do you wish me to stay more often?"

He stared at his stubbled face in the mirror. "I don't mind you being around."

She was staring at him, but he didn't look back at her for some reason. "That is not the same."

He turned. "Now, that right there might be the most damned woman-esque thing you've ever said." She cocked her head at him, a curious question unspoken. "It was the sort of thing a lady might say to lay a trap for a fella to step right into."

"What kind of trap?"

"The kind meant to prompt a man to say something she wants to hear," Hendricks said, turning back to the mirror. He had a few bruises on his neck where she'd broken some blood vessels sucking on him. Thank God she hadn't put that much effort and suction on his cock, because the way she was putting miles on that thing, he needed it in top condition. She'd wear and tear it in a different way.

"What do you think I want to hear?" She said it more softly than usual.

He studied a long bruise that extended to his collarbone. He vaguely recalled her making that one, though it was kind of a blur. Hendricks figured it had come during that second, longer fuck when she'd been straddling him, riding him like a bucking bronco, pausing and going shallower in order to nibble and bite at his neck. It was a hard screw, filled with hunger and empty rhythm, desire without a lot of pleasure during parts of it. He liked it overall, but it had some weird, hollow moments that made him not so sorry when he'd finally hit his climax.

"I figure you want to hear …" he started, but stopped when he heard a knocking in the distance. It started faint but grew in intensity, and he turned his head, looking around.

Starling was gone, without a trace as always. Not even the smell of her sweaty skin and that faint hint of her sex was present.

Hendricks stepped out of the bathroom, looking toward the door. Another knock sounded and he looked around. Starling was definitely gone, and someone was thumping at it.

He edged over and snatched up his coat, putting it on over his naked body, then picked up his sword. "Who is it?"

"It's Duncan," came the muffled voice from the other side.

Hendricks froze. "What the hell are you doing here?"

"I came to get a glimpse of those packaged goods you're barely hiding under your coat, flasher. Get dressed and answer the door, will you?"

Hendricks chuckled and dropped the coat, searching for his boxers. No point in dirtying another pair when he was all covered in Starling and his own dried ejaculate.

"No, I said get dressed. Don't answer the door in the damned buff," Duncan said faintly from the other side.

"You shut up or I'm answering the door right fucking now," Hendricks said, balancing on one leg while he shoved the other one into the leg of his boxers.

"I've seen your ass and your junk before when we were roomies out in that abandoned house," Duncan said. "Also, I'm a demon; I don't really care about your little snail hose or that pinched hole between your buttcheeks. Your anatomy doesn't impress me at all."

"Oh, yeah? Well, you're the only one it doesn't impress then," Hendricks muttered.

"I doubt that." Duncan had heard him perfectly.

Hendricks pulled on his jeans and forewent the shirt, walking over and throwing the door open. "What do you want, shell game?"

Duncan just squinted at him. "Is that supposed to be a nickname? Or are you calling me the operator of a cheating street game?"

Hendricks gave him a shrug right back. "I dunno. I just thought it sounded cool, since you've got a shell instead of skin." He leaned a shoulder against the door frame. "What are you doing with your neck all up in my woods?"

"It's a pretty small woods around here," Duncan said. "I caught a blip out in this direction."

"Blip?"

"You remember I can sense things?"

It was Hendricks's turn to squint. "I remember you could for a while. Thought you were all constipated with that or something."

Duncan didn't react visibly, at least not in the obvious way a human might have. He did, however, fidget. "I am, though that's a pretty clumsy and anthropomorphic way of looking at it. My sense ... it's clouded, something is pressing in on it. Those talismans the screen has been selling aren't helping, but there's more, now. Something deeper. More powerful, maybe."

"Sounds a little sinister," Hendricks said.

Duncan kept a straight face. As always. "Doesn't need to be. Some forces of our kind are just so powerful, they blot things out when they get near."

Hendricks nodded. "I expect I might have that problem if Kate Upton were to get too close to me. Where's your lesser half? Washing her hair? Painting her toenails?"

Duncan shook his head. "You're kind of a pig, Hendricks."

"These days, pig's just code for a guy who has the balls to occasionally say the rude shit that comes to mind," Hendricks said. "So ... this blip—where is it and why are you knocking on my door?" He looked back. "Wait, it wasn't in my room, was it? Because I could maybe explain that—"

"No, it didn't have anything to do with the squirming redhead you've been exuberantly shoving your pickled mini-hose into every chance you get," Duncan said. "The blip I got—it's close. Figured you might want in on the action, especially since, uh ... Guthrie is otherwise occupied."

Hendricks strolled to the bed and snatched up his dirty shirt, shedding his coat and stretching it on over his head. "Not gonna tell me what she's up to, huh?"

"Just getting acclimated to her new shell," Duncan said. He could have been telling the truth; it wasn't like there was tension in his voice that betrayed the lie. But when it came to Guthrie, Hendricks wasn't so sure he trusted anything about the newly returned OOC.

"How?" Hendricks asked. "And seriously, if you say toenail painting—"

"I didn't see any full-service nail salons around here, did you?" Duncan asked. "Besides, our toenails don't grow. What you see is what you get."

"That true of your hair, too?"

Duncan nodded. "Ours, yes. Our shells don't really come with that feature built in. There are demons who do grow hair and toenails, just like there are demons who have certain spots on their bodies that can feel a little more sensation than I do."

Hendricks got a little queasy at the words. He was pretty sure he knew what Duncan was alluding to; he just wasn't sure why he would have gone there—and now, especially. He didn't say any of this though, instead going with, "All right, where are we going?" as he pulled his coat back on. He looked around for his hat, and found it in the usual spot atop the dresser.

"Nowhere," Duncan said, head turned around to stare. Hendricks threw the hat on his head and rejoined the OOC at the door in time to see a thin man shuffling across the parking lot toward what looked like an old hearse. "At least not yet."

Hendricks stared at the guy. He wasn't looking around, just making his way to the car. He got out the keys and unlocked it, then slipped inside. His movements were fluid, graceful—they kind of reminded Hendricks of a bird, a really big one. The hearse's engine roared to life a moment later, and the car started to roll toward the Sinbad parking lot's exit.

"Okay, now we're going," Duncan said, heading for Hendricks's car.

"I like how you just know I'm going to want to drive," Hendricks said.

"You're kind of a control freak, Marine," Duncan said, slipping into the passenger seat. Hendricks never locked the doors. Why would he? Demons would kill you, but car theft in Midian was probably pretty flat at zero once you controlled for all the GTA he'd been doing himself.

"I let Uncle Sam sit in the driver's seat for a couple years," Hendricks said. "Now that I'm out, I do like to occasionally exercise a little control over my own self, when I get the chance." He started the car. "That guy? Pretty sure I've seen him before."

"Where?" Duncan asked.

Hendricks took a deep breath. "I want to say he was at Alison's funeral, but I'm not a hundred percent sure."

"Well, that's interesting," Duncan said. "Because he's got an aura about him."

"Aura?" Hendricks put the car in gear and backed out in a quick turn, gunning the vehicle toward the parking lot exit. The hearse was already rolling back over the interstate bridge toward town, and Hendricks took care not to squeal the tires to draw attention. His purloined SUV had some miles and was pretty common. He might be able to blend in, even in these low-traffic country roads.

"You know," Duncan said, "I get a bad feeling about him."

"Shit," Hendricks said, turning out onto Old Jackson Highway. "In this town, that could mean anything." And he headed off slowly after the hearse, trying not to attract the attention of the thin man behind the wheel.

*

Lauren was awakened by the thud of a heavy pillow across her face, and it had the effect of startling her out of a deep sleep and making her feel like she was under attack all in one. She jerked to wakefulness and sat up on the sofa bed she'd been sleeping on these last few nights like someone had zapped her with a bolt of lightning, looking around for the threat just in time to catch a pillow to the kisser again.

"Oh, good," Molly said dryly, whacking her with the pillow again for good measure, "you're awake."

"What the fuck is up with the low-key murder attempt?" Lauren growled, feeling bushwhacked, irritable, and not all that well rested. Sleep had been like her mother when she was a teenager—a total bitch, always harassing the shit out of her but never making her feel particularly happy to see her. Lauren cringed as that comparison crossed her mind, and she silently caught herself asking forgiveness for the uncharitable thought from a higher power she didn't even really believe in. Old habit, she supposed, from an easier time in her life.

"You wanted me to wake you up for work," Molly said. She was still wearing PJs, probably because it wasn't like she was registered for school down here in Chattanooga. "Voila. You're awake." She wore a look of what Lauren judged to be supreme teenager-ness, filled with angst and rage, expressed not-so-gently through a pillow this morning.

"I figured you could shake my shoulder, or say, 'Mom, it's time to wake up,' in that honeyed voice of yours, or maybe—and this is kind of a throwback—just come running into my bed and dive-bomb me like the olden days of yore."

"I'm a little bigger now," Molly said. "I'd probably rupture your spleen or something."

"Yeah, well, medically I could deal with that."

"But a smack to the face with a pillow is beyond your ken, Doctor?"

"Smartass," Lauren muttered. Molly disappeared out the door of the small attic room they were sharing, and Lauren rubbed at her eyes, trying to salvage some of those sleepy feelings she'd been indulging just a few minutes earlier, before the rudest of all rude awakenings that didn't involve a demon.

But it did involve a teenager, and those were sort of like demons.

Lauren grabbed her cell phone; twelve missed calls, eleven messages. That was par for the course, and made her glad she'd muted the damned thing before bed. She could have set the alarm on that, of course, but she'd figured Molly would do a slightly less annoying job of waking her for her shift.

She stared at the clock display. At least her daughter had gotten her up. An hour after she was supposed to, but still ... Lauren smiled, but it faded quickly. She still knew Molly. Sort of.

With a stifled yawn, Lauren stood, feet against the cool wood of the attic floor. This place belonged to a friend from work, and she'd need to find a place of her own soon. They'd only been here a week, and while Molly was clearly not adjusted—not within miles of it, actually—Lauren was feeling good about her decision. Other than her daughter's murder-by-pillow attempt this morning, neither of them had been in mortal peril in almost a week.

It was just better this way. Safer. All she had to do was her work and raise her daughter. And that was plenty enough to be dealing with at this stage of her life, she thought as she headed toward the bathroom to start putting herself together for the day.

*

Aaron Drake savored the last bite of the barbecued meat. It was a radius and ulna of a human being, smoked gently in the Kamado for hours and then checked by a digital thermometer to be sure it was just the perfect temperature. He'd seasoned the whole body with a dry rub he'd made himself from a recipe online by a very famous chef. He'd patted it gently on, not removing the skin before cooking, then placed a full beer can in the rectum, which entered directly into the empty body cavity. It had boiled during cooking and imparted a lovely flavor that melded well with the dry rub. After the meat was done cooking, he added a little small-batch barbecue sauce from an outfit near Memphis that was really on to something with their exquisite flavors.

All told, it was juicy, lip-smacking meat, and he practically sucked it off the bone, it was so tender. This arm had belonged to a young fellow named Morgan Davis. Drake had quietly broken into Davis's home and discovered him and his girlfriend sleeping quietly in bed only last night. He'd quickly taken them, breaking Morgan's neck almost before he could open his eyes, and then smothering his girlfriend with a pillow as she struggled and screamed into the feathered down. He was still running A/B experiments with meat and the flavors caused by dying in a panic, but it was sooooo difficult to decide. One time he'd be certain that yes, adding in the fear definitely gave the meat additional flavor. The next he was certain that, no, the adrenaline gave it no seasoning at all. He'd done some reading online in some of his fellow demons' culinary sites, and they seemed to be rather torn about the whole thing.

Drake discarded Morgan Davis's radius and ulna, and they clattered to the plate with a rattle, still joined by a piece of cartilage at what had been the elbow. He'd hungrily slurped the meat from between the bones, his tongue flicking out and stroking it clean in an act of almost sexual pleasure. For Drake, it nearly was; flavor profiles excited him much more than the silly lusts exhibited by these humans or his fellow demons who were capable of such appetites.

No, his was a more sensible appetite. The closest to nirvana a demon like him was capable of experiencing was a satiation—a full belly, ideally, one that had been filled while sampling delectable flavors. Drake sighed. His latest excursion—a home invasion—had produced good results and little resistance. He was quiet on his feet, and had chosen a house without an alarm sign, killing the dog first and silently—it had all gone to plan. He wasn't sure it always would, but this time it seemed his calculated risk had paid off. Paid off handsomely enough that he'd follow through again tonight, after he'd had a chance to cook up the girlfriend and eat her this afternoon. He was all about the farm-to-table concept, and the idea of the meat lingering more than a day after slaughter was simply unacceptable to him and his culinary ethos. He shuddered at the mere thought.

No, he'd need more meat—and soon. In fact, in keeping with that ethos of freshness, he had already started contemplations about how best to ... stockpile living humans, to keep them before the slaughter for maximum freshness. Humans could be caged, after all, it didn't affect their flavor as near as he could tell, other than perhaps an increase in that adrenaline he'd been experimenting with.

The thick sauce of regret was still hanging over him, though, regarding the boy who had gotten away after his first kill on that back road. Sure, it had been delicious in the moment he had acceded, letting the child run off without having to give further chase, but the flavor became too rich by half afterward. He had thought of the boy over and over since, wondering if he had simply poured on the speed, gone after him a little harder, maybe now, almost a week later, the question would be settled in his mind: what does fresh veal taste like? He'd never had it before, because it tended to be highly frowned upon in most of the demon channels. If OOCs took it personally when you sold adult human meat, they were merciless at the attention drawn by the slaughter of children.

But now Aaron was in a place where the rules no longer seemed to apply. A better place, really, but one that required a bit more effort on his part than if he'd had pieces delivered to him in New York or LA or DC. He'd found he'd enjoyed the kill, the sensation of 'farming' his own dinners, making it an organic part of the whole culinary process. It was nature, it was beautiful, and so richly rewarding.

"I need more," he muttered, sticking a fingernail in his teeth to dislodge a piece of Morgan Davis. Drake knew he'd go out again tonight. His appetite required feeding, even though, strictly speaking, his stomach didn't. That lingering regret, too, was eating at him the way he'd gnawed at Morgan Davis's bones just now. He needed to try one of the little ones, to sample that flavor profile for himself, really taste it. After all, it might just be the taste he was looking for.

*

Arch didn't like donuts. They tasted fine, sure—good, even. But all he could think about when pushing one of those, sweet, doughy confections in his mouth was how long it'd take him to burn it off. So he tended to avoid them, leaving any that came in the front door to Reeve or Ed Fries, at least back in the days when they operated like normal cops rather than the demon-hunting force they'd become.

So when County Administrator Pike thrust the box of donuts at him, Arch took them out of politeness only, and transferred them and their sweet-smelling selves to the counter, opening the carton so that the air could get at them, make them even less appealing to him over time and, hopefully, spare him the temptation.

Because that glazed one there in the front row, all glistening ... it looked mighty fine.

"I know, I know," Pike said with a saccharine grin that made Arch want to take a step back, "donuts and cops. What a stereotype, right? But still, I figured maybe it had some little grain of truth in there, somewhere."

"Ed Fries was a big fan," Reeve said, arms stiff at his sides. Arch figured the sheriff was working to keep from crossing them in front of Pike, give the wrong—or right—impression.

"You're telling me you don't pick up a donut from time to time, Sheriff?" Pike still grinned, like he was trying to be in on the joke.

"Maybe later," Reeve said. "I just ate." That was a flat-out lie, unless he had a box of Twinkies secreted away in the back storage room. "What can we do for you, County Administrator?"

"Well, I came to get out the vote," Pike said, his grin fading a little. "I've just cast mine in favor of you, Sheriff. Been campaigning for you as much as I can in these parts—not sure how much good it'll do since people are a mite suspicious of everything at this point ... but I've done what I could."

"And I do appreciate it," Reeve said dryly. Arch had known the man long enough to hear the unsaid words: *But I would have appreciated it more if you hadn't tried to drag me out of office to begin with.*

"Well, I just hope we can move past this and focus on the crisis at hand," Pike said.

"You mean the demons?" Brian tossed in helpfully. He was still sitting at the dispatcher's desk, and had a grin to match Pike's, but for entirely different reasons, Arch was sure.

"Absolutely," Pike said with a nod. "That's exactly what I meant. Demons. It sounds funny, and it's tough for people—voters—to wrap their brains around, because I know it was for me, but ... demons. Yeah. We gotta focus on what it's going to take to bring this county through this crisis, this demon crisis—together. And I'm just glad this election is going to be over after today, with the result—I hope—being you still sitting in that chair, Sheriff." He nodded at Reeve. "But I know even if things go awry, you're still going to be front and center helping us on this, because I truly believe that you're the only man that can."

Arch felt like he needed hip waders, it was getting so deep in here. He didn't say anything though, waiting for Reeve to respond, because it was his malarkey to respond to, not Arch's.

"Well, that's mighty kind of you," Reeve said, showing some hint of loosening up. Arch wondered if it was because of the pretty words or because he was fighting against his nature and trying not to show himself as an enemy to Pike right now. "I—"

"Here we go," Brian said as the dispatch phone in front of him rang. He clicked a button and said, "911, what's your emergency?" He stared off into space, concentrating intently. "Whoa, whoa—slow down. I can't—ohhh, oh shit." He covered the microphone boom that stretched over his mouth, apparently missing the mute button hanging from the cord that dangled in front of his chest. "We got a pack of hellcats terrorizing Mary Wrightson."

"Got it," Reeve said, springing into motion so fast his coffee slopped over the edge of the mug. The sheriff ignored it and headed for the door, sweeping up his sword in the process. "We're en route." He shot a look at Arch. "You coming?"

"On your six," Arch said, then wondered why he'd said it that way. Hanging out with Hendricks too much, probably. Then again, the way the cowboy swore, hanging out with him for any amount of time was too much.

"Let's go," Pike said, scrambling and opening the front door for Reeve.

Reeve missed a step, almost coming to a stop. "You can't be serious."

"Hey, we're all in this together," Pike said, smarmy smile gone in the urgency of the moment. "I want to see what we're up against. I owe to it the voters. Maybe I can even help."

"With what?" Reeve asked.

"Come on, Sheriff, it's Tennessee." Pike raised his suit jacket and half-turned. Visible inside the waistband of his pants was a holster and a pistol. "Anyone who ain't packing around here right now is a damned fool, and I only consider myself a mediocre fool, at worst."

Reeve looked ready to argue, but Brian said, "How many?" And they all turned to look at him. He covered the mic again and said, "Fifty or more. You might want to hurry. They're massing out there, running through the fields."

"Shit," Reeve said, and motioned for Pike to come along. "Whistle up some help, will you?" he said to Brian. "We're going to need it. Nobody goes in until ordered. I want this done tight, you know? If they're coming en masse, we need to also."

"Got it," Brian said. "I'll set the rendezvous point for just up the road from her—say Orville and Edith Milner's place, end of the driveway?"

"That works!" Reeve shouted behind him as he headed out the door, Pike in tow. Arch was a step behind them, the sound of Brian reassuring Mary Wrightson that everything was going to be all right fading behind him, and he wondered, given how many of those hellcats were out there, just how right his brother-in-law would turn out to be.

He slid into his car as Pike was saying to Reeve, "I'll ride with you," not even asking.

Reeve's jaw tightened, but the sheriff kept his composure. "I don't know when I'll be getting back here. You may want to drive yourself."

"Hell, no," Pike said. "I'm not sure I'd feel safe without someone who knows what they're doing in this situation."

"You got a gun," Reeve said.

"As I understand it from what you've told me, those only delay this enemy," Pike said. Well, shucks. Turns out the County Administrator wasn't a total buffoon, not that Arch had ever taken him for one.

"Get in," Reeve said, and they both disappeared into Reeve's car, Pike flashing a last look of triumph as he did so.

Arch just shook his head and shut his door, starting up the big Explorer, which he had today. He didn't want to be part of the conversation that was about to be held in the sheriff's borrowed car. Funny how they fell into patterns; Reeve hadn't even asked Arch for the Explorer back after his cruiser had been shredded by one of those hellcats. He'd just gone to the square and taken a dead man's car for his own use, a big Toyota 4-Runner that sat a ways off the ground. The sheriff started her up and Arch let him lead. He didn't need to hear any complaints about how he drove like a grandma, not today.

He pulled onto Old Jackson Highway just behind the sheriff's 4-Runner, turning on the sirens and lights to clear a path. He'd stick relatively close to the sheriff's bumper, and he could already see through the moisture-covered rearview window that Pike was turned and talking to the sheriff. No, he didn't want to be part of that conversation at all, but then, there were quite a few of those conversations he'd been avoiding of late. Braeden Tarley had wanted to talk—to do all the talking, actually, after the encounter with the shadowcats in the woods. He'd jabbered for hours; Arch had heard him through the walls of Barney Jones's house long after he'd gone to bed, barely shutting up for two seconds to allow Jones to say anything.

Then there was Jones himself. He'd been trying to catch Arch for days, but Arch had dodged thus far. He had a feeling he knew what the pastor was going to say, so he'd been carefully structuring his time to avoid the man. He felt some residual guilt at avoiding an envoy of the Lord, but he had a purpose he was called to, and it was crossed with what Barney had in mind, he suspected. No right or wrong there, just a lack of clarity on the pastor's part. He was called to save; Arch felt called to destroy in the name of God. Hard to reconcile those two points of view, Arch supposed, but hadn't people been telling him for years that real life was muddier, less clear than he'd always thought? It wasn't black and white, no—but in this case, it sort of was.

Arch glanced at the file sitting on the seat next to him. It was a thick manila folder, filled with witness statements he'd been taking these last few days. Three calls over four days, all the same thing—missing persons. What had started with Nora Wellstone was becoming a pattern. A lady assaulted and kidnapped from her car. A man missing from a local park when he went to walk his dog near sundown. The dog came back dragging his leash; no sign of the man. And then there the lady who went out for groceries at Rogerson's and apparently disappeared from the parking lot. They found her car, loaded with groceries, but she was gone, her purse lying underneath the vehicle.

He'd seen the work of demons these last few months. Up close. Too close. They were messy creatures, vile, disgusting beasts that worked in the name of evil. He'd seen one that burned people up from the inside, seen ones that ripped people apart and tore them to bits after coming into their houses. He'd even seen ones that ran people down on their bicycles.

But in all that time, in all these cases, he hadn't had a lot of missing persons reports. Demons tended to kill people right where they found them, not a lot of runaround, no playing hide-the-corpse.

They'd found nothing of these missing folks. Not a fingernail, not a sign, nothing but the blood smeared on Nora Wellstone's steering wheel. It was a bone Arch felt he had to pick, trying to find the meat. Because these folks could still be alive for all he knew, and it didn't sit right with him that he not try to find them.

He looked ahead into the sheriff's car. Pike was nodding animatedly to whatever Reeve was saying. No, Arch didn't need those complications, that conversation, or any of the other ones people were lining up to have with him. "I got this," he said, and he was sure of it. He knew what he had to do.

He'd keep fighting, doing what he needed to in order to kick back these demons. He'd find this kidnapper, whoever he was, making people just disappear out of the lives of their loved ones without a word, without a trace. Arch swallowed hard; that thought got to him, and it wasn't hard to guess why. "I can handle it," he said, and he meant it. Because he was sure he could.

*

Erin got the mass text and saddled up immediately. It didn't take long for her to get dressed and sweep her hair back in a ponytail, grab her gun belt and bat and hurry to the car. It was a misty cool morning in Midian, the kind that prickled the skin even if you were wearing a jacket. Her cruiser's windshield was covered over with condensation, a thick layer that turned the world into a massive distortion as she slid into the seat and started her up.

With luck, this wouldn't turn into a bad day, but that was all pretty fucking subjective these days.

Her cruiser's engine roared as she took her out onto the road, bumping as it crossed over the storm gutter. She turned the wheel hard to the left, heading for the sticks—again, subjectively. Mary Wrightson's place was outside the city proper, though well inside the town's boundaries. This was how these things were going lately, caterwauling their way through the countryside but not approaching the neatly laid street grid of Midian itself. They'd gotten a few calls and picked off a few stragglers, but killing a half-dozen hellcats wasn't exactly making a difference in the world, or the county, or whatever.

She'd seen that swarm of fuckers with her own eyes. She could aerate a hundred of them and not make a dent.

Erin was still working the problem. Everyone was, but it wasn't a problem with the kind of solution that just jumped out at you. Thousands of demons that moved like a pack of ... well, demon wolves or something, and they weren't small. Even with the army that the watch was assembling, they weren't going to be easy to put down in combat. She had a vague vision of massing a bunch of people on a hilltop with spears and lances and battle standards, like something out of a movie. It always ended in an abject clusterfuck, because those goddamned hellcats would come charging in and keep coming, and because she doubted they could muster a thousand people to fight that kind of battle. Maybe a hundred or two if really pressed. That made the numbers very uneven. Worse, there weren't exactly an abundance of holy weapons yet, which made things even more lopsided in her epic battle vision.

Every way she sliced it, it always seemed to end in a slaughter for her side. Even if they were really, really fortunate, Sam Allen-type casualties would turn the fucking ground red wherever they decided to fight. And the mobility of these damned things ... it practically guaranteed that if for some reason they were able to turn the tables, the hellcats would just run away, like they seemed to every time the watch showed up.

That stunk like a trap to her, if these things could think and assess risk at all. She deemed the threat of the watch to be pretty fucking low to this pack as a whole, but maybe they didn't see it that way. It was better for her if they didn't, because a skittish enemy beat the shit out of one that knew it was too badass for you to handle. Nothing would embolden the hell out of these things better than the feeling that they were unstoppable.

And it was all the worse because, as near as she could tell ... they kind of were, at least in these numbers.

Erin went rattling over the interstate bridge with her sirens blaring and lights flashing, undeterred. Hell, just because there didn't seem to be a hope in hell of beating the things didn't mean they should just surrender. She'd go out there, put a hole in the fuckers as best she could, hopefully wear them down eventually. Because what was the alternative? Bug out like the doc? Hell no. That wasn't her way. That wasn't her way at all.

*

Brian was killing time, the call from Mary Wrightson over with. He'd have stayed on with her, but she got skittish and went to watch at the window. Apparently she hadn't invested in one of those newfangled cordless phones, because she'd hung up on him to do it, in spite of his entreaties to maybe go upstairs, bar the doors, hide her face. Mary Wrightson had never struck him as the sort of soul blessed with an overabundance of brains. Not that most were, compared to him, but still ... stupid. Really stupid to show her face at the window with hellcats running around outside. They weren't the sort to shy away from coming after a body. Quite the opposite, in fact, from what he'd heard.

"Hey," Casey Meacham said, door ringing as he entered the station house. He looked sweaty and disheveled, which was about normal for Casey. "Sorry I'm late."

"It's fine," Brian said, shedding his headset. He frowned at the appearance of the taxidermist; he'd need to break out the rubbing alcohol later, maybe give the microphone and earphones a scrub before he put them back on next shift. Casey's fingers kneaded nervously at his jeans, and they looked ... sticky.

Brian held in a sensation of general disgust at the man's appearance. God only knew what he'd been doing or who with, but it was probably pretty kinky and probably involved Ms. Cherry. Brian had nothing in particular against Ms. Cherry; in fact, if his own personal dry spell of lack of sex continued much longer, he might have considered putting a few sweaty bills in her hand himself in exchange for some form of relief. At least, before he had the point driven home over and over that she traded with Casey on the regular. That had been a blow to her glamorous image. He'd always known she'd fucked for money, but seeing who she fucked destroyed any illusions he'd had about the profession and made his own hand seem like a real classy, sensible, STD-free option.

"Just got the text," Casey said. "Everybody else on the way?"

"Yeah, you might need to coordinate some," Brian said, peeling himself out of the chair, a layer of sweat coating his pants to his ass. How long had he been sitting here? He hadn't even noticed until he tried to stand up, but his legs felt uneven. "Someone always ends up calling in for directions, even when you send them in the text."

"Well, not everyone's as bright as you and I," Casey said in all seriousness. He licked his lips, which looked chapped, and a little bloody at one end. "Any word from the doc?"

Brian shrugged. "Not that I know of. We keep leaving messages, presumably she keeps ignoring them, unless she's one of our missing persons, but ... Reeve says her cell's active in Chattanooga, so ..." He shrugged again. "She left. Sensibly."

"Still a shame," Casey said, sitting down in the chair and rolling it around in a circle once with a squeal. "She's a MILF-y one, ain't she? And I swear she and Molly feed every mother/daughter fantasy I ever had."

"Dude," Brian said, barely keeping himself from taking a step back in revulsion. "She's sixteen."

"I know, I know. I wouldn't do nothing," Casey said, winking. "Not with the daughter, anyway."

"I doubt you'd do much with the mother either," Brian said.

"She's a fiery one," Casey seemed to agree. "But that's okay. I like a little fire."

Brian blinked. "Take up smoking then. It'd be healthier for you than making a pass at Lauren Darlington. I would guess, anyway."

"You may just be right," Casey said, nodding. "But you know what they say about that."

Brian didn't. "Uhh ... that the heart wants what the heart wants?" He felt stupid after it came out.

Casey just chortled, low and sleazy. "Nawww. That a dick ain't got no conscience. And lemme tell you ... I think about 'em all the time while I'm—"

"Shiiiiiiit," Brian said, cringing away.

"Ain't got to feel guilty, son," Casey said, cackling and turning his back, putting on the headset. "They don't know they're involved."

"I don't know how it is that you can make shit that's sorta normal, like a sexual fantasy you have in the privacy of your mind, sound so goddamned creepy, Casey," Brian said.

"You're overthinking this," Casey said, fiddling with the headset and then with the cell phone used for contacting the watch. He slid it over the surface of the table, making an irritating scraping noise as the smooth surface of the plastic raked against the faux wood of the desk. "You gotta do what feels right to get yourself even, brutha." He winked. "You know what I mean?"

Brian just stared at him. "I don't think just randomly hittin' some ass is going to make things right, Casey. Our town is being invaded by demons, dude. Getting laid isn't going to solve the problem. Getting high isn't going to do it, though God knows I wish I could right now." And boy, did he. "It's just crushing pressure, twenty-four seven, like trying to go to sleep after you've watched people die and knowing there's an axe hanging over you. It's the sword of fucking Damocles—" He sighed, turning away. "You don't know what that means."

"Sure I do," Casey said. "Man sitting at a banquet after he made wise with a king about how happy or prosperous or whatever the man was, and he's got a sword hanging over his head dangling by a single hair." Brian turned and looked back at the taxidermist. "I done some reading in my life, you know. I ain't just a pretty face. And the lesson is—happiness hangs by a thread, right?"

"Yeah," Brian said, a little taken aback. "That's ... yeah, that's basically it."

"You gotta grab all the happiness you can in the moments when you can, son," Casey said. "If that means filling your glass with some shine, you oughta get to drinking. If it's weed, hell, man, smoke it up. Me, I prefer a strict regimen of all that plus ass. Lots of ass. Keeps me level."

"Gee, I'd hate to see what you're like when you're ... unlevel," Brian said.

"I'm a fucking mess," Casey said. "Like you. But still better looking." He flashed Brian a grin. "That's why I do these things, you know. I gotta be effective in my work life, in my personal life. That means finding those stress relief valves and twisting them motherfuckers to let the steam out however you got to. You wanting to be out there today?"

Brian was listening vaguely until the question, then felt like he'd been smacked between the eyes by a football. Which he'd had happen to him more than a few times as his father was trying to teach him about his favorite sport. "Uh ... no, actually." He leaned back against a desk. "I don't belong out there."

"Ain't what I asked," Casey said. "I said do you *want* to be out there. You know, one of the boys, gun in hand, sword in hand, whatever—"

"I got a limp now, Casey," Brian said, trying to keep that frozen smile on his face. "And I wasn't exactly mobile and effective before—"

"But do you want to be out there?" Casey asked. "You know what I mean. Like Braeden Tarley—wait, bad example, he's had shit go wrong on him no one wants to. Like Percy Olson? Good ol' boy, factory worker, been showing up some lately to whoop ass. Neck as red as a fire ant bite, swings a lead pipe like you said something bad about a biker's momma. You put that boy in a softball game with one of them aluminum bats and he's going to hit him some home runs and piss off some steady drinking motherfuckers in the outfield because he's making them run."

Brian just closed his eyes and shook his head. "What the fuck are you talking about, Casey?"

Casey just stared at him a second. "Do you wish you could be like Percy? Be out there in the fight?"

"No, I don't want to be like Percy," Brian said, staring back. "I don't need to be out there."

Casey stared back at him. "You sure? Percy's been fucking Daisy Lenzen for about three years, and I don't know if you've seen her lately, but that girl has matured into a hell of a woman. I mean, she's a peach. Not like a Georgia peach, but pretty fucking good—"

"Later, Casey," Brian said. "I gotta go to the hospital."

"Hey, whatcha doing later?" Casey called after him.

Brian had almost made the door, and was regretting he didn't just walk right out. "I told you—I'm going to the hospital."

"All day and all night?" Casey asked. "You not coming home tonight?"

Brian almost answered, "Nope," but he hadn't slept in his own bed in a while, and had a feeling it was starting to show. It was definitely starting to be smelled. "I don't know, maybe. Why?"

"Because I'm getting off shift here at four o'clock. Figured you might want to do something to unwind."

Brian nearly pushed the door without answering, but instead he stood there, frozen. Had the town weirdo just asked him on a ... man date?

And if so ... why was he hesitating to respond with a resounding "NO"?

"I don't want to visit Ms. Cherry's with you, Casey," Brian said, taking a breath. Mostly true. Except for that wiggling few inches below his belt that hadn't gotten laid since college. But like Casey had said, that thing didn't have a conscience.

"Wasn't talking about that," Casey said. "I wanted to show you my other favorite place. Give you a chance to blow off some steam all real-like. You know?"

Brian tried to unwind that sentence and was fairly sure he'd gotten the gist but still missed something. "Uh ... doing what?"

"I'll show you," Casey said, eyes glinting. "Ain't nothing you'd find objectionable, don't worry. I get your boundaries, and I ain't gonna expose you to nothing that'd send you squealing in the other direction."

Brian surveyed him with a wary eye. "What the hell do you know about boundaries, Casey?"

"That while mine might extend to letting Gus Terkel give me a little love in the backdoor every once in a while when he's desperately on the outs with his wife, most of y'all would find that objectionable," Casey said, all his humor gone. "And it ain't gonna be nothing like that, so don't worry. Just meet me here at four, and we'll work on getting your head straight."

Brian just stared at him with a cocked eyebrow. He opened his mouth to protest and then shut it. What the hell else was he going to do? Sit at the hospital all night again? Besides, knowing Casey did have a basic understanding of boundaries was ... strangely reassuring. "Yeah ..." Brian said, and pushed through the door.

"So I'll see you at four?" Casey called after him.

"Maybe," Brian called back, unwilling to commit to more than that right now. The sunshine and cool air hit him in the face as he stepped into the parking lot, the high humidity making it feel chillier than it was. "Maybe you will." Because why the hell not try something different?

*

Jason Pike was enjoying the ride, surprisingly, even though Reeve was driving like a bat out of hell. Well, it wasn't like it was the first time

Pike had gone a hundred miles an hour down a back road. It was, however, the first time he could recall doing it legally.

"I just want to point this out. We seem to be rushing there in an effort to get to this rendezvous point so we can wait," Pike said.

"Yep," Reeve said.

Pike just nodded. "Why not come at this a little slower, knowing we're going to get there and have to wait for the others?" Reeve's jaw moved tightly, but he said nothing. "I ain't objecting, you understand," Pike said. "Just trying to understand the 'hurry up and wait' philosophy we're embracing here."

"We're doing it this way because I'd rather be close by, so we can rush in to help Mary if need be rather than get a screaming emergency call and not be able to get there for another half hour." He kept his eyes nailed to the road ahead, and the siren wailed from the cruiser behind them. "So yeah, we're going to hurry up and get there, then wait for the others—unless we get the call that it's all gone to hell; then we might charge in early. You understand now?"

Pike nodded once and smiled, to show he was cool with it. "Yep. I think I got it."

"Well, good," Reeve said, just dripping with sarcasm, "because that's what I'm here for. To explain to our County Administrator the stuff he plainly don't get."

Pike whistled. "Damn. How long you been holding that in?"

Reeve looked pissed, mostly with himself. "I'm sorry. That was—"

"Pretty damned reflective of how you been feeling for months, I'd say." Pike grinned. "And I can't blame you. I been a real pain in your ass."

"That's something that sticks in my craw," Reeve finally admitted after a few seconds silence. "You know what a pain in the ass you've been. And you've proceeded to do it anyway."

"Look, if I'm a pain in the ass—and I freely admit I am," Pike said, "it's because I don't serve you, Sheriff. I serve the same people as you." That was a lie. Pike didn't serve any people, except maybe Darla. Unless you counted the occasional foray into cannibalism. Then he'd definitely served a person or two. "That means I got them to answer to. Now, if it was just you and me and all the money in the world, hell, I'd raise your budget sky high and no one would give a shit. But Calhoun County ain't exactly the most prosperous place, and when we go over our budgets, we start having to talk to taxpayers about raising property taxes, the sales tax, the wheel tax … Things no one wants to hear about."

"Yeah, and I get that during normal conditions," Reeve snapped.

The sheriff seemed to be losing his composure, trees whipping by outside the window past his face, which remained resolutely locked on target through the windshield ahead. "But you've been aware for a while that we are not operating under normal conditions right now. And I have a hard time giving a good goddamn about blowing a hole in your budget while I'm trying to keep this town, this county, from being destroyed by demons."

"Well, if you'll forgive me for saying so," Pike said, "this feels a little like a World War II metaphor is in order. You know how they used to sell war bonds?"

Reeve sighed. "Yeah, I do."

"They used them to fund buying bullets and paying for tanks and—well, hell, everything else that needed to be bought, because it wasn't like people could just work for free the whole war through. Refineries had to pay their workers so their workers could eat, otherwise everybody'd end up starving while you're fighting the war."

Reeve frowned. "You suggesting we sell demon war bonds or something?"

Pike hadn't been going that way, but … "I've heard worse ideas. But it wasn't my point. My point was that the part of the war you hear about is Omaha Beach. Normandy. The Bulge. Okinawa. The soldiers on the field are heroes, and rightly so. Not heroes—the fucking accountants behind the scenes that made sure they had guns in their hands."

"That'd hold a little more water with me if you'd actually been trying to get guns in our hands before now," Reeve said, "instead of the opposite."

"Now look, you can throw all the damned acrimony my way you want," Pike said, "for how I acted before. But I have come to you now, expressed my contrition, and am trying to work with you to solve the problem, okay? If you want to just keep throwing shade my way, well, that'd be fine if it was summer. But if you'll forgive me, it's fall now, it's getting chilly, and we all need to gather 'round the campfire."

"'Throw … shade'? What the hell does that mean? How you gonna throw—"

"Never mind," Pike said. "It's just an expression. The point is—I'm here. I'm asking how I help you, Sheriff. Is it just money?"

"Well, that sure as shit wouldn't hurt," Reeve said. "Because although I'm sure it'd be great to get some war bond sales going, I'm not really sure I have time to organize that right now. And we've just been running through the accounts of one of our wealthier members of the watch. But he took a bullet to the head a week or so ago, and …" The sheriff got quiet for a few seconds. "Anyway, I don't know how long that's going to last. I'll drain my accounts if that's what I have to do to get us through, but dammit, I ain't a rich man."

"And you shouldn't have to anyway," Pike said. "The county can take up some of this burden. Now, I know you don't necessarily get this, but being in touch with people, I know that, uh, over near Culver—"

"Yeah, I don't need to hear about the politicking of this," Reeve said. "I get it. The county's long. Not everyone's feeling a demon pinch at the moment the way Midian is."

"You got the idea," Pike said. "But I been working on them for you—" Reeve snorted. "It ain't been easy, I might add."

"I imagine not," Reeve said. "Seems like someone else has a problem, why would you want to get involved?"

"Well, they're your neighbors," Pike said. "*We* are, I should say, since that's where I call home. I'm trying to get us all in this together, but—" The car cornered hard onto a dirt road, gravel rattling against the wheel well behind Pike.

"You'd have an easier time damming up the Caledonia River with your own body," Reeve said, grudgingly.

He was starting to get it. Or maybe he'd gotten it all along, but was too deep in his silo to want to look up over the edge at Pike. That was fine, because at least Pike knew where to dig for him. "I agree, it's a hell of a difficult task. Like a labor of Sisyphus. And it ain't made easier by me having worked so hard to drag your ass out of office these last weeks. I probably look like an idiot, in fact, but hey—I'm trying. I'm doing the Whitman thing about shouting all the truth I know today from the rooftops, even if it contradicts everything I said yesterday. This is too big a problem, too huge a cause, stakes higher than the damned sky—we can't lose."

"We got a point of agreement there," Reeve said.

"We got a lot more common ground than maybe you've given credit for up to this point," Pike said. "And that's fine, because I know why you've done what you've done to protect people, Midian, the county. Just understand—I can't maybe fight the fight the way you can, marshaling an army. But I'm gonna try." As lies went, that one was a whopper the size of Russia, but Pike delivered it with a smile and boyish charm. "In every way I can."

"Help is surely appreciated," Reeve said again, grudgingly. "And sorely needed."

"I'm going to get you all the help I can," Pike said. He thrust out a hand. "We're in this all the way, all the way to the end."

Reeve eyed his hand for a second like it was emitting radiation, then took it as he pulled the car to the side of the road, giving Pike a handshake that fortunately stopped short of bone-crushing force. "I'm sorry if I'm come off strong, especially if you mean what you say. But you'll have to forgive me for being skeptical."

"You're a virtuous man, Sheriff," Pike said, and caught the upraised eyebrow. "Protecting the people the way you do, plunging through the personal tragedy you've endured recently … that's a virtue of the old kind. The sort of drive to duty they used to sing songs about."

"Well, I don't imagine there's going to be a whole lot of songs sung about what we're doing here," Reeve said dryly. "Unless they're funeral hymns."

"'Amazing Grace' always did have a nice ring to it," Pike said, turning his head to look at the mailbox just outside his window. It read MILNER. "But I don't think I'm ready for it to play at my funeral just yet."

"Good," Reeve said, "because I've been to enough damn funerals this week." Reeve gave him a dark smile, and Pike matched it with that rueful one of his own. It was working, slowly. Maybe he'd move the man in the direction he needed yet. Maybe.

*

Hendricks listened to the buzz of the watch phone again and rolled his eyes. The hearse was still ahead of them, and finally he'd had it, so he looked over at Duncan and said, "What's the deal?"

"All call," Duncan said, looking at his own phone. "Hellcats on the prowl outside of town."

"Shit, fuck, damn," Hendricks said.

"That sounds like a hell of a Saturday night," Duncan said. "Maybe fuck before you shit?"

Hendricks cracked a thin smile. "What about the damn?"

"Seems we're heading that way, doesn't it?" Duncan didn't smile much, but he had a thin one right now too. "Should we give up following this guy and go render aid?"

Hendricks thought about it. "You think this hellcat army is massing up for a big assault?"

"Hard to imagine a coordinated one," Duncan said. "They're not a hive mind. They run in small social circles—or at least they did. I guess I've seen some new behavior from them since I got here."

"Do they have documentaries on these kind of demons somewhere?"

Hendricks asked. "Because all I got was a lousy handbook, and if there's a channel where I can On Demand this shit, I'm telling you, I'm gonna be so pissed at—" He cut himself off.

"At her?" Duncan was smiling now, for sure.

"Who?" Hendricks played dumb. "Starling?"

Duncan rolled his eyes, but he kind of sucked at it, so they went sideways. "You know that's not who I'm talking about."

Hendricks kept his head down, hunched over the wheel a little tighter. "It amazes me how, even with your senses supposedly constipated, you can still have a pretty good read on some of this stuff. How do you know about her?"

"She's a player," Duncan said. "The Office of Occultic Concordance would be pretty shit at our jobs if we didn't know who's breathing down the other end of your phone at night, given what she's got going for her."

Hendricks shot him a sideways look. "How much do you know about her?"

"Everything." The reply was even, knowing, and more than a little frustrating in its lack of specificity.

"Forgive me if I don't leap right into believing that just cuz you say it's so."

"Doesn't matter to me what you believe about that," Duncan said. "It's not even the question at hand anyway." The phone buzzed again and he held it up. "What do we do about this?"

"Well, what can we do?" Hendricks asked. He nodded at the hearse in front of them. "We have a definite lead in the hellcats, and then we've got a … I don't even know. A feeling, I guess?"

"Pretty much."

"What's one more car in that clump out there?" Hendricks asked. "I mean, we could go slay some hellcats, but …" He shook his head. "We're starting to get into the realm of the stupid for the fights we're undertaking, with that kind of shit. Those things …" He shook his head. "They're not a game-changer, they're a fucking game-breaker. They find their balls and go tearing through Midian all at once, this is fucking over, man. There won't even be anyone left to cry."

"Agreed," Duncan said.

Hendricks gave him a double-take look sideways. "'Agreed'? Isn't it your job to keep these things under control?"

This time Duncan shrugged. "Sure. Lots of things fit in that purview, though. Busting the shells of a thousand or so hellcats is a little outside my abilities, though."

"So much for demonic pest control," Hendricks said. "What the fuck good are you OOCs against that, then?"

"Not much, I guess," Duncan said. "Not in our current numbers."

"So, stupid question then," Hendricks said. "Why don't you have more numbers here?"

Duncan stayed silent. Scarily silent, Hendricks judged. "Good question," Duncan said.

Hendricks felt like a grenade had gone off in front of his fucking face. "One that you don't have an answer to? Or one you've got a shitty answer to?"

The OOC just sat there like a stone, or a corpse, and when he finally stirred, it was a simple hand motion, putting a palm up. "A little of column A …"

"And a little of B?" Hendricks slammed a palm against the steering wheel. "I'm used to my hotspots sucking, but shit, man. We pulled back the tide on this place how many times now?"

"Lots."

"And it's creeping in hard," Hendricks said. "I get that your office doesn't give a fuck about every flyspeck that has a hotspot flare, but JFC, man. When you see the train coming toward the wreck in slow motion, you'd think they'd want to do *something* about it."

"I don't know that they're not doing something about it," Duncan said. "I just have no idea if the thing they're maybe doing is even something we'd want them to do. If that makes any kind of sense."

Hendricks felt like he'd need a few hours to untangle that fucking knot. "How on the outs with the office are you?"

"Pretty out."

"And is Guthrie … 'in'?" Hendricks asked delicately. Well, for him.

"Hard to say." Duncan looked over at him. "You were hoping to hear the beating of the cavalry's hooves?"

"Maybe literally in the case of your peeps," Hendricks said, white-knuckling the wheel. "I ain't never counted on a demon to solve my problems before, so no—I wasn't expecting your … folks … to do anything for me. *To* me, maybe, but not a goddamned thing *for* me. Just seems weird, every time I try and wrap my head around your mission. Keep the order, but you know, don't actually worry about the order—"

"I think you're laboring under a false assumption that my people care about your so-called order," Duncan said. "They don't. They want to maintain the status quo, keep things hush hush. That doesn't mean no fatalities, no towns going to hell and disappearing off the map—it just means few enough that people don't start noticing and making a fuss. Acceptable losses. They could give a fallookandresh's turd if you and everyone in this burg goes down the craw of the nearest helghar'lac, so long as it doesn't reach a tipping point."

Hendricks held tight to the wheel, then spun the SUV about hard, flipping a bitch and taking the vehicle around into the opposite lane. He brought her about and hit the accelerator, squealing the tires and heading back in the opposite direction.

Duncan was quiet for a few seconds, then said, "So … solidarity, then?"

"Seems like I'm the only long-term demon hunter in these parts," Hendricks said, nudging the MPH needle up toward 100. "And that means the only professional doing something about this, so … yeah, I guess I should be there for whatever they got going."

"Good," Duncan said with something faint approval.

"Why?" Hendricks asked. "Don't you care about catching the Thin Man back there?"

"The undertaker can wait," Duncan said. "There are bigger priorities."

"Like hanging together?" Hendricks asked.

"Better than hanging separately," Duncan said. "Because honestly … you got no chance of getting out of those nooses on your own."

"Fucking reassuring," Hendricks said, then added grudgingly, "but … thanks for at least being honest about it."

"That may be all I have left to give you," Duncan said. "That and a baton for a few demons." He didn't smile, didn't look at Hendricks, just stared straight ahead through the window.

"Well, that's fucking unnerving," Hendricks decided after a moment's thought.

"I agree," Duncan said, "and I don't even have nerves."

They rode in silence the rest of the way, that thought causing Hendricks's guts to churn as they raced to meet up with the watch.

*

"He's stable; let's move him upstairs to the OR," Lauren said, pulling her stethoscope off the patient's chest. If he'd been conscious, he might have been whining about how cold it was as she pushed it against his sternum, but he was dead out, and a few inches from actually dead, so he didn't say a goddamned thing, which was good. Because she'd just saved his life temporarily, and bitching about it might have compelled her to slap the shit out of him.

"Moving." One of the nurses rolled the gurney, and another doc went with, heading for the elevator upstairs. Lauren snapped off a glove, pretty confident she was done for now, and if not—well, Dr. Stevens had this one until they got to the OR.

"Nice work," Alanna Castle said. She was a career nurse, and one of those mother-bear types who bridged the gap between docs and nurses when it came to the back and forth. She treated the ER like it was one big, happy family, which it often wasn't, especially around contract negotiation time. "Welcome back."

"I'd say it's good to be here, but you know bullshit when you hear it, Alanna," Lauren said.

Alanna's smile was as snide as Lauren's comment, and just as knowing. "I got three teenagers; I don't just know it when I hear it, I can smell from a mile off. Still, welcome back." She stripped off her plastic gown and trashed it, tossing the gloves in the bin with it, and went off to her next patient.

Lauren took a breath. She was probably due to check in with another patient soon too. The ER's tempo was manageable, but damned sure not quiet. Every time it got quiet, staffing cuts tended to follow, because why pay for doctors and nurses you didn't need? Management didn't tend to think about things like long-term demand, not when it hit the bottom line.

She took a few steps out into the hall, looking down at the worn white tile. She hadn't spoken with Molly after the unpleasant wake-up, and that was potentially a problem given that her daughter was going to be sitting around Elise's house all day without anything to do but think about how much she disliked the current situation. And maybe read a book or something. But probably mostly stew.

Lauren could understand that. She wasn't happy about the way things were right now either.

But what the hell else was there to do? Head back to Midian, with its fucking endless streams of demons, toss her daughter into a human-sacrifice situation in the name of—what? Home? Was that the primitive god she would be willing to give her daughter's life for? It was like some fucking caveman territorial instinct, the desire to protect the ground they considered theirs at the risk of Molly's life and her own, and that just didn't sit right with her higher brain functions.

Her gut told her a different story, but her brain? It was all in for staying the fuck away from Midian.

Lauren looked up when she heard her name called. It was a calm, male voice, and for a moment she thought maybe it was her boss about to give her grief for wandering aimlessly. Well, shit, her mother had just died and been buried; she was entitled to a little aimlessness, wasn't she? She turned, about to snap at him—

And shut the fuck up right then. It wasn't her boss at all.

"Hey," Brian Longholt said, hand up in a little wave. He looked like shit rubbed in dirt, a few days of pathetically thin beard stubble on his cheeks and upper lip, his clothes looking like they'd been slept in for weeks, and his hair—well, it had never been that impressive, but it was especially bad now, like a faux hawk gone terribly wrong, the point apparently having been directed sideways in his sleep.

"Jesus," Lauren breathed. He was only ten feet away.

Brian looked skyward for a second, like he was thinking about his reply more carefully than normal. "No, it's Brian, but that's a common mistake—oh, who am I fucking kidding? No one makes that mistake but me."

Lauren found her hands on her hips, and she was surveying him like a serious fixer-upper she'd been charged with rehabbing. "What the hell happened to you?" The words slipped out before she could rein them in, regret following hard on their heels.

"So, I guess I must look like the post-crucifixion Jesus then," Brian said, the ghost of a smile hiding beneath that stubbly lip. He'd never been the most put-together guy, but for fuck's sake, he'd gone downhill in a hurry.

"Just about," Lauren said, tugging at the scrubs that rested uncomfortably on her hips. "I mean ... how long has it been since you've had a full night of sleep?" The dark circles under his eyes looked like they'd been rubbed on by a football coach ... which was an impossibility, because if Brian had ever played football, Lauren would eat the entire biohazard bin in the ER.

Brian thought about that, too. A bad sign, because the Ivy League grad didn't usually have to think too long before snapping out an answer. "A while," he finally decided on. "Better question—how are you doing?"

"Not as badly as you," she said, edging in a little closer, hovering out of pity. Part of her wanted to wipe at the smudges on his face, to mom him, though she suspected his mother would probably do that if she got close enough and was ... well, still functional after all the shit their family had gone through.

"Well, you certainly look better," Brian said with a wan smile.

Lauren put a hand on the back of her neck and played with her ponytail self-consciously. "I'd ask you what you're doing here, but ..."

"Yeah, you already know," Brian said, looking down. He'd lost a lot of the smartassery that had defined him. He'd been such an irreverent, all-knowing kind of dick. Seeing him like this ... shit, if pride went before the fall, then the fall Brian Longholt had taken had probably jarred loose a few other vitals as well upon the landing. "Dad's ... the same, basically."

"I don't know if I said it yet—" Lauren started, rushing to her default.

"Yeah, we exchanged condolences, all that," Brian said, looking sideways. "I think. I mean, it's hard to keep track; there's been so much of it flying around, you know."

"Yeah, well ... I'm still sorry," Lauren said. "You got a double whammy."

"Triple, if we're counting," Brian said, and when she looked at him questioningly, he said, "I pulled the trigger, remember? So we had Alison, Dad, and ... the guilt."

"I think Molly's going through a little of that last one," Lauren said. "You know, losing the grandmother who raised her plus ... doing it herself at the behest of—of those—"

"Those things, yeah," Brian said with a nod. "Lots of that going around too, thick as the funeral invites and obits in Midian. I can't decide whether the people who didn't see this coming, who didn't know about demons before ... whether they have it worse or better than those of us who were in the know."

"I don't think it's a competition," Lauren said. "Or if it is, it's the kind everyone loses."

"No shit," Brian said and lapsed into silence. She was just trying to figure out a way to tell him goodbye without sounding like a bitch when he said, "So, I'm guessing by the million ignored messages you just don't want to talk about it."

She almost said, "Talk about what?" but held it back. She stared at him in silence for a few seconds that felt like a year. "Not particularly," she finally replied.

"I get that," Brian said.

"I doubt it."

"No, really," Brian said. "You're out; you probably feel like I'd try and drag you back in."

She gave him a wary eye. "Because you would. Drowning people tend to drown other people. Not because they want to, but because they try to cling to you for dear life and you can't really fight the tide plus another person unless you really, really know what you're doing. And the people who know what they're doing in this demon invasion are limited to—well, to the cowboy. And even that's questionable."

"I'm not drowning," Brian said, brow puckered in a frown. "Okay, wait ... I'm sort of drowning, but maybe not the way you think—shit,

I'm ... this metaphor is like—"

"Been a while since undergrad, but I'm pretty sure 'like' is a simile, not metaphor."

Brian stopped, smiling. "This is a, uh ... complex situation. Comparisons are difficult."

"I think I nailed it with the drowning thing."

"Yeah, maybe," Brian said, letting out a soft sigh and running his hand through his tragic mess of hair. He paused, frowning again as he ran his fingers through it, apparently discovering the state of it. "Look ... can we talk?"

"I think we just did," Lauren said, looking over her shoulder. Where was her boss, telling her to go back to work?

"For real," Brian said. "No drowning, no entreaties to bring your daughter back to hell or anything, just—you know, real talk. Between people that have been there."

Lauren held her breath unintentionally. "Brian ... what the hell else is there to talk about? I can't go back. My daughter—"

"I'm not going to ask you to," Brian said. "I just ..." He lowered his head, lowered his voice. "Okay, fine ... I guess I am drowning—"

"I'll thank you not to drag me down with you."

"Not that way," Brian said, and when he looked up, the wan humor was gone and his eyes were deep wells of loneliness. "I'm just ..." He took a breath. "I'm starting to think ... you made the right choice." He shook his head. "Never mind. It's good to see you, Lauren." He gave her another look. "You look ... good. I'll, uh—"

"Wait," she said, regretting it even as she said it. "Maybe we can ... get a coffee in the cafeteria."

Relief washed over his features, and it seemed to take a weight off him. "You sure?"

"Quick," she said, grabbing him by the upper arm and pushing him toward the elevator, "before I change my mind or my boss comes looking for me."

*

Erin had parked in the line of cars forming at the end of the Milner driveway, Arch ahead of her and Reeve two up, someone in the passenger seat who looked like County Administrator Pike. "Goddamn," Erin said, lips constricting in a rictus of distaste at the thought of what Reeve was probably being subjected to right now. She viewed politicians with distaste, and the thought of treating with one was about as appealing as having intercourse with a hot poker.

She watched another couple cars come sliding into the line behind her, followed by a third a minute later. She could see Father Nguyen in one, Mike McInness and one of his patrons behind that. She couldn't tell if the next one back was Larry Saunders, but Chauncey Watson was definitely the one after that. She lost track after that, cars rolling in every one to two minutes, filling the road around the curve.

"That ain't no good," she muttered under her breath. Hell, pretty soon the tail was going to get so stretched out no one would be able to tell if the back of the line was getting ripped apart by those fucking hellcats.

She was just about to dial up Reeve to say exactly that when someone knocked at the window on the passenger side and she just about shit herself jumping, hand already going for the gun on her hip. She looked over to see a dark face grinning in at her, and when she flipped the unlock button Amanda Guthrie slid in next to her.

"Lerner," she said as the black woman slammed the door after slipping into the passenger seat.

"You know, calling me by a white man's name is a microaggression," Guthrie said with a smirk.

"You prefer I call you by your demon name?" Erin tossed back. She knew full well that demons didn't share names. "Because it's the only real one you got."

"I always admired your skill with repartee, dear," Guthrie said, and here she completely departed from Lerner, who would have come off sounding like a pretentious, paternalistic ass if he'd delivered these same words in that Boston accent. Coming from Guthrie it almost sounded sincere. "How are you doing this fine morning?" The question was delivered with definite precision, eyes focused on Erin, who was keeping hers straight ahead.

"Fi—" Erin started to say.

"'Fine'? That's all you've got?" Guthrie snorted.

"Why are you in my car?" Erin asked.

"Well, because we're longtime gal pals, of course," Guthrie said, holding a hand over her heart, mock-wounded. When she saw Erin's skeptical glare, she said, "Oh, come on. We went over a cliff together. Also, I caught a ride here with Father Nguyen, and you can't expect me to sit in a car with a holy man. That's like asking any woman on the planet to sit next to Harvey Weinstein. You know what even setting foot in his church does to me?" Guthrie shuddered. "So … I needed some sanctuary. A safe place. And I saw you."

"You think I'm safe?" Erin kept her eyes ahead again.

"Well, we went through—or over—some shit together," Guthrie

said breezily, "so ... yeah. You'll do, gal pal." Guthrie settled back in her seat and feigned a deep breath. "So. What should we talk about?"

"I dunno."

"How about vagina stuff?" Guthrie asked, looking right at Erin with a big grin. "Because lemme tell you, these things—"

"Oh, God, what the fuck?" Erin felt like clawing her way out the window without even opening it first.

"Yes, the fuck—let's talk about fucking," Guthrie said. "This body got an upgrade. Cuz I'm gonna tell you—that old one? Seriously lacking in the pleasure centers. This one is new hotness though, and they really improved the interface for experiencing the big O if you know what I mean—"

"I'd like to not know what you mean," Erin said, clutching helplessly at the door handle. She didn't pull it, but God, did she want to.

"Hey, I just figured given how much you and the cowboy used to roll around like a couple of angry hamsters, you might be able to give me some advice," Guthrie said, "maybe some pointers. I haven't spent a lot of time pondering sex since it was, uhh ... kinda pointless, actually, in my old body. Home Office neutered us, big time, in terms of what made it through those shells. But now, it's like a fucking symphony up in my—"

"Lalalalalalala," Erin said, putting her hands over her head. "You're a demon. I don't need to know about what you're doing with your demon snatch."

"Fine, be that way," Guthrie said, folding her arms over her chest. "I'll find someone else to talk it over with later." She stayed silent long enough for Erin to withdraw her hands from her head. "So ... what do you want to talk about then?"

"I don't, really," Erin said.

"What about your family?" Guthrie asked.

"Uh, no—"

"I heard they all came swarming to town when you got hurt," Guthrie said, keeping a neutral expression. "Weren't you raised here?"

"Yeah, why—"

"So did they just bail on you the second you graduated or what?"

Erin just sort of sat there, blinking. "Not—I mean, yeah, shortly after, I guess. My parents never intended to stay here as long as they did, so when I graduated—yeah, they moved over by Nashville. My brothers were already gone—"

"Oh, cool, where'd your brothers go?" Guthrie asked.

"One's in Cleveland, Ohio," Erin said. "He helps run a factory up there; been working there since he graduated college. Another is a captain in the army—"

"So they left and never came back," Guthrie nodded. "Is that a trend? I feel like that's a trend I've read about. Brain drain, I think they call it? Where the smart, ambitious people leave little towns for prospects elsewhere?"

Erin flushed. "Does that mean I'm not a brain, since I haven't been drained?"

Guthrie just shrugged. "You can get all offended by it if you want, but I'm not casting judgment on you, nor aspersions on your choices. Just stating a fact as expressed by someone else. Seems like your family left this little berg and you stayed, for whatever reason. I'm curious about why."

"Because I like it here," Erin said, feeling a little defensive.

"Pre-demon, I assume you mean. Unless you're really into brimstoning us, which—I wouldn't blame you. There's some fun in popping demons."

"No, I don't particularly enjoy popping you like zits," Erin said. "I liked the town the way it was before. I knew everybody. Everything was … familiar. I grew up here. My parents didn't. My dad came for work, and stayed because it was a decent, quiet place to raise a family. Once his family was raised, he didn't see a reason to stay, so he and Mom left. They offered to have me come with them, but—come on, I'm a grown-up … ish," she added, blushing. "I didn't want to follow them to some new place where I didn't know anyone."

"See, I read towns like this are dying," Guthrie said. "That they usually have this one big employer—"

"Yeah," Erin said. "Ours is a paper mill."

"Right," Guthrie said. "So when that one big employer goes, this town of a thousand, two thousand, three thousand—it throws like a quarter, half the workforce out of work. Suddenly all this money that's flowing into that employer stops, the paychecks from the employer stop, all the money those employees are spending stops—"

"Thanks for the high-school economics lesson."

"—and the town just dries up," Guthrie went on. "Shops croak off—you know, the ones that weren't already torched by Wal-Mart. The square ends up a hollow shell of closed-down businesses. People leave if they can, stay if they can't, or if they're … overly attached." She didn't look at Erin as she said this, but Erin felt the burn of accusation even so. "Hope sinks, and so does the town."

"And then demons move in and make things oh so much worse," Erin said.

"That does happen sometimes," Guthrie said with a nod. "Hotspots don't tend to happen in economically booming areas for some reason. I've pondered that one, but it'd take someone with a lot more knowledge of how that world works to come to a conclusion, I think." Her eyes twinkled, and Erin got the feeling she wasn't saying all she knew.

"Feels like that might be intentional," Erin said, her face starting to cool down a little.

"Maybe," Guthrie said, "but as they say, 'correlation does not equal causation.' Meaning—"

"I fucking know it means they might be unrelated, asshole. I may not fit your definition of a brain, but I'm not an idiot."

Guthrie grinned. "Sorry. Talking down to an audience is part of being a demon, you know. Our opinion of humans isn't all that high."

Erin rolled her eyes. "Last I checked, you guys live in our society, not vice versa, and I don't see you creating the internal combustion engine, the internet, or cell phones." She looked at Guthrie pointedly, expecting she'd know the answer to this next question before she asked it. "Do they have cell phones in hell?"

Guthrie made a whoosh noise. "I must give credit here, because that was a quality burn. It wasn't quite to the burn level of flesh in the pits, but—damn, girl, you have struck true. No, demons didn't have much to do with any of those things, and all we use cell phones for in hell is in this one room where all they do is ring all day long, different phones. Or they're just out of reach of someone who wants to check their email—because they're at a low level of conscious thought, and it's this instinctive kind of drive to get that phone in hand." Guthrie cackled. "It'd be sad if it wasn't so damned funny. You people enslaved your conscious thought to machines in less than twenty years. I thought the TV was bad, but these things—anyway, yeah. Way to go with that little innovation. You should totes be proud of what you accomplished with those."

"Jokes aside, I kinda am proud," Erin said, "to be part of a species that innovates, that shares knowledge at the tips of our fingers—"

"Yeah, that Kylie Jenner Instagram account is a real boon to humanity."

"Manufacturing and the automobile created pollution on an industrial level," Erin said. "If Kylie Jenner's Instagram account and the rest of the Kardashians is the worst side effect of the digital age, I think we're going to be okay."

"I knew I chose the right car to get into," Guthrie said. "So, here's something I've pondered—"

Brake lights flared ahead of Erin, catching her attention immediately. Guthrie shut right up. "Looks like it's go time," Erin said.

"Bummer," Guthrie said. "I was just about to regale you with my treatise on the notional divide between rural and urban America in these times."

Erin rolled her eyes as she put the car in gear. "Shit, I'm out of the fucking loop by a mile, and I can tell you that this is a topic that's already been beaten to death."

"But that's the thing about whatever's in the zeitgeist," Guthrie said, "everyone has their take. And I like to hear them all."

"Later," Erin said, putting her foot gently on the accelerator. "We've got to get moving now." And she eased the car off the shoulder, following Arch's bumper as their little convoy headed down the road. She wondered what they'd find—if anything—when they got there.

*

Brian kept his head down, staring at the surface of the hospital cafeteria table, cup of coffee steaming in front of him, a small mountain of unstirred sugar somewhere in the depths. Cream had turned the dark surface a blotchy cocoa color. He'd stuck a wooden stir stick in it, but had yet to twirl it. He did so now, and it flared along the surface, the color blending under the steam that rose off it, the deep aroma of coffee filling his nostrils.

He could feel Lauren's gaze, burning into the top of his head, but he kept his down, focusing on the coffee. He'd gotten her here and—now what? What the hell was he supposed to say? He'd caught her with the intention of presenting some sort of case for the watch, and now that she was here, sitting right in front of him, the buzz of the cafeteria all around them …

What the hell was he supposed to say?

"You know what happens when someone drowns?" Lauren asked, breaking the silence and causing Brian to jerk his head up to look at her. She was cool and impassive, the doc in her professional environs, her scrubs and her jaded expression marking her as someone who belonged here, among the stress and the fear, among the patients and their anxious loved ones and the overworked staff.

Doctor Darlington leaned forward, her own coffee black as the Midian night. "It's not like in movies, and it's not like what you'd think it looks like. They're in panic mode, no upper brain function. It almost looks like they're playing, but really they're trying desperately to keep their head above water. And if you go in there, after them, they will cling to you, drag you, not even knowing they're doing it. Easiest way to drown is to try and rescue someone who's drowning."

Brian cleared his throat. He looked up and found her staring straight at him. "Are you saying … we're drowning?"

"Yes," Lauren said simply. "You, the watch—you can feel it. Midian's sinking, the ground beneath you is gone, and you're just—dipping below the surface of the waves. You haven't really felt the ground in a long time, haven't gotten a good breath in a while—of hope, I guess? I dunno, it's not a perfect analogy. But you're drowning, Brian, you more than most, and I think—if I let you talk me into what you want to talk me into—I'd get dragged back in and drown with you. With the town. And my daughter too."

"Shit," Brian said, taking a sip of the coffee. He just barely kept from embarrassing himself by spitting it out. Four creams, four sugars, and it still tasted like bottom-of-the-pot grounds dipped in ass.

"You saying that because you believe I'm wrong?" Lauren asked. "Or because you know I'm right?"

"I don't … I'm not saying whether I think you're right or wrong," Brian said, lying. "I know that's how you see it—"

"It's how anyone with a halfway clear head and a pair of eyes sees it, Brian," Lauren said, leaning in closer. "Do you know how many of those things there were on Faulkner Road? How much destruction they caused? One of them ripped a police cruiser to pieces, pretty much by accident. They slashed Sam Allen into guts and cutlets. Whatever's left of him, you might as well throw into the mess in the square, because putting him back together? You'd have an easier fucking time with Humpty Dumpty. There are hundreds of those things. Maybe a thousand or more. What are you going to do? Grab a bunch of swords and play hack n' slash?" She brought a hand up and put it over her forehead. "I just … can't believe it took me seeing that, living in a whorehouse, burying my mother … it took all that for me to realize …" She shook her head.

He knew what she was going to say, but he wanted to hear it anyhow. "Realize what?"

"Midian's fucking lost, Brian," Lauren said, now whispering. She looked around self-consciously, but there was no one near enough to hear them. "It's sinking, you're sinking, and the sooner you guys realize it, the sooner you can do something sensible, like evacuate the place. Get out while you can, because staying is going to equal dying."

"I don't believe it," Brian said, shaking his head. "We beat that—

that Rog'tausch thing, that giant demon wrecking ball, we beat that legion—"

"Yeah, well, we beat more than that," Lauren said, "but fighting the last war is a good way to get yourself killed, and I'm telling you—we got nothing when it comes to this. And things are just getting worse. I mean, does anyone have any idea what happened to that Mack kid? Or his mom?"

Brian looked back down at the table, at his steaming, corrosive, acidic coffee. "We think the hellcats got him. No idea about his mom though. Kid claimed a guy got her. Some other folks have been disappearing; they might be related—"

"So you add that together with the shit that happened on Crosser Street," Lauren said, "where all those people got eaten like a fucking buffet, the—the hooker that got burned from the inside out, the bicycle victims, and I bet you've had other stuff pop up since then—shit, Brian, they keep coming up with new demons and new ways to kill us. Who knows what's coming tomorrow? How long do you want to keep trying to see the next way that town's going to fuck with us—"

"It's not the town that's doing the fucking," Brian said, looking up at her with a fresh determination. "It's the demons."

"Does it matter?" Lauren asked. "Think about how many have been killed. How many different ways they've died. Yeah, it's demons, I get it. But as nasty as it's gotten there, does it really matter if we differentiate? Because the people are just as dead. And if you're living there, staying there, in the midst of—of all the shit that's going on—how crazy do you have to be? At what point do you look at what's staring at you out of the dark, licking its lips ravenously, and say, 'Yep, that's my limit. I quit'? And how stupid are you if you don't ever hit that point?"

"Ouch," Brian said, leaning back in his own chair, head still bowed and focused on his coffee. "You're basically just saying—"

"I'm saying it's over for me," Lauren said, folding her arms across her chest, clutching her coffee in one hand. "The town is sinking. For me, it's past the point of sunk, and … I don't want to drown with you, Brian." She stood up, chair scraping across the cafeteria's old tile floor. "I've got a daughter to worry about. A life, maybe, if I can rebuild it … I don't know." She shook her head. "And if I were you … come on. You're a bright guy. You never wanted to come back to Midian after school. Get out while you can."

Brian sat there for a long while after she left, staring at his shitty coffee but not daring to take another sip. He couldn't bring himself to; the taste was just too unpleasant for him to digest. Not unlike Dr.

Darlington's words, which were almost as unpalatable. And yet he knew, somehow, just like the coffee—which he took an experimental sip of and made a face; God, it was fucking gross—he needed it, and so he took another sip, and mulled over everything she'd said, and with time, it got easier and easier to take in.

*

Arch followed the sheriff's car, lights no longer blazing. He rode in silence, the Explorer's tires ripping at the dirt and gravel driveway as they took the turn into the Widow Wrightson's place. Thick trees had canopied over the path to her home long ago, and overhead he could see the leaves had turned, the last vestiges of summer green given way to autumn oranges, red and browns as they fell, one hitting him squarely in the middle of the windshield.

If that wasn't a metaphor for the death and dying all around them, Arch didn't know what was.

"'To everything there is a season,'" he muttered to himself, remembering Ecclesiastes 3. "'A time to be born, and a time to die …'"

Felt like the season for that was approaching pretty quickly. Heck, it was in the air, wasn't it?

The road stretched in front of him, telescoping as his heart thudded in his chest. He wanted to get to the widow's house, but he also didn't. He hadn't seen a text update from Casey while he'd been waiting with the others, and now that they were moving, he wouldn't have dared check. Others probably would though. Even with the tightening embrace of evil wrapping itself around Midian like a python, Arch didn't truck with texting and driving.

Besides, he hadn't heard the buzzing to indicate one had come in.

He took the last corner, and the trees started to open up. Ahead he could see the sunny skies, a meadow past the woods that led up to the Widow Wrightson's small, white house, situated in the middle of those fields of grass …

Or, at least, it had been when last Arch had been here.

There was no house there now; just a foundation where a house had been, debris spread out for a hundred yards to the east, as though a tornado had plowed right into the structure and ripped it up by the roots. Boards and sections of roof were laid out unevenly along the path, torn from the house and spread like a picnic buffet across the field.

Sheriff Reeve tapped the brakes, then stomped them, and Arch brought his car to a sudden stop. He'd left enough following distance that it wasn't a problem, but felt the telltale jerk of Erin hitting his bumper as she came to a stop, a whole lot less warning because she'd been riding his tailpipe. He turned around, the light thump of the impact still rocking its way through him, and saw her throw up her hands in a *mea culpa*-type gesture. Someone hit her from behind as well, and Arch felt the thump of that impact roll through to his Explorer, though somewhat reduced, and sighed, then turned back to look at the spectacle ahead.

"My goodness," he said. Because what else was there to say?

*

"Holy fucking shitballs," Hendricks said. He'd just knocked bumpers with the car in front of him, and why not? The shit he'd just seen was crazy as hell, a farmhouse ripped into pieces like it had been slammed into by a swarm of demons and then shredded like fucking lettuce for a taco. It had been just spread across the field, all in one direction too, which suggested bad fucking things to him.

"That's ugly," Duncan said, "and unexpected."

"Well, goddamn, I fucking hope it's unexpected," Hendricks said. "If you were expecting this shit, I hope you would have told me it was coming."

Duncan just raised an eyebrow. "If you had seen this coming, would it have mattered?"

"Maybe," Hendricks said, but they both knew a "no" was buried in his tone. "I could have known to clear the fuck out of town before the demon tornado hit."

"You've known a lot worse than a demon tornado has been coming for a long damned while now," Duncan said, still staring out the window passively. "I haven't seen you tuck tail and go yet."

"Any day now, I'll wise up," Hendricks said, waiting for the line of cars ahead of him to move. "Any fucking day now, I'll grow a damned brain and get while the getting's—well, before it at least gets too damned bad."

"Liar," Duncan said.

"I thought you couldn't read shit anymore," Hendricks said.

"I can't read much, but I can still tell a lie at a hundred paces, cowboy," Duncan said, "and as fucked up as it sounds, your ass wouldn't go running from this shit even if you knew a demon orgy tornado was blowing right toward your hotel room—"

"Sounds kinda like a conga line of demon banging."

"—and you were pinned with your wrists bound to your ankles, bent over without a stitch on," Duncan finished. "Your crazy ass is in for the long haul, that's what I'm saying."

The cars ahead of him started to move, and Hendricks took his foot off the brake and allowed the SUV to creep forward slightly. "Maybe," he allowed, not wanting to commit. "Maybe."

*

They parked in a nearly literal circling of the wagons, Reeve directing it as best he could from the front of the pack. It wasn't the sort of thing he'd imagined orchestrating, a tight circular formation around a spread-out field of debris that was the wreckage of Mary Wrightson's house, torn apart by a pack of demons who'd—well, hell if Reeve could figure out what they'd done to it, other than maybe run into it all at once and just torn through like it wasn't even there.

He opened his door tentatively, Pike next to him with gun drawn, and—thank God—the sense to point the firearm straight up rather than at something valuable, like Reeve's head. Still, bullets sent into the air had a nasty way of returning to earth. "Mind pointing that toward the ground? Just to be sure."

Pike did just that, angling the barrel off toward the woods as he lowered the piece, still leaning toward Reeve's side of the car, not looking too eager to step out. "You see anything?"

"Shit load of building materials that'll probably be sold at an extreme discount," Reeve cracked. He felt bad about it after he said it; Mary Wrightson had been an all right enough lady, and here he was, being an ass at the site of her probable grave.

Well, hell, if he didn't embrace gallows humor right now, he'd never fucking laugh.

Pike smiled tightly. Maybe he was thinking the same thing, maybe he appreciated being in the shitty situation, who knew? "What do you have in mind here?"

"Covered search and rescue," Reeve said. "We take a quick survey of the house, see if we can find our 911 caller, and then we hightail it out of here before these things come back."

"I've seen *Jurassic Park*," Pike said. "I don't know that your plan is going to turn out real well."

Reeve frowned. "Well, I haven't seen that movie, but I have to assume it's about dinosaurs, and we're dealing with demons here. These things aren't as big as a T-Rex."

"They apparently ain't got to be in order to tear down a house," Pike said. "That's a mite concerning, wouldn't you say?"

"I am concerned more than a mite," Reeve said, bringing out his sword. "But that's why you came, right?" He kept a straight face, twisting the knife. "To watch my back, right?"

If Pike knew he'd been challenged, he didn't give any sign of umbrage, nor of backing down. "I'll give you a shout if I see anything coming." And he turned to watch the fields, opening the door a crack and getting out, weapon still at low ready, almost like a professional. Almost.

Reeve headed for the house, ducking his head down like incoming fire was going to start whipping at him at any second, or maybe he was running for a chopper.

"You expecting to find Mary Wrightson in this mess somewhere?" Arch called after him, catching him in no time flat. Reeve had always admired the man's speed, even back when he'd been on the football field. Now, perhaps, even more than then.

"I don't know what I'm going to find," he said, looking over at Arch, who was running with his sword out too. They'd be fools not to. Their eyes met and Arch seemed to get what he was thinking at the same time. Reeve said, "I don't reckon running with sharp objects is our smartest move ever."

"Smarter than running without 'em around here," Arch said, proving that yep, he was thinking the same thing.

Hendricks met them both shortly, doing his own awkward, sword-at-the-side run, accompanied by Duncan, who was wearing a suit and tie again. Reeve would have thought it uncharacteristic, but Duncan had been doing some posing as a fed lately to keep the citizenry from asking awkward questions about demon law enforcement and what role it might have in this whole mess. It seemed simpler than trying to explain everything at once, like drinking from the fire hose. *Yes, there are demons, and they do seem to be evil, but there's also a demon law enforcement agency that's doing us a few favors of late, and—wait, no, they're not necessarily evil—*

Best to avoid the explanation, Reeve figured.

"This is going to be an interesting dig," Hendricks said. "Duncan, you think these things will come back?"

"Well, I haven't correctly predicted anything they've done so far," the OOC said, "so ... let's go with yes, since if I'm wrong again at least we'll be prepared for the worst."

"Shit, man," Hendricks muttered, "that's awfully complicated." He shook his head and grabbed a six-foot section of siding, shoving it aside with one hand.

"I like how no one is complaining that this is fruitless," Erin said, lifting the shattered remnant of a window frame by her lonesome. Broken glass tinkled free, and she grimaced, taking a step back as she let the wreckage fall. It made a shattering noise as it landed.

"I don't know about fruit," Arch said as the big man waded in, grabbing a section of a dislodged subfloor and lifting with both hands, his sword back on his belt, "but I don't think this is going to end with much point."

"I could do without any point," Guthrie said, looking meaningfully at Arch's sword. "Not for me, not for any of these things, because I hope they decide to beat feet for the fucking hill country after this, never to return."

"That seems kinda unlikely," Recve said, wiping his head. He'd just moved a piece of a shattered armoire. These demons had done a damned fine job of spreading the damned house out, that was for sure. If a house fell over—something he'd seen a time or two in old, abandoned homes—then it all ended in a massive pile, like a Jenga from hell. It became a sort of new structure all its own, and removing pieces resulted in other shit falling down.

This, though … this was just a spread-out mess of wreckage, no structure to it at all. Oh, sure, some of it was attached to something else, and moving a section of roofing here meant that the dresser beneath was going to rattle and slip a little lower. But it couldn't go much lower, because the wreck of the house wasn't very deep, thanks to the thorough job the hellcats had done of ripping it apart and spreading it out over a hundred-yard segment of the property.

"I think I'm coming around to Arch's way of thinking," Hendricks said as he tossed aside what looked like it might once have been a TV, one of the old, thick, heavy ones with a cathode ray tube instead of those fancy new flatscreens. It rattled, the lump of twisted plastic that was all joined together, pieces of glass and electronics hanging out of the middle. "This lady has gotta be deader than Osama Bin Laden."

Erin shook her head. "Yeah, I don't think we're going to find—"

A rumble caused everyone to freeze, and Erin stopped talking mid-sentence. A little chill warbled its way down Reeve's spine. He started to ask, "Did anyone hear that?" but it was obvious by the way they were all listening, waiting, wondering from whence it had come that, oh yeah, they all heard it too.

No one spoke, the moment stretching into an eternity. "Hey, you guys!" Keith Drumlin called from the perimeter of cars circled around them, and the guard waiting with them. "Did that come from y'all's way?"

"I don't know," Reeve called back.

"Maybe we should get back to the cars," Erin said, but damn, she sounded uncertain, like she was more afraid of making the wrong call than of getting caught out in the open by the things that had done this to Mary Wrightson's house.

"Because they'll protect us from demons who tore apart a house like it was cabbage in a Cuisinart?" Arch asked, shaking his head. He had his sword back in his hand. When he caught the funny look from Reeve, he said, "Don't tell me your momma never made coleslaw that way."

"I don't reckon she did," Reeve said with a faint smile, "because I don't think they had a food processor like that back when I was a kid."

Another small rattle jolted them all, and Reeve turned, listening. This time he knew it came from the debris. "Shit," he said, taking up his own sword and readying himself. "You think one of these things stayed behind?"

"Nastier things have happened here lately," Duncan said, his baton like a black beacon shining in his hand.

They were forming a circle around the movement in the wreckage, this little group of them. Reeve glanced around; it was funny how they'd unconsciously formed the group—it was the two OOCs, Reeve, Erin, Arch and Hendricks over here. All the newer folks who'd joined the watch were in the perimeter ring, with the cars. Here it was all the old-timers, the ones who'd been working this thing since before the town square had blown it up in a big way.

The creak of wood somewhere in the pile caused Reeve to snap his head around. "Could just be debris settling," he said, strangely hopeful. He'd seen what one of those things had done to his car. The last thing he wanted to deal with right now was one springing from the wreckage and eviscerating three of them before they could scramble the fuck out of the way.

"That ain't the way our luck runs around here," Arch said, and shit, he sounded dour in a way Reeve couldn't recall hearing him before. Arch had always been a little more ... restrained, but he'd never been morose. Reeve made a mental note to check on him. Hell if he hadn't been through the goddamned ringer of late. Reeve mentally cursed himself for not thinking to check on the deputy sooner, but ...

Well, they'd both lost, hadn't they? And they both had this duty sitting in front of them too, this thing keeping them from focusing on all the pain and loss that'd probably be burning a hole in them otherwise ...

That was who they were though, wasn't it? Reeve didn't cotton to all this touchy-feely nonsense that men went in for nowadays. They bled their feelings everywhere, these skinny-jeans-wearing nancy boys, ejaculated them all over the place like one of those sick pornos he'd heard about where the men squirted their jizz places he couldn't even imagine. That wasn't Reeve, and it didn't seem to be Arch either. They were steady, traditional, buttoned-up, coloring between the lines types. There were only a few appropriate places to show those feelings, and it was almost entirely with their w—

Dammit. Now wasn't the time to get sentimental. Or weepy.

Siding crackled as something moved, again, in the rubble. It sounded like scratching had been added to the mix, maybe demon claws against wood, and Reeve readied himself. His fingers pressed into the leather wrapping of his sword hilt and a faint sheen of sweat started to form on his fingers.

Fear crept in with the uncertainty. Seeing one of those hellcats bursting out would be better than this quiet waiting. He'd seen one chop Sam Allen into pieces like he was a dead deer in need of processing in the middle of hunting season. It was almost definitely one of those damned things; why couldn't it just show its fucking face so they could get on with it?

"Get on with it already," Hendricks said, earning him a nod of Reeve's approval. The Marine might have been a pain in the ass, but he had the stoic thing down too. You didn't see him crying everywhere, even after the shit he'd apparently gone through at the hands of that demon duchess. He kept it all tight inside. Sure, he was a dickhead every now and again, but at least he wasn't weeping like a little millennial bitch and pouring his feelings out anywhere. Hell, even Brian Longholt wasn't doing that shit, and if anyone in this crew had the disposition for it, that Ivy Leaguer who hadn't done a hard day's work in his life was the one he'd have put his money on.

"That ain't us," Reeve muttered, and his words were obscured by another round of rubble shifting, debris clinking as broken glass moved in the layer of housing material spread over the green grass.

He inched closer to where the noise was coming from, at once tentative about one of those things leaping out like a breaching whale with fucking claws and shearing him in half, but also pissed that this just kept dragging on, like one of those boxing matches where they couldn't seem to wrap up the bullshit and stop hugging long enough to beat the hell out of one another properly. "Let's get to it," he said.

"Let's get right to being ripped to pieces by demons?" Erin asked, catching his eye. "How about … no? How about we hang back, wait for this thing to show its face, and give it a good poke with something sharp and holy?"

Reeve stalled in his approach. He'd been easing forward, but that stopped him right in his tracks. "Uhh … you got a point there, Erin. Thank you." He'd been building this thing up in his mind, getting impatient, and he'd just about lost his head on that one. She gave him a casual nod, and they both turned back to the shifting wreckage.

Another noise made it out of the ruin of Mary Wrightson's house, something softer, something lower, faint, and it took Reeve a moment to realize it was a voice, pushing its way up through the cracks in the debris. "Y'all gonna just stand out there and jabber like a bird in a damned tree, or are you gonna help me out of this?"

Reeve stood there, eyebrow cocked like a pistol, brain trying to decipher what he'd heard for a second—

"Shit, Mary," he said once it broke through, and he was off, throwing that sword back in the sheath and hustling up unsteadily over house wreckage. A piece of wall shifted uncertainly beneath his feet and he stopped himself from keeling over hard, throwing out his arms as he scrambled to get to the moving debris ahead.

Arch beat him to it, more sure-footed over the shifting landscape of wreckage. He grabbed a piece of concrete a good foot wide and tossed it, then removed a busted sink, staring at it curiously for a half-second before breaking out of a trance and throwing that too, water raining out of it as he cast it aside.

Others were out there now, Duncan and Hendricks, digging down where Mary's voice had made its way out of the rubble, tossing aside pieces of her house—busted photographs, a medicine cabinet that showered broken glass shards—and then, as they all heaved aside a segment of wall—

Out popped Mary Wrightson, covered in white dust and looking about as pissed off as he'd ever seen the woman. Her hair, which she had probably dyed for years, was coated in white drywall dust that extended down her face and her shoulders, giving her a look like she'd coated herself in baby powder—but without the pleasant smell.

"Took you long enough," she said, rising out of a small well in the ruin of the house. Reeve stared down into the gapped space she occupied for a second before realizing it was a wooden cabinet, the kind that had probably held the sink Arch had tossed. She'd been literally hiding under the damned sink. Out with her came a sawed-off—beyond illegal—double-barreled shotgun, which she offered to Reeve. He took it, and then she grabbed Arch's hand and climbed out of the cabinet. Busted shards of wood fell out of the folds of her shirt, and even under the dust he could see she was pissed off. "What the hell were you doing? Holding a damned parliamentary debate?"

"Well, yes," Reeve said, handing her back the shotgun once she was out. He damned sure didn't want to get stuck holding it in case the hellcats came back looking for a fight. Especially since it wouldn't do a damned thing against their demon shells.

Mary snatched the shotgun out of his hand, jaw sticking out, lips puckered. Oh, she was pissed all right. Reeve had once gotten a call out to Fast Freddie's and found Mary there with her late husband—this had been a decade ago, before he'd died—and she was standing over Jacob, her hubby, who was holding a broken jaw, and Larry Knox, who had an ice pack on his head, dazed from a concussion with his eyes all floaty. When he'd asked what happened, the bartender told him that Mary had knocked the living hell out of both of them for getting pissed at each other, then getting lippy with her when she'd tried to settle them down. Larry Knox had been in the hospital for days for observation. Hadn't talked right for months after that, tripping over his damned words.

Mary had just stood there, seething. Neither had pressed charges, of course. Probably too damned afraid to. Reeve hadn't known quite what to do about it, but had seen the aftermath of both Larry and Jacob getting in fights before, and considered Mary's damage to be infinitely preferable to the two of them crashing through tables and windows and all else in their damned quest for drunken superiority. He wrote that one off as a win and didn't even book Mary or take her into custody.

But that didn't mean he wasn't wary as hell of her every time they met from then on out. He could see it in her eyes too; she knew, but was too polite by half to say so, unless her ire was up. It was sure as shit up now, and once she got done poring over the shotgun, she took Reeve in with one good look and said, "You're thinking about me busting Larry and Jacob's heads right now, aren't you?"

Reeve just shook his head, keeping his sword pointed forty-five degrees low. Yeah, they were out hunting demons that had ripped apart Mary's house, and he was still minding his P's and Q's in front of her. "Now, why did you have to go and bring that up?"

Mary had a double chin, and when her mouth settled into a hard line and she looked up at him, he could see where the folds had protected her from the dust; in there, her flesh was almost the normal color. "Because I'm thinking what I did to Larry and Jacob that day is going to be a damned light touch compared to when I get my hands on the things that just smashed my house to ribbons."

"You get a good look at them?" Hendricks asked.

Mary took one look at the cowboy and said, "Where the hell did you dig this boy up? Texas? You bringing in the herds, son?"

"Yeah," Hendricks said with a slick grin. "I'm riding herd on the things that just tore up your residence. That and worse."

She didn't look impressed. "I doubt you're going to do much more than end up a squashed turd in a hat after those things come tearing through your precious little ass." When Hendricks raised an eyebrow at her, she went on. "Yeah, I noticed. Don't think it'll get you anything from me though; I'm too old to give a shit."

If Hendricks had a reply to that, he kept it buttoned down, which seemed wise, since Mary was still holding a shotgun and not looking too reticent about using it at the moment. "We should get the fuck outta here," he said instead.

"Best idea I've heard all day," Erin said, and once more, Reeve caught a transmission of looks between her and the cowboy—something grudging, almost like she was admitting he was right without having to say it too explicitly. "Since we got a whole lot of no plan for dealing with these things."

"Yeah," Reeve said, echoing them, "let's head for the hills. Quick-like." And he waved toward the cars in the circle around them.

"You don't have to tell me twice," Duncan said, and he shuffled toward Hendricks, hot-footing it around the wreckage in the cowboy's wake.

"Arch, you want to take Mary with you?" Reeve asked, already starting back toward his car. Pike was waiting there, craning his neck to see what was going on down in the pile. He looked away when he caught Reeve looking at him, pointing his gun uselessly toward the empty, rolling hills beyond.

"Sure," Arch said a little tightly. But that was how he said everything these days.

"You foisting me off on your underlings, Nick?" Mary asked, giving him a narrow-eyed, pissed-off look. "Is this because I voted against you this morning?"

"Well, that having happened in a quiet voting booth where I couldn't have known about it until you told me ... no," Reeve said. "But now that I do know, it ain't highly incentivizing me to change my mind."

"You shitbird," Mary said, clutching the shotgun across her body as she fell in behind Arch. She was taking care not to point it at his back, keeping it well off to the side and skyward.

"See you back at the station, Mary," Reeve said, hustling the last few yards to his car and slipping in as Pike jumped in next to him. They slammed their doors at the same time and Reeve started it up.

"Looks like a successful rescue," Pike said. He still had his pistol drawn, like he expected something to come through window at him. Not a baseless fear, Reeve knew, after seeing how these hellcats worked.

"Yeah, we got her out," Reeve said, "or rather, we got her out, and she bitched at us all for not doing it quicker."

Pike just chuckled. "Sounds like a normal day for me."

Reeve eyed the Glock in his hand. It was small, looked like one of the new 42s, maybe even a 43. Fancy. "Pistol and all?"

Pike glanced at the weapon as Reeve put a foot on the accelerator and started them back up the driveway. The others were all moving too, no one wasting a damned bit of time in getting going and getting out of here. "Well, that part's maybe a little new," he said hastily and finally holstered the gun, slipping it back inside his waistband. Reeve let out a little breath as the County Administrator did so. Reeve had been around guns his whole life, and didn't much mind handing someone like Mary a double-barreled shotgun, knowing she'd show the weapon the respect it deserved.

Letting a Johnny-come-lately like Pike handle a Glock in his presence, though? Something about it gave Reeve little chills down his spine. Maybe that was just the thought of the hellcats descending on the watch while they'd been rescuing Mary Wrightson, though, because once he was back on the road and heading toward town, it felt like he should have been able to breathe clearly again. But he didn't. Like a catch in his lungs, one that persisted the whole way back to the station.

*

"Well, I never," Mary Wrightson said as she got in the passenger side of Arch's Explorer.

Arch waited, then just gave up and said, "You never what?"

That wasn't the thing to say. "My house just got wrecked," she said, and it was clear she was looking to do some unloading. The woman looked like she was wearing whiteface because of the plaster dust all over her, but Arch refrained from commenting on that fact. He doubted it'd help. "And here Nick goes, sending me off with you instead of dealing with me directly."

Arch threw the Explorer into gear, and followed behind as Reeve started them out of the gate like he was intending to have a race to get the heck away from the wreck of the house. "You see who's in the car with him?" Arch asked. He wasn't too nonplussed by Mary Wrightson's offputting manner; she'd just lost her house, after all. It'd be strange if her teakettle wasn't boiling at least a little. She'd probably lived there for double Arch's lifespan, maybe more.

Mary squinted ahead, and after a minute, asked, "Is that County Administrator Pike I see?"

"It surely is."

She spat right there in the floorboard of his car, and Arch physically recoiled at the action. Mary Wrightson seemed to realize what she'd done a second later, because she reached out and patted Arch on the arm. "Sorry. Sorry, son. I didn't mean to do that. It's just habit, you understand?"

"It's your habit to spit in my car when you see the sheriff riding with a county administrator?"

"No, it's my habit to spit, period, whenever I see that greasy son of a bitch," Mary Wrightson said, shaking her head, brushing some of the plaster dust loose onto Arch's seat. A week ago, he might have cared a lot more about the spit and the dust. "He is a worthless turd, the sort you don't even dare spread on your farmland for fear it'll kill your crops."

Arch raised his own eyebrow to that. "That's ... quite a statement."

"It's all true, I assure you," Mary said, patting him on the forearm again with a hamlike hand. "Maybe you ain't had cause to deal with sumbitches like Pike afore—" She was laying it on thick.

"Oh, we've had dealings," Arch assured her.

"Then you know what I mean," Mary said, finishing her patting of his wrist and relinquishing it. Now she stroked the barrel of her shotgun like she was reassuring herself that it was there, or maybe reassuring the shotgun that she was there for it. It was hard for Arch to tell.

"Sort of," Arch said after a moment. "You realize he was the one behind the recall on Sheriff Reeve?"

Her eyes moved subtly, flicking side to side. "I did not realize that, no. And now I feel particularly foolish having voted for it."

Arch looked out at the sun, which was just barely above the trees. "You've already been out and voted?"

"Polls open at six a.m." Mary Wrightson fluffed her hair, dislodging another mess of plaster dust. "I even got up early and did my hair. Can't you tell?"

Arch felt like a bug someone had trained a magnifying glass on during a particularly sunny summer day. "Uhm ... why, yes. Yes, I can. It looks ... lovely." The pang of guilt for lying tweaked Arch right in the heart a second later, and he made a face.

Mary Wrightson just stared at him. "You are a lying sumbitch," she pronounced. Arch didn't feel obliged to argue.

*

"Look at us," Guthrie said as the road bucked hard under Erin, the cruiser leaping up onto the pavement as she jerked the wheel sideways, following the convoy back onto the road. "Big fucking heroes again."

"We did all right, I guess," Erin conceded. She wasn't going to breathe again until they were the hell out of this stretch of woods, watching the loping hills roll outside the window. There was none of that now, just a steady flash of bare tree trunks rolling by outside, sun snaking its way through every crack between them, threatening to blind her until she snatched her sunglasses off the holder on the visor and put them on.

"Awww, there you go minimizing your accomplishments," Guthrie said. "What's the deal with you, Erin? You're so stiff lately. Someone push you off a cliff or something?"

There was just enough bite in the smartassery that Erin's cheeks flushed. "I'm not testy about that, so don't bother poking me over it. I made my peace with what happened there, okay?"

"So what's crawled up your ass then?" Guthrie asked. "Seriously. For real. Girl talk."

Erin gave her a nasty look. "You're not a girl."

"Neither are you," Guthrie said. "You're a full-on woman now. A sulking, pissy one, but still—look at you, a woman, roaring and everything." She narrowed her eyes. "This isn't just about the cowboy."

"Nothing is about him, dumbass," she said, then added, "or nearly nothing. I don't have time to give a fuck about Hendricks right now. Do you not see what's going on here? People disappearing, houses being ripped apart by herds of demon animals—who gives a shit about the cowboy and his moody ass in the midst of all that? People are dying, Guthrie—"

"People die every day, sweetheart." Guthrie yawned, as if to illustrate how pedestrian an activity it was.

"I'm having déjà vu," Erin said. "Like I've heard this before."

"It's a common theme around here, isn't it?" Guthrie asked. "When you're standing at the edge of the abyss, looking down, why would you be talking about anything but the drop?"

"This isn't about a drop," Erin said. "You're basically arguing that people die, so why should we fucking care about saving people?"

"Not saying you shouldn't care, fleshbag," Guthrie said with a grin. "You're human. Of course you should care. But you shouldn't be surprised when you and your fellow meat sacks end up rotting in a few days, weeks, years, whatever. You can feel however you want about it—feel, feel, feel—but it's what it is. You die. It's your defining attribute. If you lasted a little longer, maybe you'd understand that fact a little better. Then again, maybe not, because you people feel way more than you think."

That caused Erin to burn a little. "You just shit all over everything we are, as people."

Guthrie shrugged. "I delivered a cold assessment of the facts. If you got offended by them, that's your business, and it's probably because the truth hurts like a kick to the tit. Which, damn, I mean, it does not feel good, does it? I had no idea."

"What the hell does that have to do with—"

"Everything," Guthrie said. "Your feelings ... I didn't attach any judgment to whether you feeling more than thinking made you better or worse as a species. I just said if you lived longer, you'd think about it differently. And you went all tomato red." She pointed at Erin. "Yeah, like that. Does that hurt?"

Erin tried to control the flush, but failed. "No. It just feels hot. Why are you saying these th—"

"Because they're in my mind," Guthrie said. "I've had a lot of time to contemplate the human condition, you know. Sharing them with Duncan is pointless, so ... congratulations. I'm guessing by how bad it's burning you that you think I'm right."

Erin turned away from Guthrie. "I don't ... I mean—"

"You don't have to answer, toots," Guthrie said. "Like I said, it's just an opinion. Probably an accurate one, but who cares? You shouldn't. I'm a demon, after all, and it's not like the world rises and sets in my flawless ebony ass crack. You should cling tight to your world view about what gives you value as a species. No point in upsetting your emotional grocery cart right now, especially when you've got a lot of shit to do."

And with that, Guthrie lapsed into an empty silence, one that Erin swore to herself she wouldn't break until she had a really good, searing counter argument.

She still hadn't spoken by the time she got back to the station.

*

Reeve pulled into the station, a goodly portion of the watch's convoy having bled off by the time he got there. That was, of course, how they worked—mostly people still trying to carve out a little portion of their old lives while dealing with the reality inherent in how Midian was working these days. Volunteer army? Town guard? Something like that.

"You've put together a real impressive rallying force here," Pike said, nodding along as they bumped into Reeve's spot at the station. There were a few cars following behind still; Arch, Hendricks, Erin. The old pros were coming in for a meeting ... or maybe just because they had nothing else going on at the moment.

"You still ain't seen a demon yet," Reeve said, opening up his door once he'd killed the ignition. Reeve had figured Pike would talk his ear off, maybe make mention of the fact he'd still not actually seen a demon, at least not in the shell, but Pike had said nothing and they'd driven back in silence.

"I've heard enough stories from the survivors," Pike said with a shake of the head. "And I did see that house bulldozed to the ground. Well, 'bulldozed' isn't the right word. A bulldozed house would have been a lot cleaner than whatever happened out there."

Reeve cocked an eyebrow at him. "You ready to believe me now?"

"Been ready for a while now," Pike said with an easy grin, coming around the car. He extended a hand. "I've been trying to help you, remember?"

"Well, maybe it was tough to see that helping hand while I was busy trying to fight off demons and keep myself from getting dragged out of office," Reeve said, eyeing Pike's hand. He was about ready to take the man's hand, but he couldn't resist getting one more good lick in. Pike had certainly put him through enough to warrant it. Hell, he wasn't technically even done, at least not until Reeve won his recall—if he did win.

"I don't know how many times I can apologize for that," Pike said, hand still hanging out there.

"Well, let's hope it ends up being no big deal," Reeve said and shook his hand. He felt slightly dirty doing it, but he couldn't be real choosy about where he got his help right now, could he?

"It's my most sincere hope that a year from now, we're sitting on a front porch around sundown, sipping a couple sweet teas, talking about how glad we are this bullshit is behind us," Pike said. He seemed to mean it, but who could tell with a politician? He sure pumped Reeve's hand like he was serious.

"Let's hope so," Reeve said, breaking off. "What are you up to now?"

"Back to the office," Pike said, nodding as he stood right where he was. "Gonna see what else I can shake loose for you from the county budget. Don't reckon the parks department is going to need the allotment for that playground we had planned in Culver—you know, if the county goes sliding into hell or whatever."

"I'm hoping that don't become a reality," Reeve said, catching sight of the others filing into the sheriff's station, Mary Wrightson giving him a real sour look as she passed through the doors. He figured he was going to get an earful from her. Another delightful perk of being a public servant.

"I'll let you get back to it then," Pike said, waving. "Keep me in the loop, Sheriff. Let's knock these bastards back, all right?"

"We'll do everything we can," Reeve said, waiting until he'd turned to roll his eyes. Did the fucker think they weren't already trying to? Well, at least he was showing up and seeing for himself now, and not just pissing on them without even bothering to lie and tell them it was raining—which was what he'd been doing before that.

*

"We seem to have lost the thread we started on this morning," Duncan said as Hendricks walked in the door, the OOC a few steps behind him.

"No shit," Hendricks said, a nice little blast of warm air catching him as he passed through the inner door to the sheriff's station. He'd just followed the convoy, more out of habit than anything, and Duncan hadn't said much on the drive, like anything to remind him they had been up to something when this particular shitshow had started. "What do you want to do about it?"

"I've got a vague idea about where to sniff," Duncan said.

Hendricks frowned, stopping just short of the counter. Erin was already stomping around back behind it, looking pretty fucking surly, Guthrie grinning to high heaven at Casey Meacham, which gave Hendricks a little chill. "Why didn't you say that before we got here?"

"Reasons," Duncan said.

"What fucking reasons?" Hendricks asked.

"What are you two going on about?" Arch asked, a somewhat menacing look on his face as he loomed into their conversation, lunging in awkwardly as that cranky lady they'd dug out of the house appeared behind him. She looked like a real bitter pill to Hendricks's eyes, a battleaxe that was looking for somewhere to swing herself. Or maybe a ballbuster looking for some testicles to turn into jelly.

"We were following a lead earlier," Duncan said, "and were about to head out again just now."

"I'll go with you," Arch said, pushing himself into the conversation between them and making it a little triangle of people. Well, people-shaped entities anyway, what with Duncan not really being a person. Arch hadn't even made it sound like a suggestion. He was just coming.

Hendricks tried not to grin at that. He'd been wanting to catch Arch by himself for a while. It wasn't funny, really, not at all. He figured the two of them had things to talk about, and had been surprised—but not that much—when the big deputy hadn't sought him out after the square. Well, he'd had other things on his mind, Hendricks reckoned.

"Yeah, let's head out," Hendricks said, waving Arch and Duncan toward the door.

They passed Reeve, who looked wary, like he knew he was about to skydive onto a bed of nails without a parachute. "Where are you fellas headed?"

"Getting some lunch," Hendricks said. He glanced back at Arch, who didn't even roll his eyes at the lie as he normally might have. "You want something from that diner on the square?"

"It's called Surrey's," Reeve said. "And in case you ain't found this one out for yourself yet, don't get the burritos."

"I have heard tell of the epic diarrhea those tend to prompt," Hendricks said, nodding sagely. "I definitely don't need any of that interfering in my evening activities." He grinned, and the sheriff just nodded, still wary as fuck, probably knowing he was strolling into an ass chewing of epic proportions from that angry old biddy they'd pulled out of that house wreck. Hendricks tossed another look over his shoulder; she'd gone and picked up the phone and was using it without so much as a by your leave. Shit. "Let's roll, bitches," Hendricks said, and sprang for the door.

"What are y'all after?" Arch asked as they hit fresh air again.

Hendricks cast a look over the unmowed, vacant lot next to the sheriff's station. Grass was getting long there, and starting to brown for the coming winter. "Not sure," Hendricks said. "Duncan?"

"Also not sure," Duncan said. "Got a little hint of something through my demon senses. We were following a guy."

"What'd he look like?" Arch asked, fingering the hilt of his sword as they walked across the parking lot.

"Thin," Hendricks said. "Drove a hearse. Wore a black suit." He hesitated, then, "I think he was at Alison's funeral."

Arch froze in his tracks. "Tall fella. When he smiles, you get the feeling he's doing it because he doesn't know what else to do."

Hendricks shook his head. "I dunno. I didn't get him to smile at me."

"Maybe he didn't think you were pretty," Duncan said.

"Motherfucker, everyone thinks I'm pretty," Hendricks said. "Look at this chiseled jawline."

"It is the like of which they used to carve into marble," Duncan conceded.

"You would know," Hendricks said, then to Arch, "You remember this guy?"

Arch was looking pretty pissed now too, like it was a communicable disease he'd picked up riding with the old lady, though Hendricks guessed it went back farther and deeper than that. He was considering how he felt about an uninvited demon crashing his wife's funeral. "I remember him." He shot a forceful look at Duncan. "You sure he's one of your people?"

"You mean an Enshelled-American?" Duncan cracked. "Because 'you people' is offensive for many reasons, the least of which being that we're not really people." Hendricks nodded along in amusement.

"Answer the danged question."

"Hard to imagine he's not," Duncan said. "Don't get me wrong, my senses pick up some human activity at times, but what I got from him definitely felt like a demon vibe rather than the low-level lust of, say, Hendricks about to get his pickle tickled."

Hendricks blinked. "You can feel that?"

"Smell it, more like," Duncan said.

Hendricks waited a second to take that in. "What … does it smell like?"

Duncan kept a straight face. "Bacon."

Hendricks had a feeling his leg was being pulled, but hell, who wanted to argue with an answer like that? "Goddamned right. Let's go."

*

Pike was already dialing his phone before he was out of the sheriff's station parking lot. It rang as he headed down Old Jackson Highway, that familiar dinging echoing through the cabin of his vehicle, the hands-free projecting the sound of the call out of the car's speakers so he could hear it and talk without having to hold a damned phone up to the side of his head. That shit was dangerous, after all.

"Hey, baby," Darla said when she answered.

"Darling Darla," he tossed back, out of habit and to get the pleasantries out of the way so he could get out what he needed to say. "I just spent a little time with Reeve's crusaders."

"Is that so?" She paused on the other side of the call. "Mera, don't smear food on the table, sweetie, put it in your mouth. You were saying?"

"He's forged himself an effective little demon fighting force," Pike said. "I saw them do a quick rescue after some cats or something ripped down a house out in the boonies. They were ready, steady, all that."

"Cats ...?"

"Never mind," Pike said. "It was some low-level vermin type shit, except lots of them. The point is—"

"Reeve's got his shit together," Darla said. "Jay, sweetheart, we don't throw spoons or knives or forks at our sister. Put it down. Put. It. Down. Thank you." Then, without the sweetness, "So, what do we do about it?"

"I don't know," Pike said. "No clue where we're going to end up on this recall—"

"You voted against him, right?"

"Of course."

"But you told him—"

"Lied and brought him donuts, just like you suggested," Pike said with a grin.

"Attaboy. I voted against him too. With these little shits scrabbling around my ankles the entire fucking time." Her voice got tight, then loosened up. "Maybe he'll lose."

"That ain't gonna solve our problems," Pike said. "Throw a little monkey wrench into things, maybe—though who'd notice in this town? But it ain't gonna solve anything."

"Mmmhmm." She was thinking. Or maybe wiping up spittle from one of the babies. "You campaigning against him behind his back?"

"Hell no. Town this small, word would get back to him in a second. I'm just keeping my mouth shut; figure influencing the vote one way or another doesn't matter enough to risk pissing him off while I'm trying to get this bucking bronco back under control."

"You're going to find that an impossible task," Darla said. "Tell me about him and this army. How'd it go with them?"

"Reeve whistled them up and out they came, neat as you please. They circled the wagons, had a perimeter—"

"They took orders from him? Did what he told them to do?"

"Yep."

"Hmmm," Darla said, and the clanging of something in the background of the call drew a hiss from her. "Jay, I told you not to throw your silverware!" A slap of flesh against flesh was followed by a startled cry, then an extended whine that built as the realization swept through the child that his mother had struck him. Pike had seen it enough times to know when Darla got pissed it was best to stay out of arm's reach. "That'll learn you, as they say around here."

"I get the feeling Reeve is going to be a thorn for us for a while," Pike said. "He's dug in now, like a tick. And we're not getting the top predators around here, not yet. Lots of this little vermin bullshit, enough to bust up a house or two but not bring any real power to this burg—"

"Don't let's worry about Reeve right now," Darla said. "We're behind schedule, and things aren't going that swell, it's true, but we can always turn it around. If we're not getting the high-wattage demon stars we're looking for at this hotspot, then maybe it's time to re-ring the dinner bell you planned on at Halloween."

"You imagine a scenario where Reeve's little crew ain't going to roll in and fuck that up for us?" Pike asked.

"I imagine Reeve's little circle jerk is going to get tired sooner or later," Darla said, and he could imagine the smile on her face. "They don't have the stamina for a long war. They won't know what it's going to take when things really amp up around here. They'll start peeling off in ones and twos, deciding discretion is the better part of valor. They'll pull up stakes and leave. Some of them will get tired and sloppy, and a demon will take them down, especially if we can get some real power summoned around here. Jason … we need a ritual. Maybe more than one. We can keep it quiet, but … it'll start drawing the power to us we need, and move the gears on this machine."

Pike didn't quite blanch, but he did frown and evince his disgust to the empty car the way he might have when thinking about praying the Rosary as a kid. "If you say so," he said, but his heart wasn't near in it.

"I say so," Darla said. "If we're not getting the fish we're here for, let's switch bait. Or hell, chum the waters and get some damned sharks coming this way. Put some good blood in the water and they'll show up."

"What ritual were you thinking?" Jason asked. He knew of a couple she'd been keeping under her hat, but … damn. They weren't just not for the faint-hearted; they weren't for anybody who didn't have an ironclad stomach and ice water in their veins. One of them even made him sweat with discomfort at the mere thought of performing it.

"Blood and sex," Darla said.

Pike let out a little, "Whew."

"That doesn't mean we won't, later—"

"Yeah, I know," he said, brushing his hand against his forehead. "I'm just not savoring the thought of—"

"Jason," she said softly, "this is about power. Real power. Eternal power, not the silly shit you're doing as a County Administrator. This is real influence we're talking about, not stupid backwoods Tennessee podunk horse-trading bullshit. We're steps away from the big game. Don't let them see you sweat now, and don't fold like a little bitch because you see a table full of fat chips, okay?"

"Yes, ma'am," Pike said.

"Gotta go," Darla said. "Somebody needs a nap." She hung up unceremoniously.

Pike just sat there, blinking. "Hell, I could use a nap." That didn't seem likely to be on the agenda for today though.

*

"Mary," Reeve said, trying to dodge her and get over to Casey, who was sitting at the dispatcher's desk, wearing an expression that said he might, just maybe, have something interesting to say. It was a thin thread on which to hang his hopes, but Reeve was quite willing to discuss something unsavory with Casey—hooker sodomy, maybe—in order to get the hell away from Mary Wrightson, whose expression was not nearly so benign as the taxidermist's.

"Nick," Mary said, stopping him in his tracks because her voice had an *I got a bone to pick with you* quality to it. "What's all this I'm hearing about demons?"

"Oh, you're just now hearing about demons?" Reeve said with great sarcasm. "I would have thought the shit-ton of them plowing into the front of your house might have clued you in that they're real and they're here."

"Don't give me that bullshit," Mary said. "I didn't know what I was seeing. I thought maybe it was a herd of buffalo."

"A herd of buffalo?" Reeve let his jaw go slightly slack. "In East Tennessee?"

"I hear they're farming 'em now," she said. "I went out to Knoxville last year to visit my boy Larry, and he took me to this burger place where they had buffalo burgers. It ain't out the realm of possibility that they'd be farming some around here, and that they might slip loose."

"Well, now that's something," Reeve said. "But yeah, it was demons, not buffalo."

"They seemed a little small for what I imagined a buffalo to look like," Mary conceded. "And they had long tails too."

"We call 'em hellcats," Reeve said, trying to get past her. Casey was just sitting over there, feet away, like a human lifeline he couldn't quite reach.

"Why ain't I heard about this until now, Nick?" Mary asked as he attempted to squeeze by again.

"I honestly don't know," Reeve said. "I'd always figured you hear everything, Mary. Not sure how something like demons invading the town could slip your attention, especially since we've had meetings about 'em—"

"You know I don't truck with that meeting bullshit."

"—we had that whole Halloween massacre; posted some flyers afterward at Rogerson's—"

"Like I'm gonna stop and read a flyer on that bulletin board, Nick. Honestly, now. Half that shit is people from those companies selling soap and shit—"

"—we put it in the newspaper, tried to let people know that way—"

"I don't read that crap. Half of it's lies and the other half is bull-larkey I don't care about."

"—figure maybe somebody would tell you, failing all that. I mean, your boy Gary is still here in town, I know."

"Please. That little shitbird barely calls."

"Well, I don't know then, Mary," Reeve said, throwing up his hands in exasperation. "Sounds like you're about cut off from all human contact. I have no idea how you might get the word about demons short of us coming up to your house and door-knocking like one of them Jehovah's Witnesses from the temple over on Bilmore—"

"You know I'd never open up my door to evangelicals, Nick."

"Then I ain't got a clue how you'd hear about demons, short of them rip-shredding their damned way through your house at high speed."

"Hmph," she said. "Sounds to me like you're doing a pretty shit job of communicating, Nick."

"Well, riddle me this," Reeve said, still trying to find the most expedient way to get out of this conversation, "how'd you hear about the vote today, then?"

"Saw it on a sign as I was driving past the precinct a few days ago. Had to exercise my God-given rights, you know."

"Well, if you didn't know about the demons," Reeve said with a fierce squint, "or the murders, or any of the other shit that's been going on around here ... why'd you vote against me?"

"I just don't like you," Mary answered immediately. "You always got that look in your eyes like you think I'm about a second away from whacking you upside the head."

"Wonder where I got that idea," Reeve muttered, shaking his head. That headache was only getting worse as the day wore on. Was it too soon to take another round of Tylenol?

*

"Let's have a talk in here," Guthrie said as Erin followed her into the depths of the jail, Mary Wrightson's strident conversation with Reeve echoing along the corridor behind them. Erin didn't really want a piece of that discussion. She didn't care for the thought of trailing along after Arch, Duncan and Hendricks either, mostly because of that last one. They said they were heading to Surrey's, because it was about that time, and while she might have thought it rude a few weeks ago if Arch had gone to lunch without asking her if she wanted something, it was a new world now, and Hendricks had bowled through and fucked shit up too, and that meant she was just as happy to not be asked now.

Well, mostly.

"Why in here?" Erin asked, following him toward the sealed door that led into the confinement area. She didn't know who was on duty in this part of the jail, but she'd be finding out pretty quick.

"I've been pondering about this fella in here," she said as she stood by the door. "I wanna see him for myself."

"I've seen him," Erin said as Guthrie waved through the little window to the jailkeeper. "Ain't nothing going on behind the curtains."

"Oh, yeah?" Guthrie cast him a smirk. "Do they match the carpet?"

Erin frowned. "What?"

Erin pushed through into the waiting area. They stepped inside, and there was Chauncey Watson, his eyes magnified by those massive glasses he wore. "Hey, Erin," he warbled in greeting, raising his hand to her. He had a few metal miniature figures on the desk in front of him, and the air smelled of acrylic paint. She wrinkled her nose in response.

"Hey, Chauncey," Erin said. "You're looking mighty settled in."

"It ain't exactly the most mind-intensive duty," Chauncey said, grinning weakly. His cheeks were covered in a dark layer of scruff, like he hadn't shaved in a day or two. "I pretty much just sit here for a few hours, then go home. Maybe push the door to buzz somebody in a couple times."

"Sounds lonely," Erin said.

"Huh?" Chauncey blinked. "Awww, no, it's wonderful. It's a lot better than my day job."

Guthrie scratched at her head. "Wait … isn't it Tuesday? If you've got a day job …"

"Oh, I called in sick," Chauncey said. "Somebody had to watch this critter until Sam gets done with his shift." He looked down, a set of tiny paint brushes laid out on a paper towel in front of him. "Reckon he'll be here to spell me after a while."

"Uh, Chauncey," Erin said, "Sam died last week." She stared at the unblinking eyes behind the Coke-bottle glasses. "He got ripped to pieces by those hellcats we ran into in the woods."

Chauncey just stared for a moment, then thudded back against the seat's rest, slowly, like he'd been knocked over by a feather. "Well, shit. Last week? I swear I had a conversation with him yesterday!"

"Unless he's a ghost, no," Erin said. "You really didn't notice he's been gone?"

Chauncey stared, deep in thought. "You know, I thought my shifts here had been going a little longer. And Bernie's been relieving me instead of Sam, come to think of it … he used to be the shift after me … I didn't even notice." His lip curled. "Well, damn. Did I miss the funeral?"

"Yeah," Erin said gingerly. "You did. But I wouldn't worry about it." When Chauncey cocked his head, clearly asking without asking about what she meant, she said, "Lotta people been missing funerals lately. It's kind of a thing."

"Well, this is all very lovely," Guthrie said, brusque as ever, "but while you work through your five stages of grief and eventually get back to nerding—" she pointed vaguely to the miniatures on the desk in front of Chauncey "—would you mind letting us in before I keel over of boredom?"

"Oh, sure," Chauncey said, apparently either not offended by the shot Guthrie had taken at him or just oblivious to it. He picked up the key and unlocked the door, opening it for them.

"Thanks, darlin'," Guthrie said with a smirk, and then winked at Chauncey, who appeared to miss that too. Guthrie headed through the door into the prisoner detention area and waited until it closed to say, "What a fucking idiot."

"Chauncey's a good guy," Erin said with perhaps a little excess defensive zeal.

"Good does not equal smart," Guthrie said. "The two qualities are, in fact, almost completely unrelated. See for evidence—evil geniuses, and morons with a heart of gold. Like Dan Rather."

"Which one of those is he?"

"Your mileage may vary," Guthrie said, then nodded at the specimen in front of them. "Speaking of drooling morons—look at this sad motherfucker. An empty vessel, all the wine poured out." She looked back at Erin. "You ever wonder what it's like to have your whole life taken over and run for you by powers beyond your control?"

"Well, I'm still technically a teenager, so I have a pretty vivid memory of what that's like, since … strict parents." Erin's cheeks burned as Guthrie grinned back at her in undisguised amusement. "How long do you suppose he was possessed before he ended up … this way?" She'd searched for a better way to put it, but all she came up with was *like a fucking vegetable*, or, appealing to her darker instincts, the kind of shit she'd only say when really hammered, *like Bill Longholt?*

Guthrie was perhaps too interested in staring at the man in front of him—or the empty shell of a man—to pick up on her discomfort. "I'm guessing at least a hundred years. I mean, he probably receded into nothingness before that, but—I'm guessing they used his body for over a hundred years, judging by the state of his teeth."

Erin frowned. "What? His teeth?"

"Take a look at 'em," Guthrie said, sidling over and opening the man's mouth. They were in pretty shit shape; Erin didn't take a step back, but she was tempted to. "See, they're not in total disrepair, and being possessed by a demon essentially stops the clock on things like abscesses and infections, turning you into a shell for your new host. No sickness, no disease, none of that during the period of possession, these little elements of demon physiology layered over your physical form. So this shit with his teeth? It predates his possession." She ran a finger over his front teeth; they were yellowed, plaque-stained, and whitish deposits covered the cracks. "Being a possessed person sucks, but at least the dental plan is pretty good." Guthrie shot her a smile. "Stasis and an end to the pain."

"So … did his teeth look like this the whole time he was possessed?" Erin asked. "And what makes you think a hundred years?"

"Well, because he's not entirely lost them all, and looks to be thirty years of age," Guthrie said. "That means dental hygiene wasn't totally medieval, but it wasn't exactly in an advanced state either. Ergo, a hundred years or more. Unless he's just a hillbilly." She gave the man a little slap on the cheek. "When were you born? What year?"

He actually blinked from the tap, which looked to have been just sharp enough to cause some pain, disturbing the tube that ran up his nose, wiggling it along its length. The man moaned lightly, as if discovering his voice.

"What the fuck?" Now Erin did take a step back. "He's never reacted like that before, at least not that I've heard."

"You people are all pussies, that's why," Guthrie said, and drew back to slap him again. She didn't draw back far, but then, she didn't have to. Demon strength meant she could keep her hand an inch from the man's face and still snap his head around with the force of impact.

"What the fuck, Lern—Guthrie!" Erin started forward to stop her.

Guthrie just grinned, letting him have it, then stepped away as the man toppled over. He made another sound. "You idiots are content to just let him sit in here like a vegetable."

"Unnnnhhhh," the man said, face now against the floor. He didn't move, just moaned.

"Because torturing a fucking prisoner is inhumane," Erin said.

"Yeah, well, so am I," Guthrie said. "And if you want this guy to come out of a hundred or so years of being crushed under the weight of a million demons in his head, you better do something to kickstart his reactions. Hunger ain't doing it."

"We've been feeding him," Erin said, looking at the pile of a man lying on the ground like he was going to spring up and slap her for Guthrie's misdeeds. "That's what the tube in his nose is for, I guess. Aren't those supposed to be painful?"

"They're no picnic, I'm sure," Guthrie said, "but if you want to bring this guy back to life, you're gonna need some sharp relief for what ails him. His brain's muted, and dull aches ain't gonna draw him out. You need the snap, the hit, the sudden, jarring pain to make him feel wherever he is in there."

"I can't let you beat him," Erin said, letting her palm rest on her gun. It was stupid not to bring her baseball bat in here, she realized now. She'd inadvertently trusted Guthrie.

"If you can't beat 'em," Guthrie said, and motioned to the man, his ass up in the air, "I guess you could always join 'em."

Erin froze. "Is that—did you just suggest a course of action, or were you just repeating a cliché?"

"Little of both," Guthrie said, "though I wouldn't suggest trying to join the demons around here if you can't beat 'em. Because the only thing you'll be joining is your death to their total lack of mercy." She nodded at the man on the ground. "Seriously though. Let me slap him a few more times, we'll get him back to functioning on a basic level."

"What—no!" She drew her gun now, and kept it at her side. "You can't do that."

"Why not?"

"Because you can't hurt someone who's in custody and completely unable to defend themselves!" Erin gripped the pistol, carefully keeping her finger off the trigger as she argued with the demon. Her heart was thundering, caught in this confined space with someone so dangerous. How could she have been so stupid as to be lulled by Lerner—Guthrie?

"Funny thing about that," Guthrie said, folding her arms in front of her. "Something no one really thinks about, but—surgeons do gross bodily harm to people every day. They cut them open, invasively, sometimes without their permission. Car accident happens, lady gets a ruptured—I dunno, what ruptures on you people? Spleens? They bust, right? Lady gets a ruptured spleen and gets wheeled into a surgical bay where a doctor cuts her wide open, leaving a massive wound. It'll take weeks, months, maybe even years to heal fully—if you heal fully at all. If a street punk did the same damned thing to you with a knife in an alley, we'd call that assault with a deadly weapon, and they'd get punished for it. A doctor does it … ehhh, let's just overlook this gross bodily harm we did to this person without their permission."

"Because it's to save their life," Erin said. "They're doing it to—" She looked at the fallen form of the man, who had gone silent once more.

"Exactly," Guthrie said. "And I'm not beating a helpless person for the kicks, okay? I could do that in any city in the world and probably get away with it, if I were so inclined. Why, I'm almost virtuous." She grinned. "I'm trying to help this poor bastard come back to us. I'm like a surgeon, focused on the result rather than the fact I'm ripping into a human being with a knife and causing gross bodily harm. Why won't you let me help this poor fucker?" Guthrie settled into a look of pure amusement, mingled slightly with the satisfaction of knowing she'd just rhetorically bitchslapped Erin.

Erin felt the sting of it too, and it ached her brain slightly, knowing she'd gotten pushed to a conclusion she found … distasteful. "You're not a doctor."

"Pffft, I could have been," Guthrie said, "as many medical shows as I've watched over these years. My point is, though, you're all focused on the means rather than the desired result. 'Ohhh, it's hurting him, the poor prisoner.' You don't think being a vegetable is hurting him more? I'm talking about bringing him back to life, and all you can focus on is how he's feeling an ounce of pain as I perform a surgery to bring him back to whole again." Guthrie leaned toward her. "Stop focusing on the pain. Start looking at the desired result."

Erin paused. She was holding her breath and didn't even realize it. She swallowed, her face feeling hot. "You could really hurt him."

"I could really hurt a lot of people, sweetheart. But I don't."

Her words just didn't sound right to Erin. It was like the old Lerner was peeking out from beneath the facade.

Erin holstered her gun, barely realizing she'd done it. She swallowed again, feeling like she'd taken down an apple whole, and it had lodged in her throat. Who the hell was this guy, anyway? How had he ended up with a demon legion in him? These were questions that had rankled her for a while. It was the same shit that bounced around her mind when she thought about how she'd ended up in the path of the demon legion, how she'd become a tool for them to do … all the vile shit they did.

"No," she said, and to Guthrie's credit, she didn't do more than sigh and roll her eyes. And with that, Erin beckoned toward the door, and Guthrie went first, rapping on it to get them out. While they waited, Erin helped pick up the man on the ground, dragging him back to sitting. There was no movement in his eyes, nothing, and as she left him behind, she wondered if—just maybe—she shouldn't have let Guthrie try things her way.

*

Archibald Stan is the man who will bring about the end of the world. Those words popped into Hendricks's head as he drove, Arch in the passenger seat, looking restless at not being in control of the vehicle, and Duncan behind him, not making a goddamned peep. Hendricks just had to keep steering the car as that unsettling, shitass feeling washed over him again, same as it always did whenever those words came to mind.

"Your head is not a fun place to be," Duncan said.

"No shit," Hendricks tossed back. It was really fucking annoying how he did that, and extremely shitty to contemplate how much the demon could read. Probably another reason why Duncan kept it to himself of late. He was a little more in tune with the stuff that unnerved humans than Guthrie seemed to be. Or more circumspect about it, at least.

"You reading his mind?" Arch asked.

Hendricks didn't think Duncan could actually do that—or maybe that was just wishful thinking on his part. He'd heard the explanation at one point, but it all sounded fucking vague and full of caveats. It seemed to be like a condom; when it worked, it just ruined the fun, and when it didn't, it had the chance to ruin everything.

"Not exactly," Duncan said. He didn't elaborate, and Hendricks tried not to sigh in relief. Until he waited a few seconds and sort of did: "Your bodies aren't some mysterious thing, you know. And neither are your brains."

"My brain seems like a total fucking mystery to most," Hendricks cracked, trying to get the OOC to shut the fuck up.

"Your brain is neurons. Physical reactions. Chemicals. Synapses—"

"Thanks for the biology lesson, Bill Nye minus the bowtie," Hendricks said. "What does that have to do with you and your special soul-sensing powers?"

"These are physical phenomena," Duncan said. "They can be measured and charted. Maybe not by your scientists, entirely, just yet, but they're there. They exist. They can be perceived, with the right instrumentation."

"And you're the right instrument?" Arch's deep voice sounded interested.

"Sometimes," Duncan said. "Sometimes … not."

"So when you're perceiving this demon that we're chasing all over the place—" Hendricks waved to the road ahead—they were bumping along a back road surrounded on either side by fence posts strung with barbed wire "—you're not actually perceiving his mystical, magical essence or whatever the shit? You're really just using the equivalent of a built-in demon radiation detector to track him?"

"Something like that," Duncan said.

"So how do those things—those talismans we pick up from dead demons—how do they interfere with your sense?" Arch asked. He seemed to be really engaged, which was something Hendricks hadn't seen much from the man of late.

"That's a good question," Duncan said quietly. "You should ask Guthrie."

"Why the fuck would I go out of my way to have a conversation with Guthrie when you're sitting right here?" Hendricks asked. "Do you just not know?"

Duncan didn't blink. "No. I don't know. And I haven't given it a lot of thought."

Hendricks actually exchanged a look with Arch, then went back to the OOC. "Why the hell not? You've got this special power but you don't think about it?"

"How often do you give a lot of thought to how your sense of smell works?" Duncan asked. "I mean, you clearly can smell things. Rotten eggs. Roses. But how does that work? How do you perceive—"

"Cuz I just fucking *do*," Hendricks said, feeling the exasperation before the realization cracked down on him. He really hadn't given much thought to how particles or whatever of smell made their way into his brain. Because who thinks about that shit when there was so much else to do?

"Exactly." Duncan didn't wear smug very often, but when he did wear it, he wore it well.

"Interesting," Arch said, but he said it so neutrally Hendricks couldn't tell if he actually thought it was interesting, or if he was just saying it to make a comment and close the conversation.

Either way, it shut everybody up until Duncan said, "Turn here," at a sign for a new subdivision that looked like it was still under construction. There wasn't even one house standing in the place yet, just a few wooden skeletons of partially framed buildings, no sign of workers on the site and the machinery parked and silent.

Well, that was understandable. Who the hell would want to build in Midian right now?

"Looks like the local construction companies are experiencing slumping demand," Hendricks said, steering the car down the road, which was littered with some old wooden pallets and probably five times as dusty as a normal street thanks to all the ground being torn up to make the vacant lots ready for building.

"Guess they'll have a rough quarter," Duncan deadpanned, then nodded. "Somebody's still here."

Hendricks followed the OOC's gaze and saw that, yeah, there was one work truck still here. It was fairly easy to tell a construction work truck; they were always wider-bodied, the big Fords and Chevys, the occasional Dodge or Nissan or even Toyota, though those seemed to be rarer. Toolbox in the back, sometimes a King cab if it was someone having to a haul a crew, or maybe kiddos on weekends. Scaffolding type shit hanging out of the bed seemed to be a dead giveaway, a few torn cloths and an old plastic shopping bag dangling in the breeze.

"Ghost town," Arch muttered under his breath, and Hendricks wondered if he'd even meant to say it aloud.

Hendricks brought the SUV to the curb, which was a good inch above the first layer of asphalt, the one the construction company had laid down in order to get trucks and concrete mixers and all that shit rolling out here. They definitely hadn't put a final layer on yet, though, because the nearby manhole cover jutted out of the street a good inch or two above normal, a nice little navigational hazard that he'd had to roll over.

They got out, Hendricks being real gentle when he shut the door. "Think there might be some hellcats lurking around?" he asked. This was a little ways out of town. Nice spot for those fuckers to tear into shit without getting too public. Not that the hellcats worried about that sort of thing, but they had seemed to avoid humanity en masse so far, keeping their activities out of the town proper.

"Could be something else," Duncan said. "Remember, I didn't bring us here because I was sensing those things. I'm having trouble getting a bead on them, which is weird for a low-thought demon like that—"

"Someone actively interfering with your abilities?" Arch asked. He already had his sword out, the deputy standing there like an old knight about to go to battle.

"There are rituals that can interfere with my sense, yeah," Duncan said. "Sort of a broad-based version of those talismans, the equivalent of throwing up a cloud of hot pepper to mess with my smell."

Hendricks was staring at the partially constructed house that the truck was abandoned in front of. He reached down and gently brushed the tailpipe. It was plenty cold.

"What's that for?" Duncan asked.

Hendricks smiled. "For exhaust."

Duncan didn't sigh, but Hendricks could sense his displeasure nonetheless. "Why are you feeling it up? Is there something missing in your sex life that compels you to stroke it like that?"

"It's got a nice-looking hole right there," Hendricks said, "just about the right size for—"

"That's enough." Arch's disgust bled out. "Construction guys would start early. That thing would be long cold even if they had just come to work here today."

"Yeah, but construction guys ain't quiet," Hendricks said. "Especially ones that are carrying scaffolding and lumber in the bed of their truck. You oughta hear hammering and shit. Electric drills. Something."

"They could be masons," Arch said. "The slap of a trowel doesn't make much noise."

Hendricks scanned the aborning subdivision. "I don't see any houses ready for brick, Arch. This stuff is all in the framing stages. That means heavy machinery and guys bolting shit together. Noise. Lots of noise."

"Should we keep jawing or go take a look?" Duncan asked, stepping up on the curb. The lawn was a patchwork of weed and blown seed grass, the sort of stuff that wouldn't look good no matter how often it was watered. It wouldn't ever grow into a proper lawn either, because it looked like some grass fairy had spread a patch here and there and then a weed demon had come along behind her and shit copiously before wiping his ass all over the ground. What didn't have green or weeds was dry damned dust, ground that looked like it hadn't been rained on since the Big Bang.

"Of course we're going to take a look inside the partially framed house," Hendricks said, starting across the "lawn." "Because we're stupid like that. Or heroes, maybe. Can't decide."

The house looked like it was built on a hill, a basement maybe sticking out the back following down the hill's grade. They might have dug in, tried to give it a little extra square footage by following the curve of the earth here. Hendricks had seen plenty of that; it was a pretty common thing in the Midwest. He hadn't given much thought to what kind of basements they might have here, if any at all. Hell, why would he? Housebuilding was for people not engaged in a war with demonkind. He didn't know many demon hunters who had wives or families or houses. It was pretty much an all-consuming occupation, and not a lucrative one that allowed for peaceful private villas elsewhere in the world.

As he approached the house, Hendricks tried to tune out Arch's soft footsteps next to him. The big man had automatically gone into quiet mode too, figuring it was better to scare the hell out of a construction worker or two than have the hell beaten out of you by some demon or twelve who heard you coming.

The floor was in, but just barely, dried cement showing in a few places where they'd poured subfloor. In others it was straight wood, but kinda patchy, because he could see some nice drops right into the dark of the basement below. It was hard to tell how much of a basement there was; he suspected by the slope of the land it was partially buried, maybe a few egress windows or something at the back of the house, but it was tough to tell from the front, especially with most of the floor installed and occluding his view.

"Hm," Duncan said from a step back. "You see that back corner over there?" He pointed at the rear left of the house.

Hendricks hadn't noticed it until now, but it did look a little funny, like someone had stacked a few beams off to one side, and that maybe one of the floor joists had fallen in. "Either something big brushed aside some of those supports, or else ... this is the shittiest construction job you'll find this side of Sochi."

"I'm inclined toward the former," Duncan said, "because I'm sensing something ... right down below us." He kept a steely calm, but it was still enough to stop both Hendricks and Arch in their tracks.

"Sensing ... what?" Hendricks asked. "Tell me it's a couple teenagers with a blanket playing hide the salami in the back of the basement."

"Why, you want to watch a really, really amateur porn?" Duncan asked. "It's not teenagers. Or human at all."

"Shit," Hendricks muttered. "This our boy in the suit? The funeral crasher?"

"What's Will Ferrell got to do with this?" Arch asked, and when he caught looks from both of them, he said, "Y'all aren't the only ones who can make stupid jokes."

"That movie was about two guys who tried to sneak into weddings to screw vulnerable chicks," Hendricks said. "Feels like that'd be a little too sinful for you."

"I didn't rent it." Arch was stiff as a board, shoulders looking like they had enough tension built up that he might not be able to swing the sword, and it only took a second for Hendricks to get the message: Alison rented it.

"I don't think this is our funeral crasher," Duncan said. "Feels rougher. Bigger."

Hendricks froze. "How much bigger?"

Something scraped against the floor below, and the entire wooden framework of the house rippled. The fierce smell of sulfur came wafting up between the boards, and a piece of concrete subfloor broke loose and fell into the basement below, shattering on impact, reverberating through the confined space like a thundercrack.

"However much space is below there," Duncan said as the basement started to collapse in, "that's the size of the thing."

"Helpful," Hendricks said, taking a step back as the meager framework of the house began to fall in on itself. "Really fucking helpful." He had his sword out, trying to get himself ready for whatever was coming.

Duncan started to say something, but he didn't get to finish. Something ripped through the back corner of the basement nearest them, climbing up the foundation to their right. Hendricks backed off, Arch a couple steps behind him and Duncan leading the field in getting the fuck back. The first thing to emerge was a paw—there was just no other way to describe it—and it had three big claws, each probably the size of Hendricks's shin, emerging from the broken boards. There was fur too, dark and straight, like porcupine quills but with the unmistakable aura of something unnatural.

It showed its face a moment later, pushing up through the wooden supports and breaking some of them in half easily. Hendricks realized that this was where it had made its den, and it was using that rear corner to enter and exit the structure. Now it had foregone the simple entry because there was prey nearby, and this thing was a hunter.

It had glowing orange eyes that burned like someone had lit a campfire in each of them. That worried Hendricks when he saw them sticking out of the domed head, but it probably would have been positively fucking pants-shitting scary if he'd seen them glowing in the dark from inside the basement. "Kudos for Duncan's danger sense," Hendricks muttered, taking another few steps back. He was not alone in this at all; neither Arch nor the OOC were being stingy about getting the fuck back.

"I wish it had been a little more clear," Duncan said, almost plaintive. He was fussing with something, baton in one hand and—a cell phone, Hendricks realized after a second look—in the other. He was dialing, and then sticking it up to his face. Hendricks didn't hear an answer, but Duncan said, "GPS my coordinates and get the watch out here now. I've got a stray—" He said something else here, something in demonic gibberish, something Hendricks couldn't have repeated back unless maybe he cut out his own tongue. Probably not even then.

The beast was still clawing its way out of the basement, but making a pretty good job of it. Now it seemed to have emerged up to the belly, stepping out. It was at least as big as that construction work truck, and Hendricks no longer wondered what had become of its occupants. He had a suspicion they were on the big monster meal plan, and it had probably come as a bigass surprise to those poor bastards to show up for work one morning and find that fucking thing already on the job site.

It had a funny shape, he realized as it cleared the house, pulling itself out like a snake from its den. Its head was a dome, and its body below the arms or forelegs or whatever was almost chubby, like a raccoon or a possum, that slick fur running the length of the body and something like scales or really dry skin covering the belly. It popped its backside out, and of course it had a tail behind shorter back legs that lifted the body out. The claws were covered in concrete dust from where it had scaled its way through the block wall.

"I'm not even gonna bother to ask what you called that thing," Hendricks said to Duncan. "But I would like to know what it can do."

"You don't recognize it?" Duncan said, a little more tautly than the OOC usually spoke. "It's in that book of yours. Funny name, but the tribes of—" Here he said something else, something Hendricks maybe could have said with ten years to practice "—call it something else. Loosely translated, it's a fire sloth."

Hendricks snapped his finger. "That's what it looks like. I was trying to figure it out. A fucking sloth. Those claws! The face! It's a giant demon sloth."

Arch raised an eyebrow at him. "You may be fixated on the sloth part … but I'm a little worried about the demon part. Does that mean it can—"

The fire sloth opened its mouth, bellowing toward the heavens in a show of pure, territorial animal bravado that Hendricks recognized from countless documentaries he'd seen. Following that horrible howling noise came a wash of fire so hot that he felt it even fifty feet away.

"Yep," Duncan said, and took a step forward. "Hellfire, in fact, straight from the depths. Just like your pal Gideon, actually." He held out the baton. "I wouldn't expect it to back off; it won't give up, and it's not going to present much of a target to us—at all—if it can avoid it. These things are smart and dangerous, and if it can cook us from a distance and then eat us all crispy, it will do so."

"So it's like Erin then?" Hendricks quipped. And the fire sloth, either hearing this and becoming offended or else simply running out of patience, bellowed again and charged, shaking the earth as it came after them.

*

"So, what are we doing out here?" Brian asked Casey as they jolted down a country road. The ride wasn't just bumpy, it was like his seat was spring-loaded, firing him at the ceiling of the truck every few seconds, the old seatbelt not exactly doing a great job of holding him down.

"You'll see," Casey promised with a gleam in his eye. He hadn't made a peep about where they were going during the whole car ride, ever since Brian had rejoined him at the station house. Instead, he'd launched into a graded assessment of the asses of the women of

Midian, and even thrown in a couple of guys for good measure. That was wearing pretty thin for Brian, but he'd yet to say so, instead looking intently at the road ahead, trying not to get carsick.

The inside of Casey's car smelled like the man enjoyed a cigarette every now and again, faint traces of smoke seeped into the upholstery and even the faux-leather dashboard and linings of the doors. It was slightly sweet, like maybe pipe smoke would be. Not weed, Brian reflected with a careful sniff. He didn't want to get caught smelling the seats for fear that Casey might think it weird. Or worse, that he wouldn't think it weird at all, but rather take it as an invitation to something stranger.

"Great," Brian said under his breath. He'd committed to go on a dude date with the weirdest man in the watch. At least Casey had seemed like he wanted to cheer Brian up, had engaged with him as a fellow human being. Everyone else seemed too mired in their own misery to do anything other than offer him a brief comment, a nice little pat on the head for his grief: "Such a shame, they were such good people, you must be suffering, you poor thing." And then they were back to caring about their own business, their own grief, their own worries.

Brian got that. There was no shortage of misery or worry floating around Midian these days.

But it sure did conspire to make him feel more lonely and cut off than ever. At least when he'd been hanging in the basement and getting high, he was actively choosing to cut himself off from humanity. His daily discussions with his father—lectures, really—so hated at the time, had been an unintended source of warm-ish human contact.

Now ... he only wished he could be on the receiving end of one of them again.

Instead, his dad was languishing in a persistent state of near vegetativeness.

"Hell of a way to spend the rest of your life," Brian muttered.

"In Becky Stordal's ass? I reckon that would be a little like heaven," Casey said, nodding along.

Brian blinked. He'd unwittingly interrupted Casey Assman's Top Forty. "No, not Becky Stordal's ass. I was talking about my dad being permanently—well, you know."

"Brain damaged? That's a motherfucker, all right." Casey scrunched up his face, and hesitated for a moment. "Say ... never mind."

Brian leaned his head back against the seat, breathing in that long-buried aroma of cigarette. "What?"

"I just thought of something, but it ain't important right now." Casey had a gleam in his eyes, fixed straight ahead.

"What?" Brian pushed a little harder. He hated when people did this shit: brought something up, acted like it might be good or interesting, and then withdrew it like they were pulling the bait back. "What is it?"

"I was just thinking when I said 'motherfucker' ... hey, your mom's a stately lady ... and now that your dad's down, she might get lonely ..."

"Fucking shit," Brian said, rolling his head to look out the window. "Jesus Christ, Casey."

"Look, I know she's got a period of mourning to go through. I was just thinking, you know ... she might need some comfort at some point, and I have a wonderful shoulder to cry on. And then, after—"

"Jesus! Don't say it!"

"I have an excellent penis to bounce up and down on—"

"Fucking—fuckety—that's my mom, asshole!"

Casey stared at Brian, seemingly infinitely perplexed. "Well, then don't you want her to be happy?"

A little bit of gruesome sick feeling washed over Brian, and it wasn't from the winding of the roads bouncing his inner ear. "Of course I want her to be happy. Which is why I don't want her having to deal with you or your bizarre, sick fuck, horny old dog turned up to eleven ass, while she's mourning her daughter and caring for her husband." He put a hand over his eyes, enjoying the faint darkness. It was hardly complete, but when combined with thick boughs of the trees overhead gave him a break from the sunlight flooding him.

"That's okay, I understand," Casey said. He sounded like he said, "unnerstand." "She needs some space to grieve. I'm happy to give her that. Just figured maybe she needed a strong man—"

"She needs the space," Brian said, closing his eyes under his hand. It was soothing in the dark, strangely. "Light-years of space."

Then, suddenly, it wasn't so dark anymore. Brian opened his eyes and the woods before him were gone, replaced by an old gate that was plastered with a couple faded NO TRESPASSING signs.

Casey brought the truck to a halt and hopped out. Brian watched him walk in front of the vehicle, straight up to the gate, and just swing it open as pretty as you please. Then he came back up to the truck and vaulted back in over the running board, grinning to beat the band.

"Where the hell are we?" Brian stared at the road ahead. It seemed to rise up to a hill and then go right or left to either side, not forward at all.

"You'll see," Casey said, and he was driving again, the truck bumping up and down the disused gravel path. It was clear this particular road hadn't been cared for in a long time, the gravel washed out enough to leave large potholes.

Brian braced himself against the dash with his left hand and the *Oh shit!* bar with his right. It didn't help that much; he still bounced around like a pea in an empty bag as Casey floored it and took the truck over the uneven-as-hell road. "Fuck!" Brian breathed as Casey swung the truck to the left at the intersection and they started to head down as the road curved.

Looking left, Brian finally realized—or suspected—where they were. "Is this the old quarry?"

"Yep," Casey almost chirped with glee. He pushed the truck hard down the old road that led down into the quarry. Brian could see the bottom; it looked drier than a jar of moonshine the morning after a redneck party.

"What the hell are we doing here?" Brian asked.

"You'll see," Casey said, pushing the truck down the path.

The quarry was—objectively speaking—fucking huge, acres and acres of fill having been ripped right out of the earth for all manner of construction projects. They'd probably even used some of the gravel to build that road back there, and the rock, in general, was used for—well, hell, whatever rock was used for. Asphalt, among other things. It stretched the length and width of several football fields. Brian had heard that they'd shut it down because it was practically an artificial lake at this point, but there damned sure wasn't a lot of evidence of that.

But then, rain had been hard to come by of late, though no one had said much about it. The harvest was over, and rain wasn't nearly as critical as it had been during the summer months. No one was fussing about it now, especially with all the other shit they had to worry about in Midian.

Casey brought the truck to a skidding halt down in the floor of the quarry, yelling, "Yeeeeehaw!" like some stereotypical redneck. Brian, although pretty fucking busy holding on for his damned life, had a second to reflect on this choice by Casey, and he had to wonder whether the taxidermist was genuinely yelling it out of enthusiasm, or whether he was using it ironically. Hard to tell. Irony and sarcasm had ruined, almost permanently, genuine enthusiasm.

"All right," Casey said, and opened up the door, stepping out like he was jumping out of a plane for a sky dive. He left it open and stalked around to Brian's side, ripping the door open as Brian sat there, still clutching the dash and the *Oh shit!* bar. "Let's go."

"Go where?" Brian asked, finally deciding it was safe to start letting go of the things he was clinging to for stability. The truck probably wasn't going to start driving like a bat out of hell without Casey at the wheel. He checked to make sure it was in park though, just to be certain.

"You're gonna drive," Casey said, pointing at the driver's seat, like that cleared it all up.

"Drive where?"

"Right here, dumbass," Casey said. "Around the quarry."

Brian only had to think about this for a second. "Look, man, if I thought making turns in a confined space was fun, I'd be a huge fan of NASCAR, but I don't. So I don't see what the point is—"

"The point is, slide over into that driver's seat and let's get started." Casey brought up a hand as though he were going to touch him. "Don't make me move your ass myself. Because I'm not just going to push it; I'm gonna cop a feel and add you to the ratings matrix at the same time." He grinned. "Make my day."

"Shit." Brian slid over without hesitation. He put his hands on the wheel; at least it would provide some stability, and he could avoid going ninety miles an hour around this quarry while in the driver's seat.

"Attagirl," Casey said, and hopped up into the passenger seat. He slammed the door shut and put on the seatbelt, then put his hands in his lap. "Get your door closed." Brian obeyed, leaning over and feeling like he was going to fall out of the giant truck to do so. "Okay, let's rock out with the cock out!" Casey said.

"That's kinda sexist," Brian said, wishing he'd kept his mouth shut as soon as he said it.

"We're dudes," Casey said, staring at him blankly.

"Yeah," Brian said lamely. "But ... still."

"Fair point, I guess," Casey said. "All right, I got the ladies covered too—Let's roll out with your hole out!"

Brian stared at the steering wheel, wondering again how he'd been talked into this. The sun was beating down on the truck from overhead, the mighty engine idling, and his foot was on the pedal. "For fuck's sake," Brian murmured.

"Well, come on then," Casey said, grinning widely. "Let's do this."

"Do what? There's no one to race, there's nothing to—"

"It ain't a race," Casey said, like this was the stupidest comment in the world. "It's about getting out there, letting yourself run wild. Run free! Like our ancestors, unfettered by the craziness of the day. It's about finding yourself by letting loose!"

"I don't know that 'letting loose' is going to help me right now. Because I have very serious problems that aren't going to be solved by racing a big old truck around an abandoned quarry."

"You say that, but you ain't even touched the pedal yet. Come on."

Brian sat back against the seat, smelling the aroma of tobacco buried in the cloth like it had been released by his gentle push against it. His stomach rumbled, and the faint taste of the coffee he'd had hours and hours ago lingered on his tongue mixed with the bile that seemed perpetually ready to work its way up in the back of his throat. "I don't want to."

Casey just sat there in silence for a minute, then nodded. "You need to unwind, brutha." He shifted his head toward the glove compartment in front of him. "I got some weed in here, just for you. Let's smoke out and tear some shit up, get some dust on these tires."

"I don't—" Brian sagged farther into the seat. "I shouldn't."

"You need to cut loose, man," Casey said. "Get some of the kinks out of your soul. Smoke up, me hearty, yo ho." His voice took on a pirate accent.

"No," Brian said, shaking his head. He'd been through this, hadn't he? It might feel better in the short-term, but getting high wouldn't fix anything that was wrong, tempting as it was.

"Well, you need to relax somehow." Casey seemed to ponder in the silence. "I got whiskey in the glove box too."

"No." Brian didn't really like the feeling of being drunk.

"Well …" Casey leaned in. "Ms. Cherry's?"

"No."

That provided a moment of blissful silence. Then Casey said, "There's some condoms in the glove box, if you want a little piece of what I let Gus Terkel have."

"Jesus, do you have a full BDSM kit in there too?" Brian nodded at the glove box. He stared at Casey for only a moment as the taxidermist smiled. Before the man had a chance to answer, Brian said, "You know what? I'll just take the weed. The weed's fine."

"What about—"

"No, I'm good on everything else," Brian said, pushing his eyes straight ahead. "No offense, Casey, you're just … not my type." He stared out across the dusty ground, feeling the hard blush. "I'm sure Gus Terkel is a very, uh, lucky man …"

"I'd say so," Casey agreed. "You seen his wife? Pshaaaw. Wish I could be in the middle of that sandwich."

Brian stomped the pedal, hoping it would stop Casey before he could go into too much detail about what that might entail.

"Yeehaw!" Casey shouted again as the truck surged into motion, kicking up a cloud of dust in the rearview. "And you aren't even high yet! This is gonna be great!"

The back end of the truck started to fishtail, and Brian fought it back under control, remembering what his daddy had taught him about not overcorrecting. Casey howled with excitement next to him, pumping his fist in the air. "That's right, boy! You show this fucker who's boss!" Brian wasn't quite sure who he was referring to, but as the truck accelerated along the empty quarry, bumping hard on the uneven surface, he realized he didn't really need to know. He had a vision of the internet comic where the dog was sitting in the middle of flames and thinking, "This is fine." He found himself laughing, uncontrollably, as he brought the truck into a sharp turn.

"What?" Casey asked, as they hit a bump that almost put his head into the liner of the truck roof.

"I was just thinking ... 'This is fine,'" Brian said, and the truck bounced hard again, hard enough it felt like the bottom might have touched the ground. Casey howled his enthusiasm. "This is fine," Brian muttered again under his breath. And for the moment, it was.

*

"Let's go, let's go, let's go!" Erin bustled out into the bullpen, hauling ass as fast as her ass would be hauled. "Got an emergency call from Duncan down at the Whistling Pines construction site off Bullock Pike!" Guthrie preceded her by a few steps, demon speed aiding the OOC's passage out of the confinement area where they'd been extricating themselves from the cell block with John Demon Doe.

"Shit," Reeve said, spurred to immediate action. Benny Binion was manning the dispatch station, and Reeve pointed a finger at him as he started to run for the door. "Get the word out!"

"You got it, bossman," Benny said. He was a middle-aged guy, most of his hair gone but covered over by a cap, a few days of scruff settled on his cheeks. He worked out at the mill, drank at Fast Freddie's sometimes, and had a wife and a couple kids at home. He started pounding away composing a text message on the emergency phone the second he picked it up. He pecked a couple times, said, "Shit," and then hit the delete key. "Shit," he said again. "Goddamned technology."

Reeve slowed as he got to the door. "You gonna be okay there, Benny?"

"Fine," Benny said, still pecking away, all his attention on the phone. "Shit. Goddamned autocorrect." He looked up. "Go, go! I got this!"

"All right," Reeve said, sounding a little skeptical.

Erin was right behind him and Guthrie, and then she felt a shove at her elbow. She looked to her left and there was Mary Wrightson, the look of fierce determination on her face reminding Erin of a bulldog. She looked up at Erin and said, by way of explanation, "I wanna see."

"Mary, you should wait for your son here." Reeve didn't stop moving through the doors in order to tell her this, almost like he knew arguing with her was like arguing with a stone wall.

"Fuck that," Mary said, brandishing her sawed-off shotgun. "I'm gonna see what this demon shit is all about."

"Didn't you see what it was all about when those hellcats ripped your house down?" Guthrie asked, almost innocently.

"I saw a swarm of shitbats flying my way," Mary said, her head still covered with the dust of her ruined home, "like a fucking storm of meteors, tearing my crap all apart. You watch a curio box that's been in your family for generations get shredded like cabbage for slaw as a black shadowy cat-looking motherfucker comes leaping through, it changes your perspective on life."

Erin bit the bait on that one. "From what to what?"

"From thinking, 'Hey, I'm old enough I got this thing figured out,' to, 'Holy fuck, I don't know my ass from a glory hole,'" Mary replied. "So, I need to see the glory hole, as it were, get the world right in my head afore I need to take a dump, lest some poor bastard ends up with an unpleasant experience. Or maybe an awakening one, I don't know."

Erin snorted as she hit the parking lot. Something about that was funny, but she couldn't quite sort out what.

"What are we dealing with here?" Reeve asked as he made for his car. Mary followed him, of course. Erin had a trace of regret about that, because naturally Guthrie followed her.

"It's a—" Guthrie stopped, like she was puzzling through. "It's a fifteen-foot-tall demon sloth that breathes fire."

"That ain't making my ass no clearer from the hole," Mary said. "A what?"

"You'll know it when you see it," Guthrie said, diving into the passenger seat of Erin's car just before she got there.

"Which one?" Mary called, wobbling her way to Reeve's passenger side. "My ass or the sloth?"

"Both, I hope," Guthrie said, then, to Erin, "Human appetites are annoying. I don't know how you humans put up with all these physical demands—water, food, excretion, sleep, sex. How do you get anything else done?"

"Some of us, that's all we do," Erin said as she started the car. She floored it into reverse and her phone dinged with a text alert. She ripped it out of the case and slapped it into the holder on the dashboard, where the screen lit for a moment with the text message. It was from the emergency phone:

DAEMON SITED AT WHISTLING POONS CONSTRUCTION SIGHT. ALL WITCH REPORTAGE.

"I'm no expert on the English language," Guthrie said, "but I don't there's more than a word of that he got right."

"Text him back that he's a goddamned idiot," Erin said, throwing the car into drive and beating Reeve out onto Old Jackson Highway. "And then send the correct address. This ain't the time for a colossal cock-up."

"You're telling me," Guthrie said, already futzing with the phone. "Fire sloths? They do not fuck around. At all."

"Great," Erin said. "And our people are stuck waiting for help because Benny fat-fingered the fuck out of his phone."

"Hey, what girl doesn't love a good fat-fingering?" Guthrie smirked.

Erin steamed in silence as she put the pedal to the floor, flipping the switch for the sirens and lights and praying that everybody got the hell out of her way, because in this mood, in this moment, she might just run them off the road if they didn't.

*

"Haul ass!" Duncan screamed, and the three of them bolted, Arch galloping away from that furry, fiery thing just as it let out another breath of flame so hot it felt like the breath of Satan himself licking at his backside. It warmed up the brisk day, set him to sweating down the back of his neck, maybe from the heat and the fear combined. Arch did not care to have his biscuits burned.

Hendricks had darted back to the car, but Duncan laid a hand on his collar and twisted him, pulling him toward the partially erected house next door. It had TyVek up, the plastic coating covering its wooden bones. The sloth screeched behind them and Arch adjusted his course to follow Duncan and Hendricks.

"Why—" Hendricks started.

"Because while you start up the car to go, you'll get cooked like a chicken in a smoker," Duncan said as they all three hot-footed it toward the partially completed house next door. "And it'll snack the meat right off your bones."

"What'd happen to you?" Hendricks asked.

"Nothing good. Move it!"

Arch was unclear on the plan, but hoped someone else had one other than, *Run!* It didn't look like anyone did, though, because Duncan steered them toward the open door of the incomplete house and in they went, each of them leaping to clear the place where the front porch steps concrete hadn't been laid yet. Arch dodged inside, first in the line, and looked back in time to see fire burning its way through the TyVek wrap at the corner of the house next door. "This ain't gonna stop him for long."

"Thread the needle, man," Duncan said, taking the lead and running through an unfinished wall toward a staircase covered in plywood that led down to this house's basement. He jumped down to the landing and Hendricks shrugged, following him. Arch just took the steps fast, falling behind in the scramble once they'd gotten inside the door. The air smelled of sawdust, and as he booked it down the basement stairs, the air got a little cooler.

Duncan's shoes slapped against the concrete, still hauling butt toward the daylight shining in from the back of the house. The demon jumped out a back window even as the sound of wood splintering came from behind them and upstairs. Arch chanced a look back; he could see the floor buckling under the fire sloth's weight, and the smell of smoke hung in the air. He was definitely following them. "Heck fire," Arch muttered.

"Hellfire, goddammit!" Hendricks shot back as he booked it out the back of the house, Arch on his heels. The cowboy veered wide toward the open rear door instead of leaping out the window the way Duncan did. Arch followed the OOC and tried to hurdle out. His scabbard hit the wooden frame of the window space and stopped him. Arch's pants ripped, two belt loops popping off as he felt like someone seized him by the waist and tried to drag him back in. He landed clumsily. It was clear why Hendricks had gone wide around. "Gotta watch the scabbard, man," Hendricks said with a grin as Arch lurched back into motion.

"Make for the woods!" Duncan said, already heading for the vegetation behind them. "Post-haste." And he sped away as the sounds of crashing and thrashing behind them got worse.

Arch outpaced Hendricks again, and as he passed him, Hendricks said, "You think you can outrun a bear?" between puffing breaths.

Arch didn't laugh, but he did feel a faint smile pop up in spite of everything going on now, and everything that was weighing on his mind. It was the setup to a joke that he actually did know, because it was clean. "I don't have to outrun the bear," he said. "I just have to outrun you."

"Bravo," Hendricks said as they reached the tree line and Duncan grabbed them both, yanking them behind a bush and to the ground.

"Shhhhh," the demon said, applying his weight to the backs of both.

Arch wasn't out of breath, but Hendricks was puffing a little. He got it under control fast, like he was holding it in fear of being heard. They all sat there, Duncan on top of both of them, staring back the way they'd come. The house they'd just escaped was already puffing smoke, the fire sloth having done his thing. The snapping of wood carried to them loud on the wind. The fire sloth was fighting his way through a house that was collapsing under his weight, the rear studs already buckled and fallen. The sound of the lumber breaking under its weight was quite fearsome, and Arch listened as though his very life depended upon it.

The fire sloth poked its head out of the timbers of the fallen house, writhing to get its shoulders free. It screamed, burning up the splintered beams trapping it and provoking more to fall. It was like watching a hairy, angry, demon baby being born from the rear of a fallen house.

"And now," Duncan whispered, "we wait." He lay upon them as though trying to protect them from outward attack.

"Uh huh," Hendricks muttered. "While I got you here, Duncan ... is that a banana in your pocket, or are you just happy to be lying on top of us?" Arch stifled a giggle, and it felt ... strange. He couldn't see the cowboy's face, but he knew that son of a gun was grinning. What a time to try and make them cut up laughing. But it almost worked, because Arch had to bury his face in the dirt in order to keep from chuckling out loud.

The screams of the fire sloth extracting himself from the fallen house grew louder and more frantic as they waited to see if he would pick up their trail.

*

"You don't look so good, Nick," Mary pronounced as they rattled along behind Erin's cruiser. Reeve's foot was glued to the pedal, partly because he needed, needed, needed to get out to Whistling Pines fast to deal with this situation and—based on Reeve's prior experience—save Hendricks's and Arch's asses. The other reason was so he didn't take his foot off, lift it over the center console, and give that annoying old bitch Mary Wrightson a good kick out the door while the car was in motion.

"Oh, yeah?" Reeve ground out.

"You're looking haggard," she said.

"Like Merle, I hope," Reeve said. "I always liked him."

"You're looking like something the cat dragged in," Mary said. "On his ass. Through a briar patch. And some nettles too, maybe—"

"Thank you."

"I just can't believe Donna let you get to this state," Mary said, shaking her head sadly. "If my Larry walked out the door in this state, I would whop him upside the head for disgracing our family."

"You don't think he looked like hell that time you creased his damned skull?" Reeve asked. He felt agitated and combative, and not really in the sort of mood required to admit that his wife was dead. He'd rather argue with Mary Wrightson than, God forbid, receive her pity.

Mary seemed to think that over. "You know, you got a point there, but … he was needing it."

"Don't we all, sooner or later," Reeve said, intending to clam up and let her sit in silence. Instead, somehow, the words sprang out of his lips: "Donna's dead, Mary. Died two weeks ago." When Mary didn't say anything, he felt compelled to add, "Demons got her," for some reason.

"Well, Jesus, Nick," Mary said. "You got every reason to look like hell then, I guess—if you want to be one of them goddamned millennial children that wear their emotions on their sleeves." He looked over at her. "You and I come from a different generation. These kids nowadays may go ejaculating their emotions everywhere like in those movies my Larry used to watch when he thought I wasn't around, but we don't do that shit. We were the types that lived through 'Nam and Korea and World War II, and you could take a bullet to the leg, and you'd just grin and say, 'Nope, I'm fine.'"

Reeve wasn't sure how to take that, but after a moment he chortled. "You got a point there, Mary," he said. "And I ain't gonna tell you about my feelings—"

"Good, cuz I didn't fucking ask."

"—but I will say, while you were—off on your property doing whatever the hell it is you do to fill your days—"

"Well, I got a garden, Nick."

"It's fall."

"And I got my programs."

"Soap operas?"

"And my boy Gary stops out every once in a blue moon. You know him, right? He's the one in the wheelchair?"

Oh, Reeve knew Gary Wrightson. Everyone did. "I do indeed. Anyway, my point is, while you're checked out from town life—"

"Politics around here are always the same bullshit, and the same bullshit people. I bet Keith Drumlin is bitching about something somebody did to his house, just like his daddy used to do—"

"Yeah, I think Nate McMinn took a shit on his front porch or something, but—I dunno, they ain't complaining much lately. They're both in the Watch." Reeve quieted for a moment. "Keith lost his family here recently."

"Well, shit." Mary only waited a beat. "'In the watch' what?"

It took Reeve a second to get what she was asking. "The Watch. It's what we call the group that deals with these demon problems."

Mary wrinkled her nose. "That's a dumbass name. What dumbass came up with it?"

"That cowboy, I think?" Reeve racked his brain. He really didn't know; they'd called it that since he'd been onboard.

Mary nodded. "There's a motherfucker who's got a finely apportioned sense of the dramatic. Look at that coat. You ever seen anyone in a getup like that outside of Montana?"

"Reckon I haven't."

"Hmph." A few moments of silence proceeded. "Well, I won't ask you how you're feeling, Nick, because that ain't my bailiwick. But I will ask—how are you doing?"

"I won't tell you how I'm feeling then, Mary," he said, "but I will say I got a goddamned headache, and I feel like that thing the cat dragged in through the briars and the nettles. Except I'm too tired to want to scratch the itches. It ain't the kind of sleepy tired, either." He felt it now, keeping the car around seventy on this road, barreling along behind Erin. "It's the soul-deep kind, the kind that you fall into bed at night and wonder how you'll ever sleep. But sleep comes for you, sooner or later, in that … that morass of thoughts—"

"You're getting dangerously close to talking about feelings, here. I might have to pop this door and jump on out if you do."

"That ain't much of a threat to me, to be real honest."

"Oh fuck you. I'm a delight."

"I got a task," Reeve said, hunching his shoulders. They felt tighter than hell. "Got a job to do. It keeps me going."

"That's good," Mary said, a little quieter. "Men who don't have work to do, well—they tend to die real quick."

Reeve let out a laugh, and he felt that all the way to his toes too, over that soul-weariness. "I reckon I'll hold on for another hundred years, then—or at least 'til this demon business is over." His face tightened. "Unless one of them eats me first. And I don't rule that out."

"Eat you? I reckon it'd find you so ornery it'd spit your ass right out," Mary said definitely, like that settled the subject. Reeve chortled, because what else was there to say on the matter? He didn't have anything, and his head was already shifting out of this short interruption—back to what was waiting for them at Whistling Pines.

*

The smoke whirled faintly up out of the joint as Brian held it in his fingers, keeping in the hard hit he'd just taken. His lungs felt like they were going to explode, he'd held his breath so long, trying to get the alveoli to take as much of the sweet THC into his bloodstream as possible. When he couldn't hold it any longer he let out his breath and coughed slightly. Like a fucking rookie.

He hated to be picky, especially since this was the first weed he'd had in weeks, but goddamn. "Where did you get this ditchweed, Casey?" he asked, looking over at the taxidermist as he proffered the joint. They were sitting on Casey's tailgate in the middle of the quarry, not a fucking soul in sight.

"I ain't exactly a connoisseur of marijuana, you know," Casey said, picking it out of his fingertips gingerly, eyeing it like it was going to explode in his hand, and finally pressing it to his lips. He took a half-hearted hit, coughed, and then handed it back. "Pussy, ass, mouth—those are my drug of choice. Everybody knows it. You can keep this inhalable shit; I feel like I'm going to die every time I try it." Casey puckered his lips, rubbing his tongue in and out of his mouth, like he could scrub the taste out. He fell silent for a beat, then asked, "Brian ... why ain't you smoked lately?"

"I gave it up for Lent."

"It's November."

"Been a long time then."

Casey snickered. "I doubt you been going that long."

"No, you're right." Brian took another hit, enjoying the natural conversational pause it offered. Casey didn't interrupt his moment of bliss. He let it out and enjoyed the sensation of his head feeling a little floaty. "It hasn't been that long. Since ... whenever that destroyer thing came ripping through town. That was probably the last time, that night."

"A few weeks then," Casey said, then let out a low whistle. "I don't know if I could do celibacy that long, to tell you the truth. I like to get my dick wet two, three times a day."

Brian stared at him through the drifting smoke. "That's gotta be an expensive habit, if you're always going to Miss Cherry."

"I don't always go to Miss Cherry," he said, lowering his voice. "There's places around town—women, you know—"

"And Gus Terkel, apparently."

"Oh, there's more than Gus Terkel," Casey said with a gleam in his eye. "It's out there to be had, is the point. People wanting to be … intimate with people. Miss Cherry, she's a treat though. Most people are amateurs. Some gifted, some not so much. A few I think—well, I know it might be pity, but I'm okay with that. Pity ass is better than no ass."

"I think one of the great philosophers said something similar."

A goofy grin spread across Casey's face. "Really?"

"No, probably not."

"Bummer." He deflated a little. "But you know … sex is life. People want it. Even the people you wouldn't expect. Maybe mostly the people you wouldn't expect … it's such a buttoned-up affair—"

"Not literally, I assume."

Casey ignored him. "—we get so hung up about it, you know? Dudes, on average, got a drive to get fucked or get to releasing their seed at least once a day, most of us. It's a biological imperative. Women? Ehhh, on average, less so. Don't get me wrong—there are some women who will match the horniest sailor fuck for fuck, and lick for lick—but on average, I'm saying, most women—they just ain't got the carnal urge like the average man. We're different. We used to realize that. Hell, a thousand billion jokes sprung out of it. We don't talk about that much anymore, probably because of this 'equality' push."

Brian raised an eyebrow. "You think people being equal is a bad thing?"

Casey flushed. "No. No, I'm just saying that equal in law and life and whatever else, that's fine, but we still ain't built the same. Equal is one thing—someone can have the same chance as me to do whatever, and that's cool; *same* is another thing entirely. Men ain't all packing the same size cock, you know. Women ain't all receiving an equal distribution of bosoms from birth—though doctors are doing some fine work in this area, the field of tit equality."

Brian snorted, flubbing just as he was about to take a hit. "'The field of tit equality.' That's good." He coughed. "I mean, uh ... that's ... really inappropriate and objectifies women."

Casey just shrugged it off. "I don't mean to. I see women as women, and I ain't never been with a woman who didn't want to be with me. I don't like to go where I'm unwanted, personally. I want someone who's into it, or at least acting like it." He went quiet for a second. "My point is ... I need it more than most, and I know that. Because it's my—my thang. My solace." He looked right at Brian. "I wish everybody felt that way. I wish every woman needed it as much as I do. Or maybe that I found just one who really did. My point is ... you got a lot of ... stuff in your head. In your heart. Lots happened. So ... why not just smoke out before now?"

Brian coughed lightly on his exhale. "Because my dad never approved, you know." He stared at the floor of the quarry beneath their dangling feet. "He didn't say much about it. Snide remark every now and again when I was blazing up in the basement every day. But since I started doing this, well ..." Brian sniffed, the rich marijuana smoke wafting into his nostrils. It stank, he knew it, but it still felt like ... home, strangely. Sweet, even though it wasn't at all. "I don't want to say he was proud of me, because for all I know, he wasn't. But to start this up again ... it feels ..." He stared forlornly at the joint. "Well, a little like I'm betraying him."

Casey just stared at him for a second, and then reached up and slapped Brian across the back of the head so fast that he didn't even have a chance to react. He dropped the joint against the hard stone quarry floor and blanched. It didn't hurt too bad, but it stung, and Brian's jaw fell open as he reacted to the sudden stimulus of a whack to the back of the skull. "What the fuck?"

"Sorry," Casey said, nonchalant, like he hadn't just physically assaulted Brian. "I heard dumbassery and I had to deal with the dumbassery. My bad."

Brian held his hand over the back of his head like it could protect him from the slap that had already been delivered. "How is that dealing with it?"

"So you admit it was dumbassery?"

"I was telling you how I feel," Brian said, nursing the sting from the slap. It smarted. "You can't just—whack it out of me."

"I whack out bad feelings all the time," Casey said, making a motion like he was stroking an invisible dick from his lap. "Literally. You know when you cum, it sends a shot of endorphins in your brain. Changes your mood, because mood is just a chemical thing, you know?"

"Yeah, I guess I knew that," Brian said, finally starting to withdraw his hand from the back of his head.

"Slapping you in the back of the head changed your mood, am I right?" Casey chuckled. "You get hit, that releases chemicals too. Pain receptors fire up. Mood, feelings—they're all just chemistry in your brain."

"What the fuck does this have to do with slapping me?"

"Getting high changes your brain chemistry too," Casey said. "Lightens your mood. And right now, under the influence of grief and all the shit feelings that brings—you need to lighten your brain chemistry. You think your dad would be mad about that? That you're soldiering on over his lamed body? Shit. If he was really your daddy, he'd want you to be happy as you could be given what's happened. And he'd want you to keep going. And if that meant changing your brain chemistry through a little pot, you think he'd give a shit? If he didn't stop you from doing it when you were just sitting on your ass in the basement doing jack shit, you really thing he'd be pissed if you elevate your mood out of the dumps while you're going through this crap pile? Hell, I bet he wouldn't even give a damn if you took a beej from a dude like me right now." Casey arched his eyebrows.

"Maybe," Brian said, then quickly added, "Let's not test that assumption though." He felt compelled to add further explanation. "You're kinda ... awesome and all, Casey, but you just slapped me and it stung, and I don't want you to take that sting away by—uhhh, whatever means you're considering."

"It's called a blowjob, stupid ass," Casey said, "and that's fine if you're too homophobic to accept one from me."

"Hey, I'm not h—"

"It's fine, it's fine, I get it," Casey said, his feathers all ruffled. "You can take the small-town boy off to a fancy college, but you can't erase the small-town thinking—"

"What? I am so open-minded—I have no—I mean, I have supported—"

"These are all just pretty words from your pretty mouth. Get right down to it and you feel the same as—"

"Jesus! I'm not gay, Casey! I'm not homophobic; I'm just not into ... dicks ... in my orifices."

"Uh huh, sure. I can see the hate of me in your eyes." Casey snorted laughter. "Hehehehe. That was fun. Seriously, though, I'd blow you. We could talk reciprocity later, maybe after two, three times, once you got a little more comfortable—"

"Please," Brian said, holding up a hand and stooping to retrieve the joint. "I'm not—"

"Yeah, yeah, I'm just yanking your crank cuz you won't let me yank your cock," Casey said. "I get it. You ain't feeling it. And this ain't exactly my first time being told no, I expect you realize. But back to the topic at hand—you think your daddy would be mad at you for taking a break and doing whatever it took to get over the shit in your head, in your heart—and get back to work? We ain't machines, man. And that brain chemistry I was talking about? It's hard to make things happen when it's stacked against you. You end up with real problems," he said, soberly, "serious ones. Like the inability to maintain an erection."

Brian made a face. "I, uh ... haven't had that problem."

"Well, let me tell you something—you get down enough, it could happen." Casey coughed. "I've heard. I wouldn't know personally, of course. But this is why it's so important to get your head right. How useful do you think you're gonna be to the watch if you got your skull up your sphincter? Anal, not oral sphincter, just to be clear. Because those are two different muscles, and they feel totally different, obviously—"

"Stick to the point, Casey."

"Right." Casey nodded. "People talk about fitness. Gotta keep your body in shape. But you gotta keep your head in shape too. And if you ain't got no way to blow off steam, to balance your brain chemistry so it ain't all overworked and whatnot—"

"You're a real expert endocrinologist and neurologist here, Casey."

"—I know you're making fun of me, but this is all just common sense stuff, man. Your head ain't right, you ain't right. Simple as that. And your body falls with you. Know what I mean?" He picked up the lighter out of the pickup bed next to him and proffered it to Brian. "So toke up. We're in the fight of our lives here, and you don't need to be so wound up, man. Get high every once in a while. Get laid—"

"No."

"—by a girl, if that's what you need," Casey said, rolling his eyes. "I think you know I am plenty partial to pussy. I get that. Just get right, you know? Even out, man. Because I get the feeling—" and here he leaned in conspiratorially "—this thing? This fight? It ain't gonna be like Gus Terkel—by which I mean ten seconds and done, if you get me?"

Brian lit the joint back up and took a long inhale before he answered, letting the smoke blow out slowly. "It'd be pretty tough to miss a point as boldly stated as that one, Casey. Yes, I get you." He took a breath, letting the feeling of warmth, of lightness creep up into his head. It felt good. "And yeah ... I will let loose a little." He looked at the glowing end of the joint, the ember fading without oxygen to feed the little flame. "Wouldn't want to burn out, after all. Not now."

*

Pike was sitting back in his chair when Darla came into his office. The kids were out in the receptionist area with Jenny, already busy talking to her, which was something they viewed as a great novelty. Jenny was good with kids. That was definitely one of her pluses, that warm, personable personality.

Also, she could suck a monkey through thirty feet of garden hose. That was a bigger plus than her way with kids, at least as far as he was concerned.

"I got a babysitter for this afternoon," Darla said as she breezed in, closing the door behind her.

"Is it Jenny?" Pike asked, leaning back in his chair.

"No," Darla said, features pinched with amusement. "She'll be working late with you."

"Oh," Pike said, then the realization of what she meant dawned on him and he said, "Ohh."

"How can you get Reeve up here?" Darla asked, sliding onto the surface of the desk in front of him. She was wearing yoga pants, and when she sat down, the desk flattened out her leg in a line where it met. It looked funny under the stretchy material, and he found his eyes strangely drawn to it. Darla's legs were never one of his favorite features, but they weren't bad. A little hammier than he might have liked, even before two kids, but she made up for it upstairs, in brains and tits.

"I don't know yet," Pike said, bringing his eyes up. She didn't get mad when he stared at her body, but she did roll her eyes and make fun of him if she caught him. Underneath it all, he wondered if it was because secretly—in spite of her protestations to the contrary—all her witticisms about how kids had fucked up her body were really just cover for her being pissed about it.

"Glad you're finally looking at me," she said, and leaned over, dropping a hand into his lap. She caught the tip of his cock in a pincer grip with her right hand, and he flinched until she lightened the pressure and gave it a little rub between her fingers. He took a breath and she rubbed it again, thumb and forefinger finding the spot where his tip met the shaft even through his underwear and his Dockers. "You fucked Jenny yet today?"

"Not yet," he said. She wasn't doing a whole lot for him with two layers of clothing between their skin, but it was better than nothing.

"Okay, you're going to need to do it later," Darla said, all instruction. "You'll need to blow a load in her pussy, okay? You think you got that much in you?"

"I think I can manage that."

"Watch some porn on your phone if you have to. Get a little slow burn going, build up some interest—but don't finish yourself off, okay?" He nodded, and his gaze fell down to those yoga pants again, and where they met the desk. "Jesus, Jason, it isn't even going to be difficult, is it? You're hard already." She twinged him a little between her fingers. "Also, you should look at a lady when she's talking to you."

"I'm looking at your thighs where they meet the desk," Pike said, looking up with a smirk of his own.

"I'm not my thighs. Or my ass. Or my tits, because I know that's where you'll look next."

"I'm still on those yoga pants, really," Pike said, admiring the curve of the top of her thigh.

"Still up here, jackass."

"If you didn't want me to look, maybe wear something looser?" He shifted his gaze to her tits, because dammit, she pretty much asked for it, but mostly to get her goat. He smiled as he met her eyes again. "Come on, Darling Darla. You're sitting here talking to me about getting fucked like I'm a hungry beast. Don't get mad when I start appetizing on what's in front of me."

She snorted, still rubbing his tip under the cloth of his pants. "I'm just giving you shit. Do whatever you have to do to make this happen. I've got everything planned on my end. You have two jobs—get Reeve here, and get ready to nail Jenny's ass. Just get 'em done." She stood.

"I'll be all over that as soon as you leave," he promised, and then watched her yoga pants ass retreat toward the door. She shook it a little extra for him, smiling as she did so. He really did love that woman.

*

Lauren came into her friend's house quietly, like the guest she was. Elise was a doctor too, but she'd moved on to private practice and the wealth that came with it. Meanwhile, Lauren was doing her time as an attending at Red Cedar, and not receiving much in the way of wealth. But it was still better than med school, where she'd been actively paying rather than earning.

The lovely front door had a glass, ovoid window that was partially frosted and distorted in the rings where it wasn't, making it difficult to see inside. She refrained from calling, "I'm home!" to see if Molly would come running. Spoiler alert: she wouldn't, because they were still barely speaking.

She closed the door behind her, taking her time, keeping the noise to an absolute minimum. She slid out of her shoes, parking them on a mat that lay over the beautiful teakwood floor, and padded down the hall. She could hear faint voices ahead, through a push door in the kitchen.

Lauren paused just outside, listening to the conversation within. She could hear Elise bustling around the kitchen, probably fixing herself an organic kale smoothie or something.

"You settling in?" Elise asked. She wasn't working today. She only worked like three, four days a week—and still lived in this renovated beauty near downtown Chattanooga. It would be enough to make Lauren jealous, under normal circumstances.

"Well," Molly said dryly, "last week we lived in a whorehouse and this week we're here. Before that, we lived at my grandmother's house—you know, until she was murdered." Lauren could almost feel Elise flinch even though she couldn't see her. "So I guess you could say ... no, I'm not settled, really. I'm unsettled."

"What a coincidence. Me too, after that answer," Elise said. "Here we are. Two unsettled people. In a kitchen. Yay."

"Yes, but you're unsettled as in your tummy is a little queasy with pity, because you don't know what to say to me." Molly speared Elise with unerring accuracy, and Lauren cringed because ... ouch. "I'm unsettled like the state of Oklahoma right up until people didn't have anywhere else in the US to expand."

"I saw that infographic," Elise said. "Poor Oklahoma."

"Ever been there?"

"Yep."

"Then you know why it was last."

"Well, it was also supposed to be reserved for the Native Americans, but ... yep." Elise's tone changed. It was still stilted. "Well. Maybe I should leave you to—"

Lauren brushed into the kitchen, the door squeaking as she pushed through and let it swing back. She stepped clear, taking care that it didn't come back and whack her heel, which had happened before when she'd stood in its swing radius for dramatic effect. "Molly," she said warningly. She actually sounded like her own mother, and Lauren wanted to curse herself for it.

"To be honest, I preferred the whorehouse," Molly said. She had been sitting on one of the stools at the kitchen's island, and she got up, heading off to the staircase and up, without even a backward glance at her mother.

"Good talk," Elise called after her. "We should do this against tomorrow." Molly didn't react. "She's so much like you it's creepy," Elise said once the sound of a door slamming came from upstairs.

"Thanks, I guess," Lauren said, taking Molly's place at the counter.

"Her freeze-out game is on point. That shit was tense," Elise said, sliding in front of her and leaning over like a bartender—except with a green, cloudy drink in front of her. It smelled of apples and something bitter. Kale, probably. "Like your shoulders."

"That obvious, huh?" Lauren felt for her right shoulder and—yep, sure enough, knots like a ship's line.

"Obvious like a meteor striking you in the middle of the street just after you've changed your undies," Elise said, and when Lauren gave her a perplexed look, she said, "because afterward you're going to need to change your undies again."

"Wouldn't you be dead?"

"I assumed a small meteor. The better to make you suffer. Maybe a good head wound, concussion, loss of con—"

"Stop it, Doctor," Lauren said, cradling her head.

"How was work? Miserable as ever?"

"It was pure delight," Lauren said. "I got sent home early."

"What? Did your boss grow a heart? A conscience? A pair?"

"Some human decency, maybe. He kept mentioning that he lost his mother last year, so who knows?"

"I'm surprised he had a mother," Elise said. "I figured he was grown in a lab somewhere from rejected scrotal tissue samples." She let the last joke hang for a second before moving on. "So … your kid's pretty pissed."

"She's turning into a really maladjusted child," Lauren said.

"Bet you're wishing you'd gone into psych now, huh?"

"I don't know that there's a category of study for …" Lauren's voice trailed off. She hadn't told Elise the raw truth about what was happening in Midian because … well, hell, if Elise had come to her with that kind of story, their roles reversed, Lauren wouldn't have believed it, either. "For whatever we went through back there."

"Your mom dying is tough," Elise said with that kind of mostly-sympathy that lacked empathy, the cold voice of distance that told

Lauren she maybe was trying to understand, but didn't get it on any level. That was Elise; she was the poster child for *ooh!-ing* in sympathy whenever someone got hurt, but when it came to feeling the pain of others, she didn't. She was way too busy feeling her own self-indulgent emotions and planning her social calendar. "Especially since she basically raised your daughter. It's gotta be weighing on Molls."

"I'm sure it is, and don't ever call her that to her face," Lauren said as neutrally as possible. How could she explain that what happened would be weighing on Molly more than it would have if, say, her mother had died of old age, or cancer, rather than a knife wielded by Molly's own hand? That wasn't the sort of thing she could easily walk Elise through, step by step. *Oh, and then the demon took over Molly's body, and used her to strike back at me for my part in an anti-demon organization trying to save our hometown ...*

"Well, I gotta go," Elise said abruptly, counseling session over. "Got late lunch plans with Cara—you remember her from med school, right? She landed at a radiology practice in North Carolina, can you believe it? But she's back in town for a few days, so we're going to go eat at Puckett's in downtown Chattanooga. I think after that I'm going to indulge in a little retail therapy before my spa appointment this afternoon. I have this wonderful massage therapist named Kelly. You should book with her—but not today, because I need her to work out some knots. And then, later tonight, I've got one of those parties where my friend Jana is getting us together to drink wine and sell us stuff. Essential oils, maybe, or dildos? I dunno. Honestly, I hope it's the dildos, because the last one I went to was essential oils, and I'm kinda over that whole thing."

Lauren watched her as she spoke, prattling on about such insignificant shit that it was hard to keep from picking up the garlic press on the counter and throwing it at her just to shut her up. This was what Elise spent her day doing? Lunches with old friends and parties with dildos and wine? Brunches on weekends, long days at the office followed by dinners out and then a return to her immaculate yet empty house?

Lauren felt the urge to swallow a lump in the back of her throat before she fully registered that it was there. She'd always complained about the ER, and then about the shit she had to do with the watch, but ... damn. At least what she was doing meant something. When she was raising Molly, it was putting her time and effort toward something beyond just herself and what she wanted to do. And once she joined the watch, well ...

Sitting at her mother's kitchen table, smelling the biscuits baking, gravy bubbling on the stove ... she missed that, the simple, homey feeling on the days when she wasn't rushing around trying to keep a kid from dying after an ATV accident that split his head open and crushed his chest.

That ... had meaning. Those stolen moments after a fight with demons, or after a long day at the hospital ... they had meaning because they existed in the time between when she was fighting against some invisible onslaught, either of disease and injury or the very literal demons that had invaded Midian.

They had meaning because what she was doing mattered.

And as she listened to Elise prattle on about her day, every single action she was taking oriented entirely toward making sure Elise enjoyed herself ... it made Lauren a little sick for ever envying her—whether for her wealth, her freedom or even her cushy job.

"Well, I'll see you later, okay?" Elise waved on her way out the door, already back to thinking about what was next in her day. "I'll bring you some leftovers from Puckett's, maybe, depending on what I get."

The door slammed and Lauren was left sitting in the kitchen, pondering her life and trying to figure out which mattered more—meaning? Or saving her and her daughter's lives?

*

"Well, this fucking sucks," Hendricks opined from beneath the weight of Duncan, who was pressing into his back and felt, well, weighty.

The fire sloth, visible through the thin layer of vegetation that guarded them from his sight, was still bellowing flames into the air. The bushes weren't that thick here, but holding still had kept them safe so far, while the giant demon thing just burned shit in a rage. Three of the houses under construction were lit up now, the damned thing destroying its own den and a few potential others in a mad rush of what looked like pure anger.

"Shhhhh," Duncan whispered and gave Hendricks a little poke to the back of his neck. Hendricks shut his mouth, but if the goddamned fire sloth could hear him over its own bellowing and the crackling of the flames now racing through the wooden framing of those three houses, hell if he didn't deserve to catch them like a goddamned king-shit apex predator.

"I'm about to have a claustrophobic reaction to you smothering me," Arch said, causing Hendricks a dash of relief. At least he wasn't the only one feeling squished by the OOC.

They all three froze as the fire sloth swung around, screaming and bellowing, loosing another blast of flame straight up. It glowed against the black smoke that was already rising into the sky, and Hendricks stared. He could feel the heat coming off it even at this distance, like he'd taken a peek inside the oven while something was cooking. It damned sure wasn't warm cookies or his mother's meatloaf either.

The fire sloth's black eyes floated over the woods, like it was dimly considering that there might be prey hiding in the trees. Hendricks held his breath as he watched that fucking obvious expression cross the thing's face, and so it didn't exactly surprise him when about two seconds later it sprayed a nice, long, hot tongue of fire into the woods ten feet to their right.

Hendricks held his goddamned tongue, even as the underbrush ignited, going up in a big fucking WHOOSH! of heat and flame. Out of the corner of his eye, he kept his gaze on the growing conflagration, trying not to move his head.

"We should probably move," Duncan said under his breath. He spoke in a muffled way that suggested he wasn't moving his lips. "So you two don't cook to death."

"Mmhmm," Arch said, clearly trying to keep quiet too. "Where do we go?"

"All it takes is one fucking stab into this thing's paw and he's toast," Hendricks said, violating his oath of silence. He was overheating, and not just because the fire to his right was rising up the trunks of the trees and spreading into the dry branches and whatever leaves were left alive.

"All it takes is one good breath of that hellfire and you're toast too," Duncan said. "Just keep that in mind." He paused. "Unless—"

"Fuck this shit," Hendricks said. He pushed out from under Duncan's body and surged ahead, readying his sword to make a big lunge. If he could just sink it in before the fire sloth realized … "He may be big, but he's going to get the fucking air let out of him like any other motherfucking one of you sons of bi—"

The fire sloth snapped around as Hendricks was three steps into his run, and as he saw the glow rising in the demon's mouth, he knew for a fact he wasn't going to make it anywhere near where he could plunge a sword into it before it burned him into a little pile of ashes.

*

Erin shot past two parked cars just up from Whistling Pines—Poons, now she was thinking of it, goddamn Benny all to hell—and watched the cars roll back onto the road after she passed, a couple members of the watch waiting for reinforcements before charging in.

That was smart, but it annoyed the fuck out of her right now.

She turned the corner into the development and damned near sideswiped a pallet of bricks, tires squealing as she came around in a hurry to avoid smashing it. "Whoa," Guthrie said mildly at the sudden movement, "let's not have a repeat of last time."

"There's no cliff this time," Erin said tightly. "At worst, I'd roll this bitch, and we'd climb out. Unless you cracked up again, which, if you did—I mean, that's kinda on your weaksauce ass."

"What are you saying here?" Guthrie asked. "You calling my new shell like … a pussy shell?"

"Well, it does have one," Erin said. She still wasn't smiling, because it wasn't that funny.

"Heh." That was the sort of shit Guthrie would find funny, naturally. "Oh, fuck."

The fire ahead, though? That wasn't the shit Erin found funny, nor Guthrie either, apparently. It was streaming into the air, a five-alarm blaze if they'd had five fire departments in the area to respond. Black smoke was already clouding up the sky on the right side of the street, and Erin eased the car up against the curb, drawing her bat as she got out.

"Don't go charging in like a Marine with a black coat," Guthrie said, getting out her side. "I was serious about these fire sloths. They breathe hellfire."

"Looks like regular, ordinary fire to me," Erin said, holding the bat up as she got up on the weed-strewn dirt stretch where a lawn would probably have gone in better times. "What's the difference?"

"This fire comes from hell."

"Nice fucking answer, asshole."

Guthrie shrugged expansively, baton bouncing in her hand as she held it. "I don't know what else to say. Hellfire is different than regular fire because it comes from hell. Water doesn't exactly put it out; it just kind of mutes the heat. You've seen it before."

Erin tried to think back past a cavalcade of demons these last couple months. "I have?"

"Yeah. That squashed turd, Gideon the serial masturbator, he was breathing it," Guthrie said.

"Squashed—?" Erin started to say, and a bellow of fire blew high in the air, coming from behind one of the burning house frames, like something had started up an oil rig fire back there. It stank, too, like sulfur and an old truck stop bathroom combined.

"I think we found the problem," Guthrie said as a couple other watch members hit the ground next to them, jumping up onto the weed-strewn grass. Erin gave 'em glance; it was Nate McMinn, Keith Drumlin, Bart Creasy—a local well driller—and bartender Mike McInness, his SM Lines ball cap pulled down over his eyes and a baseball bat of his own in hand.

"I think a blind fucking monk could find that problem," McInness cracked as he stopped his ass with the rest of them. No one seemed eager to charge into this, and Erin couldn't blame them. Three houses were already on fire, and whatever the hell was doing it sounded pretty pissed. They'd have to go sashaying down between the burning houses, hoping the black smoke pouring out of the foundations wouldn't blind them all to whatever might be waiting down there.

Another bellow cut through the air and everyone was just lingering there on the front lawn. *Shit,* Erin thought, *if no one else is going to do this, I guess I'll—*

Reeve came bounding up just then, his car squealing to a stop in the street. "What the fuck are y'all sitting around here gawking for?" He stormed up into the dead yard with his sword, Mary Wrightson a step behind, still brandishing her sawed-off double-barrel—like that would do a fucking thing against a demon—and he charged on down ahead of them, leaving them all in the damned dust. A second later, he'd been swallowed up by the black smoke like a pebble dropped in a lake.

"Well, shit, I ain't gonna sit back here and do nothing while there's fighting going on," Nate McMinn said, and off he went down the hill too. Keith Drumlin and Bart Creasy followed, bellowing out their own cries that got lost in whatever the fire sloth was howling about past the smoke and flames.

"Watch all these dumb menfolk go running into trouble without a thought in their damned heads," Mary Wrightson said, walking with a little bit of a hitch in her step. "Me, I'm gonna take my time and try not to go sprinting headlong into something that'll rip it off." And off she went down the hill, a little bit of a waddle to her stride accented by the uneven slope she was navigating.

"You hanging back for a reason other than unmitigated sanity?" Guthrie asked, sidling closer.

"I was gonna suggest we charge too," Erin said, "right before Reeve said it."

"He steal your thunder?" Guthrie made a face. "Boo hoo."

"Fuck off," Erin said, and off she went, down the hill, bat in hand. It didn't take more than a few steps before she couldn't see a damned thing through the smoke.

*

Aaron Drake was ready for his next culinary experiment, and his regrets for what he was missing in the realm of human veal were hardly staunching his appetite. His movements of late had been unlucky: a string of houses that failed to yield even a single child, as though the people of this sunny, hell-blighted hamlet had done what the Londoners in World War II had done and sent their children away to be raised by others. He knew this was not so, that he had just chosen poorly in his recent string of attacks, but still, it rankled him to be confined to culinary experimentation with only adult meat, when his palate cried out for more tender, refined options to enhance his table.

Still, there was meat in hand, and that was better than where he'd been before all this, trapped in this burg with little to show for it in the way of creative dining options save for these insipid little diners and roadside chain restaurants.

Meat, he had, and plenty of it. The basement was filled with fresh possibilities, some live, most dead, and enough that he would be sated, belly full for the next few days. Three houses, six cattle—people were his cattle—of which the youngest was probably in their twenties and the oldest ... well, it didn't bear thinking about the grey-haired ones he'd dragged in. They were dead anyway, and he was letting them age a little further now that they were cleaned.

The youngest of them was a man of his twenties who had been living in his parents' home. Drake had been so excited to stumble upon him when he'd found him, but the ecstasy turned to disappointment in such a brief flicker of time; this one was an adult like the others, in form if not in maturity. A full-grown bird that simply hadn't left the nest yet, not tender and succulent yearling. It was like ashes in the mouth, this disappointment.

Still, it was better than nothing, Drake thought as he stared down at the boy—young man, he supposed. The cutlet waiting to be transformed, the dish nearly ready for serving. The ingredient.

"Please," the protein said, adopting a tone of begging, as though that might help. "Please—"

Drake just frowned, his shell contorting in the manner necessary to evince this subtle emotion. "You must be joking." Why was he dignifying it by speaking to it? Butchers occasionally talked to their cows, he supposed. He reached down and seized this creature by the neck, lifting it up. It wasn't difficult; the protein was neatly bound, hand and foot. It had had a ball gag shoved in its mouth until Drake had removed it, casting it aside on the cold, stone basement floor before the watching, squealing eyes of the surviving three ... cutlets. Cuts. No. Sides of meat? He struggled with proper nomenclature with these things, having never done the butchery himself. Farm-to-table was new to him, but thus far he'd been eminently pleased with the results.

"What are you doing?" it squealed as he lifted it, almost dragging it along as it failed to cooperate fully. It was probably trying to keep up, he realized vaguely, and he gave it a moment to regain its footing. It did so, and he led it up the stairs as the floorboards creaked ominously beneath them. Did it know that it was marching to its own doom? Surely not. He hadn't slaughtered the old ones in front of these ones, so any cues it might have picked up on would have to have been subtle, like when he brought the steaks back down to the basement, properly seasoned, to begin their dry aging.

"Taking you upstairs," Drake replied with ease, going slower now. Yes, that was the ticket. It had no idea it was being led to the slaughter. Best not to agitate it now.

"And then?"

"Why, releasing you, of course." Drake had made an error here, and he saw it now. It was a small one, but still, an error. He'd removed the ball gag in anticipation of placing an apple in the mouth of this roast, but he'd left the apple upstairs. That meant, theoretically, it could scream loud enough that someone might hear it in one of the neighboring houses before he could get the apple properly placed. That would be unfortunate. Probably for them rather than him, but still ... unfortunate.

"Really?" it asked, dull as dirt. How stupid could it be? Drake led it upstairs, into the kitchen.

"Absolutely," Drake said, walking past the kitchen island, strewn with spices and rubs that he'd prepared. He picked up the apple as he passed, dropping it in a bowl of the rub. He glanced at the protein; it was naked, of course, and ready, save for the apple and ... one other trifle. "Come with me." And he continued to lead it by the rope around its neck toward the door to the back yard of his rental house.

The fire was crackling out in the backyard, faint smoke rising up into the midday sky as Drake led it, hand on the rope, rough twine against the surface of his shell. He didn't drag it along; he took his time and then stopped when they reached the fire, looking back. Drake took no malicious joy in the roast looking over the two heavy iron forks placed on either side of the fire, the spit just waiting, leaned against a picnic table.

"What is th—" it got out before Drake shoved the apple in his waiting mouth and then slapped it in the back of the head, killing it instantly, like one of those pneumatic spikes that farmers used. It dropped, plastering its face in the dirt.

"Oh, good," Drake said mildly, and rolled it face up. He took a few minutes to dress it right there, cutting out the guts from the esophagus to the anal sphincter, tying them off and tossing all the waste in another waiting pail, where it slopped, stink filling the air.

He strung the body up and let it drain as he coated it thickly with a honey and barbecue marinade, then dusted it with a lovely, salty and spiced rub. It had a tang to it, one that he was sure was going to taste truly excellent once the fire crystallized the honey with the rub in it.

Drake took a lick of the marinade and rub, and … mmm. Yes, this was going to be good.

He fetched the spit. It took a few minutes to position the roast correctly, binding its limp arms tightly to the pole, then the feet. Once he'd finally strung it properly, dead, waxy hands bleeding where he'd opened some wounds to let it drain while it cooked, he draped the carcass over the fire, and set the spit to turning on its own, electrical motor at the far end guiding it as it rolled the carcass over the open flames.

Drake, for his part, just sat back and watched it go. The flesh began to cook, and he seasoned it here and there, throwing a little extra rub and marinade on as needed. Fire didn't bother him so much, after all. He rubbed it into the flesh, taking care to spread out the coals so as to avoid scorching the skin. The best part of the searing would come late in the cooking process, once it had a chance to roast properly and all that marinade carmelized on the skin, turning it into a sweet, crackling treat that would soak into the meat.

All that done, Drake just let the spit turn, the roast cooking on its own. It turned, eyes wide and dead, staring off in different directions. Drake stared into them for a few seconds, blue irises finding his on every rotation, staring back with every turn.

He wondered how they'd taste. Probably not well, but he'd try them anyway.

Before long, he'd have to put some vegetables on. He had corn and potatoes, figuring he'd turn this into his own version of a real Southern barbecue. And he even had a Southerner to barbecue. He chuckled about that as he went to check his spices for the vegetable prep. This was going to be a sumptuous meal.

*

"NO!" Arch leapt up in a hurry, seeing his chance. Hendricks was about to become barbecue, deep fried without the batter, and he couldn't, in good conscience, just let the man die.

Especially when he could do it himself.

Arch threw himself in front of the fire sloth, shoving Hendricks aside. His hand slipped on the cowboy's coat, the cumulative sweat from hiding in the dust under Duncan's weight coating his palms. The smell of the greenery burning around them as the fire sloth put the torch to the woods disappeared as it, instead, engulfed Arch—

His clothing flared up, singed from his chest and back. The sword in his hand should have melted, shouldn't it? But it didn't, instead remaining cool to the touch within his grasp.

Arch blinked, flames shrouding his vision, billowing into his eyes. Shouldn't he be ... burning? Like his shirt.

His pants were on fire too, but he didn't feel a bit of it.

"Oh," Arch said after a moment, and then, a little more crossly as the flames covering him completely, "son of a gun."

*

When Reeve came down the hill, emerging from the black cloud of smoke, he did it in time to see something he damned sure never thought he'd see—a sloth breathing fire at Arch Stan, a full frontal barbecue of the big deputy.

Arch was just standing there, hands spread wide in front of him as the fire consumed his shirt and left him bare-chested, then started to work on his pants ...

And didn't seem to do a damned thing to the rest of him.

"What in the pig's ass of hell fuck is this?" Mary Wrightson cursed as she ambled out behind him between the burning houses and burning woods.

"It's a sloth the size of a VW van," Bart Creasy said, looking cockeyed at the fire sloth as it breathed, well, fire at Arch Stan. In fairness, though, Bart Creasy looked at everything cockeyed; his left eye was perpetually squinted thanks to some sort of accident from his youth that Reeve couldn't recall the details of.

"What did you think fire sloth meant?" Reeve asked, trying to regain his composure as he watched his deputy burn to death, because that damned sure had to be coming. People didn't just sit in the middle of flames, unburnt. Or at least they didn't used to.

"Look at this guy, always showing off how impervious he is to hellfire," Guthrie said as she and Erin emerged onto the field of battle as Reeve started forward, raising his sword.

The fire sloth whipped its head around at his motion and out streamed a long breath of lipping flame that Reeve was forced to dodge. As he did so, he noticed a long series of streaks along the fire sloth's flank, like claw marks against its side.

Putting that out of his mind, Reeve scrambled sideways as he watched Arch mutter something from within a whirlwind of flames that seemed to swirl around him. The big deputy was not charring, not turning into ash; he was just scowling at the huge demon—albeit nakedly, now that his clothes had burned off.

"Oh, my," Mary Wrightson said from behind him. "Is it warm out here? Why, yes, yes it is. Also, Archibald Stan is standing there nekkid as a jaybird and fit as a fiddle. It's a damned good thing my cardiologist checked me out a couple weeks ago, I'm thinking, because otherwise I'd say I was experiencing a palpitation here."

"It's a demon the size of a minibus, and you're getting fired up because of the deputy's junk?" Guthrie asked. "I mean, I see it too, and it's good and all, but … seriously, I think you humans are fucked up."

Flames whirled and swirled around the fire sloth, and Arch stepped up to it, out of his flames, keeping his attention squarely on the thing, and as it brought a clawed hand around to swipe at him—

Arch just swung his sword. The paw and the blade made contact in front of both of them, and for a brief moment there was almost a silence, save for the crackling flames.

Then a hissing noise rushed over them, and the smell of sulfur came rolling out hard enough to make Reeve feel like he was going to gag up all those Tylenols and ibuprofens he'd wolfed down that morning. The fire sloth stretched and went black, and a couple seconds later it was gone, pulled back into hell where it belonged.

"Well, now that that's over with …" Mary Wrightson said, "we can admire Mr. Stan's fine musculature and even finer tallywhacker, can't we?"

"You're old enough to be his grandmother," Reeve commented with all the patience God had given a parent with three jobs and four sick kids: none.

"I'm old but I ain't dead," Mary cackled, as some more folks straggled their way out of the sweltering black clouds. One of the frame houses collapsed behind them, turning everybody's head.

"Why's everybody just standing around, watching things burn?" Barney Jones asked, loping along with Braeden Tarley beside him. Tarley had a tense scowl, like he expected something to launch out of the burning woods.

"Because nobody's got a fire engine down the front of their pants," Hendricks quipped.

"That's cuz Arch ain't got no pants to hide it down," Mary said, still grinning. "But he's got a—"

"I reckon someone needs to call Benny and tell him to whistle up those boys from the fire department before the whole woods burns down," Reeve said, marshaling his thoughts. The smoke was getting heavy. "And the reason we're all standing around is because Arch just slayed the biggest goddamned demon ever." He caught motion out of the corner of his eye and turned to see Hendricks and Duncan both shaking their heads. Guthrie's shoulders were shaking with silent mirth. "That wasn't ...? Fuuuckk."

"There's a lot bigger stuff out there than fire sloths," Duncan said. "But hopefully not around here."

"That thing," Reeve said, gesturing to where it had stood, and where now the grass still showed the churned-up impression of its feet in the dust, "it had a bigass scratch down the side of it, like a scar. You don't reckon it got in a fight with something bigger?"

Duncan just stared at him. "I hope not. You know, for your sake."

"Shit," Reeve said, and shook it off. "Someone go call Benny. Get the fire engine out here."

"Go pee on the flames, Arch," Mary said. "Settle it all out before they get here."

Arch just pursed his lips. "I don't believe that'll do what you suggest it will." At least he wasn't running off in shame or something. Reeve damned sure would have, but then, he didn't have Arch's physique. Then again, maybe he wouldn't have bothered either, because people probably would have averted their eyes to avoid his old ass rather than looking. Except for Mary. She seemed like she still might have looked anyway, just out of curiosity.

*

Erin was already on her way up the hill, dialing Benny Binion on the phone. When he answered, she said, "I need you to roust the volunteer fire department."

Benny sounded like he was in a wind tunnel. "What's that, Erin?"

She had a fair amount of noise to overcome herself, what with another house coming crashing down next to her, sending ashes and embers into the air. The wind caught some of them and sent them her way, and she scrambled up the hill as the ground behind her caught them, sparking a few little patches to light up. "I said I need the fire department, Benny. Right fucking quick, because Whistling Poons is burning. And don't text 'em either; I want you to call Marty Ferrell—he's the captain. His number's on the call sheet next to your desk, and he always answers or calls back within five minutes."

"I'm surprised the fire department ain't left town," Benny said, papers rustling in the background of the call.

Erin was sweating, the damned flames overcoming the chill of the day. Shit, she was sweating, and she smelled like wood smoke from all those burning timbers. "Thankfully they ain't, because we need 'em right now in a bad way."

"I'll get right up on that, Erin," Benny said, and hung up.

A shadow moved in the smoke, and it took Erin a few seconds to distinguish who it was. At first she thought it was probably Guthrie, dedicated to hounding her to the ends of the goddamned earth, but no, a few seconds later Duncan emerged, the black smoke streaming off him like he was in danger of lighting up like a match himself. He picked his way up the hillside past patches of flaming weeds and came to lean on the car next to her, as casually as an OOC probably could. Or at least as casually as Duncan could, which was to say not fucking casual at all.

"What's up?" Erin asked, eyeing him with a due amount of suspicion.

"Not much," he said. "What's up with you?"

"Chaos," she said. "Chaos is up with me."

"It has been a busy day."

"Day? It's hardly noon."

"So it can only get better from here." Duncan didn't exactly smile, but here he came close.

"I like your optimism," she said. "Wish I shared it. But that'd buck the current trend real hard."

"Trends don't stay trends forever," he said. "I mean, look at parachute pants."

"I'd rather not."

"Most people would rather not look at parachute pants, but still, the point stands."

She settled back against the car next to him. "I just don't see how it gets better from here, Duncan. I really don't."

"That's what most people probably said about parachute pants, and look. Now they're gone."

She chuckled under her breath, less from the joke and more from the fact that he'd chosen this moment to try and be funny. She felt herself lighten up a degree or two. "What's going on with Guthrie?"

There was an almost imperceptible shift in Duncan's posture, but Erin caught it. "You've been hanging out with her. You tell me."

"I haven't known Guthrie for a century or ten or however long you two have been gal pals," Erin said. "How long has it been, anyway?"

"Long time."

"Cheerful, that answer."

"I don't know that I recall," Duncan said. "But you're right: it's been a spell, as you might say around here."

Erin stewed for a moment. "She's changed."

Duncan didn't move this time. "Yep."

"A lot."

"... Yep."

"... Better or worse?"

Duncan didn't stir, except to look at the burning houses as another load of timbers came crashing down with a terrible rumble and smoke billowed into the air. "Not for the better, I think. Not for the better at all."

*

Hendricks wasn't too excited to sit around and watch the woods burn and the framed houses collapse, but that was what he was doing, because every other idiot seemed to be doing exactly the same. Besides, the frames had done most of their collapsing now, and the wind was such that they weren't getting a face full of smoke anymore. Points for that.

Still, these sit-and-waits were growing kinda old, because they seemed to be happening all the time lately. When he'd first gotten here, he could have spent whole days in his motel room, catching some HBO between the various shitshows of demon activity that cropped up in a hotspot like this. *Westworld* was a favorite, when he caught those reruns.

Now, he'd be lucky if he could get through half an episode of *Veep* before something fucking broke loose. At least nothing had happened while he was pounding Starling's vag. Yet. Given the pace at which this shit was picking up, though, he'd be balls deep in her and get a call, soon.

Fortunately, he already had a plan for that: ignore the hell out of it and bust his nut. If things got serious, there was always time to join in later, after all, and he wasn't going to be much use to the watch if he was tripping over his own boner and readjusting for blue balls, was he? That was how he justified this pre-made decision in his head.

"Howdy there," someone said, sidling up to his elbow. Hendricks looked back to see Arch's preacher standing there, smiling politely—maybe more than politely, for all he knew.

This was the second shitty thing about the stand-and-wait shit. Sometimes you could get into a real good conversation, like he had last week with that Sam Allen guy about the heyday of the WWE Attitude era—before the poor dumb bastard had gotten chopped to pieces.

And others, you'd get trapped nodding as Casey Meacham spent twenty fucking hours regaling you with personal reviews of all the sex toys he had tried out in the last month. Hendricks had eventually called Arch over on that one, and when that didn't dissuade Casey, he'd summoned over Guthrie. That hadn't stopped the taxidermist either, but it had given Hendricks cover to bail the fuck out and leave those two holding the bag.

"Howdy back," Hendricks said, wondering why the preacher was talking to him. He was immediately suspicious, of course, because his natural belief was that a man in a collar like Jones's wasn't truly happy unless he was inflicting his religion on someone else, especially a perceived heathen like Hendricks.

Jones was quiet for a second, keeping his smile on as he worked himself up to talking out what was on his mind. He looked sincere, but looks were deceiving. After all, Erin hadn't looked like a crazy ex-girlfriend when he'd first met her, but here she was. "Have you talked to Arch lately?"

Hendricks almost let out a sigh of relief. "Not in what you'd call detail."

"Mmhm," Jones said. "He's been avoiding heart to hearts lately." The pastor looked around for Arch, and, finding him some distance away, now covered in someone's flannel sweatshirt—inadequately—from the waist down, went on. "I don't think he's in a good place."

"Speaking from experience," Hendricks said, watching the big man try to knot the flannel sleeves to cover his genitals, "losing a wife to demons ain't the sort of shit you just get over, Reverend." He'd have been better off just tying them around it, like a fucking bow on a present.

"You lost a wife to demons?" Jones asked, crossing one arm over his body and propping the other up on it, fingers resting just below his lips.

"Once in life, and over and over again in my dreams for years afterward," Hendricks said.

Jones seemed to look him over as if trying to see something he might have missed before. "I was going to say you seem to have adjusted, but ... given what you've devoted your life to, I don't reckon you have, have you?"

"Oh, I don't know about that," Hendricks said airily. "This life of killing demons seems to fit me right to a T. Hopeless causes keep me busy, you know."

"I don't think Arch is a hopeless cause," Jones said. "He's a good man, and he deserves better than to see his wife die and his town follow after."

"Well, what we deserve is a funny thing, Rev," Hendricks said. "I feel like I deserve a blowjob, but if the woman I feel like I deserve it from doesn't feel the same, I ain't getting one, am I?"

Jones didn't flinch from Hendricks's analogy, but he did put on a disapproving frown. "You think you're going to shock me by talking like that, cowboy? I was a Navy chaplain in Vietnam. I've heard shit that'd turn you whiter than a jug of milk, boy."

Hendricks let out a loud guffaw. "Well, I was in the Sandbox for a couple years and been in this particular fight for more, so ... I think my days of paling at the sight and sound of horrible things? Probably over."

"I'm sure you and I, we could get into a pissing contest all day long, the sort of thing that'd please nobody but maybe Casey, and nothing'd get done about Arch and his state of mind." Jones looked over at Arch. "I'm concerned about him as a friend. I thought maybe you were too."

Hendricks looked over at Arch again, and, sure enough, he'd just given up, leaving the sleeves of that flannel knotted in front of his junk. It was doing a pretty half-ass job of covering him up, and Hendricks figured a couple weeks ago, that would have mattered to the big deputy. A lot. But his give-a-fuck was clearly busted, and that was ... worrying. Hell, it'd been the reason Hendricks had been trying to sidle his way into a conversation with the man for a couple weeks now, not that his strategy was working. "Yeah, I'm worried," Hendricks said. "Maybe I'll just ... head on over and see if I can bring something up." And he started to do just that, working his way, casually, through the scrum of locals, toward the man who was wearing a flannel shirt like some kind of fucked-up kilt to keep his dick from swinging out in the breeze.

*

Arch wasn't real pleased about standing around with his twig and huckleberries dangling out in the breeze, but what else was there to do? They were sitting around watching the Whistling Pines development burning its way to the ground, and the woods were lighting off now too. It wasn't looking too good, in his opinion, but he wasn't going to head back to town while everyone else was sitting here. He hadn't forgotten that there were still packs of those shadowcats out here, and the last thing he wanted was to hear about everybody else getting into a fight with those things while he was off putting some clothes back on.

The smoke shifted directions with the wind, and Arch waved a hand in front of his face like someone had cut the cheese. It didn't do much against the smoke, but there wasn't too much heading his way—yet. There sure was a whole lot to be had though, black clouds piping toward the sky. Nobody seemed real sure about what to do save for just hope the cavalry would be arriving soon in the form of a fire truck.

Hendricks sauntered his way over, a little too casually. "Casual" was tough for a man dressed like Hendricks was to pull off, which was maybe why he failed. Something in the train of that long black coat didn't quite cover the intent within his movements. Either way, a few seconds later the man was standing near him, somber, and not too terribly comfortable-looking, neither.

"Thanks for, uh … saving my life back there," Hendricks said. Sounded like a tough thing for him to cough up.

"No big deal," Arch replied.

"Well, I almost got burned to death by a demon the size of one of those delivery vans, so … it was a big deal to me." Hendricks kicked at the ground with one of his boots, stirring up some dust in the process.

"Anyone would have done the same." Arch adjusted his flannel shirt. The breeze kept disturbing it, leaving him feeling even more exposed. The sleeves, knotted as they were, didn't do squat.

"No," Hendricks said, quiet and measured, "no one else would have jumped in front of a fire sloth bellowing flames the way a virgin spits out a mouthful of cum, okay?" He quieted for a second. "And damned sure no one else who would have survived it like they'd just gotten a little hairspray on them or something."

Arch froze, wondering if that was why he was feeling a little stiffer in the pubic hair. Nah, that had to be the heat. "Don't mention it," he said.

"Well, I feel obliged to mention it," Hendricks said, "because—like I said—you saved my life. And if you'd been wrong about that thing breathing hellfire, you'd have died in the process."

Arch shrugged. "I've been through hellfire before. Gideon. It was pretty hot up in old Ygrusibas too."

"Yeah, lucky you remembered how those turned out," Hendricks said dryly. "What amazing presence of mind you had."

Arch frowned at him. "You trying to say something?"

Hendricks looked ready to argue for a moment, and then backed off. "Nah. Look ... I been where you been, Arch. You know that. When Renee died—"

Arch cleared his throat. "We don't need to be talking about this right now—"

"Dammit, Arch," Hendricks said, "I'm the one guy here who would understand what you're going through. Lost a wife to demons? Boom. I'm the guy."

Arch stood there, looking down at him, straight-backed. "Sheriff Reeve lost his wife to demons too. Reckon the grief's fresh for him as well. Maybe you ought to go spend this counseling time with him."

Hendricks waved a hand back over his shoulder dismissively. "Arch, I haven't been hunting demons since I came into this town with Reeve. Shit, I barely know the man, and I'm kinda answering to him right now, like a new CO that you follow because your buddy said he's good." He lowered his voice, getting serious. "We've been in this since the beginning, and I'd think that'd have bought me a little credibility with you. We've been in the trenches together, and I'm telling you—I know what you're feeling. That reckless desire to jump in front of a fire sloth? To have it maybe be over? Done that. Several times. And only by the grace of—well, whatever you believe in—and maybe the skin of my damned teeth am I here to talk to you now." He settled down. "Don't keep shoving it all down inside you, okay?"

"I'm fine," Arch said, crossing his arms in front of him. "I'm sure you went through a real struggle. And I can't pretend it's been easy. But I've got this problem under control."

"Is that so?" Hendricks asked, not bothering to hide his doubt. "Doesn't look like it from here, pal."

"Well, maybe you're a little myopic," Arch said, feeling like he was getting near to thundering at the man. "You went through the grief alone, believing in nothing but yourself. That ain't me."

Hendricks's reply was devoid of his usual insolence: "You mean because of your Lord?" He sounded somber, almost sad.

"I do," Arch said, staring at him, looking for a sign of that sass. He was feeling pretty close to snapping at the man, sick up to the ears of everything he'd said in this vein. "It's different for me than for you. I've got this. I can do all things through Christ my Lord, who strengthens me."

Hendricks didn't look like he was feeling particularly argumentative about it, but he did open his mouth to reply. A few different ghosts of emotions passed behind his eyes, but all that came out his lips was, "I hope you do. For her sake … and yours." Which was more than Arch might have expected, really.

And with that, the cowboy wandered off, on up the hill back toward the road.

*

"I'll tell you," Casey said, back at the wheel as he steered the big truck up the path out of the quarry, "it feels like they don't want men to be men anymore. Like, I get it, there's bad parts of being a dude, historically speaking." He was waving a hand, and Brian didn't really care, listening only because he was stoned enough that Casey's diatribes were vaguely interesting. "I mean, we do raping like 99 times more than women do. That's bad. Some of us got a real stupid head on our shoulders, and we're too aggressive, and—"

Brian just nodded. The sins of man were plain to him too, like the nose on his face. Which he was totally looking at right now. He'd once heard that the brain filtered out the sight of the nose most of the time, for some reason or another. Made sense to him, because looking down the side of it was kind of trippy now that he couldn't seem to look away.

"—anyway, my point is, there's bad. No doubt. But there's good, too! You know? And it feels like all of it, good and bad, is just trying to get stamped out, baby and bathwater, you know? Crazy stuff. Like that law that says you can't fire a gun while giving your partner an orgasm—"

Brian stopped staring at his nose. "I think that's apocryphal." Casey looked at him blankly, past the tip of his nose. "Made up. Bullshit. You know."

"Really?" Casey nodded, seemingly mollified by this. "Good. Because not being able to shoot a gun while having sex kind of flies in the face of everything America stands for. Freedom! Fuck yeah!"

"Fuck yeah," Brian said, nodding along. "I want to go fire a gun while getting somebody off right now." He pumped his fist, then caught a sidelong look from Casey. "Not you. A woman-shaped person."

"I could put on a dress—"

"Stop trying to make this happen, Casey."

"Okay, okay. I get it. I'm just a little too much man for you—"

"You're way too much man for me, Casey," Brian said, blinking his eyes, which felt really dry. Like dryer than Sauron's, probably. "A hundred percent too much man for me, in fact."

"There's always Ms. Cherry's. She's very understanding, and that redhead, Lucia—"

"Is very lovely, I'm sure," Brian said, really feeling this weed, even though it was not among the very best he'd ever had. "Though I've met her alter ego, and I'm not sure I could get the thought of her out of my head enough to … y'know, get hard." Where had it come from? Grown in a ditch somewhere in Appalachia, watered by piss? Or had they imported it from somewhere like Colorado or Washington? He shifted uncomfortably in his seat, because he realized very suddenly that he was pinching one of his balls between his leg and the seat and wanted it to stop. "I just like it when a woman … you know, actually wants me."

"Don't we all," Casey said, sighing like he was talking about some great lost love. "Don't we all."

Brian shifted again, and this time the discomfort didn't have to do with his balls.

*

Hendricks looked back at the fire that was growing in the woods, eyeing it and shaking his head. Left unchecked, he reckoned that was trouble with a capital T, but kinda not his problem yet. The houses were mostly burned out on their own, still belching smoke skyward, all the good lumber reduced to kindling in the biggest bonfire he'd seen since he'd left Amery, Wisconsin, where those boys knew how to build one right.

He sauntered his way up the hill, figuring his discussion with Arch was a lost cause—for now, at least. It hadn't exactly gone the way he'd planned it, not that he'd put a lot of thought into it. Maybe that was the problem. Arch wasn't him, he wasn't Arch, but he was saying things that he'd maybe have found comforting at the time of Renee's passing.

Didn't matter though, ultimately. Arch was going to do what Arch was going to do, he told himself. Though he had a strange knot in his stomach that suggested his attitude was not nearly as laissez-faire as he wanted to believe.

Coming up to the road at the top of the hill, he caught sight of his car and started to head for it. Someone called, "Hey, cowboy!" and brought him up short.

Shit, it was Duncan. With Erin. Standing around her squad car. She was more of the reason for the "Shit!" than the demon or the squad car, though.

Ignoring his good sense, he sauntered his way over, ignoring the smoke that was blowing hard this way now. Waving his hand in front of his face like a choice fart had been ripped right in front of him, he got a hacky-gaggy feeling that came from the smoky aroma forcing its way up his nose and into his lungs. After a minute the wind stopped, and suddenly he could breathe again.

"Christ," Erin said, doing a little waving of her own. "That shit'll overpower you."

"Yeah, it shoves its way down your throat and chokes you like ..." Hendricks paused, then dismissed that one. "Y'know."

"A dick?" Erin said, clearly unamused. "Stay classy, Wisconsin."

"Or whatever," Hendricks said stiffly, then turned his attention to Duncan. "You got a read on that skinny guy from the funerals?"

Duncan just shook his head. "He's out of my sight. Or feels."

"Best not strain yourself too hard trying to find him," Hendricks said, "or else you'll end us up in some other fiery hellhole like this."

"I'd say I was sorry, but I'd be lying," Duncan said. "Killing this thing was an unvarnished good."

"I don't think the developer here would agree with that," Erin said.

"They were never gonna sell any of these right now anyway," Duncan said. "People are getting the message: Get the fuck out of Dodge before you can't dodge anymore."

"Pretty sure the 'Dodge' in that saying comes from Dodge City, Kansas," Hendricks said. "Not dodge as in, GTFO of the way."

"I was playing with the English language, Tex Dick-man," Duncan said. "You leaving?"

"If you've got no line on that skinny, bitchass funeral-director-looking motherfucker from the motel ... yep," Hendricks said, hiking up his belt a little. Damned thing always sagged with the weight of a sword and a 1911.

"Got a spicy redhead to go fuck?" Duncan's eye glimmered just a little as he said it, and the wind came blowing back through right then, smoking them out. Hendricks launched into a coughing fit that didn't alleviate when the wind stopped.

Erin's coughing stopped almost immediately after it did though. "The fuck?" she said, half-gagging. "You and Starling? Really?" She sounded more disbelieving than pissed.

"I dunno," Hendricks said, keeping his pissed-off answer aimed right at Duncan. "She didn't show up to this little party, so she might be busy."

Erin got a nasty smile. "Probably letting Casey plunge his cock in her whore ass for a twenty. Over and over, you know."

Hendricks found himself strangely unmoved by that suggestion. "Who knows? But seriously, thanks for fucking nothing, Duncan." He added the dash of sarcasm that it required, and headed for his car, getting in and starting it immediately. He burned rubber and got the fuck out of there before he had to look Erin in the face again.

*

Erin felt a strange clenching feeling in her chest, and it wasn't from just breathing in a fuck-ton of black smoke, either.

"I thought you should know," Duncan said. He was still wearing that blank, dull expression.

"Fuck, I don't care who he does in his off time," Erin said. "I'm just glad I was the girl before the actual whore, not after. And I'm over him anyway."

"Nah," Duncan said, as fucking indecipherable as ever. "But you'll get there." And he turned and walked off like that was fucking that.

*

Pike was enjoying the preparing of his preparations, his role in the next steps of all this. Enjoying it very finely, pushing his dick into Jenny's pussy, over and over, her sweet, tight little ass bent over the desk in front of him, moaning her pleasure softly into the desk calendar. Drooling a little too, making a mark on early November. Lucky that was already past.

Her ass was a nice little back end, looked good in jeans, good in those black work pants. He'd started screwing her after he made a stupid joke: "Do you wash your clothes in Windex? Cuz I could see myself in your pants."

Darla had suggested it, said the type of person Jenny was, she'd find it funny. And she did—she laughed and laughed, and then, when she came up, face red from laughing so hard, she said, "I don't know if you could fit in 'em, but I'd let you try."

And by God, he'd tried her just about every day he could since.

Some of the little moments were the ones he'd remember best when this was all over. Sitting on a stupid conference call and she'd tiptoe in to bring him something. He'd be waiting, zipper down, cock hanging out, and when she came around the desk and saw it she'd get that mischievous glint in her eyes. She knew what to do, and she'd get down on her knees and put her head in his lap, and he'd tilt his head back and just enjoy the sensation of her lips slipping around there, hand doing a yeoman's work giving his balls the right amount of pressure. He hadn't had to teach her much, but he'd got her that information, how important a good grip on the balls was. Too much and you'd make a man want to lose his lunch. Too little and your fingers were just sitting there, might as well have been cloth boxers brushing against them for all the good it'd do.

Jenny had a fine pussy too, and a nice, smooth back with a little mole a quarter inch from her spine on the left side, right in the middle. It was the only mark on her other than that tramp stamp of a butterfly. He'd cum on that thing more times than he could count, given the wings a splash of white like he gave Jenny's face or her tits, sometimes.

God, this felt good. Pike could do this all day, that simple back and forth. She was moaning, really into it, and why shouldn't she be? He'd had enough lovers, knew how to satisfy a woman, and she'd been with almost no one, and certainly no one who knew what the fuck they were doing. She'd confessed to him, after the first few times, when she started to really initiate the sex, and he asked her, "What do you like about me?" Her answer was, "You're the only guy I've been with that tries to make me cum."

His dick had blown up like a virile puffer fish that day, and he'd gone after her snatch again and again, trying to prove her assessment right by pulling screaming orgasm after screaming orgasm out of her sweet, cocksucking lips.

He put his hands right on her hips, pushing his dick all the way up into her, letting it swell inside there for a second as he held it hard. He could imagine the tip expanding up in there. Then he slid it out and put his hand around himself, giving the shaft and head a stroke on its way out. That felt good. Do that a few times and he'd get this show closer to over, quicker, because he didn't have all day to just enjoy himself.

Jenny moaned quietly. She always drooled when she was good and heated up, like she was melting out of her mouth. He pushed her legs closer together—thank God she was kinda tall, so he didn't have to squat down to fuck her from behind standing like this—and started going back at it again, the little O around his cock formed by the circle of his right thumb and forefinger giving him that little added touch as he pushed in and out, in and out …

He was getting real close now. Pike took his hand away from where he'd been stroking himself when he pulled out and thrust in, figuring he'd just let Jenny's pussy do the last of the work. Shouldn't be long now, he knew, given how close he was …

Reaching down, he slid open his top right desk drawer as he leaned harder against her and took her off balance. She grunted as her abdomen collided with the corner of the desk, but he got a deeper thrust and it felt good, so he ignored her pain and pushed hard, letting the tip rest up in there for a second, giving it a little shake as he reached for the thing waiting in his desk drawer. It shone as he picked it up, so fucking close …

He could have just ground his dick up in her at maximum extension for another minute, and he probably would cum, great heaving squirts coming out the tip, buried so deep in Jenny's snatch she could probably taste it in the back of her mouth. She might even feel the warm white spray as it pumped out of him.

Well … not today, maybe, but … any other day …

Pike was close, so close, but the distraction of reaching for the knife had set him back; his orgasm slipping away like it was over the next hill one moment, and he started to crest it, and when he got to the top he saw it slipping over the next hill yet. Slippery thing, orgasms, and he wanted to gallop after it, but Jenny was starting to moan in real pain now; he'd thrust about as far up her as he could go, and she was nice and wet, felt wonderful, but just—not quite tight enough …

He just needed her to clench real fast, just a real tight jerk of the muscles so he could get there. He thought of this thing he'd heard of, always wanted to try … and hell, it wasn't going to matter here pretty quick, was it?

Pike clenched the knife tight in his right hand and gave her a punch in the back of the head, making hard contact right at the base of the spine. She let out a yelp and every muscle in her body went tight at once from the shock of the blow. She was perfectly clenched, if only for a second, and he hit that peak like a race car going over the top, pushing his shaft in and out madly, making sure he got there, and got there good. He could feel the ejaculation starting, and he held her down over the desk, leaning over, so she didn't just slide down like a damned jellyfish, because he'd knocked her the fuck out with that punch ...

He finished cumming in her now-loose-ass pussy. "Whew," he breathed, giving his brow a wipe. It was slick with sweat, because they'd been going at it for over a half hour without a break, and he had some cramps in his legs. In his twenties they wouldn't have been a big deal. Now he'd probably be feeling them all night.

The door opened with a pop and Pike almost shit himself; if he hadn't already cum he'd have lost his erection for sure, that door swinging wide and hard, someone standing there for a second, grinning wide at him—

"Well hell," Darla said, grinning, "looks like you had fun."

She came strolling into the room as Pike sagged, dick still in Jenny. "Damn, woman. Good thing you didn't come in a minute earlier; you'd have ruined everything."

"I heard you make your O sound while I was listening at the door," Darla said, closing it behind her as she came in. She was wearing a black dress that fell to just above the knee, fancy to the nines. He'd watched her hike that dress up before and straddle him in the front seat of the car, banging the hell out of her back on the steering wheel as she banged the hell out of him. She leaned over the desk, went face to face with Jenny, who was now drooling openly on the calendar, limp as a dishrag, and Darla looked up at him with annoyance. "You shitbrick. She's not dead."

"Well, I was gettin' there," Pike said defensively. "You said that as long as it happened after I came—"

"You fucking donkey punched her? Was that what that was?" Darla snorted derisively. "Shit. Glad you decided to try that on her and not me."

"I know which side my bread is buttered on," Pike said, dick still up Jenny's snatch. It was oddly comfortable to be having this conversation with Darla in exactly this state. It wasn't the first time they'd had a marital conversation while he was balls deep in another woman in front of her.

"Well," Darla said, shrugging as she got up off the desk, crossed her arms in front of her, and gave him an expectant look. "You're done, so ... get *it* done."

Pike hesitated. "And I have to do it before ..."

"Before you pull out, jackass," she said with distinct lack of amusement. She waited a tick, and then said, "You aren't chickening out on me, are you? Because it looks like she's the one with the pussy, not you."

"I'ma do it," Pike said, steeling himself. He'd even figured out how he was going to do it. He'd originally planned to plunge the knife into the base of her spine at his climax, but ... He'd always wanted to try a donkey punch, and hell, there was no telling what the knife would do if he'd done that instead. He might have gone to his grave still wondering what a donkey punch felt like. Now he knew.

And now he also had to finish the job.

"Okay," Pike said, dick withering away inside Jenny as he stood over her, groin pressed up against the base of her ass. He could almost imagine that anal sphincter, ready to loosen up after death, the way he'd heard it did—

"Shit!" he said, and almost jerked out. Darla was behind him now and threw her weight against him to keep him from pulling out.

"What the fuck are you doing?" she growled, her head against his spine in the center. "Kill her ass before you pull out, you dumbass!"

"She's gonna shit and piss on me as soon as I do," Pike hissed, trying to recoil but finding his wife blocking his escape. She was really putting her weight into it.

"So what?" she asked. "You've had worse done to you, dumbass. Hell, you've begged me to do worse to you."

Pike steadied himself. That was true, sort of, but ... still ... he didn't want to get shit on right now ...

"There's nothing for it," she said. "Be a fucking man, not a little bitch, and slit this cunt's throat so we can do this ritual and get on with the main event." She patted him on the bare ass, not letting up on him.

"All right, all right, all right," Pike said, brain running away with him. He held the knife, the hilt's rough edges scraping his palm. This wasn't the way he wanted to do it, but it was still doable. He took a breath, raised the blade—

And he brought it sideways into Jenny's throat, almost retching as he did so. She stirred only slightly as he drove it in the side of her neck, thanking a God he hadn't ever actually believed in that he didn't have to do this to her fucking face. He couldn't even really see the damage he was doing, shoving the knife in blind. He jerked it around, hoping he was doing what needed to be done, twisting it where it was buried in the side of her throat. It felt gross and wrong, like he was trying to saw through a stick steak—

"God, you pussy," Darla breathed in his ear. Her hand cupped his, and he felt Jenny's blood between them as she guided him, opening the throat with one good, strong motion, sawing the blade out. Jenny jerked, and Pike felt his pecker sag even worse inside her, little crust of hardening cum drying painfully inside her, like he'd superglued his dick into her. Her ass jerked and dropped. Even though it was probably only an inch or so, it felt like a tectonic plate shift.

He was still holding her up, but Darla was helping now, leaning in against him. She pulled his hand free, warm, red blood covering their hands, hers atop his, the once-silvery knife blade covered in the thick blood of life. Pike breathed heavily, raggedly, as Jenny sagged, limper and limper, against the desk. She had no fight left in her; all the strength had gone out of her legs after the punch, and now she was near the end.

"Stay in her," Darla said, and slapped him on the ass. It had a Pavlovian effect on him, except instead of him drooling at the sound of a bell, his dick spasmed, trying to swell in arousal. Here it fought against the fact he'd just blown his wad and also, he thought vaguely, murdered a fellow human being after fucking her. "You keep your dick in there until I tell you otherwise." Darla's voice held that hard edge of command. "You hear me?"

"I hear you," Pike said, trying to catch his breath. He'd killed before, a time or two. Schemed more than that. But murdering a lover right after coitus?

Nope, that was new.

"God, this is hot," Darla breathed. "We should have done this years ago to spice things up."

Pike turned his head to look at her, eyebrows cocked, head and stomach somewhere between revulsion and horror.

The look on Darla's face was pure, unsubtle amusement. "Trolled ya," she said, and broke into laughter.

"God, you did," he said, shaking his head. She slapped him on the ass once more, and his dick did that involuntary spasm. It was shrinking, but still not flaccid enough to fall out on its own, thankfully. "You got me on that one."

"It's all for the greater good," she said, pressing her hand flat against his ass, cupping it as she leaned in and rested her chin gently on his shoulder. "Well, the greater good of us, anyway. Fuck everyone else."

"Fuck 'em all," Pike agreed. He could feel the sweat drying, sticky on his skin, and couldn't wait to pull out. That hadn't ever been true before, but now—oh, hell, now? This was bordering on necrophilia.

"Just a minute more," Darla breathed, sticking her tongue in his ear. She didn't plunge it in like a diver into a pool; she took it in slowly, the way he liked it, then backed it off to bite the lobe. Pike shuddered; it worked. Reversed the blood flow, got it heading back downstairs.

Jenny gave one last good shudder, and then she relaxed totally. "Shit!" Pike said as her bowels released on him. Darla shoved herself against him, hard, and stymied his inadvertent jerk.

"Just take it, fucker," Darla said, like a brick wall at his back, keeping him on course. "Take it and grin. Learn to love the scat play. You can shower later, but now we make fucking magic. Blood magic."

It was over a few seconds later. Darla was still against him, but Pike knew—beyond a doubt—Jenny was good and dead. She'd gone limp as a damned rag, no hint of movement anywhere on her body. Once again he was thankful he'd not chosen missionary today, imagining himself with her legs coiled around him on the desk, leaning up over her, plunging in and having to sit there, stare at her eyes, see the betrayal as he slit her throat—

"All right, motherfucker," Darla said, and the pressure released at his back. She took a few steps back and waited. He turned around, slowly, naked as the day he was born, and about as covered in feces as the day after, he reckoned. Darla stifled a laugh. "Yeah, you got shit on, all right."

"I feel like a baby who soiled his diaper," Pike said, looking down at the disgusting mess that covered him, brown stains from the pubic region on down. He would have vomited right there if this had happened about five years earlier, but the fact he'd been changing diapers these last few years had strengthened his stomach.

"You should be thankful Jenny's a vegetarian," Darla said with dark amusement. "Probably could have been a lot worse if she'd been on a high-protein diet." Ever the pragmatist, that woman.

"I don't think it really matters that much about the consistency of the shit," Pike said, "at least not when you've been shit upon."

"Oh, it matters," Darla said with the practiced aura of someone who had been shit upon a time or twelve. "Hit the showers, champ." She grinned. "This part's done. I'll take care of the rest."

Pike eyed the disastrous mess of his office—blood, piss, and shit everywhere, across his desk and the carpet beneath. Oh, and there was the little matter of the dead girl on his desk. Jenny slid loose and hit the ground as they stood there, dead, glassy eyes staring up at him accusingly.

He stared back, wondering if he'd feel something ... but no. Dead doll eyes, that was it.

Pike put his attention back where it belonged. "You're gonna clean this up?"

"Aren't I always cleaning up this family's messes?" Darla asked with a sigh. She didn't seem amused. "Hurry up and get done, and get back here, will you?" She leaned in and bit at his ear.

"Shouldn't I help you first?" Pike asked, holding up his bloody hands, and indicating his mess of a—well, the rest of him. "You know, before I get clean?"

Darla just barked a laugh. "We're not going to clean up," she said, licking at his ear again. "We're gonna get down and dirty right on top of her. For the ritual."

Pike just swallowed, looking over the corpse, the shit, the piss, the smells—oh, and his dick, hanging limp as a squeezed-out tube of frosting, covered in crap up to the pubis. Hell, he'd be lucky if he ever got a hard-on again, he thought, but that'd be a lie. After all, this was what they'd worked for. Still, now? "Damn, Darling Darla," he said. "Ain't you ever heard of a refractory period?"

*

"Sadly, this ain't even among the worst of the clusterfucks I've presided over in the last few weeks," Reeve admitted, almost as much to himself as Mary Wrightson, as he watched the fire department working to get the blaze under control. They'd been lucky, he figured, the developer of this place having cleared some land near the woods in order to build back a little ways deeper in the trees, and they'd already put hydrants in. The woods had been going up pretty quick thanks to the dry spell they'd been experiencing since the rains quit back in summer, but who had time to worry about a damned drought when you had demons wrecking the town? It was just another worry piled on a ton of them, and not a particularly big one. Droughts came and went, and hopefully someday soon they'd say the same about these goddamned demons.

"You ain't exactly making me want to vote for you in this election here, Nick," Mary said. Her lips were thickly pursed like she had a wad of chew in them. Though she probably didn't. It was hard to say for sure, knowing Mary.

"You already cast your damned ballot, Mary," Reeve said with only a little irritation. He didn't have much left to spare for her at this point.

"You're a shit campaigner, Nick," she said with folded arms. "If you lose, this is why."

Reeve laughed mirthlessly. "If I lose, it's because the town's going straight to hell in a handcart, and there ain't much I or anyone else can do to slow the process of entropy."

"Fancy word," Mary said. "Most people'd just say it's all going to shit. Or taking a dive in a septic lagoon."

Reeve furrowed his brow. "Septic lagoon?"

Mary frowned right back. "You youngins. Don't know anything."

"I know a fair amount," Reeve said. "Don't recall hearing about a septic lagoon though."

"It's a septic tank without a top on it," Mary said. "Not much to know."

"That's pretty damned gross, if you ask me," Reeve said, taking a look at the billowing black clouds still hanging over the woods. He couldn't see any fire now, but that didn't mean anything given how much smoke was hanging in the air. "Why not just cover it up?"

"Well, we all ain't wealthy enough to afford covers for our septic systems," Mary said with great sarcasm.

"I gotta be honest, I didn't think capping a septic was that expensive at this juncture in our civilization," Reeve said dryly. People were trickling off now, the watch disassembling again. That was how it went, wasn't it? They'd come together, fight something, then dissolve before the next damned thing happened.

How long would that last? Because Reeve was already feeling the burn of responding to some five-alarm craziness every hour. He rubbed his eyes. The headache wasn't getting any better either, just staying at a low thrum of pain behind his eyes.

"Well, I guess that makes you somewhat ignorant, doesn't it?"

"Been called worse," Reeve said, pulling his hand away from his eyes and letting the cloudy light flood in again. The headache had subsided just a pinch when he'd covered his eyes, like he was suffering from the light sensitivity that followed a hangover. Maybe going in the back room at the station and closing his eyes for a spell would cure him. If not, maybe a nap. Or coffee. Or both, if he could squeeze it, though he doubted he could. "Just today, probably."

"I tell you, I ain't seen anything quite like it," Mary said. She spat, and sure enough, a brown tinge to the saliva was evident as it hit the ground. "I mean, you had a flame-breathing thing the size of a shed out here, and a pack of—I don't even know quite how to describe them—running nightmare lions, I reckon—"

"Colorful."

"Nah, they were black as a tire," Mary said, missing the point. "Scary as hell. The noise they made? Worse than a coyote. Creepy things. And when they hit the house? My daddy was in the navy, and his ship sunk during the war." Reeve did not bother to ask which war, for fear the answer he'd get would be that he served on the CSS

Hunley. "That house going down was exactly like what he described. Shuddering, crashing, things falling every which way—it was a hell of a thing, Nick. This is all—it's a hell of thing."

"On this we can agree," Reeve said, and felt the buzz on his belt as his phone rang. "Just a minute, will ya?" He picked up the phone, glanced at it, and sighed. "What can I do for you, Mr. Pike?"

"Oh, I'm calling about what I can do for you," Pike said, and he sounded like he might just be on speakerphone. "You mind stopping out by my office when you get a chance?"

"Sure," Reeve said, committing to it but planning to punt it way out—say, eight football fields away. "How about tomorrow—"

"No, no," Pike said, "you're going to want to get on this right away. Tonight. Hell, this afternoon, if possible."

Reeve felt that weary sense of resignation tugging at him. What were the odds Pike had something useful for him? Actually useful? Only one way to find out. "I got a lot on my plate right now—" he said, figuring he'd fish for more info before going for a meeting this eve.

"I got that money loosened up for you," Pike said, "and that ain't all. Come by tonight. Please?"

Well, that was something, at least. Paying the watch might make all the sacrifice and endless calls they were getting at the moment a little easier, maybe even motivate a few of them that were hanging pretty loose at the moment, struggling with the hours they were putting in and the whole lot of nothing they were getting from it.

And if Pike had something else … well, the money would cushion the blow if whatever the other thing that had Pike all excited turned out to be a dud, since he wasn't saying what it was. A tick on his balls, for all Reeve knew. That goddamned Yankee would probably enjoy having a bloodsucker working his little cock.

"You want to say what this other business is about?" Reeve said warily. He still didn't have an overabundance of trust in the man or his judgment.

"Not over the phone," Pike said. "Come see me."

Reeve looked at his watch, looked around. They almost had things wrapped up here, and the County Administrator's office was in Culver, only about twenty minutes from here. It was likely this was the closest he'd get in the next few days, barring some other wildass call in this direction. "I'll be by in a bit," Reeve said with a sigh, and hung up without bothering with pleasantries.

"You sound so overjoyed," Mary said as he slid the phone back into its cover.

"Well, you see how it is," Reeve said, feeling a little spike of pain at his temple. Was it too soon to take down some more Tylenol? "Just one goddamned thing after another."

*

Pike hung up the phone and put it down on his desk, taking care to avoid the spots recently soiled by blood. He turned to look at Darla, and a grin broke across his face. Jenny's corpse was now in the closet, and the desk was more or less clean, but the stink of shit and piss hung in the air. "He's coming," he said, feeling the grin tug at the corners of his mouth. "Didn't say when he'll be here, but ... he bit the bait. He'll be along."
"And we'll be waiting," Darla said, with a smile of her own. He could see it in her eyes, could feel it in a quiver down his leg.
It was all coming together now.

*

Hendricks opened the door to the hotel room expecting to find her there, and he wasn't disappointed. She was lingering just inside, hair backlit by the glow of the bathroom light. It gave her tresses a fiery look, like the flames that had shot out of that fire sloth's mouth, and it was a good look on her. Her curves showed up in the silhouette too. She was stripped down to a seafoam green bra and panties.
"You almost died," she said, keeping her distance.
Hendricks put his back against the door and just admired the look of her for a minute. Goddamn, she was hot, even in shadow. She had just a little meat to that ass, and he liked it. Her belly had just a little extra layer to it too, a little more than when he'd first met her, like she was getting healthier over time, and he liked that. It gave him half a chub just to study her nearly-glowing pale stomach in the dimness. It was smooth and flawless, and he had a sudden desire to blow a load of white cum on that pristine belly, though he knew he'd change his mind in the heat of the moment, stay to the pleasure and keep it in her until he finished. "You weren't there," he said, trying not to sound too worried over it, "so I guess I wasn't in that much danger."
"I was otherwise occupied," she said softly.
That stuck in his craw, but not too much. "Well, I guess I better hope you're not meeting a client next time my ass is headed for the chipper-shredder. Or into the furnace, I guess, like this time." He hadn't thought he was that close, but then again, if Arch hadn't jumped out in front of him, he'd have gotten the full blast of hellfire.

That would have kicked his day in the ass. Hell, it would have made it his last, and that would have been an unsatisfying end, to say the least.

"You should not joke about such dangers," Starling said, still quiet, but she took soft steps across the motel carpet toward him. He watched her small feet move, just as pale as the rest of her, just as bereft of flaws and marks. She was young, a little younger than him, but the girl had some miles on her. Whatever was in her head had lived, man; shit, had it lived. He'd seen the face beneath this one, the hooker named Lucia, and she wasn't appealing, really. Sure, she had the same body, the same curves, but she was a fucking shell compared to Starling, this face, those eyes he couldn't get a bearing on save to see that they were darker than the room around him.

Hendricks brought his eyes up slowly, taking in those perfect calves, those widening thighs that tapered to that perfect ass, hidden beneath the seafoam green bikini underwear. She was close now, close enough to reach his hands out and put them on her hips, to hold her there for a second while he stared, drinking her in. She smelled good, a little sweaty, like Starling had caught Lucia just after a job, but he didn't give a fuck about that. Something in it spurred him on, like he had to have her, had to claim her for his own—reclaim her, maybe—after catching the scent of a lesser stag. He was all fucking man, after all, and she saw that, he knew, as he pulled her close and pressed his lips to her.

She pressed back, fiery and full of life, a passionate gasp escaping her when they broke. She dove for his neck and buried her face in it, nibbling along the skin, working from his earlobe down. Hendricks tingled and shucked off his coat. Once his hands were free, he wrapped them around her and found her bra clasp. He fumbled with it, but got it undone, and her tits burst free of the bra, poured out like a sweet Leinenkugel's on a hot day by the lakeshore.

Starling pressed her chest against his smoky t-shirt, and he caught that smell of her again as she worked against the side of his neck. He was full-hard now, poking into her belly, thinking again of just cumming right there, making her flesh even paler; give her a little ivory spot next to the belly button, a pool of slow-sliding white that would stream down her skin like honey down a wall.

She kissed him again, and again, her lips hungry against his. Her hands fumbled with his belt and undid it, found his button and zipper and practically ripped them down. His pants sagged under the weight of his gun and sword, dragging them down as Starling's hands tugged at his boxers, sliding them over his hips and letting them drop, too, as she grabbed his cock in hand and pulled back her face so he could see the freckles on her cheeks for just a second before she dove down—

Her lips found his cock and gave it a sweet tickle. She didn't just dive right into the deep throat, or even put it in her mouth at all. She just slipped her lips around the head and left it there, moving subtly for a couple seconds as Hendricks shuddered with pleasure. Then her tongue moved across his tip, and he shivered again. It felt like she was tonguing the hole in his urethra, and it felt surprisingly good. She worked it a couple times, moving under the tip, running it smoothly along the underside, across the scarred skin where the evidence of his circumcision remained. He'd heard someone talking in the corps about how, really, circumcisions were cruel because they took off the most sensitive part of the penis.

But they made you last longer in the sack, according to that know-it-all jackass, so that was something.

Starling slid her lips down his mast and Hendricks let out a low moan, throwing his head back against the motel room door. It made a satisfying thud, and he felt like the blood was leaving his brain. Sucked out, almost, and little lights flashed in front of his eyes. Didn't hurt enough for him to stop focusing on that sensation rolling up and down his dick, centering on the band of skin that lay right under the head of his cock.

She worked it slow and steady, nothing flashy, nothing too fast. She took her time, red hair highlighted in the light of the bathroom flooding out across the motel floor. Hendricks's bare ass rested against the smooth wood door, and her lips ran up and down his woody. He arched his back as it continued to rise in him like a tide, subsiding slightly every now and again like he'd hit a peak and then went down into a valley before it started to rise again. He could feel the Mount Everest of his orgasm in the distance, getting closer all the time.

Starling brought a hand up his leg, smoothly stroking the inside of his thigh. It wasn't exactly on the level of what she was doing to his cock, but it felt pretty good. She cupped his balls, giving them a pleasant squeeze as she drew back. She never pulled it fully out; she'd just take it in all the way to the back of her throat and then bring her lips up to just below the head, apply a little suction, then slide back down again. Now with her hand on his testicles, she upped the tempo a little, just slightly, and it was like she'd punched the damn throttle, and Hendricks was flying toward cumming.

He looked down at her, and for a split second he imagined the red hair was gone, replaced by blond hair and crystal blue eyes, staring up at him mischievously, looking like a million bucks with her cock in his mouth, and he said, "God, I love you, Alison."

To Starling's credit, if she noticed what he'd said, it did not slow her down in the least. She kept at it while Hendricks's cheeks burned like they'd been set on fire. He threw his head back so he wouldn't have to look at her, not now, while she finished and he hit that last peak. It wasn't as intense as it would have been if he hadn't fucked up like that, but it was good nonetheless, and he could feel himself buck between her lips, the head swelling as she ran a hand up the base of his shaft and emptied him into her mouth.

It felt like heaven, like the sweetest waves of pleasure lifted him up and carried him high, high up in the air. His eyes were squeezed tightly shut, and he was still imagining a blonde down there, doing what Starling was doing, and he didn't care if she knew now. He didn't need to care, because she probably didn't either. She didn't quit on him until he let out the last gasp of air and sagged, his jizz all spilled out and consumed. She'd fucking devoured him and he loved it, like he was wanted more than he'd felt in ... well, forever.

She was off his tip a second later, gently, like she knew it'd almost hurt if she'd pulled it out with a squeeze or something. Starling was still kneeling there, looking up at him with those dusky eyes, and Hendricks stayed still, ass and back planted against the hotel room door for a few seconds longer until he felt that burn in his cheeks again, shame setting in for having said the shit he did aloud. He reached down and pulled up his pants, fiddling with the boxers first and then dragging the heavy belt up, zipping and fastening and buckling so he could look at that instead of the redhead who was still there, making him feel awkward as fuck even though she'd just swallowed him like he was a ten-course meal. "I think I'm done for now," he said, feeling like he pretty much was.

He waited for her to say something, but when he looked at her again, she was already gone, an empty space there where the naked redhead had been only seconds earlier. But wasn't that every man's fantasy? Pretty girl who takes care of business, doesn't say much, and leaves when it's over? He adjusted his belt, unfastening it again, and letting it drop. He kicked off his boots, put down his hat, and stripped off his t-shirt. There was already a lagging cum-spot in his boxers, and it'd be fucking sticky later. That shit dried like concrete in his pubes and leg hair, but he didn't give a damn right now.

Once he was down to nothing but his boxers, he threw himself on his bed. His weapons were all right there in arm's reach, but he lay on the cool sheets. The smell of sex was still on them because he hadn't had housekeeping in for a good long stretch. Who gave a shit? It was the smell of his sex, not some stranger's, his and Starling's, and he wasn't done doing it with her.

Hendricks stared at the gaps between curtain and window where the light snuck in, and then leaned off the bed to fish his phone out of his pocket. He felt callous about sex now, at least since things had blown up with Erin. It was just a physical thing to him at this point, just a reaction to years of not treating his boners with anything but self-medication. He needed to relieve the pressure, and if it was with Erin, back when she was pleasant, good. Now that it was with Starling, with no strings, that was fine too. It was all he needed, really.

Or at least that was what he told himself, ignoring that dark voice in the back of his head that suggested otherwise, the same one that had said the wrong name. *Fuck that voice,* he thought, and tried to put it out of his mind.

It didn't work.

*

Drake sunk his teeth into the brisket, the pectoral muscle of an adult male. It had been roasted low and slow, smoked with the thick seam of fat on top to caramelize and melt down into the rest of the meat, all the juices pooling and collecting in the bottom of the Kamado in a drip pan set up on the indirect ceramic holder just above the fire. He'd run it for something like six hours at 250 degrees, letting it go the last hour in a marinade, wrapped in foil. Then he'd rested it for two whole hours wrapped in fresh foil, in a cooler, before taking his first bite.

It almost melted in his mouth. Brisket was a tough cut, and the only way to make it good was to do it low and slow, really allow time for the meat to steep in the juices and soften up. It maybe had been a little tough to get right, but it was good meat, and that was all that mattered. Properly cooked, properly prepared, given a reasonable amount of time to slow cook, and now—

Now it was soulful bliss, a flavor he could feel seeping into his essence. It was so delicious, another culinary triumph, and it filled him with a sense of rightness. When he bit into these foods, it was as though he was properly asserting himself in the food chain where he belonged. And he was under no illusions about where he belonged: right at the top.

The juice of the meat flowed down Drake's lips, and he licked them. The meat oozed with sweet flavor. It was well spiced too, given a wonderful rub from some Tennessee barbecue house that he'd found in a display of local products. It felt right to use it—locally sourced meat called for locally made spices, after all.

And it had translated very well to this meat.

Still ... it was a triumph, but not *the* triumph. No, the veal ... that still evaded him. He could taste the texture of the brisket as he chewed. It wasn't quite what he was looking for. It might have softened in cooking, but it still wasn't *soft*.

He needed something so tender it would nearly melt off the bone. This came close; it was certainly easy to pull it off given how long it had been in the slow cooker, but the meat itself ... it was still just a little tough in parts.

Drake sighed, putting the brisket down, his hunger not sated but thoughts—that unstoppable craving—giving him pause. Was this the culinary height for him? He wanted a child to sample, but with every house he'd broken into so far, he'd found none. Perhaps staking one out specifically, or looking for one with a swingset out back ...

Something had to be done. This curiosity, it was only growing by the day. And as much as he enjoyed this meat—and he did, tremendously, he reflected as he took another bite—until he got his hands on a piece of human veal, maybe even more than one—it would, forever, be the rarest thing, the one that eluded him, like that boy that had escaped into the woods.

The one that got away.

*

Arch had gotten a ride from Barney Jones. Tucking himself in the back of the pastor's car, he sat, flannel shirt still wrapped around his waist, the cloth delicately placed so as to cover him as much as it could. The car had a nice smell to it, like Olivia's perfume lingered in the seats. It didn't evoke memories of Alison because Olivia wore a perfume that suited her age. Alison had liked something younger. Arch couldn't even remember the name anymore.

Braeden Tarley was riding shotgun, and Arch was happy to let him do so. Sitting naked in the back was more comfortable than in front. Not that either of the men riding with him hadn't seen the male anatomy before, but it was more comfortable to keep these things under wraps as much as possible.

"I heard you saved that cowboy's life," Barney said, breaking the silence that pervaded the car. He sounded engaging, conversational. Like he always did.

"That's really something," Tarley said. "How'd you do that?" Tarley glanced back, then averted his eyes quickly. He didn't ask how Arch ended up naked.

"Stepped out in front of that fire sloth to try and keep it from burning him," Arch said simply. It was, after all, true.

"Looks like that fire sloth torched everything it could," Barney said, looking in the rearview back at Arch. "You're lucky to be alive."

"I don't reckon luck had much to do with it," Arch said. "I think God might have intervened on my behalf."

Tarley made a snorting noise, then quieted himself and got serious, smirk dissolving. "I, uh ..."

Barney caught it, and he smiled at Tarley. Arch could almost feel the heat that was about to be turned on him go another direction. "Now, Braeden," Jones said, still smiling, "we've talked a lot these last few days about faith, and what it might mean to each of us. You told me you believed in the Lord, and in a greater plan."

"I do," Tarley said after an interval of what looked to Arch like internal struggle. "I just ... I don't know, Reverend. God saving a man from flames?"

"Something which has Biblical precedent," Jones said, still smiling.

"Yeah, sure, in the stories. I guess I just don't ... think about it happening in the modern day, you know?" Tarley shrugged, but it was plain by the flush on his cheeks that he was embarrassed to raise such a subject here and now.

"How can you believe in God but not think He might throw a miracle down every now and again?" Jones was smiling again, the sweet self-satisfaction of knowing what he believed. Arch knew a little of that.

Tarley, however, didn't seem to quite get it. He retreated a little into himself, his neck retracting into his shirt an inch or two. "I dunno, Reverend," he muttered.

"Braeden," Jones said gently. "I ain't mad at you, son. You got no cause to be ashamed right now." Arch could see in Tarley's eyes that he didn't quite believe that, but he nodded nonetheless. Jones found Arch's gaze in the rearview and held it. "Arch ..."

Arch could feel the preacher's intent burning him down. Still, he answered, "Yes?"

"You remember the Lord's commandment about not committing murder, right?"

Arch's brow almost furrowed of its own accord. "Of course."

"You know," Jones said, "that includes throwing yourself to your own death too, don't you?"

As if Arch didn't know that. "Of course," Arch said, "and I haven't."

I threw myself in front of that thing to save another."

"Mmhmm," Jones said as if he didn't believe it. "'Greater love hath no man than this, that a man lay down his life for his friends,'" he said, mostly for Tarley's understanding, Arch figured. "You using the word of God as a shield from the world, Arch?"

"From the sin of the world, maybe," Arch said.

"You sure about that?" Jones asked, and he was staring back at Arch something fierce. Arch was looking at the window now, though. "You sure you aren't using it like a sled to go wherever you want to go? Because if you are, there's only one direction it'll take you."

"Downhill," Tarley jumped in, like he was trying to get points for the correct answer, or maybe make up for his earlier embarrassment.

Arch felt himself burning in a way that he hadn't when that fire sloth was breathing down on him. "This is a fight we're in, Reverend. What was I supposed to do? Let the cowboy burn? Because that wouldn't seem to me like the Lord's will."

"Oh, you're worried about the Lord's will," Jones said, and he had that air of mock sincerity, heavier on the sincerity but the mocking was there all the same. "I do apologize, Arch. I thought perhaps you were exercising your own."

"I thought maybe the Lord's will and mine coincided in this case," Arch said hotly, "since He put me in the path to help."

"You got free will, son," Jones said, "so I don't think the Lord shoved you into those flames. He may have protected your knucklehead from harm while you were in 'em, but he didn't push you in. You went a-jumpin' in all by your own self. And maybe you did have good intention, Arch. I don't know your heart; I leave that to Him. But you just keep in mind that He does—and if you go leaping into something else with your head not quite right, it's Him you're going to have to answer to if you're lying to yourself about whose will you're really following."

Arch started to open his mouth to say something, but Jones cut him off. "Why don't you just think on that a while and we'll talk about it later? I think Braeden might have some things on his heart."

Tarley blinked a couple of times, and said, "Well ... yeah, I ... I do have a couple things I wouldn't mind ... talking about."

"Well, go on then," Jones said, steering them up to a four-way stop and waiting.

Arch just sat in the back, steaming. He felt like he'd been whacked with a shovel right between the eyes, and he didn't care for the sensation at all. It burned him worse than anything that fire sloth had done, that was for sure.

*

The fire was mostly under control now, and Reeve stared at the last few hot patches. The ground nearby was ashes with a few embers, water running in thick patches, puddling here and there in the low points. Smoke was still steaming high into the air, but the fire had petered out when it ran up against a section of ground cleared for a transmission line.

"We got pretty damned lucky here," Marty Ferrell, the local fire captain, told Reeve, his face covered with smudges of soot. He'd been on the front lines of this thing. 'Course, he was a member of the watch too, though it seemed like he mostly got out here on only a few calls. His first love was firefighting and first responding, and that was fine with Reeve. He'd reckoned on making this happen with a lot of people doing a little, and a few doing a lot.

"In that the woods didn't burn down entirely, I agree," Reeve said, looking off into the smoky distance. The air was tinged heavily with wood smoke, but it wasn't nice and atmospheric like a burning fireplace. It was thick and heavy to the point that he felt like he was choking on it.

"Got a couple of places I'm still keeping an eye on," Marty said, "but I think for the most part ... we're done."

"All right then," Reeve said, stretching, lifting his ass off the hood of his car. He'd moved back up to the road a while ago, figuring that lingering in the back yard of those burnt-down house shells wasn't real productive and maybe even hampered the work being done by the real firefighters. "Guess I'll be moving along then, unless you need me for anything else." He caught the almost pitying look from Marty, and he knew: they hadn't needed him in the first place. "Thanks," he said, and the fireman nodded and moved off.

He saddled the OOCs with Mary and tasked them with taking her back to the station. They'd complied, Duncan as stoic as ever, and Guthrie wearing a sourly amused look. They hadn't complained, though.

Which left Reeve free to do the thing he had to do now.

The thing he really didn't want to do now.

He had to go see that son of a bitch, Pike.

Reeve rubbed his head, the steady ache behind his eyes spreading to his temples. This ... this was not going to make his headache any better. At all.

*

Erin pulled into the parking lot at the same time as Father Nguyen, and when she got out of the car, he was dragging himself out of his own vehicle. He had a ragged look in his eyes, the bags beneath them looking a little like a ... well, a baggage claim's worth, at least. She thought about just saying, "You look like shit, Father," but thought the better of it and went with, "You look a little tired, Padre," instead.

Nguyen caught up to her on the way through the door. He was shorter than she was, but not by much. "You can say that again," Nguyen said, tousling his black hair. His collar was stiff, but the black—outfit or whatever they called the priest's uniform—was wrinkled as hell. "I've consecrated so many weapons these last few days it feels like I've got the entire ritual memorized now. I need to take a break, or I'm going to lose my mind and start speaking Latin in my sleep."

Benny was behind the counter, running dispatch, and looking heartily bored. "How's it going?" Erin asked.

"All quiet since the fire," Benny said, looking back down at a well-thumbed copy of *American Rifleman*. Erin glanced at the pages; looked like a profile of a big rifle. Not quite as big as Alison had toted, but it was black and mean, and she wouldn't have minded having someone covering her with one of those while she swung away with her ball bat.

That was a problem in her head; this herd of hellcats was going to get worse, she was sure of it. Rampaging across the landscape, ripping apart houses like Mary Wrightson's—if they came into town like that, it'd be fucking carnage. She'd thought the Rog'tausch was bad, ripping its way through in a swatch.

If these things came to town? The chaos they'd cause would make the Rog'tausch look like a bullet to their nuclear bomb damage. They'd just shred whole streets at a time, locusts on the crops. And human lives would be the harvest.

She was about to voice one of these thoughts aloud when the door jangled, the bell above it clanging as it opened. "All I'm saying," Casey Meacham's voice reached her, that slight whine to it, "is that once you try it, you're going to love it."

Brian Longholt came in a step behind him, face like carved stone. "Then I guess I won't know, because I'm not trying that, Casey."

"It'd loosen you right up," Casey said, making a clicking noise and winking at Brian, who seemed to strain himself, butt cheeks puckering.

"Let it go," Brian said, and then turned his attention to Erin. "What's going on?" he asked, measurably relaxing when he saw her.

"We had an incident involving something called a fire sloth," Erin said. "It was about the size of one of those big SUVs, and it breathed—"

"Poison gas?" Casey leapt in, drawing every head toward him. He cracked a smile. "Just kidding. Fire, right?"

"Primo guesswork, Ace," Erin said with withering sarcasm. "Yeah, it breathed fire. Burned down that new Whistling Poons—I mean Pines—" goddamn Benny; everyone was chuckling at her for that one "—development out on the end of town. Torched the clothes off of Arch—"

"Is he okay?" Brian asked, face suddenly frozen, almost stricken.

"I knew a girl with a whistling poon," Casey said, suddenly introspective.

"He's fine," Erin said. "Apparently he's the chosen of God, so he's immune to hellfire."

"It made a sound like—actually, it reminded me a little of that part in the Kid Rock song, 'Cowboy,' where he's—"

"Shut the fuck up, Casey," Brian said, giving him a slap to the chest. "We're talking about hellfire immunity here."

"Hmm," Casey said, seeming to give that some thought. "I wonder if that means Arch is immune to gonorrhea too?" When he caught the others gaping at him, openly, he added, "What? It burns like fire."

"Yeah, he's probably immune to that," Brian said calmly, "since he's never slept with anyone but my sister, and I don't see him embracing the whoring life now."

"Wow, that's loyalty," Casey said. "I don't know how he does it. I mean, Alison was pretty and all, God rest her soul—"

"You know what, Casey?" Erin asked, catching the not-subtle hardening of Brian's features. "Probably best you just stop it right there."

"All right then," Casey said with a shrug, then clapped his hands together in front of him. "So ... what else are y'all up to?"

"I'm just checking in," Nguyen said. "And then maybe I'll collapse for a while, unless someone wants to start a poker game." When Casey cocked his head at the Father, he added, "For toothpicks only. I don't gamble."

"An unjust gain of toothpicks still seems like gambling to me, Father," Brian said with a thin smile.

"God, you all are such a bunch of gossipy, catty, worrying little bitches," Erin said, blowing air between pursed lips.

"Whooo," Brian said. "Shots fired."

"Yeah, at your manhood," Casey agreed.

Brian looked a little put out. "Yours too."

"Mine's big," Casey said with admirable self-assurance. "It can take the hit."

"You're sitting here backbiting," Erin said, building to a head of steam, "when we were all out there dealing with a truck-sized menace that blew hellfire at us. Where were you clowns?"

"Brainstorming," Brian said.

"Getting high and putting dirt on the tires at the quarry," Casey corrected him. When he caught the PO'd look, he shrugged. "She ain't your mom, dumbass. You ain't got to lie to her about smoking weed."

"No, but she's a cop, Casey," Brian said in a low growl, "and do you have any idea what the penalty for possession of marijuana is in Tennessee? Spoiler alert: it's not among the lightest sentences in the US."

"I don't give a fuck about your weed," Erin said, still steaming. "You can toke up out of dick-shaped bongs for all I care—"

"Done it," Casey said calmly.

"I'm starting to get a little pissed about the lack of commitment around here," Erin went on. "I thought we formed this watch so we could get serious about this demon shit going on around here."

"I thought it was a survival mechanism," Father Nguyen tossed in. "Hang together or hang separately?"

"It is that," Erin said, toning it down a notch and throwing a little acknowledgment the Father's way. "But you'd think, given everything on the line, people'd be all in by now. They'd be showing up more to stuff." She threw up her arms. "People are still fucking going to work at the mill like it's just another normal day."

"Yeah," Casey said, "don't they know that worrying about a demon eating you is more important than a bank taking back your house? Or your kids starving?"

Erin just let that hang there. "Dammit, Casey, that ain't—"

"He's got a point," Brian said, sounding like he was conceding something he did not want to concede. "People are acting normal about this because … fuck, Erin. Who wants to acknowledge this for what it really is when they can maybe turn away from the truth for a little longer?" He put a hand through his hair. "They're clinging to their lives because they don't want to give up everything. It's like charity. People are starving across the world, but you don't see everyone give away everything they have and keep only the minimum to survive for themselves, do you? No, they give a little extra every now and again, to assuage their conscience, and go on living their lives. Because the alternative is to admit that they're doing all right while their neighbors—local or global—are fucking dying."

"That's not exactly right," Casey said, frowning. "They go on living their lives, dumbass, because if they gave away everything, what the hell are they working for?"

Brian slipped him a silky smile. "The good of our fellow man." *Duh!* wasn't said, but it was obvious to everyone in the room he meant it.

"People ain't wired that way," Casey said, shaking his head. "We ain't all Mother Theresa, and we don't all get our satisfaction from giving everything away. You tell a man he gets to go home with his paycheck stripped down to nothing but the bare minimum to survive, why the hell is he going to go work harder?" Brian shrugged, already checking out, probably feeling like he'd made his point well enough. "People don't work at the mill cuz it's fun, Brian. They work there cuz it pays the bills, lets them live their life, feel like they're contributing." He paused. "And maybe lets 'em afford the payments on a sweet-ass bass boat and a new F-150." He looked right at Erin. "You take that away from 'em, what the hell are they working for? What the hell are they fighting for?"

"I get that, under normal circumstances," Erin said, trying to avoid thinking about the fact that Casey fucking Meacham had just made a reasonable point. "This ain't normal circumstances, Casey."

"Yeah, it ain't normal," Casey said. "But they want it to be normal, Erin. The guys around here, they'd love nothing better than for it to be back to fucking normal, you know? They ain't looking for high drama, and most ain't looking for this fight. They just want to live, man." He put his thumbs in his belt loops under his greasy, sweaty shirt. "Just live. Have a few bucks in their pockets. Maybe take the kids to Disney every few years, hit up the Redneck Riviera with the family once a summer, and spend their weekends in the boat when it's warm and the woods when it ain't, and get football when they're not doing either of those things. They don't want your demon bullshit rolling through their main street, and they'll fight to push it back, but … you can't blame 'em for keeping their heads down and hoping the problem mostly goes away on its own, so they can get back to their business." He leaned forward slightly on the balls of his feet. "Cuz they all got business of their own, and only the real adrenaline chasers or the ones who lost a shit-ton—like your friend the cowboy, or Braeden Tarley, or maybe Keith Drumlin—want this thing to go on a second longer than it has to."

Erin sighed, and looked up at the ceiling. Yeah, he had a damned good fucking point, and she hated every bit of it. "Okay," she said.

"So, how do we get 'em more involved?" She wondered if Reeve was still at the scene. Surely these were things he'd been pondering. "And ..." This was the one rattling inside her since she'd seen Mary Wrightson's shattered house: "How the hell do we kill that herd of hellcats?" She looked right at Brian.

"Uhhh ..." he said, shrugging his shoulders. He did look like he was a little high, maybe. "I have no idea."

She looked to Father Nguyen, and he said, "Unless it involves me sleeping for the first time in a couple days ... I have no idea."

Benny Binion shrugged. "I'm just the radio man."

"Well," Erin started, "we should keep thinking about—"

"Okay, actually, I have an idea," Casey said.

Erin braced herself, deciding whether or not she even wanted to ask. Finally, figuring it best to just get it over with, she said, "All right ... what is it?"

*

Reeve eased his car into the parking space at the County Administrator's office and let out a deep sigh. It may not have been his least favorite thing ever, but meeting with Pike was right up there, regardless of how contrite the greasy little shit was about what had happened about Halloween, and however much he protested he was ready to help.

Help? Shit. Even if the bastard could have made the demons go away with a slap of his ass and one good fart, Reeve would have been hesitant to ask the goddamned Yankee carpetbagging son of a bitch for help.

"Once burned, twice shy," Reeve muttered under his breath, still massaging his head. Ibuprofen, Tylenol, coffee—not one of these fucking things had made a dent in the throbbing pain Reeve was feeling in his skull. It had adopted a sort of bass echo in his ears now too, which made his disposition less friendly. Not that Reeve necessarily gave a shit, but Pike might if he ended up bearing the brunt of his orneriness. "Feels like that burn might have happened right behind the fucking eyes."

There was nothing more for it though. Reeve looked out the car window and up at the second story of the old brick building. What genius had decided to put the County Administrator's office out here near Culver when the sheriff's station was all the way back in Midian?

A genius of the first order, of course, because it meant that Reeve didn't get caught up in the bullshit day-to-day politics that Pike embraced like a horny teenage boy jumped on the first hot slice of naked chick that came his way. If Reeve could have gone back in time, he might have professed his thanks in any way possible to the architect of that decision. He wasn't a sappy man, and certainly not inclined toward the same sex, but he might have conceded a handjob or twelve would be a worthy price to pay for the limited amount of contact he'd had with Pike up to this point in his career.

Reeve had seen County Administrators come and go, of course. A sheriff or two as well. But he couldn't quite recall seeing one like Pike, poached out of somewhere too far north for Reeve to ever trust him. It wasn't that—as Erin had once accused him—Calhoun County was the end of his world; it was more of a general feeling that when someone moved halfway across the country and left their home behind to try and carve out a career in county government, leaving most of their family behind to do so—that person might just be a little toward the snake end of ambitious. And if that wasn't enough to raise your eyebrow and make you keep your attention on them, Reeve didn't know what would.

Deciding he'd sat his ass out here about as long as he could get away with, Reeve sighed once more and gave up the hope of massaging that headache away. It never did work, regardless of where he rubbed. But he still kept trying anyway.

Popping the door open, the brisk autumn breeze came rushing in at him as Reeve stood up, leaving the comfortable car's seat behind. He let out a light groan and stretched, something that was becoming more and more necessary as the years went on. His lower back was pissed at him for standing so long at the fire site, and now his hamstrings were mad as hell that he'd been sitting for a half hour. If he could ever just get his damned body to get all in agreement about a course of action, Reeve felt like he'd have accomplished almost as much as organizing the watch.

But there was always at least one complainer, and now his damned bladder, upset at the long-ish drive out here, chimed in as well.

Reeve went for the door and found the building more or less empty. Hardly surprising, given the day, given the hour, given that there was a special election today, and given that the County Administrator's office was not a polling place. He stopped off in the men's room just inside the first floor, not seeing a soul at the receptionist's desk. The other offices on the floor looked empty too, which suited Reeve just fine.

Reeve stood at the urinal, zipper down, dick out, straining against his already throbbing head. He'd held it a little too long, and now his piss was refusing to come out. Son of a bitch.

"I wish I knew what it'd take to make your ass happy," he said to his bladder, voice echoing against the tile in the small men's room. It was immaculately maintained, even though it looked like this place had been built in the forties. Janitorial took their shit seriously here, because it was fucking spotless. He wished the cleaning crew that worked the sheriff's office had a quarter of this group's work ethic and talent. Probably cost five times as much.

It felt like little pinpricks in his urethra for a second when Reeve finally got things going, and the spray squirted to a stop a moment later. "Goddammit," he said, louder than he intended. Why was everything these days such a damned ordeal?

Because it just fucking had to be, of course. Nothing could be easy, not even taking a piss. Reeve put a hand on the cold tile above the urinal, listened to the silence, or near enough. An air conditioner was faintly humming in the background, pushing cool air through the building. Or maybe heat, given it was chilly outside. Either way, that distant sound wasn't near enough to drown out the throbbing of his heart, the pulse of which provoked an actual reaction in Reeve's head, like an aneurysm building up to blow.

He took a deep breath, tried to make it soothing, but it just came out ragged, like he'd run a few miles. He'd done nothing of the sort, but he could smell the smoke from the fire on himself, seeped into his uniform, could feel the tension of dealing with—hell, all the shit he'd dealt with these last few weeks and months—ratcheting through his muscles. His left hand seemed like it might have been shaking, with his penis clutched in it and refusing to open the damned floodgates.

"For fuck's sake," he breathed, tired of exerting himself here. A funny thought flashed through his mind—how long had it been since he and Donna had had marital relations? It'd been a few weeks before she died, hadn't it? It was so infrequent these days, not at all like when they'd been young. He could almost see her in front of him. She was sagging, true, about as much as he was. They both had a gut, and took pains to hide it in their clothes. Her breasts weren't nearly as pert as they'd been when they'd first married … but he hadn't cared. They'd gotten old together, and she still looked good to him. He'd been with her more than any other woman in his life, and it was almost like he was that dog of Pavlov's he read about in his youth, conditioned to drool every time she took off her clothes. Of course, he didn't get fed every time she got naked, but it happened enough that he still got revved up, even though he knew for a fact if she'd come to him naked as a jaybird when he was a young man, he'd have thought twice, three times, maybe, but said no nonetheless.

Now, he jumped on that every time he could.

Or he had.

A little spray came drizzling out of the tip of Reeve's dick. Just a few drops at first, but somehow picturing Donna naked had taken some of the starch out of his muscles, relaxed him a little. He imagined her laugh, and another little squirt came out, splattering the back of the urinal with a gentle tinkling sound against the porcelain. It ran, tracing a yellow waterfall down to the pink, scented urinal cake, the smell of which was barely there under all the smoke on Reeve's clothes.

"I got all the time in the world," he told himself, and imagined Donna again. He thought about the two of them in bed, and strangely, that really got things going. He was letting it all out now, peeing up a storm in front of the urinal thinking about his dead wife. It should have felt disrespectful somehow, this idea that he was thinking of her and it was letting him piss, finally, after all that strain and trying came to naught, but he didn't care because he could almost feel the water level in his bladder dropping, and it was a sweet goddamned relief.

Pretty soon it pinched off, and Reeve felt a lump in his throat. The regret was setting in, now that he was done. Thinking of those sorts of memories had been relaxing at first, but of course there'd be a cost. He'd been running from this shit for weeks, burying himself in thoughts of demons, of saving the town. It had been all he'd thought of, the cause of his present headache and his fatigue. He leaned hard against that hand that braced him against the wall, and gave his dick a shake, then again. It dripped the last few stray drops, and he carefully navigated it back inside the zipper.

Another unwanted thought presented itself—would he ever use it for anything besides pissing again? He had his doubts. Nick Reeve was getting up there, and even with Donna it was becoming more and more infrequent. Hell, he'd even failed to rise to the occasion last time she'd offered, a humiliating retreat if ever there was one. The fact that that was their last sexual experience together …

Well, that, as his grandkids were so fond of saying, really sucked.

He zipped up and pushed off the tile wall, making his way over to the sink. Reeve stared at himself in the mirror. His face was red from the exertion of trying to pee around—stressed muscles, an angry prostate? Hell if he knew. It wasn't helping the headache though, that much was certain. He looked at himself in the mirror, and …

Man, he'd gotten old. Those crow's feet had really dug in around the eyes, like someone had gotten in there with a shovel and started entrenching. He turned the knob on the faucet and started to wash his hands in cold water, feeling the chill seep through to the old bones and stay there. Winter would be here soon enough, and he couldn't take those like he used to either. He and Donna had talked about spending their winters down in the Redneck Riviera after he retired, that stretch of the Florida panhandle where Tennesseeans and Alabamans and Georgians all drove down to vacation. It'd be warmer there, maybe a chance for his old bones to thaw out.

He'd figured he'd only had maybe five good years left, maybe less, as sheriff. The old *Lethal Weapon* line rang true, and he was getting too old for this shit, even before the demons showed up.

"Got work to do," he told himself, trying for a pep talk. He stared at the face in the mirror and, not for the first time today, remembered his name was on the ballot in a special election to decide whether or not he got to keep his job. Sure, he could have said it didn't matter, that he was going to keep on fighting anyway, but that wasn't entirely true, was it?

Losing Donna hadn't fully sunk in yet. Losing his job because the people who'd elected him, trusted him, invested him with the power of the law, the authority to try and keep them and their families safe? Having them say, "Nah, no thanks, you're doing a shitty job here," no matter how undeniably true it was … it would be a blow, even if he'd keep fighting.

Reeve didn't like to play the blame game. He'd kept his eyes shut to the fact that demons were walking his town for entirely too long, and he knew it now. He wished he could go back in time, slapped the ragged, lined face looking at him in the mirror, grab that man staring back by the shoulders a few worry lines ago, and said, "It's demons. Stop fucking around worrying about Arch and get to the real problem."

But there was no use crying over it now. He turned the faucet back on, cold water running down the white, immaculate porcelain, and he splashed some on his face. "I am going to keep fighting," he promised the face in the mirror, "regardless of how this election comes out."

He was readying himself for that gut punch. He had a feeling it was coming. The headache was maybe the worse of the problems right now, but his stomach felt like it was chewing itself up too. If there was another man who wanted his job, Reeve just about figured they could have it if they'd just take the goddamned brain aneurysm and stomach ulcer he seemed to be developing with it.

Staring at himself in the mirror, he wasn't sure what he saw other than an old man. Tired, sure. Haggard, yep. A little unshaven? Without doubt. Time was, he'd be looking in a mirror to shave and Donna would wander past behind him. He'd smile at her, she'd smile back at him in the mirror, and he knew there was pride in her eyes. That she was proud of her man, the sheriff of Calhoun County—the mightiest law enforcement man in their world, the steady rock the people of Midian and the outlying areas could count on no matter what.

But now Donna was dead.

Midian was getting fucked. People were dying.

And he was about to go into a goddamned budget meeting.

"What is there left to be proud of?" he wondered, and a little scrap of poetry from his youth came jumping out at him. "... and though We are not now that strength which in old days Moved earth and heaven ..." He took a breath, trying to remember the rest. "... that which we are, we are."

He pushed off the sink, and went for the door, opening it up. The lines kept rolling through his head; he'd had to memorize this back in high school, and they'd stuck for some reason.

One equal temper of heroic hearts,
Made weak by time and fate but strong in will
To strive, to seek, to find, and not to yield.

Reeve crossed the empty lobby and headed up the stairs, coming out in an open hallway. There were a few offices here, all shut for the night, and down the way he could see a woman, blond and pretty, though she was starting to show a little age, her glasses thick around the frames, look up and meet his gaze. She smiled, and he smiled back politely.

"Aren't you Mrs. Pike?" Reeve asked, stepping up to the receptionist's desk. It was neatly organized except for a book that this lady had out. It looked old, but she had a piece of paper out and covering the pages, so Reeve could only see the edges. It could have been a first edition of Shakespeare, or a collection of poetry that included the verse that was rolling unbidden through his head.

"Howdy, Sheriff," she said, putting on a Southern accent that was as fake—and terrible—as George Clooney's. "And yes, I am. My husband's secretary is gone, so ..." She smiled. "I stepped in for a few hours."

"Well, that's mighty kind of you," Reeve said. "My Donna used to do that too, a little secretarial stuff around the office when we needed it." He drew up, all serious now, thinking about her again, goddammit.

She'd done that all unpaid, like this lady probably was. "I believe your fella is expecting me."

"He surely is," she said, still with that fakey Southern accent. Reeve concealed a grimace. The woman was a Yankee, for fuck's sake; everyone knew it. Why bother trying to blend in by using such a tone-deaf approach? It almost sounded like mockery to him, but he smiled through it. She pushed a button on the phone and said, "Jason? Sheriff Reeve is here to see you." She smiled back at him. "He'll be right with you."

Reeve glanced up at the door. He could hear a little movement inside, and sure enough, Pike opened the door a second later, grinning expansively, lit by the windows behind him. "Sheriff," he said, sounding almost ... pleasant, like he was greeting a long-lost friend. "I do appreciate you coming out here this afternoon. I know it's not a short trip."

"Well, you came out to me this morning," Reeve said, trying to conceal his stiff unease. Something about Mrs. Pike annoyed him, and it wasn't just the accent. The smile was fake too, and her clothing wasn't quite right. She was wearing a blouse that was a little low cut for his taste, and sleeveless. In fall. "Seemed only fair I came out to you, and ... I was out at that fire anyway."

Pike's eyebrows knitted in a thin line across his face. "Fire?"

"Yeah, we had a fire demon hiding out in that new development, Whistling Pines," Reeve said, putting Mrs. Pike and her irritating flaws out of his mind and heading over to the man himself, still waiting at the door. "Burned down some houses in construction, damned near set the woods on fire." He caught a hint of concern from Pike. "It's all out now," Reeve said, trying to put the man at ease. "Under control. For the moment."

"That's good," Pike said quietly. "Why don't you come on in?"

*

They walked on inside, and Pike sat down behind the desk, trying not to grin. Reeve ambled in after him, a hair slower, and paused in front of his desk. Reeve's nose prickled; he was getting the scent of something, probably the smell of Jenny soiling herself after death.

"Had one of my kids in here this afternoon, and we had a little accident," Pike said. That was damned easy; he just thought about how many times he'd smelled shit in the last few years and it sprang out, pretty as you please.

Reeve seemed to accept that with a nod, a little stiff, but then, he was like that a lot. "I remember those days." He was wearing a real tight smile. "Seemed like we were dealing with diapers forever and then one day, shit, they were off to school and moving away."

Pike had learned over the years to smile and nod his head while people said boring-ass shit. "How old are your kids?" he asked, playing polite politician again.

Reeve's face clouded up. Something was bothering him there. "Old enough I don't have to worry about wiping their asses anymore," he said, trying to paper over it. "You wanted to talk about something? Budget? Money?"

"I do indeed," Pike said, as Reeve winced and touched his forehead. "You, uh ... got a headache there?"

Reeve's eyes were slightly squinted. "Yeah. Bad one. All danged day."

It's about to get a fuck-lot worse, Pike just kept himself from saying. "You want Darla to get you some Tylenol?"

"I've taken a few. Doesn't seem to be helping," Reeve said, removing his hand from his bald scalp.

"You know what the best cure is for a headache?" Pike asked. "An orgasm."

Reeve just stared at him stonily. "Well, I don't reckon I'm going to be having one of those anytime soon, so ... maybe I'll just take that Tylenol after all."

Pike just grinned at him, and called out, "Darla—Sheriff Reeve's got a headache. You mind bringing him that Tylenol in the drawer?"

*

Reeve's headache was spreading like—well, wildfire, if it wasn't contained by Marty Ferrell and his boys. It seemed like it was moving down his spine. Sitting across the desk from this jackass wasn't helping, listening to him try and make politician small talk.

It didn't help that the whole office smelled like shit. Shit and something else, a little below that, something he couldn't quite place over the screaming fire in his head. Reeve shut one eye; cutting out the light helped a little, at least temporarily.

He heard the scuff of a footstep behind him and there was Mrs. Pike, holding out a bottle of Tylenol. He took it from her and said, "Thank you, ma'am," with a polite nod, and she was turning around and walking off again. He hesitated, then added, "Do you have a water fountain I could—?" and held up the Tylenol bottle.

"Oh, she can get you something," Pike said quickly and then

nodded to his wife.

This was the slow grind of hard pain, like someone had taken ice picks and shoved them in Reeve's temples, twirling 'em like they were trying to stir his brains up. Fuck, there was no joy in this. And talking to Pike about whatever this jagoff wanted to talk about? Not a help. Orgasm's the best medicine for a headache? Shit, who the hell did he think he was talking to?

Reeve hadn't been with another woman since he'd married Donna. And now, after thirty-something years, he wasn't interested in branching out again. It had been a funny thing; he had figured—worried, really—that when he got married, things would get scary at some point. You couldn't look around at all the older, married women and not notice a disparity between them and the young woman he was marrying at the time. And sure as shit, his wife had aged. Her bottom had gotten bigger, gravity had taken hold upstairs.

But he hadn't given much of a shit. Those pretty things he'd chased in his youth, stuck his dick in whenever he'd been offered the opportunity—they seemed to get younger and younger while he got older. They started to get ... less appealing, almost, especially after the kids started coming along.

He'd wanted Donna every chance he could get his hands on her, and that hadn't changed in all these years. Oh, sure, he could still appreciate the beauty of some tuned-up supermodel with an ass the size of a paper plate if she walked by, but he didn't crave them the way he might have when he was nineteen. Maybe he'd gotten old. Or maybe he'd just grown in the direction of wanting what he had.

"... you know what I mean?" Pike asked, and Reeve was lightly jolted back to reality, and to the office that smelled like shit.

Reeve blinked a couple times, and looked at Pike's desk. It was covered over in papers. He hadn't been to the man's office too many times—only a few—but every single one of them, he'd found Pike's desk meticulously neat. Now there was shit strewn everywhere, almost papering over the surface. He stared at that for a second, then dazedly drew his attention back up to Pike's face, intent on him and awaiting his reply.

"I'm sorry," Reeve said, touching the side of his head again. "I ... I'm having trouble concentrating today." *Because you're boring as shit and so full of yourself I'm surprised you don't have your own dick in your mouth all the time.* He retained the sense not to say that aloud, but only barely.

"Oh, yeah, I understand," Pike said, nodding sympathetically. It could have been false sympathy, and Reeve wouldn't have known. He expected just about everything this man did was false. That was probably why it was so goddamned galling that the prissy fucker was sitting between him and something he needed. Reeve had some pride, and this was straining every bit of it. "Oh, here comes Darla now with your water."

Reeve nodded, turning to see her. Mrs. Pike came on up again with a glass, tall cylinder filled to the brimming with tap water. Reeve took it with a grateful nod, and found himself looking at her ass as she turned to walk off. He didn't mean to, but his gaze lingered a second longer than he intended. She had the hips and the ass that told him she'd spit out a couple of kids. It was a strangely compelling feature to him, and he looked a little longer than he needed to. When he came back around, Pike was smirking at him.

Caught, Reeve reckoned. Not that he much cared.

"Thank you for this," he said, raising the water cup and putting it on Pike's desk gingerly. That done, he opened the bottle of Tylenol and poured a few out. Carefully, he replaced the cap, then put it down on the desk and threw four extra-strength pills in his mouth. Picking up the water, he tossed them back, feeling the Tylenol roll down his throat, striking the sides like pinballs on the way down. The water sluiced on down his throat, room temperature but a little like heaven, honestly.

He set the water down on the desk, a few sips left. "Thanks," he said again. He knew it'd be a while before it started to work, but there was a psychological effect of relief he felt like he was receiving already.

Pike leaned over the desk and picked up the Tylenol bottle. "Isn't it amazing?" He brandished the bottle.

Reeve just sort of waited, wondering where the hell he was going with this. "It's a bottle of pills."

Pike grinned. "This was something that they couldn't have comprehended a couple hundred years ago. The modern pharmaceutical industry, I mean."

"They also would have had some trouble understanding indoor toilets," Reeve said. What the hell was wrong with this asshole?

Pike just grinned bigger, and raised his index finger, wagging it. "See, there's this failure among us modern folk to really appreciate progress. Because we've always known things to be this way, we don't appreciate something as small as Tylenol for the miracle it is. If you went back in time just a few hundred years and asked people about the nature of matter, about the universe, science—the answers you'd get would convince you that these people were all primitive idiots— even the ones that were the most brilliant of their time, titans that helped change the world." He was still grinning like a fucking idiot, and Reeve felt it best to just let him go on. "I like to remember that whenever I get to feeling too smug—" *That must be all the goddamned time then,* thought Reeve "—because I figure in a few hundred years, if humanity survives, we'll be the same kind of ignorant, unknowing idiots to our descendants." He tapped the side of his head. "The benefit of perspective."

Reeve just sat there uncomfortably, praying for the Tylenol to work and for Pike to shut the fuck up, and he wondered if he'd see either of those happen in the short-term. He kind of doubted it. "Well, that's an interesting way to think of things," he said, trying for diplomacy and a little too pained in the skull to give a fuck if he missed the mark wide.

"You don't agree?" Pike templed his fingertips together and leaned back at his desk.

Reeve tried to string a couple thoughts together to avoid sounding like an idiot when answering. "I don't reckon I give much thought to how I'm going to look a hundred or two hundred years from now when we're sitting here fighting for our lives. Probably the same way primitive man didn't give a shit about vegetarianism or TV repair. It didn't apply to him surviving the day."

Pike chuckled. "You got a point there. You're a man focused on the immediate needs of the town. And that's what makes you so vital to this effort." Pike leaned in, the squeak of his chair like another icepick thrust into Reeve's head. "You've organized the townsfolk against this demon invasion. No one in this county has more credibility than you, which means when you step up and say, 'Hey, there are demons here,' people actually believe you instead of thinking you've gone batshit crazy the way they would if some new deputy were to come in and tell people to cast aside their deeply held beliefs about the way the world works. And make no mistake, that's what we're up against." Pike's eyes seemed to go fuzzy. "Can you imagine the massive gap in our scientific knowledge, not having seen demons coming? They've been here for as long as we have, and we just ... missed them."

Reeve stared at him, concentrating. Pike had gotten on this demon train now, it seemed. He was on it enough to be admitting that they'd been here all along.

This news should have come as a relief, but for some reason, it made the hairs on the back of Reeve's neck stand up. Or maybe that was the headache talking. "I'm glad to hear you say that," Reeve said, trying to temper his response. "It seems to me that they didn't get 'missed.'"

"Oh?" Pike leaned back again. "How's that?"

"We've got accounts of demons going back thousands of years," Reeve said. "The Bible talks about 'em. Probably a few other holy books, though I'll admit my knowledge of ... well, any of 'em, honestly ... is a bit thin. But I did go to Sunday school when I was a kid, and I've gone to church, uh ... maybe a little unenthusiastically over the years, preferring to worship at the TV when the Titans or Vols were on." He forced a smile; surely this limpdick city slicker could understand that. "But it talked about demons. Ancient knowledge, and a head-on confrontation with modern reality. This is the shit we don't believe anymore because it don't fit into our—our 'modern framework.'" Reeve avoided using air quotes, because he didn't feel like he was that kind of a guy. "It's like the death of common sense in favor of pie-in-the-sky unproven theory that sounds nice. I'd be the first to admit that I ain't gonna follow large tracts of the Bible, but ... damn if there ain't some useful things in those pages that hold true to this day. Even an old lapsed Christian like me can see that some of the thoughts they held that seem a little quaint to our modern sensibilities—they weren't rooted in some far-out idea. Some of them were just ... useful observations about how human nature worked, and how best to be a good person."

Pike nodded, face screwed up in thought. "That's an interesting perspective," he said, and Reeve heard, *That's total bullshit, but I don't want to argue with you.*

"I don't reckon any of that's all that helpful in the moment though, is it?" Reeve asked, allowing himself to crack a smile.

Pike's eyes seemed to flicker. "No, you may be right. Maybe ... in our headlong rush into progress, in our eagerness to move forward and make things better, we lost touch with a few fundamental truths, tossed 'em aside to make way for the new order." He looked introspective, and Reeve got the feeling he liked to bloviate like this fairly often. Ought to introduce him to Guthrie; that lady seemed to like to bend an ear and talk philosophy. Pike smiled again. "How's that headache?"

Reeve could feel the strains of it in his skull, still throbbing, radiating outward from a central point like someone had dinged him right in the dead center of the brain with a sledgehammer. "Still feels like my head's in a vice. It takes like forty minutes for these things to work, you know—"

He stopped abruptly, because he'd just noticed something on one of the papers on Pike's desk.

Little dots of red, four or five of them, wet, and spreading through the paper.

He sniffed again, and put a smile back on his face. He was pretty sure he'd tensed, and he tried to put that off. "This headache, I swear," he said, faking it, blinking his eyes, as if that would help.

Blood. There was blood on those pages. Little spots of it, sure. It could have come from a paper cut, except—

He could smell the undertones of blood under the shit and piss stench. That was the thing that set his head to tingling even harder, and Reeve cursed this goddamned headache. If it hadn't been drill-pressing into his skull, he would have picked up on it sooner, that familiar stink, because he knew it from every goddamned crime scene he'd ever been in where they'd had a bleeder, that coppery, metallic, distinctive smell that—now that he was paying attention—shit, it was as obvious as the smug on Pike's face.

Those droplets were not from any paper cut, and that smell of piss and shit wasn't from any kid's accident.

It hit him like the roof had caved in. Someone had died in here, someone had been killed, and they'd done what a dead person did—they bled, they pissed, they shit, and they'd …

He let his gaze drift down, and then coughed, hard, a couple times, and bent over to pretend to be polite.

Fuck. There were dark stains on the cheap blue government carpet, and when he put his foot down he could feel the squish. Someone had soaked the motherfucker, trying to get it to come clean.

Reeve coughed again, and let his hand fall to his chest, then, when his head came up, he let it linger there. "Jesus, I'm sorry," he said, trying to cover his shock with the aftermath of the fake coughing fit. It wasn't that fake; he did feel like he had a frog in his throat after the fire, and it was all scratchy in the back. "Think I must have breathed in enough smoke back there to put the mill to shame."

Pike made a face; the mill did stink. "I don't envy you that."

Reeve let his hand drift down from his chest to his belly, rolling along that right side. If Pike had killed someone here, who would he have—

His secretary. Of course. Mrs. Pike—stiff-assed bitch—no way would she have been caught dead answering phones and fetching water for visitors. He'd met the woman a few times, and she was the kind of—*I'm sorry for the language, Donna*—he thought; couldn't help himself—*cunt* that wouldn't have been caught dead waiting on another person. She was a high and mighty if he'd ever met one. No way she thought her shit smelled like anything other than fresh apple pie—though maybe even that would be a little too middle-America for this—this cunt, and her pussy-ass coward of a husband, who Reeve was suddenly sure had overpowered and murdered his goddamned secretary.

Reeve let his hand rest on the right side of his belly and blinked his eyes again real quick. He grabbed the water cup from the desk with his left hand, downed it in one as he was staring right at Pike, and then, as he swallowed, held it up again. "You mind if I go get a refill?" He was trying to decide which direction the danger was coming from, and he deemed County Administrator Pike, the dickless weasel, the bigger threat than Mrs. Pike, the cunt. It was about 80/20 in his mind, but he didn't want to turn his back on either of them, and if he could get out the door and put both of them in front of him, that'd beat the shit out of where he was sitting now.

"Oh, Darla can—"

"No," Reeve said, shaking his head and trying to clear his throat. "I think I need to—" He gestured with the cup, trying to make a face of pure misery.

Shit, here she came. He could hear her stepping, and he turned to look at her.

A loud thump from behind him jerked his attention back to Pike at the desk, and away from Mrs. Pike—Reeve couldn't help it; he did it on instinct, jerking his pistol at the sound—

Pike had thumped the desk with his palm, and when he saw Reeve draw, his face went fucking white, seeing the Sheriff's gun aimed right at him from the hip. Reeve stared at the man for only a second, saw his hands, both of them on the desk, empty of weapons, and then turned his head—

The thunderous blast of a gun came only a couple feet from his face, and Reeve caught the round right in his forehead as he turned. The bullet came crashing into his skull like a nail driven in, like an icepick crushing its way through, and—strangely—made a lot of the pain disappear as the bullet passed through and blew out the back of his head.

Reeve jerked the trigger of his own gun as he sat there for a second, stunned, the nerves in his hand firing off one last time. County Administrator Pike jerked and the window behind him spiderwebbed with cracks as Reeve slid off the chair and lost sight of them both, his hands useless and his vision blurring around the edges.

Damned if she hadn't cured his headache. Mrs. Pike leered over him, smiling a smile that was a hundred times—a thousand times—as smug as her husband's. Reeve couldn't fully process what he was seeing, but he knew that face, the one standing over him, framed by that blond hair. He knew and he hated it, instinctively, down to the bottom of him. The fact that she was pointing a gun down at him, well, that would have been the icing on the cake, if he'd been able to actually think about what it was he was seeing.

But the world was darkening around him, and Reeve's face squished against the wet carpet. He'd have known the smell was blood, if he hadn't been fading, would have known that some of it was his and some was older, from the last person these two had killed right here in this spot. He was past all that now though, and all he could focus on was the face staring down at him from above as the pain—and his life—receded.

He thought of Donna, for just a second, and then she faded away. He'd see her soon, maybe, if he was lucky. The light was blotted out, darkness rising. He fought to keep his eyes open, but they fought back, winning the struggle.

One last word popped in as he closed his eyes, and that headache went away, along with everything else, forever.

Cunt.

*

"Jesus Fucking Christ, Darla!" Pike was on his feet, holding his ear. Not only had the sound of those fucking gunshots—first hers, blasting a hole in Reeve's head right in front of him, and then his, in response—deafened him, but the sheriff's had taken off a piece of his goddamned ear!

"Don't whine like a little bitch or I'll slap you like one," Darla said, turning her smiling face from Reeve to him. She pursed her lips in fake concern, blood spattering her face from brow to chin. "Pull your hand away from it for a second." He did, grimacing all the while. "You're fine, you big baby."

"Really?" His hand came away bloody, but it wasn't gushing. That was good, right?

"You don't even look like one of those kids that stuck those fucking plates in their earlobe to stretch things out," she said, waving the gun at him illustratively. "It's a little nick. They seem fine with those giant things in theirs, and you'll be fine with this little baby scratch on yours." She shrugged like he hadn't just been fucking shot. "Come on, pussy," she said, slinking over to him and setting the gun on the desk, letting it rattle. She grabbed him by the crotch and ran the thumb along his shaft, hidden beneath the zipper. He felt it move a little. "We've got work to do."

"Uhm, hello, I just got shot." He pointed at his ear, letting off a little steam heat as he spoke. His ears were still ringing pretty fucking fiercely.

"Yeah, I was watching." She nuzzled in on his neck. She had blood on her, all along the side of her body, and his hand found it as she leaned in to him. "But you're gonna be okay, and we've got a ritual to complete." She brought her face up to look at him. "So … get naked, honeybunch." And she gave him a slap on the ass, then grinned, picking her way away from him and over to the closet, which she threw open.

Jenny came tumbling out, stiff as a fucking board, bent in an L shape and a rictus of horror on her face. Her eyes were rolled back in her head, and she was purple. Darla unbuttoned her bloodstained blouse and put it gently on a chair in the corner of the office, one of the only places that wasn't covered in blood. She then stooped down and rubbed her hand along the back of Jenny's head, coming up with it smeared in blood. She undid her bra with the hand that wasn't bloody, and Pike admired that she could do it so easily; he still fumbled that motherfucking latch to the honey jugs every goddamned time he tried. Darla tossed that off too, her tits swinging free, unbound and unconstricted, and she let out a long breath before rubbing Jenny's blood across her nipples, which were already erect.

She dotted her chest with red and then turned to favor him with a look. "Chop chop, hon," she said, false sweetly, "we don't have all day. The babysitter's waiting and we have a dark, sexy ritual to perform." She smiled at him, impish in a way that he didn't feel right now, standing in a room with two corpses and watching his wife strip.

His dick didn't exactly thrill to this environment. For fuck's sake … there were corpses in here. And he'd just gotten his rocks off with both Jenny and Darla in succession. She was the one running this show, and he didn't want to tell her how to conduct her business or anything, but he had his doubts he was going to be able to perform in this instance, even if he hadn't already been fucking wrung out.

But Darla was stepping out of her pants, as she folded them over the back of the chair. She was muttering under her breath, too, as she smeared more of Jenny's blood on her belly, then picked her way over to where Reeve lay, almost facedown, pointed headfirst toward the door. Pike would have figured he'd have fallen backward, but no, he'd actually taken a nosedive toward Darla after she shot him, like the bullet passing through his head didn't push him back hardly at all. She was stepping out of her panties now, that folded ring of flesh he called her muffin top being drenched with blood as she covered the belly overhang above her pubic region with Reeve's blood.

"Blood of a righteous man," she said under her breath, then looked at him. "Blood of my lover's lover." She glanced back at Jenny with a contemptuous little smile. She smeared her thighs with Reeve's crimson lifeblood, then stood, and clapped her hands together. "Come on, sailor, get out of those fucking pants and get red."

Pike didn't normally consider himself squeamish, but in this case, he was willing to take his time and cop to it. "I don't know how much luck I'm gonna have here." He vaguely thrust out his pelvis as he took off his shirt. "I mean, I think you drained me pretty good earlier."

She rolled her eyes as he stepped out of his shoes and unzipped his own pants, letting them fall behind the desk. He felt chilly standing there in his boxers and socks, but his wife was in less. "You know, most of the time, I admire the fact that you sort of let me steer the ship. It's refreshing to be with a man who's not so focused on himself that he can't get out of his own way when I want to shove a hand up your ass and work you like my own personal puppet." She was working her way around the desk, and she had a look of pure intensity.

"It's nice that we've evolved as a society," Darla went on, "to the point where I can lead us in this endeavor, and know that you're following me. That I'm not worrying about who's wearing the pants, because we're on the same page, and mutually supportive, and all that other happy bullshit." She sidled up to him and yanked his boxers down with one hand, sending them to his ankles. She reached out for him with her wet hand and smeared his ass with blood, both Jenny's and Reeve's, and pulled him close, kissing him with a fervor that made him worry that she might bite his lip and then, possibly, just chew it off. Instead, she broke away. "I like that you're secure in your masculinity." She rubbed that bloody hand on his chest. "That you know I'm the brains of this operation, and that the only reason you're up front is because the misogyny of this world would never let me lead here, in this shithole Southern dump of a town, where we have to be." She brought her bloody hand down, leaving a trail from his chest to his belly to ... lower. "But every once in a while," she said, leaning in and whispering, as she started to sink to her knees, "I wish you would just take charge and be a fucking man in the old way. Just get shit done." She gripped his balls and squeezed them, lightly but enough that he felt it, and then she put his dick in her mouth, her lips running over the tip and then swallowing him all the way to the back of her throat, before pulling him out again before looking up at him with blazing eyes. "Every once in a while, I just want you to lead,

Jason." Her eyes were burning, and she sucked him again. "Now, don't you dare fucking cum in my mouth, or there's going to be three bodies on the floor here." And she went to work.

"I'll let you know when I get close," he said, already hardening in spite of the fact he was smeared with blood and standing in his office, getting a hummer from his wife while surrounded by two corpses, one fresh and one getting pretty sour now. He just closed his eyes and blotted it out, opening them every once in a while to look down at his wife, smeared in the blood of their enemy and his last girlfriend as she moved his cock in and out of her mouth to warm him up. She gripped him by the ass, and started to put a finger up there. He didn't cringe as she smoothed it down inside him, working the prostate and giving his erection a little extra oomph as it unfurled.

Once he was good and hard he beckoned her up, and, taking her advice, bent her over the desk like he'd bent Jenny. She sighed in pleasure as he entered her, already wet with anticipation, and he started sliding in and out. He came quickly, before she'd really had a chance to get close herself. Normally, this might have bothered him, and she'd have cussed a blue streak at him for failing to get the job done.

Here, though, she just stayed bent over as he felt his dick sting with overuse. She'd had to practically force him to get a hard-on, and then worked him so long in her mouth that he'd almost been over the top when he'd entered her. He was just lucky she hadn't gotten too wet or too excited, because then he might not have got off at all.

Pike lay there, gasping, pressed with his pubic bone against a woman's ass for the second time this afternoon as she lay draped over the surface of his desk. Darla's mouth was open and a little drool trail had fallen out across the papers they'd scattered to cover up the blood. Darla had her head sideways, blond hair fallen all down her neck and partly obscuring her face, but he could see the tight line of her mouth and one of her eyes, just staring at the open closet, where Jenny had come tumbling out.

"Whatcha thinking?" Pike asked, leaning over on her. He could smell the sweat, the sex, her ass right there in front of him. Her anus was puckered tight, tighter than his probably was right now.

"Just burying my disappointment," she said, stroking her own hair back behind her ear. "Whatever. At least you came, which—surprise, this fucking ancient ritual is misogynist too—was the point, I guess."

What did you say to that? "Yeah," he said, kinda shrugging. He just stayed there, because she wasn't pushing him and wasn't standing up yet.

"I heard what you two were talking about," Darla said, face still against the desk. She arched her back enough to get up on her elbows. "Reeve bought into that ancient wisdom bullshit, it sounded like."

"Seems like," Pike said.

She spat on the desk—actually spat, right over the edge of his desk and at Reeve's corpse. She hit it too, dead center on the back, staining his khaki uniform in one of the few places where blood hadn't already done the job. "Fucking dinosaur. We're going to sweep your bullshit away, you pig. You probably kept your wife at home like a caged bird, afraid to let her out while you were fucking around with anything that moved. Fuck you to fucking death. I'm not sorry I blew your goddamned caveman brains out, I'm only sorry I didn't do it forty years ago so your wife could have had a fucking life without you heaving over her like a dead weight while you were trying to fill her with your backward ass seed so she could be a goddamned baby factory for you and nothing else."

Darla was breathing heavier now, like she had gotten her rocks off even though she plainly hadn't. Or maybe because she hadn't, he thought. He waited a second, then said, "You done?"

She stirred, bare ass brushing against his pubis, sticky from the sweat, the scent of her sex, well used this afternoon, wafting up at him. He found it distasteful now that the deed was done, like he never needed to smell pussy again. That'd change, of course, as it always did, but for now ... he'd be glad to get clean and into fresh clothes.

"Yeah, I'm done," she said, letting her head sag back down onto the table. She reached back and shoved him so that he exited her, and he grimaced at the sting. She was dry, now, and it was like raking his cock across the desert sands. "Get the fucking book and let's finish this," she said, standing up. She was drenched with drying blood. "I want to get this over with so we can set this goddamned building—and that fucking fossil over there—" she pointed right at Reeve's corpse "—on fire." Darla adopted a sneer so fearful Pike took a step back. "Let's burn this place to the ground, Jason." She didn't look at him, preferring instead to keep staring at her handiwork, the dead sheriff, facing toward the empty receptionist desk. "Let's burn this building down, then burn down the goddamned town, and then—" Now she did turn on him, and the furious sneer she wore just about chilled his blood as cold as the two corpses in the room. "Let's burn the whole fucking world." And she meant it, too.

*

When the ritual was done, Pike felt a rushing sense of relief that he hadn't felt when he got his rocks off. Darla had even smiled, something he'd wondered about her doing, since she seemed mad enough when she missed her orgasm that he'd been real hesitant to go looking for trouble by opening his mouth around her.

"That's blood and sex magic," Darla said, belly damp where she'd ripped down the curtains from his office and soaked 'em in the sink, wiping them over her body to clean up the blood. She'd just about got it all now, a little here and there staining the white skin, a little seeped into her stretch marks, working their way into those little ditches like runoff after a storm. She smiled darkly. "That's the good stuff."

"You know, after we burn this place down—" and he pointed straight up at the ceiling "—where am I supposed to work during the days?"

Darla got a nasty smile. "Don't you want to work at home, with our little monsters running around all day?"

Pike felt like he'd been struck by a runaway train, even though he knew she was joking. "Not particularly, no."

Darla let out an ugly laugh. "I think you're going to have bigger things to worry about soon enough, don't you?"

Pike eyed her. "Like what?"

"I think you should kill the whole damned fire department next," she said, buttoning her blouse. "Every last one of them, if you can, or at least enough so they can't operate their engine." She was focused on her blouse, talking casually. "You take them out, and suddenly there's a lot more chaos, especially if other counties follow the Fed and State lead of ignoring the fuck out of Calhoun County's demon problem." She looked up at him. "When this thing comes down, it's gonna mostly fall on Midian anyway. The sooner we isolate them, the sooner we can kickstart the finale here and just get Midian burned to the ground—maybe literally."

"This might not stop at the outskirts of Midian," Pike said. "I mean, what we're talking about here—this hotspot—it could go bigger. A lot bigger. Maybe the whole county."

"Who gives a fuck?" She stopped midway through pulling up her pants and favored him with a look that probably reflected how stupid she thought he was being at present. "I don't even like it here. I don't like these fucking backward people. They're all, 'Bless your heart—'" she made an ugly face, stretching her lips downward and wide, sticking her tongue out "—and pretending to worry about you. And they said to me, this one cunt down at the coffee shop in Culver, 'Oh, the people are so much nicer down here.' Bullshit. Fakeass nice. It's not really nice to point out how nice you are, fucking assholes." She looked right at him. "This place is just a way station for us. Let's get what we came for, the blessings of—well, you know—all we can, okay? Every bit of lower-realm favor we can walk out of here with. Let's stockpile it. Then we go home." She fastened and zipped her pants, then took a couple steps back to sit in the chair while she put on her socks.

"Yeah, all right," Pike said. He was just about done dressing in clean clothes too. Good thing Darla had brought fresh ones. Always thinking ahead, that woman. "We're going to have to call 911 eventually once we light this place up. The fire truck was just a few miles down the road earlier, so ... we probably ought to wait a little bit for it to get all the way going."

"We'll fake having passed out just outside the entrance in the lobby. Lie down on the ground there and just wait a little while before we make the call, in case anyone passes by." Her eyes were darting as she slipped on her shoes. "We'll need to really make sure we get things going hard, though."

"The county records room should be where we start it then," he said, nodding. "Lots of paper. I think they used to use carbon paper, and that goes up quick. We hit the old records, light a few filing cabinets. Douse the place good ... let it spread a little." He considered for a second. "We can kill the sprinkler system too. Turn off the water main. They'll never find that, especially if, uh ... Marty Ferrell happens to go missing at some point in the next week or so."

She grinned at him, standing. "Now you're thinking. I'll get the gas cans."

"You didn't buy 'em just this afternoon, did you?" he asked, that nervous thought occurring.

"No, I loaded up a couple weeks ago, before this all started," she said. "Back when we knew it was coming. Figured we might need to do a fire ritual, but I didn't want to worry about having a gas can purchase and fill-up fresh in anyone's mind." She made another sour face. "And I damned sure didn't want to have to drive anywhere else to do it. I mean, fuck's sake, this place is so goddamned far from anything."

"Well, we ain't going to be here much longer," he said, and a shadow crossed her face. "What?"

"Ain't 'ain't' a word," she said. "Start speaking properly again, for fuck's sake. You sound like one of these goddamned backwoods hicks."

"Yeah, I'll work on that," he said, "right after we burn up these bodies of people we killed and call the authorities, knowing that they hopefully ain't going to even realize there was a crime, let alone prove it was us." He gave it some thought. "How do you want to handle Ferrell?"

"I don't really know him very well. Do you?" Darla asked.

"Well enough," Pike said. "He's the kind of guy that'd help anybody he could."

"Find out when he gets off shift," Darla said, eyes moving like she was thinking rapidly. "I've got a babysitter for as long as I need tonight. Provided he gets off before midnight, I'll park my car on the path this guy would take home, pretend I'm stuck. If he's an actual nice guy—" she made a nasty inference there "—he'll stop and help me." She smiled slowly. "I'll make sure to put the body somewhere it won't be found before the demons get to it."

"And you don't want my help on that?" he asked.

"I might, depending on what you're doing," she said. "But I can handle it myself, if I have to." She picked her way around Reeve's corpse, still splayed on the floor. "If you're still here, dealing with the fallout, I'll take care of it myself. If you're not ... we'll get him together."

"Whew, that's an exciting date night," Pike said.

"Yeah, I wish there was time to use him as a sacrifice too," Darla said, with actual regret. "But I don't want to chance it with something this potentially dicey. I'll shoot him in the head like I did Reeve, and quickly, while his back's turned." She nodded once, like it was decided. "If there's anything I can work into before or after ... well, I'll see. But the important thing is to cover our tracks and make it look like a demon did it."

"Okay," he said, and leaned in to give her a peck on the lips. She accepted it coolly, and then they parted, her looking around the room significantly. Enough time had elapsed; it was about time for them to get to work. "All right, let's light it up and make the call."

*

Erin was sitting at the desk in the cell bank, head resting on her hand. She'd taken over for Bernie Stout, and was now just outside the door of the unspeaking man, Mr. Voiceless, browsing her phone while she waited. Who was supposed to take over here? Bernie had told her, but she'd already forgotten. Reeve would be back before too long, and if the pattern held, he'd come do a quick inspection of the station, and she'd ask him when he passed through. He wouldn't really give a fuck about the prisoner, but he'd make a show of it.

She'd seen the look in his eyes whenever he passed this way; it was mere formality. Every time he looked in the cage-like window at the man housed behind her, she knew what he saw.

The death of everything he'd ever loved.

That bothered her on a few levels, the nearest one being that she'd had some of the demons in her head for a while too, just like the fella in the confinement behind her had. The only difference was time, and that she hadn't done a hack and slash on Donna Reeve. If she'd been in on that …

Well, odds were good the sheriff would be looking at her—or avoiding looking at her—just the same as he was this guy.

She sniffed the musty air in this part of the jail. They were caught somewhere between turning the heat on, with its dry, hot stink, and the air conditioner. This was the part of autumn where things hit an unpredictable in-between. Sometimes you'd start the morning with the heat on and move to the AC in the afternoon. This being November, they were more or less past that, but every once in a while, like today, a warm afternoon would sneak in on them. She might have enjoyed it if she hadn't been sitting outside the jail cells, watching a man who didn't really move to make sure he didn't escape.

Not that she was actually watching him. She was half-reading a gossip site on her phone and wondering why she should give a fuck now about the latest celebrity split. It was the sort of thing she would have loved to read just a few months earlier. Now, though …

Well, there were more important things to do, weren't there?

Someone unlocked the door in front of her and came in; she saw dark hair in the little window, caught a flash of a face.

Brian.

He held the door, like he was waiting for her to get up and come toward her. His face was clouded over; wasn't he supposed to be heading for the hospital soon? That was his pattern, wasn't it?

"What—" she started to ask.

"We got a fire call," Brian said, "out at the County offices. 911."

She flushed and stood. "The sheriff's out there. Was it him—"

Brian shook his head. "It was County Administrator Pike. He said something started the building on fire, said it was burning down—"

"Shit," she said, and went past him in a rush. The sheriff was there, and he hadn't called. That meant—

Fuck.

Her mind sped, trying to get to the logical version of the conclusion her gut had already reached. If the sheriff was still there, and the building was burning, and Pike had been the one to make the call—

Reeve could have been trying to save people. That's the kind of guy he was. He would have delegated Pike to 911 duty, for sure, while he—

But that other possibility tore at her as she burst out into the bullpen and found everybody except Casey already heading for the door. Her phone buzzed, but she didn't look; they'd already called the watch and this was the message.

Because the other explanation ... was that Reeve was still there.

And he was either fighting what caused the fire ...

Or he was dead.

*

Hendricks woke to a buzzing and the realization that he didn't have morning wood, or afternoon wood, as the case might have been. Starling might just have sucked him dry for a while, he realized as he came out of a deep REM sleep, might have left him flaccid for a day or two until his libido recovered. It never tended to last long, but it was interesting to him that it was just sitting there, not fully retracted but not wild and hard, like it would have been if he'd been ready to go again immediately.

Sometimes when he woke up like that, she was already here, in bed. Presumably her alter ego had nothing going on at those times, the early-morning crowd not a thing in the brothel business.

Suited him fine; not that he'd ever caught a hint of Starling being in anything other than mint condition when she'd come to him. Something about the changeover, he reckoned. He wanted to believe it included a total body sterilization. Like someone hosed her off and put a mint air freshener up there before he went to work on her.

Leaving that thought aside, because it wasn't exactly stiffening him, Hendricks rolled over and fetched the phone. He clicked the screen on and got the message: FIRE AT COUNTY OFFICES. SHERIFF REEVE LAST KNOWN WHEREABOUTS AT THAT LOCATION.

"Shit," Hendricks said under his breath. He'd had about enough of fire for this day, but tossing in that last bit got him moving. He stumbled out of bed and started to dress, determined to get the hell out the door in less than five.

After all, Reeve was basically the CO here. And no matter what a butterbars your LT was, you didn't leave his ass to twist, especially when he was one of the competent ones, and especially when it might be a literal fire of someone else's making rather than a figurative, shitstorm-type one of his own.

*

"Check that, would you, Braeden?" Barney Jones asked as they crowded around the kitchen table. Olivia Jones had put on another feast, and Arch had just bitten into a biscuit after they'd finished saying grace when the buzzing had sounded. They left their cell phones on the counter during meals, which on the whole Arch approved of. But with three of them on the watch, it wasn't as complete a break into isolation as it might have been in a normal family, under normal circumstances.

But they weren't normal, were they? Arch thought, chewing that doughy biscuit. He hadn't even buttered it, it was so rich. And they weren't really a family either, other than in the family of Christ.

Tarley nodded and put his napkin down on the table as he got up, taking care not to set it in his gravy. Arch watched the man go, thinking on all they'd been through. No, they weren't a family. Two out of the four of them had lost their families. Had lost them hard. And—

"Motherfucker," Tarley said, face lit by the screen.

"Braeden," Olivia said in the voice of a mother terribly disappointed in her son.

"Sorry, ma'am." Tarley was appropriately chastened for the second it took him to turn around, and then Arch saw it on his face. "Fire at the county offices, and Reeve was heading that way last anyone talked to him—"

"Dadgum," Arch said, mind already moving ahead, making those assumptions. They'd already turned up one of those fire sloths today. Was it really that much of a stretch that a few minutes farther out, another would rear its ugly head?

"Let's adjourn to the car, gentlemen." Jones was already on his feet, kissing Olivia. "Sorry, my dear."

"I'll put your plates away," Olivia promised, "and make sure y'all can heat 'em back up later tonight, when you get home."

"That's mighty kind of you," Braeden said. He was still torn up about swearing in front of Olivia, Arch could tell.

Arch grabbed another biscuit for the road, heading out the door a few steps behind Braeden after pocketing his own phone and seeing that, sure enough, he'd gotten the same message. Barney was the last one out, and the screen door slammed behind him as Arch slid into the back seat of the Buick.

"Shit," Braeden said under his breath as he bent himself into the passenger seat. Arch rolled his eyes; he was upset about swearing in front of the lady of the house, and here he was swearing again. Apparently he didn't possess the hindsight to see that if he stopped the habit of swearing entircly, he wouldn't have had the problem to begin with.

Barney slid in, a little slower than either of his charges, sinking into the seat and then reaching out, leaning hard to shut the door. He started the car without a word, and then backed up out of the driveway at about a hundred miles an hour.

Arch let out a creative word of his own at the speed of the movement, but, as per habit, that word was "Dadgum!"

Jones threw the car into gear and stomped on the accelerator. "When one of your people gets into the soup, you come a-running, even if there's nothing you can do," the old pastor said, not taking his eyes off the road as he explained, very matter-of-factly, why he was driving like he'd never driven before in Arch's experience.

Arch just took that one in; Tarley didn't say nothing either. If it was true, though, and there really was nothing to be done, and they were racing there just to be racing there …

Well, better that they were there and not able to do a thing to help than to be elsewhere, too slow, and unable to help when it was needed.

*

Erin let the sirens scream, let the pedal kiss the metal, kept the squad car floored and ripping along the back roads. She was hitting a hundred, hundred and twenty on straightaways and going eighty into blind corners. Sure, she'd gone off a cliff like this not that long ago, she thought as she swept into a hard turn, feeling the gravity tearing at her, and sure, she'd kill somebody and probably herself in a head-on if she didn't slow the fuck down soon, but …

Dammit, this was Reeve.

The man could be in danger. And help, though coming, was slow. She didn't even know where the fire truck was, though she'd heard somebody say something about it on the squad radio. It had just buzzed right past her, not even registering.

Her hands were on the wheel, white-knuckled, tight against that fakeass leather, and she was two turns away from the County offices in Culver. She was squealing her way around one now, sure that any second now she'd meet some hay truck or something on the curve and that'd be it, she'd be worse off than the time she tumbled down Mt. Horeb's winding roads, but unable to ease her foot off that goddamned accelerator because—

It was Reeve, for fuck's sake.

She iced the last corner at almost ninety, running off the road and fucking up the grass next to the shoulder. She slowed it down in the curve itself, but she'd come into it hard and came out of it hard, in the left lane, relying a little too much on the grip of the cruiser's tires. Back on the pavement once more, she hit the goddamned pedal again, setting the tires squealing.

Culver was lit up ahead, about a hundred lights just shining as night started to descend, but …

The town had faded beneath the black smoke blotting out the purple sky in a steady cloud, and what looked like a massive bonfire going on just up ahead.

Erin eased off finally on the approach, done blistering her way up the highway. It was like seeing the conflagration gave her permission to stop rushing. Or maybe it just stunned her, she realized as she pulled the cruiser into the parking lot, wheeling up, and looking around for—

There was no sign of the bald head shining against the licking flames that were billowing their way out of the flat roof of the county building. Smoke poured out of the second floor windows, like black water rolling upward in defiance of gravity.

She let the cruiser coast into the parking lot, managed to regain her presence of mind and hit the brakes right before she collided with the fire truck, already deployed and just starting to get the hoses going. They'd probably been here a while, but she knew, dimly, that it took some time to charge the hoses and all that. They were starting a stream now, water falling into the black smoke and into the structure itself as Erin put the car in park and stepped out.

The air was thick with smoke, that chemical stink of something other than wood burning. She coughed a couple times, then covered her nose with her upper arm, but that didn't do anything but make her realize she'd either rushed out the door this morning without remembering her deodorant or else it had failed, miserably, after a taxing day.

Erin looked around, and found one thing—County Administrator Pike sitting on the bumper of a car with a blanket wrapped around him, his wife next to him. She was watching the blaze, and as Erin came up, she could see the fire dancing in the woman's eyes, a kind of intensity in the flames that made Erin wonder if she was in there at all.

They both had a little soot caked on their faces, like they'd rubbed charcoal on them. Pike coughed as she approached, and Mrs. Pike blinked her surprise away, locking her eyes on Erin.

Erin didn't have to ask; Pike told her: "Sheriff Reeve—he's still in there." His voice was hoarse, like he'd breathed in a fair amount of smoke.

"Jenny's in there too," Mrs. Pike said, her own voice a little wobbly. When Erin just stared at her, she went on, "Jenny's his administrative assistant."

Erin just stared at her. Nobody called things what they were anymore. She looked at Pike, and he nodded. His secretary was still in there?

She turned back to the blaze, and it was glowing orange in every one of the first floor windows now, fire kicking out from every single one. If the secretary was still in there ... if Reeve was still in there ...

"They're fucking dead," Erin said, as the squeal of tires turned her head, announcing the arrival of Hendricks in his stolen SUV, and, a second later, Barney Jones, Braeden Tarley, and, in the back seat, Arch. She'd have to tell them, she realized, feeling a little cloud settling over her like the black smoke filling the skies was twisting downward to funnel right onto her. She'd have to tell them all.

Sheriff Reeve was fucking dead.

*

Brian was killing time, tapping his fingers against the desk as he sat there in the holding cell area. He didn't want to get up, didn't want to go look at the thing—that empty vessel in the next room that had carried more death to this town than any other demon so far. Staring in there didn't seem like a sound plan, especially since he was still coming down off his high with Casey.

So he sat and tapped his fingers, and found it strangely rewarding. He could have fucked around with his phone, sure, but he'd done that, and staring at a small digital screen for a long time was kinda unappealing when he was lit.

So instead he tapped his fingers, and found it strangely soothing, both in the sensation at the tips and also for the steady cadence and noise it brought, ringing in his senses.

Something buzzed, and Brian sighed. There went the phone. He fished for it, coming up with it and staring at the burning phosphorescent screen, white and bright as the text message came through.

SHERIFF REEVE IS DEAD.

"Holy fuck," he whispered, gut sinking like someone had kicked him in the balls.

Was this for real?

*

Arch had waited around with the others until the fire died down. No one had said much of anything once Erin had gotten out her news, because … what was anyone going to say?

So they'd waited in silence until the fire department had done their work, and the building was barely smoking now. It still stank to high heaven, but there were no embers coming out of the windows like fireflies in the night, and the hoses weren't squirting to their fullest, the streams dying down now.

The first firemen went in a few minutes later, and came out a few more after that. Arch was standing with Marty Ferrell, waiting to see what he'd say.

It didn't take long for Ferrell to make his way over, his grey hair matted down with sweat. Marty was in his late forties, and he had that jaded look that cops tended to pick up after a year or two patrolling. Ferrell split his attention between Arch and Erin, like he was delivering news of a car accident death to a married couple. Arch realized he might have done the same a time or two in his career, and felt mighty strange about it.

"We think we found them," Ferrell said, his mask hanging off.

"I need to see," Erin said.

For just a moment, Ferrell looked like he might argue. But then he shrugged, and said, "The building seems structurally sound, so … okay. You'll need a mask." He nodded at one of his men.

"I'm going too," Arch said, just to eliminate any doubt. The chief nodded.

"Me three," Hendricks said, and the man shed his coat, tossing it to a fireman, who caught it, looking sour at the catch and then, a second later, surprised at the sight of the pistol and the sword on Hendricks's belt. Maybe some of these guys were from Culver, not Midian, and didn't know what had been happening.

It took a few minutes to suit up, and they did this in silence too, except for the occasional acknowledgment of the fireman's commands. Arch had his head in a mask the first of all of them, carrying one of those oxygen tanks on his back, a fireman in close attendance.

"If this goes sideways," Ferrell said, and his expression was plain even though he had his mask back on, "you will follow us and haul your asses out of there. Follow my commands exactly, you understand?"

"Yes," Erin said, and Arch echoed her.

"Yes, Mother," Hendricks said a beat after them.

If Ferrell took umbrage to Hendricks's remark, he didn't let on. Instead he lifted a hand and signaled for them to follow.

The downstairs didn't look anything like what Arch was expecting. He figured the whole place would be gutted by fire, but it wasn't. There was damage, sure, but to his right it looked like the fire hadn't even made it down there. Just an inch of standing water that seemed like it might have washed in during the flood a few months back. Papers were floating, sodden, on top of the waters, and a small desk trash can on its side drifted past in one of the larger puddles.

Black soot clung to every wall, giving the entire place a shading. They made their way through toward the staircase, and passed a bathroom. "Anyone need to piss?" Hendricks muttered, spiking Arch's annoyance. He didn't say anything though.

"Up the stairs, and be careful," Ferrell said, muffled through his mask but talking loud enough to be heard.

They circled up the stairwell, borrowed boots squishing in the wetness and squeaking once they went up a step, leaving the standing water behind. Here, thin smoke still clouded the ceiling, and Arch eyed it nervously. He knew that the big danger in a fire was smoke inhalation, not necessarily being burned to death, and it made him leery of the stuff lingering above.

"This way," Ferrell said, as he pushed through the door at the top of the staircase.

Here, the evidence of a fire was in full flower. Black scorched the walls from the ground up, dark ebony scoring telling Arch that the flames had had their way here. A charred desk in the corner of the room suggested to him that this had maybe been an office, though it was hard to tell in the haze. Water dripped down from the ceiling, catching him on the shoulders and wetting the bright yellow coat he wore over his clothes.

"Jesus," Hendricks breathed.

Erin made no sound, but led the way behind the chief, ash and water splashing underfoot. She turned and he saw a grim look through her plastic mask, the quiet determination that suggested to him she was focused, taking in everything or maybe almost nothing—excluding anything from her sight that didn't fit what she was looking for.

"Over here," Ferrell said, waving them over. They went on through a room that had the same black scorching as the walls. It was obvious this was where the fire had been at the hottest, and Arch could see clear through to the sky above. "This old building was made out of cinder block and the subfloor's pretty strong, but … better we don't linger here too much, okay?"

Erin stopped in the door, Arch a step behind her. He could see over her just fine, so he didn't need to ask why she stopped.

There was a body in the floor in front of another burned-out desk. It looked like it had gotten the worst of the fire, scorched and charred, almost kneeling like it was praying.

"Shit," Erin breathed, and a second later, he saw it. He saw quite a lot, actually, but this …

A piece of metal hanging from the body, a six-point star reduced to slag that hung, deformed, from the blackened remainder of clothing on the left breast. It was no longer readable, but based on where it was located on the body, Arch had no doubts …

That was a sheriff's badge.

This was Sheriff Nicholas Reeve.

"Fuck," Hendricks breathed behind him. They were all whispering like they were treading on holy ground.

The face was no longer recognizable as such. Arch had seen folks die in a fire before, and sometimes they even came out of it looking like nothing had happened.

This was not the case here.

Reeve's face was gone, black and charred, not a square inch of visible skin that didn't carry a thick layer of carbon, the face and skull charred beyond recognition.

Erin finally moved, turning, pushing past Arch, on her way out. "Move," she said, sounding like she had gravel in her throat.

"There's another body in here," Ferrell said, and Arch turned back to deal with him as Erin bustled past. Hendricks hesitated, then Arch heard him turn his heel and splash off after her, a little slower.

"I'll take a look," Arch said, and he did, stepping into the room. It might once have been a sunny office, but now he was afforded a view of the trees outside, not seeing a heck of a lot except the smoke oozing its way out. There was another body, sure enough, and he gave it a quick look. It was a little smaller than the one before, and he nodded once he'd given it the once-over. "Probably the secretary."

"That's my guess," Ferrell said with a nod, face blurred by the mask.
"You got a guess on how this came to happen?" Arch asked, trying to picture the scene in his mind. He hadn't quite run across anything this bad.
"Fire started down the hall—I think," Ferrell said. "Old records room, highly combustible. Can't say for sure how it happened, just that it spread quickly." He hesitated. "I need to look around more before I make a judgment. But anyway, looks like these two were maybe overwhelmed. By the time they got warning about the fire, it was already blocking the stairs." He shrugged under the fire coat. "That's all speculation, of course."
"The sprinklers didn't work?" Arch asked.
"Apparently not," Ferrell said. "It's an old building, but ..." He shook his head. "We'll take a closer look."
"Shouldn't the fire alarms have warned them about this?" Hendricks spoke from behind him, and Arch turned in surprise to see the cowboy standing there, hatless, coatless, watching intently beneath the mask. "You know, before it trapped them and burned them alive."
"You'd think," Ferrell said, tension betraying him. "Like I said, I need to look around more."
"Could have been a fire sloth," Arch said. "Maybe shot a blaze right in here."
"He just said it started in the records room," Hendricks said.
"I said I think it did," Ferrell said. "I need to actually investigate. It could have started in multiple places for all I know. One of those things y'all killed, breathing in the window? That'd explain how it lit up so fast, because that fire it used down at Whistling Pines? Was damned hot."
"'Damned hot' is the right way to describe it," Hendricks said dryly. And then he turned and headed on out.
"You let us know when you figure it out, okay?" Arch asked, taking one last look at the corpse, burned like it was praying, right there in front of the remains of the desk.
He turned away from the bizarre tableau, thinking he might ought to do some praying of his own, post-haste. Beyond that ...
Sheriff Reeve was dead.
Arch tried to come to grips with that reality on his way down the stairs. He still hadn't, even when he took off the mask out in the parking lot, and breathed in a long breath of smoky night air.

*

Erin was struggling with what she'd seen inside. She knew what it was she'd seen, but her gut didn't want to believe it. It felt like one of those times when you looked in the mirror and didn't quite recognize the face looking back at you. Dazed, she shed her fire coat and mask, handing them off numbly to a fireman who took them, unspeaking, and wandered across the parking lot.

"Yo," Guthrie's voice reached out to her, like a beacon in the dark, and Erin found herself drawn toward the demon. Duncan was standing next to Guthrie, the two of them just waiting, like they'd gotten the message and come running—

Of course they had. That was what they did.

This was what the watch did.

Erin's legs were numb and carried her over, her head down, dully staring at the webwork of hoses that crisscrossed the dark parking lot. She was staring at the individual pebbles, then lifted her eyes again. Guthrie was nearly inscrutable, severe, but Duncan—

Duncan knew.

He wasn't looking up anymore, he was staring at his own feet in those whiter than white, perfectly gleaming tennis shoes. When had he even found time to get a new pair of shoes?

"You look like someone kicked you in the jimmies," Guthrie said as she got closer. "Or the ovaries, I guess." She traded a look with Duncan, who was glaring at her. "What?"

"Who else showed up?" Erin asked, looking around the parking lot. Other than the fire department volunteers, it didn't look like many in the watch were here.

"I don't know—" Guthrie started to say.

"We're it," Duncan said, "for now."

The chill autumn air prickled at Erin's skin. Dusk was settling heavy on this place. It was suppertime, and she glanced over to her right. The Pikes were standing there, still wearing their heavy emergency blankets. Braeden Tarley and Barney Jones were standing off from them a little ways, Jones watching her.

Erin picked her way over, Guthrie and Duncan trailing along in her wake a little ways back. When she got close, Mrs. Pike—damned if Erin could remember her name, in spite of having met the spiteful cunt a few times—looked up at her. There was no flash of recognition, but there was a flash. She elbowed her husband, and County Administrator Pike got up on his feet, trying to look solicitous as he did so, she reckoned.

"Hey there, deputy," Pike said, voice all scratchy and low. Smoke inhalation, she figured. "Did you find—"

"We found him," she said, with a simple nod. "Sheriff Reeve is dead. The other woman who was in there—"

"Oh, God, no," Pike said, slumping back down onto the bumper of the car as his wife placed a hand on his back, rubbing it soothingly. "Jenny."

"This is so terrible," Mrs. Pike said, a little flatly for Erin's taste. She bore a big cut on her left hand, an open wound that was bleeding slightly.

"Yeah." Erin didn't know what to say other than that. "Can you tell us what happened?"

There was a scrape of a foot behind them, and Erin turned to see Arch and Hendricks making their way over, Hendricks slipping back into his coat, the hat already back on his head. Arch had a dulled look, no surprise there, and neither of them acknowledged anyone in this rapidly forming little circle, just hung at the edge, listening to the Pikes.

"Something came out of the woods," Mr. Pike said, giving a thousand-yard stare at the ground and shaking his head slowly. "All I saw was fire come blazing in the window. I jumped and ducked, but … it was everywhere."

"I grabbed him by the collar and we crawled," Mrs. Pike said, as she looked into Erin's eyes. "On the ground, as fast as we could."

"She just hung on to me the whole way," Pike said, looking at his wife with those glazed eyes. "If it hadn't been for you …" He kissed her on the cheek, a wet smack in the growing darkness. Then he looked at the building and shuddered.

"So no one else made it out alive?" Mrs. Pike's lip trembled.

"I'm afraid not," Erin said, feeling like the fire had burned out her insides, like it had scorched through the dead underbrush in her soul, and everything had just washed it away in the flames. There was nothing left now, not even the professionalism it took to remember what questions she should ask here, nor the sense to get some distance from it so she could recall.

All she could think of was that damned giant flaming sloth thing this afternoon, and how shit-tacular it was that now there was another one of them, a mate, maybe, all pissed off that its other half was dead. She glanced in the direction of Culver. Lucky it hadn't decided to go on a rage through town, because that would have been a catastrophe.

"Thank you so much for your help," Erin said dully, then looked at Arch. "You got anything you want to ask?"

Arch just stared, like he'd put on the spot. "I can't think of anythin—"

"What were you talking to Sheriff Reeve about?" Hendricks asked, shoving his dick right into this. The brim of his hat was down, head cocked, and she could just barely see his eyes as he stared fiercely at the Pikes.

"I was going to talk to him about budgetary issues," Pike said. "About getting y'all in the watch paid."

Hendricks just stared at him, like he was a duelist on a Wild West street. "Is that so?" There was something real hard about the way he said it, and his hand was lingering a little too near to his Colt—

"Come on, Hendricks," she said, bumping up against him as she turned to leave.

"I got questions—" Hendricks started to say.

"You're not a deputy," she said, just as fiery. If he wanted to have a pissing contest right here, she'd drop trou and water the ashes at the back of the building with him. She was feeling so full of pressure right now, she would win in a heartbeat, she knew that much. He wasn't going to be his dick self right now.

Not in her county.

A little flame lit in his eyes and he looked right at her. "That's how it is, huh?"

She stared cool as ice back, frosty as the coming winter. "That's how it is. Let's leave these nice folks alone. They've had a trying day."

He looked like he might whip it out and give a spray right here, but then it was like he visibly disengaged from the process, turning away, long black coat rippling dramatically behind him as he stalked off across the parking lot toward his vehicle.

"Were he and Sheriff Reeve tight?" Mrs. Pike asked as Hendricks got in his car and started it, headlamps flaring. He backed out of the parking lot onto the road and gunned it, squealing tires as he pointed the car toward Midian and raced off.

"Not particularly, no," Arch said.

"As far as I know," Erin said, staring after him, "they didn't really get along at all." She shook her head. "He's just got a burr up his ass." She motioned to Arch, and the two of them sauntered back toward where Barney Jones and Braeden Tarley were waiting, not far away. Guthrie and Duncan trailed in their wake, joining the little circle in the parking lot once they'd come to a halt.

"Did you find the body? Do we know for sure he's dead?" Jones asked in a low, hushed voice. Respect for the dead. That was novel, Erin thought, compared to Hendricks's fly-off-the-handle-at-everything reaction.

"Yes," Erin said, when Arch didn't answer for her. "We …" The next words came to her naturally, like someone had handed them right to her. "We need to get the watch together. All hands. They need to know."

*

Lauren was about ready to call this one a day. Not a great day, obviously, because they didn't really have great days anymore, not since the demons had come and treated her life like a metaphorical Hummel cabinet and sent everything crashing to about a million pieces. But she lived in hope that each day would at least fall into the category of "marginal," or maybe even "not totally shit." Lauren figured modest goals were best for now.

Molly had not said a word to her all evening and was avoiding any room she was in. Elise was still out, probably sitting at one of those fancy restaurants for dinner now, eating a buffalo wing lollipop or pork belly bao bun or whatever the hell the present fancy culinary trend was, and talking about awesome shoes and awesome living with her similarly unattached friends before going to a concert and listening to cool new artists perform in small venues where you could almost reach out and touch them.

"Marginal," Lauren reminded herself. Modest expectations. Maybe try not to be jealous of her high-flying single friends who hadn't had children in their teenage years—or had their hometowns invaded by demons in their thirties.

Lauren was slowly getting ready for bed. Flossing was the chore it always was, and brushing her teeth was a lot less easy since she left her sonic toothbrush behind when she refused to actually ever go home again after her mother was murdered in front of her eyes in the bathroom. It probably had blood on it anyway, but …

She missed her toothbrush now. It was a symbol of everything that had been ripped away from her, she thought, as she stood in front of the mirror, the familiar, soothing hum of the toothbrush no longer there.

Kind of like how Midian wasn't there for her now. She drove the streets of Chattanooga and everything felt …

Well, not like home.

Unfamiliar. Cold, even. Which was sad, because she'd been coming to Chattanooga her whole life and always thought it was cool and fun and exciting. She would have loved to live in Chattanooga at almost any point in her life.

Until now.

Now she wanted to live somewhere she couldn't live.

The dull bristles scratched against her teeth. God, this was so much work compared to the sonic toothbrush. Sure, it sounded like an angry Waterpik rampaging across her teeth, but it was her angry Waterpik, and it was a piece of home. She looked around Elise's guest bathroom. Everything was so finely appointed, so beautiful and artisanal and gorgeous and thoughtfully done. There was even a wooden carving of Tennessee with a heart where Chattanooga was, hanging above the toilet. It said "Home" above the heart, and it was so cute that Lauren thought she might die of diabetic shock right there.

The heart was in the wrong place, she reflected grimly.

She'd stopped brushing, and without a sonic toothbrush, this was a problem because now the damned bristles weren't doing anything for her. She started brushing again, and spat, and called it quits. Brushing her teeth was not going to get her full attention. Not tonight.

Lauren sighed, and headed over to the toilet, dropped her soft cotton pajama bottoms and did what she had to do. She wasn't staring in the mirror anymore, but she knew she wore a grim look, filled with sad from front to back. There was no papering over how she felt. She'd been forced from her home, and now she was bunking with a friend, and her daughter flat-out hated her—

"Mom." A soft knocking came at the door, and Lauren scrambled for her panties and pajama bottoms.

"Uh, just a sec," Lauren said. She hadn't even realized she'd been crying, softly, on the toilet. How pathetic could pathetic get? Was there a natural bottom? "I'm just—" She pulled her pants up and hit the flush button (there was an actual button on the back of the tank, with one inset for pee, and one for … larger items. How eco-cool was that?). "I'm—coming—"

Molly was coming to talk to her! For the first time in what felt like decades. She almost tripped on the tile floor trying to get her pants up as she scrambled to—

Lauren unlocked the door and opened it to find Molly standing there, phone in hand, a look on her face somewhere between disgusted and … something else.

"Mom …"

Lauren felt the floor fall out from below her stomach. Something bad had happened, she could just tell. Someone had died. There was no doubt in her mind by the look on her daughter's face. She managed to squeeze out one word, shocked, like she was pushing out a bomb: "Who?"

Molly's lip wobbled, but she managed to get it out. "Sheriff Reeve." She sniffled, and the first tear ran out of her left eye, tracing a course down her cheek. "He's dead."

*

Pike watched the little meeting after they'd all shuffled across the parking lot, trying to keep that traumatized look on his face, the dusky sky overhead like a purple neon shining down on them. He stayed silent until they were out of earshot to not chance anyone overhearing. Darla rubbed her hand up and down his back, like he was a good dog.

He didn't look at her as he spoke. "I think we did it. I think by killing Reeve—we fucking got 'em."

She waited a long few seconds to reply, but when she did, she sounded as satisfied as if he'd given her the biggest orgasm she'd ever had instead of petering out last time. "Oh, yeah," she breathed, deep and throaty, but low so no one else could hear. "We got 'em."

*

Erin trudged into the sheriff's station about an hour later. The sun was gone, sundown coming on quick with autumn's arrival, so unlike those long, lazy summer days when it had been hesitant to go. Now it fled quickly; here's your hat, what's your hurry? And was already gone even though it was barely six o'clock.

"Can you believe Thanksgiving is only a couple weeks out?" Casey Meacham was saying. The bullpen had a smoky smell to it, Erin realized as she came in. They'd sent out a text message to assemble as much of the watch as could come, and here it was, what they had of it. Her eyes flitted over the counter that separated the waiting area from the beating heart of the station's operations—there wasn't a lot of room, so the counter was all the separation there was—and saw the people haphazardly arrayed about. Brian was in place as dispatch, head down. Meacham didn't seem too fussed, and Father Nguyen was pretty stoic. McMinn and Drumlin were there too. They were both wearing their reflective vests from the plant, their hair mussed from wearing safety helmets.

The scene was a study in human misery, everyone up their own asses in thought. Erin wrinkled her nose as she passed behind the counter; she'd beaten the others back from Culver because she'd put pedal to metal and given zero fucks about speed limits or other bullshit. She'd needed to clear her head.

Hadn't worked.

"Erin," Nate McMinn said, looking up. He had a hangdog look, that motherfucker, kinda shy until you got to know him. "What happened?"

Erin took a breath, caught that smoky aroma in the air again. Was that weed, or the smoke that was left on her own clothes? Didn't matter. "We think another one of those fire sloths must have hit the county offices," she said, voice about as subdued as could be without shooting a needle full of heroin right into her arm. At least that'd dull the shit out of the pain that was running through her right now like a forest fire, burning up everything of substance within. It had felt hotter a little while ago. Now she just felt hollow, like her feelings really had room to echo around. Almost numb.

Father Nguyen did one of those long, slow shakes of his head. "A real tragedy."

The bell above the door jangled behind her. "Fucking right it's a tragedy," Hendricks said, coming in. His cowboy boots rang on the old white tile floor like he'd come in shooting. His head was down and he looked steaming pissed, hat brim hiding his eyes as he cruised along, like a shark cutting through the waters. "What are we gonna do about it?"

That produced a moment of silence, and not the honorable, thoughtful kind. "Well, what the hell do you think we should do about it?" Erin asked, drenching the question—unintentionally—in sarcasm. She didn't actually care what he thought, or if she did, it was buried under a six-layer cake of bitter fucking pissiness of the sort that Hendricks seemed to both inspire and use himself.

"I think we ought to go right after the motherfucker who did this," Hendricks said. "We go find this fire sloth, if that's what did it, and tear that motherfucker up."

That produced another moment of silence, and Erin, of course, found herself speaking up again. "This isn't the only problem we've got, Hendricks. There's still a goddamned pack of those shadow cats out there, the ones that wrecked Mary Wrightson's house—"

"Hey, where is Grandma, anyway?" Hendricks looked around. "She disappear as soon as Arch put his pants back on or what?"

"She went home with her son," Brian said. "She asked Benny to put her boy on the text list." He shrugged. "Guess she got a taste for fighting, but I assume she must have been tired or watching *Wheel of Fortune* or something when the call went out tonight, cuz ..." He swept an arm around the place. "Of course, people are still dragging in."

STARLING

The bell jingled again, and Erin turned. Guthrie and Duncan were next to enter, the stately black lady whistling like she didn't give a fuck and Duncan a notch more subdued than usual. "These are some sad sack motherfuckers," Guthrie pronounced, really leaning into the accent and almost making a joke of it.

"Hey, show some respect for the dead," Nguyen said, the little priest coming to life, frown heavy on his forehead and weighing down the corners of his mouth.

"If I did that," Guthrie said, "I'd never get a chance to be flippant, because you people are dying all the time."

"There are an awful lot of us dying lately," Keith Drumlin said, his voice just dead. His eyes were fixed, staring at the floor.

"There are a lot of you fleshy bags of farts dying every day," Guthrie said, sidling up to the counter and plopping down her elbows. "I don't hear you crying about it most of the time; just when it comes geographically close to you. You know why that is?" No one answered, either because they were too surprised to, or because no one had rallied the rudeness to shut down the rudest motherfucker of all, standing right in their midst. "Because your brains are programmed tribally. If it's too far outside your little circle of trust …" She mimed a head exploding motion, even making a "Tschhhh!" sound.

"Bullshit," Erin said, her cheeks burning. She took that personally. "When we see a tsunami hit Japan, for instance, people donate money—"

"Because you can see it," Guthrie said. "On the news, on the net, whatever. It's visible now in a way it wasn't before."

"It's not because we see it—it's because we care for others, you dick," she fired back.

"Maybe," Guthrie said. "I wouldn't exactly call that an evolutionary adaptation, though. In a state like the one we're in, you're going to get a lot farther by thinking tribally than trying to go into a fight worrying about the puppies of Cambodia and the poor unfortunates of the Oregon coast."

Brian blinked. "What … what happened on the Oregon coast?"

Guthrie looked at him. "Have you been there lately? They got a homeless problem you wouldn't believe. All these small towns, filled with bums …" She quieted for a second, pausing for dramatic effect. "… smoking weed all day, not doing a damned thing." She loosed a quicksilver smile at him.

There was a silence where you could have heard pants drop. Well, Guthrie had sure shown her ass. A second, it lasted, and then

McMinn let out a snicker, followed by Drumlin, both looking sidelong at Brian, who was red as a USSR flag.

"Hilarious," Brian said from behind that suffocating crimson on his cheeks.

The bell above the door dinged again, and in came Ms. Cherry, not a hair out of place, her makeup Grade A, wearing stilettos and a coat that kept her rack under wraps. Erin felt a little tiny surge of envy, because every man in the room looked as she came in. "I just heard," Ms. Cherry said, coming up to the counter and leaning over on it. Every man's eyes widened, watching, but the coat thwarted them.

"Let me ask you a serious question," Guthrie said, peering at her. "Do you look like this all the time? Because I'm guessing it takes some serious effort to put on a face like that. Like an hour or better. Am I right?"

"It takes effort, yes," Ms. Cherry said coolly, "but this is hardly the time for makeup tips, darling."

Duncan laid a hand on Guthrie's arm, and Guthrie said, "What? I'm asking, okay? Curiosity didn't kill any OOCs that I know of, just pussies—y'know, cats. So don't be one."

"I think curiosity kills boners sometimes," Casey Meacham said, just drifting right out of his lane and into that conversation. "Lucky thing hard-ons get produced on an industrial scale." He arched his eyebrow, and Erin looked away.

"What do we do now?" McMinn asked.

"Well—" Erin started to say.

"Revenge," Hendricks said.

The bell rang out, and Erin turned. Here came Arch, with Barney Jones and Braeden Tarley in his wake. Arch didn't look too happy.

"Grandma finally got here, kids," Guthrie said, looking at Barney Jones. "What, were you traveling at three miles an hour the whole trip?"

Jones wasn't swayed. "It wasn't an emergency, so I didn't figure on risking our lives just so we could listen to y'all chew the fat for a couple more minutes."

Arch sauntered up to the counter, a real heavy air about the man's personality. "What'd we miss?"

"Guthrie being a cunt," Hendricks said, head still a little low under that hat brim. A few people gasped, and Jones looked at him with stern disapproval, shaking his head. "What?" Hendricks looked like he didn't give a shit, which, to be fair, he probably didn't. "She's not even a real she, you dumbasses. Don't go getting all offended for her sake."

"I was more offended for my own," Ms. Cherry said, shooting him a smoldering look that Hendricks shrugged off.

"We got a lot of people disappearing under mysterious circumstances in this town," Arch said, getting back on track. "Seems like somebody ought to look into that."

"Another precinct heard from," Guthrie said. "I swear, you people and your opinions." She looked around. "What? I'm black now; I get to say 'you people.' Anyway, you people—you fleshy bags of feelings—this is just crazy. You should really invest in some antidepressants, stop feeling so fucking much, and *do* more." Guthrie shot a look at Duncan. "Do you remember the human race being so emotionally incontinent when we first showed up? Because I feel like they had their shit together a little better before. I don't know what happened, but it's like the idea of being stoic and getting shit done fell by the wayside in favor of having tantrums and doing jack diddly shit while basking in your sad feelz became in vogue."

"The demon commentary on the human condition is super helpful, but—" Brian said.

"Oh, good," Guthrie cut right over him. "Because I've got bales of this shit, pothead."

"That's enough," Duncan mumbled.

Erin saw Duncan put a hand on Guthrie, who eyed it, the pale hand across her ebony skin right at the elbow. She gave him a surveying look, cool, maybe a little pissed off—it was hard to tell with Guthrie—but she just said, "Fine," and actually shut up.

"So what the hell we gonna do now?" Casey asked, looking around the room. "And where is everybody else?"

"There's a football game tonight in Athens," Barney Jones said. "Half the town's probably there. Midian versus—"

"The entire underworld," Guthrie said under her breath. Everyone heard her anyway. That shut everybody up for a minute. Duncan must have squeezed her arm, because then: "What? Oh, right." And she quieted again.

"It seems we have several problems," Nguyen said, "in addition to Sheriff Reeve dying. Which one should we focus on?"

"What—or who—killed Reeve," Hendricks said.

"The missing persons," Arch said.

"These shadowcats," Erin said. They'd all spoken at the same time, and exchanged uneasy looks. Well, she and Arch did. Hendricks didn't look like he gave a rat's ass.

Brian's voice rang out over the bullpen. "Oh, good, we've got clear priorities."

"Shut the fuck up, stoner boy," Hendricks said, tilting his head to look at Brian under his hat brim. "I could smell you before I saw you. Way to honor your daddy by bucking up and being a man. Do we need to get you some Mary Jane chewing gum so you can ease off the habit, you fucking burnout?"

"Jesus, cowboy," McMinn said, snorting with a barely controlled laugh.

"He's throwing the heat," Drumlin agreed.

Something about that made Erin see red. "What the fuck are you on his back about?" She cast a look at Brian, whose face was flaming and whose mouth was shut tight; the Marine had embarrassed the biggest brain in the room into silence. That was Hendricks though, the biggest asshole in sight, even bigger than Guthrie, and something snapped in Erin, and she just wanted to see his big fat fucking ego take a broadside and sink. "None of us are your girlfriend Starling, so why don't you stop trying to fuck people in the ass?"

"Holy shit," Drumlin said, and let out a low whistle.

"Wait, so is he actually fucking that crazy redhead?" McMinn asked, sotto voce.

"This isn't productive," Ms. Cherry said. "We should focus on—"

"You jealous?" Hendricks said, taking the air out of the room as he stared at Erin. "It's been a while since I rode your back, and I know you enjoyed getting a finger or two dipped in your ass."

"I'd rather fuck Duncan at this point, now that I know what you are," Erin fired back. She was in no mood to put up with his bullshit tonight.

"Go get some," Guthrie said, elbowing Duncan. "She's ready for you."

"Shut. Up," Duncan said forcefully.

"Both of y'all need to shut up," Arch said, and the big man had stormclouds over him. "I've heard about enough of this lover's quarrel—"

"Hey, when I need relationship advice from the saddest man in town," Hendricks said, his voice crackling with fury, "I'll fucking give you a call, Arch, at your reverend's house."

It was like someone had hooked an industrial-grade vacuum superpump to the air conditioning and sucked all the air out of the room in one big burst. Arch looked like a thunderhead swelling. "Excuse me?" The restraint was evident, cabled steel over his response.

"Hendricks—" Duncan said warningly, but this time Guthrie clamped a hand down on his arm, and he shut up mid-thought.

"Jesus H. Christ," McMinn breathed.

"Did you just go after this man's wife?" Barney Jones said, his own countenance darkening, maybe more than Arch's.

"No, I went after him," Hendricks said, not letting wisdom or discretion keep anger from carrying him away. "Alison's problems are over; now we're dealing with Arch's issues—"

"He just lost his wife," Keith Drumlin said in a near whisper, face white as a cotton ball.

"Yeah," Hendricks said, subtle as a gunshot to the belly, "and he's coping real well with it."

Erin just blinked, not really sure what to say. She saw red again, and realized that whatever needed to be said, she didn't fucking care anymore; she just wanted to go low and hit Hendricks so he'd shut the hell up. "You should talk. When your wife died you basically became a soulless, demon-hunting son of a bitch. And look at you now," she almost crowed. "What a fucking prize, sticking your dick in a redhead hooker every night. Bravo. You're really doing great things, douchebag."

Ms. Cherry stirred at the counter. "Please don't insult my Lucia like that."

"When she's Starling, she ain't your Lucia," Erin fired back at the madam. "I don't know if you've noticed," she spat at Ms. Cherry, whose eyes narrowed as she stared back, "but your employee ain't exactly operating like a normal human being, or even a normal hooker."

"Cuz she's got, like, an angel riding shotgun in her head, right?" McMinn asked, drawing every eye in the room toward him. "I mean, that's what she is, right? Come down to save our asses from whatever?" He looked straight at Guthrie and Duncan.

Duncan just stayed still, but Guthrie was cool, almost disgusted. "Don't fucking ask me about those things like I know any of them."

"Sorry you all had to see Erin get jealous of who I'm fucking now, guys," Hendricks said, almost laughing, the motherfucker.

"Good grief," Arch said, disgust rolling off the big man like smoke off a fire. "You really think it's about that?"

"I think it's either about that, or that some of you delicate little flowers are losing your nerve," Hendricks said.

Arch's face looked like someone had closed the door to any lighter emotions. Only fury emanated from him now. "You think I'm losing my nerve?"

"No," Hendricks said, in what probably passed for delicate for him. "I think you're fucking up in relation to how you're dealing with

Alison's death, but given that you suicidally threw yourself in front of a fire-breathing demon this afternoon—no, nerve's not what you're lacking, Arch."

"You know nothing about me," Arch said, and he got right up in Hendricks's face, so close he almost knocked the hat right off the cowboy's head.

"I been where you've been," Hendricks said, not backing down a fucking inch. "You sure I don't know a thing or two?"

"None of this is helping the situation," Barney Jones said, trying to interpose himself between Hendricks and Arch by putting a hand on each of their chests.

"A man died tonight," Father Nguyen said. "I don't think Sheriff Reeve would want us all to fight over these petty things."

"No, but he's hung around us enough by this point that he wouldn't exactly have to pick his jaw up off the floor," Hendricks drawled.

"Why are you such a sack of fuck all the time, Hendricks?" The question escaped Erin before she could contain it.

Hendricks surveyed her with a cool gaze. "I'm just saying it how it is, and some of you are getting pissed about it."

"That's what I do too, kid," Guthrie said. "No one appreciates a truth-teller. I mean, think of the noble history—Cassandra, Joan of Arc—what happens? They put you up on a cross and pound in the nails."

"Jesus Christ," Drumlin said, putting his head down and covering his eyes.

"Yeah, exactly." Guthrie grinned.

Hendricks rolled his eyes at the demon. "All I'm saying—we should saddle up and get revenge on whatever killed Reeve."

"So I can jump in front of your dumb butt again before you get cooked?" Arch asked, still inches from Hendricks's face. "Maybe I don't feel like losing another set of clothes this time."

"Well, then I guess you're going to fail your Lord as well as your pregnant wife," Hendricks said.

It was like someone picked up the entire room by the neck and throttled all the goddamned life out of it. You could have heard a bead of sweat drip to the floor in the silence. The slow tick of heated air through the ducts was the only sound for a long moment that seemed to extend into infinity ... then snapped back as everyone in the room spoke at once.

"Holy living fuck," McMinn breathed.

"The hell did you just say?" Braeden Tarley ground out a raspy question.

"Arch …" One of Barney Jones's hands was on the big man's swelling bicep, the other on his chest.

"What … the … fuck …" Brian whispered, now on his feet.

"This is some sweet, prime, human drama right here," Guthrie stage whispered to Duncan, who slapped him on the wrist again.

"Shit," Hendricks said, and his lips were pursed, face pale. "Arch … I'm sorry, I shouldn't have said—"

The punch was like a roaring train coming out of a hidden tunnel, no choreographing to it, just a straight uppercut from the waist that pitched Hendricks back. The cowboy hit the counter and bounced off, hat askew but still on his head, lip split wide and a trickle of red already working its way down his chin. He staggered and caught his balance, then put a hand to his lip and checked. It came back bloody. "Yeah," he said after staring at it smeared on his finger, "I deserved that."

"Damned right you did," Arch breathed, in a voice darker than midnight. He seemed to be barely holding himself back from doing a lot worse. Jones's hand pushed against his chest, but not too hard.

A bell rang behind them, tinkling loudly in the dead quiet of the bullpen, and in came Benny Binion, wearing a smile, almost ear to ear on his broad face. "Hey," he said, peppy as if he'd just dipped his lily. "Did you guys hear?" He didn't even wait before he let loose the news. "Reeve won the recall election! Beat the piss out of it, 62% to 30%." He guffawed. "We won." He looked around, and his face started to fall a little at a time, picking up on the state of the room. "What?"

Ms. Cherry let out a little sniffle, and the rest of them hung in silence until Brian broke it. "Benny … did you not check your messages?"

Benny stared for a second, then fumbled for his phone, fishing down in his pocket and dragging it out. "Y'all sure do seem …" He stared as the screen lit his face, and then he stared harder. "Awww … Jesus Christ …" He looked up. "Y'all ain't serious …"

But it was true, and he knew it was true, Erin could tell. She just hung her head.

Reeve was dead. And as she looked around the room, it almost seemed to her that if they couldn't get their shit together, and put this fighting behind them …

The watch might not long survive him.

*

Drake opened the Kamado grill's lid, admiring the links of sausage smoked within. They'd been cooking at a touch under 160 degrees for about three hours, with a nice Jack Daniel's wood chip sprinkled in for flavoring among the premium lump charcoal. He still had the whole human roasting on the spit, but that'd be hours before it was ready. This was a little something he'd started up a while ago, figuring to try it out.

The heat rose, smoky and pleasant, when he lifted the circular lid. It hit his eyes, drying them, not that it mattered. They weren't real eyes, after all, but he could feel the smoke in them nonetheless. He spared a fleeting thought for how these cattle reacted to such stimuli. Cooking them on the grills that they made? Delicious. Both the irony and the meat. But their eyes probably ached to take in such smoke, drying out those delicate membranes.

He'd eaten eyes before. They weren't his favorite. There were prime cuts of meat and then there were the scraps. Eyeballs were the scraps in his opinion, much like the brains. Perhaps a very innovative chef could find use for all the parts, in the name of sustainability or some such, but Drake knew what he liked, and he wasn't too proud to simply state it—some cuts were better. Some cuts were decent, and could be prepared beautifully.

And the rest was only worthy of throwing out. Which was why he needed a steady supply of meat.

This sausage smelled wonderful. Rich, delicately flavored, and carrying the hints of the smoke. He'd spent extra on the charcoal, and of course the grill itself was a marvel, with its cast-iron cap and bottom vents to allow control of the temperature in the coal bed. It was really quite the innovation, and Drake found himself smiling as he made the simple adjustments and watched the temp slowly climb on the circular thermometer face on the front of the grill. It had a smooth yet dimpled skin to it, and he ran his fingertips over it, his shell enjoying the tactile contact and flaming heat. It was like a dragon's egg, a hot reminder of the awesome power that humans had discovered when they'd harnessed the ability to use nature's own tool to cook their food.

Drake pulled a skewer off the grill with his bare hand; no need for grill gloves for him, his skin not really skin, his flesh not edible the way these beasts were. Delicately popping the end of the sausage into his mouth, he took a bite.

Fatty juices poured out, and Drake felt a little stir of joy within. It was subtle—no, not subtle—glorious. The fatty marbling made scraps into greatness with the aid of wood chips and fire. Maybe there was some use for scraps after all, albeit limited. It was a delicacy, after a fashion, but not one he'd enjoy every day. He took a second bite, but already the pleasure was fading. Now the juices seemed a little less sweet, the flavor just a little less succulent.

No, he decided, putting the skewer back on the grill, this wasn't for him. It was comfort food, not culinary greatness. A fun novelty, but not the new heights he was seeking.

He had enough choice cuts to keep him in good meat for quite some time, and there was a certain comfort in that. But there was a sense of stagnation too, like he was trapped in the grill with the hot, suffocating air, like one of the cattle. Drake frowned, something he didn't do often, as he pondered the problem.

It always came back to the veal.

Demons had been eating children for thousands of years. It wasn't new per se, but it was new to Drake—and Drake wanted it.

He craved it. It was the forbidden fruit, and he hungered for it.

But how to get it? How to get not just a little, but a lot of it? There were places, of course, in cities, but here?

Rural Free Delivery of children seemed unlikely, even from the Class A suppliers back in the major cities. Why hadn't he sought this before? Why had he always restricted himself to human food until now? When such lovely opportunities had abounded?

Probably the taboo. The fear of getting caught. It was against the Pact, after all. That the Pact was violated every day seemed a small matter, now that he was in the heart of this ... this movement. He'd never been to a hotspot before, and watching the rampant fall of this town was opening him to new possibilities, new horizons.

He wanted to eat the meat of a child, dammit.

But how? They were still here, in this town, of course, but ... not readily available. Guarded? Well, by their parents, but ...

He'd surely killed parents by now. He'd preyed on some older folks. Preyed on some younger ones too, but it'd been his bad luck not to pick a house that had a tricycle outside or some similar sign, in his huntings.

But ...

What if there was a way to get more, all at once, without the frustration of constantly missing? A soft target, one that would provide ample ... rewards?

Where did children go where they weren't protected by angry parents who would throw themselves into the path of danger for their children?

Ah.

Of course.

Drake's frown disappeared as the delicate hints of a plan formed, like the wisps of blue smoke wafting out the cap of his grill. They rose, drifting off and becoming a part of the very air, the very world around him—just like his plan soon would.

Interlude, Too

Two Years Ago

"Do you feel safe at home?"

The dark-haired doctor read the question off the form to Lucia. Lucia kept her eyes down, right around the doctor's chest, where she wore one of those pure white lab coats that had the name "Darlington" printed across the right breast. Lucia kept focused on that, her hair brushing against the rough pillow in this hospital bed. Her ribs, pain radiating from the bones, a steady ache in her head, and her eyes—

She just kept them focused right on that name: Darlington.

The doctor's voice was soft, and she asked the question again: "Do you feel safe at home?"

"Home's fine," Lucia said, and her voice sounded dead even to her, quiet and distracted. "It's ... fine."

The doctor shuffled foot to foot, cleared her throat. "Doesn't seem like that's the case."

Lucia would have shrugged, but it would have hurt too much, so she just kept her voice low and sullen, though not intending to. "It's fine."

The doctor had been standing at the side of her bed, and now the dark-haired woman leaned in closer. "Lucia," she whispered, and looked at the door behind her, which was closed. "There's no one here but the two of us. You don't have to lie to me."

"I'm not lying," Lucia said in a monotone.

"Did your boyfriend really beat you up?" the doctor asked. "Is that what happened?"

"Nothing happened," Lucia said. "I don't have a boyfriend."

The doctor let out a sigh, frustration just oozing out of the woman.

She was young ... ish. Younger than most doctors, Lucia thought, but a lot older than her. Worlds older. "I can't help you if you don't talk to me, Lucia."

"I'm fine," Lucia said. "I don't need help."

The doctor sunk back slightly. "You're beat all to hell. This, to you, is fine?"

Lucia still couldn't shrug. "It'll be all right."

The doctor just stood there. Lucia couldn't see her face. It was white, that much she could tell, white against the beige walls, and she had a little perfume on that overcame the smell of disinfectant that this hospital reeked of. Michael and Karen had hovered over her in the ambulance the whole way. Oh, they'd looked concerned, but she knew why they did it—so that she couldn't answer any questions without them hearing her answers.

It didn't matter though. Lucia hadn't answered a one in any way other than ones Michael and Karen would have approved of.

The doctor must have decided she wasn't going to get anything out of Lucia, because she said, "I'll be back later to check on you. Think about what I said? Nobody can help you if you don't tell us what's wrong."

"Nothing's wrong," Lucia said, and thank fuck she left after that.

Lucia watched TV some during the day, because she didn't have anything else to do. She wasn't exactly the crossword puzzle type. The days were long and boring.

Lunch came. It was a chicken breast covered in salty gravy. There was tapioca pudding on the side, like jizz in a little bucket. She didn't eat it, and thought of Ray. Her pussy still hurt, just like the rest of her, but not nearly as much as it had. The painkillers helped, and they had her on a nice drip of them. She pushed the tray away.

Lucia lay her head down for a little bit. Darkness flowed in around the edges of her consciousness, but sound stirred her back when she started to drift off.

There was someone at the door. Dark hair, bright eyes creased with concern.

"Lara?" Lucia asked, blinking out of her sleep. She couldn't tell at first, but the figure resolved into the young girl, Lucia's best—sometimes she'd felt like only—friend back in Fort Oglethorpe. She blinked again; it felt like some remnant of her old life, the one where she had actual parents and a house of her own, had crossed into this new reality of pain, of disconnection, of feeling...

Worthless.

"Hey," Lara said, in that quiet manner like she was afraid the sound would break Lucia. She drifted in tentatively from the door.

Her mother followed after. Lucia didn't really know Ms. Black all that well. They'd met a bunch of times when Lucia had gone to Lara's house, but ... she didn't really know her. Just nodded or talked for a second while passing through from door to living room, or vice versa.

"How are you feeling, Lucia?" Ms. Black asked. She was a very definite Ms. She had a lighter shade of auburn hair, completely unlike Lara's. Hers was full of life, almost glimmering. Lara's hair hung in limp ringlets. Ms. Black sounded a little more alert, like she wanted to be there, than Lara did.

"Fine," Lucia lied again. It was getting to be easy to say.

Lara eased up to her bedside; Ms. Black didn't hesitate, following her daughter right up and lingering. She brushed Lara's hair back and Lara seemed to struggle to find something to say.

Ms. Black didn't. "We came to see you a few days ago too, but you were sleeping. Good to see you're awake." She smiled down at Lucia, and it felt a little funny—

Like she was genuinely, sincerely happy to see her.

Lucia looked down. "Yeah. I'm sleeping some." Like it was her fault. Well, it kinda was.

"You need rest," Ms. Black said, just taking right over when Lara didn't say anything. "To make a recovery." She had a big purse, and it hung from her arm. "Have the doctors told you when you might get out?"

"Umm, I don't know," Lucia said, looking down. She hadn't asked. Maybe they'd said and she hadn't heard. She wasn't exactly in a hurry to get back to Michael and Karen's and the smoky air. It felt like she would choke to death in it.

"Oh." Lara's voice was soothing and encouraging, like, "Oh, you got a passing grade on your algebra test."

"Oh," Ms. Black said, and hers was more like, "Oh, I know you're lying, but I respect you enough not to call you on it right here in front of your bestie." Her eyes told more of the tale than the "Oh."

"Did you talk to my doctor?" Lucia asked, feeling the faint buzz of nervousness like a bow drawn across strings. She thought of the sound it made from when she had taken band, before she'd moved in with Michael and Karen. Before the crash.

"They don't talk to anyone but your legal guardian about your health," Ms. Black said warmly, and yet ... there was a point—a little sting buried in there. Lucia didn't think it was aimed to her, but ...

"That's okay," Lucia said. She couldn't think of anything else.

"Lara," Ms. Black said, brushing her daughter's arm, "would you be a dear and go get me a cup of coffee?" She reached into her purse and came out with a ten. "At the cafeteria."

Lara's brow knitted in a rumpled line. "There was a machine just back—"

"I know," Ms. Black said, smiling down at Lucia. "Those machine coffees taste like someone shit in the filter. Go get me one from the cafeteria?"

Lara stared at the tenner for a second, then pulled the rumpled bill from her mother's stubby fingers. "Okay." She shrugged and went for the door, disappearing into the hallway and beyond.

Lucia had been tempted to call out to her, not really sure why Ms. Black didn't just get her own damned coffee; it wasn't like she knew the woman, after all …

"Welp," Ms. Black said, once Lara was out, walking slowly over to the door and pushing it shut before she turned back to Lucia and gave her a flat stare. "You look like hell."

"Uhm." Lucia didn't know what to say to that, either.

"You know how you answered earlier?" Ms. Black sidled back over to the bed, bulging purse still hanging on her arm, creasing it neatly and fading the skin on either side of the leather strap. It was like a thin strip of pale white between the leather and the sun-kissed rest. "'Fine.'" She said it in a slightly higher-pitched voice, then shook her head. "Gah!" A noise of frustration burst loose. "I remember answering people like that. Fuck." She closed her eyes.

Lucia just froze. "I … don't know what—"

"Yes, you do," Ms. Black said, eyes springing open and finding her, coolly. "Somebody beat the hell out of you, Lucia. If I had to guess, I'd say your foster parents." She watched Lucia carefully. "Foster dad, maybe? Did he get handsy?" She was watching like an interrogator.

"N-no," Lucia said, shaking her head like a bad twitch. Then she realized maybe she didn't deny the first thing hard enough because she was focused on the second. "They didn't hurt me—"

"And you're *fine*," Ms. Black said, still staring at her. "Totally, absolutely, completely fine. Goddammit, Lucia." She hung her head for a second, putting a hand over her face before raising it back up again to look Lucia in the eye. It sparkled, just a little bit, a little moist. "Let me tell you a story."

"I—"

"No, you just lie there and be quiet for a sec," Ms. Black said. "When I was a teenager, I had a stepdad that I had to call 'Dad.'" Her eyes narrowed. "His name was Rick, and I wanted to call him Rick, but I had to call him 'Dad' because my momma made me.

"Well, one night not long after I started having to call Rick 'Dad,' he came into my bedroom in the middle of the night, and made me do shit that my real dad never did before he died." Her jaw hardened. "When I told my mom about it, she slapped me. Called me an ungrateful brat. Said I was just trying to ruin her life so I wouldn't have to call Rick 'Dad' anymore." Ms. Black leaned in. "I never said a word to her about it again, and she never said anything to me about it either."

Lucia stared at her; Ms. Black's eyes were a deep brown, and they stared down at her like two glowing orbs, near-black in their luster. A little droplet came sliding down out of one and dripped onto Lucia's thin sheet. "I ..." Lucia sniffed.

"I lived with that son of a bitch for five years," Ms. Black said, standing up straight. Now she looked commanding. "Five years of fucking hell. No one ought to go through that, not for a real dad or a fakeass motherfucker like Rick." Her fingers twitched; she smelled of faint, stale cigarette smoke. She looked down at Lucia once more. "You know what I was thinking those five years? 'I want to fucking die.'"

Lucia just blinked. Because she didn't know what else to say.

"You know why I was thinking that?" Ms. Black leaned in again. "Because I couldn't find any way out. I felt more trapped than I've ever felt in my life. My teachers couldn't help. My mom didn't give a shit. Was I supposed to call the cops, hope that they'd believe me? I was a stupid shit; I'd already been in trouble with the law by that point. I figured they'd lock me up, and Rick made plenty of suggestions that I was worthless and anyone I told about 'our little secret' wasn't going to believe me, and hell if my mom hadn't gone and proved his fucking lech ass right once already." She shook her head, raw, bitter anger twisting her face. "I mean, if your momma won't even fucking believe you ... goddamn, I need a cigarette." She shook her head again, then looked down at Lucia. "You know why I'm telling you all this?"

Lucia felt frozen, paralyzed in the stare of some massive predator walking through. "I ..." Guilt broke through, washing over her for all the horrible things she'd done, the things that had happened; they were her fault, weren't they? She deserved the beating, she deserved the pain that Ray had given her, she deserved ... all of it.

Because it was her fault, what had happened to her parents.

All her fault.

"I can see what you're doing right now." Ms. Black looked thinly unamused, almost scornful. "I wonder if I looked like that to people when I was thinking like you are. Because what I was thinking when I was in your shoes? 'It's all my fault,' even though I hadn't done a goddamned thing to deserve Rick using me like his personal fucking cum catcher. And I'm telling you—and you won't believe me—whatever you think you've done that's awful in this world, it ain't a reason for whoever has hurt you to have fucking hurt you. Being an asshole to people, making mistakes, whatever it is you think you've done … you're not as big a girl as you think you are, and your foster parents—I fucking bet it was them; it was, wasn't it?—they got no cause to do this to you, because you are a kid, and they said they'd protect and raise you when they took you in." Ms. Black balled a fist. "Goddammit."

"I do deserve it," Lucia said, in the softest whisper she'd ever managed.

"No, you fucking don't," Ms. Black said, and she seemed to struggle for a moment, unballing her fist, like it was a real labor. "Whatever you think you've done … you probably didn't do—"

"I got my parents killed," Lucia said, numbly.

"No, you didn't." Ms. Black shook her head. "No, you didn't."

"They were arguing because of me—"

"I fucking argue with people all the time. Hell, I argue with everybody all the time. If I got my cell phone in my hand and I'm fucking arguing with somebody while I'm driving, that's on me, not you, because the driver ought to know better." She leaned down. "A parent—a real one, not a fakeass parent who'd abuse their kid—I don't care about blood here either, I'm talking about somebody who really loves you, who really cares, who's really gonna take care of you—they're not gonna fucking do what Rick did to me, regardless of how guilty I am of bad shit in the past. And your foster parents … fucking steamy goddamned slimy shits—they got no cause to punish you for shit you did or didn't do before they even met you, you hear me?"

"But it's like karma, isn't it?" Lucia sniffled.

"Their job is to parent you, not be fucking karma," Ms. Black said, her big eyes glistening with moisture as she leaned down. "They're supposed to take fucking care of you." A tear slid down to her chin. "That's what a parent does."

Lucia turned her face away. "I … I'm f—" There came the feel of almost a snap in her head, and cool relief rushed over her as though someone had poured water over her.

"Don't say you're fine," Ms. Black whispered. "You're not fine. It ain't gonna be fine."

She looked back to Ms. Black and tried to smile, that cool feeling resting over her. She didn't need to cry anymore, she was just … numb. And Ms. Black was just trying to help, but … "I'll be okay. Thank you for worrying about me." Then she looked down.

Ms. Black hovered over her still, like a tall tower. "I probably would have said the same thing when Rick was …" She sniffled. "It fucking sucks how long I called him 'Dad,' and believed I was the one that was wrong." She rummaged in her purse, the things in it making shifting noises as they were moved. Eventually she found something, pulling out a bound black book. "I finally went searching for answers somewhere else—went searching for a father … somewhere else." Lucia didn't answer, and Ms. Black seemed to take that as invitation to keep talking anyway. "There's help out there for those who ask … if you know how to ask in the right way."

Ms. Black took Lucia's hand. Hers was big and rough and calloused, and she lifted Lucia's and slipped that little black book into it. Lucia glanced down and saw the words HOLY BIBLE written on the spine.

"I already have one of these," Lucia said, trying to give it back to her.

Ms. Black pushed it toward her, toward her chest. She was strong, and Lucia didn't fight back. It thumped lightly against her breastbone, and Lucia stared at it. "Read it. It might just have the answer you need … at the moment you're ready for it."

Lucia stared at her with blank eyes. "Okay." She didn't even look at it.

"I know you're barely hearing a word I'm saying—" Ms. Black blinked, another tear slipping down to her chin "—but you trust me on this one. If you read this when you're looking for answers … you will find your answer, and your salvation. And it's not going to be what you expect." She pushed it at Lucia again, and the leather binding dug into her breastbone through the thin hospital gown. "Keep it. Trust me. I've been where you've been. Just … read it." And she stared at Lucia, looking her right in the eyes, and nodding, like she could get her point across that way alone, now that all the words were spent.

"Okay," Lucia said again, because there really wasn't anything else to say.

Ms. Black's strong hands relinquished their grip on her and she stood, sniffing and digging in her purse again. She pulled out a tissue and wiped her eyes with it, and started to make her way to the door.

Lucia watched her go, kind of sauntering her way out. "Thank you." She remembered her manners just before Ms. Black left.

Ms. Black paused at the door, opening it back up. The sounds of the hospital corridor filtered in, the steady thrum of equipment and chatter, of life. "Don't thank me until after you read it." She sniffled. "But seriously … hang onto it, okay? If you don't do anything else … hang onto it until you need it."

"Sure," Lucia said. She would hang onto it. Ms. Black seemed nice enough, like she wanted to help. Keeping a simple book wouldn't be anything other than being polite, on the level with hanging onto that shitty Mr. Potato Head that her uncle Andrew had given her once upon a time. Hell, she'd kept that thing until her teenage years just to be polite, her mom making sure it was displayed anytime Andrew came to town.

Keeping a Bible wouldn't be a big deal. She'd just put it on the shelf and leave it there. She stared up at Ms. Black, who nodded at her once, and then walked out.

Lucia let out a little breath she hadn't realized she'd been holding, and then turned her face away. She let go of the Bible and it rested there on her breastbone, just sitting there, an uncomfortable weight, but she didn't really have anywhere else to put it. Eventually she didn't really notice it at all, and off she went to sleep.

Day Three

"... so, anyway, this old bastard, I think he's ninety-four, and richer than shit, and this woman's suing because they were lovers for a long time and—hell if I remember his name, but he runs some big company—anyway, in this lawsuit, all this—whaddyacallit? Deposition? All this shit comes out, basically," Keith Drumlin said, the hose in hand, a hard spray nozzle on the tip now, gushing toward the sidewalk outside the old tire store on the square that shut down back in the eighties.

"Mmm hmm," Nate McMinn grunted. He was a good listener.

Keith stood there, letting the hose pressure press against his fingers, satisfying in its way, as he sluiced that cold water against the concrete. Nate was going to come along behind him, give it a good scrubbing. "So one of the things that sticks with me is that his girlfriend, who's like forty, she says that all he wants every day—and this motherfucker is in his nineties, keep in mind—is steak and fucking. Every single day."

Nate grunted again, eyebrows rolling back in a display of respect. "That's a man with his priorities straight."

"Damned right, that's what I said." Keith adjusted the nozzle to hit a bit of caked-on internal organ that had dried up on the sidewalk. It was getting harder to wash this shit off as time went by. It'd been three weeks since the Halloween massacre and everything was congealed now, sticky and impossible to fucking dislodge without the pressure spray the nozzle was giving him. It'd get cold in the night, then catch the sun's rays all day. It stank to high heaven, and stuck to everything.

Keith looked around, tracing his gaze around the square. They'd cleaned maybe—maybe—three quarters of it by now. As far as he could tell, he and Nate were the only ones working on it. Everyone else had fucked off and gone back to living their lives, avoiding the shit out of this place, letting the police barricades be their guides and just detouring around the mess.

But not him and Nate. They came here every morning and worked at it faithfully, trying to clean a little more sidewalk, a little more road, to expunge a little more death and rotting tissue and blood and shit. Some of it wasn't ever going to come up, not now, not since it had hardened every which way.

But, he reflected as a little chunk of—was that lung, maybe? Fuck!—brownish tissue broke loose of its clinging place on the sidewalk and washed down into the drain, the square was kind of a metaphor for the town, wasn't it?

Things weren't ever really, fully, going to be the same around here.

"I hope Andrea and I are still fucking every day and eating steak at ninety-something," Nate said, a bristly, wide-head broom ahead of him as he tried to scrape where Keith washed.

Keith scrunched up his face. "Are you fucking every day right now? And eating steak?"

Nate sagged, but kept pushing the broom. "No. Shit. We ain't fucked every day since … I don't know? First year of marriage. After we had kids, we were lucky to go once a week."

"Once a week ain't bad," Keith said, and when Nate gave him a *You must be fucking crazy* look, he added, "When Nancy was pregnant, she got this thing where she got excessive lubrication going up in there. It was like …" He looked around just to be sure the square was empty. It damned sure was. "Like dipping it into a bucket of warm spit. Fucking useless, man. I went months getting nothing but head." Keith felt a little twinge in his chest when he thought about that period. It seemed so damned long ago.

Nate frowned. "I've gone about a month before. That sucks. I'd still do it every day if I could, you know? I damned sure want to."

"It's all about time," Keith said. "Your time, your wife's time … getting those two to match up."

"Exactly," Nate said. "The problem is that, you know, when you first get together, you're the only two in your lives. Maybe there's a job to work around, but that's it! Then you start adding kids, and suddenly it ain't just you vying for her attention. So she's dealing with the kids who are crying out at night at one year, and five years, and fuck, maybe 'til they're twenty-five, it's starting to feel like—"

"It's like, how do you get laid when you're fighting against the motherly instinct, right?" Keith was nodding. "And they're tired—"

"All the goddamned time!"

"Because, you know as well as I do—kids are fucking tiring! I'm tired, and I don't really get up with them but maybe one time in five when they call out." Keith shook his head. Something about that caused an itch in the back of his head. "And then you get groused at for that—"

"See, when I get woke up in the middle of the night," Nate said, nodding, "if I get up and walk around—I'm for up like, hours. She just cruises right on back to sleep. So my options—my shitty options—are to wake up and take care of the kid myself, and then I'm too tired to have a hope of sex the next night, going to sleep at like seven, you know? Or else I let her get up with the kids, and hope I slide into that window of five minutes or so between when we get the kids to sleep and before she conks out." He held his thumb and forefinger a centimeter apart. "It's a tricky business, trying to get into that window."

"Yep. Spend most of my life trying to get in there." Keith nodded right along, but something about it jangled within him, a discordant little thought that didn't match up with what had been said.

Nate snickered. "That's an old joke, you know." Keith just shook his head; no idea what Nate was on about. "That when a man is born, he comes out of a vagina and spends the rest of his life trying to get back into one. That ninety-year-old fucker sure is proving that, ain't he?"

"He's giving me hope for the future, that's what he's doing," Keith said. "He's a fucking thought leader, that's what he is. Ninety-something and still giving it to a woman fifty years his junior." Keith saluted, over-exaggerated and yet still meant as a sign of respect. "This is a great man, there, with great stamina."

"Probably just takes them blue bombers," Nate said with a chuckle.

"Whatever you got to do to feed the beast, man," Keith said.

They settled into a steady silence for a few minutes before Nate spoke up again. "That guy's probably gonna die in the next few years."

Keith only gave it a moment's thought. "In his nineties? Probably. Though if he's still craving pussy and steak, maybe not."

"He ain't even dead," Nate said, adopting that pensive look he got sometimes, "and people are sifting his guts, you know?"

Keith didn't quite see where this was going. "I guess ...?"

"Because that's what they do after a great man dies," Nate said, probably thinking out loud, "they sift his guts. What did he do? What did he accomplish? What did he feel? You seen some of those biographical movies nowadays? Like the one for Ray Charles—"

"Yeah, I saw that," Keith said. "'Georgia On My Mind' is one of the greatest fucking songs of all time—"

"You're goddamned right," Nate said, nodding furiously. "But did you see how they portrayed him in that? Drug addict, asshole, all that—"

"They did the same thing to Johnny Cash," Keith said. "Fucking sacrilege. I mean, shit, we all know Johnny Cash wasn't a damned saint—"

"Right, exactly," Nate said. "But nowadays they lean in hard on the shit part of your story if they do a biography. 'Oh, he was a drunkard who abused his wife every fucking night' when you maybe got mad, had an argument and threw a glass at the wall one time—"

"I don't think Johnny Cash got fucked up just one time."

"You know what I mean," Nate said. "It's this relentless drive to embrace the negative. We crawl in there and really rummage through a person's flaws these days when they die."

"Not everybody's," Keith said. "I mean, you don't hear about half the nasty shit that LBJ or FDR did, or at least it ain't taught in school."

"But it's out there," Nate said. "You could learn about how many women John Kennedy was fucking while he was in office, if you were of a mind to. And that ain't the substance of the man, but nowadays it's the stuff we dig into. We get right in there, right in the guts. If biography up to the last twenty years or so was climbing into the head of our heroes, nowadays it's gotta be more like a 'climb up their ass and see all the shit' approach."

Keith nodded, thinking that one over. "You might have a point there."

"Yeah," Nate said, and paused for a second. "I kinda like that trend, though."

"Why's that?" Keith turned the hose to a stubborn, clinging piece of refuse. It was anchored on the sidewalk like it had been glued. Looked like ... hell, who knew at this point?

"Because it feels like in a lot of ways," Nate said, "the people who rule over us these days ... they're almost like a substitute for gods." He had a pensive look. "Back in the olden days—no, think about it—people had pantheons. Household gods. They had all these deities that they worshipped, and each of them did different things. And most of that went away with Christianity, but ... it's almost like people still need gods to believe in. And we don't think about, y'know, gods of fire, or thunder, or whatever ... now it's 'the distinguished gentleman from Arizona,' or 'the junior Senator from

Pennsylvania.' Or the Supreme Court Justice of choice, or whatever." Nate shook his head. "Your favorite TV personality. Your sports hero."

"Peyton Manning," Keith said with an air of almost romantic admiration. He was well aware of what he sounded like.

"Damned straight," Nate said. "For some people, their god is sports, for some it's politics. They've got their household deities, and they go to their church, whether it's their Sunday morning news shows or Sunday night football. And we worship—"

"But come on, Nate," Keith said. "Lots of people go to church and then watch the game afterward."

"I ain't saying it's bad or good, just saying it's so," Nate said. "Especially politics. You can hate a sports team—"

"The fucking Cleveland Browns. Fuck them. What a sorry-ass bunch of losers. I hope the Titans crush their fucking bones."

"—and it's gonna have very little consequence on the long-term effects of your life or anyone else's," Nate said. "You may hate the Browns and their fans, but y'know, it's just you being crazy about your hobby. When politics takes on a religious importance, shit is hitting the fan—"

"Why?" Keith asked. "How's that any different than sports?"

Nate stopped brushing the broom, the scraping sound of the bristles fading into the quiet morning and the emptiness of the town square. "Because the NFL doesn't have any actual influence over your life if you don't want it to. You turn off the TV, and so long as you don't get snared in the traffic going to or from the game, or have a family member playing, your relationship with them motherfuckers is over. But Washington, DC … they got their fingers in your ass whether you watch 'em or not, and there are an awful lot of people with power over politics and policy, and these a-holes got sway over your life whether you want 'em to or not." He shook his head. "I'd prefer *not*, personally."

"Well, what's the alternative?" Keith asked. "You get ruled from DC or you get ruled from Nashville. Which would you prefer?"

"Honest to God, I'd rather be ruled from Nashville," Nate said. "I could at least drive the three hours or so over there and yell at those dickheads if I were so inclined. DC's a long damned ways, and those people don't know me—"

"That's kinda the point of sending a representative or a senator, ain't it?"

"I can't watch everything they do," Nate said. "I don't want to watch everything they do. I don't want politics to be *my* religion. I don't want my government to have that much power. I want them to leave me the hell alone so I can do the things I want to do without them fucking it up. Is that too much to ask?"

"Yeah," Keith said.

"Shit," Nate said, sighing. "Don't I know it. So instead we get ruled by gods who are damned near unaccountable, pretty well untouchable, whose names we know from legend—well, TV; same-ass thing these days—that are spoken of in awe or hate, depending on which side of the pantheon they're sitting on—and they get to rule over us. A thousand miles away—might as well be on the moon for all the connection they've got to us and what we've got going on."

"I bet if you did move governance out of the federal system and devolved the power to the states, you'd just end up with Nashville feeling like it was on the moon."

"I already feel like Nashville is on the fucking moon," Nate grumbled. "I was there last year. Walking down Broadway, I ain't never seen that many man buns in my life. I wonder if there's any testicles left in that town ain't carried in a man purse."

Keith chuckled. "You best stay away from Brooklyn or the left coast, my friend, if man buns offend you."

"They don't *offend* me," Nate said. "I don't give a fuck how you wear your hair. But it seems like there are easier ways to signal that you're looking to be penetrated anally. Maybe a Grindr ad." He paused. "That's the gay one, right?"

Keith just shrugged. "Hell if I know." He did know, but he didn't want to admit to it.

"So you've got these unaccountable elites," Nate said, "and you got the watchers slobbering all over them in worship, and it's all one big circle jerk. Or a daisy chain, if you'd rather think about it like—"

"I do like watching a daisy chain every now and again," Keith said, nodding slowly. God bless the internet.

"The problem is …" Nate said, "think about how much they've fucked up the last few years. How many things they've missed. And now we found out there are demons? That we never knew about? And the press don't report on that shit. How can you be that wrong and still want to consider yourself some kind of knowing god? Or better than God? To rule over man, because you know we idiots out here in the flyover can't figure out which one's our ass and which one's a hole in the ground." He pointed at the grate where traces of red were washing down from where Keith was spraying the sidewalk. "They don't really seem that elite to me. But they sure as shit know everything we're doing wrong, while they're doing nothing wrong, it seems like."

"Maybe," Keith said. "Maybe you're missing the parts where they say what they're doing wrong. I tend to notice the shit that offends me more than the shit that don't apply to me."

"You know what the worst part of it is?" Nate asked, leaning the broom against the wall of the old tire shop and sauntering over the cleanest section of curb. "I keep hearing how people are voting their interests. How these folks in DC just want to make things better. For the poor. For us, maybe; who knows?" He looked up at Keith. "I don't have a lot of illusions left. Whether I was ruled from Nashville or from DC, you're right—they ain't gonna know me. Maybe if it was done locally ... it'd be different. They'd have to look me in the eye at a county or a town meeting as they fucked me over." He shook his head. "Or maybe it wouldn't matter a damned bit. All I know is, they ain't—any of them, federal, state, or even county, at this point, I'm starting to believe—gonna miss us when we're dead. They ain't even gonna notice." Staring off across the empty square, Nate leaned back, surveying their handiwork of the last few weeks ...

And he frowned. "We ain't even a number on a spreadsheet to the people who are voting and making our decisions for us at this point. It's been going on like this for all my life, but I've only really noticed it these last few years. And that ... scares the shit out of me more than I care to think about, most days." Nate's shoulders sagged, and he stared at the stained ground. "Who knows what else we're missing?"

*

Pink Floyd's "Comfortably Numb" was playing on the radio when Erin's alarm clicked on. It was somewhere in the middle of the beginning, and she moaned in her twilight state, not just upset in general about being awakened, but being awakened to a song that wasn't really designed for full consciousness.

It launched into one of those long, trippy, dragged-out sections of the chorus, and Erin summoned the presence of mind to slap the damned snooze button right as it started to marshal its way to a half-hearted conclusion of the verse.

"Fuck Pink Floyd," Erin said, slitting her eyes and seeing light streaming in through the cracks of the blinds. It didn't hurt, but it was annoying. It would have been better if it had hurt, because then at least she'd have had the luck of being hungover.

But Erin didn't get hungover any more, because Erin hadn't had a drink in weeks.

Sure, she would have liked to have taken a deep dive into the bottle after Sheriff Reeve's funeral a few days earlier, but that would have been ... irresponsible or something.

The sad thing was, she'd actually bought a bottle of whiskey and poured one in a glass. She'd sat there at her kitchen table for something like an hour—or maybe five minutes that felt like an hour, who knew—staring at the amber glass, wishing she could just tip it back.

But she knew if she did, it wouldn't be the only one. And that she'd be hurting in the morning.

Forcing her eyes open, Erin came back to herself, back to the world ... and she knew she had no time to be hurting. Not this morning, not any morning.

She sat up, surrendering the last clinging vestiges of sleep that wanted to anchor themselves to her eyelids. No time for that. No time for any of this. It was go time, and she needed to move.

The station awaited, she reflected as she stood, ignoring the faint after-echoes of a headache. She needed coffee. Coffee was a manageable addiction for a deputy in the middle of a demon war. Whiskey wasn't. With that in mind, she headed for the coffee pot, figuring on getting it started, appeasing her brain through at least giving it a sniff of the good stuff while she went through the motions of getting ready.

And maybe, by the time she got a cup down and everything else done, she'd actually feel alive—a feeling, she thought grimly, that an increasing number people in Midian weren't feeling these days, and never would again.

*

Hendricks was getting rode like a fucking bronco, his ass buried in the motel bed, Starling's crotch grinding against his, his hard-on swollen and buried so deep in her pelvis he felt like the tip had to be kissing her cervix. It wasn't, but damn if he didn't feel like she was riding him hard enough to push it up there when she let her leg muscles go and dropped that ass down on him.

She was in the reverse cowgirl—an appropriate position, he thought, and damned sure one of his favorites—so he had a prime view of her ass moving up and down on him. Her back was in shadow, the red hair dangling down behind her, and he could watch his dick sliding in and out of her as she tensed her legs and rose up, showing the snake sliding out of the hole, and then back down—whoosh, it was gone to the fucking pubic mound. She wasn't doing it like a frenzied madwoman either, she was taking it slow, and the pressure had built over time to fucking insane levels. His dick was so swollen, he was so close, that he thought it might launch off like a bottle rocket. Then it really would hit her cervix, probably end up lodged in her throat or something.

"Fucking A," Hendricks said, settling his head back on the pillow and closing his eyes. He didn't need to watch to get turned on at this point, though it didn't hurt matters. He dipped off into his imagination for a minute while Starling just kept on going.

It was a weird thing, getting to climax. He almost equated it to driving around on a racetrack, over and over, the speed getting higher with each lap, most of the time. There was an exit on the last turn though, and that was orgasm. Sometimes you'd come around on a lap and somehow miss the exit, and it was like you had to rev your speed back up to take it right the next time.

He'd seen someone diagram out the male orgasm at one point, like a steadily rising mountain peak. Women were different, but that was a man for you—an almost perfect rise to climax. He could vouch for that, but every once in a while you'd hit that minor peak and come down—miss the exit and go on another lap—and that happened to him now, as he slipped his focus and lost track of where he was for just a second.

He'd been just about to cum too, which was a damned shame.

"Fuck," he said under his breath, but whether Starling heard him or somehow just knew what he needed, she sped up again. The frenzied tempo of her sweet snatch sliding up and down his glistening, veiny pole increased, and he watched the snake slither in and out a few more times, mentally imagining that peak getting closer ... and closer ... her ass riding up and down, his cock sliding in and out of her perfectly shaven slit of a pussy ...

He put his hands on her hips and slowed her ride as he came in that last stretch. He moaned, breathing heavy, even though he wasn't exerting himself at all. It was close ... close ... he could barely breathe, now ... felt like his tip was going to blast off ... any second ...

Hendricks flew off the track, blew his wad, and Starling sagged down on it, sliding up and down less heavily, keeping it lower when she'd go up, just massaging him through his climax. And when he was done, he put the pressure on her hips and she slid to rest on him, his dick buried up to the balls in her.

For his part, Hendricks let her sit there, splaying out his arms to either side and letting his head sag onto the pillow. "That … is the way to start a day," he said, because damned if it didn't beat the shit out of coffee or reveille or a ten-mile run or anything else.

She didn't say anything, just let him rest his cock in her. He didn't really want to move her yet, because all was sweet in afterglow, and her weight didn't bother him much. She tipped forward onto her hands, causing his dick to slide out only a little as she changed angles. He grimaced slightly, that extra sensitivity across the body of the cock dragging a moan out of him. Not a pleasurable one, either. Well, maybe like 10% pleasurable and 90% FUCK FUCK NO AIGHHHH.

"Are you finished?" she asked after another minute.

He could feel his hard-on shriveling up like one of those retractile garden hoses that went flaccid when the water was drained out of them. "Yeah," he managed to grunt out, because he was done, at least for this morning. She'd got him last night going to bed and this morning waking up, and that was pretty close to Hendricks's limit for now.

She dismounted and there was that 90/10 feeling again, but it only lasted a second and she was off, standing beside the bed. He wondered if she'd wander to the bathroom. She never really had before—Starling didn't seem to need to answer the call of nature, unlike other women he'd been with—but there was a first time for everything.

But she just stood there, back to him, not looking anywhere near him, and finally, she said, "You buried the sheriff."

"Not me personally," he said, eyeing her, kinda torn between getting up, showering, getting dressed, and going into the station—fuck, that sounded like a lot of work—or just riding the post-climax sleepy feeling back to unconsciousness. The path of least resistance had been winning until she'd started talking. "But yeah. We had his funeral already." Hendricks stared at the bumpy wall, then at Starling's little ass, tight as a lug nut that had been drilled on. "His kids didn't show up. I guess nobody told 'em their mom and dad are dead and their childhood home burned to the ground. What a fuck job, huh?"

She didn't answer that, of course. "It is a shame," she said instead.

"Yeah," Hendricks said. "A shame." What was even more of a shame was, "You know they don't even seem to want to hunt down the thing that did it?" This was still burning his ass like seven straight nights of acidic diarrhea. You just didn't leave a fallen comrade unavenged. "I wanted to track down that fire sloth motherfucker, but they're all—'No, we'll wait until we get a call, we shouldn't go wandering in the woods with the dangerous demons.'" He snorted. "I get that and all—hell, I championed it when we were going after those hellcats—but … goddamn. This was Reeve, for fuck's sake. We ought to make this thing that burned him to death pay—"

"He wasn't burned to death," Starling said, standing there naked. "He was dead before the fire."

Hendricks had let his eyes drift shut, but they suddenly sprang open. "What did you just s—" He sat up.

Starling was gone.

"Of fucking course," he muttered to the empty room. The darkness was not complete, not nearly, but she was plainly vanished.

The knock at the door nearly scared the shit out of him, and Hendricks just about leapt out of bed at the sound. All thought of pleasant, basking afterglow was gone, and he was on Red Alert right away. "Who is it?"

"Knock knock, motherfucker," came the voice of Duncan from beyond the door. Hendricks shuffled over and unlocked it, throwing it open without bothering to put his pants on. The OOC just stared at him. "You're going like that?"

Hendricks blinked at him, the morning sun streaming in and nearly blinding his ass. "Going? Where?"

"I got that old familiar feeling again," Duncan said, chucking a thumb over his shoulder. "Something's up." He glanced down at Hendricks's groin. "And it ain't you, plainly."

"You missed it by five minutes," Hendricks said.

"Lucky me. You gonna cover up? Because I'm guessing you'd have a hard time keeping your belt from sliding off relying on that alone, especially right now."

Hendricks responded with a rough laugh. "Gimme five and we'll ride." And he shut the door.

*

Arch awoke to the sounds of the house, the quiet hum of electricity and conversations in the distance. A clatter of pans shocked him out of unconsciousness, but it took him a few more seconds to process what he'd heard.

Olivia was making breakfast, he realized as he turned over and buried his face in the sheet. The smell of fresh detergent was powerful, and he rolled away again. It wasn't whatever brand Alison had used to wash their clothes.

Alison ...

He put his head back down in the sheet again and inhaled the detergent Olivia Jones used. He had heard things got easier, but no, they did not. Or they hadn't for him. It was getting toward the end of November now—the calendar for the month would be turning over in another week or so—and he was still living in the last of October. Hendricks, that son of a gun, throwing that little detail Arch had missed right in his face. Not that it had been easy before that either ...

How could he have been so stupid? As soon as the cowboy had said it, he'd known the truth of things. Alison, pregnant. Well, why not? They hadn't exactly been careful these last few months, so far as he knew. He'd sort of forgotten about them trying to have a baby in all the rush of the demons coming into town, and she hadn't gone out of her way to remind him.

Something about that information was a kick right in the pants. It was a wake-up when he wanted to sleep more, a piece of grit in his eye he couldn't ignore, like a drill that was eating its way right down to his heart. Didn't feel like it would ever stop, either. He wanted it to, but grief was like an endless well, never going to run dry ...

"Oh, Lord," Arch said, closing his eyes, hoping he could complete a prayer and maybe drift back to sleep for a while, "I do not know the mysteries that you know ..."

He let the words drift off, sinking into his own head as he prayed.

... I don't know why you chose to take my wife from me, but I trust in your plan. That was a little bit of a lie. He wanted to trust in the plan, but it was something he was struggling with. He wanted to believe it was for a good cause, but he was having one devil of a time seeing any cause at all. It looked more like a cause and effect to his eyes—demons came to town, he and Alison tried to fight them off and help people, Alison died. And that was ... somewhat more understandable. Because to him it being chalked it up to collisions of free will rather than plan of the divine; capriciousness on the part of that demon mingled with Alison's desire to do the right thing ... there was something brave and noble about that, something that put the actions squarely in their court rather than assigning this terrible deed to the Almighty.

The idea that there was a plan, some greater good to be served, some higher ideal they were pursuing? Well ... Arch wanted to believe in that too. But he was struggling with believing these days, and it started with the smaller ideas and stopped there—for now. He worried about that though. After all, when the foundation crumbled, the roof wouldn't long survive it.

"Oh, Lord," Arch said, talking out loud again. "I worry. I worry, and I fret. I obsess about that which is already over. I add no hours to my life by doing so, but I worry nonetheless." When you had such a solid, tangible grip on the way things were, and loved the way things were, how could you not latch on in your mind to how things had played out? How could you not wish for a referee—the referee of the universe, perhaps—to call foul on the play, cost the other team some yardage, and reset the downs so you got another chance?

"I wonder how you could have given me so sweet a gift ... only for life to take it from me." He knew life was transitory, that he was obsessing about something temporary instead of the eternal, but ...

He'd played this game of mortal existence, and he'd been invested in the play. That this one had gone hard against him ... well, that didn't make it any easier to let go of than it had when he actually had played football. That he'd poured more emotion into his life with Alison than any game, any obsession, anything else in his life ... it had been his marriage that had weathered it all.

And curse Hendricks for opening his eyes to a new pain that he hadn't even realized was there, like figuring out after the adrenaline faded that you didn't just have a bruised foot, you'd broken the danged thing.

Soft footsteps scuffed just outside the door and a knock thumped, jarring him. "Arch," Olivia's voice came through, "breakfast is going to be ready in about five minutes."

"Be right there," Arch said, and his prayer just sort of ended. He hadn't been sure what he was going to say anyway.

*

Brian awoke to the beeping of the breathing machine. His neck had a fierce crick in it. He hadn't meant to sleep here, but he'd gotten too tired to drive home, and the hospital had a reclining chair with some sort of plasti-leather cover that didn't breathe too well. Which wouldn't have mattered in normal conditions, but he'd gotten hot and sticky during the night, and moved his head to the side, lolling off in search of a way to keep the back of his head from sweating balls. Who would have thought someone would turn the damned heat up so high in a hospital in November that it'd feel like fucking summertime?

Brian massaged his neck. Hopefully this would dissipate shortly, because otherwise ... ouch. He doubted it though. It wasn't like he was a two-year-old anymore. At the last family reunion he'd seen a distant cousin of that age go to sleep sitting up, tilted forward against a pole. It looked like the most uncomfortable damned position he'd ever seen, and yet the kid awoke later without a whine, like it was nothing.

"Oh, to be young again," Brian muttered, letting loose a fierce yawn. Not that he was old, but that neck ...

He sat upright, sliding the reclining seat down so that his legs came back to the floor. Other than the sweat-inducing material, this chair wasn't bad for sleeping. He would have preferred to be back in his own bed back in Midian, but ...

Well, maybe he wouldn't prefer that at this point. Not that there was much good here, but it was better than the sounds of an empty house. He'd spent a night or two there while his mother was at the hospital, and the noises—the empty house noises—worked at him, waking him in the night. It was a restless, fitful sleep, and he'd run out of patience with it.

His mother stirred in her sleep across the way, another one of these rolling recliners in her corner. It looked like a normal enough chair when you sat in it. You had to do a little jockeying to unlock it and get it to lean back, but when you did ... whew. Comfort.

His father was making a *Mmmm, mmmmmm* grunting noise in his sleep and twitching, head jerking to one side.

Brian lifted his head up and set about converting the recliner back into a chair. It was habit by now, the nights of sleeping in this thing and the mornings of waking up having turned him into an automaton, setting things up for visitors in case anyone showed up while he was gone. Because he had to get gone; he had his shift at the station to get to.

Because ... well, because he had to. Just another area where he was going through the motions, following the now-familiar routine.

Stiffening, Brian looked over at his father. His face was lined, way more lined than it had been before all this shit came down. Brian had taken Casey's advice lately, trying to unwind a little more, trying to find that centering point in himself. It wasn't easy, but the weed did seem to help ... well, some. It at least gave him a reason to go on, those brief moments when everything felt different and better. The rest of the time was sitting around a hospital bed or a desk, waiting for emergency calls to come in.

"This is my life?" Brian asked himself, standing at the foot of his father's bed. He didn't even really feel like he was making a difference at this point. Trying to fight demons had been a thing he'd taken on wholeheartedly back when he'd first stumbled into this mess. He'd seen the value after the Rog'tausch had gone tearing through Midian—and thank God he'd finally figured out how to dispose of that damned thing in a manner that wouldn't cause it to be an EPA hazard. Or, hopefully, ever be found again.

But now ... the price for this demon business was getting too high. He turned for the door, the antiseptic smell of the hospital particularly strong today. He needed to get out for a while, go to the office, answer some calls, maybe head home and smoke a J, then shower and take a night off from visiting the hospital. Maybe spend a night in his own bed, restless sleep be damned. He'd earned it, hadn't he?

As he came out of the stairwell on the ground floor he looked to his left and saw a flash of dark hair turning the corner. He got a glimpse of the profile of Dr. Lauren Darlington, but she hadn't seen him, which was just as well. He thought about chasing after her, but what was the point, really? Let the woman have her life, he thought, turning to head toward the exit and his car. She didn't need to get sucked back into this Midian bullshit.

Hell, really, no one did.

*

Lauren was behind in her rounds, but that was okay, because her boss was still treating her with kid gloves. She probably didn't need that treatment, but by God she'd take it, especially since she kept getting the mass texts from the watch. So her phone blew up every once in a while. Or every day. Several times a day. Like now.

She glanced down at the text: MAAASIVE DEMONS SITED AT HICKORY LN.

How in the hell did you even mess up the word 'massive' that badly? Autocorrect had gone badly astray.

Lauren put her phone on nighttime mode, knowing that the pager she wore on her belt would guide her just fine. She'd just disregard, maybe ask Molly to help her block the watch number later tonight. Because Molly was speaking to her again, in small doses.

Or maybe she'd just Google how to block them. It didn't seem like a wise idea to provoke her daughter by bringing up the watch, not when things were finally starting to defrost between them.

*

Erin felt the buzz and was instantly on high alert; if her cell phone was going off, odds were good it was something important. She fiddled to grab it, slipping as she took the car into a turn to enter Jackson Highway, and managed to check it without fucking up too badly—like, say, ramming the car into a semi as it went by. Near thing, though.

She got the phone up to the steering wheel and it lit, automatically.

MAAASIVE DEMONS SITED AT HICKORY LN.

Erin wasn't much of a pedant, but she spied a few things wrong with that sentence. Instead of texting back a thoughtful reply about spelling, though, she flipped the switch that activated the lights and sirens and whipped the car around, cutting off Mort Grammer in his pickup. With an apologetic wave in his direction, she hauled ass toward Hickory Lane.

*

Drake had planned this for a week. He had the recipes, he had the ideas, and he had it in mind to do great things. All he lacked ...

Was the meat.

The veal.

Human veal.

Drake's hands gripped the steering wheel tightly, his eyes focused on the little house across the road from where he'd parked. It was an in-home daycare, according to the ad in the yellow pages. He didn't even know there still were phone books, but he found one in the drawer of his rental house, thin, almost the length of a reasonable novel. Such an anachronism in this modern age. Not that he was complaining.

The ad boasted that the daycare had been open for thirty years. Well, that was good. Experience. Also, a person in charge who probably hadn't seen his like before. He eyed the white house with the colonial-style porch and sniffed. It wasn't to his liking at all. Too old, too provincial. He liked the sleeker style of modernity, not this old ... stuff.

But he wasn't here to live in the place, he was just here to pick up the ingredients for his next culinary masterwork. All that mattered was securing them.

With that in mind, he picked up the knife from the seat next to him and took a short breath. He didn't care if anyone got hurt, really, so long as he got what he wanted.

It was time to take the next step.

*

Brian walked in the front door of the sheriff's station and found Benny Binion at the desk. He'd gotten the text; he should have known. For all his myriad faults, Casey knew how to spell and construct a sentence reasonably well. Also, autocorrect wasn't his mortal enemy.

"Hey, Benny," Brian said without enthusiasm. "Any idea what's going on out on Hickory?"

"Something big," Benny said. "You shoulda heard the call. Penny Frye sounded like she was about to shit a brick. Said it was big and black—"

"That's what people say about my brother-in-law," Brian said.

"Bigger than Arch," Benny said. "Bigger than a house, according to her."

Brian just stared at him. "And you didn't think to mention that to the watch?" He scrambled and grabbed the cell phone from in front of Benny and hurriedly composed a text. Even without him trying, it was better spelled than the last.

*

Hendricks was driving again, happy as a pig in shit to be in charge. Duncan didn't seem to mind, since he was a little demonic pussy gelding, content to let others drive. Not that Hendricks hadn't had a long period of that, but it was mainly because he didn't want to deal with the maintenance issues of having a car. Now that he'd come to Midian, though, and was dealing with a hotspot laid out over a full-sized American county—or most of it—the advantages of having an automobile were undeniable. It wasn't like this was some quaint, one-street European village with excellent public transportation, after all.

Which was good, because he liked having the .45 strapped to his hip, no matter how little it did to demons. He fucking hated leaving it behind on the rare occasions when he traveled internationally. And getting the sword through customs? A cast-iron bitch, it was.

"What are you feeling?" Hendricks asked, looking over at Duncan. So far all the OOC had told him was to head into town. The thin man, whoever he was, had not come back to the motel after their initial sighting, at least as far as Hendricks knew. He'd been watching—at least a little between sleeping, fucking Starling, and watching *Westworld*—and no dice on seeing him. He suspected that the bastard had probably taken a room in town somewhere. Maybe he'd seen them, who knew? "Other than yourself." He nodded at Duncan's crotch.

"I don't really do that," Duncan said, concentrating.

"You let Guthrie do it?" Hendricks asked.

Duncan just stared out the front window. "Guthrie's got his—her—whatever—Guthrie's got no need for me."

Hendricks wasn't sure how to take that reply and didn't want to probe further for fear of what it might upturn. So he didn't.

For about five seconds. "Is Guthrie fucking someone local?"

"You mean like you?" Duncan asked, finally favoring him with at least a sidelong look.

"I know she ain't fucking me," Hendricks said. "I'd remember a cranky demon wearing the shell of a middle-aged black lady crashing into my crotch, and that ain't happened."

"What *has* happened?" Duncan asked, and Hendricks got the feeling he was trying to divert attention away from not answering the question. "You and a—whatever Starling is—"

"You guys have a hard time copping to the fact that she's on the other team, huh?"

"I don't know her and I don't know what she is," Duncan said. "And neither do you, other than a good lay."

"Sounds like almost every relationship on planet Earth," Hendricks said. "Plus or minus the 'good lay' thing. So I'm kinda ahead with that."

"You didn't even believe in the 'other side,'" Duncan said. "But now you believe—"

"I don't believe in God," Hendricks said, "in the same way I don't believe in Zeus or Odin or whoever the ancient peoples of the world worshipped. That doesn't mean I don't think there might have been people by those names who were—I don't know—ancient heroes or something that ancient man elevated into gods. I mean, think about it, maybe some guy got crucified two thousand years ago, and his followers put on a scheme to pretend he came back. The ultimate stage one of the grief process, you know?" He shrugged. "We humans have funny ways of explaining the events of life to ourselves. I could easily believe someone takes a story about some scary army up against their virtuous one and turned it into something about frightening, demonic anger—them—versus our saintly, sweet army of pure defense who never did a cross thing ever—us. Boom, there's your Christian myth in a nutshell, because let's face it—everybody needs a devil to hate."

"Well, you people do a fair amount of hating of us devils," Duncan said. "And speaking as one of them, I wish you'd pick your targets better."

"Speaking as one of the hunters," Hendricks said, "I do—as evidenced by the fact you and I haven't gotten in a scrape yet." He jerked the steering wheel slightly to avoid an oversized truck coming down the road toward him.

"I like the 'yet,'" Duncan said.

Hendricks did his best to shrug without upsetting the wheel. "You seem all right, but let's face it—you work for somebody other than the watch. You've seen what's happened among us humans over the last week, without Reeve to steer the ship. Our intentions are all toward trying to get things righted around here. Yours are to police demons, probably. But your Home Office—"

"Which I've been ignoring." Duncan didn't quite bristle, but maybe his low-key version of it.

"—they've got other aims," Hendricks said. "Now maybe you stay with us all the way up to whatever end we make of this thing, and maybe you decide to follow your original loyalties. I wouldn't care to speak for you in that."

Duncan actually turned and looked at him, but he was inscrutable. "That's . . . probably wise." It sounded like a concession.

"Do I turn up ahead here?" Hendricks asked. As much as he wanted to continue the conversation and stab home the next point he'd come up with, he was just driving down Old Jackson Highway without a clue where he was going.

"Stay straight," Duncan said. A buzzing filled the air as their phones went off. Hendricks started to go for his, but Duncan beat him, grabbing his own first. "Eyes on the road. I'll read it to you."

"Maybe mine's different than yours," Hendricks said.

"'I need you now,'" Duncan said. "It's signed, 'Starling.' You're right; this one is probably just for me."

"Dick," Hendricks said. Duncan was reading his own phone; there was no way he got a text from Starling. Plus: "She doesn't even text, you fucking shelled asshole."

"I bet Starling sexting would be super hot," Duncan said, still staring at his phone. "'I will bring the hot pussy unto you this eve. You must bring the rigid cock, and together we will grate our nethers against one another until climax is achieved.'"

"You're giving me another boner here," Hendricks said. "What's the message actually say?"

"It's borderline illiterate, but it says there was a massive demon sighted out on Hickory Lane. Why do you people bother having rules you don't even follow?"

"What the hell are we talking about?" Hendricks asked, kinda confused.

"The speed limit is 45 through here," Duncan said, pointing at the needle. "I don't mean to be pedantic, but you're doing 55."

Hendricks confirmed that he was indeed ten over. "And?"

"No one drives the speed limit exactly," Duncan said. "It's more like a speed guideline, and they only tend to nail you if you get, like, ten over."

"Yeah, I doubt they'll do that around here, because we work with them, and they're busy with other shit," Hendricks said. "But I get your point."

"Why have a law nobody follows?" Duncan asked. "Also, turn left at the next traffic light."

"We getting close?" Hendricks asked.

"No. The square's been closed since Halloween, remember?" Duncan pointed ahead. Yep, Hendricks could see the barricades, still up. "I guess the county hasn't hired an official clean-up crew, and you people seem averse to driving on the splattered remains of your own, so …"

Hendricks cringed. "Yeah. Somebody ought to get to cleaning that shit."

"Drumlin and McMinn are on it." Hendricks stared at Duncan blankly over those names. "I dunno," the demon said in answer, "they're two of the new guys on the watch."

"Pffft, FNGs," Hendricks said. "You expect me to remember all these Johnny Come Latelys?"

"I don't expect anything of you except for you to keep sticking your boner in a redhead you don't exactly understand," Duncan said, "but then again, I've probably got a Hobbesian view of human nature."

"Cute. What's that supposed to mean?"

"It's dim," Duncan said. "Very dim. Take a right and follow this past the square."

Hendricks did as he was told, mainly because he didn't have an active GPS to do the guiding for him. "So … massive demon out near Hickory Lane. Wherever that is."

"I guess," Duncan said. "I'm not feeling it."

"You think it's a false alarm?"

"Maybe. Or maybe I'm just not feeling it. Either way, I want to follow this up."

"Because the skinny guy here is dangerous?" Hendricks asked. He'd stabbed a few demons of late, but there was always time in his day to stab another.

"I don't know," Duncan said. "He's no innocent, hanging around this town and stirring up my demon-dar."

It took Hendricks a second to get it. "Like demon radar."

"Bingo."

"That wasn't real clear."

"Sometimes I like to make you get off your lazy, redhead-fucking ass and work for it."

"Maybe if it was a better joke …"

"Turn in here," Duncan said, sitting up abruptly. He pointed at a squat building that was on a side street, a small parking lot out back. It wasn't terribly big, maybe a couple times the size of a normal house in town.

Hendricks obeyed and pulled in, driving past the building into the rear parking lot and finding an open spot. He shifted into park because Duncan didn't tell him not to, nose up like a bloodhound, ears perked like he was hearing something. "What is it, boy?" he asked, thinking of those black and white reruns of Lassie that he'd occasionally catch as a kid when at his grandparents' house. "You hear something?"

Duncan didn't move. "I'm not a dog, and if you fall down a well, I'm leaving you there. Also … obscure."

"Like I made you work for it?" Hendricks cracked a grin and caught some more side-eye from Duncan. "You've been around a long time. Figured if anyone got it, you would." He chucked a thumb over his shoulder toward the building. "This it?"

"Yeah." Duncan nodded. "What is this place?"

Hendricks turned at the waist, looking over his shoulder. "Funeral home. Say, didn't we run into this guy at—"

"Funerals," Duncan said, now turned around himself, squinting back at the building. "Hmm."

"What's that supposed to mean? 'Hmmm.'"

"Could be a lot of things," Duncan said, opening the car door. "Mostly, though, it means we're going to have to go inside for a closer look, because it'd be impossible to tell from here."

Hendricks checked his phone, catching the text message from the watch. The spelling wasn't that far off. At least it was readable. Got the point across. He'd probably done worse. "And our comrades in arms? You reckon they'll be fine while we go put a holy point in this skinny fuck?"

"More of them are going out there to check out this 'MAAASIVE' demon than are going in here with us," Duncan said, pulling out his baton and cradling it, undeployed, in his hand. "If you're asking me to guess who's in more danger, I say us."

"Pffft," Hendricks said as they started across the parking lot. "'Ain't skeered.'" But he kept his hand on the hilt of his sword nonetheless.

*

Drake made his way carefully up to the front door of the house/daycare. He wasn't sure exactly how many of the little creatures to expect, and it didn't really matter. He would pick the choicest cuts.

His wingtips thumped against the aging floorboards of the porch, and he tilted his head sideways in order to look into the tall pane window just to the left of the door. He put a pleasant smile on his face and rang the doorbell.

The wind picked up and blew past him, ruffling the tail of his suit jacket and his hair, which was very carefully styled. He looked in the window, past his own reflection, which he barely noticed, and saw movement in the shadow projected by the glass. A woman with a wide smile and age lines at the corners of her eyes made her way to the door, little shadows following at her heels. A satisfying click heralded the door's deadbolt being undone, and then the handle lock rattled.

The door swung just a foot, and a woman's face appeared, stuck out a little.

"Perfect," Drake said, and the woman frowned in confusion.

He slipped the knife from his belt and ran it across her throat before she even had a chance to react. That done, he shoved her hard back inside, looking swiftly left and then right. There was no one on the surrounding porches—probably a little too chilly—and so he was alone out here, unwatched. Once he'd pushed the older woman out of the way, hearing squeals as she stumbled over some future cutlet lingering behind her, Drake entered the home daycare and shut the door behind him.

The old woman was gasping, flopping, trying to hold her throat. She'd also fallen atop the cutlets, and so he heaved her off, tossing her bodily through the air. She crashed against the archway of a door leading into a playroom where another few children were playing with a colorful variety of toys, and then crashed back to the floor, head thumping soundly against it upon impact. She lay still, a pool of red spreading out onto the carpet from her neck, her skull caved in squarely in the back.

Drake did a headcount. One, two, three, four, five—six. Six little animals. It wasn't perfect, but it was better than nothing, and would at least let him answer the big questions. "Hmm," he said, and unlooped the rope he'd put on his belt. He leaned down and picked up the one caterwauling next to him, dragging it to its feet. It did not wish to stay on its feet though, which was most annoying. He wrapped the rope around its midsection and then moved on to bind up the next, leaving it to cry—for now. He had six more to rope, after all, before he could get moving.

*

Brian felt the semi-warm air come rushing down at him as the station's heater kicked in. Thank God the heat worked here. Not that it was freezing outside, but it wasn't exactly balmy out there.

"Now that that's done," Brian said, putting down the cell phone, "you're pretty much relieved, Benny."

Benny just frowned at him. "I think you relieved me when you took the phone away, Brian."

Brian shrugged. "Just wanted to make sure they knew what was coming."

Benny looked at him for a moment, then shrugged. "My wife's always busting my ass about my spelling. I'm telling you, autocorrect did it this time."

"Autocorrect made it so you didn't remember to tell them exactly how big the demon they were going out to investigate was?" Benny's face took on a sullen expression. "I mean, uh ..." Brian tried to think of a way to dig himself out, but it didn't come immediately.

"See you later," Benny said a little huffily, and threaded his way through the bullpen's assortment of desks, around the counter and out the door. Brian still hadn't thought of something soothing to say by the time he walked out, and so he just mentally shrugged and got on about the day. Wasn't much he could do, after all.

*

"Well, ain't this a fucking grandiose display of hell come to earth?" Nate McMinn asked as Erin stood on Hickory Lane, trying to keep her jaw from banging against her clit. Maybe even her ankles, it was so close to the ground.

Her skin prickled, and it had zero to do with the chilly air. The breeze came up and rustled its way through the trees still standing on the street, shoving aside the branches like a pissed-off running back shoving off a tackle, then two tackles, then more.

Hickory Lane was a fucking devastated mess. Twelve houses used to stand here, and now …

It looked like a hurricane had run through, shingles at Erin's feet, entire buildings caved in, a disaster scene out of the *Earthquake!* movie, or maybe any one of a dozen others she'd seen over the years lately, where the endgame was always utter devastation.

That was what she was seeing here. One house had an open gas line burning, shooting flame up in the air like the fires of hell. She'd talked to Wyatt Pressler—Marty Ferrell's replacement, now that he'd gone and disappeared—and he was already on it, trying to shut off the line for the entire street, because every front lawn on Hickory Lane was so covered in debris, every house so fucking devastated to the foundation that it wasn't like they could reach the gas shutoffs for any of the former residences.

This was Mary Wrightson's farmhouse writ large; this was getting toward epic in its scale of destruction, and it made her sick. She'd been there the night that the Rog'tausch had started tearing through Midian, but that had been one big guy-shaped demon that had pounded its way through town, like a wrecking ball leaving holes in walls and smashing cars.

Here, though … here it was an army of wrecking balls, ripping their way through whatever they wanted.

"How the fuck do we even fight this?" Keith Drumlin asked. He and McMinn were tight, almost like they should have been holding each other for comfort, Erin thought. Normally, she might have gotten a giggle out of that idea.

Not here. Not now.

Instead she listened carefully for any sound out of the woods that surrounded Hickory Lane. Not a thing was moving though, and once she was sure it was so, she pulled her cell phone off its place on her belt and dialed up Father Nguyen. He answered after a few seconds with a sleepy mutter: "Hello?"

"Did you finish yet?" she asked, hoping—hoping—goddamn did she hope—that he had.

"Yeah," he said, and she pumped her fist, looking at the wreckage of the debris field in front of her. "The last one is done. Did you run into—"

"Yes," Erin said. "The text is on your phone. Get whoever you can together and meet us out here. We'll do a little mapping and then …" She hung up on the suggestion, staring at the wreckage of one of the houses. She hadn't needed to say the rest; Nguyen knew exactly what was coming next anyhow. They'd been planning it since the last shadowcats had come running through and ripped up Mary Wrightson's house.

*

The 911 line rang, loud and jangling, the sound of a different time. Brian scrambled to pick it up as quickly as he could.

For a while, this had been outsourced to some call center because of how much volume they were getting and how little help they had. No more; now they had people from the watch on call 24 hours a day, and the volume had softened, because a lot of the crazy, worried calls had seemed to evaporate when the knowledge that it was demons doing most of what was happening to Midian had almost seemed to make most people more afraid to call in. Even after Halloween, if they had to call in and admit they were seeing a demon, people would almost internally combust. Fear of ridicule was holding some or a lot of them back, Brian suspected, from seeking the help they needed.

Which was why, when he said, "911, what's your emergency?" he was surprised to hear on the other end of the line: "A demon just broken into Millie Falkes's house. Just walked right up on the porch and slit her throat."

"Excuse me?" Brian hesitated, trying to process through what he'd just heard. The voice had a local accent, but he didn't recognize it.

"A demon just busted into Millie Falkes's house," the lady said. An older lady by the sound of her voice. "He's in there right now."

"Okay," Brian said, trying to mentally manage his way through this. He didn't have anyone to dispatch, since everyone was pretty well at Hickory Lane. "Let me take down your information and I'll send someone over as soon as we can—"

"You don't understand," the voice came back more urgently. "Millie runs a daycare in her house. There are children in there. And there's a demon—"

"Oh, uh, well—that's bad," Brian said, trying to agree just to get this over with. "What's your address, and I'll try and send someone over immediately."

"319 Bilius," the woman said. "That's Millie's address."

"And whom am I speaking to?" Brian asked.

"This is Kay Bland."

Brian remembered that name from fifth grade. "Ms. Bland, this is Brian Longholt."

There was an impatient noise. "You still wasting your potential, Brian?" She said it as only a disappointed teacher could.

"Uh, well, I ended up going to Brown," Brian said.

A pause. "What'd you get your degree in?" Aura of suspicion hung in her voice.

"Uh … philosophy."

She made another disgusted noise. "All that brain power you had and you're just going to sit around all day and make shit up about the universe," she said. "I ought to kick you where the good Lord split you. What a waste."

"Hey, I'm answering 911 calls now, trying to help out," he said.

"You are playing so far below your potential," she said, and he could almost hear his former teacher shaking her head on the other end of the phone.

"Wow," Brian said, "this is new. Getting lectured when someone calls 911 to report a demon incident."

"Well, what are you going to do about it?"

Brian paused before replying. "I mean, I'll probably sort of internalize the criticism, stew on it for a while, emotionally—"

"Not that, you jackass! The demon in Millie's house!"

Brian sat up. "Well, uh, we've got all units out responding to a report of devastation on Hickory Lane. I don't have anyone I can send just now—"

"Dammit," she said, and there was shuffling in the background. "I told you it's a daycare and—my God." Her voice grew hushed.

"What?" Brian stood, though there wasn't a damned thing he could do about it or anything else, standing in the station house.

"He's bringing out the children. My God, Brian, he's bringing out the children and—they're roped up." Her voice was in quiet awe. "He's got them tied up like animals and he's—he's dragging them out."

Brian felt a strange, cold tingle. He hadn't quite believed the demon call, and there wasn't much he could do about it right now other than take down the address and call in the watch, but if they had their hands full with the maaasive demons …

Children being led out of a daycare by a man, roped up? What age were the kids who went to daycare, anyway?

Brian started scrambling, fumbling for the cell phone, and when he found it, he dialed a number in its memory, waiting for it to ring with his breath held, hoping he'd get an answer.

*

Arch was in the car with Barney Jones and Braeden Tarley, rolling along toward Hickory Lane but still a ways off. They'd gotten the call in the middle of breakfast and had to put it all down, grab whatever they could carry—Arch had scooped some egg and ham onto a biscuit—and let Olivia wrap things up in hopes of finishing them later. Even now Arch could still smell the egg, that slightly sulfuric tinge, lingering in the air. He might not have been able to detect it a few months ago, but with all his exposure to brimstone of late, sulfur seemed to be a smell that tripped his trigger no matter how small the quantity, now.

"I don't truck much with the ideas of the Calvinists," Jones was saying, part of a longer talk he was having with Tarley that Arch had mostly tuned out, "but—"

Arch's phone rattled in his pocket, clicking against some change. He pulled it out and answered it, seeing it was the watch cell phone back in the station. "Hello?"

"Arch," Brian's voice came rushed, "we got an incident out on Bilius Street. Millie Falkes's daycare might have just been hit by a demon."

"Whoa," Arch said and leaned forward, thumping the seat back in front of him. "Head to Bilius Street."

"Rerouting," Jones said, like he was one of those GPS things, not even questioning as he steered the car into a right turn.

"Any idea what we're dealing with?" Arch asked, clinging on to the phone tight.

"No, it's—hang on," Brian said, hushing up for a minute before his voice dropped precipitously. "My God."

*

"I'm going out there," Kay Bland said through the phone, huffing in Brian's ear. "I got my husband's old rifle—I ain't letting this sonofabitch walk off with those kids. He just put them in a van, and—my Jesus."

"No no no," Brian said, a phone in one hand, but speaking into the headset wrapped around his head. "Kay, do not—demons are not affected by bullets—"

"I don't give a damn, Brian," she said, and she was fired up. "He ain't getting away with these kids. I wouldn't have let some sonofabitch get to you when you were in my class, and I'll be damned if I let some scrub so-and-so get these little—" She grunted, opening a door with a loud squeak. "Hey! You! You stop that right there!"

"No!" Brian shouted. "You might hit the kids!"

"I know what a backstop is, Brian!" she shouted back at him. The shot rang out with astonishing clarity over the phone line, followed by two more. "You son of a—"

"What's going on?" Arch asked in Brian's other ear, the one not being deafened by gunfire. At least the receiver helped blot out some of the sound made by the shots.

"She's giving 'em hell," Brian said, cringing away from the noise. He was standing in the middle of the bullpen, all alone, and yet more afraid than he'd been in quite some time. "Not sure how it's go—"

"He's driving off," she said in his ear. "He's—he's—" She was gasping for breath. "I got his front windshield, didn't want to aim toward the passenger compartment of the van, because the kids—he loaded the kids up in the back, Brian. Dammit. I ain't shot a rifle since 1978. And I missed him, dammit. I missed him. I must have, because he didn't even budge. Just ran off, but those kids—oh, Brian, those kids—he got the children—"

"Arch," Brian said. "Stand by a second. Kay, which way was he headed?"

"Left on Bilius outside my house," she said, still gasping.

"South, north, east, what?" Brian asked.

"Um ..." She paused, taking stock. "The sun is over there, so—he's headed north. Took a left at the end of the street, so ... yeah, north. On Hager Avenue."

"Suspect last sighted going north on Hager Ave," Brian said numbly. "Arch, you get that?"

"On it," Arch said. "Call me if you get anything else." And he hung up.

*

"Our demon took a van full of children," Arch said as he pulled the phone away from his ear. "Heading north on Hager Avenue."

"That's a short street," Braeden said, gulping but suddenly alive in a way he hadn't been since ... well, Halloween. "Comes to a T at Burnham. He'll have to go either east or west."

"We're five minutes away," Barney said, picking up the pace and throwing them into a hard curve.

"Where are they going to go from there?" Arch said, trying to map it in his head.

"'They'?" Tarley almost snarled—but not at Arch. "That's a load of kids? 'They' ain't going anywhere they want to go, I promise you that." He thumped his hand against the car door, and it was impossible not to read that for what it was. Fire was burning in Tarley's eyes, focused, angry and looking straight ahead for the first time in weeks.

Jones saw it too, Arch knew. "Simmer down, Braeden. We're going to get them back."

"Damned right we are," Tarley said, voice cracking. Even a blind man couldn't have missed the transformation in Braeden Tarley, and Arch knew exactly where it was coming from. You couldn't lose a child like Tarley had lost his Abi and not come off the bench swinging in a situation like this. Not unless you were a completely broken man.

"Where are they going to go?" Arch asked again. "They turn on Burnham—left or right?"

"I don't know," Tarley said, head down, eyes shifting left and right like he was reading an invisible map on his lap. "Left takes you out of town toward Mt. Horeb, eventually ... but there are so many turnoffs. Right goes straight through the middle of town, through some neighborhoods." He shrugged hard. "Who is this demon? Where's he going? If we knew—"

"He's taking kids," Arch said, his own mind racing. "Might be related to all these disappearances."

"Might be the *cause* of these disappearances," Jones offered. The speedometer was pushing 60 in a residential area and Arch knew they were seconds from another turn.

"We can't do this alone," Arch said, coming to his own conclusion. He picked up his phone and started to dial.

*

Hendricks thumbed the ignore button on Arch's call as he stepped into the funeral home, Duncan a step behind him. It didn't feel smart having the OOC walk in front of him, not if he needed to draw a sword. It'd be a real shame if Duncan caught the tip instead of the thing he wanted to catch it, after all. He might even mourn for like five seconds for Duncan.

The interior of the funeral home was all warm wood paneling, aged but classic. Flowers everywhere, of course. It was also pretty empty, save for a couple padded benches along the left wall, and upon one of these benches sat the fucking thin man of legend that they'd been chasing.

"Well, well, well," said Hendricks, eyeing the lanky fuck and sauntering in, letting Duncan step up on his left side, out of the way of his draw. "Here you are."

The thin man frowned, his long face lined in concentration. "I'm sorry," he said with a trace of a British accent. "Do I know you gentlemen?"

"You're about to," Hendricks said, stepping forward, putting a hand on the hilt of his sword, "but don't worry; our acquaintance will be brief." He started to draw—

Duncan grabbed him by the upper arm and jerked him back a step. It was like a wall had been built around his arm and secured it in place, and Hendricks almost dislocated a joint trying to move while the OOC had a grip on it. "Stop," Duncan said, flat and forceful.

"Can't I stop after he's got a hole in him?" Hendricks asked, not daring to look back at Duncan, no matter how much the OOC had pissed him off with this bullshit. Here was a demon, Hendricks had a sword; put the two together and they'd be done with this shit. Why couldn't anything be easy anymore?

"Show me your ID," Duncan said, not letting Hendricks go. Hendricks didn't bother to struggle. He assumed there was a point—a fucking irritating point that was keeping him from showing this tall demon his own point, right to the fucking shell—and decided to be a good grunt and hold fire for a second.

The thin man stood, reaching delicately into his black suit and producing a wallet from which he extracted a card and showed it to Duncan and Hendricks in turn. "I don't fucking care that you're from Vermont," Hendricks said, not daring to look away from him.

"Your *other* ID," Duncan said, and the thin man produced another card, this one ... different.

Hendricks stared at it, and for a second he felt woozy, like he'd looked at Duncan's badge or something. "The fuck?" he muttered.

"Okay," Duncan said, and jerked Hendricks back another step. "We can't kill him."

"What the actual f—" Hendricks started to say. "Demon royalty again?"

"No," Duncan said, keeping that grip on Hendricks. Hendricks just stared at the thin man, who showed no emotion at the discussion about his very life taking place in front of him. "He's a law-abiding demon. And probably not a killer, either."

"Good grief." The thin man looked affronted. "I've never killed a human in my life. That's not my area of interest at all."

"Area of—the fuck?" Hendricks tore his gaze off the thin man and put it squarely on Duncan, who was looking at him. "What the shit is this?"

"*This* is a vulture," Duncan said. "They won't kill you; they'll just pick at the bones."

"Carrion eater?" Hendricks rounded on the thin bastard. "I don't see why we spare an eater of the dead."

"I don't eat the dead," the thin man said with clear revulsion, upper lip twisted in disgust. "I feed on the sorrows of humanity, not any sort of literal destruction. I crave the wreckage of the soul."

"Like Gideon," Hendricks said, itching to pull the sword.

"Gideon got a rush out of death," Duncan said. "This guy lurks at funerals and feeds on the negative emotions of the mourners. The sorrow, the sadness, all that. He's harmless. Actually helps a little, leeching the despair away."

"Despair is a rich sauce in this town," the vulture said, his long nose looking a little like a beak to Hendricks.

"I thought you demons were coming to town to destroy it," Hendricks said, no longer tugging on Duncan's grip. What was the point? He liked to slaughter demons every chance he got, but as much as he enjoyed that, he didn't go out of his way to wipe out the ones that weren't doing shit to people.

"I wouldn't care to destroy your town," the vulture said, no trace of amusement. "I'd much rather keep things on their current clip or even move it back a pace or two. Too much death and the despair gets … impossible, really. Too much for even me to bear. Rather like overseasoning a meal. You can only eat so much cake, you see …"

"Our grief is your cake?" Hendricks wanted to pull the sword again. He threw Duncan a look. "Seriously, you don't want me to kill this guy?" Duncan shook his head. "Because he obeys your laws?"

"And yours," the vulture said archly. Resignation came over him. "Still … things are reaching a state in this town where it won't be safe for even me much longer, as your mere presence here suggests."

"Where will you go next?" Duncan asked.

The vulture sniffed. "Another large city, of course. There are so comparatively few that aren't taken up by my people these days, though."

"Too many ticks, not enough veins," Hendricks said. "One sympathizes."

"It's not quite like that," the vulture said. "We help. If I had a few more of my brethren here, even you—watchers or whatever you call yourselves—might have an easier time of things." He was looking down his nose at Hendricks. "Do you know how desperate people are getting here? How little hope remains?"

"I have some inkling, yes," Hendricks said, looking at the vulture with narrowed eyes. His phone buzzed again, and he reached for it, shaking off Duncan's grip. Now that he had found this to be a dry hole, there was no point in not seeing if something interesting was happening elsewhere. "Are we on speaking terms again?" he asked when he answered.

"We got a problem," Arch said, ignoring his remark. "Demon hit a daycare, made off with some kids, killed the proprietor. We're trying to chase 'em down."

That one hit Hendricks like a brick in the face. "Jesus. Where?"

"In town. Heading toward Burnham Street. We're trying to figure out which way they went."

"Good heavens," the vulture sniffed. "That's appalling."

Hendricks spun around on him. "You talking about this or the floral arrangements here?"

"Stealing children is a loathsome practice," the vulture said, looking very put out by the whole affair. "They don't even have fully developed emotions yet." He sniffed, which was apparently his preferred expression of distaste. "A terrible waste."

"Your objection to them being kidnapped is that they can't feel grown-up feelings yet?" Hendricks stared at him coolly.

"Who are you talking to?" Arch asked, sounding like he was edging closer to panic.

"Just a sec," Hendricks said, getting an idea. "Can you feel these kids' feelings? Their pitiful little sad, non-adult, not-of-interest to you feelings?"

The vulture blinked at him a few times, then closed his eyes. He opened them again. "Yes. They are … quite afraid, at least in their … limited … terms."

Hendricks looked at Duncan, who nodded at him once. "Can you lead us to them?"

The vulture almost sneered. "I could, but why would I want t—oh."

Duncan had turned his back, rather obviously and theatrically. "I can't see what's going on here."

"You don't have eyes in the traditional sense," the vulture said, voice rising with irritation.

Hendricks drew his sword and pointed it at the vulture. One good leap and he could nick the sonofabitch, put a nice hole in him. "I've got nothing in particular against you, but leeches piss me off. So, freeloader … you want to suck the grief-blood of this town, you're not doing it for free."

The vulture made a noise of disgust, then composed himself. "And once I've done this thing for you, you'll let me go back to my business?"

"Of sucking the shitty feelings out of funerals?" Hendricks asked, smiling broadly. "Sure. Maybe you'll even make a dent in some of that 'Too much spice even for me' despair you were talking about." He nodded toward the door, and Duncan opened it for them. "Come on. Let's go for a ride." He put the phone back up to his ear. "Arch, we're on our way. I've got a guy who can lead us to the kids."

"I'm not a bloody GPS," the vulture said, lurching toward the door on his long legs. "More like a divining rod."

"Well divine me a path to those kids," Hendricks said, "or you're going to be facing the not-so-divine hereafter. And I'm told it's quite unpleasant for you fucks." He jerked his head toward the door and the vulture sniffed once more, passing through it behind Duncan. Hendricks followed a second later, keeping his hand on the sword the whole way.

*

Erin was staring at a topographical map of the area when the phone call came buzzing through, pissing her off at the interruption. Didn't people know she had shit to do at this point? "Yeah?" she asked when she realized it was HQ.

"Hey, it's Brian." He sounded jumpy.

"Kinda in the middle of something here," Erin said, tracing a line on the map laid out on the hood of her car with a finger. "What do you need?" *Make it snappy* was what she meant.

"We had a demon hit a daycare in town," Brian said. "Arch and his crew are on it, but—"

"What the fuck?" Erin muttered. "A daycare?" She put a hand over her exposed ear and jammed the cell phone closer as Father Nguyen arrived, the sound of his vehicle's engine like the fucking carpocalypse all down Hickory Lane.

"Yeah. Whoever it was, they marched the kids out all roped up," Brian said. "And like I said, Arch is on it, but it's—I mean, they got a head start."

Erin just listened, mind racing. "Well ... we're setting up here for—"

"I know."

Erin sagged. "What do you want me to do about this?" How the hell was any human being supposed to make these choices?

She looked over the remains of Hickory Lane. She hadn't had the heart to join the search; her crew had been digging in the wreckage of the houses, looking for survivors. Unlike Mary Wrightson's place, it hadn't been quite so satisfactory in its results. This road, a nice little cul-de-sac, had a dozen houses on it. She knew at least two families on the street, but not whether they'd been home at the time this had gone down, and she was doing her level best not to contemplate it.

She was doing her level best to make sure it didn't happen to anyone else.

"I'm sending out a text blast to everyone," Brian said. "I know—I know what you've got going on—" there was a little hiccup in his voice "—but … this …"

"We're saddling up in like five, okay?" Erin said, running her fingers through her hair now that Nguyen had shut off his damned engine and she didn't have to cover her ear anymore. "I can't spare anyone here. I need basically every person I've got to do this, and it still might not work. You send out that mass text and it peels off any of the people I really need …" She didn't finish the thought, but it was laced with menace. "We haven't had a line on these things in a week, Brian."

"These kids, Erin," Brian said, and he sounded like he was about to cry. "Can you even imagine—"

"I don't need to fucking imagine right now, okay?" She closed her eyes and shook her head violently. "I need to kill these hellcats. Let Arch handle that, and he can rope in whoever's not with me. But I need Casey, I need Nguyen, I need Drumlin and McMinn, Ms. Cherry, and Chauncey Watson and—"

"I hear you," Brian said, almost choking it back. "I'll try and hit some of the people with it that we haven't seen in a while. I'll stay away from—whoever you got, okay?"

"Please do," she said and hung up, staring out at the ruins of houses, pieces of them all sticking up out of the ruin—wood and stone, shingle and nail, a grave for whoever had been home at the time, an almost certain doom.

Just like she might have sent those kidnapped kids to by what she was doing now.

"Goddammit," she said, squeezing the edges of the phone in her hand. It bit into her palm, the smooth edges, and she almost threw it, but couldn't bring herself to. She needed it, after all, for this job.

"Erin?" Nate McMinn's soft voice reached her where she was standing, and she kept her back to him for just another minute while she tried to get her shit together. "We're about ready here. Just need an idea of where we're moving."

"Yeah," she said, nodding once, and then she turned around, letting her face fall back into steely calm. She had shit to do—and no time to worry about the things she couldn't do jack about.

*

County Administrator Pike was feeling like a bit of a vagrant lately, wandering around the county visiting some of the smaller offices and working out of his home when he had actual stuff to do that didn't involve meetings. It wasn't ideal, but on the bright side, he was able to wake up and not dress up a decent portion of the time.

Not today though. He was suited up today.

"You going in this morning?" Darla asked from the stove. She was making grilled cheese sandwiches for the kids, by popular request. She wore her apron over her pajamas, her hair up in a bun that had been flattened on one side. The effect was comical, but Pike knew better than to comment on it.

"Got a meeting in Midian," he said, adjusting his belt. He'd gained a pound or two since they'd burned down the office, shot Reeve in the head, and killed Jenny while he was fucking her. Of all of those, it'd been Jenny shitting all over him when she died that had caused him the most stress. It'd made it hard to get a boner since then without thinking about it, too. Put a kink in his sex life. Now he was down to basically Darla and his own hand for relief, and her thoughts this last week had been … elsewhere. "Should be back by noon."

"Good," Darla said, flipping a sandwich. She beckoned him forward, and he half-expected a kiss. Instead, she whispered in his ear, "These little shits are driving me nuts."

Pike turned his head to look at the kids. They were both parked in front of the TV, not a care in the world for their parents, who were discussing boring adult stuff behind them while Doc McStuffins was doing her thing on the screen. "They seem all right to me," he said.

"For now," she said, "but the minute it goes off—boom. They're going to be all up in my area." She let air hiss out between her teeth. "I'd send them to daycare, but …" She rolled her eyes. "On a County Administrator's salary …"

"Yeah, well," he said, "when these rituals we've been doing start paying dividends, salary's going to be a little less of a worry."

"I know," she said with a thin smile. "But the waiting sucks sweaty, unwashed cock." She reached over and slapped him in the ass. "Get out there and accumulate us some more power, okay?"

"I'm all over that," he said with a smile of his own as he adjusted his tie. With a peck on the cheek, he was out the door, and about the business of reshaping this sorry-ass county in the image he had in mind for it. Probably not the one the residents would have preferred, but who gave a shit about these unwashed hillbillies, anyway?

*

Drake stopped at the intersection of Burnham Street, peering left and right before pulling out onto the road with a slight squeal of the van's tires. He was obeying the rules of the road scrupulously, not daring to break the law, even though his windshield was a spiderweb of cracks. That probably wasn't street legal, but it wasn't as though Drake had asked someone to shoot at him. It certainly wasn't his fault.

Nor did it matter. The van was rented and couldn't be tied to him, and he had his veal, all loaded up and whimpering in the back. He was quite deaf to the noises they were making. It was all the moans of cattle and goats to him. So on he drove, ignoring all the pitiful sounds from the small creatures behind him, continuing toward his destination—and his culinary destiny.

*

Lauren had just finished up the intubation of a heroin OD and had received a pat on her back and an attagirl when she decided to stop by her locker on her break. Her mind was still on the twenty-something—just a kid, really—that she'd spared from death with a generous dose of Narcan, when she checked her phone. She liked to do that about twenty times a shift, just to make sure that she hadn't missed any important messages from Molly. Something like, "I accidentally burned Elise's house down, please stop by the police station with bail money," or, "I had sex with a well-sculpted set of Bohemian triplets and now I'm pregnant with their Eastern European children." The essentials, only.

So when she snapped off her gloves and reached into her scrubs for her phone, she expected maybe something from Molly. She should have some of those myriad messages from the watch, but for some reason she didn't.

There one was though.

KIDS TAKEN FROM MILLIE FALKES'S DAYCARE. ALL HANDS NOT DEALING WITH HICKORY LANE INCIDENT PLEASE REPORT TO BURNHAM STREET FOR SEARCH IMMEDIATELY!!!

"Oh," she said, a sick feeling in her stomach welling up as she processed the message before her eyes, like it was written in blood—Molly's, she thought for some reason. "Well. At least it's all spelled right." It was a sick thing to say, to think ... but it was all she could come up with.

*

Brian sent the message and then slumped back in his seat. He was loose against the back of the chair, feeling like spilling those words out through the keys of the phone had drained him of life.

It wasn't the texting though, was it? No. He'd sent a billion texts in his life. It was the content of the fucking thing.

Child trafficking? He knew, dimly, that it happened, on a small scale, even here in the US. Maybe even on a bigger scale than he'd ever want to admit. But it happened out of sight, easier to ignore.

Shit, lots of things happened that way. He slid his hand along the sharp edge of the desk, and it felt like a dull sword blade against his palm, a distant threat of a cut.

This happening here though, now ... a demon kidnapping children, maybe killing a daycare provider ... hell, they couldn't even spare anyone to go check on Millie, because they were all too busy chasing after the kids right now.

How fucked up were things in Midian right now? This incident was about as emblematic as Brian could imagine.

He stared down at the phone in front of him, wondering if maybe somehow he could go out to—but no. He didn't know how to transfer the incoming 911 calls, which had to be answered ... because they didn't have anyone else to do it ...

And, he reflected ruefully, it'd be a real shame if they missed an important one right now, even though there'd be not a damned thing he could do if one came in except sit there and sympathize with them over the phone, hoping things would work out all right.

*

Hendricks was in the back of the SUV, the vulture riding shotgun, Duncan in the driver's seat. It wasn't his preferred method of travel, but he'd deal, sword in his hand and threateningly close to the vulture's side, the demon looking distastefully back at him. He imagined that was how an English lord would look down upon his subjects in times of old.

The vulture sniffed, and Hendricks grinned at him. "What's the matter?" Hendricks asked. The SUV hit a bump; Duncan had it cranked up around fifty and was tearing through town trying to get to the damned rendezvous with Arch.

"I appear to have been drafted into the service of humanity," the vulture said, looking straight ahead once more. Duncan took a corner hard, tires squealing, the car feeling like it might just tip. At the last second it hugged the ground, though, so it all worked out.

"You too good to serve?" Hendricks asked. He'd heard that shit before, usually preceded by, *I would have joined the military, but blah, blah, blah.* "Blah, blah, blah" always translated to, "Because I was a pussy," at least in his head.

The vulture wisely did not answer his loaded inquiry. Hendricks shrugged it off; having a demon provide excuses as to why he didn't want to help humans wasn't exactly something he needed in his life anyway. "How far out are we?" he asked Duncan instead.

"We're not," Duncan said, and brought the car to a screeching stop. Hendricks had braced his knee against the back of the driver's seat, but still he almost went flying. He managed to plant his left hand at the last second, which was the only thing that kept his sword from coming forward and turning the vulture into a cloud of free-floating stink.

"Nice fucking driving," Hendricks said, throwing open the rear passenger door and stepping out. Duncan was doing the same.

"I thought so," Duncan said, then looked over at the vulture's side of the car. The door opened and stayed that way, the lanky creature springing out and breaking into a run. "Seems we've got a prison break."

"Bullshit," Hendricks said, and jerked his .45. He put two right in the vulture's back and the demon wobbled a little, a little squeal escaping him as Hendricks circled around the car and caught him, laying the sword tip right on his buttock.

"This is a custom Brooks Brothers suit," the vulture said, both pained and clearly upset at the same time.

"And it'd still be fully intact if you hadn't decided to be a jagoff and run," Hendricks said. "Life's about choices, bitchnuts. Don't make the wrong ones unless you want to eat a shit sandwich of consequences, the least of which being your fancy suit springing a couple of holes."

"What in the fires of Hades is going on over here?" Arch called, popping out of where he'd been sitting in Barney Jones's car.

"First-world demon problems," Hendricks called back, careful to keep the point of the sword good and resting on the vulture's back.

"What the hell are you doing?" another voice called, harsher and higher, and Hendricks turned to see that Guthrie was sauntering toward him. She didn't look pissed—yet—but that'd probably change if she sussed out what the vulture was and what Hendricks was doing.

"Coercing, probably," Hendricks said as Duncan fell into line next to Guthrie. The OOCs looked like an unusual pair, Duncan cool as a cucumber and Guthrie scowling. "Trying to get a little help from our local citizenry in apprehending this dangerous kidnapper," Hendricks said, keeping his voice level as he tried to decide how best to jump this particular hurdle. Guthrie wouldn't play as fast and loose with the rules as Duncan, no fucking way. She'd come down on the side of this vulture, for sure, and that'd mean their one good lead for tracking down the kidnapper would either get away clean or else have another chance to escape while he and the others fought Guthrie to the death over this fucker. In that situation, Hendricks wasn't sure whether Duncan would end up on their side or that of his putative partner, and that was cause for worry because these OOCs could fight.

Arch came on over too, along with Braeden Tarley, the mechanic looking like someone had finally lit the pilot light under his ass. Hendricks gave him a once-over and that was all, preferring to keep his attention on the vulture and where his sword was pointed. Safer that way. Still, he couldn't fail to miss the flush to the cheeks this particular threat had seemed to awaken in Tarley. About damned time, in his opinion. Hendricks had lost before, but never a child; still, it seemed to him, the mechanic was going to gutter out if he didn't get to burning soon.

"This guy," Hendricks said, gesturing with the sword at the vulture, "can sniff out our missing kids. But he requires a little … persuasion."

Tarley came at the vulture just then, raising high his wrench. Hendricks thought maybe by now it had been consecrated, but who knew? Nguyen was busy as a horny priest in a room full of altar boys. "I'll persuade him," he said, and the vulture flinched back without Tarley making it within five feet of him.

"What kind of demon is this?" Guthrie asked, face all clouded with suspicion. She was looking over the vulture with a wandering eye, and not the good kind.

"Saskavon," Hendricks lied so Duncan wouldn't have to; the chubbier OOC gave him a grateful look behind Duncan's back. Saskavons could read proximity to prey, including the size of said prey.

Guthrie shrugged, though the vulture favored Hendricks with an offended look that he gave very little in the way of shits about.

"Let's get this party started," Tarley said. "Time's wasting and the trail's getting colder by the moment."

"All right then," Hendricks said, nodding to the vulture. "Let's saddle up, and you start telling us which way to go."

The vulture blinked at him for a moment, apparently gauging his chances of dodging out of this. He must have given up, because he picked a direction and pointed. It was left. "That way."

"Let's go, let's go," Hendricks said, and jerked his head toward Tarley. "You want this fuck to ride with you?"

Tarley smiled, and it was a malicious damned look. "Damned right. I'll make him talk."

"Just keep in mind, one good poke and he's ashes," Hendricks said, wondering about the look in the man's eyes. "That happens, those kids are gone, okay?"

"He won't get the hard end unless he gets difficult," Tarley said. The vulture swallowed, his thin neck bobbed. Neat reaction, Hendricks thought as he made his way back to the SUV alone, Duncan throwing him a glance as he walked away with Guthrie. It almost made the vulture look human.

*

"Let's move, let's move!" Tarley urged as he slid into the backseat of the car next to the demon and Arch took the front seat. Barney already had it running, and they were off almost before Arch got a chance to close his door. It clunked shut and held, but he could tell it wasn't fully latched. He gave it a good pull and it clicked. But a second later he almost hit the windshield as Jones slammed on the brakes to avoid hitting a minivan, and Arch regretted not getting his seatbelt fastened first.

"Come on now, you so-and-so!" Jones shouted, making a motion with his open hand. He accelerated into the temporary gap left by the minivan's sudden halt just as they started to go, and it clunked his bumper. He didn't seem to care, whipping the wheel to the right then back to the left, going straight ahead in the direction in which the demon had pointed them, hitting his horn as he passed.

Arch saw a woman staring open-mouthed at them as Jones sped them past. It was Brigitte Durst, and he expected she was powerfully shocked to see Barney Jones driving like a bat out of Hades. Jones, for his part, didn't seem fussed.

"Now," Braeden said from the back seat, as menacing as he'd ever heard the man, "I expect to hear from you frequently and without any of this 'last minute turn' shit. You let him know a ways off, y'hear me?"

"I hear you," the demon said in a kind of classical English tone. It sounded like he was ready for a stage performance or something, not a high-speed pursuit of a demon kidnapper. But, Arch reflected as he grabbed hold of the bar to stabilize himself as Jones took another corner at high speed, the old car not really taking to it very well, that just wasn't the hand they were dealt. Any of them.

*

Erin was poring over the map, her decisions nearly made, but a couple of final things to run through. The topographical map spread out over the hood made things easier, giving her a pretty clear idea of the path of these demons. It would have been really useful back when they'd faced them at Mary Wrightson's, or on the night of the missing persons incident out on Faulkner Road, when these things had streamed out of the woods like water running over the bank of a river.

But she had them now, and it was telling her exactly where they had to have gone in the last hour or so since the call had come in. "They couldn't have done anything but skirt the line and head this way, up the side of this hill." She looked around, pointing in the distance to the top of a rounded hilltop nearby that was covered in high trees. "They go around it the other way, things start to get mighty rough and they'd run into that house—which—you can still see the chimney, so it's probably standing, you know?"

"What if just the chimney's standing?" Father Nguyen asked, leaning over the map with her. Ms. Cherry was next to him, McMinn and Drumlin were just down the line, and Casey Meacham was staring over Father Nguyen, kind of peeking over his shoulder.

"We're going to have to take that risk," Erin said. She'd thought of that herself, but she hadn't wanted to waste the time bringing it up just to defuse it like she was now. "If I'm wrong, I'm wrong—this is a guessing game, and we're trying to pick the most likely path. And the most likely path—" she traced a finger down the side of that hilltop ahead, and the one next to it "—is that they funneled this way, into Shade's Hollow."

"Man," McMinn said, "nobody liked to go into Shade's Hollow before this. With those things running around I'm doubly disinclined to visit."

Erin rolled her eyes at that bit of local color. He wasn't totally wrong; people didn't like to go into Shade's Hollow, that much was true, mostly because the Alder family pretty much treated it like their own personal fiefdom of assholes. Erin knew a few of them, and they were all right once you got to know them—she'd gone to school with a couple of the Alder boys—but few bothered, because they were rough, tumble, and backward as hell. She'd heard someone joke that any day now, they were going to get dial-up internet in Shade's Hollow. She thought that was a pretty dick thing to say, mostly because Bobby Alder had had an iPhone before almost anyone else in town. That he probably stole it and almost certainly used it in the commission of his various crimes was beside the point.

"Well, that's where we're going," Erin said, and she pointed out a line. "This area's been logged, so it makes a kind of natural highway into the hollow." She didn't pronounce it "holler," like so many she knew did. "We'll roll through the woods and see if we can join up with it there." She pointed on the map. "This is a swimming hole that the Alders used to use. It's an old quarry."

"I been there," Casey said, nodding. "Not all that big, for a quarry, but … it could work, we run 'em in there."

"And if it doesn't?" Ms. Cherry asked. "Won't we be boxing ourselves in there?"

"She's not wrong," Casey said, running a dirty finger over the squarish mark on the map indicating the quarry. "It's got one good entry and exit, and the back half is underwater a decent portion of the time."

"But we ain't had a rainfall since the summer," Keith Drumlin said, blinking his eyes at them. "It's gotta be dried out by now, ain't it?"

"For sure," Erin said, staring at the quarry mark. "That's the place."

"Do we have a backup plan?" Ms. Cherry asked, a little tentatively. "In case things go awry?"

Erin didn't have to think about it very long to answer, because she'd been thinking of this answer for the entire time. "We fight 'em wherever we have to. Do as much damage to them as we can. Make 'em hurt, make 'em pay. Knock off as many as we can before things bust loose. The quarry'd be better, but … we'll fight them however we need to." She grabbed the map and started folding it up. "Now let's get to work."

*

Pike drove into Midian, admiring his handiwork. There was a house boarded up, probably the result of some family deciding either to barricade themselves in, or pull up stakes. Either worked for him—scared and tender prey for the demons, or one less enemy in this fractured watch. Then on the left, here was a car that had gotten shellacked and vandalized sometime in the last couple weeks, a good example of the trickle-down effects of chaos. Maybe demons had done it, or maybe it had just been shithead kids, but either worked for him. It all served the greater societal breakdown, after all.

He turned the car left on Vickers Avenue. He had a plan to meet a demon for a late lunch, a little sacrifice to discuss some business. He hadn't told Darla about it because … well, he was getting an inkling based on how much she'd known about the rituals they'd performed with Jenny and Reeve that she'd perhaps dipped more than her toe in these dark waters. He'd read some shit in books that she kept off the shelves, things that had been marked, ones that made him wonder if she hadn't been doing some things on the side as well. Scratch that; he knew she had, and not said boo about it. The question was which things she'd done …

He suspected her of partaking of one of the rituals for sure, a demon gangbang kind of thing. She'd had some bruises, been moving a little gingerly the last few days, cringes of pain when she thought he wasn't looking …

Pike put that thought out of his mind, because it made him a little sick to his stomach. He wasn't really the jealous type—well, maybe a little—but the thought of her doing that behind his back skeeved him out. Darla was seeking power, would probably do anything to acquire it, but the fact she'd hoarded that to herself rather than share with him …

Well, he'd just have to get a little creative and go looking for his own alliances as well.

And to that end, he was steering toward an old abandoned industrial building just off the square. It had been a cola bottling plant back in the sixties, abandoned when operations for the major companies had gone through a round of centralizations. Some retailer or another had picked up the lease every now and again, but the last of those had moved out years ago, so now it sat dormant in a section of town every damned body was avoiding.

Seemed to Pike like the perfect place to do some business.

So he took that last turn, all full of self-assurance and a little muted excitement. The last ritual had turned out pretty damned well. He'd gotten away with it, not a single hint of suspicion from those impotent little hick fucks in the sheriff's watch. This would be a small meeting, but a good one, a down payment on a future sacrifice. It was time for him to start making his own inroads, start greasing the wheels of his new constituency on the corpses of his old, and this was the next step.

*

Hendricks felt a little weird driving on his own in the SUV. Arch and company were ahead of him two up, Guthrie and Duncan emoting like a sullen married couple just ahead, and he was following, watching the drama play out.

He didn't really feel like he necessarily had a real interest in the fight, more of a detached interest in not seeing Guthrie go asshole and ruin their mission to recover these kids. Just another magnificent day in Midian. He looked out at the cloud-lined sky overhead and drove on in silence.

Still, something was nagging at him: this vague sense that everybody was chasing different things for different reasons. He should have been happy about that—it was how he'd operated for years, after all—but it didn't please him. It didn't even leave him indifferent.

It left him ... cold.

But here he was, chasing this trail because ... he needed to. Didn't he? There were kids at risk here, and he should be all over that, right?

Hendricks squeezed the faux leather wheel. He should have been all over it. He should have been gung-ho. He damned sure stuck his pig-sticking sword in that vulture's direction quick enough when the chance presented itself. These were little babies, and anyone who went after them was the lowest of the fucking low.

And he should put a hole in them. End of story.

But ... how many damned demon hunters did it take to track down one stupid demon and poke them with something holy?

Hendricks sighed, making the pleather wheel squeak as he gave it some pressure. It felt smooth and a little softly pebbled in his grasp. This was the problem with running with a pack—Arch was on his thing, Erin was on hers, but Hendricks ... he was a lone wolf. Always had been, up to now. When he'd started in this with Arch, it was a partnership. They were going to fight the tide together, here in Midian.

But the tide wasn't exactly going out, was it? And the watch, which had looked like it was going to swell, to go not just big but huge, had decided to mostly go home instead. Sure, they had a core of people, but Dr. Darlington, Sheriff Reeve, Bill Longholt, Alison ... shit, they'd taken some fucking losses, the kind that'd make a lesser man—

probably some army pussy—weep like a bitch during a sappy movie.

And here he was, riding in with the cavalry like days of old. Except ...

Hendricks had left the Marine Corps a long-ass time ago. He didn't ride with a squad anymore.

"This shit is for the pigeons," he said, thinking of a flock. They'd go wherever the trouble was now, and then where it was tomorrow, and then the day after ... like demon hunters, sort of, but so tied to this place they couldn't see objectively what was happening ...

They were fucking losing this war. All the way to the streets.

As if to drive the point home, he passed by a car that had been spray-painted and vandalized, something that never would have happened in this town when he'd first come to it. Kids were being stolen out of daycares, the public got slaughtered out on a square during a festival ...

"You despair," came a voice from beside him, and it nearly sent him into the fucking ceiling. It took Hendricks a second to unclench; if he'd had a pencil up his ass it would have snapped cleanly in two just now.

"Things are going straight to shit," Hendricks said, keeping his hands on the wheel and not bothering to give his red-headed sudden co-pilot a glance. "Doesn't seem to be anything I can do about it, even if we save these kids."

"What if there was?" Starling asked, cool, calm, robotic as ever. "Something you could do about it." This she asked lower, and maybe a trifle less cool.

That seemed to wake up a little something in Hendricks, made him sit up a little straighter. Keep following this convoy, or do something else, something that actually made a difference in the long run? "Shit, I'm in on that," he said, giving her a look. She didn't respond with a smile or anything, because why would she? This was Starling.

*

Arch was wishing he was behind the wheel for the first time in a while. Not because he thought he was a better driver than Barney Jones, but because—just maybe—he might have been a safer one, at least at the moment.

Something about the thought of kids at risk had turned the pastor into a madman, because he was going, going, gone in his crazy. Every direction the demon who acted as their guide pointed, he was heading, and all at top speed.

"Left ahead again," the demon said in that stuffy accent, reminding

Arch of when Alison used to make him watch *Downton Abbey*.

Jones took the corner at sixty, and again Arch was left wondering if they'd get there in one piece or in pieces. Tarley swore in the back seat. This was going to get worse before it got better.

*

As immune as Drake was to the squalls and the pleas, they did get annoying after a while. These little creatures couldn't really even talk—couldn't construct a sentence, which made them not dissimilar from their parents, Drake thought with a sneer.

He wheeled the van carefully around a corner. They were in a neighborhood now, not terribly far from his rental home. Already he could imagine the grill, lighting the coals, smelling the white smoke that would come first before it worked its way to clear blue. He had a little paddock set up, a containment pen for these specimens, to keep them fresh. They'd go swiftly, of course, being so small, but he had four or five recipes in mind for them, experiments he wanted to try involving their meat. He was practically salivating already at the thought.

Tires squealed behind him, and Drake looked in his rearview. The autumn clouds were heavy and grey in the sky, and a long Buick had just turned the corner beside him. Drake frowned. He was going the speed limit, but this madman was driving like a bat out of—well, Drake knew where. The best course was to simply slow, maybe even give this lunatic clearance to pass. There were no telltale signs of police lights to indicate that he was in any sort of trouble, which, to him, suggested he was home free. He hadn't seen any sign of pursuit thus far, and this wasn't a police car, so …

Drake looked ahead. He was approaching a bridge abutment, and an embankment lay to his right, sloping down a hill into a backyard. It passed, and suddenly he was confronted with a cemetery just out his window. He sighed. Such a shame that all that delicious meat went to waste, buried under the ground.

*

Jones was pulling the car closer to the van, in sight now just up the road. "We got a problem," he said, and Arch's ears perked up.

"What?" Tarley asked from the back seat, gruff and hard, hand reaching up to grasp the soft leather seat between them.

"There are babies in the back of this van," Jones said, lifting a hand off the wheel to point ahead. "How am I supposed to get this demon to pull over without hurting them?"

That produced a moment of silence in the Buick. "You can't ram them," Arch said, thinking of the things he'd learned in the police academy. There weren't any gentle ways he could think of that would allow for a stop, especially given this was a demon. It was unlikely he'd respond to shouts of "Pull over!" or even a police car running up behind him with lights flashing.

"I got an idea," Tarley said, leaning forward toward them in the front seat, his wrench still pointed at that demon in the back with him. "You come up alongside to pass, and I'll open the door and lean out, give his tires a quick poke with a sword." He nodded to Arch. Arch just stared at him; the idea carried a whiff of insanity. "We pop one of them, he'll have to stop pretty quick."

"He's going to see us do that," Arch said.

"I don't think he's going to miss almost any approach we take," Jones said. "For example—if you were to shoot out his tires—"

"I can't do that with kids in the car," Arch said.

"—he'd hear that as well," Jones said. "Anything we do, it's going to be obvious."

"He could swerve the car right into you," Arch said, looking back at Tarley.

Tarley's eyes were alive with fire and fury. "Yeah, I know."

Arch didn't want to argue with those eyes. "All right then." And he carefully lifted his sword up over the seat and handed it to Tarley. He didn't see a better way.

"I'll come alongside," Jones said, still gripping the wheel, "you open up and ... we'll just do this thing." He nodded ahead. "We've got a couple blocks to the next stop sign, and he's not going more than about thirty. This is probably the safest it's going to get."

"When it pops, he might swerve toward you," Tarley said, "unintentionally or not. I'm aiming for the left rear, which will make him fishtail if he's not careful. If somehow I get smashed in the door by him hitting us, you keep on his ass." Tarley's voice was aflame. "Don't worry about me. You get those kids back, y'hear?"

Arch took in Tarley's words, but more the tone, which was like the man coughing up his heart in front of all of them. "We hear you," Barney said, casting a quick look over his shoulder. "You're a good man, Braeden."

Tarley didn't say anything for a second, then: "And you, demon—if you use this moment to try any shit, we're going to smear your God-forsaken guts into the damned atmosphere."

"I shan't be a problem," the demon said. Arch almost heard him gulp.

"Here we go," Jones said, and the atmosphere in the car seemed to thicken.

*

"Turn left here," Starling said, her dusky eyes nailed straight ahead, focused on the task before them. Hendricks was gripping the wheel like it was his life preserver, which—metaphorically—it kind of was, given what he was heading into. He'd wanted something uniquely his, something he could go and do, and here Starling had answered him, leading him into the old brick buildings off the town square, all of which looked …

Well, they looked like hell. Abandoned for decades, it seemed like.

He'd seen the town square—hell, he'd fought a demon in it the first night he'd come here—and it was looking rough even before Halloween and all the hell unleashed on it there. But this was a different beast still, this decaying industrial and commercial sector off the square. Here he was in the dying heart of Americana. Back when America had had half the population, these places had flourished.

Now it had twice as many people, and so many of them had moved to cities and left these dead places behind like scars.

"Here," Starling said, and she indicated what looked like it might have been an old factory once. It looked like two different names had weather-stained their way over lighted lettering, and now all that remained were the pockmarks where electrical wiring hung where the last had been stripped off. Broken windows dotted the front of the building. To Hendricks, the whole place radiated a *Nothing but trouble here* vibe.

He pulled into the parking lot and brought the car around the side, brick wall slipping slowly by on his right as he drifted along the side of the building. When he reached the back he found a parking lot and a lone car, a nice little sedan, not too old. He pulled in next to it and killed the ignition.

"Anything I need to know before we go in?" Hendricks asked.

"If you do not do this thing, no one will," Starling said, still staring straight ahead.

"Good enough for me," he said, and opened the door. It wasn't quite good enough—yet—but they were getting close.

He didn't have to force entry; the door was open, and it didn't squeak when he pushed through and entered an old office space. The carpet was threadbare and ancient, and he ignored the strips of it that were coming up or simply rotted away. There was almost no furniture left, just a bunch of walls that looked like they'd been stripped of all wiring. It wasn't the first building in this county he'd seen like this, and he wondered what industrious asshole had adopted this pastime.

The air was stale, but a few degrees warmer than outside, and Hendricks strolled through the office quietly. He could hear something, faintly, ahead, like chanting.

He came to a huge, heavy door that must have once done its best to keep the factory noise out of the offices. It was propped open, and he paused at its entry, taking a second to look back at Starling, who trailed silently in his wake. Once he knew she was still there, he took off his hat and peeked out.

The chanting was full-bore now, a man's voice echoing in the wide space, talking some demon language, hands wide and voice full of passionate expression. It was a ritual, Hendricks would have staked his life on it, and the man was mid-stream on it, looking like he might start into the chicken dance or something right here, communing with the spirits of evil.

"Good enough for me," Hendricks whispered, and now, it was.

Standing out there, trying to summon the enemy, was County Administrator Pike.

*

Drake had been keeping an eye on the car that had raced up to him, another car following close behind, then suddenly slowed as it came alongside.

This was a two-lane town street. Not a freeway. A car shouldn't be coming alongside him.

But there was a turn lane, Drake realized, his eyes back on the road as he approached the stop sign ahead. He slowed as required, staring out his cracked windshield, foot on the brake pedal and feeling the loose tension it offered him in return.

Then he saw movement in his driver's side mirror and one of the Buick's rear doors opened, and somebody moved behind it. Something happened, there was a flash—

And the van jerked slightly, as though someone had bumped it.

"What was that?" Drake asked over the mewling cries of children who were in varying stages between whimpering and all-out screaming. The screaming one needed to go first, because the sound was all over Drake's fucking nerves.

No matter. He'd done his obligatory stop, there was no cross traffic. Drake pushed down the accelerator, and the van started to move. But—

The vehicle was sluggish, struggling to respond. The vehicle pulled to the left, hard.

What was this?

Looking back, Drake could see men in that car. Several of them. Was that normal?

They were watching him.

Drake panicked, gunned the engine—

The van squealed, the left rear tire like a giant drag, keeping him from moving, as though someone had anchored it in place. He stomped the accelerator, wanting to get away from them. He jerked the wheel to the right in a desperate bid to get away from them, these men—

He pulled the wheel too far though, and hit the pedal too hard.

The van mounted the curb to his right and Drake let out a little gasp of panic. Beyond that was a steep slope, and the van went over it as Drake froze. The bottom of the van ground against the curb, mechanical screaming like an angry metal demon ripping his vehicle apart from beneath.

"Oh shit, oh shit!" Drake gasped as the van went over the embankment and down, down the hill. It bumped, he almost hit the ceiling, and the cries of the children escalated to shrieks.

The van slid ten feet down the embankment and came to a rest with its nose in a drainage ditch that was empty of any moisture. It was cracked reddish soil, the vehicle nestled at an angle that didn't lend itself to motion. Drake floored the accelerator, but—

Nothing.

The van was wedged, solidly, at a forty-five-degree angle. He opened the door and hopped out, trying to gauge—

The back wheels were off the ground. The nose of the van was hard against the broken soil and sparse grasses in this drainage ditch. Ahead he could see the back of a brick building, no entry, no doors, no windows even. To his left the embankment climbed back up to the road, as it did behind him.

Drake circled the vehicle, trying to get some idea of what to do. He could see the men up top now, just above him, could hear them talking—about him. About …

Children?

"Oh shit, oh shit …" Drake muttered, reaching the other side. It was no better. He could see a door at the far end of the back of the brick building, but it looked like solid metal. He might be able to break through it, but ...

Wait, was that?

In the hillside behind him there seemed to be a culvert, like a door under the ground. Maybe it led to the other side of the road, maybe ...

It was a thin hope, but it was all that Drake had. Throwing the side of the van open, the cries of the whining cutlets reached his ears once more, and he seized hold of the rope, dragging them out. That started a whole new round of crying from the ones that had finally started to settle, and he gathered them up in his arms, these tasty little pieces of meat, and started to run for the culvert, his only means of escape.

*

Pike was in the middle of a good chant, and according to the book, only two lines away from summoning the demon Asgorath, who was of fire and brimstone and death, but also liked to make deals, especially ones that allowed him to possess human beings. Pike wasn't planning on letting himself be possessed, but he was perfectly happy to provide some sacrifices to Asgorath so he could wear human skin for a spell. It wasn't exactly a hard thing to kidnap someone, scare the shit out of them, have them read a few words of apparent gibberish, and boom, Asgorath had a new temple of flesh to defile for a while. The books all said he had a predilection for possessing teenage girls— something about liking to entice older men to take their virginities. Then Asgorath would slit the old men's throats post-coitus.

Pike didn't judge. He didn't really care if a few old guys bit the dust. It wasn't like he was real attached to anyone in this community anyway. If they didn't want to die that way, they should probably keep their dicks out of teenage girls possessed by Asgorath. Or maybe out of teenage girls in general, because Southern daddies didn't take too kindly to that sort of shit, he knew just from general conversation with the locals.

One line away from finishing the chant, Pike heard something in the empty warehouse. It echoed off the walls like a slamming door, except it wasn't.

It was artificial, metallic, and loud, and it made him pause for a second to turn.

The demon hunter in the cowboy hat came strolling in, and over his shoulder was the red-headed hooker from Ms. Cherry's establishment. What was her name? He'd never been there himself, but Darla had checked the place out once and fairly raved about—

Lucia. That was it. She could apparently eat pussy with the best of them, or so Darla said. It had made him a little jealous, which Darla had enjoyed thoroughly when they'd fucked afterward.

"Summoning a demon in the middle of Midian right now," the cowboy said—Hendricks, was that his name? Pike thought so. "Not exactly sending up a flare that you're a good guy, *County Administrator* Pike." Hendricks put a lot of sneer into the title.

"How do you know I'm not summoning somebody to help?" Pike had to disguise a smile. There was a gun on the cowboy's belt, but he had his sword out, which told Pike a lot about what was going on here. If he'd been a hundred percent sure Pike was doing bad, he'd have come at him with the gun drawn.

"Because I just do," Hendricks said, certain as the fucking sun setting in the west. He had the moral authority of a young person who was damned sure he was on the side of good.

It was going to be fun to yank that from underneath him, Pike thought, still keeping the smile off his face only through long practice. All he had to do was keep this dumb, hillbilly sonofabitch talking …

*

Arch was standing at the top of the embankment, looking down at where the van had gone over. It was nose-to in a drainage ditch and not going anywhere anytime soon, not that that mattered. The danged demon had grabbed up the kids and hot-footed it for a tall culvert just down the way, and Arch would have cursed if he could, especially as he watched the man—no, not man, *thing*—disappear into the storm drain.

"We'll get him on the other side of the road," Guthrie shouted, starting to turn back to run back over the road. Because she didn't know, plainly.

"There's no exit on the other side of the road," Arch said. "There's no exit for six blocks. That's the municipal storm drain system."

"The what?" Guthrie asked.

Jones and Tarley knew, both of them showing the same weary, wary distaste Arch did. Everyone local knew the storm drains. Kids played in them all the time. Mostly they weren't dangerous. It wasn't like you got flash floods here very often, and even during a hard rain you had plenty of time to get the hell out before they filled. If they filled at all.

"It's drainage," Jones said. "For most of the town. Also provides access to the city sewer for municipal workers. It's a warren of drain tunnels built under the hilltop part of Midian. Six square blocks of tunnels, a perfect playground for kids during a drought."

"Perfect demon hiding place now," Tarley said, still standing next to that other demon, the stiff British one. He looked right at Arch. "You ever play in these as a kid?"

Arch nodded. It hadn't even been forbidden, really, or he might have steered clear. He only got warned away when bad weather was coming, and that was more precautionary than anything. "I know my way around them."

"Me too," Tarley said with a nod. "There's another exit comes out on Briar Lane. Unless he doubles back, that's his most likely escape point. I'll go there."

"We ain't all going to be able to cover every exit," Jones said. "We're going to need some help."

"Someone needs to send a text letting everybody know where we are," Arch said, mind whirling as he started down the hill toward the massive culvert. "I'm going in after him."

"Same," Duncan said, pacing right beside him within a step.

"Well, I ain't staying out here with you fancy fucks," Guthrie said, coming one more behind them.

"Three of us, three branches on this entry," Arch said. "Left, right, center," and he pointed at each of them in turn, giving Guthrie left, Duncan right, and him the middle. "Barney, you go to Truman Street, over by Barry Manley's house. There's another exit just below his backyard."

"I know it," Jones said with a light in his eyes. "I used to play in these when I was kid, though I don't think it was Barry's house back then. The Manley family—aww, never mind that now." He waved off the memory and disappeared up off the embankment.

"Hey, wrench monkey," Guthrie said, and tossed Tarley her keys. "You wreck it, you buy it, you hear me?"

Tarley caught them without effort. "I can fix anything I fuck up." And then he disappeared over the top of the embankment with a, "Come on, fuckstick. Let's go block this shitbird so I don't have to open you up instead."

The thin Brit demon gulped again, and followed obediently behind him. The roar of an engine starting a moment later was obscured as Arch stepped into the square box of concrete culvert. It was rectangular, tall end up, like a door under the road, and he barely had to stoop to enter. It stretched out before him, curving off in three paths.

He headed right up the center, into the dark, squinting. He could hear the cries of children somewhere ahead, though he couldn't tell which branch it was coming from. He broke into a run, leaving the two OOCs behind, sword at the ready for whatever came.

*

Erin hit the switch on her radio, listening to the click override the steady hiss of static usually present in her ear while it was stuck in there. "This is Harris, testing, testing—we are go."

"Meacham here," Casey's voice crackled. She could see him driving that big truck of his a few cars back in the rumbling line. "Go."

"We should have call signs," Nate McMinn said. "Why did we do away with the call signs? I want to be BIG MAC."

"This is Ms. Cherry," Melina Cherry's cool voice broke in. "I would like my callsign to be HOTNESS instead of HARLOT."

"We did away with them because it got so confusing with so many members of the watch," Erin said, bumping off road. Greenery was passing around her, tree branches that hung low occasionally scraping the top of the police Explorer Arch used to drive. She'd taken it over with his blessing, specifically for this. "If we go back to it, I vote for Casey to be designated PERVERT."

"Don't be hatin'," Casey said.

"This is Chauncey," Chauncey Watson's staticky, awkward voice came through. "Bringing up the rear." A pause. "Though I guess that's where Casey wanted to be."

"You people know me," Casey said, almost laughing. "You really know me."

"This is Drumlin," Keith Drumlin broke in. "Man, the going sure is slow. You think they've been through here?"

Erin stared out the windshield at the path ahead. The ground did look trodden, at least to her eyes, the fallen leaves crushed and crunched in a way that suggested to her a herd of something had passed this way. Branches hung off trees in a few places like they'd been hit by something big running through low. "I think maybe, yeah. Seems to me something's been along this path recently, though it'd be easier to tell if we'd had a rain anytime in the last few months." She hit the button to roll down the window and tried to listen for anything, but all she could hear was the rumbling of her little convoy—especially Nguyen's vehicle.

"Nguyen here," Father Nguyen finally crackled in. She guessed that talk of Casey and being in back hadn't exactly made the priest feel super comfortable. "I have a higher view than most of you—I don't see anything ahead. I'm hitting a lot of tree branches, though." A clunking noise made it through the mic, and he said, "Like that. Did you hear that?"

"Yep," Erin said, looking to her left. There was a sharp slope up the side of the hill, and ahead the path started to bend down toward Shade's Hollow. She had a feeling this was an old logging trail, something the Alders had used when they'd had men come in and take their lumber for money. That was what the Alders did, sell off parts of their resources, because damned if most of them ever worked an honest job. A few did, but they usually tended to escape Shade's Hollow if so. She knew three of the cousins that got out and worked in the mill, but they all had houses in town.

Erin came up over a small rise, and there she could see endless trees, all the way down. This perspective gave her the suggestion of interlocking branches, like the forest was a flat, 2D thing, a painting that all ran together. She knew it wasn't so, that it was miles of trees that just looked like they were all smooshed together in a great brown and green canvas, but either way it formed a nearly impenetrable wall of forest that she couldn't see through. The road wended through it, making it tough to discern much beyond the next couple turns.

"Okay," she said, maybe trying to get her own courage up as she pushed down on the accelerator. They weren't going outlandishly fast, because rushing into this felt like suicide, but they were trying to keep a good clip going, trying to catch these things before they got too far ahead. Her eyes flicked to the offroad settings. She was still on the sand, dirt, grass setting, and it was treating her all right. The car was probably using its all-wheel drive.

It bumped down the uneven trail, divots washed into the ground long ago now empty, perfect places to catch her tires and send her thumping from side to side. Erin gritted her teeth at some of the bumps, bringing the Explorer around in a solid turn to match the trail. It reminded her of an ages-ago moment where she was racing down a different hill a lot quicker, and to a much more perilous finish.

She came around a gap in the trees and saw a shadow down the hill, closer to the hollow. It was just a brief movement. She almost thought she'd imagined it for a second.

Then she came around another corner, and deeper into the hollow, she saw it again—shadows moving into the trees, fading into them. Small things, dotting across her view, darting between the trees.

The last corner and she came into a straightaway, and then there was no doubt.

They weren't shadows.

"Holy hell," Casey said. "You seeing this?"

"I'm seeing it," Father Nguyen said. "The small ones are like a swarm. But ... those big ones ... does anyone see—?"

Oh, Erin saw, all right.

It wasn't just the little shadowcats they'd been dealing with all this time. There were bigger ones, ones that were the size of her Explorer, and bigger still. They were galloping along and suddenly they all sort of ... bristled; looked over their shoulders and saw Erin and her little convoy, coming down the hollow after them.

"Game time," Erin said to herself as she stomped the pedal to the metal and tore down the trail toward them.

This was it.

*

"You know I'm a human being, right?" Pike asked Hendricks. Hendricks, for his part, listened to the man, not quite ready to charge. "You saw your little friend give me a cut on the hand?"

"I saw it," Hendricks said. He had seen Alison give the man a little slice to the hand, but that didn't mean much to him. He'd been in Iraq, had dealt with insurgents who'd lie right to your fucking face while they dealt under the table with any number of assholes hostile to US soldiers.

"So what are you doing here?" Pike asked. He sounded smug; the fucker couldn't sound anything but smug, could he? Hendricks doubted it.

"Watching you try and summon up a demon," Hendricks threw right back at him. He had his sword clenched tight in hand. He had a feeling he knew what was coming—Pike would try and talk him out of doing what he was heading toward doing. Hendricks was okay with him trying, because he'd never yet killed a human being on American soil and he'd long drawn that line pretty effectively.

But then, he didn't often run into humans who were plainly giving aid and comfort to demons.

"That's what you think you're seeing," Pike said, keeping his hands out at his side. "But I'm telling you that ain't what's happening. So ... whatcha gonna do?"

Hendricks watched the man stare him down, and he knew— knew—Pike thought he was going to talk his way out of this. Why wouldn't he, after all? The fucker probably hadn't ever met a situation he couldn't talk his way out of before.

*

Drake was already sick of the dark and he hadn't even been here that long. The smells of this storm drain, the echoes down the dry corridors, they were like poison to his cultured soul. He wanted to be back at his cooking station, working on the perfect slices of cutlet ...

He had them strung around him now, the cutlets. The ... *children*, he thought grudgingly. They were so loud, so obnoxious, but he didn't want to soil their freshness by killing them yet. It might come to that, if he had to silence them to get away, but thus far he was running, running away from the people in pursuit of him. He wasn't sure, but he thought he might have caught a whiff of OOCs, and definitely a few very perturbed humans.

He supposed that was what happened to any animal when you threatened their young.

Drake had the children draped over him, the rope aiding him in keeping them together. Some were suspended around him, some were under his arms—he had them all over, the six of them, and he was willing to yield exactly zero of them, even though they were weighing him down.

This would be his Beethoven's Fifth, he knew, his masterpiece of culinary achievement, meat that would melt in your mouth, and he wasn't going to let some OOCs or angry humans keep him from greatness.

Footsteps behind him sounded thunderously, making him pause for only a second to take stock of what was coming, and then Drake was off again, hurrying faster, needing to find an exit and make his escape before they caught him, caught him and stopped him from doing what his very essence called out to do:

To make art of these children—and consume their flesh.

*

"That motherfucking hellcat is the size of a single-wide," Nate McMinn said dully into Erin's earpiece. The car was bumping along hard down the last hundred yards of the trail into Shade's Hollow. She could picture the map in her head, how it was laid out. The quarry was probably a quarter of a mile ahead.

No chance they were going to get to it without a fight now. Not with these shadowcats turning around.

"Looks like a pure black cattle drive from hell," Keith Drumlin said, a little bit of awe leaking into his tone over the staticky channel.

They were all out there, hanging between the trees, looking back at her as she looked at them. Almost like they were scenting the wind, trying to get the read on what was after them. These were creatures that had torn through houses in great fucking herds, just run through Mary Wrightson's house and Hickory Lane and others. They'd torn up the sheriff's car on that night in the woods, ripped right into it and made it into a wreck.

"They killed Sam," Erin said under her breath, then gunned the engine.

One of the house-sized ones was turning now, and damn if it wasn't the size of a double-wide. Maybe bigger. It was snaking its way along on legs the size of a bridge support, and powerful too, as it started to spring at her, turning the herd her way.

"Here they come," Ms. Cherry said over the channel.

Erin froze for just a second, seeing the herd start to come for them, ripping up the trail toward her, streaming around the trees on their way toward the new target—this line of cars that was pursuing them, trying to turn the hunters into prey.

She stomped the pedal. The engine raced. Dirt spun beneath the tires, then they caught and she was off.

Erin gripped the wheel tightly, going for them. She didn't bother to signal the others; they'd wait and see what happened to her. But she wasn't going to sit there and wait for them to charge.

She was going to go right for them.

"Heeeeeere we go!" Casey said, sounding a little thrilled about it all.

"Dude, you sound excited," McMinn said. "We're about to—"

Erin tuned him out. She was running down the road, engine throttled up, going about sixty. She didn't want to go any faster than that for fear of what might happen if things went really wrong.

Hell, with this many shadowcats racing at her, she didn't even want to think about how she might define "really wrong."

The biggest hellcat was bounding toward her. It had the scent of danger in its nose, and it must have sensed she was unafraid. She couldn't read its dark eyes. But she wanted to believe it sensed …

Not prey. But not a hunter either.

And it was right. Erin might have been a cop, but she was no hunter.

She'd sat a desk for two years. Until the demons had come to Midian.

She'd done every shit detail the sheriff could come up with. Been the low girl in the totem pole.

Last bird on the lowest wire.

Not because Reeve hated her, but because she was new.

And now—she might be just about all there was left of the sheriff's office.

Definitely the only one facing this.

"I'm gonna show you, motherfucker," she said as the black hellcat stared her down, coming at her, head down—

And hit the ramming bar mounted on the bumper that Father Nguyen had sanctified.

She burst out the other side of the shadowcat like it hadn't even hit her more than a jarring blow, skidding slightly before she got the Explorer under control. She coughed, the stink of brimstone heavy. The car slewed a little, and she straightened it out.

"Erin, are you okay?" Father Nguyen called over the radio.

"Yeah," she said. "Might want to put your air on recirculate though." She coughed lightly. "But ... yeah. It worked."

She turned her head to look at the herd of shadowcats ahead of her; they were tentative now, unsure.

The big one maybe thought it could smell her fear.

But now ... she could smell theirs.

She threw a look back over her shoulder. The others were parked back there, still in a line, though Ms. Cherry was starting forward now, her Range Rover covered with another rammer welded to the bumper, Casey behind her with a pickup similarly doctored. McMinn and Drumlin had just affixed some holy blessed objects to their grills with duct tape; some knives and swords.

But Father Nguyen ... he'd borrowed a monster truck from a parishioner and sanctified the whole thing—including each tire, according to the sleepy priest, who'd told her this with a grin.

Now they were charging down the hill, toward the waiting shadowcats.

And yeah ... she could smell their fear.

"SUNDAY, SUNDAY, SUNDAY!" Casey called with glee over the radio. "It's a demolition derby, live from Calhoun County! Come on down and watch the fiends from hell catch a car up the ass! HAHAHA!" He broke loose from the pack and shot down a side trail, blowing past Erin and plowing into a thicket of them as they spooked and started to move, running back downhill.

"Fuck yeah!" Drumlin shouted over the radio. "You messed with the wrong fucking people, assholes! We are rednecks, and we will not put up with your demon shit! Vehicular mayhem is our jam, you bunch of cheesedick shitbirds!"

"Damn straight," McMinn hooted. "Let's get these fucks!"

"Y'all made a big fucking mistake coming to the South if you thought we were just gonna sit back and take this shit," Erin said, gripping the wheel. The shadowcats were running now, spooked like cattle or some shit. "Drive them toward the quarry! And let's end this," she said, determination running from the top of her head down to her foot on the pedal, which she punched down even harder, the Explorer howling along after the damned cats from hell.

*

Arch found himself in darkness, wondering what he was thinking.
 No, scratch that. He knew what he was thinking. All he had to do was listen.
 Kids were crying in the distance. The echo in the tunnel was so bad he couldn't tell exactly which direction it was coming from, but he could hear them.
 It might have been the saddest sound he'd ever heard.
 It made him remember John 8:12, and he spoke it aloud: "'Then spake Jesus again unto them, saying, I am the light of the world: he that followeth me shall not walk in darkness, but shall have the light of life.'"
 Something about that reassured him, and Arch picked up the pace, running flat out into the darkness of the tunnel, knowing that somewhere ahead were children he could help.
 Children he could save.
 The way he hadn't been able to save his own.

*

Pike still kept from grinning. It was tough though, smelling the indecision on this dumbass. Here was a man who had one purpose in life—to be the lackey for others. Pike had met a million like him.
 They stood in the warehouse, quiet pervading as Pike took a step, his wingtip scratching its leather sole against the bare concrete. "What are you going to do, cowboy?" Pike asked, keeping his arms wide and unthreatening. It wasn't like Pike had a weapon on him, so there was no point in acting like he was going to draw on the man. In addition to the sword, he had a gun, plainly. "I'm standing right here. You going to go ahead and shoot me for chanting some weird words in a warehouse? Without even taking into account my side of the story?"
 The redhead behind him spoke up, then, and in a voice that was … all too familiar.

"I think we did it. I think by killing Reeve—we fucking got 'em." It came out in his voice—Pike's voice, loud and clearly, words he'd said to Darla without anyone else around to hear them.

Hendricks didn't even look back, kept his eyes right on Pike.

And the bastard smiled.

Pike just stared. The redhead hooker had just perfectly voiced him—had he said that? It sure as hell sounded familiar. "Now wait a second," Pike said, feeling the heat rising in his face. "That's not—it's—"

He saw the look in the cowboy's eyes.

He wasn't buying a thing Pike was selling.

"Shit," Pike said, and threw down the last few words of his ritual, raising his hand—

The smell of brimstone blew out in a black cloud from the floor as Asgorath the demon rose from a hole in the floor. Coal-colored skin, glowing red eyes, horns—he was the picture of a perfect demon. He floated up out of the ground and stood easily a foot taller than Pike himself, clenching a six-fingered fist to let sharp protrusions on his knuckles be seen. Ugly things, looked like they'd tear a human being apart with a good punch ... and he was pointing them right at Hendricks.

Pike looked at the cowboy and smiled. "You should have killed me when you had a chance."

*

Arch stopped at another intersection, faint grey light streaming down from above. A storm drain was up there, a mail-slot-looking opening to a street. He couldn't see much other than a leafless tree and grey skies, but it gave him a second to rest in the light, then turn his eyes forward.

Something moved ahead, and the squawling of children was much closer. Arch knew now that he had picked the right passageway. He brushed against one of the corrugated steel grooves that made up the pipe, leaning against it for support as he made his way along.

He came to another cross passage, looking for that shadow that had moved. It was so dang dark, how could he even tell? The crying seemed like it was coming from up ahead, just a chorus of pitiful wails that sent his heart pittering in a way he hated. He wanted to find those babies, snatch 'em up, make them feel safe, get them out of here.

Arch broke into a jog. He had his sword clutched in hand, tight, fingers digging into the leather that wrapped the hilt. He had to—

Something hit him from the side and sent him wheeling. He slammed into the side of the tunnel and his head flashed with unnatural light. He spun back around, swinging wide, clumsy, and didn't even see it when something clipped him again in the side of the head.

"You couldn't just leave me alone," a voice said, quiet and effete in the darkness. He was a little overweight, gut overhanging his belt, clad in jeans that didn't fit him well at all. They were far too tight, but the man—demon—had a prissy, angry look on his face. He lashed out at Arch with a kick, hammering him down.

Arch hit the ground hard and thrust the sword out again, but it was knocked aside easily. The demon caught him with a punch to the mouth that sent Arch back against the wall. The corrugated metal thumped against the back of his head, aiding that swirling feeling he was getting. His mind spun. He felt like he was floating, legs rising up over his head, as though he were weightless and floating in space.

"I just wanted to eat in peace!" the demon shouted, echoing down the corridors. "I just ... *need* ... to eat ..." And it was sniffing him, smacking its lips in his ears. "Maybe a little tartare before the veal ..."

*

Even though Hendricks had heard Starling perfectly ape Pike's voice, that might not have been enough for him—if Pike hadn't gone and basically proven himself guilty a breath later.

Then the damned sonofabitch went and summoned an armored-shell demon.

Hendricks wasn't looking forward to this one. The thing looked flat-out mean, had glowing red eyes, and basically what looked like blackened hull armor from an Abrams tank over every single surface inch of his fucking shell.

About to swear aloud, Hendricks waited just a quarter second, and then the demon spoke.

"Whoa," the demon said, "am I interrupting something here?" He sounded like a fucking Valley Boy, and even with the horns and the hellacious look, it totally ruined it for Hendricks. A fucking support corps puke wouldn't have been intimidated by this bitchass.

"Yeah," Hendricks said, staring him down, "so why don't you fuck back off to wherever you came from and let us get on with it?"

"I've summoned you to offer you sacrifices," Pike said. The man's confidence and smugness had grown even further since the arrival of the demon, which Hendricks did not regard as a good thing. "Exactly the kind you prefer—human possessions of a certain age and gender, if you know what I mean." Pike was practically winking at the fucker. "I'll even help you set up the dates."

The demon nodded at him. "You'd do that for me? Extra mile, bro. I like that." The demon offered a fist like he was going to bump with the shitheel.

"You will leave this place now," Starling said, and the armored demon did a double-take at her.

"Whoa," the armored demon said. "Uhm. Yeah." He looked down at Pike. "I'ma have to decline your deal, bro. Lataz."

And poof, he was gone again, a black cloud of smoke, and when it cleared—nada.

Pike just stared at where the demon had stood, and the smugness evaporated like a drop of water on a hot sidewalk. He looked right at Hendricks, and his face fell. "Well ... shit."

Hendricks just grinned at him. "You got that right."

"Hey, maybe we could make a deal—" Pike started to say.

Hendricks drew his 1911 and plugged Pike with it in the chest three times fast, three quick strokes of the trigger that caught that cunt of a County Administrator in the chest. He staggered back a couple of steps, but Hendricks didn't let it rest like that.

"The shit did you—" Pike wheezed.

Hendricks caught up to him and drove the sword right into his belly where one of the rounds had already gone in, stabbing him straight through, holding the pistol to his neck as he did so. "The shit I did was kill your ass," Hendricks said, staring him right in the eyes. It wasn't the first time he'd killed a man up close, but it was the first time he'd done it with a sword. He pulled it out and plunged it right back in again, a little higher, right in the second bullet hole. He repeated it a third time with the last gunshot wound, covering his tracks by impaling the bastard hard, really moving the sword around in the wounds.

Pike gagged, and blood came flooding out, running down his neatly shaven chin. The bureaucrat fell to his knees, his dress shirt completely sodden with red as Hendricks withdrew the sword and took a step back.

"You ... motherf—" Pike gasped, really trying to get it out, but the blood flowing out with the words. "Darla ..." He gagged on his own bodily fluids.

"That's for Sheriff Reeve," Hendricks said, and wiped his bloody sword right on the back of Pike's shirt as he hung there, on his knees, upright for a second before he toppled over onto his face. "Oh, and just to be safe ..."

Hendricks raised a booted foot and brought it down on the back of Pike's neck. The crunch of bone sealed it for him, but in case that wasn't enough, he could smell it—the bastard had shit his pants.

Hendricks circled around and checked, just to be sure.

Pike was dead. His eyes were unfocused, staring at nothing in particular. Hendricks stooped just to look him in the eye. No breath. He touched the neck. No heartbeat.

Yeah. That fucker was toast.

Hendricks started to say something to Starling, but when he turned, she was already gone.

"Figures," he said, holstering the 1911. He made a quick sweep and picked up his shell casings, putting them in his pocket. He didn't figure this would end up being a big deal, but there wasn't a hell of a lot of point in making this any easier if there was an investigation.

Then he walked out, leaving Pike in a pool of his own blood.

*

Erin wanted to shift gears, not because she actually needed to—the Explorer was an automatic transmission—but for a FUCK YEAH! point of emphasis, because it would look cool if she did.

Instead, she settled for planting her grill through a pack of shadowcats at sixty miles an hour. Even the recirculate feature couldn't keep the stink of sulfur out of the car. Whew.

"YEEEEHAWWW!" Father Nguyen shouted through the earpiece, really leaning into the redneck fun of this. She saw his truck go streaking by outside, just a massive thing, tires the size of her and replete with all these dirt-digging spikes. She thought about him prescribing penance in the confessional, something like, "Twenty Hail Marys, an Our Father, and, uh ... you have to let me borrow your truck," and was beset by a case of the giggles as about fifty shadowcats went *poof!* under his tires.

"This is the shit!" McMinn shouted, zipping along beside her.

"Don't get too crazy," Erin said. "Remember, if you flip your vehicle, they'll tear your ass to pieces lickety split."

"If I had to go out, this is the fucking way to do it!" Casey shouted. His truck bounced over a rut to the side of her and landed on two shadowcats, turning them into nothingness.

Erin looked out soberly as her little driving brigade—Holy-Armored Cavalry?—sped down into the hollow. "Keep an eye out for the quarry; it's gotta be coming up soon. Ms. Cherry, get up on the right and try to steer them toward the middle—"

"You want me to herd them?" She punched it left and spiked a couple cats, her Range Rover dirtier than she'd ever seen a shiny, pretty car like that. "Okay. I can do that."

"Casey, take the left," Erin said, and she saw him cut in front of her wildly, wiping out a dozen cats with the sudden move. It was like the running of the bulls, and they were right in the middle of them. "If we miss this, they keep running free, and there has to be like ... a hundred or more of them still." She looked over the pack. They'd killed a lot of them, probably more than were left, but still ... this was a sizable threat. Enough to kill another street, enough to kill the whole town.

And damned sure enough to kill *them* if Erin wasn't careful.

They were spooked and scared, but she didn't count on that to last. Casey was coming at them from the left, bopping one of them into making a shrieking noise when he hit it with his vehicle. It didn't pop, which illustrated the flaw in her plan, because he'd caught it with a flat door panel, going sideways, not nearly fast enough to bust its shell.

Now that they were running, matching speed, the only way to get them was to crush them with their holy tires or catch them with a sharp corner of the pronged ramming bar. Just hitting them with the bumper, flat and smooth as they were, wasn't going to kill one of these fuckers.

"Nate, Chauncey, Keith, Father Nguyen ... take up position at the back of the herd. Keep 'em running," she said, and gunned the pedal.

"What are you going to do?" Nguyen asked.

"Try something," she said, surging forward as she watched the others move in behind her, creating a nice little herd box.

She raced ahead, right up through the middle of them. She had to do it quick; couldn't lay off the horses, because if she did, they'd just part for her.

So she revved up to a hundred miles an hour and plowed through. Shadowcats hit the front of her car like they were a swarm of flies and she was a big swatter.

"You look like you just wrecking balled them!" Casey shouted with glee as Erin tore through them, blasting out the front of the pack and into the lead. She didn't slow down once she was through, either. The trees were thinned here, pretty near gone, leaving behind only the little traces of saplings, stumps and a sandy, rocky slope down into the hollow where the loggers had made a hell of a mess. The quarry had to be—

There it was.

They were heading into open ground, and Erin was leading the way, probably close to a quarter mile out front, and still charging ahead. She needed to be sure that there wasn't anything blocking the quarry. The Alders weren't the kind of people who'd waste their money putting up a fence, so far as she knew—probably embraced more of a Darwinian philosophy, even with their own kin—but the last thing she needed now was an obstacle in the way of their plan.

She raced closer, and said, "It's coming up. Tighten them into a formation. Get 'em herded. Once they're in here, there's no escape."

"Roger that," Ms. Cherry said formally. Erin wondered where she'd picked that up.

Erin shot into the quarry, which was a spiral road down into the deeper ground. It wasn't a very big thing, not like miles across—more like a hundred yards or less. She followed the road down, down the curve, and found herself in the bottom. When she got there, sure enough, it was bone dry, rock and dust and the occasional near-dead cluster of weeds the only thing waiting.

"Quarry's clear to the bottom," Erin said. "We're good to go." She gunned it again, spun the car around and started heading back up.

"They're coming in!" Casey shouted. "Watch yourself!"

Erin would have sworn, but what was the point right now? This was what she'd wanted. Instead, she said, "Well, hot dog," without a lot of enthusiasm.

She revved the engine harder. She didn't want to meet a shadowcat going twenty up this slope; if it merely hit her car without breaking its skin, it wasn't exactly going to do a ton of damage to the damned thing. More likely the damage would be to the surface of the Explorer at that speed.

Erin pushed up the speedometer to sixty, seventy, on a tight curve, and she felt her heart jackhammer. This was what she'd done up on Mount Horeb just before she went flying over the edge. The mere thought made her hands close hard on the wheel, made her white-knuckle—

They came flooding around her just as she drifted into the turn, the sound of the shadowcats slamming into her grill and poofing like a hard rain on the outside of the car, like the most hammering fucking storm she'd ever driven through. It was weird and intense, and she slid through it, tires catching, shadowcats catching hell, and little clouds of black appearing and disappearing in front of her grill as she killed the fucking things.

She slid out of the curve as the last of them were clearing through. "Made it," she muttered, almost triumphant, as she watched the last of them coming at her. All she had to do was make it through and they'd turn around, charge down and mop up—

One of the last shadowcats leapt when it saw her steamroll their fellows. Its thin legs pinwheeled through the air as it flew toward her, slipping sideways in its comical last-minute stop and jump. It hit the windshield ass first and smashed through, showering her with beads of safety glass and sliding into the vehicle. It hit the cage at the back of the driver's seat and burst right through, landing half its ass in the prisoner area in the back seat and the other half still sticking out at her.

Erin couldn't breathe for a second, staring out the wrecked windshield at the cars of her little pack ahead, at the entry to the quarry, waiting for her. She was almost there, but she'd let her foot off the Explorer's pedal when the shadowcats came thick and heavy and she went into the turn.

Now they all seemed impossibly far away. She was stuck out here, dim, frozen, a moment of peace before the panic hit.

She was trapped in her car with a shadowcat.

And then the damned thing howled, and started to struggle, the sound of the metal squealing as it fought against the only thing holding it back from tearing Erin to pieces.

*

Desperation practically dripped from Drake's pores. The hunger. It ground at his essence, ate away at him. His throat was tight, his lips up against the skin of the human who'd followed him. His cutlets were steps away, just up the dark storm drain.

Meat. Tender, delicious meat. This was what he wanted. What he strove for. Ached for. Craved.

He was so hungry. All the time. It was beyond hunger now; it was an unquenchable voraciousness to feed. But every bite he took just made him crave *more* …

More food, more flavor, more to satiate.

He sniffed the human in police clothes, licked the skin, leaned back to take a bite—human tartare … maybe tasting it uncooked would soothe the cravings …

*

The shadowcat was going nuts next to Erin, wild with frenzied anger, shrieking louder than the speakers at any concert she'd ever been to, ripping through the cage in the back of the Explorer, writhing its front end trying to free its back end, black shadowy paws swiping left to right.

"Fuck!" Erin scrambled for her seatbelt, trying to get loose. This was the shit she feared, the shit she'd had nightmares about ever since she'd gone off that cliff.

She was going to die in a fucking car.

The seatbelt whipped loose and Erin threw her back against the door. The shadowcat was lashing blind, trying to writhe itself free of where it was stuck in the metal cage barrier to the back seat. It looked like a meteor had struck the damned thing, a shadowcat meteor that just lodged there and sprung to life, pissed as hell about its current status. It lashed at her, and she missed getting ripped open by about a half inch.

Where the fuck was her bat?

Erin's looked over the car, desperate. It clicked—passenger seat well.

Her gaze flew to where the bat had been resting. It was gone, gone like—

No.

It was there, but it had fallen completely into the well, and there was a goddamned shadowcat between them. The cat was trapped ass-first, but those back claws weren't fucking playing around, were they?

Hell no. She caught one of them, she'd be hurting, maybe dying.

"Erin!" someone shouted in her earpiece. It was a distant voice.

Erin's back was pressed against the door, the armrest punching right into the middle of her back. Her head was against the window, as far as it could go without starting to spiderweb the damned thing as she tried to force her way out. Or at least that was how it felt.

"Get down there and finish these fucks," she breathed into the open mic. "Don't let 'em get away."

"What about y—"

"I got this one," she said, with a fiery confidence she damned sure didn't feel.

Then she ripped the earpiece out of her ear and fought to get to the door handle.

She fell out backward when she found it, catching herself, shock running up her arms from where she landed on the dusty, rocky ground. She caught a rock in the elbow and didn't give a fuck. The pain shot up her arm.

She didn't give a fuck about that, either.

Erin kicked her legs, getting back to her feet. "I'm not fucking dying in a car," she said, as Ms. Cherry flew by her on one side, her door missing by a neat few inches, stirring her uniform as she blew by. Erin broke into a run as soon as she was clear, hellcat shrieks and revving engines her soundtrack.

She swept around the rear of the Explorer as the hellcat writhed within, wrenching its way free of its little prison. It'd get loose soon, that much was sure.

Erin came around to the passenger door, hauled it open with a hard tug on the handle, and bent low, snatching up the bat—

The cat broke loose just then in a squeal of metal as it hauled its ass out of the barrier and got the dashboard with a good swipe that ripped through plastic and metal, shattering the radio in the middle of the console.

Its back paws landed on the seat and ripped through the cloth, shredding and tearing up pieces of white stuffing as it twisted, working its way toward her.

Erin fell over backward, screaming pain radiating out from her tailbone as she lay there, bat in hand. The hellcat burst out of the car, getting traction at last like her coming out of a turn with the Explorer, and it leapt at her, those ebony jaws open wide and coming for her throat—

She managed a wide swing around, like she was back in softball again. The barb-wire-wrapped bat caught the thing right in the side, and it burst in a black cloud that lasted only a second, then vanished into nothingness.

She was left lying there on the quarry floor, rocks poking up in the back of her neck, against her back, for a second before she slapped a hand down and pushed herself up. On unsteady legs, she worked her way back to the driver's seat, tossing the barbed wire bat right into the hole that the hellcat had made in the seat with its claws. It rested there, upright, braced against the busted dash, well enough for her purposes—which were to make sure she had a weapon handy in case she needed one again.

Erin slipped the earpiece back in just in time to hear Casey say, "Fuck yeah!"

"We got 'em on the run?" she asked, shifting the car back into drive. She took a slow breath. Cool fall air slid into the car from above, in through the windshield. She reached out and brushed some of the pebbled glass out of the way, dislodging the last chunk remaining on her side so she could see clearly.

"Hell yeah, Erin," Chauncey Watson said. "You make it through that okay?"

"Me one, that sonofabitch zero," she said, still breathing. She'd made it through all right—by the skin of her teeth. She never wanted to be that close to death again, but down there …

She had a busted windshield. Another one could get wise and jump on up, and she'd be in even worse straits than before.

She could wait here. Catch strays, maybe, if any came. It sounded like—engines roaring around the bend—they had it in hand. She could just chill, catch any that came, or—

Fuck. No.

Erin laid on the accelerator and heard the engine rev. It raced her pulse too, made her fear for a second that she was back in the old hell, flying over the cliff.

But she wasn't. This was something new. And her baggage—her high school years, her teenage boredom, her stupid drinking, the car crash, the guys she'd slept with, all the way up to that shithead Hendricks—none of that fucking mattered now.

"Town before everything," she said, under her breath, slewing the car around to face downhill. She let off just enough to let the wheels catch, and she was off, racing, down into the quarry to finish this with the rest of them.

And she wouldn't let up until they were done.

*

Arch was feeling fuzzy. Something was licking him, tasting him. It was so dark, his perception of things like a tunnel he'd slid into. He wanted to close his eyes, but something told him not to …

Arch …

Alison. It was like she was breathing in his ear again. Right there, close as life, his blond-locked angel. She brushed his skin, and he felt like he was on fire. Her kisses were like ice down the side of his cheek—

Arch …

Her voice was so soft, so sweet, and she nibbled at him. It was sharp, filled his senses, the daydream, the darkness, the pain eclipsing it all in a way that—

Arch …!

She wasn't whispering anymore, she was shouting his name, in the distance, where he could just barely hear her. Something was closer—her breath was in his ear, her hands touching down his sides. Arch didn't want to wake up, didn't want to come out of this tunnel of darkness. She was right there with him, for the first time since—

It all crashed in with a moment of clarity so profound it was like the Lord Himself did reach down and rip Arch's eyes open and command him: *"SEE."*

There was a demon at his neck, foul sulfurous breath that he'd somehow mistaken for Alison in his delirium. His head ached fiercely, it was so dark, bands of light coming from the distance to either side, spare, lower than twilight, and his skin crawled like bugs were everywhere on him.

The voice was a lie. An effect of the delirium. Alison wasn't here; just this *thing*. This baby stealing thing. And it was licking him, tasting him, about to eat him whole—

"ARCH!" someone shouted, feminine but loud and angry and urgent—

Someone hit the demon and sent it reeling just as it was about to open its mouth and take a chunk of him. He saw a flash of dark hair and a length of pipe, and Dr. Lauren Darlington rocked that demon and sent him flying off of Arch with a perfect golf swing the like of which would have sent the sonofagun's head arcing off to the green if he hadn't been a demon.

The good doctor stumbled a little after her hard swing, almost looking like she might go pitching forward from overdoing it. But she caught her balance and looked back at Arch, her white lab coat swinging in her wake. She looked right at Arch and shouted, "Get up!" and he felt compelled to obey.

"I'ma do it," he muttered, barely making sense to his own ears as he hurried to his feet. Dust and little pebbles of rock crunched beneath them as he used the metal tunnel edge as a brace. Something glinted in the dark, and he hustled over to retrieve it—

His sword.

*

Lauren couldn't believe she found him, especially since all she did was run straight into the tunnels after she'd gotten the text message and gone straight ahead, forgoing the left or right branch and running right up the center. She'd driven like the fires of hell themselves were sweeping in behind her, from Chattanooga to here, and she'd made it. Looking at that text, somehow, she'd known where she was supposed to be.

Here.

And she'd made it just in time to save Archibald Stan's life.

"Thank you, Doctor," Arch said, a little muffled, as he scooped up his sword. He sounded like he might have a head injury; she'd need to check him later to be sure. She couldn't see him very well in the dark, but she could hear the confusion in his voice. "How did you find me?"

"Just ran right in," she said, now fixed on the demon ahead. Her tire iron wasn't consecrated, and the demon was working back to his feet, too.

Arch saw him move. "Now listen here, you—you ain't taking these babies." And he stepped to the side, interposing himself between the demon and the children, whose cries Lauren could hear, whose cries ripped at her heart. She shuffled to the side like Arch, working her way around to form a wall with him against the demon. She couldn't really see his face, and his shape was obscured as it lay in the shadows down a little side spur. There was no light in that direction, but it was cut off nicely from where the children were.

Lauren stepped right next to Arch, bumping shoulders with him. "You want them? You're going to eat holy steel, motherfucker." Arch stiffened at her side. "I mean," she said, suddenly flustered. "You heard me." To Arch she whispered, "Sorry." She actually was, for once.

"It's all right," Arch said, and she could tell by his voice that it was. "Couldn't have said it better myself."

"You don't understand," the demon whined as it staggered to its feet. "I have to eat. I have to try. To sample." Its voice was a shuddering mess. It stepped toward them out of the spur tunnel, and she caught a glimpse of a face racked with desperation. She braced herself; if desperate people did the craziest things, she didn't want to know what desperate demons might do. "I need them ... *I NEED THEM—*"

The demon rushed them, and Arch met him, a hard slash greeting the demon, who squealed and flinched back, lacking an arm. The arm fell to the ground and thumped on the dry dust, stirring up a little cloud as they all stood there, status quo ante—well, almost. The demon was now missing an arm.

"I will butcher you like a spring lamb," Arch said, holding his sword out front. "Take you piece by piece if you're a greater, if that's what I have to do. You aren't getting those babies." The cries of the children were subsiding.

The demon was almost crying with them, his breath coming in sobs. The desperation was matched by pain now, the arm missing, a reminder of his mortality, maybe. She caught a glimpse of his eyes in the shadowy light, and they were wild. He stood there, staring at them, one more second, then he broke and ran down one of the tunnels. His cries were pathetic, like a wounded animal, and Lauren almost—almost—felt sorry for him.

But the cries of the children behind them convinced her otherwise.

She lowered her tire iron once she was sure he was far enough gone. Then she hurried over to the children, kneeling next to them. They'd been bound together by a rope around their little torsos, and she checked pulses, checked each of them. She couldn't even see faces hardly, in the light, but what she did see were tears, streaking tears, big eyes, watery and scared. "It's okay," she whispered, and the sobs came again, renewed, like hope had given them breath in their lungs.

"It's going to be all right." Arch was there next to her, and he was patting the child that thrust itself into her arms. A little boy, she thought, clamoring for comfort. Here came the others now, still crying, starved for love in the last minutes, so scared by being dragged and herded and taken from a place of loving care and pulled down here into these tunnels. They had to know on some instinctive, animal level what it was doing.

"Holy shit," Duncan's voice cracked over them as he skidded out around a corner. "Doc?"

"Yeah, it's me," Lauren said, stifling her emotions. She was the doctor now, and she made a cursory exam of one of the toddlers. No serious injuries, no obvious broken bones. No blatant traumas. She'd need to do this for every single one here, before they could move them. "The demon went that-a-way." She pointed where it had gone.

"We might need Duncan more here," Arch said, trying to scoop up as many of the kids that were crowding around him as possible. He was enfolding them all in a hug, his sword put down behind him to avoid any injury to the children. They smelled, diapers filled, so sad, so scared. Lauren's heart broke for them. "To watch our backs while we get these kids out."

"Right," Lauren said, going about the business. She was checking one of the children for a hernia. Why? Because it was her job.

And it felt good to be back to doing what she was supposed to be.

"How'd you know about this place?" Arch asked, toddlers crowding in his arms, crying over him, and he was holding them tight, whispering softly between his questions to her.

Lauren blushed in the dark. "I, uh ... lost my virginity down here."

"You tell him this in front of the children?" Duncan sounded darkly amused.

"We, uh …" Arch didn't sound amused. He sounded like he wanted to change the subject with rapidity. "We probably ought to get them out of here."

"You find them?" Barney Jones called out, coming around the corner with his weapon out. He took one look at them and sagged against a wall, putting a hand to his heart. "Thank the Lord."

"It's not safe down here," Duncan said, touching Arch on the shoulder. "We need to—"

"Get out, I know," Arch said, and looked right at Lauren. "Can we move these children?"

She was wrapping up her feeler exam. It was hardly conclusive, but she wanted to linger around the storm drains like she wanted to stick her ass in a demon's mouth and wait for it to take a bite. "I don't think any of them are hurt badly. We should be able to move them." She tucked the pipe awkwardly in her coat and grabbed up two of the toddlers, one in each arm, and stood, balancing them on her hip like she used to do with Molly. They were still crying, of course, because she was a strange woman to them, but she made a soothing sound—like she had for her daughter—and one of them quieted. "It'll be okay." And she meant it, all the way through.

"Come on then," Arch said, and handed off one of them to Jones, who didn't relinquish his weapon, but took up the weight of one toddler easily, perching him against his shoulder. Arch beckoned to Duncan, holding out one of the children. "You too, Duncan."

Duncan brandished his baton. "I can't."

Arch just stared him down, baby in hand. "You're stronger than any of us. You can carry one and beat a demon off with the other if need be."

Lauren held in the snicker at Arch's unintentional faux pas. He didn't know what he'd said.

Duncan seemed to consider it a second, maybe braced for argument, but ultimately, he leaned down and accepted the child that Arch offered him. When he stood, Lauren caught a glimpse of his face; it was infused with curiosity, a kind of quiet wonder, as the child stared back at him.

Both toddler and demon were utterly quiet.

"And I'll get the last two," Arch said, sheathing his sword and rising, two children cradled in his arms. The noise was quieting down, the children—not soothed, perhaps, but not as fearful as they had been minutes earlier. "Come on," Arch said, and started to lead them out of the darkness, the three adults and the six children, heading toward a distant pinprick of light that, to Lauren's eyes, heralded safety.

And home. Home lay beyond the light. How curious, she thought, a child on each hip, that she'd forgotten for so long what home had felt like.

*

Drake staggered toward the end of the tunnel, the grey sky glaring in at him, an unfathomably bright light. He was blinded, in pain, his arm gone—carved off like he was no better than the meat he served.

Something about that moment had charged him, inflicting a desire for self-preservation like nothing else ever had. The little cutlets were no longer top of mind, his desire to be sated giving way to desperation to live, for he knew charging that man with the holy blade—that tasty man; he should have taken a deep bite and ended him when he had the chance—that he, Drake, would die.

There was nothing for it now but to escape. There would be other days, other days when he could claim a cutlet of his own. He wouldn't stop. He'd just flee, retreat, find another place to lay low for a spell. He staggered out into the light, the cool air prickling at his shell. Yes, he'd be back for a child sooner or later. He'd eventually get that taste he craved—

Something struck him from the side and it was as the coming of death upon his head. A cracking sound evinced itself within his shell and Drake tumbled to his knees. It sounded as though he'd just split open a human ribcage to get to the succulent organs within, roasted and ready, as though someone were dressing a meal for him.

"You like taking children, you sonofabitch?" A grubby man stood over him, wearing a mechanic's overalls with the name *Tarley* on a white patch over the left breast pocket, stitched in red thread. Spots of oil dotted the denim, and he brandished a wrench over his head and brought it down again and again, rocking Drake with each hit, his greater shell cracking and shattering with the blows. "You like taking children? You motherfucker!"

Drake cried into the ground, his sobs disturbing the dry dust between his fingers. He just wanted to eat … to be filled …

A rain of blows fell upon Drake, and the mechanic shouted, "This is for Abi, you godless piece of shit!" And he smashed him again.

Drake could taste a fine meal somewhere in the distance, but coughed dirt. His face was in it now, and there was an oily residue that hung in the air. "For Abi!" he heard, and another blow rained down on him, and another, shattering his shell in the back, the neck, the buttock, the leg ... he could feel them all taking the hits, and he thought about a meat tenderizer being applied to his flesh. It was a little poetic, wasn't it? He thought so, with what thoughts he had left. But it was getting hard to think. Drake didn't bother, instead recalling a pleasant rump roast from a week prior. Or was it two weeks? He couldn't recall. But the spices ... the delicate flavor of the meat ...

It was all to die for.

*

Arch emerged from the tunnel first to find Braeden Tarley beating the snot out of the one-armed demon. The mechanic had gone to town on the thing. Its clothing was torn, cracks were present all over the shell, black shadowy substance threatening to leak out. "Holy smokes," Arch said, pausing in the grim autumn light, and trying to shelter the eyes of the toddlers from the scene.

"I guess that's a little poetic," Barney Jones said, holding his sword at one side, and trying to shy his own toddler's eyes away as well.

"Aren't you going to counsel against wrath or something?" Lauren asked. For her part, the doc looked to Arch like she was more horrified than surprised by the scene unfolding before them.

The cracking noises were sickening, reminding Arch a little of the time he and Alison had gone to a seafood restaurant in Chattanooga for their first anniversary. She'd showed him how to crack the crab claws, busting open the shell and pulling out the sweet meat inside.

There wasn't any sweet meat being revealed here, just pooled shadowy essence, but Tarley was surely exposing a lot of it. The demon was whimpering.

"Goodness," the other demon whispered—the tall, British one that had led them here. "This is ... quite appalling."

Tarley paused in his downward swings, and looked over his shoulder at the thin demon. "You get the fuck out of here, y'hear?" The Brit blanched, maybe at the perceived threat, maybe at his crass use of language. "Go the fuck on ... or you're next." And Tarley hoisted the wrench again, and got back to just beating the tar out of the kidnapping demon.

The tall, sniffing demon didn't have to be told twice. "As you say," he said, and off he ran, blazing fast.

"What the fuck is this all about?" Guthrie emerged from the darkness behind them, passing Lauren and scowling at one of the kids that she caught looking at her. She turned in time to see the tall demon beating feet across the street. "We're letting that one get away, huh?"

"He did help us," Arch said, by way of explanation.

Guthrie just shrugged. "Okay then."

"You like that, you motherfucker?" Tarley screamed, and everyone watched as he seized the demon and rolled it over. There was almost nothing identifiable or human about it anymore, the shell cracked in a thousand places like a boiled egg that had been busted but not stripped yet.

"Go on, Braeden," Jones said quietly. "Finish it. Go for the heart."

"Wrath, wrath, and more wrath," Lauren muttered.

"Braeden is just delivering us from evil, that's all," Jones said, but he didn't seem to be enjoying it too much.

Tarley raised the wrench high, and then jammed it down with a hard thrust into the demon's face. The shell spread and broke apart, and he shoved it in deeper, like he was force-feeding it to a newly created orifice. It was an ugly, brutal thing, and for some reason it didn't please Arch the way it might once have.

But it didn't bother him either.

There was a final cracking noise, and the demon lurched. Then Tarley ripped the wrench free, raising it above his head—

With a desperate sucking sound, the demon collapsed in on himself with a vortex of noise and hell, louder than a normal demon, but disappearing all the same. When it was over, there was nothing left to mark the passage but a scorched section of ground, blackened grass and dust.

And in that moment, with nothing but the heavy breathing of those around him in the quiet fall air ... Arch knew it was over.

*

Brian had heard the last battle at the quarry, faintly, through the radio. He'd pumped a fist in exultation, cheering quietly for the victory. The shadowcats were done, their wrecking reign of destruction brought to an end in a uniquely Southern way. He could get behind that, and definitely wanted to applaud Casey for the idea.

His phone buzzed; a text came through: CHILDREN RETRIEVED. ALL ACCOUNTED FOR. ALL SAFE.

Brian slumped against the back of the chair.

They'd done it.

And by "they," he meant ... everyone but him.

A strange sort of self-pity took hold of him then. He should have felt more excitement. They'd won, after all—a rare victory these days.

In the three weeks since the Halloween massacre on the square, hardly a day had passed without more losses. They'd lost dozens of townspeople, maybe even a couple hundred. It was impossible to tell without going door to door—and nobody had proposed that yet.

All they had to go on were the calls that came in. And he had a sheet in front of him listing them all. Right at the top was the daycare, because they'd yet to send anybody out to that. A dozen more followed after it, from a call of strange noises from a house on Tavern Drive all the way to the last one, which came from downtown.

Brian lowered his head, taking the list in with despair. The question occurred—the same one he kept coming up with, time after time.

Was any of this ... making any kind of difference?

Of course. There were parents that would get their children back tonight because of what the watch had done today, people whose houses and lives would be saved because they'd wiped out those goddamned hellcats.

Of course they made a difference.

But he looked over the list again, and realized ... the watch might be making a difference, but ...

Coldly, analytically ... *he* was making zero impact.

That might have bothered him more, but he looked up at the clock and saw he only had twenty minutes left until his relief showed up. He'd go to the hospital again tonight; his mom needed a break, had already texted him that she'd left, so he'd go relieve her. Sit with his dad for a spell, stare at the ceiling, smell the disinfectant, listen to his father's grunts if he was awake.

Did that make a difference?

Probably not, no. But he'd do it anyway.

He gave that list of crimes in front of him another look. As soon as the watch got back, he'd start farming these out to them. From the nuisance calls to the last one, that one about someone screaming in an old factory off the square ... they'd get looked at, every one of them. Checked out. Investigated.

Because this was what the watch did.

They might not solve all the problems, but they'd sure try. And that was all the difference Brian could hope for, he realized grimly, as he counted the minutes until he could leave.

*

The elevator doors opened on the 4th floor at Red Cedar, and Brian stepped out, head down, humming to himself. It wasn't a happy hum—the smell of this place tended to put him into a quieter mood. It was more born of desire to break the chain of gloomy thoughts that had hounded him on the drive to Chattanooga.

And they had hounded him, too. Right into the elevator, following like a mangy and flea-bitten stray dog, ready to transfer some itchy misery right to him.

He raised his eyes to make sure he wasn't going to run into anyone as he navigated the beige hallways, passing right by the waiting area where he'd killed more hours than he cared to count. Then he let his gaze droop again. He didn't look up much anymore. Why would he? People here were mostly grim, mostly glum. A few spots of light here and there, but … these were people whose family members, friends were seriously ill.

Where was the bright spot in that?

It was kinda like Midian in that way. Smiling, happy people in the streets? Yeah, once upon a time. They might have been having a hell of a time if not for this whole demon swarm that had come down on them like a fucking apocalypse, but—

"Mr. Longholt?" A soft voice caused Brian to stop, mid-step, and nearly trip over himself. He blinked and looked up to see a woman standing. He hadn't even heard her approach. She was wearing a long white coat. One of his dad's doctors, probably. He'd met a few but didn't remember all their names.

"Yeah?" Brian asked, voice a little raspy. He rubbed at his neck. "That's me."

The doctor's face was expressionless. "About your father …"

Brian perked up. "Yes?" Could there be some good news at-fucking-last?

"He went into cardiac arrest about an hour ago," the doctor went on, as calm as if she were placing a lunch order, "and despite all of our efforts, we were unable to resuscitate him."

Brian blinked, taking all that in. "You … what?"

The lady doctor looked at him. She was somehow blurry now. "I'm so sorry for your loss."

"My … loss …?" It didn't quite make it through the first time, but it was starting to sink in now.

Brian just stood there, numb. She probably said something more, but he couldn't hear it.

His dad … dead?

Something snapped in him, and even though people were talking, he ignored them all, plunging past the elevator and to the stairs. Urgent cries followed him, but he heard none of them—and all of them. He went down the four flights to the lobby and was out, out the door and on his way back to his car, had started it up and was on his way back to Midian only moments later.

And through the cloud of emotions, all pressed on mute, he knew at last what he had to do.

*

"I can't protect you from life," Lauren said. It was her opening volley to Molly. Heh. "Volley to Molly." It even sounded funny in her head.

Molly was just staring at her as they cruised down the Chattanooga street, head tilted to the side. "Uhm, okay. What does that have to do with my trig homework for the new school?" She stared blankly at Lauren. "Which is due tomorrow, and we don't seem to be heading back to Elise's house." She kept her eyes fixed on Lauren but shook her head slightly. "Hello? Mom? Anybody home?"

"I'm here," Lauren said, turning her attention back to the road. It was only a quarter mile to 75, and she needed to pay attention so she didn't miss the turn. "Just … trying to tell you something I figured out today." She thought about carrying those toddlers on her hips. Once upon a time she'd carried Molly like that.

Now all she could do was carry her daughter in a car. She was way too big to lift.

"Ooookay," Molly said, in full sarcastic teen style, leaning back and looking at Lauren, waiting for her to go on.

"If all I teach you is to run when things get really bad," Lauren said, easing back into the conversation she'd rehearsed in her head when she'd driven back to Chattanooga, "what the hell am I really teaching you?" She hit the turn signal; I-75's northbound on-ramp was coming up.

"I don't know," Molly said, sounding pretty checked out. "To be a track star?"

"Well, I don't think you have much of a future as Usain Bolt," Lauren said, "because I've seen you run, and frankly, you're more dangerous to yourself on those gangly legs than you are safe."

Molly's face darkened. "Gee, thanks. I wonder who I inherited being a klutz from, 'She-who-trips-on-moonbeams'?"

Lauren shrugged. "We're not graceful. It's genetic. But that's okay, because you know what we are?" She looked right at Molly as she took the turn onto 75. "We're fucking fighters, daughter of mine."

Molly frowned, then turned to look out the windshield. "Are we going …?" She pointed toward the freeway ahead as Lauren sped up, preparing to merge. Traffic was light; Midian was less than an hour away.

"Yeah," Lauren said, and saw Molly's eyebrows rise. "We are. We're going home."

Molly swallowed, and there was a moment of conflict. "Good," she said with a pleasant, cheek-rosying bout of enthusiasm. Then, after a pause: "So ... where are we staying? Back at Ms. Cherry's? Because—"

"No," Lauren said, shaking her head. She'd had enough of living in a whorehouse. Not that Ms. Cherry wasn't sweet, but that environment made her skin itch like she was courting crabs. Which was probably unfair, but when it came to her daughter ... fuck fair. Fuck fair right where Casey fucked the girls in that house. "Like I said ... we're going home."

This time Molly gulped for real, but she didn't say anything. She just held her peace, lapsing into a quiet. Lauren could read it, could tell the fear was still there, the thought of confronting what they'd left behind ...

"It's on my mind too," Lauren said, reaching over and brushing Molly's arm. Her daughter nodded once, then swallowed visibly again. "And it's going to be tough. But we're going to face it together, okay?"

"Okay," Molly said, and she nodded, a little more forcefully. "Okay." It wasn't, of course—not yet.

But Lauren knew that it would be.

Because they really would face it together.

*

Hendricks got the call and responded, dragging his ass out of bed and coming to the station. He'd half-expected Starling to show up while he'd been killing time back at the motel, but she hadn't. Lucia must have been busy. The thought didn't bother him, but not getting his dick sucked kind of did.

He walked into the station, pushing through the Plexiglas entry and into the bullpen. It was pretty quiet, save for Casey behind the desk. The taxidermist was dicking around on his phone, and Hendricks caught a glimpse of Candy Crush as he passed. How long had that shit been going on? He started to say something, but Arch poked his head out of the sheriff's old office and waved him in.

Hendricks cocked an eyebrow at that as Arch disappeared back inside. But he shrugged, threading his way between desks and heading toward the office door, where he paused briefly when he came around the edge and saw who was sitting in the chair.

"Come in," Erin said, stern as fuck, the vision of every pissed-off law enforcement professional he'd ever seen.

Hendricks felt a tingle of doubt at whether he should abide by that "suggestion" or not. It didn't seem real friendly to him, but then, nothing she did seemed friendly to him these days. He glanced inside; Arch stood to his left, just inside the door, arms folded.

The whole thing made him uneasy.

But he didn't say a damned thing, just walked right in and gestured to the door behind him. "Is this an open door or closed door kind of meeting?"

Arch reached over and shut it, answering that one.

They stood there in silence for a few minutes, Arch with his arms folded, Erin sitting in Reeve's old chair, staring at him impassively, so Hendricks took his cue from both of them and hitched his hands behind him in "at ease" position. He could outlast the fucking end of the world like this, knees loose and eyes forward. He hated that it might seem like he was waiting for orders or something, but he knew himself, and knew he could sit like this until Midian was nothing but a mosquito bite hole in the face of the globe. Which would probably be about three weeks from now.

The minutes dragged on, and still Hendricks said nothing. If these fuckers wanted to have a stubborn-off, he'd show the hell out of them. He could out-wait them, fucking amateurs—

Arch finally broke the silence. "Why didn't you help us with the demon today?"

Hendricks didn't bother to look at him. "Which one? Yours—" he pointed to Arch "—or yours?" He pointed to Erin.

"You were right behind us," Arch said, answering again without actually dignifying him with an answer. He unfolded his arms, coming off the wall. "And then, when we got to the end of the chase, you were gone."

"Didn't think you'd notice," Hendricks said, still in at-ease position. "Flattered that you did." He looked sideways at Arch. "Seemed like you had it under control, so I just went on home."

"Why do I doubt that?" Erin asked, cool, still just sitting there.

"Because you hate me?" Hendricks offered, somewhat lightly.

She just stared him down, no hint of reaction. He'd baited her a few times lately, and she always showed a sign.

This time? Nada.

She leaned forward. "We got a 911 call while our respective chases were going on—"

"Just one?" Hendricks raised an eyebrow. "The demons must be napping."

"Someone reported screaming from an old factory downtown," Erin went on, apparently undeterred by his interruption. "When we got there, we found County Administrator Pike. Dead." She added the last like a punctuation mark.

Hendricks just stared at her. "That's a shame," he said flatly. He didn't put much feeling into it one way or another.

"The man looked to have been damned near gutted," Arch said, moving up behind him. "Something sharp got him right across the torso, ripped him open."

"Scary things, demons," Hendricks said. He could see which way this wind was blowing, and it was straight from the latrines toward him.

"If this was a demon, yeah …" Erin said, just staring him down. He stared right back, not going to give her an inch. "But it wasn't a demon, was it?"

"I guess you'll just have to ask your crime scene unit once they get done investigating it all," Hendricks said.

"Cut the crap," Arch said, and now he got right up in Hendricks's left ear. "He had bullets in him. .45s. And the wound channels were destroyed by something sharp—like your sword."

Hendricks cocked his head to the side to look at Arch. "Prove it."

That brought about another silence before Arch exploded into it again: "We don't kill human beings, Hendricks—"

"That's flatly untrue," Hendricks said, still maintaining his cool. It was hard not to under this level of stupid questioning. He tossed a nod toward Erin. "She killed a human. Back when the Rog'tausch came through town. She shot down Kitty Elizabeth's manservant, who was an actual man, remember? Reeve hushed it up, buried it under a John Doe bullshit name." He stared at Erin, who stared back. Now they were both impassive as hell. "I remember, even if you don't."

"I remember," Erin said, staring him down. "That was an accident though."

"No, it wasn't," Hendricks said, pulling out the full scoff. "You damned sure meant to kill him; you just didn't realize he wasn't a demon at the time."

"We knew Pike wasn't a demon," Arch started to say. He was getting fucking overheated, and Hendricks knew why, a second later. "Alison—"

"Something new is happening here," Hendricks said, stretching a little because he was tired of dealing with this bullshit, jagoff inquiry without at least flexing his body. He was stiff from a rumble with a couple hesper'antu a few days earlier, the biggest physical challenge he'd had lately. Pissy little shits—both the hesper'antu and Erin and Arch at this point. "People are starting to work with demons. I mean, it does happen from time to time, but ... given us partnering up with the OOCs, that vulture motherfucker who led you to the kids ... it was inevitable, I guess, that people were gonna make some pacts with the enemy. It's happening. Right here, right now."

"How is that new?" Arch asked, still seething. He looked like he had a leash on it for the moment, but Hendricks knew it was just a matter of time before the fury he was wanting to turn loose on Hendricks found its outlet, and it'd come racing back for him at that point. "You told me when everything started that people prayed to demons and such."

"I've never seen it happen at a hotspot though," Hendricks said with a shrug. "Never *seen* it, period."

"That's what you're saying happened with Pike?" Erin was leaning forward now. "That he was ... working with demons?"

"I couldn't prove it," Hendricks said with a shrug, "but think about how he was trying to shut us down back during the buildup to the Rog'tausch. How he set up Halloween, trying to recall Reeve. If Alison hadn't cut him with a holy knife, we would have all sworn he was a demon." Here he looked right back at Arch. "And I bet—I just bet—if you pulled Reeve's corpse out of the ground and had some mortician with half a brain give it the once-over ... I bet you find signs of foul play, on him and that secretary."

His bit said, Hendricks shut his trap. He wasn't going to incriminate himself, but he wasn't going to let them build up Pike as some kind of fucking hero either.

"If you thought that was the case," Erin said, about ten degrees cooler than Arch, "why not say anything to either of us?"

"I just did," Hendricks said, shrugging again. "Not my fault somebody already dealt with the motherfucker in question."

"I just bet," Arch seethed. He stared Hendricks down for a minute, then said, "You didn't even like Reeve. Why would you go out of your way to avenge him?"

"Who says I did?" Hendricks tossed back. "My question is—why didn't you? He was one of ours. He was your—both of your—mentors. But you just bought this bullshit story Pike threw out about a fire sloth, even though we haven't heard a whisper of a second one of those slinking around since we wiped out the one in that development." Hendricks slung his arms wide. "They're not fucking quiet, okay? That first one ate some construction workers, I guarantee it. I know a lot of people are getting lost in the shuffle around here, but Jesus F. Christ, stop and smell the bullshit. Pike just parroted back what he'd probably heard from Reeve that same afternoon. He clipped him, clipped the secretary, probably sacrificed them both to demons, and you all showed up like the goddamned Army cavalry, so full of yourselves and the rightness of your cause that you didn't even bother to ask yourselves if these were civilians or insurgents." Hendricks leaned forward. "Let me help you out, because I've seen both: Pike was working for the enemy. No doubt. I'd stake my life on it."

"Or at least his," Arch threw at him. Hendricks ignored it. "He had a wife and family—"

"His wife was probably in on it," Hendricks said. He didn't have any doubts to assuage. Pike had confessed to someone, after all, based on what Starling had played back to him.

Erin just stared at him, but he could see the wheels spinning. "You can't just deal out justice however you see fit. Not here. Not now. You can't just go killing people—"

"I wish everybody in town, demons included, would get that message," Hendricks said, looking right at her.

She looked back. Didn't back down an inch. "They will."

Hendricks could think of only one thing to say to that, some stupid *Game of Thrones* quote that bubbled right up: "'I wish you luck in the wars to come.'"

"I wish you would get your head out of your ass," Erin said, standing up. It was almost hilarious how hard she was staring him down, but damn if she didn't do it well, almost like a drill sergeant. "Or else … just get out, period. We don't need your moody, maverick bullshit while we're trying to save this town." And with a last burning look, she walked to the door and out, closing it behind her.

"Get yourself under control," Arch said, clearly still seething. He started for the door, but Hendricks wasn't done yet.

"I was thinking about …" Hendricks started, and Arch slowed his roll, listening. "It's been like an endless succession of days lately, since Halloween, with all the calls we've gotten. But …" He paused, things on his mind spilling out of his mouth. "You remember that kid, like two weeks ago? The one we saved from the hellcats in the woods on the day of hunting opener—"

"I remember," Arch said stiffly. "Mack Wellstone."

"Yeah, Mack," Hendricks said, staring out the window behind Reeve's desk. It was getting darker outside, twilight seeping out from behind the clouds in the form of a darkening sky. "We saved him ... and then we lost him again. Then we lost Reeve ... so much has happened in these last few months, but it's all stepped up these last three weeks since Halloween. Every day a crisis. But those two things stand out, Mack and Reeve. We've seen a lot of people die—"

"Or disappear," Arch added quietly, all the anger bled out of his voice.

"But some things ..." Hendricks stared out that window, at that scraggly field outside where the even the weeds were starting to go brown for the coming winter. "Some things just stick with you, you know? For you, I guess, it's the kids." He glanced back over his shoulder and saw Arch nod. He didn't have to guess why Arch had latched onto that thing. "For Erin, the hellcats; for me ... I don't know. I guess it was Reeve, sort of."

"You didn't even like the man," Arch said. "And he sure didn't much care for you."

"In the Corps, you don't get to pick your squadmates," Hendricks said. "There were a few guys I really hated. Fucking assholes, the kind who—it doesn't matter. Way worse than any beef I had with Reeve, let's put it that way." He turned to look at Arch. "But when we went into Ramadi, those assholes were my brothers. They had my back, I had theirs. And if some motherfucking insurgent blew their head off, his was following without mercy as soon as I could get my barrel lined up, I don't care if I'd been arguing with the sonofabitch he killed two seconds earlier."

He rounded on Arch. "This shit right here? This is us versus them. If Pike turned on you, was selling you guys out to demons, he deserved what happened to him and worse. I don't give two shits what excuses he has. He betrays our side, he's on theirs, and needs to have his guts exposed to the air just like any other asshole demon that crosses the line."

"Who decides that?" Arch said, and he was back to being a rock wall that Hendricks's words would just bounce off. Which was a shame, because Hendricks would have liked him to understand. "You?"

"Who else was available?" Hendricks asked. "You were saving kids, Erin was saving the town ... what do you do when you get the call? Evil's afoot. Let it live, it spreads. Maybe it summons a demon, uses it to cause more havoc, kill more people, sacrifice more lives." Hendricks shrugged. "What do you do, Arch? Just shrug your shoulders and let it be? Because he's skin-covered and not shelled?"

"I don't know," Arch said, "and you shouldn't know either. It shouldn't be one man's decision. This ain't some lawless town out of the frontier, where you're the sheriff and the law."

"I know I'm not the sheriff," Hendricks said. "He's dead."

Arch got stonefaced. "There you go again, dodging out of all responsibility. This ain't going anywhere—"

"Damned right it isn't," Hendricks said.

Arch held up a finger, pointing it right at Hendricks. "Erin was right. Get your head out of your backside—"

"You can say ass; I won't tell anyone."

"—or just get the hell out of town," Arch said, and he finally lost it, voice rising to a yell. "We got no use for you if you can't put a leash on yourself!" And he stormed out, not nearly so reserved as Erin.

Hendricks, for his part, stood and stewed for another minute before he decided he'd had enough of standing there. "Fuck this," he muttered to himself and left as well, figuring he'd rather stare at the walls in his motel room than here.

*

"You ready for this?" Lauren asked, Molly at her side.

The lawn was overgrown, because who was going to bother to mow it? Albert Daniel, their neighbor, had died just over there, Lauren recalled, killed by the demons that had possessed Molly. She could remember his face. She'd lain right there, shuddering in despair, as the blood had spurted out of his head from a gunshot that rang out on the quiet street.

The chill wind felt like it was cutting through them, opening up her skin to force in a reminder.

But Lauren remembered.

So did Molly; she could tell by the way her daughter's gaze fixed on that spot on the lawn. It was on her mind, clearly, and why wouldn't it be?

They'd both been violated here, in different ways—and yet the same. The things that had happened hadn't just resulted in demons seizing them, each, bodily, but taking away her mother—Molly's grandmother—and—

Their home.

It stood as it ever did, the house Lauren had lived in all her life. It was forbidding from down here, a two-story that wasn't all that big but wasn't all that small. She'd had memories here—her own, and then those with Molly. Growing up, getting pregnant, having a baby, going to med school, raising Molly—all those right here in this home.

And they didn't change just because some asshole pack of demons decided to come to town for whatever reason and piss all over everything.

"If we don't face this," Molly said, almost as much probably to herself as to her mother, "this place isn't ours anymore." Her daughter's resolve visibly hardened. "It's theirs."

"When did you get all sensible and grown up?" Lauren murmured, putting an arm around Molly's shoulder. She didn't shrug it off, which was good. Lauren felt like she was at peak vulnerable right now, and pulling Molly close to her helped as they took the small, manageable infinity of steps up to the front porch.

When they were up there, they paused, by mutual accord, both staring at the door. It was closed, some kind soul who'd brought them their clothing and effects surely having done so. Lauren took a breath, then leaned down, and tugged at the handle.

It squeaked, that old sound that always greeted her when she came home from a long day at the hospital, and then relinquished its grip on the lock, and started to swing open.

Darkness waited within as it swung wide, the faint grey of the sky overhead streaming in to light their path.

Molly was the first to take a step forward, over the threshold, but Lauren matched it, stepping in on the rug behind her.

They stood in the silence. It wasn't like she remembered it—full of laughter and joy and happiness and wonder and arguments and TV shows and all else.

It was different.

Empty.

She squeezed Molly tighter, and felt her daughter do the same to her. It wasn't the same, but … they hadn't expected it to be. Because things were different now.

Everything was different now. And it always would be.

"Well," Molly said, and her voice came out warbling and uncertain, then strengthened, "we're home."

*

Arch was still thinking about Hendricks as he gathered up his stuff from the spare room in the Jones house. It was a tough thing to fathom, what Hendricks might have done to Pike. It shook him right to the core of what he thought of the cowboy, what he'd always thought of the man—turned his opinion around in the worst way. He didn't know what to do with those thoughts, those—feelings, really.

Especially not giving everything else he'd already worked through.

He'd felt strangely alive again after bringing those children out of the drains. It was almost like he was crawling his way back to life. He'd prayed in the dark, prayed for the light, and he'd seen it again, somewhere in there as he got shellacked and nearly eaten by a demon.

Answered prayers were a funny thing, but he wasn't sure this was something he'd even asked for. At least not in this way.

"Going somewhere?" Barney Jones's voice was quiet, almost wry. Arch turned to find him at the door, leaning against the jamb, watching.

"I think it's time I moved on out," Arch said. "Seems to me that there's work to be done, and a room at the station that's empty, so ... I'm going to head on over there, be a little closer to the center of the action."

Jones pursed his lips. "You sure that's a good idea?"

Arch lowered his voice. He knew the man's concern, could see it plainly now in a way he hadn't before. "I know you're worried about me. And a week ago—heck, a day ago—you were right to be. I ain't been handling this well. But ... I think I got my head on straight."

Jones raised an eyebrow, cocked it at him accusingly. "That so?"

"I think it is," Arch said, nodding slowly. "Everything I've gone through lately—part of me was praying for deliverance from it like it was something directed specifically at me. Alison dying, her not telling me about—well, you know—I took it all personally. But it wasn't."

Jones watched him quietly for a moment, then nodded. "Go on."

"The world's a tough place," Arch said. "People make choices. Choices have their consequences. Alison chose not to tell me—and I can see why. That demon that ... killed her ... he ... they, whatever ... they made choices too. She chose to fight for her town, for ... me, I guess. All this while, I wanted to make it about me. I did make it about me—in my prayers, in my mind. But it wasn't about me." He nodded. "I see that now."

"We all suffer from a little self-centeredness every now and again," Jones said wryly. "But thinking about yourself at the worst of times—how this thing hits you, when others are suffering—it ain't good. We think about ourselves, crawl up our own heads, we tend to turn to rage and revenge as a solution—like Braeden." He lowered his voice and looked over his shoulder. "Now maybe that beating he dealt out will do his heart some good, maybe it won't. Either way ... it ain't pure as a motive, that's sure."

"No, it's not," Arch said. "I don't believe that just being angry, that striking back ... that these are the things that will heal a heart." He shook his head. "I could march into that jail tomorrow and put a sword right through the heart of that man that carried the demon that killed Alison ... but it wouldn't do a danged bit of good. She gave her life, the last minutes of it, to save us—and save him, really." He bowed his head. "Now, I want to use my time, however much of it there is ... making good her efforts."

"That's a reasonable cause," Jones said, "expressed in reasonable words. But ..." He tilted his head, looked expectantly at Arch.

"I'm not doing it just so I can go meet the Lord and see Alison again," Arch said. "I'm not aiming for that to happen anytime soon, is what I'm saying. I expect if we get through this ... I might end up living a whole life after Midian." He paused. "Though that's feeling like a mighty big 'if' these days."

Jones nodded. "I could see it in your eyes, you know, that loss of hope. You weren't looking for a reason to live, Arch." He lowered his voice to a whisper. "You were looking for a reason to die."

Arch felt the burn of shame on that one. "I know ... and I'm ... I'm not proud of it."

"Good; you shouldn't be," Jones said, coming off the jamb and on into the room, putting a hand on his shoulder. "But you got a lot of good you could still do. Here, and elsewhere after this is over, if ... like you said, we make it out."

Arch thought about that a second. "Do you think we will? Make it through, I mean?"

Jones just smiled—wry, again, but with a gleam in his eyes—and said, "I know who's on our side, and I've seen who's on theirs. And you won't see me switching, even if it's just us against them all."

Arch nodded slowly. "It ain't just us, I don't think. You going to the meeting?"

"I'll be there," Jones said, "but Olivia's fixing dinner first. You want a meal before you go?"

"Wouldn't mind still being able to stop by for one every now and again even after I go," Arch said, throwing in a little wryness of his own.

Jones burst into a big grin. "You're welcome anytime. You know what she says ..." And he put his arm around Arch's shoulder as Arch picked up his bag and started toward the door. "'I only fixed what I thought y'all'd eat'! And you know what I add to that?" The preacher guffawed. "'Yeah—what you thought we'd eat in fifty years of digging in!'" He laughed at his own joke. "Anytime you want to stop, Arch, we'll always have plenty. You just drop on by."

Arch felt a warmth over his shoulder where Jones's arm rested, and lower, a little catch in his throat. It was good to have people you could count on. "I might just do that. I might just."

*

Erin called things to order just past six. She didn't have a gavel or any such thing, just thumped her palm against the podium in the meeting room in the municipal building, which was filled to the brimming with people who'd professed their loyalty to the watch only a few weeks earlier, after Halloween. She'd stood in this room while Reeve had done the same thing—called them to order, tried to organize them, to draw the strings of a system in place to protect Midian—

And failed. Three weeks of floundering had proven that much.

They'd seen untold chaos in these weeks. The hellcats, the demon kidnapper—they'd found his hideout, and it ended up being a truly grotesque set of discoveries that Erin wished she could unsee—and other shit, of course. Never-ending rivers of shit, lately.

And Reeve. Of course, Reeve.

Well … she'd seen about enough of it. That was why she was standing here, in front of this group of people who'd said they wanted to save Midian. They'd said it, some of them had dipped their toe in it, some had gone all in, whole hog, and others …

She hadn't seen some of their asses since.

But here they were now, most of them. There were a few notable absences, but she couldn't trouble herself for those. She was dealing with people, after all, and people were flawed. They fucked up. They lied, sometimes even to themselves.

She looked over the crowd as she waited for the last of them to settle. No sign of Hendricks.

She tried to figure out how she felt about that, but ultimately … there was a bare prickle of relief. She didn't know how to handle the cowboy at this point. She'd been so sure of how she felt about him during the summer, sure enough to go off a cliff for him …

But now? Maybe it would be better if he really didn't show up to this. Or anything else either, if he couldn't stop being the world's biggest asshole.

"I call y'all to order," Erin said, almost jokingly, and it got a couple chuckles. "Seriously, though … thank you for coming. I don't want to take up your whole evening, but …" Here she got serious. "But I will. If I can."

That sent a little rumble through the crowd. They'd been invited to a meeting, no doubt assuming it would be a standard progress report.

They hadn't had one of those since Reeve had died. Some probably were coming just to hear whatever sort of spin would get thrown out about the sheriff's death.

Well, Erin didn't have time for that shit.

"We stood here a few weeks ago," Erin said, looking through the faces in the crowd, gripping the sides of the podium for support, "and Sheriff Reeve—God rest his soul—asked y'all to make a commitment to help with the shit going on in this town. It was a small commitment, in most cases; a show of hands kind of thing. He wanted to see who would fight for Midian, and some of y'all really came through.

"And some of y'all," she said, trying to keep the next part low-key to avoid being a Hendricks-level ass, "ain't done a blessed thing since then."

That caused a little hum, and she held up a hand to stay it off. "I don't blame you. Y'all are busy. Got lives to lead. Maybe you ain't been hit by this personally; maybe you're ignoring it all, hoping it'll go away. But I'm gonna say it now, and we'll have it out, and if you want to tell me to take a flying leap of fuck off after this, then you won't hear from me again. But ... y'all have got to see that shit is spiraling down around here." She put her heart into her voice, tried to put the plea into her eyes. "People have been dying left and right. In the woods, in the neighborhoods, in the streets. We got a demon problem, and it ain't going away.

"Those of us that can fight—well, we've been trying. Trying real hard." She looked around and saw Chauncey Watson nodding his head behind those big glasses, and Ms. Cherry, nodding a little more subtly in the second row, looking her right in the eye, practically telling her, *You go, girl*, with that look. "But we can't do it alone, those of us in this fight.

"It's come time for some of y'all to shit or get off the pot," she said, and that caused another uncomfortable murmur. "We are failing this thing, failing this town, because we just don't have the people. So I'm asking you for a big-ass commitment. I'm asking you to come in on this with us, and treat it like a damned job—to be like volunteer firemen, only a volunteer army."

"The demon fighting minutemen," Mike McInness said, and a low hum of agreement met that statement. "And women."

"Exactly," Erin said. "We tried this with a few, but we need to get in the fight with many. They stir shit, we show up with forty, fifty, a hundred people, and lay their demon asses out." She thumped a closed fist down on the podium, rattling the wood. "We can't keep having this half-hearted army try and save things. You either need to get in on this, with us, trying to save this town—

"Or you need to get the fuck out of Midian before your ass gets killed by demons," she said, and that shut up any buzz and sucked all the air out of the room.

"We're failing because we don't have an army, and they're picking us apart a little at a time," Erin said, looking over the quiet room. Some faces were nodding. Some were looking real hard at their laps. She couldn't tell what anyone was thinking. "I know this shit is scary and unprecedented and—and I know we all wish that Reeve was here to lead us through it."

She got a little something caught in her throat just then. "But he's not. And we need 100% from all of you who are willing to give it right now. Nothing less is going to save this town. It's them versus us, and it will only work if *us* works together as a team." She paused, and choked up, just for a second again. "Like Reeve would have wanted it."

Erin took a couple breaths. They were all listening. Hard to tell what they were thinking, but they were sure as shit hanging on her every word, even the shamefaced ones looking at their damned shoelaces.

"Maybe some of you think this is just going to taper off, that things will get back to normal." She shook her head. "That we'll win the battle and win the day. Well, I'll tell you—we've won days—but the damned war grinds on, and it's going to keep going until we kick every last demon sonofabitch out of this town." Nodding heads greeted her. "Now that's not going to happen today, that's not going to happen tomorrow. Best settle in for a long war. But with your help—we can actually fight it. Get together, build ourselves into an army, and cram holy steel up every demon ass in this town until there is not a goddamned one of them left." She stared out over the quiet crowd, wondering if she'd just killed them all with that one. "Now ..." Her mouth went dry. "Who's with me?"

A long pause.

Silence.

And the room erupted in a chorus of "I am!" and "We're with you!" and everything else imaginable that indicated a yes. She could barely hear it all, it was so loud.

But they were in, she thought, staring dumbly at the crowd in front of her. They were going to do this—for real, this time, no half-assed efforts.

And she was going to lead them.

*

Hendricks sat alone in his motel room, staring at the walls.

He'd got the text telling him about the meeting, but fuuuuuuck that. He'd already had enough meetings for today.

So instead he'd settled in, shirt off, back against the cold wood headboard, watching TV. That Key and Peele movie about the cat was on again, and he was half-watching it, mostly lost in his own damned head.

"I don't belong here," he muttered, thinking out loud. It had been rattling around since he'd gotten out of his meeting with Arch and Erin earlier.

He really didn't need this shit. How many hotspots were there right now? Less than when he came to the town, but still … there were surely some out there, firing. Always demons somewhere in the world, getting up to no good.

The phone rang, the one that belonged to the motel, and he leaned over to answer it. "Hello?" he muttered, surly as he could get.

"It's me," the melodic voice came.

"Haven't heard from you in a while," Hendricks said coolly. "How's things?"

"Things are … proceeding." She didn't sound particularly pleased one way or another.

He looked around the messy room. "Yeah? Well, things are 'proceeding' around here too. In a southerly direction up the ass of a south-facing muskox."

She didn't answer for a moment. "Is that so?"

"Not literally so, no," Hendricks said. He always had to explain this shit to her. In that way, she was kinda worse than Starling. But she had paid his bills for a long time, so he dealt with her occasional bullshit and gaps in learning. "But it's pretty bad."

She didn't seem to answer that, at least not right away. "That seems reason enough for you to stay, doesn't it?"

He didn't bother to ask her how she knew he was debating leaving. "They've got it under control. Or at least as under control as a spiraling hotspot can be," he amended, not really keen on the taste of his own bullshit when it was that flagrant.

"You know that's not true."

"What I know is true is that I've had enough of this fucking town," Hendricks said flatly.

"Language."

Hendricks started to light into a long string of curses, but held back at the last second. "I don't want to be here anymore," he said instead.

"You have a role in this yet."

"So did Archibald Stan, remember?" Hendricks tossed back at her. "He was supposed to bring about the end of the world?"

"And still will."

"Yeah, I'm kinda doubting that," Hendricks said, not exactly rolling his eyes—because you didn't really roll your eyes at this lady—but came close. "They're putting together an army. They're fighting back. They don't need me, and they don't want me."

"I want you there."

"Well," Hendricks said, his jaw getting tight, "I know I've worked for you for a while, but … you don't own me. Find me a different hotspot, and I'll go there. This one? It's played out for me."

"That's not—"

He hung up, because it was pointless to argue. The phone rang again, and he ignored it. It rang again after that, he ignored it again. It went on like that for a while, but he just turned the movie up and then, finally, unplugged the damned phone from the wall.

"Starling," he called out to the empty room.

No answer.

"Starling! Show your ass up." He looked around, toward the darkened door to the bathroom. "We need to talk."

Nothing.

"Fuck," Hendricks muttered, leaning back on the bed. He closed his eyes, wondering if Lucia was just busy being fucked like a—well, like a hooker on retainer or something.

That thought settled a little less easily on his mind, and he kept his eyes closed, hoping he could just fall asleep. The movie ended after a while, and he still hadn't opened his eyes.

He didn't get to sleep for a long time.

And she never did show up.

*

Brian was almost done packing when he heard his mom's car pull into the driveway. He'd loaded up the back of his old beater, sticking the last few things in the trunk when she stepped down from the big SUV she drove, silver hair catching the dim moonlight barely shining through the clouds, and the house lights that were glowing orange behind him.

Brian's breath stuck in his lungs. She looked weathered as hell, tired as hell, making her way toward him one step at a time. She caught him around the chest with a hug, pulled him tight, and he let her, laying his head down as far as he could reach—not quite to his mom's shoulder anymore.

"You left the hospital before I got there," she said dully.

"I didn't want to stay," he said. "Sorry."

"There were things that needed to be decided," she said in a vaguely reproachful tone as she pulled back from him. There were smudges at the corners of her eyes where her mascara hadn't survived what he was sure was a tearful onslaught. "Funeral arrangements and whatnot."

He just nodded. There wasn't much he could say to that.

Her gaze drifted to his open trunk, all the things packed inside. "What's all this?" she asked, after she had a moment to really take it all in.

Brian swallowed. "I'm leaving. Tonight." She turned her head to look at him, blankly, uncomprehending. "I called a buddy of mine from college who works in New York and … he said I could crash on his couch for a while, so … I am. Going to, I mean." He sort of nodded without looking at her.

She blinked a few times then looked down at the ground. "You're just going to leave me here then?"

"You don't have to stay here, Mom," Brian said.

She looked up at him again. "Midian is my home, Brian."

He swallowed again, thick knot in his throat. "I always said I wanted to get out of this town as a kid. Just … get the hell out, to whatever bright spot on the map I could find that was away from here. I didn't want to end up like the other people I knew who were born in the local hospital and ended up dying there, too." He shook his head. "I can't do it, Mom."

"Oh, Brian," she said, taking a step back and looking at him, "what would your father say?"

"I don't know," he said, dully. "He's dead, so I'll never know what he says again." He swallowed, hard, seeing the look on her face at that. She just crumpled. "Mom …" he said softly, "I don't want to be next."

That left a stinging silence, and he decided to fill it himself. "I kept thinking … after what happened to him, what happened to Alison … I kept thinking that maybe I … I was strong. Sheriff Reeve told me so. I kept thinking … I'm wandering my way through this, and I'm holding on. Maybe I am strong." He looked right at her. "But I'm not, Mom. I'm weak. Weak as fuck. I don't want to live like this anymore, here where everything is falling apart. Midian was your home, it was Dad's home, it was Alison's ... but I never belonged here." He pursed his lips. "And I don't want to be here for the end. Because it's coming. And nothing we've done has seemed to make a damned bit of difference."

She stared at him a long time in the porch light, then nodded once and hugged him again. There seemed to be a thin veil of relief over his mother's face as she looked at him. "Drive safe," she said, and stepped back.

"I will," he said, feeling strangely unmoored now that she was no longer close to him. He wobbled his way to his driver's side and got in. His mother was still standing there, in the rearview, as he started the car. He looked at the road ahead, and not her, though, as he drove off—because he was afraid if he looked back, he might not find it in himself to leave.

*

Lauren breezed into the sheriff's department, figuring it was beyond time for her to stop by and do that thing that needed to be done. She wondered who'd handled it the last couple weeks, and found herself—somewhat grimly—considering that maybe she'd find a real mess when she came to visit the prisoner, a starved man down to skin and bones.

So she was pleasantly surprised when she found him in reasonable order. Chauncey Watson had let her into the cell without any question, like her showing up was the most regular thing for anyone to do, even at this late hour.

She was about halfway through checking his vitals when the door squeaked open and she turned to find Erin Harris at the entry to the cell. Chauncey dutifully locked it behind her, leaving the two of them here in the cell by themselves.

"Hey," Lauren said, turning her focus away from the job for a little bit.

"I'd heard you were back," Erin said, "but we didn't get a chance to talk yet, so ..."

Lauren smiled. "I heard you were in charge now. Congratulations. I think." That was dicey.

Erin smiled, taking it in the spirit in which it was intended. "Yeah. It's a little heady, taking over the watch. Big shoes to fill, what with Reeve being a hard act to follow ..."

"Don't try and fill Reeve's shoes," Lauren said, a little slyly. "They're way too big for you, and yours are way more stylish. Be yourself. You know what needs to be done. Do it your way. Or whatever way works. Don't get trapped into thinking you have to do it the way Reeve would have."

"Sage advice," Erin said, nodding along. Her tan uniform looked like it might have gotten a little sweaty around the underarms, and Lauren concealed a smile. Leading people was pretty tough on the antiperspirant. She'd found that out the first time she'd had to deal with interns. "In that vein, I asked people for a lot bigger commitment than they've given thus far."

"Pretty good idea," Lauren said. "You get it?"

"Mostly," Erin said. "A lot of hooting and hollering. We'll see if it lasts until morning, or later tonight, when the calls start rolling in heavy. Been kinda quiet so far, except for ..." Her voice trailed off.

Lauren froze. "What?"

Erin stuttered back to life out of a daze. "Hm? Oh. Addie Longholt called. Said Bill didn't make it. And Brian decided to leave town, head to New York."

"Sorry to hear about Bill. He was a good man." Lauren stared back at her, thinking it over. "I can see that about Brian though."

"Oh?"

"Last time I talked to him, we talked about how desperation kinda ... drowns you," Lauren said. "And how you can drag others with you." She shook her head. "That's the soul-sucking part of this thing, isn't it? You see things that defy description. Worse even than most cops deal with on a daily basis. And they never let up, really. It's just bad all the time. You stay in Midian long enough as things start to get worse, and you don't have a really clear reason why you're doing it?" She blinked, thinking how close she'd gotten to this very edge. "I think it would eat you right up."

Erin's eyes flicked around. "What would?"

Lauren blinked back at her. "It—it's just a metaphor. The town, desperation, that sort of—"

"Hell."

The word came as a whisper, the kind that sent a chill right up Lauren's back in an uncontrollable shiver. Jarred by the sound, she stepped away from the speaker, the man who was sitting, dull-eyed, to her left, retreating closer to Erin, who was watching the man with her eyes as wide as trash can lids.

"What did you just say?" Erin asked, hand resting on her pistol.

The man sat there, looking at them both dazedly. "Hell ... will eat you," he said in a low, raspy voice.

It didn't sound like a threat. It sounded like a statement of fact.

"Hell ... is going to eat us?" Erin asked. Now she had the jaded look of someone who'd heard something they didn't come close to believing. "I hope it starts with my pussy then, because I could use someone to really go down there and work the clit for a while—"

"Hell is here," he said, sounding like a crazy itinerant street preacher who'd once accosted Lauren on the streets of Atlanta, raving about the end of the world. "The gates—here, in this place," he went on, rasping, "it's what draws them—like flies to death, the gates of hell— hell and its analog on the other side—oh yes, they're both here, and make this the place of battle to draw in all manner of evils—"

"Wait ..." Lauren said. "Did he just say—"

"I think so," Erin said, eyes moving back and forth. "But ... was he serious? Or is he mad as a hatter?"

"The gates of hell await," he said, his own eyes wide now, looking at them both. Lauren didn't know much about hell, or heaven, or even life on Earth, lately—but she knew one thing, as he finished his thought. "And heaven as well. Here. In this place. And there will be a great battle with great destruction wrought ... and it will settle the matter ... for good and for always."

She listened, and she heard, and although she didn't know if he was crazy or not, she did know ... "He believes every word he's saying," she told Erin, who nodded along. "Every damned word."

Heaven?

Hell?

... Gates?

"Oh, fuck," Lauren said.

Interlude, the Last

Two Years Ago

It was happening again. Lucia was bleeding, she was hurting, she was in pain—it was all happening again, again, like it happened every time these days ...

"Get your slutty cunt ass back in here!" Michael roared as Lucia staggered down the hall. She left bloody handprints down the hallway, staining the beige walls. That was going to cost her later.

She made it into her room and locked the door, shoving it closed just a second before the first hammering began. It was inevitable, she knew. Mike and Karen would bust the damned thing down, him kicking it loose, her crowing and laughing in his wake. That much was certain. They wouldn't stop, no chance.

Lucia was bleeding from the lip, from the mouth. Her stomach ached from where he had hit her. She'd stayed on her feet this time, but only barely.

She looked around the room. There wasn't much left. Mike had trashed so many of her things, taken away so many more.

The hammering came again, harder this time, the bedroom door rattling in its frame. "Open up this door or I'm going to have him take it out of your cunt ass!" That was Karen, loud as a foghorn, right outside the door.

Lucia backed away, slowly, looking, eyes sweeping, desperately, for something, anything she could use as a weapon. "I need help," she whispered. No phone to call for it—and she would have called for it, this time.

Her eyes flew to the window—but no. It was too small. No way could she get it open and squeeze out.

The door rattled again, more swearing followed. It wouldn't have been so bad; she could have listened to it all day if not for what always followed it.

Lucia's eyes flew to the bookshelf again, one last time, and fell on ...

The Bible?

She snatched it off the shelf, desperate, smooth leather cover rubbing across her palm. She didn't even know why she did it; it was just a book. But she was desperate. Looking for help, any help, Ms. Black's entreaties popped into her head and she snatched it up. She flipped to the marked page and found herself reading.

Lucia stopped after a few lines. What ...?

What the hell was this?

Mike smashed against the door outside, and Lucia's heart sank. It was coming. And soon.

Her eyes darted over the page one last time. It was ... a prayer?

She read the words:

In hours of darkness summon me;
Call my servants or invoke my name
Hate your enemies
And I will see them destroyed
In your hour of despair
Speak the words and cry out my name

Below it was a name, and she read it, aloud, and—

—and something seemed to pause; the door quieted, and then—

Everything seemed to burst loose at once, and Michael was shrieking and Karen was screaming and there was more screaming, and anger, and blood and—

Lucia woke, and she was miles away. Sitting on a bench, in a bus depot. The walls were dull, and night had fallen outside. A janitor came by, slopping the floors with a dirty old mop. He didn't even spare her a look.

Lucia looked down. Her clothes were clean, she was clean—save for one little dot of red under her right index finger's nail. Like a warning.

She could see flashes in her head, remember—just vaguely—what had happened.

Opening the bag at her side, Lucia stared.

The Bible was up top, with a bus ticket just next to it. She took in the bus ticket with a glance, and picked up the Bible.

She paged through it again, and this ...

... this wasn't like the Bible she remembered.

Leaning back on the bench, she shut the Bible back in the bag.

On the overhead speaker, she could hear them calling her bus. Dazed, she stood.

This was what was left for her. Something had happened. Something bad. And she needed to get out of Chattanooga.

On stumbling legs, she walked to the bus and stood in the door as the hydraulics let out a powerful hiss.

"Ticket," the driver said as she stepped up. He looked her over once, maybe gave her a look of appreciation, and then did his thing with the ticket. "Midian, huh? That's just down the road."

She didn't answer, just shuffled off to a seat. Midian? She'd never heard of it. But there it was, printed on her ticket.

And something about the name ... told her that was where she was supposed to be.

Go.

So she went.

Who are you? she asked, the quiet question coming in her own mind.

Starling, the voice said.

It wasn't the name that she'd called in that room, with everything falling apart around her, but for some reason ...

It was enough.

Day Four

"Starling!" Hendricks called into the empty motel room. It was six o'clock in the morning.

No answer.

His bag was packed, and he was dressed. He was calling out as one last attempt. Figured he owed her that much for giving him all those orgasms. Like an obligation—try to talk to her one last time, murder an evil guy when she tells you to. It was payment for saving his life a few times too.

The orgasms probably weighed more in his calculus, though, if he was being honest.

"Fuck it," he said, and meant it, slinging the bag over his shoulder and heading for the door.

He didn't bother with a last look. The Sinbad motel was a shithole, and one he'd grown pretty damned tired of, cumshots to Starling's vagina notwithstanding. He'd seen enough of Midian, Tennessee to last a lifetime, and when he tossed his bag in the SUV, he didn't feel a need to do anything dramatic, like look around or cut a figure or pose or some shit.

No, he just got in the car and started the engine.

He pulled up the GPS for his new phone and entered an address. He looked at the different options, the different ways he could skin the cat of this journey, and decided to go for the scenic route, the one that bypassed the freeways.

That in mind, he pulled onto Old Jackson Highway and headed into Midian, because that was the direction it told him to go.

"Fuck it," he said again, and couldn't tell whether he was talking about this town, or the people in it, or maybe—dimly—even himself. But he definitely meant it, whoever it was aimed at. Fuck them.

He pointed the car toward Midian, and realized it was like a metaphor for all this too. He'd have to go right through the heart of it in order to get the hell out of it to his scenic route. Neat little symmetry there, he thought.

Hendricks opened a window and let the wind in. He'd ride it out of town, to where he was going, lie low there for a while, and then maybe—just maybe—figure out his next move. "Fuck it," he said again, passing the sheriff's station.

He still didn't know who he was talking to.

But it still felt right.

*

"Okay, go," Keith Drumlin said, and he and Nate moved the barricade out of the way, opening up the last road into the square. It was heavy, and they took faltering steps. Mostly it was him moving and Nate just keeping the other end up while he did it, but soon enough he'd gotten it the hell out of the way, and now ...

Now, the Midian town square was open again.

"That was a hell of a thing," Nate said as they set the barrier down again. Keith knew what he was talking about. The barrier wasn't light, but neither had been the restoration of the square.

And it still wasn't exactly pristine. There were stains everywhere on the concrete. Blood didn't wash off so easy, after all. But at least it wasn't a total fucking wreck anymore.

"That was a hell of a thing," Keith agreed.

Nate looked at him funny. "We talking about the same thing?"

Keith brushed his sleeve against his forehead. Even in the cool, morning air, it was damp from their labors. "The cleanup?"

"I was talking about Erin's meeting last night," Nate said. "She got me all gung-ho to kick some demon ass, man. That's why I was here half an hour early. I couldn't sleep last night, I was so fired up."

"You were here a half-hour early?" Keith asked, eyebrows up. "I didn't know. I would have shown up early too."

"Yeah, man," Nate said. "I scrubbed the last of that shit off the walls over by the diner too. Used that Works stuff from Walmart. The wife uses it for cleaning toilets, but it's cheap as shit and takes just about anything off of anything. For example." He nodded in the direction of the wall.

"Well, how about that," Keith said, staring at that wall in the distance. It did look cleaner. "So ... what's left now?"

"Kicking demon ass, I reckon," Nate said.

"On the square, shit for brains," Keith said.

"Well, there's that area over there," Nate said, pointing at the sidewalk around the monument. "Seemed like we kinda skipped over it, but it's just stain work, mostly."

Keith just nodded, feeling the chill rustle through him. He didn't look too hard at the place Nate was pointing; he knew it pretty well.

He'd been avoiding it for the last three weeks. "Stain work it is," he said with a hard swallow.

They were both at it a few minutes later, working on the sidewalk that circled the monument. They worked in a companionable silence, as they inevitably did, until one of them broke it. This time, it was Nate. Keith couldn't have gotten himself to say anything right now without pouring his guts out on this bloody sidewalk, so he hadn't.

"Soo ..." Nate said, brush running up and down a particularly brown stain. Shit? Blood? Who knew at this point? "Seems the going rate for grabbing Taylor Swift's ass is $1." That got Keith to chuckle, the joke a nice substitution for thinking about ... well, what had happened on this particular piece of real estate. "Seem like a bargain to you?"

"I think it cost that dumbass a lot more than a dollar to give her a grope," Keith said, the levity fleeing quickly. He stared at the water, running out the tip of his hose onto the red ground. This was where it happened, wasn't it? "Who even does that shit, anyway?" he asked, trying to keep his mind on the conversation and off ... other things. "Grabs some random woman's ass unasked? Who thinks that's even okay?"

"A real douchebag, I reckon," Nate said, brush still running up and down. "I mean, I could see it if you were on a dance floor with a girl, dancing real close, and your hand kind of wandered down, giving her enough time to shift away—"

"Right, right."

"But a grope during a photo op?" Nate made a pffffft-ing noise. "That's some animal shit right there. Savage as fuck, and not in a good way."

"I reckon he's going to be on the outs of polite society for a good long while," Keith said. He was dousing a stain pretty hard, drowning it, but the red ... it wasn't coming up. "Who's going to hire you when a Google search turns up the fact that you grabbed Taylor Swift's ass?"

"Hmm," Nate said, nodding as he scrubbed. "I guess it probably did cost him a lot more than a dollar."

"Mmmhmm."

"Hey, Keith?" Nate asked after a few more minutes of quiet.

"Yeah?"

"D'ye reckon Erin Harris knows what she's doing?" Nate threw that out there, sounding the least bit unsure. Maybe more than the least bit.

Keith gave it a thought or two, looking up in the sky, away from that stain—that fucking stain, the one that wouldn't go away. It was like a personal nemesis. He'd certainly been avoiding it long enough, dreading it long enough. "Does anybody know what they're doing, really?"

That shut him up for a minute. Not that Keith was aiming for it, but he wasn't complaining that it happened. "Some people sure do act like they do," Nate said at last.

"Well," Keith said, "she did manage to lead us through that demon pack of hellcats. That's gotta be worth something." That had felt good. Real good, in fact. Best Keith had felt since …

"That's a good point," Nate said. "Not many people would take an idea Casey Meacham came up with and turn it into victory. But she sure did."

"She did," Keith said. "Yeah, I think Erin's about as good as we could ask for at this point. She's young, but you can tell she's really into killing these fucks. She's lived here her whole life. Probably believes in this place like nobody's business." He nodded again. He understood that motive. Understood it real well. He looked away from the stain, but it didn't help.

He could still remember standing over it on Halloween …

Watching his family die right here.

Keith just swallowed, trying to bite back hard on that emotion.

Nate went on, oblivious. "Yeah, I think we might have an actual chance with her in charge, and getting real serious about getting people in or out."

The low hum of a car motor caused Keith to look up. A sweet distraction at last. He listened; something was definitely coming.

An SUV cruised into the square a few moments later, window down, and he could see the cowboy, hat on, staring straight ahead as he followed the road up past Surrey's Diner and onward, not even giving them a sideward look.

"Where do you suppose he's going?" Nate asked, nodding at the SUV, now fading in the distance.

"Who knows?" Keith said, shaking it all off. His voice sounded low and gruff. He didn't mean it to.

He was just trying to hold it all in. Just like he had the last three weeks.

"Hey, it's that cowboy," Nate said.

Keith could see him now too, in the window of the car as he steered through the square. He never had got a real good read on the cowboy. "Maybe he's off to fuck that Starling chick somewhere." It was the first thing that came to mind.

Nate paused. "You think?" He sounded like he might be interested in hearing more.

"Who cares?"

Nate shrugged it off, then started scrubbing again. "You know what a starling is?"

Keith just stared, dazed. "A redhead, about yea high—" He started to hold up a hand.

"Not that like, cheesedick! The bird, I mean."

Keith didn't. His head felt like it was floating. "Nope."

"Well, it's a bird. A real nasty bird, too."

Keith made a face at him. "Nasty?"

"Yeah. My uncle told me about it," Nate said, head bobbing with the scrub brush. "See, a starling ain't like other birds where they lay their eggs in a nest and sit on them, nossir. You see, a starling will come in to the nest of other birds and kick their eggs out and replace them with their own. Then the other bird ends up raising the starlings as their own." He made a disgusted face. "Nasty. Just nasty."

"Mmmhmm," Keith said, scrubbing along. His mind was elsewhere. Three weeks ... it had felt like eternity, and now here he was, standing over the same spot where ... "Yeah, that's something, all right," he said, and tried to put it all out of his mind. The stain wasn't washing off; none of it would. The problems of this town didn't go away that easily; why would he think a stain would? Keith just turned his attention to the next one though, opening up the spray and washing it hard, trying to ignore everything else that threatened to overtake him like a boat on big wave—and just make his town the best he could.

Coda

Two Weeks Earlier

Mack Wellstone was running madly, trying to get away from the things that he'd heard, from the man who'd attacked his mom, from ... well, everybody at this point. His breath was coming out in gasps, steaming in the cold air, and his cheeks were so frozen and raw they felt like they'd been sandpapered down. Mack's fingers were numb, he'd been out so long, and the sky was dark, night fallen over this country road.

The sounds of the fight had long since faded behind him. Mack didn't care. He'd run for miles, for what felt like hours ... and he'd keep going until he couldn't go any more.

There was nowhere among those people that was safe, nowhere in this town that was safe. His dad had died in front of him this morning, and that man had taken his mom. He knew she was as good as dead, there was no doubt in his mind. He could smell it on that guy, knew he was up to no good.

Mack didn't have any desire to end up grabbed, to be dragged off by demon cats, to die like that. That was stuff out of horror movies, and he didn't even watch those, really. Maybe once or twice on a sleepover at his friend Finn's house, but that was it.

But this was how horror movies went, wasn't it? Always chasing a kid through the woods. No, not kid ... teenagers? Mack wasn't that old yet ...

"I'm ... getting out ... of this ..." Mack huffed, trees blazing past him like spooky fingers reaching out of the dark.

He looked back, just for a second, and started to slow. There was no one behind him.

Nothing behind him.

Mack stopped, putting his hands on his knees, trying to catch his breath. But then, it felt like he'd been trying to catch his breath all day, even when he'd just been sitting in the police station waiting for his mom to show up.

"What the hell is happening in this town?" Mack asked, steaming breath fogging the night air. The moon slipped out from behind the clouds, and something moved in front of him—

A sharp pain worked its way into Mack's belly, and he almost screamed, but something hit him in the chest, twice, once on each side, just beneath the nipple. He wanted to shout but he gasped instead, and his chest swelled with pain in the lungs.

He stared, down, vision blurry. Were those … feet? They cleared, and he saw brown shoes, small feet—a woman's feet, he realized, tapering to thin legs hidden by tight-cuffed blue jeans. He raised his head slowly, up the legs—kinda shapely; he would have stared under different circumstances—and up to tight hips and then a tank top under a white blouse, and finally dusky eyes and a sweeping amount of red hair.

She stared at him curiously, and he realized … she had him impaled on her fingers. They were just sticking into his chest, holding him up from falling, lifting him a few inches off the ground. His legs just hung there, unmoving.

Mack looked down. His belly was wet, slick with blood. Her first hit had …

The pain in his stomach ran through every nerve in his body a second later, and he tried to scream. It didn't work.

"I'm almost sorry," the woman said, her red hair aglow, eyes so dark he couldn't see the color of them.

Mack gasped, feeling something warm slide out of him. The world was getting darker; her eyes—they were—

"But I need your blood," she said as he slumped, hit his knees. She had it too, hands drenched in red. She lifted her shirt with one hand, a clean one, and smeared blood—his blood—all over her belly with the other. "I need it," she said again, as Mack started to slump. "Because you're innocent."

Mack hit the ground at her feet, staring dully at her shoe, parked right in front of his face. It had started out to be such a good day too, with him finally getting to do the thing he'd most wanted to—to go to the woods with his dad.

He never would have predicted that it'd end up like this, he thought, as the night grew even darker. This wasn't how it was supposed to go. He'd waited for years for this. This was supposed to be—

"Best day ... of my ... life," Mack mumbled through the pain, not sure it even made any sense.

No one answered him. The cold was seeping in; the red-haired woman was gone, had just up and vanished into the night after smearing herself with his blood.

Mack's brain fired its last few thoughts. It hadn't turned out to be the best day.

It had turned out to be the worst day of Mack Wellstone's life.

And, he realized as the light faded from his eyes, the night fading into black, the last.

The Watch Will Return In

FORSAKEN
Southern Watch
Book 7

Coming 2018!

Author's Note

Thanks for reading! If you want to know immediately when future books become available, take sixty seconds and sign up for my NEW RELEASE EMAIL ALERTS by visiting my website. I don't sell your information and I only send out emails when I have a new book out. The reason you should sign up for this is because I don't always set release dates, and even if you're following me on Facebook (robertJcrane (Author)) or Twitter (@robertJcrane), it's easy to miss my book announcements because...well, because social media is an imprecise thing.

Come join the discussion on my website:
http://www.robertjcrane.com!

Cheers,
Robert J. Crane

ACKNOWLEDGMENTS

Editorial/Literary Janitorial duties performed by Sarah Barbour, Nick Bowman and Jeffrey Bryan. Any errors you see in the text, however, are the result of me rejecting changes.

The cover was once more designed with exceeding skill by Karri Klawiter of Artbykarri.com.

The formatting was provided by nickbowmanediting.com.

Also, a huge thanks to Megg Jensen, who taught me how a hooker really feels (this is how she suggested I phrase my thanks to her).

Once more, thanks to my parents, my in-laws, my kids and my wife, for helping me keep things together.

Other Works by Robert J. Crane

World of Sanctuary
Epic Fantasy

Defender: The Sanctuary Series, Volume One
Avenger: The Sanctuary Series, Volume Two
Champion: The Sanctuary Series, Volume Three
Crusader: The Sanctuary Series, Volume Four
Sanctuary Tales, Volume One - A Short Story Collection
Thy Father's Shadow: The Sanctuary Series, Volume 4.5
Master: The Sanctuary Series, Volume Five
Fated in Darkness: The Sanctuary Series, Volume 5.5
Warlord: The Sanctuary Series, Volume Six
Heretic: The Sanctuary Series, Volume Seven
Legend: The Sanctuary Series, Volume Eight
Ghosts of Sanctuary: The Sanctuary Series, Volume Nine* *(Coming 2018, at earliest.)*

A Haven in Ash: Ashes of Luukessia, Volume One* *(with Michael Winstone—Coming Late 2017!)*
A Respite From Storms: Ashes of Luukessia, Volume Two* *(with Michael Winstone—Coming 2018!)*

The Girl in the Box
and
Out of the Box
Contemporary Urban Fantasy

Alone: The Girl in the Box, Book 1
Untouched: The Girl in the Box, Book 2
Soulless: The Girl in the Box, Book 3
Family: The Girl in the Box, Book 4
Omega: The Girl in the Box, Book 5
Broken: The Girl in the Box, Book 6
Enemies: The Girl in the Box, Book 7
Legacy: The Girl in the Box, Book 8

Destiny: The Girl in the Box, Book 9
Power: The Girl in the Box, Book 10

Limitless: Out of the Box, Book 1
In the Wind: Out of the Box, Book 2
Ruthless: Out of the Box, Book 3
Grounded: Out of the Box, Book 4
Tormented: Out of the Box, Book 5
Vengeful: Out of the Box, Book 6
Sea Change: Out of the Box, Book 7
Painkiller: Out of the Box, Book 8
Masks: Out of the Box, Book 9
Prisoners: Out of the Box, Book 10
Unyielding: Out of the Box, Book 11
Hollow: Out of the Box, Book 12
Toxicity: Out of the Box, Book 13
Small Things: Out of the Box, Book 14
Hunters: Out of the Box, Book 15
Badder: Out of the Box, Book 16
Apex: Out of the Box, Book 18* *(Coming February 1, 2018!)*
Time: Out of the Box, Book 19* *(Coming May 2018!)*
Driven: Out of the Box, Book 20* *(Coming July 2018!)*

Southern Watch

Contemporary Urban Fantasy

Called: Southern Watch, Book 1
Depths: Southern Watch, Book 2
Corrupted: Southern Watch, Book 3
Unearthed: Southern Watch, Book 4
Legion: Southern Watch, Book 5
Starling: Southern Watch, Book 6
Forsaken: South Watch, Book 7* *(Come Late 2018—Tentatively)*

The Shattered Dome Series
(with Nicholas J. Ambrose)
Sci-Fi

Voiceless: The Shattered Dome, Book 1
Unspeakable: The Shattered Dome, Book 2* *(Coming 2018!)*

The Mira Brand Adventures
Contemporary Urban Fantasy

The World Beneath: The Mira Brand Adventures, Book 1
The Tide of Ages: The Mira Brand Adventures, Book 2
The City of Lies: The Mira Brand Adventures, Book 3
The King of the Skies: The Mira Brand Adventures, Book 4* *(Coming Late 2017/Early 2018!)*

Liars and Vampires
(with Lauren Harper)
Contemporary Urban Fantasy

No One Will Believe You: Liars and Vampires, Book 1* *(Coming Early 2018!)*
Someone Should Save Her: Liars and Vampires, Book 2* *(Coming Early 2018!)*
You Can't Go Home Again: Liars and Vampires, Book 3* *(Coming Early 2018!)*

* Forthcoming, Subject to Change

Printed in Great Britain
by Amazon